WORLD OF DARKNESS

Robert Weinberg

Mark Rein•Hagen

Owl Goingback

Scott Ciencin

David Niall Wilson

Esther M. Friesner

White Wolf Publishing
735 Park North Boulevard
Suite 128
Clarkston, Georgia 30021
www.white-wolf.com

Contents

NEVERLAND

DEAR BEN,

BY THE TIME YOU RECEIVE THIS LETTER, I'LL BE GONE. DON'T SHED ANY TEARS FOR ME. IT'S BETTER THIS WAY. AFTER YOU READ MY DIARY, YOU'LL UNDERSTAND WHAT'S GOING ON... AND WHY I CAN'T SAY, WITH TOTAL SINCERITY, THAT I'LL FINALLY BE AT PEACE.

I AM SENDING THIS IN THE HOPE THAT YOU WILL COME TO UNDERSTAND WHAT I HAVE BECOME. IN THE LAST FEW YEARS WE HAVE NOT BEEN AS CLOSE AS WE WERE AS KIDS, AND I REGRET THAT MORE THAN ANYTHING ELSE. I WISH THINGS HAD TURNED OUT DIFFERENTLY. I WISH I COULD GO BACK.

REMEMBER THESE WORDS ARE A WARNING. LIKE DAD ALWAYS SAID, THERE ARE MORE THINGS IN HEAVEN AND EARTH THAN ARE DREAMT OF IN ANY PHILOSOPHY. BEWARE, BROTHER, BEWARE — ALL THIS IS TRUE. THEY'LL KILL YOU IF THEY FIND OUT YOU KNOW ABOUT THEM.

STAY SAFE, STAY ALIVE. TELL MOM AND DAD I LOVE THEM. REMEMBER THEM FONDLY.

WITH LOVE,

Austin

P.S. THIS AIN'T NO JOKE.

14 Quincy Ave., Los Angeles, California, 90026. Phone 213-555-8542, Fax 213-555-8543

Vampire Diary: The Embraced

WRITTEN BY
ROBERT WEINBERG
AND MARK REIN•HAGEN

ILLUSTRATED BY
DANIEL THRON
AND CHRIS ELLIOTT

It WAS ~~the best of times~~
~~It was the worst~~

The Nellie Nellie, a cruising yawl
swung to her anchor without a
flutter of the sails.
AND WAS AT REST.

CHRIST
How did Conrad
do it.

~~Dear Diary,~~
~~I feel like a~~
~~total idiot~~

so much
crap

It WAS A
DARK
A Stormy

June 28th 6:00 PM   I haven't kept a diary for years, not since I was a kid. I feel silly writing to myself this way. Like I'm a bag lady at the bus stop talking to herself

For me diaries have always been something out of Brady Bunch reruns. Something girls with crushes on Johnny Depp write... But Danya thought this might help with these INSANE nightmares I keep having. This thing is her idea

So, what the hell, I got nothing better to do might as well give it a try...

If nothing else I can just fill these pages with doodles

...maybe not

I need the practice Well, that's it for now—

JULY 1ST, 3:00AM — Been a bad boy. Haven't been much dedicated to write lately — been too busy. Boss-man has been keeping me at the wheel hard. Little shit doesn't like me much. Guess Mary feels threatened. But this is a good gig and I want to keep it. Go straight for a while ... YEAH, RIGHT.

I had the same nightmare again, the one with the wolves. I don't remember much — just mist and snow and then the kill ... screams, howls, blood ... Red on white, Red on WHITE.
RED ON WHITE

July 3rd, 9:00 PM — Danya hung out at the bar tonight, talking while I worked. One thing for sure, she's highly unique... and opinionated. I've never met someone with so many opinions about so many different things.

Music, Movies, serial killers, psychology, religion, Satanism politics, lubricants, PAIN, sex, ORAL HYGENE, LAUGHING, DRUGS. — DISNEYLAND. WHERE THE HELL DOES SHE COME UP WITH THIS SHIT?

She like to think she's punk, but she's really more of a goth. Black is her look, blooddolls are her crowd.

She tries hard to blend in with the rest of the wretches at Neverland. Black velvet dress, lace bustier, worn leather jacket, ripped fishnet stalkings. But for her its just a game.

A WILD, glamorous, exciting silly game.

I love her for that.

For all her posing, she's brighter than I am. She watches things, knows things, sees things. She knew right away what an idiot Kary is ... how he steals from the till.

I wonder if she's figured me out yet...

I sure hope not.

WHY DO WE CELEBRATE WITH FIREWORKS?

PROBABLY TO SCARE AWAY THE MONSTERS.

THE BRITS, THE INDIANS, THE JAPS, THE RUSSIANS, THE MOSLEMS.

WE MUST THINK THEY'RE AFRAID OF LOUD NOISES.

WE'VE ALWAYS HAD OUR DEMONS. THEY'RE WHAT KEEP US UNITED

WE NEED AN ENEMY TO KEEP OUR "MOTLEY CREW TOGETHER

FEAR MAKES SENSE OUT OF THINGS, MONSTERS GIVE US MEANI

WE'VE JUST BEGUN TO REALIZE HOW BIG THE UNIVERSE IS,

AND HOW LITTLE WE UNDERSTAND OF IT —

AND IT SCARES THE SHIT OUT OF US.

WE TREMBLE IN FUCKING AWE.

SO WE KILL THINGS TO FEEL BETTER.

I DON'T BELIEVE IN MONSTERS.

NOT IN OTHER PEOPLES MONSTERS AT LEAST—

I HAVE MY OWN TO WORRY ABOUT.

The wolves came again tonight. They turned on me, clawed at me, and ATE ME WHOLE... I couldn't go back to sleep. I'm so tired now, exhausted. But I gotta go to work soon.

July 5th 3:00 A.M.
     What a long night its been —
  so many damn drunks.
I talk to a lot of people every night.
there's always someone who wants to gab.
Rich and Poor, young and
  old, senile and raving,
  anyone who's crazy
  comes here

Its the epicenter
     of the
  L.A. scene
GO DUDE!
     Yeah, sure.

U.S. DEPT OF
ASSHOLES
2596-8342
KARY

Neverland has
  Potential, but right now its
     definately flat. Kary don't
  give a shit about this place
     He's gonna run it into
          the ground.

I know most of the regulars by now, but Danya's the only one who ever listens to what I'm saying. They just want to talk, and talk. They're as shallow as Micheal, fucking, Bolton.

She just walked in with her friends a few weeks ago, just after I started. (The three of them were dressed like the unholy sisters in Dracula.)

Instead of ordering red wine like her friends she asked for a white zin. She told me, winking, that she prefered albino blood... Asked her out that night, we've been hanging ever since.

She's such a freak!!
   I love it.

   Its been a long time
since I've been
   this happy.
And the way she kisses
   me on the side of
      the mouth.

      So delicate
      So,
         So sexy.

July 7th 2:30 a.m.

What a bizarre night. This scrawny poser punk found a cockroach crawling around in his nachos, and threw a hissy fit. Having coexisted peacefully with bugs for years, I scooped it up in a glass and tossed it out into the alley. When Kary asked me why I didn't just kill it, I said that any friend of Franz Kafka was a friend of mine. Danya was the only one who laughed.

Usually no one gets my jokes.

Tonight I loaned her my copy of Conrad's Heart of Darkness. She returned the favor by reading me some morbid prose by some guy, Peter Straub or something.

We both love Bogart and Bacall, Bert and Ernie, Beavis and Butthead (I'm SO ASHAMED) Neither of us finds Lucy funny. If only she appreciated Nine Inch Nails, we'd be perfect for each other.

She says I look like goddamn Keanu Reeves, which I DON'T take as a compliment (I'm not just a pretty face, I can talk too). In retaliation I've taken to calling her "Winona" — which makes her shut up in a hurry.

July 9th 3:00 A.M.
I've come clean with Danya about my dreams!
I'd told her they'd stopped, but that was a lie. That was her cue... She said that dreams reflected the thoughts of the subconsciousness. They were messages from the inner mind — so complex they could only be expressed during deep sleep. I don't know why she's into that Psychobabble Bullshit they yap about in Cosmo. It may be shit but she has a point, of sorts.

She didn't like that I wasn't writing down my dreams much — the way I said I would. We thought of a new way to do it...

I'm gonna keep the diary under the bed, and after a nightmare wake me up, I'll write it down. That way I'll actually remember it. Maybe I can figure out whats bee haunting me. At least that's what Danya says — and I'm willing to be convinced.

July 15th—cont. Claudius has been out of town the last few days. With the old man gone, Kary likes to keep the club understaffed. Not hiring as many people as he should, and not hiring a band at all, but doctoring the books so it looks like he did. The extra money ends up in **HIS** wallet. Our chickenshit manager is a first class dickwad. He doesn't seem to realize that somehow Mr. Claudius is going to find out about his skimming. I mean shit, this guy is organized crime or something. You don't fuck around with that. I'm surprized Kary's lasted this long. **I Hate that son of a Bitch.—**

for now I'm keeping my mouth shut and my eyes open— If he does get canned, I have a chance at this job. I may be a wild dream, but if the menendez brothers can get off Scott free ANYTHING IS POSSIBLE!

Wow, pretty far out.

fertilize the lawn with it. Pal

WOOF

Meantime, I'm being worked like a mule. Neverland is getting to be trendy— Some Beverly brat packers are showing up. I fall into my bed exhausted and sleep like a log. Nothing disturbs me. No dreams. For the first time in weeks I'm getting a good nights sleep.

I could just throw this thing away now, but for sure Danya'd ask me about it. Besides, I've gotten used to scribbling when things are slow. It's nice to get back into drawing.

I remember when Ben would have me draw while telling him Granpa's stories about Olle' the Sheepshooter. That was a long time ago—

July 16th, 1:43 A.
Yoo-hoo.
goodnight

July 17th 4:50 A.M.

DAMN IT ALL. HERE I AM AGAIN MIDDLE OF THE NIGHT, COVERED IN SWEAT...

I'm running through a black, black forest.
There's no moon, but I don't need it.
I move with careless grace, dodging trunks
left and right. I am a wolf, my thoughts
are not human. I AM THE HUNTER.
The BEAST IS FREE Within me.
My quarry is just ahead.

I STALK HER, PLAY WITH HER.
HER PATH LEADS ME THROUGH A COLD BROOK
AT THE CENTER OF THE WOODS. Trying to hide
her trail - To no avail.
She leads me down a stream. Trying to hide
her trail - TO NO AVAIL.

She trips
and falls.

Deep within me the beast growled
In blood lust. I Pounce,
AND I DEVOUR.

Her screams are but an echo in a padded room-
It's my own voice.

I WAKE UP.

July 21st 4:32 A.M. It's been a while since I drew professionally but that's what they looked like. From the dream. I woke up screaming. Danya took care of me. She's asleep now. **WHAT THE HELL IS HAPPENING TO ME!?**

I don't remember much, just the eyes. whatever scared the shit out of me is gone Even the memory. I'm not sure what it is,

<u>But</u> looking at those eyes gives me the wee willies.

5:47 A.M.

I'm calmer now. A couple of beers and a hot shower helped. I don't plan on going back to sleep though. I could wake up Danya to talk to her about it, but she has a job interview at one of the studios. Besides, there's no reason for both of us to suffer...

Sitting here in the dark alone, looking at those eyes. The red neon of the strip joint across the street reflecting off everything. I put my sanity in question. What I'm thinking can't be RATIONAL — HAVE I LOST IT? I wish they sold a kit in drug stores to tell if you're insane. Just like those pregnancy kits. "OH SHIT. I'M INSANE! GET ME TO A PADDED ROOM!"

BUST A MOVE

PARKING

But if the big dollar shrinks can't agree— HOW THE HELL CAN I TELL? What does crazy mean ANYHOW?

DAMNIT, DAMNIT, DAMNIT, DAMNIT, DAMNIT, DAMNIT, DAMNIT

If these dreams do reflect something in me, then I really am fucked up. They should lock me up. It's like a clockwork orange, Natural Born Killers Double feature going on behind my eyelids.

HOME INSANITY Test how do I look sane

WHACKO JACKO

DID John Wayne Gacy have these dreams DID DALMER?

Maybe DAD was right after all. Maybe I am a bad seed.

But I wont regret what's done is done Life moves on.

JULY 28th   WAY TOO EARLY
THERE'S THIS FOREST, ONLY I'M NOT A WOLF, I'M, A MAN.
I'M NAKED, BUT I'M CHASING SOMETHING. I ATTACK
THIS LITTLE GIRL, SHE TURNS TOWARDS ME, SCREAMS,
I LOSE MYSELF IN HER, I DEVOUR HER—
THERE WAS MORE, BUT I CAN'T REMEMBER
Forgot already

July 30th, 3A.M
Danya stopped
in at the club
after work today.
(she got the job,
a P.A. to some
B-movie producer).
I told her about
the dream. Had to
tell someone.
I showed her my
sketch, and she said
some stuff. It was
about Dad and religion
(or lack thereof) and

fearing the shadow. I didn't buy it, but it was interesting. She sure can talk. Funny thing is, I should be the one interpreting the dreams on account that my real first name is Joseph, and that story in the Bible about the Pharoh's dreams.

August 2nd, 8:00 P.M.

Everytime I see Danya I realize how badly I'm falling for her. I want to make love with her — its so weird we haven't yet. She knows how to thrill me, she takes a fiendish pleasure in making suffer. Tonight she ran her fingernail up under my arm. I nearly jumped her right there. I felt like dragging her across the bar and doing her on the floor.

YO-thats disgusting. I shouldn't think of her that way... but I can't help it. Danya frightens me in a way. Before it was always just sex, and never lasted more than a few months. Women are easy to find, and sex is too much fun to do the monogomy thing. Its not that way with Danya. Everythings different. She's special. Maybe I'll even call home, tell Mom. Maybe I could call Ben. Hope He's doing well.

What would they say if I brought Danya home? They'd probably hate her eye liner. It'd be hate the sin, love the sinner shit all over again. I'm **not** playing that game anymore.

August 8th. 3:00 A.M.
No dreams, and that's a good thing
Just got up for some water.

4:45 A.M. - Spoke too soon - It was the
wolves again. And I ate the carcass -
OF THE GIRL
The most horrible thing is, it wasn't so
horrible - NOT AT ALL.
A SLUMBER POWER TRIP
The sort of thing that gives
teenage boys wet dreams.

August 10th, 3:20 A.M. — When I was just a kid, back in Minnesota, before things with Dad got so bad I had to leave, I used to write a lot of songs. Poems really. I suppose most "rebels without a clue" do it. Express your teen angst in a poem! Expurge your soul!

I am filled with <u>anguish</u>,
Please baby, don't let me <u>languish</u> — I wish I kept them. Maybe Mom has 'em in one of her trunks. It's been a long since words came to me like they did then. Maybe its this diary thing.

Thing is, I want to write something about Danya. Something not crass, Something real and true and pure. These words are personal, private I can take a chance.

She is ~~beauty~~ on fire
Liquid heat
A beast of black mystery
beating beneath me
~~Her~~ Crimson succulent lips
burning with dark passion
naked beneath black velvet
A cat in heat
Nothing I say ~~of~~ nothing I do
Can pierce her proud dignity
This ~~wild~~ Valkarie queen
she calls herself Danya
~~and she hides within~~
But she cannot hide the truth
I know her real name
Her true identity
DesiRE
Yeah I languish, baby.

WHAT TOTAL SHIT!

how totally embarassing
I'm not showing this
to Danya. How did
Anais Nin get the
courage to read hers to
Henry Miller? She was
more of a writer than I
AM I guess. WHY
DO I HUMILIATE MYSELF
THIS WAY?

August 13th, 6:00 P.M. — WHAT TOTAL FUCKING BULLSHIT! I've got to pick out a playlist for tonight. Kary didn't hire a replacement for Myk, who's recovering from last night (what a trip that was), so he pulled me off of bar duty. That should slow counter service to a crawl — any extra breaks in the music will push my bar crew to the edge — There's going to be some unhappy campers at Neverland tonight. I haven't DJed in years — ANOTHER NOTCH AGAINST KARY — THAT PUNK'S GOING DOWN. I almost feel sorry for the stupid shit, but this just makes me look better. I just wish he didn't screw the bar crew. Oh well.

PLAYLIST

Bauhaus — ~~Bela~~ — "Double Dare"
Dead can Dance — that "Mr. Love groove song"
Skinny Puppy — "Assimilate" "Smothered Hope"
Smiths — "How Soon is Now"
Nine Inch Nails — "Down in It" — yawn
£U$¢ — (just to watch 'em squirm)
Swans — "Love will tear us apart"
Joy Division — "Love will tear us apart" (back to back)
Revco — "Ya think I'm sexy"
The Cure — That song from...
Sisters of Mercy — "Lucretia" "Burn" "Body"

August 14th, 3:00 A.M. Claudius is back.
Kary's gonna be in DEEP shit
when the old man finds out
whats been going on
And man, I wanna
watch

This dude
is a very cool
customer

I've never seen him angry, or even raise
his voice. He doesn't ever lose control, least
not that I've ever seen — and I've seen him
provoked. Only his eyebrows give him away.
I think it's his self control that makes him
so intimidating. NO ONE fucks with him.
he reminds me of that godfather guy,
who goes to a christening while his men gun
down every rival of his in the city. He even
looks the part dressed in his three piece
Armani suits.

Some of the guys behind the bar say
he's the most powerful mob figure
in L.A., with mucho contacts in New York.
But he doesn't look Italian, he's more
of a Scandinavian type. Those eyebrows
are out of control.
When it comes to the old man I'm not sure
what's truth and what's innuendo. Nor do I
really want to know. After Bangkok,
I'm not as curious as I used to be.
        Once dicked — twice warned.
He has a couple of bodyguards around
him at all times. Some Drake guy,
a real Hell's Angel type, and a six foot
black woman in shades who looks like
Grace Jones on steroids. NOT my idea
of a fun date.
I doubt the big cheese even knows I
exist. He's not around enough to think
about a bartender
        But that'll change
        I'll MAKE IT HAPPEN.

August 15th 8p.m. I'm sitting in Neverland,
waiting for it to open, the lights on for once.
I can't clear my head. My thoughts dart between
Danya and Clavdivs. They're so different, but they
both hang out here.

There's two types of people who hang here. It's funny I never thought about it before. While they look sort of similar, they're miles apart in attitude.

Danya and her West Hollywood friends are goths. Blood dolls, out for fun in a world with no truth or love or passion beyond Maxwell House commercials. They tend to cop an attitude, a lot of them overdo the drug thing, and they aren't going anywhere, but I sympathize with them. They remind me of myself, back before I realized that eating was more important than philosophy. They're midnight rebels - They work their daytime jobs, wearing suits or whatever, and keep their opinions to themselves. At night they come out, usally at clubs like Neverland. They dress up in black leather and lace, drink, smoke cigarettes and pretend to be dead - but their Nikilism is only skin deep. Its an act.

Claudius's crowd is the opposite. I think they actually live this shit. No matter what age, sex, or race, its obvious they don't get a whole lot of sun. They dress like its Halloween, decked out in duds ranging from glam rock freak show to dandy in a tux. Though they spend hours here, they don't drink much. I figure they must snort or shoot up in Claudius's office or in the bathrooms.

Then there's the little things. They've got a brittle hardness to their eyes, and a casual cruelty to their talk. They unnerve me. I don't know what they do for Claudius, but obviously they're all part of the same gang.

While the goths like to think of themselves as Libertines, they're souls of propriety compared to this crowd - its like what Joseph Conrad said: "The belief in a supernatural source of evil is not necessary. Men alone are quite capable of every wickedness" His posse are all real bad ass - I give them a wide berth.

August 16th 7:00 AM
Another nightmare. Gotta
get some words down—So tired
OH SHit my lips are bleeding. Must
have bit myself in my sleep. My lower
face is covered in blood, AND I can't
get the taste of out of mouth.
I want to scream
I WANT I WANT TO SCREAM
I WANT TO SCREAM!

7:20 A.M. I'm clean now
The blood is all gone. But I can't
forget the taste of it. The damage
felt a lot worse than it really was.

Weird thing is, I don't remember
making that last sketch of the eyes.
The page was empty when I went to
sleep — Things get creepy.

In my whole life I've never sleepwalked, much less
sleepsketched. Maybe this diary isn't such a good
idea after all. But I'm afraid to stop. Wish
I could wake Danya up but she's gotta go
to work soon — I'm not going back to sleep.

August 17th 3:00 A.M.

Its been a very odd,
     exhilerating evening.

I'm the full time DJ now, people liked my mix.
Even ¢$¢.
I didn't know I had that rant in me either.
Watching Danya dance inspired me,
  I guess.
I don't look at the other ones anymore,
Just her.

AUGUST 20TH 3:00 A.M. I've always been a loner. Never believed in much, certainly not in God - at least not the way Dad did. Since I was a kid, I considered life a pointless game, with no rules, no referee, and no prizes.

I'll never forget the day I was sitting in church and suddenly realized how much I didn't fit in. I thought to myself, what are all these people doing here, why are they sitting on these hard benches, why are they listening to my father talk? I realized then that I didn't belong. That I wasn't one of them.

When it finally ended, I shook Dad's hand at the door and ran all the way home - and didn't look back once. I've never looked back since.

I ran home every Sunday for the next 10 years — I had to be free.

I wish there was a God, I really do... I just can't buy it. But it's like what Ambrose Bierce said, I see things as they are, not as they ought to be.

So does that make me an agnostic or an atheist?

Having accepted that the world is utterly devoid of meaning, my only goal is to make the best of it. (with as little effort as I can) Sometimes I succeed, usually I fail.

I just want to survive, and to see the funny side of things. The club scene is my home now, ever since I got back to the States. The noise and the tension make it the only place where I feel alive. I like to feel things in my bones, and here the music's loud enough to do that. Most of my life I've been in clubs - selling things or behind the counter it's where I belong I guess. I'm fufilled here. It's not like I'm going to spend my life here. I've got ambitions. I've got plans. I haven't told Danya this yet, but I will want to own my own club. I want to book the acts, hire the help, and run the show. I want to be the guy who decides what bands are cool and what bands suck. I want talent to win for once. maybe I'll finally get my own band together.

August 23rd. 3:00 AM. Claudius stopped by the both tonight. Just as I was trying to juggle two albums out of their sleeves and winding down my rant. I nearly dropped a load upon seeing him up top. He was as polite as always. Thanked me for taking on the extra work, for keeping an eye on things for him. I didn't know what to say. but, thanks. I totally blew my chance to say something about Kary - Then he left, me still holding records and dead air comming up. But I handled it.

Call MOM - get Bens adress

Hey! I think I've been noticed!

August 25th 5:00 A.M. I am flying through the darkness. Gliding on the cool air. It's a dream. My wings hardly move, shifting only slightly to catch the smallest changes in air pressure. I feel as if I'm running, and I hold my breath.

My thoughts are not my own. I am no longer Juston; but some nameless bird. Strange desires fill my mind. My urges are not entirely human. Exactly what is I am unsure.

I am searching, hunting for something. Something other than mortal flesh. After more powerful than that.

Patterns control me. Motivate me. I am one with my heart.

Beneath me, no if on command, the clouds part and I can see the land hundreds of feet below. Bright moonlight illuminates the scene. Almost directly below me, my gaze sweeps the ground, searching for the...

I sense a nearby. Finally, I see him. A lone figure on horseback rides wildly across the countryside as if pursued. Instinctively I fold my wings and spiral downwards.

...pursued by wolves.

he is my quarry, my feast. The air whistles shrilly around me as I descend. It feels perfectly natural, something I have done hundreds of times before. As I draw ever closer, a hunger begins to burn in my belly. It feels perfectly natural, something I have felt hundreds of times before. I hunt partially for the pleasure of the chase, but also for the blood that gives me life. The blood, the life... the ecstasy. This too I accept without question.

When just a hundred feet above the man, he looks skyward, screaming in terror. He pushes his horse into a gallop and whips it, tries to... of his belt — Powder flashes, but I easily dodge the bullet. The next instant I am on him.

Taloned hands, attached to my huge wings, rip him from his mount. Thrashing out in terror he struggles to no avail. My strength is ten times his. Holding him, feeling the life throbbing in his form, overwhelms my senses. I claw at his throat, then I realize the rider's face is my own.

It is my... I

Holy Hell! — What a dream. I scribbled those notes right after bolting upright in bed. Fully awake. Totally Lucid. As with most of my nightmares, I was totally drenched in sweat. But this time my joints ached as well, as if I had writhed around in bed for hours. After I started writing, I didn't stop. It was like I was in a trance the details are getting fuzzy now, I'm glad I got it all down. I don't think I'll ever forget the look of terror in that face. IN MY FACE.

I'm going to read it to Danya tomorrow maybe she can make sense out of it

It sure as hell doesn't make sense to me.

TO DO:

Present for Danya—flowers?

Clean Bathroom

Restock Absolut and 8 cases Rolling Rock

Stop by Golden Records

TELL OFF KARY for not locking up bar.

August 26th 3:AM — I'd like to introduce the new General Manager of Neverland — Aviston Jacobson! (applause, applause) Thank You, Thank You. Yes, I am now boss of this pile of junk.

The old man said he knew that Kary was skimming, but wanted a decent replacement before dumping him. Muttered something about going into business with KIN. I figured it wasn't my place to lecture him on nepotism. I let him do the talking.

Then he made the offer to me. I was shocked. Though I don't know why - it was pretty obvious. At first I couldn't say anything. I was caught completely by surprise. Claudius told me to sleep on it, I said I would get back to him.

I can't wait to tell Danya the news. Her friends and her should be comming in soon. I think a free round of drinks are in order We're going to have one hell of a PARTY!

What a fucktastic day this is. I'm going to ROCK this CITY.

THIS IS one dream I hope never ends.

ME
GENERAL MANAGER
NEVERLAND

AUGUST 28th 6:45 AM. Writing this on some beach in Malibu. Sun is rising. So peaceful here, so calm, it feels as if I am in another world. One I wish I never had to leave. Danya's asleep beside me—more beautiful now than ever. Such a strange combination of passion and innocence. For the first time in my life I know that I am in love. And it feels great.

whoever or whatever is up there looking out for me—THANK YOU.

When I picked her up at first, yesterday noon, I barely recognized her. Without a painted face or leather, and wearing a big floppy hat and a yellow sundress that came down to her knees - she looked like a flower child. It was still her, but a different side of her — I loved it.

Once we got to the beach I wanted to read her the last entry in the diary, but she wouldn't have any of it. It was to be a day of celebration, not psychobabble. And it was— We got into her car, a black Miata, and rode off to the beach with the top down — leaving everything, including my dreams behind us.

Some moments are so perfect you want to etch them into your mind, so you can relive them over and over again. Yesterday was one of those times. It was perfect. The sun, the waves, the seagulls, the little girl in the water with her grandfather. I don't want to forget anything I want to write it all down.

We sat in the sand and talked for hours, about books, music, childhood memories, and lust. About our families, about past lovers, about our dreams for the future, about us. We were silly too. I carried her out, kicking and screaming into the water. She looks so hot in a bikini. She wrote her name in Hawaiian Tropic on my back so that I would be bound to her.

It was symbolic.
When the sun sank into the sea, we
pulled out a blanket and cuddled
underneath it. Her taut, warm
skin, pressed close to mine,
was more than I could resist.
We kissed.
At first slowly, shyly, tenatively-
like two strangers afraid
of what they are about to do.
Like two kids under the bleachers.
Our music was the water.
The hypnotic chant of the
roaring waves washed over us.
Embraced us. Brought us into
ourselves. Into one Another.—
We made love under the
Moonlight.
A harmony of souls.

FINALLY—
WE DID IT...
and it was good.

Sometimes sex works, sometimes it
doesn't. For all the spin and hype
Hollywood puts on it-it isn't always
perfect. All too often, one or both
partners feel cheated, unsatisfied, or used.

But that wasn't even an issue. Not even the stirings
of a thought. Even if I couldn't have gotten
it up, we still would have made love.

It was that far
beyond the physical.
We moved, and
felt, and loved
in total harmony
we slide into one
another
completely in rhythm,
completely in balance

I told her I LOVED her. I'd never done
that before, never said those words
At least not honestly.

This is so freaky
I feel so alive
It hurts

Now the sun has risen.
Its rays are washing away all of my guilt,
and doubts, and pride, and fear, and sorrow.
I am born anew. If only I could watch
the sun rise every day, I would be free,
and the black of the night could never
overwhelm me again.
No more bad dreams

August 29th, 4 p.m. **THE DEAL IS DONE! I AM SO STOKED!**

The contract is signed — its so hard to write when my hand trembles like this. This is nuts but I love it. I'm in charge of this place now. Hell, I've never been boss of anything before.

There are still a couple of details to be worked out, but not only do I double my salary but I have complete control. I decide what bands play. I decide how expensive drinks are. I decide who gets in.

This is very cool.

Danya has to work this weekend, some horror shoot up in Reno, but she dropped me off before she left.

better to rule in Neverland.

DOWN TOWN

The whole crew was in a state of panic. Kary hadn't shown up (of course) and no one had told them what was going on. When I said I was the boss, everyone thought it was a joke. It took a while to get myself understood.

Then I got the congratulations. Heaps and piles of it, bootlicking extraordinaire. I think they really like me though. I hope they still will after I start changing things around here. It won't make everyone happy.

As I watched the crowd surge in, I felt good about myself. It's been a while since I was proud of anything I've done. It was almost sexual in intensity. I wish Danya was here.

So here I am, a preacher's son, a farm boy, a runaway, a drifter, a slacker, and a loner — running my own show. It's a fairy tale, though I sure ain't a sleeping beauty. Hmmm...

If only Dad could see this. He swore I'd end up in the "fiery pits" and (according to Ben) cursed me the day I walked out. He won't even let my name be mentioned. I'd love to see his face when he finds out his son is running a night club.

And he will find out.

I'll make damn sure of that.

<u>Later</u> I didn't see him approach, and suddenly he was just there. I didn't expect the old man to show up tonight, usually Claudius hangs out in his office upstairs. The first moment I realized anything was when he draped his arm over my back and patted me in a fatherly way. God, his fingers were cold.

He'd been watching things, he said, and liked what he saw. Said he'd gotten good reports. He even cracked a smile, if you could call it that. His eyebrows gave him away, he was playing me, watching my reactions. I said things were good at the club and would get better, but I didn't want to get involved in his other businesses. That I didn't want to know anything.

He didn't like that much. But the smile stayed. He just said he was sure I would perform all my duties well. I'm glad we could get things straight. This is my destiny. I'm going to kick some ass in this burg.

August 30th 10:00 p.m. Kary didn't show up again tonight, but no one seems to care. No one knows where he is. Claudius wants me to fire him personally. I have no idea why.

I'm in my new office, kicking back, spinning around in my chair. I can't wait for Danya to get back.

I need to share this with someone. This triumph. If you can't share a victory, it has a hollow ring to it. I never understood that before, too much of a loner. I don't want to be alone any more.

But I'm alone now, and I'm a little melancoly I guess. Myk's back, he's playing the Smiths — "I wear black on the outside, because black is how I feel on the inside."

I've been thinking about Ben too. Haven't seen him in years I feel bad about it. I tried writing to him a couple of times, but Dad always sent back the letters... unopened. When he went to college I lost contact. I was out of the country, he was busy, we both had new lives. A few of his letters made it to me, past a long list of forwarding adresses. I wish I could call him. Last time I heard he was majoring in Broadcast Journalism.

Typical.

I wonder if he'd get into a club like Neverland? maybe he could do a story on it. wouldn't that be a bizzare turn of events.

WBEN

WBEN

— Geraldo I'm here live at a prominent LA club Neverland.

August 31st 6:00 A.M. - Another bad dream. This time its me.
I'm running down the street. It's night. Everything is
deserted. Empty.
The stores are all open, but they're totally vacant.
Lights are on, but no one's home.
The world is so barren, its a blur. Nothing is real,
Nobody is there to make it real.
For hours I look for someone, anyone,
For days, weeks, months.
I get paniced. I get lonely. I get scared.
I scream - over and over
And still I am alone.

Then things get really weird.
I go back home, and go into the bathroom - I look in the
mirror. I start to talk to myself — tell myself stories
Pretty soon I'm not alone anymore - there's more
than one of me. And I'm more than enough company
for myself... Then one of the Voices tells a story about
being all alone in a deserted world. About walking through
empty streets. Then I realize it's not me in
the mirror anymore. It's Claudius. I'm looking
at him - He's looking at me. He winks - It's REALLY
him, we're in the same dream together. And
its NOT MY IMAGINATION
        Then the Mirror cracks
        And I'm alone again.

9:00 A.M.

Just got off the phone with Danya. She spent an hour trying to convince me that the mirror thing was a warning. Dream projection she called it. When one person has such strong dreams that they are telepathically broadcast to sensative minds nearby. Right. Like Claudius and I are on the same "psychic wavelength" Though it's goofy as hell, it's hard to argue with the facts. Fact is though, no matter how real it seemed- it could be just a dream. Danya thinks I should quit and move in with her. She doesn't like Claudius, thinks he's dangerous. That she has bad premonitions. That was a new one for me. I had no idea she felt this way. I didn't want to hear any of it. I love this job. It's my big chance. Besides I can't leave just after I started. Claudius and I have a deal, a verbal contract. Danya wasn't thrilled to hear what I had to say, but she dealt with it. She'll be back soon, we'll talk then. I need Danya, I love her, but Neverland is important too. I hope I never have to choose between my loves. Hopefully she won't worry about this the way she does sometimes- it was just a dream after all. It doesn't take a lot of sense to realize that nightmare and reality are a long ways apart. Besides it's not unusual to dream about your boss. My dream just had a little twist to it. I was warning myself to be careful.

September 1st, 10:P.M.
~~DANYA CALLED BACK. She wanted to talk more,~~
~~I was busy. It was our first fight. WHAT A BITCH!~~
~~where does she get off telling me what to do with my~~
~~life? NO ONE BUT ME HAS ANY SAY IN THAT.~~
~~NOT HER, NOT MY FATHER, NOT ANYONE.~~
~~THE HELL WITH HER.~~

10:43 P.M.
Calmer now. A bit. I'm pretty ashamed of
myself. I tried to call her back, but she's
out. I should have just ripped out the
page, but I can't do it. Be like ripping
out a page of my life.

If I can't be honest
with myself, then who
else can I trust?

God, I need to
apologize —
she hates me now.
Probably never wants
to see me again.

I feel like
shit.

NO

OH GOD OH GOD

WHY THIS

WHY Goddamn it

WHY THE HELL:

WHY?

I can still taste it in my mouth. I'm Hungry

September 2nd, 3:00 AM

It's not,

I'm so, so sorry

Why can't I be dead.

I want this to be over, Over will I never wake up. Sitting alone in my loft I pray that this just another bad dream and that I will wake up soon and no breath and everything will be all right come morning, soft sweet DANYA will be there she'll hold me and then over time I'll forget anything ever happened and it will be as if it never was, never, never was

I wonder if the God of my father, the God I have always denied, listens to the prayers of creatures like me.

I PRAY TO YOU NOW. Mr. GOD save me.

PLEASE SAVE ME.

5:23 a.m. I can't sleep. I can't think straight. But maybe I can write. Maybe I can make sense out of this - a glitch, a fault, a loop, a gaping hole in events that proves I'm insane. That would be better than this.

It started last night - I was feeling shitty after the fight with Danya. Hardly noticed it was midnight. Claudius summoned me to his office, with a note. A fucking note. He was waiting for me. With a fat Cheshire smile. Sat behind his huge mahogany desk, in a carved oak chair. Like a throne. I hadn't thought anything of it before.

Told me to sit. Told his bodyguards to bugger off. They locked the door behind them. Made me nervous. I didn't say anything. I trusted him. *FOOL*.

I just didn't like being alone with him.

Everything Danya said came back to me in a flash.

For a while he said nothing, just stared at me. Just staring with eyes like flames.

Then he started to talk, slowly at first, then faster, about how long he had waited for me, for how hellishly long he had searched, and looked, and waited. How he had to be just right, right breeding, right family, right innocence, right mind, right passion, right strength, right ambition, right stuff. And how perfect a son I would make. How perfect a child.

I thought he was comming on to me.

I didn't say anything,
I couldn't.
His eyes grew till they
were the size of coasters.
Engulfing me in fire
my head filled with smoke,
I was cast adrift in a
storm of thoughts,
few of them my own.
His voice was my only
anchor.

He talked of the past, of
an age long life, of
being born anew,
of joining a new family,
a new breed.

He talked of giving me the greatest gift in existence. He talked nonsense I only dimly understood.

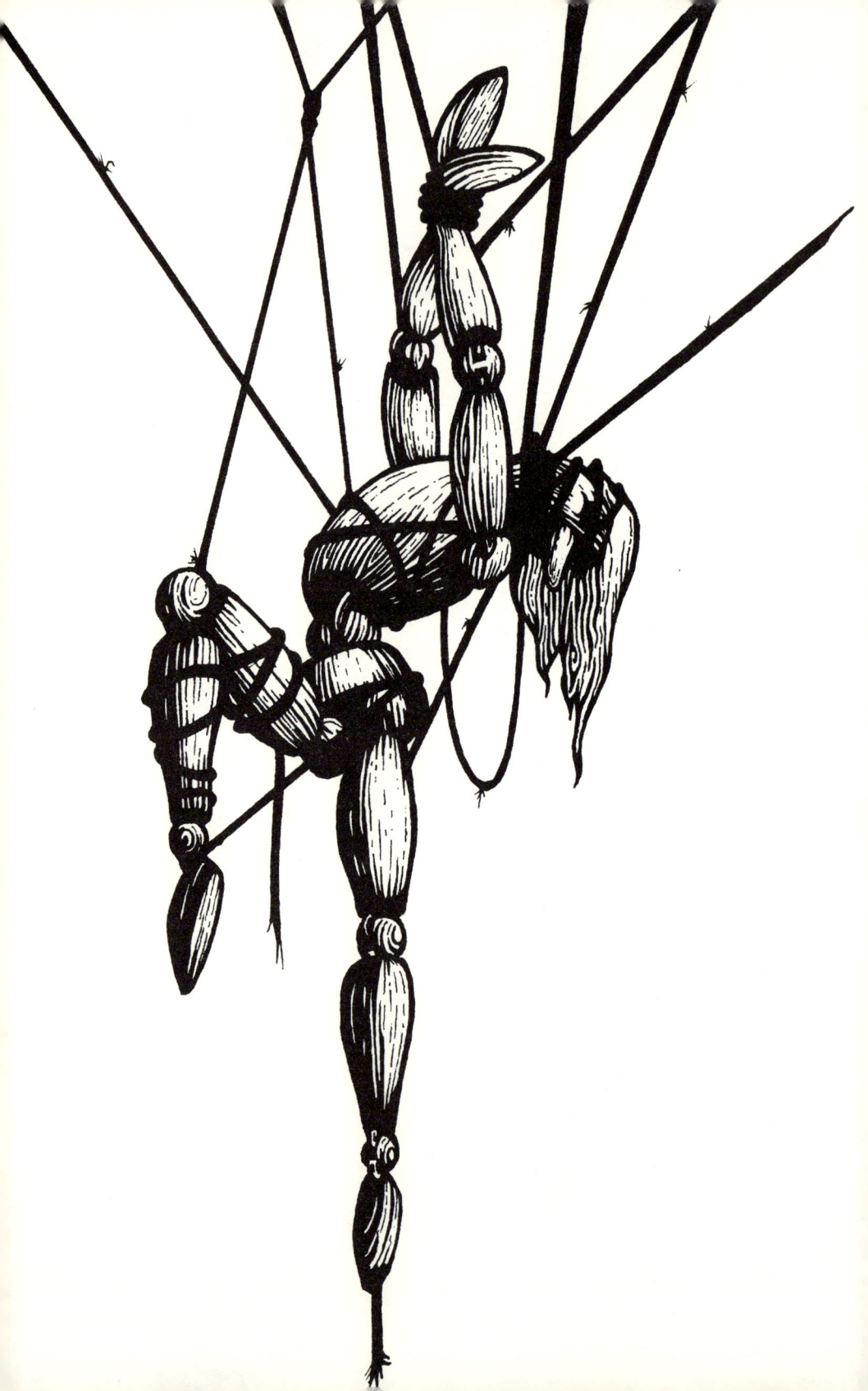

Finally he rose from his chair.
I was frozen in mine. He bid me to rise,
and like a puppet I did.

Dancing to his pipers tune.
His icy hands gripped me
by the shoulders and then
with

Oh GOD

then he sunk his teeth
Into my Neck.

The pain was horrible. Excruciating. Then it wasn't pain anymore. It was sex.

Forbidden sex — with a man. A blood right of passion. My mucles turned to jelly. My whole body quivered in ecstacy. If he hadn't held me so tightly, I would have fallen to the floor. I was a virgin vanquished, my blood, proof of my purity.

I was burning with desire, I wanted to be plundered, to be raped, I wanted it.

I liked it and thats the truth of it.

I could feel myself dying. I knew it. But I did give a fuck. I was like sex without a condom. Only the lust matters. Nothing existed except for the power and the passion. I was consumed by the exstacy as he consumed me.

After an eternity of black pleasure, darkness finally overwhelmed me. My mind plunged forward into an abyss from which there was no return. I teetered on the edge.

Anticipating the plunge.

Death beckoned me,
Not with a skeletal claw,
but with a warm tender hand.
The world retreated from me, all pain, all pleasure
gone.

A drop of molten fire seared my throat.
It was as if a burning poker had been thrust
into my mouth and stirred around. I was
chewing razor blades while swallowing battery acid.
I tried to scream, but my mouth was full.

The skin of my face crackled and
sizzled like bacon. My eyeballs exploded
in a gushing torrent of blood. I tried
to scream but no sound came forth. A
voice told me to drink deeply, and I did
I did gladly—
Stinging and salty like inside Danya
but I'm sorry—better.

And All I could think of was
the time Ben and I were climbing
the old giant oak at Nerstrand
Woods. We were way up, over 200 feet
And Ben was on the other side of the
trunk, looking for a new way up. Suddenly
there was a big cracking Noise And the branch
Ben was standing on broke loose AND plunged
to the ground — Ben Along with it. For a few seconds
I thought I had lost him. my brother dead
I was terror Stricken, Paniced, paralyzed
Then I heard a laugh — Ben
was hanging on a branch
higher up. swinging there in
the Air — just swinging —
And I had wanted to jump
Memory CAN play
such cruel tricks.
such twisted
timing.

So I drank.
And with EACH sip beame stronger.
The pain went away. I OPENED MY EYES.
I was in the chair. Claudius stood over me,
a red gash in his wrist. Blood was All over my face.
and hands. The smell was EVERYWHERE.
I gagged, and tried to PULL AWAY from him.
But couldn't. My WILL WAS not my own - BASTARD
I WAS HIS slave. He beGAN to speak, his
words penetrating my mind like the Groon of
A song. Words I CANNOT Forget, words I
CANNOT cast out.
HE NAMED The act. The EMBRACE. A sire creates
progeny, through the Bond of Blood. From
death into BIRth.
First CAME CAINE, Son of Adam, Slayer of ABEL.
Cursed by GOD. Cursed with eternal life, eterNAL
damnation, AND AN eternal Thirst. CAINE, the
progenitor. HE WANDERED Alone for An Eon, but
but At last he GREW Lonely. He CREATED progeny,
3 childeR - They in TURN CREATED 13 more.
THE NUMBERS RANG through my head like bells.

1.3.13 God the trinity. 13 At the table.

How much of what I have been taught, what my father believes without question, is actually a reflection of this acursed history? A world not of light, but of Darkness. Which reality is a reflection of the other. Where lies the truth? Where was GOD in all this?

But if this is true. If Cain really was the first then there is a GOD. Then he does exist.

And then I am most asuredly DAMNED.

The 13 of the 3rd sired the entire race. 13 clans, each the rival of the others. 13 clans manipulating history, human destiny, to their own ends. All of humanity the pawns of the Masters. Predators and sheep, sharing the same world.
Seven Laws. Traditions. Binding us together. Binding us as one. The first, the Masquerade. Do not let them know we exist. The second honor thy father, for he has given you eternal life. The third —

why does it matter

I am lost.

Its almost dawn, I must sleep.
This exhaustion hangs on me
like a stone.

8 p.m.
Sept. 3rd

I'm still out of it. Can't think. Just awoke from a really deep sleep. No Nightmares

And I don't know what to think. I don't know what to do. This book is my only escape.

Claudius spoke of his clan. He said we were of the Ventru line. We were, he said, the greatest and most powerful of the clans. He spoke of my duty to the clan, my obligations — and the power I would share with him as his child and heir. A privilege beyond any recompense —

I listened because I had no choice. His will compelled mine to pay attention. But all the time I was aware of a new hunger gnawing at my insides. Gnawing at my soul. An unnatural thirst. Ravenous and unstill. The desire was repulsive, yet it aroused me.

I wanted to feed.

Claudius saw this. And he said to me, "You must sate your hunger, it shall be your first test" then he rapped three times on the door with his cane.

The Nubian bodyguard walked in, holding some guy by the back of his neck. It was Kary. The little stiff looked a little beat up, and very dazed. In a high pitched voice he demanded to know why he had been brought here, and why was I here and not at work.

He was going to be terminated, Claudius said. His voice was flat and colder than a whore's heart. He had abused his authority, through a combination of greed and incompetance. Avarice, Claudius declared, he could forgive. It came with ambition but ineptitude was inexcusable.

Kary begged. He pleaded. He swore he'd do a better job. He promised he'd pay back every penny. Claudius only looked at him in contempt. I just kept my mouth shut. Sudenly I realized what was about to happen. What was expected of me. But I didn't care - I just wasn't thinking. I could only feel my hunger. Pity had no place in my heart. How could I have been so fucking weak - I hate this. I cant take it I cant take it.

Later...

Kary was on his knees by now. His hands clasped as if in prayer. Words tumbled out of him. Neverland was his life. Claudius was his master. He was a schmuck, yes, but he could change. I found him pathetic, every word only increased my hunger. A red mist began to cloud my vision. The terrible hunger rose up and enveloped me like a cloak. A beast rose up within me, and consumed my soul. The invisible bonds of will and volition dissolved like smoke. Reason vanished. And I leaped forward. He never realized what was coming. Not until I wrenched him to the ground. Screaming in pain, he flopped around like a fish caught on a line. I can't bear it...

I panted in frustration, my only thought was to tear at his neck with my teeth. Consumed with lust, I attacked him like a wild animal.

My fingers ripped at his skin. I tore away chunks of his face and dug deep furrows in his chest. Blood exploded from his wounds, adding to my madness. He went limp.

And then, I drank...

Blood filled my mouth. I sucked greedily at his throat. Like a child nursing at a mothers breast. Instinct consumed me. I didn't think, I felt. My mind was filled with images of the forest, of wolves running through the mist. Slowly, steadily, the crimson elixer flowed from his body into mine. It was the essence of lust, the fluid of a brutal sex. Better than the finest wine. Better than the best food. Yet this blood was not like Claudius's. This was wine, Claudius had been brandy. Perhaps this is why he required bodyguards. How old he really was, I could not imagine. When at last it was done, Claudius laughted. A harsh, mean sound, filled with no mirth. I had learned my first lesson he said. We paid a price for our immortality. The beast could not be controlled, only contained. The beast was our master, just as we were masters of the herd. Only then did I realize what I had become. Standing there, a dead man in my arms, drained of all life - by me. I understood finally how my world had changed forever.

I was no longer Auston Jacobson. What happened was irreversable. I had murdered a man. I was a killer. And I was no longer human. Everything my father had ever said about me had been proven true. The drug high ended faster than it came... and I crashed back to reality. I threw the body off of me, and stared at the blood on my hands. My thirst had not been completely quenched. It was still there. I knew then everything I needed to know. I wanted more blood. I craved the pleasure, though the need motivated me not. Claudius dismissed me. A wave of his hand, and I was told to take care of my unfinished business, and come back when I was done. I didn't know what he meant but I left. I staggered through the streets for hours. All night I wandered, until finally I found my way home. And here I am now. Alone. Struggling with what has happened to me. Fighting my hunger. My lust.

Pray God this is a dream.

But I'm a sinner. And there's no miracles for my kind.

September 4th, 4:00AM

I've been sitting here for hours. Fighting off the Hunger. I know what I must do.

I must not kill again. I am determined.

I will take only a little blood at a time. I will feed off animals if I must. I will starve myself, until I gain back some measure of my reason. The sharpness of my pain will guide me ... it will let me think

FUCK IT!

I am a monster. I have killed this is all too real. It is the undeniable truth. Knowing the truth leaves me with only one question.

September 6th 2:00 A.M. Temptation sings a siren song that I fight to ignore chirping in my ear - endlessly I've tried TV. but there's 50 channels and nothing on My CD collection doesn't have a thing in it that I feel

like hearing. I can't concentrate enough to read.
I can't do anything but sit here in silence.
My thoughts always return me to the blood. It doesn't
disgust me I crave it - the high - I'm a junkie
And they say it can't happen after just one hit.
Satan is tempting me. Just as he did Christ in the
wilderness. I must suffer mightily. Suffer for
what I did. Suffer till I see straight. See straight
I wish I could call Ben. Thank god Danya isn't in
town this would kill her every once in a while I'm
WRAKED IN PAIN MY WHOLE BODY
CONVULSES AND I GO FETAL

I think
I'm going
through
same

sort of
CHANGE.
I don't
WANT
TO THINK
ABOUT
IT.

Junkie
need blood like a
drug

SEPTEMBER 7th, 2:00 AM.

I DON'T NEED FOOD ANYMORE. ACTUALLY,
I CAN'T TOLERATE IT. NOT EVEN HAMBURGER.
EVEN WATER. OR SLEEP OTHER THAN THE
COMA THAT ENGULFS ME WHENEVER THE
SUN RISES.

BUT I CAN STILL FEEL PAIN
EACH NIGHT IT GETS WORSE
BUT ITS GOOD, GOOD FOR ME.
I'M BEING PURIFIED BY IT.

THE PHONE RINGS SOMETIMES,
BUT I IGNORE IT. IT'S DAD,
CALLING TO TELL ME I'M
GOING TO HELL.

I CAN'T TALK TO ANYONE,
I CAN'T TALK AT ALL.
I WANT TO BECOME MUTE.
I WANT TO HOLD ALL THE PAIN
INSIDE ME.

I'VE DECIDED I WANT
TO BE CREMATED.

I SLEEP IN THE BATHTUB.
TO AVOID THE LIGHT. THE SUN
BURNS, EVEN A TINY GLIMPSE
OF IT. I WAS BLINDED FOR
HOURS LAST NIGHT. I HATE
THE LIGHT, I HATE IT.

ITS GETTING DIFFICULT TO WRITE.
I'M LOSING IT. THE WORDS GIVE
ME A BRIEF HOLD ON SANITY - MY
ONE LAST LIFELINE TO MY LIFE,
TO MY PAST.

I'VE BEEN READING
THE PART ABOUT DANYA
AND ME ON THE BEACH
OVER AND OVER
AGAIN.
I WANT HER.

BUT SOMETIMES I FORGET
THATS WHY I NEED THESE WORDS
GOTTA WRITE
GOTTA Write.

My will is stronger than this hunger

I shall overcome   I am MY DRUG

I AM MY MASTER.
OWN
MASTER

I AM MY DRUG

September sometime?

I've smashed the goddamn clock. Ticking was driving me MAD and I DON'T want to go crazy...

Watching the hands creep by. second by second. Minute by minute, hour by hour was unbearable. NOW I'm free of it. I feel good

VERY VERY GOOD

I love you
DANYA
wake me up
Please

I am my
own
master
I AM MY OWN MASTER.

The PAIN IS getting WORSE.
DESERVE IT.

Yep DESERVE it.
I deserve Nothing. not even
MY OWN Pity. I WON'T EVEN give
Myself that
POOR Fucking KARY

I MUST NOT DRINK
AGAIN NEVER

NEVER ' ' '

NEVER

I AM MY OWN MASTER   i ▶

September
Nth Day of Hell

I AM
OWN -

PLEASE GOD NO NO NO N

she's dead.

By these hands

even the tears are red.

Last day of hell.

Why oh why,
oh why did she
have to come

I heard the knock. Thought I was halucinating
again. I was huddled over in the corner, my arms
wrapped about me, when she walked in. Had a key.
        I had forgotten that. I had forgotten
                a lot of things.
She walked in softly. I didn't think it was real.
    Then I smelled her, it woke me up.
Only a bare shell of me remained, all else was the
beast. It had swallowed me.
    Even with my eyes shut I knew it was her. Only
she could smell that good, only she would have blood
that fresh. The red mist rose up over me.

WHY i have blood on my hands, worse than 2nd roman
             govenor, worse than any serial killer
          i murdered my lover, and then i drank her blood
              i played in it.

    In the darkness, it took her a while to see me.
Her cry of horror broke through the walls I had
carefully built, brick by brick around my soul.
Over and over she sobbed my name, Auston Auston
Auston AUSton auSTON.
 she thought me dead.
Through the red I recognized her
voice. I awakened more, and rose up.
Then I realized the danger she was in.
Summoning what little strength
I had left, I snarled at her.
I told her to go, to leave me
alone. I ordered her out of
my loft, out of my life. I
said I didn't want to see her again, ever, that I
hated her.
But she wouldn't listen. She stepped toward me,

arms outstretched. She was so beautiful. Her form was framed in the light from the stairway. She was wearing the sundress from the beach. She carried a small envelope in one hand.

The beast howled, it bellowed, it roared in unholy rage. Danya was beautiful. She was tender and innocent. The love she felt for me was precious. But it didn't matter. The blood was the thing.

She didn't know what Claudius had done to me she said. Drugs, brainwashing, whatever — she could deal with it. She loved me, and knew I loved her. Unafraid, she inched closer. And closer. And closer.

I clenched my hands together so tightly I bled. I trembled with desire and fear. I knew I had to tell her the truth. She had to be warned, I had to set her free. I had to get her away from here, away from Claudius. Away from me. Her scent was driving me mad. Pushing me over the brink. I opened my mouth to speak. To blurt out the horrid truth, when she reached out and gently touched my cheek. I recoiled in shock. The warmth of her fingers, of her affection, burned my skin.

I could smell the blood beneath her skin. She shuddered, but did not pull back. For minutes we stood there motionless. Then she kissed me. The beast bellowed in triumph.

What happened next I cannot ——

The anguish is with me still. Not all agonies are that of the flesh. I have inflicted this pain on myself.

I feasted on the lifeblood of this woman who had come to save me. Holding her tightly in my arms, in cruel mockery of a lovers embrace, I drank deeply. Her blood was more wonderous than my own Sire's.

I reveled in her death, it gave me pleasure.

She died in my arms. At least we had that HAA.
But it need not have been the end. We could be
reunited. In death if not in life. A few drops
of my blood on her tongue would bring her back.
Back to me.

But it could not be. That thought I banished from
my mind. Danya was a creature of life, not death. She
would not think it a kindness. She would not
think of me as a savior. I had to let her rest
in peace.

It would be only for me that I would reincarnate
her. And she would hate me for it.

I could not condemn her to my fate.
Better a pure, simple, and short life than an
eternity of torment.

She died in my arms.

when it was done, I went to the bathroom and attempted to vomit up my meal. But to no avail. Her essence warmed my whole body. I covered the whole bathroom with paw prints of lust.

I sat for hours, sobbing to myself. Her body in the next room. But it didn't bring her back.

Then I remembered the envelope she brought with her. I searched the loft until I found it. Inside were two bus tickets to Minnesota. She was going to take me home.

I have no home anymore. No one will take in a creature such as me. They hunt things like me, or scare us away with fireworks.

The beast is still inside me. I have killed twice. I can kill again. I must stop this insanity.

The guilt of this will never leave me. And I cannot live with it. There is only one way out.

LATER

MY THOUGHTS ARE LUCID, I UNDERSTAND NOW WHAT I MUST DO. MY PATH IS CLEAR.

I'M GOING TO FINISH WITH THE DIARY, AND SEND IT OFF TO BEN. I COULD'N'T LEAVE WITHOUT SAYING GOODBYE, WITHOUT AN EXPLAINATION. WITHOUT A WARNING.

I HOPE DAD GIVES THE PACKAGE TO BEN. I WON'T PUT MY NAME ON IT.

I ALWAYS THOUGHT THAT SUICIDE WAS THE COWARDS WAY OUT. BUT WHAT TO MAKE OF IT WHEN YOU'RE ALREADY DEAD. WHAT TO MAKE OF IT WHEN YOU'RE A KILLER.

I SHALL BE MY OWN EXECUTIONER.

ALL I KNOW IS THAT I CAN'T CONTINUE LIKE THIS.

IN A FEW HOURS I'LL BE WITH DANYA AGAIN.

MY LITTLE STAR.

I'LL GO TO THE BEACH TO BE WITH HER.

I SHALL WATCH THE SUN RISE.

SHE WILL WARM ME,

AND THEN SHE WILL BURN ME UP.

I LOOK FORWARD TO IT.

GOD GRANT THAT I REST IN PEACE

FAREWELL

Ben is here in L.A.
at the club.
Claudius musn't get
his hands on him
I can't go now.

The Sacred Laws of the Wendigo

Gaia is the earth, your mother; from her womb springs all living things. Gaia is your mother, protect her with your life.

When you awake in the morning, give thanks to Gaia for all that you see. Give thanks for the air you breathe, the water you drink, and the food that you eat.

Respect your elders, for they are the keepers of sacred wisdom and knowledge. Speak softly in their presence, lest you offend their ears.

Love all Wendigo as you would love your brother or your sister. We are all one family. One tribe.

Great is the warrior who places his people before himself. Take care of the weak, the sick, the old, and the helpless. Never eat when others go hungry. Never allow yourself to be warm when others are cold.

Always be truthful; be a person of your word. Never break a promise that you have made to another. No matter what.

Do not touch alcohol or drugs, for they are the blackness that robs the spirit of its vision. Instead seek guidance in the sweatlodge, and through the vision quest.

Touch no Garou's medicine but your own. Such things are dangerous.

Be not afraid of death in battle. A warrior dies but once, while a coward will die a thousand times.

Do not speak of the dead except to recall their good deeds. Give your children the names of your parents, grandparents, and ancestors so they will live forever.

Garou do not mate with Garou, that is the law. The children of such corrupt unions bring no honor to the tribe.

Never forget that the Wyrm is your enemy. You must do battle with those of the Wyrm whenever and wherever you meet.

OWL GOINGBACK

Shaman Moon

BY OWL GOINGBACK

PART I

*To us the ashes of our ancestors are sacred
and their resting place is hallowed ground.*
—Seattle, Chief of the Dwamish

1

Night had come once again to the mountains of North Carolina. Cool darkness lay over the land like a blanket, broken only by the twinkling of stars and the soft glow of a first-quarter moon.

Heather Ocoee stood in a tiny clearing deep within the forest and welcomed the darkness, feeling the cool breeze wash over her skin. She hurried to remove her shoes, blue jeans, T-Shirt and underwear, for she wanted nothing to come between her and the night. Nothing at all. She stood there, naked except for a tiny leather pouch that hung from the cord around her neck, taking deep breaths, filling her lungs with the darkness.

Glancing down at her body, she laughed. At twelve years of age, Heather was just beginning to physically develop into a woman. Her breasts were small, almost nonexistent, her legs still the knobby-kneed limbs of a child. Even so, in the last six months she had spiritually and mentally matured more than most women would in their entire lifetime.

A tremor of excitement passed through the girl, causing her arms and legs to break out in quivering gooseflesh. "Not yet," she told herself, keeping her newly acquired gift in check. "Savor the moment. There is still plenty of time."

Up until seven months ago, her life had been the miserable existence of a lonely orphan. Shuffled about from one foster home to another, she had been considered little more than a servant to some people, an additional income from the government to others. Adoption had never been an option, not even when she was an infant. People didn't want children of interracial parents. Heather's long black hair and olive complexion was a dead giveaway that she was of mixed blood, half white and half something else. Mexican maybe. Or Indian.

Heather wished she knew more about her parents, but she didn't. The state of California had sealed all her records, denying a little girl even a brief glimpse into her past. All she knew was that her parents had been killed while she was still just an infant; she had been found in a trash bin a few blocks away from their bodies. She would never know the names of her mother and father, who they had been, or even what they had looked like. Nor would she ever know if she had a brother, or a sister, or even an aunt and uncle.

Hardly a day went by that she didn't think about her parents. Who were they? How had they lived? And why had they both been killed? Was their murder drug-related? Had they been gunned down during a deal gone bad? She had seen similar things reported so many times on the evening news. Or was robbery the motive? Had her mother and father been innocent victims, shot in cold blood for a few lousy dollars? The not-knowing was the hardest part.

If only someone would have told her about her real family she might not have resented her foster parents so much, running away at each and every opportunity. It wasn't that they had all been mean to her, though many of them had. She just didn't belong in a foster home—they weren't her real parents—no matter how nice the people were. After running away from her fourth set of foster parents in three years, the state of California had labelled Heather a troublemaker and placed her in the care of an orphanage. At the time, she hadn't thought anything could be worse than being in the foster care program. But she was wrong. Very wrong.

The Pentex Home for Girls was more of a prison than an orphanage. Located in San Francisco's poorest neighborhood, the three-story brick building was surrounded by a cyclone fence topped with three strands of razor wire. In addition to being infested with rats the size of alley cats, the orphanage lacked air conditioning and barely had any heat in the winter time. What little heat it did have rattled and whistled through an assemblage of twisting pipes and ducts that hung from the ceiling, sounding like the dying gasps of an elderly man in an iron lung.

Long, darkened hallways stretched past wooden doors opening onto rooms crowded with metal bunk beds. Some of the rooms didn't even have beds; the kids forced to sleep on the moldy carpeting, fighting for floor space with the cockroaches and spiders. The ceiling also leaked whenever it rained, staining the acoustic tiles a deep brown and leaving streaks down the faded floral wallpaper.

Margaret Zimbraw ran the orphanage. She was a tall, thin woman with a permanent scowl etched upon her face. The kids all called her the Iron Maiden, but only behind her back—and then only in carefully guarded whispers. Such insults spoken openly always resulted in a swift and very painful punishment. Margaret carried with her at all times a jockey's riding crop, which she would gleefully apply to the back and buttocks of a naughty girl. And it was never just one swat or two. Instead she would have two of the older girls, her personal goons, hold the offender while she used the riding crop over and over again until blood was drawn.

During such malicious punishments was the only time any of them ever saw Margaret smile. She seemed to take great delight in seeing a screaming child twitch and jump like a frog under the fiery pain of her riding crop. With each stroke she would call the child a name: "Bitch, whore, slut," gradually building up the intensity of the beating until blood flowed and the victim was left limp and near lifeless.

OWL GOINGBACK

To make matters worse, the punishments were always carried out in front of the other girls so they too might enjoy witnessing the suffering of one of their comrades. The child who laughed and cheered the loudest was often rewarded with a lighter workload the following day. Those who cried or hid their eyes usually ended up scrubbing the toilets in the bathrooms.

Maybe it was because they were forced to watch such hideous acts of violence. Maybe it was because of Margaret's sick and twisted reward system. Either way, many of the older girls became the Iron Maiden's obedient servants. They served as her eyes and ears, informing on those who didn't carry out their specific duties to the letter. To reward these "goons" for their servitude, Margaret often allowed the older girls to help out with the punishments, passing the riding crop to them so they too could spank the offending child.

But a few swats with a riding crop now and then was never enough for the goon squad. At night, when the lights were out and everyone was in bed, they would band together to inflict their own form of punishment on any girl who had met with their displeasure earlier in the day. Waiting until their victim was asleep, they would sneak into the room and throw a blanket over the helpless child's head. While two goons held the blanket tight against the bed, keeping their victim from sitting up or escaping, the others would hit her with their fists or pieces of rubber hose.

Many a girl was left black and blue by such a beating. Some even suffered broken bones. But no matter how serious their injury, they were never hospitalized. Hospitals meant medical reports and doctors; questions would be asked. Instead they were treated by an elderly physician hired by the Pentex Company, a dirty old man who took great delight in touching little girls where they should not be touched.

Heather had arrived at the orphanage on a Tuesday morning. By Friday evening of the same week she had already received two beatings for minor rule infractions. She quickly learned that the key to survival in the orphanage was not to draw attention to herself. Becoming little more than a nameless face in the crowd, she accepted the endless workload of scrubbing walls and floors and scouring kitchen pots with a silent resignation. But her anonymity ended two months later when the dreams began.

At first she thought the dreams were the result of her dreadful environment, but they were always the same, night after night. In her dreams, Heather saw herself running through a forest at nighttime, bathed in the silvery light of a full moon. She was never alone in her nocturnal visions, for with her ran several wolves. Large, powerful wolves, with thick fur and bushy tails and eyes that seemed to glow in the darkness.

She wasn't afraid of the wolves in her dreams. On the contrary, their sudden appearance from the shadows of the forest seemed to reassure her, give her strength. More than anything she wanted to run with them, play with them, even hunt with them. For the first time in her life she felt like she belonged.

Unfortunately, the happiness she experienced with the wolves never lasted. Something else stalked the forest in Heather's dreams; a foul, loathsome thing that was never seen but felt nonetheless, something so utterly horrifying it caused her to thrash about in her bed and awake screaming.

Because of the recurring dreams, because of the screams, Heather suffered the ridicule of her fellow orphans and the wrath of the goons. She was forced to scrub more floors than anyone else, even made to sleep by herself in the rat-infested basement. But no matter what the other girls did to her, or how hard she prayed for the dreams to stop, the nightly visions continued to haunt her sleep.

Along with the dreams came a terrible nausea that would strike without warning, leaving Heather sick to her stomach and trembling. When the nausea hit, which was almost daily, she was unable to tolerate the taste of most foods. Even the smell of the people around her turned her stomach. Unable to eat, she lost weight and grew weaker, making her that much more of a target for the bigger girls.

Not all of the older girls in the orphanage were monsters, but most were. One who wasn't a monster was Maria Alvarez. Maria was a Mexican girl who had spent her whole life in orphanages and homes for troubled children. She was from one of San Francisco's most notorious neighborhoods, the result of a one-night stand between a prostitute and a gangster. At sixteen years of age she was probably the toughest girl in the orphanage, which was why Margaret's goon squad left her alone. She was tough, but she wasn't mean or cruel like the others. She was also Heather's only friend.

They hadn't started out as friends. Though they knew each other by sight, they had never spoken. But one day Heather spotted Maria coming out of a small, little-used storeroom on the third floor, a place definitely off limits to the girls. Heather could have told on the other girl, which was the encouraged practice at the orphanage, but she kept her mouth shut. Two days later Maria cornered her in the hallway.

"Why didn't you tell on me?" Maria asked, sizing Heather up. There was no question about who would win in a fight. Maria was a foot taller and probably outweighed her by thirty pounds. She was also a hell of a lot stronger, as well as being a more experienced fighter.

"Why should I care what you do?" Heather said, starting to turn away.

Maria grabbed her by the shoulder and spun her back around. Heather thought she was going to be punched, but the feisty Mexican girl just smiled. "I like you. You know how to keep your mouth shut." She glanced around. "Not like the other snitches in this place. What's your name?"

"Heather Ocoee."

"Ocoee? Is that Spanish? Are you Mexican?"

Heather shrugged. "I'm not sure. I never knew my parents."

Maria looked at her closely. "Well, it might be Spanish. You look like you might have a little 'home girl' in you. Maybe you're Indian; it's really all the same." She smiled and stuck out her hand. "My name's Maria Alvarez."

Heather shook the hand offered her. Maria glanced around again and whispered, "You know that room you saw me coming out of?"

Heather nodded, knowing that Maria was about to tell her a secret. She was delighted someone actually trusted her that much.

"Good," Maria smiled. "Meet me there after dinner."

"But I'm supposed to be doing the windows," Heather argued.

"No problem. Just do the windows on the third floor. See you then," Maria said, walking away.

That night after dinner, Heather carried a bucket of soapy water up to the third floor. Making sure no one was around, she hurried down the hallway to the storeroom she had seen Maria coming out of. The door was locked, so she knocked softly. She was just about to hurry away when the knob turned and the door opened.

Maria stood in the doorway, a smile of mischief upon her face. Ushering Heather inside, she closed and locked the door behind her. Except for a set of wooden shelves that held a few dusty paint cans, the storeroom was empty. Opposite the shelves was a narrow window covered with four rusty iron bars. One of the panes of glass in the window was missing, allowing fresh air to enter the room. Heather spotted a crumpled pack of Marlboros and a book of matches on the window's ledge and knew what the room was being used for.

"Do you smoke?" Maria asked, picking up the pack.

Heather shook her head.

"Then now's a good time to learn."

Heather accepted one of the filtered cigarettes offered her, the act sealing a bond of friendship between the two girls. Now they were both committing a punishable act, so from this moment on a certain kind of loyalty would exist between them. Lighting the end of her cigarette off a match, Heather inhaled deeply and coughed.

"Shhh…" Maria warned. "Someone will hear you. And be sure to blow the smoke out the window." Heather covered her mouth with her hand and nodded, waiting until the coughing subsided before removing it. She noticed Maria had placed an old towel against the bottom of the door to keep the cigarette smell from drifting out into the hallway.

"How long have you been doing this?" Heather asked, finally able to speak again.

"Not long," Maria answered, taking a long drag on her cigarette. "It's too hard to find smokes."

"Where'd you find these?"

"I stole them out of the Iron Maiden's desk."

Heather nearly choked again. "You stole these from Margaret? How'd you do that?"

"Simple," Maria answered. "I waited until no one was around, then pried her desk drawer open with a screwdriver."

"Aren't you afraid of getting caught?"

"Naw. She had several packs; she probably won't notice one missing."

"But what are you going to do when you run out?"

Maria grinned. "I'll steal another pack."

And Maria did steal another pack. Several packs, as a matter of fact. And during the course of the next couple of months, Heather learned how to smoke cigarettes like a professional. She also learned how to cover the smell of tobacco smoke on her breath by swishing a mouthful of PineSol and then spitting into a cleaning bucket. It tasted awful, but it was better than getting busted for smoking.

As Heather's smoking skills increased, so too did her friendship with Maria. They each looked forward to their meetings in the storeroom, sneaking away only when they were absolutely certain they would not be missed. Over glowing cigarettes, they discussed their hopes and dreams, and their fear of being disciplined by Margaret's riding crop.

During one such rendezvous, Maria showed Heather how one of the bars covering the window was loose at the bottom. She wiggled the bar back and forth, promising that one day she would loosen it enough to escape from the orphanage. The storeroom was on the third floor, but the branch of a large oak tree ran just below the window. A second branch stretched over the fence. Unfortunately, Maria's planned escape would not happen until she managed to spread the bars far enough apart to squeeze through.

Making sure the loose bar was once again straight, Maria hid her cigarettes and matches in one of the empty paint cans and opened the door. They had just stepped into the hallway when two of Margaret's goons came around the corner.

"Oh, shit," Maria whispered, seeing Margaret's watch dogs.

They were caught. The goons would want to know what the two of them were doing in the storeroom. Lying wouldn't help. If the older girls entered the room, they would smell the lingering odor of cigarette smoke and know exactly what Heather and Maria were up to.

Heather was absolutely frozen with fear, visions of being beaten in front of the other children flashing through her mind. She wanted to come up with an excuse, something halfway believable. But before she could think of anything to say, Maria turned suddenly and kissed her full on the mouth.

"I'll see you later, lover," Maria said, stepping back and giving Heather a smile. She turned and winked at the other girls and then walked away with an exaggerated swing of her hips. Heather was left alone in the hallway with the goons, but they didn't even seem to notice her. Instead they watched Maria walk away, and then beat a hasty retreat back the way they had come.

Maria's quick thinking had caught the goons by surprise. So shocked by what they had seen, the girls completely forgot to check the storeroom to find out what was going on. Maria was no lesbian, but her kiss had saved the two of them from the goons and possibly from a severe beating. Unfortunately, the reprieve was only temporary.

They came for Maria later that night. Five of Margaret's biggest goons attacked her while she was sleeping. Heather heard the noise coming from the next room and quickly jumped out of bed. Inching the door open, she watched in horror as the goons carried her friend's limp body downstairs.

Knowing she would be punished if caught out of her room at night, Heather slipped on her clothes and hurried down the hallway in pursuit of the others. Her heart pounding in fear, she expected to be stopped at any moment. But the hallway was deserted, as were the stairs and the ground floor of the orphanage.

Where did they go? Where did they take her?

Heather tiptoed quietly to the other end of the building, clinging to the shadows when possible, hurrying across the brightly lit areas when not. She placed her ear against the door to Margaret's office, but heard nothing on the other side. Maria had been taken somewhere else.

Where then? Where? Where would they take someone to punish them?

The basement. Of course. They would put Maria in the darkness with the rats, as they had done several times to Heather.

Hurrying back to the opposite end of the building, she quietly approached the door that opened onto the concrete steps leading down into the dark and smelly basement. She was surprised to see the door standing ajar; Maria must not have been locked in the basement after all.

Heather was just about to turn away, when she heard a long, drawn-out scream; a cry of pain so terrifying it turned her bowels to ice and sent waves of chills racing down her spine. A voice followed the scream, the strangled voice of a teenage girl pleading for mercy. Maria's voice.

"No. No. No. Please, God. No. It was nothing. I swear it."

Heather slipped through the open doorway and started slowly down the steps, staying in the shadows. She was terrified beyond words, but she had to find out what was going on. Maria was her best friend, her only friend.

She paused as a second voice drifted up from the darkness, bringing even more chills than the scream. It was Margaret's voice.

"So you like other girls, do you, bitch? Well, we'll see about that. You pathetic slut. You whore."

Heather descended another step and stopped, frozen by what she saw. The scene below her was so unbelievably frightening it appeared unreal, like a vision from the dreams of a madman.

Maria was in the center of the room, completely naked, held spread-eagled by five goons. Basked in the amber glow of a single light bulb, her face and body were a mass of cuts and bruises from the beating she had taken. Heather took in the entire scene in an instant, her gaze locking on the woman who stood between Maria's legs, and the object that she held.

Margaret Zimbraw was dressed in a long, flowing black robe, like a witch from a bad Hollywood movie. But this was no movie; the terror and pain she was inflicting on the girl before her was very real. In her right hand, Margaret held what looked to be a flesh-colored baton, its tip wet with fresh blood.

Heather gasped when she saw the object, for she knew what it was. She had found a similar item, only much smaller, hidden in the nightstand of a former foster parent. It was a plastic penis, a dildo, something to take the place of the real thing when the real thing could not be found. Some said it was an object for pleasure, but the device Margaret held was being used to inflict pain.

"So you want to have sex with girls. Do you?" Margaret asked, the corner of her mouth turning up in a sneer. "Good. Then have sex with me."

Maria screamed as the Iron Maiden rammed the plastic penis inside her, twisting, shoving, tearing, and drawing blood. The blood ran bright red from inside her, dripping from between her legs to the floor. Heather saw the droplets of blood fall to the floor, landing in the center of a white chalk drawing. She hadn't noticed the drawing before, but now her eyes were drawn to it. It was a five-pointed star within a circle. A pentagram. The symbol for the Dark One.

Heather stared at the pentagram in horror, suddenly realizing that the abuse and torture she was witnessing were part of a more elaborate ritual. An evil ritual. Maria's suffering and blood were being used to appease the lord of darkness. A gift to a dark god from his humble servants. Heather was so horrified by what she saw, she almost didn't hear what Margaret said next:

"And when I'm done with you, I'll do the same to your filthy lover."

Heather's head shot up, the trance broken. Lover? What lover? Maria had no lover; she wasn't even gay. They could only be talking about her. The kiss that Maria had planted on her lips to keep them from getting into trouble for smoking had brought upon them a far worse punishment.

Heather nearly fainted when she realized that it would be her turn next. As it was, she had to clamp her hand tightly over her mouth to keep from screaming. Grabbing the bannister with her other hand, she turned and fled back up the stairs. Her mind clouded with fear, she moved less cautiously than she should have, crashing into the partially opened door and banging it against the wall. The sound echoed into the basement, alerting the others that their little ceremony had been seen.

"Who was that? Who's there?" Margaret yelled, her voice a scream of anger. "Get her! Get the little bitch!"

There was no reason to move cautiously now. She had been caught. Instead Heather ran through the building as fast as she could, looking for a place to hide or a way out. From behind her came shouts and the crashing footfalls of those who pursued her.

Run. Run. Run.

All the doors she tried on the bottom floor were locked, so she started up the stairs to the second level. She thought about hiding in her bed, but quickly dismissed the idea. The other kids would probably take great delight in telling on her. Even if they didn't, she would never be able to slow her breathing, or calm her wildly beating heart, before the goons came around checking from bed to bed. She would be discovered and taken to the basement. Begging for mercy would not help, for none would be given. Since hiding in bed was out of the question, her only hope was to escape the orphanage. She had to get out. Now.

Heather passed the second floor and continued up the stairs to the third. Reaching the top level, she raced down the hallway to the storeroom. Luckily, the door was still unlocked. Entering the room and locking the door behind her, she grabbed an empty paint can and hurried to the window.

Using the paint can to knock the remaining glass out of the window, she grabbed the loose bar and pushed it as far to the right as it would go. The space between the bars was too narrow for Maria to squeeze through, but it was not too narrow for Heather. Climbing up into the open window, she slowly squeezed herself between the bars.

Heather had just gotten her head through the bars when she heard shouts. The goons had reached the third floor and were starting down the hallways, checking doors as they went. It was only a matter of time—a matter of mere moments—before someone unlocked the door and found her attempting to escape. She was out of time.

Taking a deep breath, she exhaled all the air from her lungs and squeezed her upper body through the opening. Her hips and legs came next. Once through, she stepped carefully from the window sill to the branch of the oak tree which hung closest to the building. Crawling along the branch, she circled the tree's trunk and then crept carefully along another branch that hung out over the fence.

She had just reached the fence when the faces of several girls appeared in the open window of the storeroom. The goons stared in wide-eyed wonderment as Heather dropped from the branch to the sidewalk on the other side of the fence. Pausing long enough to flip her pursuers the bird, she turned and ran off into the night.

Heather Ocoee had managed to escape the terrors and dangers of the orphanage, but life on the streets wasn't much better. San Francisco was a city filled with thieves, murderers, rapists and other vile denizens who made their living preying upon the innocent. Heather had to remain constantly on guard, or she too would end up as a victim. It didn't help that her nights continued to be haunted by strange dreams, her days filled with sickness and nausea.

Two weeks after her escape, while using an old newspaper in a vain effort to keep dry from the rain, she spotted a small article about a suicide at the Pentex Home for Girls. Just a couple of paragraphs on the back page about a troubled teenager who had hung herself in the basement late one night—a teenager who supposedly had a history of violent behavior toward others. Heather cried when she saw Maria's name and read the lies told about it. The newspaper called it a suicide, but Heather knew that her friend had been murdered.

Afraid she might be picked up by the police and returned to the orphanage, delivered to a fate she dared not even think about, Heather decided to get out of the city. She wanted to put as much distance as possible between herself and the Pentex Home for Girls. But no matter how far she ran, she couldn't escape the memories that haunted her. Nor could she escape the dreams, or the nausea, which had become such a big part of her life.

Even in the country there were smells that made her sick: the sharp metallic scent of toxic chemicals oozing up through the ground from illegal dump sites, the obnoxious oily odor of car exhaust which coated the highways and dirt roads, and the foul, loathsome scent of beer cans and cigarette butts tossed from the windows of speeding vehicles. They were the smells of people, and each and every one of them made her want to puke.

Late one night on a deserted country road, during yet another spasm of nausea, she had been attacked by a hideous creature with the puny, pallid body of a man and an oversized head like a wrinkled pumpkin.

The creature was a Banth, a servant of the Wyrm. She might have died that night had it not been for Sam Nakai. He had saved her life from the Banth and the Black Spiral Dancers who chased her. Sam had also explained to her why she was having strange dreams and attacks of nausea, opening her eyes to who and what she really was.

That was six months ago. Heather Ocoee now stood naked in the tiny clearing, her body bathed in streams of shimmering moonlight. The wind caressed her skin, causing her to shiver slightly, helping to build the excitement. She smiled. Sam Nakai had lifted the veil from her eyes, showing her she was different on the inside from most people. Very different. She was Garou.

Now, she thought, unable to endure the waiting any longer. *Now.*

With bare feet firmly planted on Gaia, Heather stretched her arms overhead, reaching toward the night sky, reaching for the moon. She let down the mental guard which kept her other self bottled up inside, welcoming the change.

"Now!" she cried. A tingling of energy swept through her body like a thousand tiny fingers, seizing her mind in an orgasmic embrace.

Throwing her head back, Heather screamed with pleasure as hair sprouted from her arms and shoulders, cascading like a waterfall down her back. Long, luxurious gray hair. The hair grew thicker and became fur. The fur of a wolf.

Now. Now. Now.

The muscles in Heather's arms and legs quivered like live electrical wires as her body began to transform. Cracking and popping like pistol shots, the bones in her spine began to reshape themselves to her new form.

She fell forward as her arms and legs shortened, watching as her hands slowly made the change from human to werewolf, and finally into the padded paws of a wolf. Tonight she would travel in Lupus form, as a wolf, for she wanted to run close to the ground, taking in the sweet smells of Gaia. Tonight she would be as one with her brothers and sisters of the forest.

Heather shook her head from side to side and stretched her neck as her jaws lengthened and narrowed, becoming the jaws and snout of a wolf. Taking a deep breath, she detected a thousand smells that had gone unnoticed only moments before. The scents of animals and humans were carried on the night wind, bringing with them stories of fear, anger, pain and love.

She sniffed again and closed her eyes. When she opened them again the night had changed. The world was no longer dark, but bright as it was during the day. She now saw the forest through the eyes of a wolf, an exciting world of motion just waiting to be explored.

Closing her eyes once more, she experienced a maddening itch as her ears lengthened and reshaped themselves. Suddenly, the night erupted into a symphony of sounds. Twitching her left ear, Heather heard the songs of crickets, frogs, the hunting cry of an owl, and the lonesome whine of a semi-truck climbing a distant mountain highway. She twitched her right ear and heard the babble of a tiny stream, the rustle of leaves, the whisper of the wind, and the sacred promises of spirits.

Heather Ocoee opened her eyes. The transformation was complete. She was no longer a girl of twelve, no longer a human. Instead she was Garou, a wolf, known to her people as Wa Ya Ny Wa Ti, Medicine Wolf, Guardian of the Fang.

Flexing her muscles, Heather threw back her head and howled. And then she ran to join the night.

2

Sam Nakai sat on a lonely mountain top, staring into the flickering flames of a tiny campfire. Suddenly from the valley below came the long, eerie howl of a wolf. He looked up and smiled, the image of the teenage girl who made the howl flashing through his mind. Heather Ocoee ran with the animals and the spirits of the forest, basking in the many joys of Gaia. He longed to join her, to slip free of his human form and let the wolf in him emerge once again, but he could not. Not tonight.

The smile left his weathered face, replaced by a frown of concern. He sniffed. There was something on the night wind, something not quite right. A smell. A feeling. Maybe even a premonition of things to come. Bad things. At first Sam thought he was detecting the corruption of the Wyrm, for few places remained where the evil one had not touched. Even in the sacred homeland of the Cherokee, the Wyrm had made its presence known.

The Wyrm's corruption was carried on the wind, in the form of pollution from the factories of the big cities, and in the poisons that fouled the streams and rivers which once had run clear. Its vile darkness could also be found in the hearts of those that dumped their garbage and toxic chemicals deep in the forest, and in the glassy-eyed stares of the people who sold their souls to the demons of alcohol and drugs. Sam had spent over fifty years of his life battling the Wyrm and knew its many disguises and tricks. The scars that lined his face and body, and the black patch that covered his sightless left eye, were testimony that not all of his battles had been easily fought.

Leaning forward, Sam opened his backpack and removed his beaded medicine bag. Laying the bag in his lap, he slowly untied the leather cords that held it shut. Inside the bag were several small pouches, containing tobacco, sage and assorted dried herbs, and his sacred medicine pipe. The pipe was a little over two feet in length, its wooden stem wrapped in buckskin and rabbit fur, its red, pipestone bowl carved in the shape of a badger's head.

The badger was one of his personal totems, a spirit guide which aided him in his battle against the Wyrm and its followers. The spirit of the badger had come to Sam on his very first vision quest, during his Rites of Passage, bestowing upon him the gifts of strength and courage, as well as blessing him with the ability to strike his enemies quickly in battle. The badger also taught him how to live close to Gaia, his body and soul in constant touch with the sacred spirit of Mother Earth.

Sam was Garou, a werewolf, but in his veins also flowed the blood of the Dine', the Navajo. He had spent the early years of his life living in a six-sided hogan, on a reservation near Slippery Rock, New Mexico. It was a land of towering peaks, grasslands, deserts and blood-red canyons. A place where flocks of sheep grazed contentedly on sagebrush during the day, and where spirits and the Holy People rode the wind at night.

Just two weeks shy of his fourteenth birthday, Sam was besieged by a terrible sickness and nightmarish dreams. He begged his father, John Nakai, to call for a Navajo shaman to perform the Blessing Way ceremony. But his father refused. Instead, he took his son into the family sweatlodge, revealing a secret he had kept close to his heart for many years. Seated across the fire pit from the man he dearly loved, Sam had learned about the Garou, and the reason for his sickness and strange dreams.

While Sam's father was nothing more than a Navajo shepherd, a man of simple means who had lived all his life on the reservation, his mother had been a member of the Wendigo tribe. A werewolf. Sam didn't remember much about his mother; she had died when he was only four, killed in a bloody fight with a Black Spiral Dancer. His only memory of the woman who had given him birth, passing on the Garou bloodline to him, were the bits and pieces of a lullaby she used to sing to him. Even now, the song occasionally floated up from the depths of his subconscious, tugging at his heartstrings.

Two days after telling all that he knew about the "Wolf People," John Nakai drove his son deep into the desert. There, among the crumbling stone ruins of the Anasazi, he had given Sam, his only child, to three warriors of the Wendigo tribe, fulfilling a promise made long ago to his beloved wife. The Garou might have taken Sam away from his father a year earlier, but out of respect for the memory of his mother, who was a tribal healer, they waited until John Nakai was ready to give up his son—though they might not have waited too much longer. Sam didn't know it at the time, but he would never see his father again.

The three Garou to whom Sam's care had been entrusted were anything but gentle with him. Kindness was not something offered to a young pup, especially one preparing to undergo the Rites of Passage. Only those of strong spirit and mind survived their first transformations from "human" to Garou. Those who were weak often died from the ordeal, went mad, or became little more than helpless cripples, their pitiful lives mercifully ended with the quick snap of powerful jaws at the base of their necks. Weakness was not tolerated by the Wendigo, or by any of the other twelve Garou tribes. The survival of the pact depended on the strength of its warriors. There could be no weakness in the day-to-day battle against the Wyrm's evil.

In order to complete his Rites of Passage, Sam had undergone the stifling heat of sweatlodge ceremonies, the hunger, thirst and loneliness of a vision quest, and the pain and torture of physical tests that pushed his body to its limits. Blood had been spilled on more than one occasion: his blood, as the older Garou taught him how to fight with tooth and claw, and with weapons of silver and magic. Each lesson left a painful scar, a reminder of what was expected of him and the right or wrong way to fight. Luckily, Sam was a fast learner; soon it was the blood of his opponents that ran thick and red in the moonlight.

Holding his pipe lovingly in his left hand, Sam ran his fingers through his short, ebony hair—now more gray than black. So many fights over the course of his life, so many battles, yet the war against the Wyrm was still not won. If anything, the evil one was stronger now than it had ever been. The world was vile, corrupt; only the Garou kept Gaia from being completely consumed by the darkness.

When he wasn't fighting as a werewolf against one of the Wyrm's minions, he was doing battle as a Native American against the oppression of a dishonest government. He had been at Wounded Knee in 1973, fighting alongside Leonard Peltier, Russell Means, Dennis Banks and the other members of the American Indian Movement. He had also joined the Kanesatake Mohawks in 1990 when they fought against the government of Quebec to protect their sacred burial grounds from being turned into a golf course. But whether it was in human or wolf form that he fought, there never seemed to be an end to the battles.

Opening a small leather pouch, Sam removed a pinch of tobacco and scattered it over the ground as an offering to the Sacred Mother. A second pinch was tossed into the fire as a gift to the spirits who were constantly watching. Reaching into the tobacco pouch again, he slowly filled the blackened bowl of his medicine pipe. Once filled, he lit a wooden kitchen match and held the tiny flame just above the bowl.

Sam placed the pipe's stem to his lips and inhaled deeply, drawing the flame to the tobacco and filling his lungs with the sweet smoke. He exhaled and raised the pipe above his head, offering it to Gaia and the great mystery. Inhaling again, he offered the pipe to the totem spirits of the four directions. To each spirit he said a prayer, and from each he asked a favor.

"Oh, golden eagle of the east. You are the guardian of the land of the rising sun. The springtime. The morning. Carry my prayers up into the night sky, to the land of the Great Spirit and the Holy People. Lend me your eyes, brother eagle, so I might see the things that Gaia has placed before me to see.

"Oh, little mouse of the south. In your home dwells the noonday sun and the summertime, the time of green growing things. You have taught me how to be humble, little brother, and I thank you. Please carry my prayers through your tiny burrows, carry them deep into the bosom of Gaia.

"Oh, great black bear of the west. You are the keeper of the setting sun, the land of autumn, and guardian to the spirit world. You have taught me how to be strong, and shown me how to face the darkness that lies both in the west and in the hearts of men. Grant me the strength now so that I may look inward, to my own darkness, in order to see out.

"And finally, I offer my pipe to you, great white buffalo of the north. From your land comes the midnight and the winter months. You bring the cold that strengthens our bodies and cracks the seeds so the new plants may come forth in the spring. You are also the bringer of sacred knowledge and wisdom. If I am worthy, oh great white buffalo, I ask that you open my eyes to your wisdom and guidance. Come, share this pipe with me. Share your wisdom with me."

Finished with his prayers, Sam dug a tiny hole in the earth and filled it with the ashes from his pipe. Placing the pipe back in his medicine bag, he removed a small, black wooden bowl. The bowl was a spirit bowl, an object used when there were questions that needed to be answered. Something strange was on the wind; the spirits would know what it was.

Filling it with water from his canteen, he set the bowl beside the fire and tilted it so the glow of the flames reflected on the water's surface. Making himself comfortable, Sam focused his gaze on the fiery reflection. There was nothing to do now but watch and wait. If the spirits chose to help him, they would do so before the sun came up. Hopefully they wouldn't make him wait quite that long.

Several hours had already passed when the water in the spirit bowl began to grow dark and cloudy. Even though the fire still burned, its reflection could no longer be seen. Instead a gray fog seemed to cover the surface of the water, like an early morning mist rising up from a lake. Aware that the bowl was finally working, Sam watched closely as the fog slowly blew away to reveal the answer he sought.

At first he thought something was wrong, because the water's surface remained black. But then Sam noticed tiny pinpoints of light and realized he was looking at an image of the night sky. He watched as a miniature full moon appeared in the spirit bowl, crossing the water's surface like the real one crosses the heavens. But as the tiny moon reached the center of the bowl, it changed color from yellow to a deep crimson. The color of blood.

Sam sucked in his breath, unable to believe what he was seeing. "No, it can't be. It just can't."

The blood moon, called the Shaman Moon, came only once every hundred years or so. When it appeared, a rift formed in the invisible boundary known as the Gauntlet—a boundary that separated the spirit world, or Umbra, from the normal world of the Realm. The rift was located on top of Monterey Mountain in Tennessee. When it opened, spirit ancestors could pass freely through the Gauntlet to visit their relatives in the world of the living. Unfortunately, those who served the Wyrm could also pass through the rift into the Realm.

To keep the Wyrm from passing through the Gauntlet, the old ones had built Nee Yah Kah Tah Kee, the Sacred Sitting Wolf. A towering stone statue of immense magical power, Nee Yah Kah Tah Kee had stood guard at the rift for more than a thousand years. And in those thousand years, it had kept the Wyrm's minions from entering the Realm during the Shaman Moon.

But Nee Yah Kah Tah Kee no longer stood guard on Monterey Mountain. In 1893, just one year after the Gauntlet last opened, a group of white engineers had dynamited the statue in order to build a railroad through the mountains. They could have gone around, but they chose instead to destroy something held sacred by both Indians and Garou.

Before the giant statue was destroyed, a Garou elder, named Runs-On-Fire, broke off the two stone fangs of the Sacred Wolf. The Fangs contained powerful magic of the old ones, the very essence of Nee Yah Kah Tah Kee. Unfortunately, one of the Fangs had been lost somewhere in the Umbra years ago.

The remaining Fang had been passed down from generation to generation, from one Garou to the next. One did not volunteer to become the Guardian of the Fang. Instead one was chosen by the ancestor spirits that lived in the vast reaches of the Umbra. It was an honor to be chosen the Guardian, but it was also a curse. The Wyrm would do anything to destroy both the Guardian and the sacred power of the Fang. Anything at all.

Sam had been chosen by the spirits to be the Guardian when he was in his late thirties. The Fang of the Wolf had been passed on to him by an elderly Garou who was no longer strong enough to protect the magic of Nee Yah Kah Tah Kee. Sam would have refused the responsibility, but to do so would have dishonored his pack, his tribe, and the spirits who chose him. It would also have meant another victory for the Wyrm.

Therefore, Sam had accepted the Fang, taking on the responsibility of the Guardianship. He had become the Chosen One, dedicating his life to protecting the last remaining magic of the Sacred Wolf. The years that followed were an endless concession of battles as the Wyrm did everything within its power to destroy him. Luckily, he was very strong, as well as being a skilled fighter. He had been injured many times, but he always came out the victor.

Unfortunately, Sam Nakai was no longer the Guardian. The spirits had instructed him to pass on the Fang to another. It now resided in the possession of someone who was not so strong, and far too young to have the cunning or experience of a seasoned fighter. The Fang of the Wolf now belonged to a girl barely in her teens.

Turning away from the spirit bowl, he looked out over the valley. Somewhere in the darkness ran Heather Ocoee, unaware of the task that lay before her or the dangers she now faced. The girl was the Guardian of the Fang; she alone could seal the Gauntlet against the Wyrm. But Heather had yet to complete the Rites of Passage, or even gain the protection of a single spirit guide.

Sam stood up, kicking the spirit bowl out of his way. He had to find Heather and teach her the things she had yet to learn, before the Shaman Moon rose to fill the sky. Time was running out. The Wyrm would not wait.

Removing his clothes, he willed the transformation to come over him. He too became a wolf, at one with Gaia. But his change was not for pleasure; there was no time for enjoyment. He had to find Heather and prepare her for what lay ahead, before it was too late.

3

Heather ran through the forest in Lupus form, a wolf, at one with the creatures of the night. Her heart filled with happiness, she followed the trails made by her brothers and sisters of the forest. Putting her muscles to the test, she raced at full speed through a narrow valley between the mountains, lengthening her stride to leap over the fallen logs and other obstacles which lay in her path. She stumbled once, almost fell, looking around to see if anyone was watching. Her embarrassment was an entirely human reaction.

You are not a human. Not now. Not anymore. You are a werewolf.

A werewolf. She almost howled in laughter, her lips pulling away from her fangs in a wolf's smile. Who would have thought such a thing could be possible? Certainly not her. At least not a year ago.

Move over Lon Chaney, Jr., Heather Ocoee is here.

Not only was she a werewolf, a certified member of the furry face and fang society, Heather had also been adopted by the Wendigo, one of the thirteen remaining Garou tribes.

The last surviving Native American tribe of werewolves, the Wendigo were made up of Garou of Cherokee, Navajo, Apache, and Iroquois descent. Their ancestors pushed ever westward by the invasion of white settlers from Europe, most of the Wendigo now lived in Canada, the Pacific Northwest, and scattered among the reservations of South Dakota and Oklahoma. Most, but not all.

Refusing to be driven from their homeland, a few handfuls of Wendigo from the now-extinct eastern bands had hidden deep in the forests to escape the infamous "Trail of Tears." Living in caves high up in the mountains, they had waited until it was safe to reclaim the tribal caerns of their ancestors. While they waited, the warriors had honed their fighting skills, becoming experts at hit-and-run tactics and terrorist operations. Those tactics were later taught to their brothers and sisters to the west. The Wendigo tactic of stealthily creeping up on an intended victim several nights before the kill and softly calling out his name from the darkness, provided the basis for many horrible myths told among the Canadian Indians.

The Wendigo were just one of thirteen Garou tribes dedicated to protecting Gaia. And though each tribe had different beliefs and enlisted the aid of different totems—and despite the fact that they rarely seemed to get along with one another—they were all committed to fighting the darkness and the corruption of the Wyrm. But there was a fourteenth werewolf tribe that wanted nothing more than to destroy Gaia and unleash the power of the Dark One.

The Black Spiral Dancers were not spoken of openly in Garou society, not without a shudder and a curse. Long ago the members of that tribe had turned their back on Gaia and the other tribes, selling their souls to the corruption of the Wyrm. They were now a vision of madness itself, an enemy more dangerous than anything else the Dark One could have conjured up.

Death to all Black Spiral Dancers. That is the law.

Heather's smile faded. Laws. Rules. Being a werewolf was definitely not easy; at least it hadn't been easy for her. Ever since they had left California, through a portal opened by the Fang, she had done nothing but train and learn the laws of the Wendigo. Sam Nakai was her friend, but he was also a merciless teacher.

Every day was a day of learning, a day of putting her physical body to the test. Only rarely, like tonight, was she ever given any time off to enjoy her newly acquired gift. Most of the time it was training, training, and more training. She had to learn everything there was to learn about being a Wendigo, including tribal customs, laws, ceremonies, medicine and songs. She also had to learn how to fight, for every Garou was required to be a warrior. It did not matter if she was only a girl in homid form; there were no excuses.

Since being a werewolf was something quite new to Heather, the combat training proved to be especially difficult. She had yet to gain complete confidence in her abilities, despite Sam's constant encouragement and criticism. She had killed before as a werewolf, but that had been a matter of luck and rage rather than skill. Defeating an opponent with a clear mind was something else entirely.

So Heather continued to train each and every day, the bruises on her body growing in number as Sam taught her how to fight like a warrior. He was never gentle with her, never showed any favoritism or mercy, but he never went out of his way to hurt her deliberately either. Each and every time they fought, painful as it was, she learned a new move or trick that might one day save her life. And when they were done, he made her talk about what she had learned, making sure that the lesson had not been wasted.

Though she had finally been given a night off, Heather knew that this too was part of her training, a chance to further develop her skills as a Garou. Sam would want a full report when she returned to camp. He would question her about what she had seen and heard, and what she had smelled.

With this in mind, she brought her run to a slow trot. Sniffing the ground, she tried to identify all the different odors she encountered. Deer. Rabbit. Fox. Every new scent delighted her, for each and every one of them told a story.

Here, where the grass and weeds were trampled flat, a buck had rutted with his mate, leaving behind the musky scent of his sweat and his sex. Over there, a rabbit had stopped to nibble from the tender leaves of a bush, only to be frightened away by a large and very hungry rattlesnake. Beyond that a fox had stopped to relieve himself, marking his territory in pungent urine.

Pleased with herself for being able to identify so many scents at one time, she veered off the trail and stopped to drink from the waters of a clear-running stream. Touching her muzzle to the surface of the stream, she lapped the water noisily with her tongue. But as she drank, Heather noticed an oily, sour kind of taste. Curious, she pulled her head back and looked around. There were no picnic areas nearby, no houses or farms. The stream was in the middle of the wilderness and not normally used by people. It shouldn't be polluted, yet it apparently was.

A wave of anger surged through her as she thought about how the planet was slowly being poisoned to death. Their hearts and minds filled with the Wyrm's corruption, most people didn't even care if they were destroying Gaia, the Sacred Mother, and stealing the future of children yet to be born.

According to documented reports, an estimated 9.7 billion pounds of toxic waste were dumped into streams and rivers each year. Ground water was also contaminated throughout the country by seepage from underground chemical storage tanks and leakage from toxic land fills.

Sam had told her that he once met a man whose job it was to empty barrels of dangerous chemicals into the wells and cisterns of old abandoned farms, thus saving the company he worked for millions of dollars in storage and hauling fees. Unfortunately for the man, his meeting with Sam Nakai proved to be fatal. His body now lay at the bottom of one of the cisterns he'd polluted.

SHAMAN MOON 123

In addition to factories polluting the streams and rivers, runoffs from farms and agricultural areas were also dangerous. Of the more than 35,000 pesticides introduced since 1945, only ten percent have ever been tested. At least sixty-six of the pesticides used on produce today contain cancer-causing agents. In several states, traces of PCBs and DDT have been found in the breast milk of nursing mothers.

Heather shuddered when she thought about all the children who were exposed to dangerous chemicals on a daily basis. She had seen pictures of patients in a pediatric ward in Kellogg, Idaho, children who suffered brain damage because of a local smelter filling the atmosphere with tons of toxic lead. And the Cuyahoga River in Cleveland, Ohio, has so many combustible pollutants dumped into its waters each year the local inhabitants have to take special precautions during the summer to avoid setting it on fire.

Toxins, carcinogens, radiation. It boggled the mind to think about the things mankind was doing to Mother Earth. No place was sacred; no place was safe. It seemed only the Garou cared about what was happening, and they were fighting a losing battle.

A growl formed deep in the back of Heather's throat. They were not going to dump their poisons *here*, not if she had anything to say about it. This was her sanctuary, and she wasn't about to allow it to be polluted by outsiders. Determined to locate the source of the pollution and put a stop to it before it got any worse, she decided to follow the stream to where it started.

The stream led deep into the mountains, to places Heather had never been to before, twisting and winding like a snake through narrow canyons and rocky crevices. Gnarled oaks and towering pines grew along the edge of the water, their roots breaking through the ground to wind among the rocks, their branches stretching high overhead, blocking out the moonlight and making it appear as though she walked through a long, dark corridor. In the shadows of their leafy homes, tree frogs and cicadas filled the air with their rhythmic harmonies.

Her journey came to an abrupt halt at the base of a mountain, in a place where a narrow waterfall cascaded sixty feet down a granite cliff to fill a rippling pool. The rock cliff above the pool was much too steep for Heather to continue her search for the stream's source of pollution. Her disappointment was minimal, however, because she had found a place of sheer beauty, an undiscovered wilderness paradise that she was in no hurry to leave.

The pool of water was about thirty feet across, enclosed on three sides by the face of the cliff, fallen boulders, and outcroppings of rock. The narrow fourth side opened to the forest. Splashing noisily into the pool, the waterfall created a spray of fine mist that was carried upon the wind. Heather shook herself in delight as the mist soaked into her fur and tickled her nose. Stepping forward, she again drank from the stream's water.

The strange taste was no longer noticeable. Perhaps she had already passed the source of pollution, or maybe she had only imagined the peculiar taste. Relieved that the stream was probably not tainted after all, she lowered her snout to the water and drank deeply.

Gazing into the water as she drank, she saw the night sky and the shadowy images of trees reflected on the water's surface. It was like looking into a smoky mirror. Suddenly, the image blurred and changed. The forest reflected in the water was no longer pristine and beautiful. Instead it was blighted-looking, with withered skeletons of trees and leprous-looking vines.

Startled, Heather jumped back with a cough. She turned quickly, only to find the forest behind her as beautiful as when she first laid eyes upon it.

What kind of craziness is this?

Turning back to look at the water's surface, she again saw the reflection of the forest as it should be. But when she stepped closer the image started to change once more. Blighted trees replaced stately pines; the reflected sky turned cloudy and ominous. She was fascinated. Was the image an optical illusion, or was she having some kind of vision? Sam Nakai spoke of having visions, but she had never had one herself. Not yet anyway.

If it was a vision, Heather needed to pay careful attention to everything she saw. Every detail, no matter how small or seemingly unimportant, must be set to memory. Failure to do so could mean the loss or misunderstanding of a message from the spirit world.

Leaning forward to study the image, she noticed something besides withered trees and a cloudy sky in the reflection. There was also a house.

Clearly visible in the reflection was a small log cabin that sat back among the diseased-looking trees, almost hidden in the shadows. Heather resisted the urge to turn around and look, because she knew there really wasn't a house behind her. Instead she concentrated on the reflection, watching in awe as the cabin's tiny door slowly opened.

What the hell?

A shiver of fear danced up her spine as she watched a gnarled, little figure emerge from the cabin and walk slowly toward her. The creature was about three or four feet tall, with wrinkled grayish skin stretched tight over a bony frame. The thing shuffled along with an exaggerated walk, as though it were treading upon hot coals. For some strange reason, Heather got the feeling that the thing was trying to sneak up on her. But that was silly; it was only a reflection. A vision. Or was it?

She wanted to look behind her, but dared not take her eyes off the reflection for fear of it disappearing. Sam would be angry if she let a vision slip through her fingers without thoroughly examining it. Besides, even if it was real, the dwarfish little creature was much too small to pose much of a threat to a wolf.

Lowering her head, she continued to study the vision. Whatever the creature was, it was probably female. Even in the pale moonlight, Heather could see that it had long straggly hair and breasts. A tattered piece of fabric was tied about its waist, preventing her from seeing anything else that would identify its sex.

The creature seemed to stop just behind Heather, watching her with eyes that glowed as red as fire. There was something in its right hand: a long, pointed object that looked like a stone knife. Unable to stand it any longer, she turned and looked behind her. No one was there.

Thank God. It wasn't real.

Breathing a sigh of relief, Heather looked back at the pool. But the water's surface did not change. The reflection was only of the trees and the night sky. Disappointed that her vision was over, she turned around and started to leave.

Stepping away from the pool, she spotted something which caused her heart to seize with fear. Pressed into the soft mud near the water's edge was the misshapen footprint of someone, or something, that had stood just behind her as she stared into the pool.

The vision had not been a vision after all. Someone had been standing just behind her, someone who could only be seen in the reflection of the water. Heather resisted the urge to look back at the pool, not wanting to see what might be waiting for her in the water's dark surface. Instead she turned and ran, fleeing from something she did not understand.

4

Sam was no longer a wolf when he finally located Heather early the next morning. He found her curled up in a tiny clearing, in homid form, sleeping off the exhaustion that followed her revel. The vulnerability of her surroundings, and the fact that she had not returned to camp the previous evening, angered him. He was none too gentle when he woke her.

"If I were the enemy you would be dead," he said, grabbing her by the shoulder and shaking her.

Heather sat up, looked around, and smiled. "If you were the enemy, I would have known." She opened her right hand to reveal that she had slept with the Fang of the Wolf clenched tightly in her fist. "The Fang would have warned me."

"I doubt even the Fang could have awakened a sleepyhead like you." He tossed Heather a backpack filled with items of clothing he had brought from the camp. "I howled twice. Why didn't you answer?"

"I didn't hear you," she answered. "Maybe you should have howled three times."

"Twice should have been enough, even for you. More than that and I would have alerted any enemies in the area to our presence."

She looked around. "What enemies? There's no one here but us."

Sam clicked his tongue in annoyance. "There are enemies of the Garou everywhere. Even here. Do not let the beauty of your surroundings deceive your eyes. You must learn to trust nothing and no one."

"No one?" Heather grinned mischievously. "Not even you?"

"Not even me," he answered, turning his back on her.

"Okay then. I won't." Heather jumped up and threw herself at Sam, transforming into a werewolf in mid-lunge. She had hoped to catch her mentor by surprise, but he sidestepped out of the way and then quickly transformed into a werewolf himself.

Had Sam been wearing ordinary garments, he would have ripped his clothing to shreds when he made the change from man to werewolf. But after failing to find Heather during the night, he had gone back to camp and changed into clothing magically treated to transform with his body. He only had one such outfit, as did Heather; lucky for him that he had decided to wear it.

Turning, Heather roared and lunged again. Sam waited until the very last second, then pivoted to his right. Using Heather's own body weight and forward momentum against her, he grabbed her by the left arm and sent her flying through the air. She landed in an ungraceful sprawl, her muzzle buried in a small mound of dead leaves and dirt. Heather started to get up again, but Sam landed heavily on her back.

"Lesson one," he said to her in wolf speak. "Always expect the unexpected. Lesson two: when fighting a charging opponent, use their body weight and momentum against them. Be like the tree that bends in the wind, rather than the rock that tries to stop the river's flow."

He leaned forward and nipped Heather's left ear, counting coup on her. Had the fight been for real he would have crushed the vertebrae in her neck with his powerful jaws. "And finally," Sam said. "Lesson three: Never, ever, fuck with your instructor."

Heather felt the weight lift off her back as Sam stood up and stepped away. Thoroughly chastised, she spit the dirt and leaves from her mouth and slowly transformed back into human form.

"What about the turtle?" she asked, standing up and brushing herself off.

"What turtle? What about it?" Sam asked, pretending not to know what she was talking about.

"Last week you told me that I could learn important lessons from all the different animals. You said the turtle taught us that we couldn't get anywhere in life unless we first stuck our necks out."

"I said that?" he asked, faking surprise as he changed back into human form.

Heather frowned. "Of course you said it. Don't you remember?"

"If I said that, then I must be a really good teacher. The best. I'm surprised that of all the things I have told you, this is what you chose to remember." He chuckled. "But sometimes if you stick your neck out too far you'll get your head chopped off. Remember that the next time you decide to attack your mentor when he isn't looking."

Heather shook her head in frustration. "Stick your head out. Don't stick your head out. Be like the turtle. Don't be like the turtle. I swear, your teachings are getting more and more confusing every day. If this keeps up, I don't think I'll ever become a warrior."

Sam's laughter died in his throat. "Yes you will. All you need is lots and lots of training."

At the mention of the word *training*, Heather groaned and slumped back into a sitting position. Sam walked over and picked up the backpack, tossing it to her.

"But you won't be getting any more training today," he smiled. "Get dressed. We're leaving."

"Leaving?" She hurried to slip on underwear, blue jeans, tennis shoes and a T-shirt. "Where are we going?"

"We are going into town."

Heather started to tell Sam about her experience at the pool of water, but decided it could wait. She was excited about going into town, because it meant a break from the rigorous training imposed on her, a short recess from the difficult regimen of Garou life. If she told Sam, he would want her to show him the exact spot where the strange vision had occurred and that might mean the trip would be canceled. Besides, she could always tell him later.

Since they were only three or four miles from the city limits of Cherokee, North Carolina, they decided to walk to town rather than go all the way back to their campsite for Sam's pickup. Actually, it was Sam who made the decision to walk rather than ride; Heather figured it was his way of punishing her for not returning to camp after her revel. And since three or four miles in mountainous countryside is quite a hike, they didn't reach town until late in the afternoon.

Cherokee really wasn't much of a town, not when compared to San Francisco or some of the other places she had been to. Mostly it was just a clustering of tribal offices, gift shops, museums, gambling parlors and restaurants, preying off the white tourists who drove up from the cities to visit the mountains, gamble, and take pictures of "real Indians."

Heather thought it was funny that the Cherokee men who posed for the "authentic pictures" all wore the eagle-feather war bonnets and buckskin war shirts of the plains Indian tribes rather than wearing the traditional clothing of their own people. Some of them even stood in front of tipis, something else that was never used by the Cherokee people back in the "good old days."

While Heather was somewhat amused, Sam was quite disgusted by the cheap commercialism of Native American values that he saw, muttering a barrage of obscene insults in Navajo as they walked down the street. He was especially upset when a white couple and their three young children came out of one of the gift shops wearing souvenir war bonnets of brightly dyed chicken feathers and yelling war whoops in mock Indian fashion. Had she not grabbed him by the hand and led him away, he probably would have massacred the whole lot of them.

At the end of the main street stood a small restaurant named Watie's Cafe. It was a simple, undecorated, brown building that looked like it had seen better days. Entering the restaurant, Sam and Heather wove their way through a crowd of lunchtime customers to an empty booth in the back. After ordering burgers, fries and Cokes from a portly Cherokee woman in a stained yellow apron, they turned their attention to the other customers, watching a constant parade of tourists come and go.

Midsummer was the height of tourist season in the Smoky Mountains, especially on the reservation, so most of the customers were visitors from out of town. Adults toting cameras, maps, and armloads of souvenirs herded their restless children before them like shepherds tending flocks of sheep. Dressed in imitation leather vests and bear-claw necklaces, most of the kids were armed with rubber tomahawks, spears and plastic bows and arrows. While their parents ordered food, the children took great delight in staging mock battles in the middle of the restaurant. Heather and Sam had to duck twice when rubber-tipped arrows came sailing their way. Fortunately, the battle ended without bloodshed when the parents took the weapons away so the children would eat.

The last of the make-believe wars had just ended when the waitress returned with their lunch order, setting the plates before them. Heather leaned forward and sniffed, delighted by the aroma that rose up from her food. Squirting catsup on the plate next to her fries, she picked up her hamburger and took a bite. The hamburger was good. No, make that great, delicious. So were the french fries. Heather hadn't realized how hungry she was, and the burger and fries were a pleasant change of pace from Sam's cooking, or the rabbits she had eaten while in wolf form.

They were halfway through their meal, when an old Cherokee man entered the diner. He was short and thin, with faded blue jeans, scuffed brown shoes and a wrinkled cotton shirt. His hair was long and gray, and fell loosely about his shoulders, kept in place by an old blue bandanna tied around his forehead.

Instead of taking a seat at one of the empty tables or at the counter, the old man walked over to their booth and sat down beside Heather. As soon as he sat down, he started eating her french fries.

"Hey! What are you doing?" she asked, shocked by the Indian's rudeness.

"I am eating your food," he replied, in a matter-of-fact tone of voice.

"Why?"

"Because I am hungry," he smiled. He ate several more fries and then picked up her hamburger and took a bite. "This is good too," he said, turning to look at her. "You should try some."

Heather was absolutely furious about having her food eaten, so angry that she felt the Rage come over her. She tried to control her emotions, but it was too late and she felt herself slipping into Crinos form right there in the restaurant. But as she started to transform into a werewolf, the old man turned and looked at her. To her surprise, there was no fear in his eyes, nor did he have the glassy-eyed stare of one affected by the Delirium. He just looked bored, so bored he yawned.

The old Indian's yawn had a strange effect on Heather. It calmed her anger and quenched her rage, stopping her transformation before it could really begin. She sat staring at him, watching in mute fascination as he leaned forward and picked up her drink.

"This is also very tasty," he said, taking a sip of Coca-Cola.

Heather was still speechless, but she was no longer angry. She sniffed the air, but did not detect the familiar scent of Garou. She turned and looked to Sam Nakai for help.

"No, Joseph Swimmer is not a werewolf," Sam laughed, no longer able to keep a straight face about what was happening. "But he is Kinfolk. He's also a very good friend; we've known each other for years."

The old man smiled at Heather, then turned to Sam. "She is the one?" he asked.

Sam nodded.

Joseph shook his head. "This girl is too young; she still has much to learn."

"That's why I need your help," Sam said.

Joseph looked at Heather, studying her in silence for a moment. "Okay," he nodded, turning back to Sam. "I will help. Bring her to my place tonight. Some of the others are already there."

Joseph Swimmer stood up and shook Sam's hand. Heather thought he wanted to shake her hand too, but instead he picked up her plate of food. "No more of this, little one," he smiled. "You cannot find your guides on a full stomach."

Heather watched in stunned silence as the old man walked out of the restaurant, taking her food with him.

Guides?

5

Long ago, an old Cherokee couple lived alone in the mountains. Each morning the husband would pick three or four ears of corn from the garden for his wife. His wife would shuck the ears and then place them in the sun to dry. After dinner, she would grind the corn into cornmeal to make bread. The cornmeal was always kept outside so it wouldn't become mushy.

One day the old woman went to get some cornmeal to make the day's bread, but it wasn't there. She looked all around, but could not find the cornmeal anywhere. This upset the woman and she called for her husband.

"Foolish woman," her husband said, coming outside. "There is no cornmeal here. You must have taken it inside."

Confused, the old woman went inside to look for the cornmeal. While she was gone, her husband noticed some very large paw prints on the ground, much larger than any dog's tracks he had ever seen before. Not wanting to scare his wife, the old man didn't tell her about the tracks. He just went into the garden and picked some more corn. The next day the meal was right where they left it and they both felt better.

One week later, however, the meal was again missing. Again the old man saw the prints of a very large dog. His wife saw the prints too and knew that a dog was stealing her cornmeal.

The old couple decided they needed some help with the problem, so they went and told their neighbors about what was happening. That evening several neighbors showed up at the home of the old couple carrying hand drums and rattles to scare away the dog.

Later that night a powerful wind began to blow. The wind was so strong it made the corn plants bend to the ground. Then, as everyone watched from their hiding places, a large dog flew down out of the sky and landed near the house.

As soon as the giant dog, which was really a spirit dog, landed, it began to eat the cornmeal. The people inside the house watched in awe for a moment, then yelled, beat their drums and shook their rattles to scare off the dog. Startled by the noise, the spirit dog flew up into the sky, a trail of cornmeal spilling from its huge mouth. And instead of falling back to the ground, the meal stayed in the sky, marking the pathway where the giant dog fled.

Many today call this pathway the Milky Way, but the Cherokee know that it is actually the cornmeal spilled by the giant dog. It will stay in the sky forever to honor those who helped the old couple, and to let the people know that the spirit dog will never bother them again.

Joseph Swimmer lived in a rustic log cabin, high up in the mountains, a few miles north of the town of Cherokee. Since they had left the pickup truck back at their campsite, Heather and Sam were forced to make the trip on foot. Normally they would have traveled in wolf form, but they were too close to a populated area to risk being seen. The sight of two timberwolves racing through the forest in broad daylight would have created quite a stir, maybe even causing a panic among the tourists in the area.

To help pass the time during their walk, Sam entertained Heather with Indian legends and bits of folklore he had picked up over the years. He also told her everything he knew about the man they were going to see. In addition to being Kinfolk, Joseph Swimmer was also a Cherokee shaman and a member of the secret Ketowah Society.

Opposed to the continuing encroachment of white society on Cherokee land, society and beliefs, the Ketowahs were traditional full bloods fighting to keep the ways of their people alive through ceremonies, dances and songs. Their meetings were always held deep in the forest at night, and no outsider was ever allowed to witness them.

Valued for his knowledge of sacred ceremonies and traditional medicine, Joseph was the only human ever allowed to join the Sept of the Sitting Wolf. Composed of twenty or so Wendigo, from several different Native American tribes, the Sept considered all of the Smoky Mountains to be their private domain. They controlled several caerns, or sacred places, with the site where Nee Yah Kah Tah Kee once stood on Monterey Mountain in Tennessee being the most powerful.

Arriving at Joseph's cabin shortly after sunset, Sam followed proper Garou protocol by stopping in the front yard and howling the Song of Greeting. In the song, he introduced himself to whoever might be inside by reciting his name, tribe, clan, warrior society and pack. Heather was supposed to do the same, but being an orphan she knew very little about her past other than what the spirits had told Sam about her.

Sam finished his song and they waited in silence. A few minutes passed, and then the cabin's door opened and an elderly Indian woman, wearing a flowery gingham dress, stepped out onto the porch. Heather thought the woman might be Joseph's wife, but she wasn't sure and it would be bad manners to ask. Whoever the woman was, she recognized Sam and waved the both of them inside with a smile.

Stepping through the front door of the cabin, they found themselves in the middle of a sparsely furnished room that served as both a living room and a dining area. An old sofa was pushed against one wall, its faded brown fabric peeking out from underneath a pile of blankets and throw pillows. Next to the sofa, a gray reclining chair was strategically positioned in front of a portable television. The television set perched on top of an oval dining table that had seen better days. Several plates and glasses were also scattered across the table, but no one sat down on either of the wooden chairs to eat. Instead, the three men already in the room stood and watched with interest as Heather and Sam entered the cabin.

Heather felt a wave of nervousness wash over her as she spotted the men, because they all seemed to be staring directly at her. A quick sniff told her they were all Garou, but that didn't help calm her nerves. She didn't like being scrutinized, especially when she didn't know what was going on, or even why she had been brought to Joseph Swimmer's home in the first place.

All right then. Let's see how you like it.

Remembering one of the lessons Sam had taught her, about facing one's fear head on, she stopped in the middle of the room and turned to face the three Garou. With both feet firmly planted on the wooden floor, her legs slightly spread, Heather returned the stares directed at her in what she hoped was her most serious expression. Amused smiles unfolded upon the faces of two of the men as they realized that the tiny girl was challenging them to a facedown.

A form of ritual combat, the facedown was a contest of wits and wills in which two Garou stared into each other's eyes until one finally looked away. It was one of three different ways in which dominance was decided in Garou societies, and probably the only contest in which blood was not spilled.

Ignoring the smiles of her opponents, Heather put her fists on her hips and struck a pose of defiance. She knew she couldn't possibly take on three Garou at once, for when she looked from one to the other she would automatically lose, but she was determined to make a good showing for herself.

All three men were obviously Wendigo, probably belonging to the same sept or pack, but their physical appearance and manner varied greatly. The first Garou she locked eyes with was short and wiry, with medium-length black hair and pockmarked skin. His thin face and large nose reminded her of a weasel, or maybe even a field mouse. Dressed in blue jeans, boots and a green ribbon shirt, he looked to be in his mid to late forties. She had been staring at him for less than a minute when he smiled and nodded, allowing Heather to turn her attention to the next opponent without losing the contest.

Okay, your turn.

Her next opponent was a tall, powerfully built young man, with long raven-black hair that he wore in twin braids. He would have been handsome, were it not for the anger in his eyes. His gaze was like a fiery sword, and Heather felt herself starting to quiver beneath the force of it. Knowing she could not outstare the man, she decided to move on to her last opponent in hope of obtaining a two out of three victory.

Heather almost gasped when she turned her attention to the last man in the room. He too was tall, young and muscular; but he was also deformed, his right arm ending just below the elbow in a hideous, fleshy claw. The young man was a metis, the deformed and sterile offspring of two Garou who had broken the sacred law and mated with each other.

Garou do not mate with each other, that was the law. It was considered a crime against the tribes for one werewolf to mate with another. Such unions were often viewed as nothing less than incest. In addition to being born deformed and sterile, the children of such corrupt unions were looked down upon and considered outcasts by the other members of the tribe.

Years ago, metis children were considered a thing of superstition and evil. They were often taken from their parents immediately after their birth and killed outright, or left in the woods to die a slow, painful death of starvation and exposure to the elements. Sometimes, the parents were also punished by execution. But today, with only ten percent of the children being born with Garou blood, the tribes could no longer be picky about what shape their warriors came in. A deformed warrior was better than no warrior at all, especially considering that metis Garou were often the quickest at transforming into the terrifying Crinos form.

Heather had never seen a metis before, but she knew the tribal laws concerning them. Seeing one for the first time helped lodge the rules about mating practices firmly in her mind, even though she wouldn't be considered ready for such things for several more years. *Garou must mate with either wolves or humans in order to produce healthy young.* It was a rule she would never forget.

She was still locked in contest with the metis when the facedown was ended by someone speaking. Blinking to clear her vision, she turned and saw that it was the young Garou with the hateful gaze who had spoken.

"*This* is the Guardian of the Fang?" he asked, pointing an index finger accusingly at Heather.

Sam nodded. "She is the Guardian."

The man cleared his throat and spit on the floor, a deliberate sign of disrespect directed toward Heather and her mentor. It was an insult that usually led to bloodshed.

A hushed tension settled over the room. No one spoke. No one moved. The other two Garou stood as silent statues, waiting to see how Sam would respond to such an insult. Out of the corner of her eye, Heather could see a deep flush of anger seep into Sam's face. He was furious, yet he chose not to respond. A few moments of heavy silence filled the room, then the young man spoke again.

"The girl is much too young," he said, a mocking smile of arrogance tugging at the corners of his mouth. "How can she possibly face the Wyrm? Sam Nakai, you are still a fool. You have given sacred medicine to a child. All is now lost."

Sam stared back at the young man. "The only thing that has been lost, Michael Pathkiller, are your manners. How dare you speak so to the Chosen One? Maybe it is about time I gave you another lesson on how to behave."

The smile disappeared, replaced by a glare of hate and anger so strong it was almost a physical blow. Pathkiller tensed, ready to spring at Sam. When he spoke, his voice was as cold as ice. Deadly. "Careful, old man, lest we forget what happened last time we tangled. Maybe this time I will take both your eyes."

Heather was shocked. Not only did Sam know this Michael Pathkiller, but apparently he had fought him once before—fought him and lost his left eye in the battle. But her mentor would not lose another eye, not if she could help it.

Angry, Heather felt the Rage flow through her system, felt the change start to come over her. Sam must have known what she was doing, for he laid a hand on her arm and shook his head. Seeing Heather start to shapeshift, Pathkiller laughed out loud.

"Ha, Sam Nakai. Have you grown so old that children must now fight your battles for you?" He turned his attention to Heather, his gaze shooting icy daggers through her heart. "Careful, little girl. You may be biting off more than you can chew."

As Michael Pathkiller spoke the warning he changed, transforming into his Crinos form so fast it left Heather speechless. One second a man stood before her, the next second a muscular, gray-furred werewolf towered over her. In his Crinos form Pathkiller stood nearly eight feet tall, his head touching the ceiling. He was right, she had bitten off more than she could chew.

Stepping quickly in front of her, Sam Nakai also transformed into a werewolf. Pathkiller responded with a roar that shook the room, a battle cry, a challenge to the death. He started to lunge…

"Enough!" A shout echoed through the room, followed by a clap of thunder so loud it rattled the roof and made Heather's ears ring. Frozen in place, everyone turned toward the source of the voice.

Joseph Swimmer stood in the back doorway, his face livid with anger. He wore only a simple leather breechcloth, his thin body tanned and wrinkled by the sun. He held no weapon or magical device, so Heather wondered how he had made the thunder. Apparently there was more to the old man than met the eyes.

"I said enough," Joseph yelled again. "You are acting like children. There will be no fighting in my home. Not today. Not any day. Now change back before I get mad."

Sam and Pathkiller eyed each other for a moment longer, then they both slowly transformed back into human form. Joseph gave them a final look of warning, then smiled. "There, that's much better."

The old man entered the room, moving from one person to the next, shaking hands and giving hugs. His actions helped to ease the tension, replacing it with an almost festive atmosphere. But Heather still didn't feel at ease. If Joseph Swimmer hadn't shown up when he did, Sam and Pathkiller would have fought. She knew the confrontation was far from over; it was only postponed for a little while.

After greeting all the others, Joseph stopped in front of Heather and looked her up and down. "Sam Nakai has told me that you are now the Guardian of the Fang…"

"He told you?" Heather asked, somewhat surprised.

Joseph nodded. "His guides brought a message to me last night. They told me that you are the Guardian. They also told me that you have not yet completed your Rites of Passage. That is why you are here. You must go on a vision quest to seek your spirit guides. But before you can go on your quest, you must first purify your body in a sweatlodge ceremony. To save time, Sam has asked to use my lodge rather than build one himself. He is my friend, so I have agreed."

He turned and favored Sam with a smile, then took Heather by the arm and led her across the room. "Come, my little Guardian. The spirits are waiting for you."

6

"What's the heck's going on?" Heather asked in a whisper, cornering Sam in a tiny back bedroom in Joseph Swimmer's cabin.

"You are about to go through a sweat," Sam replied innocently.

"Why?"

"It is the first part of your final ceremony for the Wendigo Rites of Passage."

Heather was surprised. "But you said the other day that I wasn't ready for the final Rites yet, that I still had a lot more training to go through."

"That was the other day," Sam smiled. "Today is different."

Heather was confused. "I don't understand. Why is today different?"

The smile on Sam's face faded. "Things have changed since the other day. There is no longer any time to train you. The spirits have told me that you must start your final Rites tonight. Now." He grabbed a folded army blanket off the bed and handed it to her. "Enough talking. Get ready for the sweat."

Heather clutched the blanket to her chest, but didn't move. "What about your friend?"

"What friend?"

"The Garou who took your eye."

"I'll tell you later."

"You'll tell me now." Heather drew herself up to her full height and stared at her mentor. Sam almost burst out laughing at the deliberate display of boldness. Instead he clicked his tongue in mock disapproval.

"Your cockiness will get you killed one day."

"Probably," she said, relaxing her stance.

Sam shook his head. "Michael Pathkiller is Wendigo, a member of the warrior society called the Dog Soldiers. He is also the leader of the Sitting Wolf Sept, and the pack of the same name. He and his people guard the caern where Nee Yah Kah Tah Kee once stood."

"But you fought him," Heather interrupted.

"Yes, we fought," Sam nodded. "But that was many years ago."

"But you are of the same tribe," she said, trying to understand why two Wendigo would fight each other. "Was it a battle for leadership?"

"No. Our fight was not a duel to determine the leader of a pack. We are both Wendigo, true, but Pathkiller and I are of different clans, military societies, and packs. I had never even met him until after the Fang of the Wolf was passed on to me."

Heather's right hand automatically went to the leather pouch that hung from a leather cord around her neck, feeling the sliver of magical stone it contained. "You fought over the Fang. Didn't you?"

Sam nodded. "Pathkiller had just become the leader of the Sitting Wolf Pack and felt that the Fang should belong to him. He was angered that the previous Guardian had passed on the sacred stone to an outsider, so angry that he killed the Garou who had given me the Fang. Then he came looking for me."

"Who was the Guardian before you?" she asked.

"The Guardian who gave me the Fang was Michael Pathkiller's grandfather."

Heather was stunned. "He killed his own grandfather?"

Again Sam nodded. "Jealousy and the thirst for power also affects those who serve Gaia. There is little real magic left in the world; what remains is often considered of great value. The spirits chose me to be the new Guardian, but Pathkiller didn't think they made the right choice, so we fought."

"You still had the Fang; you must have won."

Sam touched the black patch covering his left eye. "I won, but I paid quite a price for the victory." He laid his hands upon Heather's shoulders. "Michael Pathkiller is not to be trusted. He will not rest until the Fang of the Wolf is his. Stay away from him; he is a killer. If he challenges you to a duel, do not accept. Despite what you may think, you are not strong enough, or skilled enough, to fight him."

Realizing he was scaring her, Sam removed his hands from Heather's shoulders. "Relax. You are still much too young to be openly challenged. If Pathkiller fought you now he would lose the respect of his pack members." He smiled. "Now hurry up and get ready for the sweat."

"I don't have a bathing suit," she pointed out.

"You don't need one," he replied. "Wear your underwear and T-shirt, or wear nothing. I'll meet you out back."

"Underwear and T-shirt it is," she grinned. Sam smiled and then left the room.

Closing the door, Heather quickly removed her shoes and socks, and then her jeans. Wrapping the army blanket around her, she left the bedroom and walked out the back door of the cabin. Sam was already outside, wearing only his underwear, a bright blue patchwork quilt wrapped around his shoulders. Joseph was also there, still dressed in his traditional leather breechcloth. He also wore a blanket.

About fifty feet behind the log cabin sat Joseph's sweatlodge. A small, squat, dome-shaped structure, no higher than a man's chest, the sweatlodge was made of bent saplings covered with blankets and old pieces of carpeting. The entrance faced the east, a narrow path of bare earth leading from the doorway to a small, circular fire pit. Inside the pit a dozen fireplace bricks had been liberally doused with kerosene and set on fire.

Stopping at the fire pit, Heather and Sam stood in silence while Joseph lit one end of a sage smudge stick with a purple butane lighter. He blew out the flame and waved the stick back and forth, allowing the fragrant white smoke to purify them. No part of their bodies was left untouched by the smoke; they even had to lift their legs so the bottom of their feet could be smudged. Once purified, they followed the old Indian down the narrow path to the sweatlodge's entrance.

OWL GOINGBACK

The three of them had to drop to their knees and crawl in order to squeeze through the sweatlodge's tiny doorway. Joseph Swimmer entered the lodge first, followed by Heather and then Sam. The entrance was deliberately made small, forcing the participants to get on their hands and knees as a sign of respect to the Great Spirit and Gaia. Crawling into the sweatlodge also symbolized entering the womb of the Sacred Mother.

In the center of the sweatlodge, another pit had been dug into the ground. Joseph sat on the west side of the pit, directly across from the entrance. Sam sat to his left; Heather to his right. They sat cross-legged, facing the pit, their blankets tight about their shoulders.

On the ground beside Joseph sat a small bucket of water, an eagle-feather fan resting on its edge. Next to the bucket was a rectangular cedar box. Opening the box, Joseph took out his medicine pipe. The pipe was similar to the one Sam carried, except that the bowl was made of clay instead of pipestone. It was a Cherokee pipe; the white clay used to make the bowl came from the mountains around the reservation.

Joseph carefully filled the pipe's bowl with his own personal mixture of tobacco and medicinal herbs, called *kinnikinick*, and then lit it with his purple lighter. Offering a prayer to the Great Spirit, Gaia, and the ancestors, he smoked the pipe and then passed it around. As the pipe was being passed, the metis Garou began carrying the heated bricks from the fire pit to the sweatlodge. He carried the bricks one by one with a shovel, carefully stacking them in the circular pit inside the lodge.

Sam Nakai explained the importance of each brick as it was carried inside. The first brick represented Gaia, the Sacred Mother, whom the Garou fought so hard to protect. She was the giver of plenty; from her womb sprang all life. Without Gaia there would be no people, animals, or green growing things.

The second brick stood for Great Spirit, Grandfather, the creator of all the universe. Known as the Great Mystery to the Indian brothers of the Garou, a tiny spark of His spirit resided in the body of all living things. And because that spark of life came from the same source, all living things upon the Earth were connected to one another. They were all brothers and sisters.

The next four bricks carried into the sweatlodge stood for the four directions of the wind, and the spirits who guarded their gates, while the seventh brick represented the ancestors who had already crossed over into the spirit world of the Umbra. Six more bricks were carefully added to the stack, making a total of thirteen. Thirteen bricks, one for each Garou tribe.

As each brick was added to the pit, the temperature in the sweatlodge increased. Heather wanted to remove the blanket from around her shoulders, but she wasn't allowed to take it off while the door stood open. Sweating uncomfortably, she watched as Sam removed his pipe from his medicine bag and filled it with tobacco. Offering the proper prayers, he lit the pipe and passed it around. After the tobacco was smoked, and the pipe safely back in Sam's hands, the door to the sweatlodge was closed and they were cast into complete darkness.

Heather could no longer see anything, but she heard Joseph Swimmer dip his eagle-feather fan into the bucket and sprinkle water over the heated bricks. The bricks crackled and hissed as the cold water splashed on them, filling the sweatlodge with a hissing cloud of hot steam.

The steam made Heather sweat even more than she already was. It also burned her nostrils when she took too deep a breath. Letting the blanket slip from her shoulders, she lowered her head and tried not to think about the heat. Her hair hung limp and heavy on her back, and sweat ran down her face to drop from her nose onto her bare legs.

Four times Joseph dipped the eagle-feather fan into the bucket and sprinkled water over the heated bricks. In between those times prayers to Gaia and the spirits were offered. Twice the door opened and a small cup of water was passed in by the metis, a child's plastic sipping cup with a spill-proof lid. No one drank. Instead, each of them poured a little of the water over the bricks as an offering to Gaia.

The final part of the ceremony proved to be the most intense. Offering a prayer to the North, to the direction from which sacred knowledge came, Joseph sprinkled twice as much water over the bricks as he had each of the times before. Heather thought her lungs would surely burn up before the door was again opened. She took small breaths and kept her head down, but even that didn't help much. It was hot. Damn hot.

Suddenly, a strange sensation came over her. It felt as through she were flying, or moving rapidly through a long dark tunnel. At first Heather thought it was just her imagination, or a feeling brought on by the intense heat, but then she noticed patches of color zipping past her at high speed. Blues. Purples. Reds. The colors blended together like surrealistic cloud formations viewed from the window of a jet airplane.

I really am flying.

Startled by what she was experiencing, Heather reached out to touch Sam's leg. But Sam Nakai no longer sat next to her. He had disappeared, vanished without a trace. She called out to him, but he didn't answer.

Somewhat frightened now, she called out to Joseph but the old Indian didn't answer either. Had he also disappeared? She started to reach toward him, but pulled her hand back in fear of touching the hot bricks. But she no longer felt any heat from the bricks, nor did she hear their hissing. Curious, Heather slowly reached out to touch the fire pit, but it too was gone. Also missing were the walls of the sweatlodge and the ground she sat on. Everything was gone, vanished.

A thought entered Heather's mind, calming her. What if Joseph and Sam weren't really gone? What if she was the one who was actually missing? Earlier, it had felt like she was flying. Could it be that her spirit had flown out of the sweatlodge, leaving the others behind? If so, then where was she?

As if in answer to her question, the darkness began to grow gradually lighter. Clouds parted in a night sky to reveal the soft, golden glow of a full moon. The light of the moon spilled down over Heather, illuminating the girl and her surroundings.

She was no longer sitting in a cramped little sweatlodge. Instead she stood in the middle of a vast prairie, surrounded by tall grasses and gentle rolling hills. But Heather could not feel the grass beneath her feet, or even the ground she stood upon, so she knew that she had made the journey to this new, mysterious land only in the spirit. Her body existed somewhere else, in another place or time.

Knowing what she was seeing might be of importance to her, or her people, Heather slowly turned around in an effort to see all there was to see. In three directions the prairie seemed to stretch all the way to the very ends of the earth. In the fourth direction the rolling hills slowly rose to embrace the rugged terrain of snow-capped mountains.

But it wasn't the mountains that captured her attention and stole a gasp from her throat. On the contrary, it was the structure that stood not more than fifty feet away from her—a framework of thin wooden poles, each fifteen to twenty feet long, that circled around and connected to a much larger center pole. The poles looked like they might have once supported a canvas covering, much like the poles of a large circus tent, but there was no covering now. There were only the poles, and the feeling of ancient mystery which enshrouded them.

Drawn to the pole framework, as a moth is drawn to an open flame, Heather was halfway to the strange structure before she even realized she was moving. And as she slipped between two of the upright poles, a profound tingling surging through her very soul, Heather knew she was treading upon sacred ground. Very sacred ground.

She stopped a few feet from the center pole, her attention drawn to the effigies of buffalos and men that were wedged between the fork near the top of the pole. Several long leather cords hung from the fork, almost reaching the ground. Wondering what they were used for, she reached out and grabbed the end of one of the cords. As Heather touched the cord, she was overwhelmed with a vision so intense it tore a scream from her throat.

Pain. Hunger. Thirst. Longing. The emotions seized her heart in an icy embrace as the vision sprang to life. Heather saw a half-naked man dancing before the center pole, his gaze firmly fixed upon the effigies that hung above him. Blood ran down the man's chest, falling freely to the ground at his feet. The blood came from twin cuts on his chest, a little over an inch in length. A wooden skewer was inserted into each cut, tied to leather cords fastened to the top of the pole.

Wearing a skirt of painted leather and a wreath of sage, the young man blew on a eagle-bone whistle as he slowly circled the pole. Leaning back while he danced, he attempted to rip the skewers from his chest, offering his own flesh as a sacrifice to his god. The vision only lasted for a few moments, long enough for her to witness the young man's pain and determination, and hear his prayers for his people. And when the image faded, Heather found that she was no longer alone.

They sat around her in a circle, silently watching the little girl brought before them by the spirits. And though they adorned themselves in feathers and beads, they were not men but animals, the spirits of the old ones. Bear sat beside wolf, who in turn sat next to fox and coyote. They were all there, all the great totems, watching her with eyes that penetrated through to her very soul.

Heather felt a shudder of fear pass through her, for she didn't know what was expected of her. Nor did she know how to act before such powerful deities. She tried to remember some of the old stories Sam had told her, for in the old legends men often came in contact with such spirits, but her mind was suddenly a blank. She could only stand there in silence, waiting to see what was wanted of her. The silence lasted for a few minutes, and then the bear spoke to her.

"Who are you, wolf child? Why have you come to the land of the old ones?" The bear spoke in the language of his people, but somehow Heather understood him. She also understood that he was the leader of all the animals, the necklace of human fingers that hung around his neck testimony to his position of power.

Heather lowered her eyes before she spoke. Partly out of respect. Mostly out of fear. "I am Wa Ya Ny Wa Ti, Medicine Wolf," she answered, giving her Garou name. "I am here because the spirits brought me."

"If the spirits brought you here, then you must be seeking something. What is it you wish to find?"

Heather swallowed, choosing her words carefully. "I seek visions of knowledge, oh great bear. I have also come here to find my spirit guides."

"And why do you seek such visions and guides?" the bear asked, his voice a rumbling growl.

"To help my people," she answered, daring to lift her head to look at him.

"And who are your people?" the bear asked. "What is your tribe? Your clan?"

"My people are the Garou," Heather answered with pride. "My tribe is the Wendigo…." She hesitated and then shook her head. "I'm sorry. I do not mean to offend you, but I do not know my clan."

A chorus of growls, snarls and howls erupted from the animals around her. To stand before the sacred totems and not be able to recite one's lineage was a great embarrassment. Heather wanted to explain why she didn't know such things, but she held her tongue and remained silent. A few moments passed, then the wolf leaned over and whispered in the bear's right ear. The bear nodded and then turned his attention back to Heather.

"You are the Guardian of the Fang?" the bear asked.

Heather drew herself up to her full height. "I am."

Again a chorus of growls, snarls and howls filled the night. The bear waited for the others to quiet down and then spoke again.

"Because you are the Guardian, I will give you this advice: you must face inward in order to see out. Look inside yourself and face the darkness that is a part of you. A part of all of us. Remember who you are, little Guardian. Remember what you are."

Raising his right paw above his head, the bear pointed at the night sky. "You come seeking visions, little Guardian. Behold, I give one to you."

She turned to face where the bear was pointing, knowing that the spirits were showing her something of great importance. She watched in awe as the full moon suddenly grew larger, brighter, changing color from yellow to a dull red. A crimson moon, the color of blood. Heather didn't know the meaning behind the red moon, but she knew it had something to do with her. Maybe it had something to do with all Garou.

The image of the crimson moon lasted for a minute or two, then faded. She turned to question the bear about its meaning, but he and the other animals were gone. Heather was alone again, standing in the middle of an empty prairie. And then the prairie also disappeared, leaving behind only the darkness. This time, however, the darkness was filled with the hissing and popping of heated bricks.

Slowing reaching out with her right hand, Heather's fingers brushed against the sweaty thigh of Sam Nakai. She was back; her spirit had returned to the sweatlodge.

7

Heather wanted to talk about everything she saw and experienced during the sweat, but Sam told her to wait until after she had completed her vision quest. Still a little weakened and lightheaded from the intense heat, she pulled the green army blanket around her shoulders and slowly crawled out of the sweatlodge.

She was dying of thirst, but knew no drinks would be offered to her. No ice-cold Pepsi to replenish the moisture that had been lost through the pores in her skin. No tea or even Kool-Aid to cool the constricted passageway of her parched throat. Even a sip or two of regular old water would have been nice, but that was also unavailable. Instead, she had to rely solely on the night wind to cool her body temperature and ebb the dryness in her mouth.

Still wearing only panties and a T-shirt, which were now soaked with perspiration, and wrapped in the blanket, Heather followed Sam deep into the woods behind Joseph Swimmer's cabin. She wondered what was in store for her, or what was expected, for the vision quest was one of the most mysterious of all Wendigo ceremonies. Those who went through the quest to receive guidance and enlist the aid of the spirits usually refused to talk about their experiences, afraid of weakening the sacred medicine they had received. All she knew about it was that each vision quest was different, and almost anything could happen.

About half a mile from the cabin, in a tiny clearing deep within the forest, a ten-foot circle had been marked out with wooden stakes and a length of rope. Tied to the rope were several small cloth sacks, tobacco offerings to the spirits, and colored strips of ribbon to mark the four directions. A yellow ribbon was used for the east, red for the south, black for west, and white for the north.

Sam walked around the circle once in a clockwise direction, singing a prayer, making sure that no evil forces had entered the circle while it was left unattended. If that had happened, the site would have to be abandoned and a new one chosen in its place. Fortunately, the circle had not been tainted by the Wyrm's darkness.

Satisfied that everything was as it should be, he turned to Heather and instructed her to enter the circle from the east. He waited until she stepped over the rope, and then handed her the sealed quart jar of water he had brought along. The jar of water was all that he gave her. Heather received no food. No weapons of any kind. Just the water and nothing else.

"You must remain inside this circle until you receive your vision and learn the identity of at least one of your spirit guides." Sam said, handing her the water.

"How long will that take?" she asked.

"As long as it takes," he smiled. "Mine took five days."

"Five days?" Heather said, horrified. "I can't last five days out here."

Sam clicked his tongue in disapproval. "You can do anything you put your mind to. Anything at all."

Heather wasn't convinced. She looked at the jar of water she held, wondering how she could possibly make so little last for so long. Food she could live without for a few days, but not water—especially not in the summertime when the temperatures soared daily into the nineties. It didn't help that she was already dying of thirst from going through the sweatlodge ceremony. If she wasn't careful, she could finish what little water she had in just one gulp.

"Will I find my spirit guides?" she asked, hoping for a positive answer to eliminate the doubts that were suddenly surging through her mind.

"If your vision comes, so too will your guides," Sam replied. He smiled briefly, then grew serious again. "This is the last ceremony of your Rites of Passage. Your final test. When you leave this place you will no longer be looked upon as human. You will be Garou...a welcomed member of the Wendigo tribe."

He pointed at Heather's feet. "Here, in this circle, you will leave your childhood and innocence. In return you will be rewarded by Gaia, the Sacred Mother, and by the spirits. Rewarded in ways you cannot possibly imagine. Do you understand?"

Heather hesitated, trying to grasp all the things that Sam had said to her. Finally, she nodded.

He looked at her in silence for a few moments, perhaps reading her spirit to make sure she really did understand everything he had said. Heather shifted uncomfortably under his gaze, greatly relieved when Sam again spoke.

"The vision quest is a hard thing, but you are stronger. You will win." He leaned forward and touched the rope. "But you must not leave this circle for any reason until after you have received what you came for. If you step outside this rope before receiving your vision, you will fail. It is as simple as that."

"But what if I have to go to the bathroom?" Heather asked, knowing it was a foolish question as soon as she said it.

Again Sam clicked his tongue. "If you need to relieve yourself you will do so in the circle. Dig a hole and go; no one will be watching."

"Can I change into a wolf first?"

"No. You were born homid, so you must stay in human form during your quest."

He stepped forward and handed her his pipe. "Since you do not have a pipe of your own yet you may use mine, but you cannot light it or smoke it."

Heather took the pipe with some reluctance. "If I can't smoke it, then what can I do with it?"

"You may offer it to Gaia in prayer," Sam said. "Maybe she will help you find your guides." He started to leave, but turned back. "One more thing: do not turn your back to the west for any reason. The west is the direction from which darkness comes, the direction of the Wyrm. It is dangerous to turn your back to the Wyrm during a vision quest, when your body is weak. If you must do so, then build a small fire first and put the flames between you and the west. The spirit elements of the fire will protect you from the darkness."

Seeing the fear in her eyes, he smiled. "You will do fine; I know it. Remember, it is your vision…they are your guides. Do not leave this circle until you have what you came for."

"I won't fail," she said, tears welling up in her eyes. Heather was not afraid of the west, or the Wyrm's darkness. Not really. She was afraid of disappointing Sam. He was her teacher. Her friend. She wouldn't be able to ever face him again if she failed her test before receiving a vision or learning the identity of at least one spirit guide. She'd rather die first.

She wanted to lean across the rope and give Sam a hug, but such things were for sentimental humans and not werewolves. She was no longer quite human, no longer a little girl. She was a Garou now, the blood of a wolf flowing through her veins. Soon she would also be a warrior. So instead of a hug, Heather nodded and promised that she would not leave the circle until after she had received a vision.

"Good," he smiled. "Then I will see you in a few days."

She stood there and watched as Sam slowly walked away, leaving her standing alone within the roped circle. And as her mentor disappeared from view, the night seemed to close in around her. Heather was on her own now, afloat on an island of hallowed ground, in a sea of darkness. She thought about what Sam had told her and turned to face the west, almost expecting to see something lunge at her from the blackness.

Was the Wyrm out there, watching, waiting for her to grow weak and careless, hoping she would turn her back to the darkness of the west? She could almost feel it, a shadow deeper than the darkness, coming through the forest toward her. Heather shuddered in fear, and then shook her head.

"I am not afraid," she said, her voice no more than a whisper. "No matter what, I will not be afraid. I will stay here until my vision comes. That's a promise."

Tucking Sam's pipe beneath her left arm, she slowly unscrewed the lid on the quart jar and took a tiny sip of water. Just a sip, enough only to wet the dryness in her mouth and throat. The water was warm, and smelled slightly of vinegar, but it was a blessing nonetheless. She wanted to take more than just a sip, but not knowing how long she would be in the forest she dared not. Replacing the lid back on the jar, she stared out into the darkness.

Five days. I'll never make it.

Four more Garou, and two Indians of Kinfolk blood, had arrived by the time Sam returned to Joseph's cabin. They sat out back with the others, around a small fire, arguing over what should be done about the Shaman Moon. Sam recognized three of the Garou as belonging to the Sitting Wolf Pack, but the fourth—a woman with long, curly black hair—he had never seen before. She might have been a member of the Shadow Lords, but there was no way of knowing without asking. And to do so now, after she had already arrived, would have been considered bad manners.

"We don't even know if the Wyrm will try to come through the rift," spoke one of the newly arrived Garou.

"It will try," Joseph answered.

"What makes you so sure?"

"Because the Wyrm tried before, but Nee Yah Kah Tah Kee stopped it."

"But the Great Wolf is no more," the Garou said, exasperated. "What's to stop the Wyrm from sending its armies into the Realm?"

"Nothing. Nothing at all," Michael Pathkiller said, his voice angry. Breaking a stick across his knee, he stood up and stared at Sam Nakai.

Though the others in the circle seemed not to notice, Pathkiller's gesture was not wasted on Sam. Had it been an arrow, rather than a stick, that he broke, it would have signified an official breaking of ties between the two men—despite the fact that both were of the same tribe. To put it simply, Pathkiller was saying that he no longer considered Sam to be a Wendigo.

The gesture was an insult, directed only towards those who had done something to hurt or shame the tribe. Pathkiller was obviously doing his best to infuriate Sam, perhaps hoping to start a fight. But Sam would not give the younger Garou such satisfaction. Not yet anyway. Instead of responding to the insult, he chose to simply ignore it as though it were of little or no importance. Infuriated, Pathkiller threw the pieces of broken stick into the fire.

"Not all of Nee Yah Kah Tah Kee's magic has been lost," Joseph Swimmer said, unaware that anything out of the ordinary had just taken place. "There is still the Fang."

"But the Guardian is just a child," one of the other Indians pointed out. "She cannot stop the Wyrm by herself."

"Not by herself," Joseph agreed. "We must help her."

"There is no time to wait while pups are weaned," Pathkiller said. He shot a hateful look in Sam's direction, then continued. "We must gather our people to stop the Wyrm."

Pathkiller turned to the black-haired woman. "Will your pack join us to fight the Wyrm?"

She nodded. "My pack will be proud to fight alongside their Wendigo brothers, though there are only seven of us—not nearly enough to turn the tide of battle. But in return for our help we want the right of free passage through your domain."

Michael Pathkiller glared at the woman. "Now is not the time to negotiate treaties and rights."

"Nor is it the time to be petty over simple things," she retaliated. "You ask us to fight for you, yet you refuse to grant us safe passageway through your land?"

Pathkiller stared at her for a moment longer, then nodded. "Very well, if you fight with us I will grant you and your people the right of free passage through the domain of the Sitting Wolf Pack."

"Your generosity knows no bounds," the woman smiled, having won the argument. "The Daughters of the Sun will fight with the Sitting Wolf Pack. I, Moon Singer, leader of the pack, give you my word on it."

Sam was quite surprised when the woman named her pack. The Daughters of the Sun were one of the packs of the Black Furies, a tribe composed almost entirely of female Garou. Originally from Greece, the Furies were a reclusive tribe that preferred to remain deep within the wilderness. Of all the Garou tribes, they were the most adamant in the defense of the few Wyld sites and creatures left in the world. They were often appointed as the punishers and avengers of the Garou, responsible for tracking down and destroying the greatest evils.

The strength and powers of the Furies would indeed be welcomed in the upcoming battle against the Wyrm. But Joseph Swimmer knew their help was still not enough. "We still need the girl," he interrupted. "She is the Guardian of the Fang."

"She is a cliath," Pathkiller spat, his anger close to the boiling point. "We do not have time to wait while she grows teeth." He turned and pointed accusingly at Sam. "Maybe if he did not give the Fang to someone so young things would not be so hopeless."

"The spirits chose her," Sam retorted calmly. "I did not."

"Spirits. Whose spirits?" Pathkiller asked, an evil smile unfolding on his face. "Certainly no totem of the Garou would make such a choice."

Sam felt a flush of anger warm his face. "What are you saying?"

Pathkiller looked him straight in the eyes. "Maybe you follow the wrong guides, Sam Nakai. Maybe it's the Wyrm's voice that you hear."

"I will not listen to such talk," Sam said, unable to tolerate any more of the younger Garou's insults. He took a step forward. Pathkiller stepped away from the fire to meet him.

"Enough," Joseph shouted, angry. "Save your fighting for the Wyrm." He waited until Sam and Pathkiller calmed down, then continued. "The girl is important. Without her we may not be able to keep the Gauntlet sealed against the Dark One. We will wait for her to seek her vision and find her guides; by then other Garou and Kinfolk will have arrived. We will need all the help we can get."

8

Three days had already passed and Heather Ocoee still had not received her vision. Nor had she seen anything even remotely resembling a spirit guide or totem. And now, on the evening of the third day, she was beginning to wonder if she had the strength to go on. Her body weakened from the lack of food, her meager supply of water almost gone, she lay on her back in the center of the roped circle and watched as the day slowly gave way to the night.

It would be dark soon. Heather longed to slip into Lupus form and run with the night, but that was not allowed. She had to remain within the circle, suffering for her vision, praying to Gaia and the spirits for guidance. Besides, she doubted if she had the strength necessary to make the transformation. Never before in her life had she felt so weak. Even during the months of sickness at the orphanage she had been stronger. A whole lot stronger.

In her present physical condition, she would be lucky if she had the strength to change even one of her hands, or a foot, into werewolf form. She almost laughed at the image of her skinny human body with a furry, oversized werewolf foot. She could just see herself clumping down the sidewalk, drawing stares from those she passed. She would be a freak, like the metis she had seen, a thing of scorn and ridicule.

Heather shook the thoughts of metis Garou from her mind, glad that she had not been born as such. Things were tough enough without having to go through life as a mutation. Looking up at the sky, she wished for the sun to hurry up and set. The day had been long and hot, her body burning even darker beneath the sun's cruel rays.

Despite being in a forest, there was little shade in the clearing where she lay. To escape the sun's heat Heather had sought shelter beneath her blanket, holding it above her head until her arms quivered with fatigue. During those times, she had fantasized about milkshakes and ice-cold drinks, praying that they would miraculously appear before her. Gifts from Gaia. When no frosty mugs floated down from the heavens on the wings of angels, she resorted to licking the outside of the quart Mason jar in a vain attempt to quench her thirst.

But no matter how many times she licked the outside of the jar, her thirst refused to go away. She didn't dare open the container and taste of the few remaining swallows of water she had left. If she did, she would surely drain the entire contents in a single gulp. And then Heather would have no water at all, nothing to get her through the day, or days, she might have yet to face.

A frown tugged at the corner of her mouth. Could she face another day? Would it be possible for her to make it through another afternoon of searing heat with nothing but a scratchy wool blanket to protect her from the sun's merciless rays, a blanket that also blocked out the breeze and made her body twice as hot? Sam Nakai had told her that his first vision quest lasted five days. Would she be able to make it that long? Could she hold out?

Heather looked at her last few precious sips of water and felt the heartache of failure settle deep into her chest. There was no way she could last five days like Sam had done, no way she could even hold out for one more day. If her vision didn't come soon, tonight, she was destined to fail.

A tear formed in her left eye and trickled slowly down her cheek. So many people were depending on her; she must not fail. She was the Guardian, the protector of the sacred Fang. But Heather couldn't help it. She was the Guardian, true, but she was also just a girl barely into her puberty. And what good did it do to be a Garou when she wasn't allowed to change forms during the vision quest? Even her stronger other self was no help to her now. Unless her vision came soon, she would fail her quest without receiving her vision or meeting even one of her spirit guides.

OWL GOINGBACK

Brushing the tear from her cheek, Heather clasped her hands together and prayed harder than she had ever prayed before. She prayed to Gaia, the Sacred Mother, asking for her help, asking for strength. She also prayed to the spirits of her ancestors, as well as to the spirits of the forest.

"Please, Sacred Mother. Please forgive me, for I am weak and no longer have the strength to go on. The spirits have chosen me to be the Guardian of the Fang, protector of the sacred tooth of Nee Yah Kah Tah Kee. But I am not worthy. They should have chosen someone stronger, someone a little older.

"Oh, Great Mother. If it be your will, please send me my vision so I may use it to help my people? I do not want to fail, but I cannot last another day here in this circle." She picked up Sam's pipe and raised it with trembling hands above her head. "I offer you this pipe in prayer, for I do not have my own. Please hear my prayer, Grandmother; send me my vision."

Clutching the pipe tightly in her right hand, Heather prayed for strength and courage, and for a vision that would help the Garou. Her people. She prayed for a tiny bit of enlightenment that might aid in the fight against the Wyrm. Finally, she asked that one of her spirit guides might make an appearance and show her the path she was to walk.

As she prayed, the sun slipped slowly behind the western horizon, relinquishing the day to the spirits of the night. A breeze came up suddenly, blowing from the north, caressing her skin and quenching the fire that burned within her body. Heather took a deep breath. The breeze was as refreshing as water from a mountain stream, killing the thirst that had afflicted her throughout most of the day.

"Thank you," she whispered, holding the pipe tighter. She knew in her heart that Gaia had heard the prayer and sent the cool night breeze to relieve some of her discomfort.

Gaia had also sent something else. For as Heather lay there, taking in great gulps of air, she heard the haunting cry of an owl calling to her from the darkness beyond the circle. The cry was followed almost immediately by the sound of footsteps slowly approaching from the south.

Someone's coming.

Startled, Heather pushed herself up into a sitting position and looked to see who approached. The sun had just set and shadows lay heavy upon the forest, but it wasn't completely dark yet. She would have seen anyone walking her way, but no one was there.

"Sam, is that you?"

The footsteps grew louder, came closer. Leaves crackled and twigs snapped as someone, or something, moved slowly between the trees. She strained her eyes to see who it was that came her way, but she didn't see anybody.

"Joseph?"

Still no reply.

A tingle of fear marched down her back on spider legs. Someone was walking toward her, someone who couldn't be seen. The sounds drew nearer, louder, circling slowly to the east.

A spirit. It has to be a spirit.

Heather sat motionless, almost afraid to breathe. The spirit that approached might be one of her guides. If so, then she didn't want to do anything that would offend it or frighten it away—if spirits could possibly be scared of anything at all.

She was still sitting motionless when something flew at her from the north. Heather caught a glimpse of white feathered wings as she ducked, a startled cry escaping her lips. She turned quickly, expecting to see the owl whose cry she had heard earlier. But it was a young man who now stood inside the circle with her.

The man was an Indian warrior, tall and thin, with sharp features and eyes that seemed to look right through her. His head was shaved, except for a patch of hair on the back of his head which was long and decorated with several white feathers. Both of his ears were adorned with earrings of shell and bone, and a necklace of tiny pink shells hung around his neck.

He wore a dark breechcloth and leggings, with a long, fringed hunting coat of tanned buckskin. Tied about his waist was a long sash of colored yarn, interwoven with beads, its ends hanging just above his right knee. The color of the sash matched the color of his moccasins, which might have been beaded but Heather couldn't be sure. Though she could see the Indian clearly, she could also see right through him. He was indeed a spirit, perhaps a guide who had come to offer his assistance.

The warrior stood in silence, watching Heather as though he expected her to say something. A feeling of panic shot through her. Neither Sam Nakai or George Swimmer had told her the proper words to say in the event a spirit should make an appearance during her vision quest. Not knowing what to say, she raised Sam's pipe with the stem pointed toward the spirit in offering. The man smiled and nodded, pleased with the gesture. She had obviously done the right thing.

No sooner had she offered the pipe to the spirit than everything around her changed. Heather no longer sat within a tiny circle deep in the forest. Instead she found herself standing on top of a mountain. The mountain was familiar; she had been there before. It was the same mountain upon which the carved stone image of Nee Yah Kah Tah Kee had once stood.

Heather had only been to Monterey Mountain once before, and that was shortly after Sam had passed on the Guardianship to her. The one and only time she had been to the mountain, she had fought and killed a Black Spiral Dancer. She had also called upon the powers of the Fang and the Sacred Wolf to heal Sam's wounds, earning her the Garou name of Wa Ya Ny Wa Ti, Medicine Wolf. She wondered why the spirit had brought her to the spot where Nee Yah Kah Tah Kee had stood, but only for a moment. When Heather turned around, she saw what it was that the warrior wished to show her. What she saw terrified her.

A bloody battle waged on top of the sacred mountain. Garou in Crinos form stood side by side with Native American Kinfolk, fighting a horde of Banths and Black Spiral Dancers that seemed to materialize out of thin air. And though they fought bravely, the children of Gaia were greatly outnumbered by the foul servants of the Wyrm. Their howls and war cries filled the night as they fought and died on top of Monterey Mountain.

Above the battle rose a full moon the color of blood, bathing those who fought in an eerie crimson glow. It was the same blood-red moon Heather had seen during the sweatlodge ceremony, only now it was no longer just a vision. What she was seeing was a premonition of the future, a glimpse of the terrifying things to come.

Tearing her gaze away from the moon, Heather looked back to the battle. The Garou and Kindreds were losing, pushed back across the mountain top by an endless horde of Wyrm-spawn that suddenly appeared as if by magic. Her breath caught as she recognized one of the Garou who had already fallen in the fight and lay dying upon the bloody ground.

"No. No," she whispered. "It can't be." But it was. The silver-haired werewolf that lay before her was none other than her dear friend and mentor, Sam Nakai.

"Dear God. No."

The scene of battle slowly faded, disappearing as her vision changed. Heather now stood in a land of shadows, a place of swirling colors and shimmering mist. She looked around, aware that everything she saw looked brighter, more vivid, than that which she usually encountered in the normal world. And though she had only visited it on a few occasions, and never alone, she immediately recognized her surroundings as being part of the mysterious spirit world, known to Garou as the Umbra.

The Umbra was a land of spirits and living memories, a place where Garou went to seek rejuvenation, guidance or knowledge of sacred things. Often as dangerous as it was beautiful, the Umbra was divided into many different regions, each with its own peculiar set of rules and laws. Some of the regions were safe for Garou, places where they could speak with ancestor spirits. Other regions were not so safe, for they were places of darkness where the followers of the Wyrm often traveled, areas strictly avoided by the werewolf tribes.

Heather stood now in one such region of darkness. Directly before her the land was split by a wide crack, a canyon of eternal night whose walls were lined with a thousand perils and whose floor was littered with the bones of those foolhardy enough to explore its secrets. Heather Ocoee stood upon the edge of the Abyss.

She wondered why her vision had brought her to the Abyss. What was her spirit guide trying to tell her? What was she to seek in the great crack of darkness? Suddenly she remembered that Sam Nakai had once told her there used to be a second Fang of the Wolf, but it had been lost years ago in the Umbra. Perhaps her guide was trying to show her what she already knew to be true, that all things lost in the Umbra eventually find their way to the Abyss. He was telling her to find the lost Fang, for its power was needed. Unless the missing Fang was found the vision she had seen would come true. Unless the sacred tooth of Nee Yah Kah Tah Kee was located before the night of the crimson moon, Sam Nakai and the others would die.

The message received and understood, Heather again found herself sitting inside a roped circle deep within the forest. Her vision over, she watched in awe as her spirit guide transformed back into an owl and flew away. On the ground where he had stood lay a single wing feather, a gift of medicine to the Guardian.

Heather picked up the owl feather and held it gently between fingers and thumb. She had not failed her quest; she had been given a vision and had met one of her spirit guides. Her final Rite of Passage complete, she would now be looked upon by the others of the tribe as a Wendigo warrior. It should have been an occasion for joy and celebration, but there was no time for such things now. She had completed the Rites, but she had also been given a task...a task she dared not fail.

Pouring the last of her water on the ground as a thank-you to Gaia, Heather wrapped the blanket around her shoulders and stepped out of the circle. Her vision quest was over, but her journey had just begun.

PART II

*I have seen the wonders of the spirit-land,
and have talked with the ghosts.
I traveled far and am sent back with a message
to tell you to make ready
for the coming of the Messiah
and return of the ghosts in the spring.*
—Kicking Bear, Sioux

9

Her body greatly weakened from the ordeal of the vision quest, Heather staggered as she made her way slowly through the forest. Several times she had to pause and rest against a tree until she regained enough strength to continue on. She walked slowly, carefully placing one foot in front of the other in a conscious effort to keep from falling. Twice she bumped painfully against a tree trunk, a silent groan escaping her lips, and once she tripped over an unseen vine and went sprawling.

Heather thought about just lying where she had fallen for the night, but only for a moment. The vision she had been given was a premonition of things to come, a warning meant to be shared with the others. She had to tell Sam and Joseph about what she had seen, before the vision became a reality.

With this bit of reasoning planted firmly in her mind, she picked herself up and staggered on. One foot in front of the other. Left. Right. Left. Keep going. Don't stop. After what seemed like hours, even days, she arrived at Joseph Swimmer's tiny log cabin.

Emerging from the forest, Heather spotted a small gathering of Garou and Kinfolk seated around a campfire, in back of the cabin; Sam and Joseph were among them. She wanted to shout out to them, warning them of the things she had seen in her vision. A danger she felt was approaching fast. She remained silent, however, for it was forbidden to speak of the things one had seen on a vision quest until after going through a second sweatlodge ceremony. Only then, when her body and spirit were once again purified, would she be allowed to talk openly.

And even if she was allowed to speak now, her throat was so parched from the lack of water that she could barely utter a single syllable, let alone describe in detail all that she had seen and experienced.

Noticing her arrival, Joseph cut short the conversation of the others with a wave of his hand. Standing up, he nodded to Heather and then hurried to heat up the bricks that would be used in the sweatlodge. Sam also got to his feet. He offered her a slight smile and then went to assist Joseph in the preparation of the lodge.

Heather wished Sam had stayed, for she found herself facing a group of Garou and Kinfolk she did not know. There was no warmth or friendship in the eyes of those who stared back at her. They looked upon her with open disdain and hostility, as though her sudden appearance had interrupted something of great importance. She had a feeling they were talking about her, and what had been said was not good.

She would have tried to prove herself by staring down those who glared at her, but Heather was much too weak—both physically and mentally—for such a contest. Instead she turned her back on the group and walked away. Finding a tree to rest against, she pulled the blanket tight about her shoulders and sat down wearily. Let them say what they wanted about her, she was just too damn tired to care.

At least they couldn't say that she had failed her vision quest. Heather had accomplished what she had set out to achieve: she had received her vision and met one of her spirit guides. Her Rites of Passage were complete. And even if she didn't feel like one just then, she was now officially a warrior of the Wendigo.

Heather was still sitting, her thoughts a million miles away, when she heard footsteps slowly approaching her. Raising her head, she saw Sam standing over her.

"Come," he said, his voice all business. She waited a moment to see if he would offer his hand to help her up. When he didn't, she leaned forward and pushed herself up with her hands. Knowing she was still being watched by the other Garou, Heather tried her best not to stumble or stagger as she followed Sam to the sweatlodge.

Joseph Swimmer was already inside the sweatlodge waiting for them. Sam entered first, followed by Heather. They sat in the same positions they had sat before, with Joseph on the west side of the circular pit. Once they were inside, the old Cherokee carefully filled his pipe with tobacco and lit it with a butane lighter. Raising the pipe above his head, he offered prayers to Gaia and the four directions. He then passed the pipe to the others so they too could pray. When the tobacco in Joseph's pipe was completely smoked, Sam filled his medicine pipe and the entire process was repeated.

After both pipes had been smoked, and the proper prayers offered, the metis Garou again appeared to pass the heated bricks into the sweatlodge. Her chin resting wearily on her knees, Heather watched the bricks being carefully stacked in the pit and wondered if she could possibly survive another sweatlodge ceremony.

The second sweatlodge ceremony lasted even longer, and was much more intense, than the first. Despite the fact that it was also a hell of a lot hotter, Heather's skin remained perfectly dry throughout the ceremony. She had gone without water for so long during her vision quest, and dehydrated so badly, that she no longer had any excess body fluids to sweat away. Running her fingertips over her chest and stomach, she was alarmed by how much weight she had lost during her time spent in the woods without food or water. She seemed dangerously thin, her skin stretched tight over a body that was now little more than bones. She would make the perfect poster child for aid to a famished country; any thinner and she would likely blow away in the wind.

Lowering her head, Heather took shallow breaths to keep the intense heat from burning her throat and lungs. She was just about to pass out when the ceremony finally ended and the flap of carpeting covering the sweatlodge's entrance was raised. A cool night breeze entered the lodge, tickling her skin like the touch of an eagle feather. A cup of water was also passed in. A real cup. Not a baby cup with a training lid like before. Heather was allowed to drink the water, all of it if she wished. Even so, she still remembered to make an offering to Gaia by pouring the first sip over the heated bricks.

Sam waited until after she had finished the water before speaking to her. "Heather, you must now tell us about everything you saw and experienced on your vision quest, both here in the sweatlodge and while you were in the forest. Leave nothing out, no matter how small, for every little detail is important."

Heather nodded, gathering together her thoughts and putting them in order. Taking a deep breath, she described everything that had happened to her on her vision quest. She took her time, making sure nothing was overlooked or forgotten. She told about seeing the crimson moon during the first sweat, and how she had talked to the bear and the council of animals. She described her spirit guide, the owl, and the terrible vision of battle he had brought to her. She left nothing out, not even the part about how she had seen Sam dying on the battlefield.

As she told her story, her eyes watered and tears slowly trickled down her cheeks. Garou were not supposed to cry, for it was a sign of weakness, but she couldn't help it. She had been through a lot in the last few days, and somewhere deep inside of her an emotional floodgate opened wide and the tears came rushing out with the words. Heather didn't bother to wipe her eyes until after she had finished speaking.

Silence fell heavily upon the three of them as her story came to an end. A few tense moments passed and then Sam nodded.

"You have done well," he said. "You should be proud of yourself. Not everyone has such a powerful vision, or meets one of their personal spirit guides, on their very first vision quest. It means your medicine is strong, and the spirits are helping you." Patting Heather on the head, he allowed a smile to slowly unfold on his face. "There is hope for you yet, little one."

Heather felt a great weight lift off her shoulders. More than anything else, she had wanted to please her mentor. Had she failed the vision quest she would have also failed him.

"But what does the vision mean?" she asked. "Why did the full moon turn the color of blood?"

Sam told Heather about the Shaman Moon, explaining that it was a magical time when a rift opened in the Gauntlet, allowing ancestor spirits the opportunity to visit their living relatives in the Realm. Unfortunately, the Wyrm could also use the rift now that the statue of Nee Yah Kah Tah Kee had been destroyed.

"It is as I feared," Joseph said, clearing his throat. "The Bear and the other animals Heather saw in her vision are warning us that the Wyrm will try to enter this world through the rift. We must do everything within our power to stop it."

"There isn't much time to prepare," Sam said, pointing out the obvious. "The moon will be full in less than a week."

Joseph nodded. "Then we must gather our forces quickly and go to the mountain where the Great Wolf once stood."

"I can open a moonbridge to get there; it will save us time," Sam suggested.

"That will work for the Garou," Joseph smiled. "But a moonbridge does not work for an old homid like me. I will take my pickup truck instead."

"How long will it take you to get there?"

"One day to gather together those of medicine who are willing to fight against the Wyrm. Another day to get there; it is a rather old pickup."

"Two days," Sam shook his head. "That's cutting it pretty damn close."

"I know," Joseph nodded. "I am sorry, but it is the best I can do. We will need an army to keep the Wyrm's followers from pouring into this Realm. It takes time to gather such an army together."

An idea suddenly sprang to Heather's mind. "What about the other Fang of the Wolf?" she asked. "We can use it to stop the Wyrm."

Sam shook his head. "The other Fang was lost somewhere in the Umbra years ago. Many Garou have looked for it, but it has never been found. I have also searched for it on several occasions, without any luck. I don't think it will ever be found."

"But I can find it," Heather said, enthusiastic. "I know I can. My vision showed me where to look. It's somewhere in the Abyss."

"Forget it. The second Fang is lost forever," Sam said, a trace of annoyance entering his voice. "Besides, it is far too dangerous for a little girl to enter the Realm of the Abyss alone."

"But I am the Guardian."

"You are a child!" he snapped.

His words stung like a slap across the face. A *child*. Is that what Sam really thought of her? If so, then why had he given her the Fang of the Wolf? And why was he wasting his time training her? She was not a child, not any more. She had passed the Rites of Passage, earning the full rights of a Wendigo warrior. She was Wa Ya Ny Wa Ti, Medicine Wolf. A Garou.

Her feelings hurt, Heather did not answer back to her mentor's insult. Instead she remained silent, swallowing her anger, listening while Sam and Joseph talked about how to stop the Wyrm from entering the Realm through the rift. Truthfully,

Heather no longer felt the need to say anything. She had already made up her mind about what needed to be done, and knew exactly what she was going to do.

A trace of a smile touched the corners of her lips. She would show Sam Nakai exactly who among them was a child. And who was a Garou.

10

A growl formed deep in the back of Michael Pathkiller's throat as he watched the girl stagger from the shadows of the forest. No one heard the growl, for they were all much too busy arguing amongst themselves. Not that he cared, for everyone knew his feelings toward the so-called Guardian. The false Guardian, she who wore the sacred medicine that rightfully should be his and one day would be his, even if he had to kill to get it.

Sam Nakai claimed the spirits had chosen Heather Ocoee as the new Guardian of the Fang, but he was an old fool guided by nothing more than the whispering of the wind. Or he was a liar. Either way, he had given the last remaining magic of Nee Yah Kah Tah Kee to a child barely out of the diaper stage, a Garou that was not worthy of the honor of the Guardianship or the responsibility that went with it.

Pathkiller had heard the stories about the girl, how she'd transformed into Crinos form and killed a Black Spiral Dancer the first night she was given the Fang. Even how the Sacred Sitting Wolf had appeared before her in spirit form, speaking to her, helping her to heal the wounds of Sam Nakai who lay dying at her feet. He had heard the stories, but he didn't believe them. They were nothing but lies to excuse the inexcusable, and to cover up the fact that a child had been given a sacred gift of magic.

Lies. Lies. Lies. His blood boiled when he thought about them. Fables created by Sam Nakai, and then repeated by other Garou with little or no sense. "Never before has someone so young, and not yet trained as a warrior, defeated a Black Spiral Dancer," they said. "This alone should be proof that Heather Ocoee truly is the Chosen One."

Pathkiller cleared his throat and spit, his anger like a bitter bile. Some Garou even speculated that the girl was much more than just the new Guardian; a child warrior perhaps, sent to aid the tribe in its time of need. Certainly none of his pack believed such nonsense, at least they dared not say so while he was around to hear it.

Lies. Blasphemy. He was the leader of the Sitting Wolf Pack. He alone was worthy of the Guardianship. The Fang of the Wolf, the sacred medicine of Nee Yah Kah Tah Kee, was rightfully his.

The growl still deep in his throat, Pathkiller watched as Joseph Swimmer hurried to heat the bricks that would be used in a second sweatlodge ceremony. Sam Nakai also stood up, and then went to help the old Indian prepare for the ceremony. That left Heather standing by herself, facing him and the other Garou.

Let's see how brave you are without your mentor, you little bitch.

Pathkiller smiled and licked his lips, focusing his gaze and thoughts on the

OWL GOINGBACK

girl who stood before him. She tried to return his stare, but faltered through weakness and lack of a strong heart. He almost laughed when she turned her back on him and walked away, showing to the others what a weak and pathetic little creature she truly was.

Maybe now the rest of Garou who had seen her weakness would come to their senses and acknowledge that he was the rightful Guardian after all. But it did not matter. One way or another, he would soon have what should have been his all along. The Guardianship would be his, Pathkiller knew, for only he had the strength and courage needed to face the Wyrm and seal the rift in the Gauntlet when the Shaman Moon rose high in the sky. He and he alone would call upon the sacred powers of Nee Yah Kah Tah Kee to defeat the darkness when it came to Monterey Mountain.

He watched Heather slump wearily against a tree, and then turned his attention to Sam Nakai. Pathkiller knew he would soon be the Guardian of the Fang; there was no doubt about it. The only question left unanswered was whom would he kill first: the teacher or the student?

11

The sweatlodge ceremony officially over, Heather, Sam and Joseph crawled from the squat, dome-shaped structure into the cool briskness of the night. She was glad to see that sometime during the ceremony, while they were still inside the lodge, the Garou and Kinfolk seated around the campfire had finished their business and left. All that remained of their council session was a small pile of glowing embers and the empty chairs that surrounded it. She was also delighted to discover that someone had been thoughtful enough to leave four buckets of cold spring water and a stack of towels sitting just outside the sweatlodge.

Grabbing one of the buckets, Heather ducked behind a tree and stripped off her grimy underwear and T-shirt. Holding the bucket above her head, she allowed half the water to pour slowly over her naked body. Once wet, she set the bucket down and used her hands to wipe away as much of the accumulated grime, sweat and body odor as she possibly could. Another rinse and she dried off with the thick terrycloth towel that smelled wonderfully of desert sage and sweetgrass.

Once dry, Heather carefully hung the towel on the lowest branch of the tree. She considered slipping her underwear and T-shirt back on, but the thought of getting back into the soiled, smelly garments made her skin crawl. Luckily, she had just dried off when an elderly Cherokee woman appeared with Heather's jeans, shoes, and a man's cotton work shirt. It was the same woman who had greeted Sam when they arrived at the cabin days ago. Again Heather wondered if the woman was Joseph's wife.

"Wa-do," Heather said, hoping she had remembered the correct Cherokee word for thank-you. It must have been the right word, for the woman smiled and nodded. She also answered with a string of dialogue that left the girl utterly confused.

"Uh, wa-do," Heather said again, falling back on one of the few Cherokee words she knew. She also knew how to say coffee, black snake and cucumber, but didn't feel that any of those words would be appropriate, or useful, to the present situation.

The woman must have realized that Heather did not really speak Cherokee, because she cut her conversation short with a laugh. Feeling quite foolish, Heather could only shrug. Luckily, no other response was necessary for the woman nodded again and then shuffled slowly back to the cabin.

"Gee, I guess I really need to brush up on my Cherokee," Heather said to herself after the woman had left. "I wonder if Joseph has a dictionary I could borrow." It was her turn to laugh. With all the things she had to learn just to be a Garou, it was doubtful if she would have any time soon to master another language.

Wishing she had thought to bring along a second pair of underwear, but not really needing any, Heather wiggled into her jeans and then slipped on the shirt, tucking it into her pants. Sam and Joseph had already disappeared by the time she was finished dressing, but there was only one place they could have gone. Entering the cabin through the back door, she found them seated around a small, wooden table that had previously held Joseph's black-and-white television.

The television no longer sat atop the table. In its place were ceramic serving plates filled with pancakes, scrambled eggs and sausage links, and several plastic bottles of flavored syrup. There was also a glass pitcher filled with milk, as well as a second one filled with orange juice. Heather felt her mouth start to water as she spotted the savory assortment of food. Her stomach also rumbled.

Seeing Heather enter the room, Joseph greeted her with a string of Cherokee words that stopped the Garou dead in her tracks. A few moments of tense silence followed, then the old man burst out laughing. "I'm sorry. My wife told me that you spoke my language fluently. She must have been mistaken." He motioned for her to join them. "Come. Join us, little one. No need to be shy. I promise we will speak only English."

Heather felt her face warm with embarrassment, but that didn't stop her from taking a seat on the empty chair that had been left for her. Nor did she waste any time filling the plate Sam handed to her with enough food to feed three people. She hadn't eaten for days and was determined to make up for lost time. A few bites of pancake, and half a sausage link later, Heather was so full she could not take another bite without popping. Worried about wasting food, and not wanting to offend the person who had prepared such a wonderful meal, she tried to force down a little more and nearly gagged. Seeing her discomfort, Sam and Joseph cracked up laughing.

"What? You're not giving up already, are you?" Sam asked, cocking an eyebrow. "You disappoint me; I had told Joseph that you could probably eat all of this food by yourself."

"Oh, little one," Joseph laughed. "It looks like your eyes are bigger than your belly."

Heather groaned and rubbed her stomach to show that he was probably right. "The food's great. Really. All of it. But I'm sorry, I'm just too full to eat anymore. If I take even one more bite I'm going to burst."

Sam nodded. "It's okay. Don't worry, no one will get mad at you for not eating. Your stomach has shrunk from going without food for so many days. It's normal. The same thing happened to me on my first vision quest. If you are full, then don't eat. It's as simple as that." He smiled. "No sense making yourself sick when you don't have to."

"Do not worry, little one," Joseph grinned. "Your stomach may be small now, but soon it will grow big again. You'll see."

Relieved that she didn't have to eat all the food she had taken, Heather pushed her plate away and leaned back in the chair. Joseph and Sam didn't speak much until after they were finished eating, and then the conversation again turned to discussing ways of preventing the Wyrm from entering the Realm through the rift.

Neither of the men asked for Heather's opinion on the subject, or made any attempt to draw her into the discussion. She should have been angry; after all she had successfully passed her final Wendigo Rite of Passage and was now supposed to be considered an adult Garou. A warrior. Truthfully, however, she was glad they didn't ask for her opinion. Her mind and body were still quite fatigued from her lengthy ordeal in the forest, and she wanted nothing more than to sit back and rest. She was also still mad at Sam for calling her a child in the sweatlodge, another valid reason to remain silent.

After breakfast, they thanked Joseph for all he had done to help, and started back to their campsite. It was midmorning by the time they left the cabin, so they decided to remain in Homid form and walk all the way back. Less risk of scaring the locals than if they had made the trip in wolf form. Heather didn't mind the long walk; it gave her a chance to ponder over all the strange and wonderful things that had happened to her during her vision quest. It also gave her time to think about what she could and would do to prove to Sam that she truly was the Guardian of the Fang, and not just a child who needed his constant supervision. By the time they reached their campsite later in the day, she had a pretty good idea about what to do to defend her honor.

Arriving at the clearing where they had pitched their tents and parked Sam's truck, Heather waited until her mentor was busy gathering together their belongings. And then, when his back was turned, she grabbed her leather traveling pack and slipped quietly away into the forest. Once she was deep in the shadows of the trees, she removed her clothes and slipped them into the pack.

Not all Garou removed their clothes before transforming into wolf or werewolf form. Most had clothing that had been specially prepared with magic and sacred ceremonies to transform with the person wearing it. Heather had one such outfit, but knew she would never be able get it out of her tent without arousing Sam's curiosity. Her traveling pack had an adjustable elastic band, allowing her to take her clothing with her no matter what form she traveled in. Walking home in the nude was one thrill she could well live without.

Fastening the pack's band about her waist, Heather quickly transformed into Lupus form. By changing into a wolf, she could move easily along the narrow trails and through the thick underbrush without having to worry about being scratched to pieces by branches and thorny vines. Four legs were also much better than two for covering great distances in a hurry.

Turning east, she followed a familiar animal trail that twisted and turned, branching out through the forest like a connecting series of arteries. She had only been following the trail for twenty minutes or so when she found the tiny stream she was looking for.

Heather hadn't told Sam about the reflection of the gnarled creature she had seen in the pool of water because she was afraid of sounding foolish. She also didn't want him to know that she had tucked tail and run away without thoroughly checking out the situation. Now that Sam had hurt her feelings by calling her a child, she wasn't about to tell him. Instead, she would return to the pool and solve its mystery by herself. After that, guided by the vision she had received, she intended to enter the Umbra to find the missing Fang. And she *would* find it. Wouldn't that put Mr. Sam Nakai in his place? He would soon find out just who was a child and who wasn't.

The pool didn't look much different in the daytime than it did at night. Large, stately trees filtered out the sunlight, cloaking the pool and the surrounding rocks in layers of dark shadows. Except for the sound of the waterfall, the forest around the pool was strangely silent. The dark shadows and the silence gave an eerie, graveyard atmosphere to the area.

Heather stopped suddenly. Raising her head, she twitched her ears and listened to the silence that surrounded her. Why was it so quiet? There were always sounds in the forest, especially during the day: the songs of birds, the chirping of frogs, the playful barks of squirrels, even the buzzing of annoying, biting insects. But here she heard none of those things. It was almost as if she had stepped through a doorway into a soundproof room. Except for the splashing, gurgling of the waterfall, and the sound of her own breathing, all was quiet.

Too quiet.

She backed up and looked around, the bristles on the nape of her neck starting to rise. Silence meant danger in the wilderness, every animal knew that. It was the first thing the forest dwellers taught to their young. Danger approaches, be quiet. Don't make a sound or you might be eaten. The birds knew to stop their melodies when a predator drew near. The squirrels knew to hush their cries and become invisible as they clung to branches and the trunks of trees, peeking out from beneath shadowy foliage. Even the tiny insects knew that silence was the golden rule when danger approached.

Something's wrong. Why is it so quiet?

Heather wondered if the eerie silence was her doing. Did the smaller animals consider her a threat, even though she was not hunting? Had a silent alarm been given to warn that a wolf was near?

She squinted her eyes and looked to the treetops, slowly turning her head from side to side. No, the birds did not pause their songs because of her. There were no birds, none that she could see anyway. No squirrels either. It was as though they were deliberately avoiding the area, staying clear for one reason or another. That was odd; an abundance of water should have drawn the local wildlife in droves. But as she looked around, Heather saw no wildlife at all. Nothing. Even the flies and mosquitos, so common in the deep forest, were noticeably absent.

Perhaps something unseen kept the forest dwellers away. She remembered the peculiar taste of the water when she first drank from the stream, and again wondered if the area was polluted. Were leaking barrels of chemical toxins, or radioactive rods, buried somewhere nearby? Those who serve the Wyrm had been known to bury such things deep in the forest in an attempt to mar the beauty of Gaia and destroy forever the things held sacred by Garou and Native Americans.

Heather turned her head and looked at the pool, a chill of fear dancing down her spine. Maybe pollution wasn't what kept the forest animals away. Perhaps instead it was something supernatural. Maybe they too feared the reflection of the gnarled little creature she had seen a few nights ago.

Sam was right. You are a child.

A ripple of shame washed through her as she remembered how she had tucked tail and run from the pool a few nights earlier, fleeing for her life like a rabbit from a hunting hawk. But Heather Ocoee was no rabbit; she was a Garou, a tribal member of the Wendigo. And now that she had gone through her Rites of Passage, meeting one of her spirit guides, she had no reason ever to be afraid again. Fear was something for rabbits and small children. She would not fear the reflection of the gnarled creature this time. Nor would she run.

With a fierce determination to prove her courage burning deep inside Heather's chest, she stepped closer to the water's edge. To further prove that she was not afraid, she transformed back into her homid form. Only a scared little girl would cower behind the strength and teeth of a wolf. She was no child.

Kneeling down at the pool's edge, she stared into the ebony water. At first nothing happened. But then, after a few minutes had gone by, the water's surface appeared to swirl and the reflection she saw slowly changed. But instead of blighted trees, a log cabin, and an ugly creature, Heather saw the reflection of an elderly woman looking back at her. An Indian woman.

The woman wore a long, fringed, white leather dress, trimmed with what looked to be pieces of shells or perhaps elk's teeth. She was slim of build and of medium height, with long white hair that cascaded over her shoulder like new-fallen snow. Her face was a road map of wrinkles, but her eyes were bright and seemed to twinkle with merriment. The old woman smiled a perfect smile, for she still had all her teeth, and Heather felt a feeling of deep calm descend over her. She had started to smile back, when the woman opened her right hand to reveal what she was holding.

"Oh, my God. The Fang!" Heather gasped, shocked by what she saw. There was no mistaking it; the old woman held the missing Fang of Nee Yah Kah Tah Kee.

Heather Ocoee turned and looked quickly behind her, hoping with all her heart that the elderly woman whose reflection she saw was standing there. She wasn't. The woman only existed as a reflection on the water's surface, which meant she had to be a spirit of some kind, a friendly spirit who happened to possess the missing Fang. With both Fangs, Heather would be able to seal the Gauntlet against the Wyrm's evil minions and prove herself once and for all to Sam Nakai.

She turned around and looked back at the water. The old woman's reflection was still there. She held out the other Fang at arm's length, offering it to Heather. A gift from the spirit world.

"The old woman has to be another one of my spirit guides," Heather said out loud, talking to herself. "She has brought me the second Fang."

In the excitement of the moment, Heather forgot many of the things Sam Nakai had taught her. Had she paused for only a moment to study the situation with a calm mind, she might have remembered that moving water was a magical element, capable of distorting, or sometimes entirely masking, the powers of others. It was the home of the Manitou, and the Manitou cared not whether you were a child of Gaia or a follower of the Wyrm.

But she did not take the time to think of such things. Instead she plunged her hand deep into the pool of ebony water, reaching for the other Fang. When she did, something seized Heather's wrist and yanked her headfirst into the pool.

Down, down, down she went, carried deep beneath the water's surface to the shadowy darkness that lined the bottom of the pool. Heather cried out in surprise, and then coughed violently as icy water rushed into her mouth and down her throat.

Closing her mouth to keep from choking, she twisted and turned in a frantic effort to tear free from the invisible thing that grabbed her. She couldn't see what it was, but she could feel it. Bony fingers gripped her wrist in a vice-like grasp, sending lightning bolts of pain shooting up her arm.

Something's got me!

Heather tried to fight back, but whatever held her was much stronger than she was. Had she been in Crinos or Lupus form things might be different, but she had changed back into Homid to prove her courage. It was a dumb mistake and she knew it. *Never face the unknown in your weakest form*; it was one of the first rules Sam had taught her. She should have known better. Now Heather's mistake might quite possibly cost her her life.

But Heather was not about to give up without a fight, not yet anyway. She kicked and clawed, twisted and turned, striking out at an enemy that could be felt but not seen. And just when it seemed that her lungs would surely burst, she felt herself tear free from the invisible grasp that held her wrist.

Air. Air. Air. Her mind screamed the command as she struggled to get back to the surface.

Kick. Damnit, kick. Don't you dare drown. Not now. Kick. Kick. Kick. Move your ass. Swim.

The surface seemed so far away. Too far. She'd never make it. Her lungs were going to fill with water and she would drown, her body sinking slowly back to the bottom of the pool. She would end up as fish food, and no one would ever know what had happened to her. Not even Sam Nakai would know of her fate.

With these grim thoughts in mind, Heather doubled her efforts to make it back to the surface. Her vision was already starting to blur with the darkness of unconsciousness when her head finally broke free from the water.

Air. Oh, thank god. Air.

Coughing and sputtering, Heather drew great shuddering breaths into her starved lungs. She was still coughing a few moments later when she finally regained the strength needed to pull her fatigued body slowly from the pool. Crawling a few feet from the water's edge, she collapsed upon the rocks. She coughed once more and then gagged, throwing up most of the water she had swallowed.

Heather rolled over onto her back and stared up at the sky. She was so exhausted that it was a strain just to keep her eyes open. Even taking a breath was somewhat of a struggle. Because of her fatigue, several minutes passed before she noticed that her surroundings were strangely different from before. Alarmed, she pushed herself up into a sitting position and looked around.

She was still deep in a forest, but it was not the same forest she had been in only moments before. Not really. The trees were basically the same—pines, evergreens, and oaks—yet they were noticeably different. Everything seemed brighter, more vivid, than it had only moments before. And the air was filled with the intoxicating scents of Mother Earth, fragrances long lost to the destructive sprawl of mankind. There was no mistaking where she was, however, for she had been here several times before. Heather Ocoee was in the Umbra.

12

Sam Nakai's heart was troubled, his spirit heavy. He had spoken harshly to Heather while in the sweatlodge, calling her a child, when he should have been congratulating her on passing her final Rite of Passage. The silence of the long walk home was proof that he had hurt her feelings. Gone were the endless questions and laughter that usually accompanied their travels together. Gone too were the girl's smiles, which always had a way of making even the gloomiest day seem brighter.

As her mentor, he should not have been so worried about bruising Heather's ego, for in truth she still was a child in many ways. When he had first become a Garou, it had taken him over two years to obtain enough knowledge and skills to be allowed the privilege of going through the final Rites, earning the respect and privileges of a warrior of the Wendigo tribe. Heather, on the other hand, had gone through the final Rite after only six months of training, and only then because she was the Guardian of the Fang and the sacred medicine of Nee Yah Kah Tah Kee might be needed in the upcoming battle against the Wyrm.

Despite his personal feelings about the situation, Sam had done what the spirits had instructed him to do and cut short the girl's training. Heather had gone through the final ritual of the vision quest, obtaining the help of a spirit guide and earning herself a place at the council fires of the Wendigo. But she was still a long way off from being a skilled warrior, a very long way off. Such things only came from years of training and hard work; they did not happen overnight. She was not yet a true warrior, nor was she qualified to journey by herself through the Umbra in search of the second Fang of the Sacred Sitting Wolf—if such a thing still existed—no matter how highly Heather thought of herself.

Truthfully, Sam doubted if a second Fang still existed anywhere. If it did, the spirits would have guided him to it years ago. Even without the help of his spirit guides, he would have been able to find the other Fang. The magic of the sacred stone he had carried as the Guardian would have led him to its missing counterpart. There was just no way that a girl of little medicine and power would be able to find something that he could not.

Unless she truly is the one spoken of in the old prophecies.

Sam shook his head and smiled. He had heard the stories shortly after becoming a Garou, tales told around flickering campfires by old Wendigo warriors whose voices were like dry leaves rustling in the wind. With solemn faces they repeated the prophecies of the ancient ones, telling of a great battle destined to take place between the Garou and the Wyrm—*an Armageddon that will leave the land scarred and bleeding. Thousands will die. Many more will be left homeless and destitute, wandering the countryside like shadows without purpose.*

But before that fateful battle takes place, Gaia will send a messenger among the wolf people to unite the thirteen werewolf tribes as one. The messenger will be a person of courage and strong medicine; a leader whose voice will call out to the Garou from the darkness, like the cry of a hunting owl. According to the legends, this messenger will also be a child. A girl.

Nonsense. It is only a legend, a silly bedtime story to give hope to those foolish enough to listen. A thing of make-believe and nothing more.

Annoyed for allowing his imagination to run away with him, Sam stuffed the rest of his clothing into his backpack and crawled out of his tent. Stowing the backpack in the back of his pickup, he turned to see if Heather needed any help gathering together her supplies and equipment. Neither of them had much in the way of personal items—a few changes of clothing, a sleeping bag, and cooking utensils—so it shouldn't take her long to get packed. But she sometimes had trouble rolling up her tent small enough to fit into its nylon sack.

Stepping away from the pickup, he was surprised to see that Heather's tent was still standing. She was usually much faster at dropping a tent than he was, especially when she chose to show off. Not only was the tent still standing, but her cooking utensils, and some of her camping equipment, lay scattered about on the ground. She should have had most of her gear already packed away; what on earth could be taking her so long?

"You need any help in there?" Sam asked, walking over to her tent. He squatted down and raised the flap, surprised to find the tent empty.

"Heather?" He turned and looked around the campsite, but the girl was nowhere to be seen. He wasn't concerned, however; she had probably gone off to relieve herself. Going on a vision quest had a way of screwing up a person's internal workings for a few days. She would be back in a minute or two.

Sam was just about to stand back up when he noticed that Heather's leather traveling pack was not among the items in her tent. The pack was used only to carry her clothes when traveling in wolf or Crinos form, a transformation that was not necessary when just going to the bathroom.

"Heather!" Sam was furious. The girl had taken off without telling him, probably because she was still mad at him. Now he had to stop what he was doing to track her down. There was no time for such foolish games. They had to get ready to leave. The Shaman Moon was only a few days away; the Wyrm would not wait.

Looking around to make sure no one was watching, Sam willed his body to transform. He didn't like changing forms in daylight, but he had no choice. He could not afford to wait for the concealment of darkness. If any humans saw him while he was undergoing the transformation from man into wolf, their minds would be affected by the Delirium. Most who saw a Garou change, or witnessed one in the terrifying Crinos form, never remembered exactly what they saw. The Delirium acted as a cushioning effect to the brain, replacing the terrifying vision with something that was easier to believe in a normal world. Werewolves became dogs, bears or even mad men. Without the Delirium, most who witnessed a Garou in his full frightening form would go quite mad from the sight of it.

Rather than risk unhinging the minds of the locals, he elected to transform himself into his Lupus form. Besides, with his nose close to the ground, it was much easier to pick up scents as a wolf than as a towering werewolf. There was also less of a chance that his anger would get the best of him while in wolf form.

Reaching his hands toward the sky, Sam allowed the wolf spirit that was trapped deep inside of him to come to the surface. A surge of pure adrenaline shot through him as his muscles began to twitch and quiver, causing his heart to beat madly in his chest and tearing a cry of pleasure from his throat. He looked at the back of his hands, watching as light gray fur sprouted faster than weeds after a summer rain. The thick fur raced down his arms like fallen dominos, spilling over his shoulders and down his back.

Sam's bones creaked and popped like a wooden ship tossed upon a stormy sea as his body quickly reshaped itself. Muscles grew taunt and firm, becoming almost as hard as concrete. Tendons took on the feel of steel cables, stretching tight beneath the surface of his skin. Teeth became fangs. Feet and hands became paws.

Once the transformation from human to wolf was complete, he only had to circle the campsite once before picking up Heather's scent. Her scent followed an old animal trail that ran due east of the clearing. Nose to the ground, Sam followed the path until it crossed a small spring. There he lost her scent.

Where? Where? Where? Where did she go? He stopped and backed up, studying the ground, looking for footprints. *Not here. Not here. Over there maybe. Look. Sniff.*

In Lupus form, Sam Nakai had the advantage of both worlds, for he could be a wolf and a man at the same time. He had the logic and reasoning of a human, yet he also had the natural cunning of a wolf.

Not here. Not here. He sniffed along the edge of the stream, suddenly picking up Heather's scent again. *Here. Here's where she crossed.* The scent led along the bank of the stream, following it upstream.

Why? Why? Why? Why follow the water? What did she see? What did she find?

Sam followed the narrow stream until it dead-ended at a pool of water fed by a waterfall. Heather's scent was all over the granite rocks around the pool, and her footprints were clearly visible in places where there was soft mud, yet she was nowhere to be found. And no matter how much he sniffed, he could not find a scent trail leading away from the water.

A feeling of dread squeezed his heart. Heather had walked up to the pool, but she had not walked away from it. Afraid of what he might find, but knowing he had to look, Sam stepped up to the edge of the pool and stuck his head beneath the water's surface.

The pool was only about six or seven feet deep, and he could see all the way to the bottom. Sam let out a sigh of relief when he saw that the pool was empty. Heather's body did not lie beneath the surface of the water. She had not drowned.

Then where was she? Heather Ocoee had disappeared, vanishing without a trace. Had she stepped sideways into the Umbra he would have known, because there would have been a lingering trace of power in the air. But Sam felt nothing. Or did he?

He looked around, noticing for the first time the eerie quiet that seemed to hang over the area. In the forest there were always sounds: birds, frogs, squirrels, even insects. But here there was only a strange, muffled silence, as if this part of the forest were devoid of any life other than his own. It wasn't right, wasn't natural. Something was wrong.

Hoping his nose would tell him something his eyes could not, Sam tilted his head straight back and sniffed. There was indeed something strange in the air, something he couldn't quite place. It was not the scent of the Wyrm, but it still gave him an uneasy feeling. Someone, or something, besides Heather had come to this pool recently. Something not of this Realm.

A spirit.

But what kind of spirit? Good or bad? And what did it have to do with the girl? If only he knew more about the spirits that inhabited the area, maybe then he would have a clue to Heather's whereabouts. Unfortunately, Sam was just a visitor to the mountainous countryside of North Carolina. The desert homeland of his childhood, a place inhabited by spirits he did know, lay far to the west.

All was not lost, however, for there was one man who could help him. Joseph Swimmer had lived all his life in the sacred heartland of the Cherokee; he would know what spirits made this land their stomping ground.

Deciding that he needed help to solve the mystery that lay before him, Sam turned away from the pool and raced through the forest in the direction of Joseph's cabin. He no longer cared if anyone saw him in wolf form; speed was essential. The Guardian might be in danger.

13

Heather jumped to her feet, quickly making the change from human to werewolf. Something unseen had taken her by surprise, pulling her into the Umbra. The pool was obviously a doorway through the Gauntlet to the spirit world, but whose magic had opened it? And who, or what, had grabbed her? She would not be so easily fooled this time. Her attacker would learn what happens to those foolish enough to attack a Garou.

She stood tense, looking around, waiting for a second attack to come. In the Realm it had been daytime, but the spirit world was cloaked in the darkness of night. It was a dangerous time for a Garou, for the Umbral moon had not risen yet; a time when those of the Wyrm would be moving freely about.

Had she been attacked by one of the Wyrm's followers? A Banth maybe? Or a Black Spiral Dancer? Heather sniffed. Yes, yes, it was there. A smell not quite right. An odor of evil that caused the skin at her temples to pull tight, and made the hair along the back of her neck stand straight up. But the smell was fading rapidly. Whoever had left the scent was gone. She was alone.

Slowly relaxing her guard, she turned to study her immediate surroundings. The pool no longer looked peaceful and inviting, as it had back in the Realm. Instead the water was oily and foul-smelling, like something dredged up from the bottom of a polluted lagoon. Large bubbles rose slowly to the pool's surface like oozing blisters of pus. Some of the bubbles appeared for a moment and then sank back beneath the slimy surface; others burst with a sickening, wet sound, releasing vaporous clouds of noxious gases.

Surrounding the pool was a forest of stunted, gnarled trees and leprous-looking vines. It was the same diseased forest Heather had seen in the water's reflection, home to a wrinkled, dwarfish creature. What she had mistaken for a reflection was in fact how the forest looked in the Umbra. It was a diseased grove of trees that had been touched by the Wyrm. A blight.

A shudder of loathing passed through her body. She was standing in a dwelling place of evil. Sour ground. She wanted to leave the area, but knew it would be foolish to wander through the Umbra without a Moon Path for guidance. She could use the Fang she wore to step sideways back through the Gauntlet, but it would take her directly to Monterey, Tennessee, to the exact spot where the statue of Nee Yah Kah Tah Kee had once stood.

Truthfully, she didn't want to leave the Umbra. Not yet, anyway. The Shaman Moon was less than a week away. If she could somehow locate the missing Fang, she would be able to seal the rift in the Gauntlet before the Wyrm could use it to enter the Realm. In her vision, she had seen herself standing before the Abyss. Heather knew in her heart that the vision was a clue to the second Fang's whereabouts. Find the Fang and she could stop the Wyrm. It was as simple as that.

In addition to the vision, she had also seen the reflection of the elderly Indian woman in the pool of water. In the reflection the old woman was holding the missing Fang, offering it to Heather. Was that another clue? Or was the woman another one of her spirit guides? She would never know if she left the Umbra; therefore, she chose to stay.

Since she needed to wait for a Moon Path to light her way, Heather decided to look around the immediate area. She wanted to find out why the ground was a blight in the Umbra, yet appeared perfectly normal back in the Realm. Circling the pool, she had only gone a few yard into the forest when she spotted the cabin.

Heather stopped, amazed. The tiny log cabin she had seen in the pool's reflection was real. It existed in the Umbra, yet no trace of it could be found in the Realm. Some powerful magic was obviously at work here. But whose magic? Gaia's or the Wyrm's?

There's only one way to find out.

She approached the cabin slowly, carefully, every sense in her body attuned to her surroundings. Even as a werewolf she had to be cautious, because the Umbra could be as dangerous as it often was beautiful. And though the dangers usually came in the form of spirits, they could still be deadly to a Garou.

Stopping while still about twenty feet away from the cabin, Heather checked for sounds, smells, gut feelings, anything which might warn her that she was walking into a trap. She clasped her left hand around the leather pouch which hung from her neck, but the Fang of the Wolf was still cold to the touch.

That was strange. The Fang always grew hot in the presence of the Wyrm. Even things touched long ago by the Evil One could produce a spark of warmth. If it wasn't the Wyrm, then what evil had touched this area to cause such a blight?

Heather studied the cabin. It was a windowless log structure with a slanted roof of rough, wooden shingles. Barely visible among the trees and vegetation, the cabin projected an air of sinister evil so strong it made her head hurt just to look at it. She was about to take another step closer when she heard the voices.

"Help me....please...help me..."

She tensed, listening, every fiber of her being flashing a message of warning to her brain. The voices came as whispered fragments upon the wind, the terrified pleas of children.

"No...please no...stop...please stop...don't...you're hurting me..."

The words gripped Heather's heart in an icy grasp and brought tears to her eyes. With the words came a sense of pain and suffering stronger than anything she had ever felt before. Even the pain and terror experienced firsthand at the Pentex School for Girls paled in comparison to what she felt now.

"Please...stop..."

Anger flowed white hot through Heather's veins as she slowly approached the cabin; she was absolutely enraged that somewhere inside the building children were being hideously mistreated. Barely more than a child herself, she knew what it was like to suffer at the hands of others, to be abused by those older and much stronger.

With a roar of rage, she ripped the cabin's door from its hinges and threw it behind her. Lunging across the threshhold, she howled a challenge to those who would dare abuse the innocence of a child. But the howl was wasted, however, for there was no one to challenge. The cabin was completely empty.

But where are the children?

Heather turned around, looking for the source of the cries she had heard. The cabin had but one room, its contents revealed in a single, sweeping glance. At one end of the dirt-floored room a pile of pine needles had been shaped into a simple bed and covered with a blanket. At the other end a set of wooden shelves lined the walls. Stacked upon the shelves were earthen containers of various size and shape.

She turned. In the center of the room, a fire pit had been dug in the ground and lined with stones. A hole in the roof above the fire pit allowed smoke from cooking fires to escape to the outside. Heather stepped closer to the pit, her blood running cold when she saw what else it contained besides rocks.

Oh, dear God.

Inside the small circular pit were a few pieces of charred wood and the bones of several human skeletons. Leg bones. Parts of arms. Fingers and toes. Jumbled sections of vertebrae. Even a hip bone or two. Carefully stacked on top of the bones were a half-dozen small human skulls—the skulls of children.

Heather stared at the tiny skulls, unable to believe what she saw. Not only had someone brutally taken the lives of several children, but they had apparently eaten them too. Even in the darkness, she could plainly see marks upon the bones—scratches, nicks, and chips—that could only have been caused by teeth. Someone had cooked the children over the fire, slowly roasting their flesh. They had then sucked and gnawed every bit of meat from the bones, breaking many of them open to get at the soft marrow inside.

"Help me..."

She spun around, her heart beating wildly. Heather had clearly heard the voice of a child, but the room remained empty. Perhaps the children were imprisoned somewhere, hidden just out of sight, locked away in the darkness. Maybe they were being kept as a snack for later. If so, then she had to free them before the owner of the cabin returned.

"Don't hurt me..."

She crossed the room slowly, her feet quietly gliding over the ground. Holding her breath, she listened carefully for the voices.

Where are they? Where? I've got to find them before it's too late.

Heather reached the opposite end of the room without finding any place where a child could be hidden. Directly before her were the wooden shelves and the earthenware containers.

"Let me go..."

The voice came from beyond the wall, from outside. She started to turn toward the door, then stopped.

It couldn't have come from outside. The voice was too clear. The child must be somewhere inside, somewhere in front of her.

But there's nothing here, only the wall, the shelves, and...

Heather's skin tightened with fear as she realized that there was strong magic at work. Evil magic. Inching closer to the wooden shelves, she carefully picked up one of the earthen containers in both hands.

"Please...help me."

There was no mistake. The voice she heard came from inside the tiny container. It was not the voice of a child. Instead it was the voice of a child's spirit, imprisoned within the earthen jar.

Holding the container in her left hand, she slowly lifted its lid with her right. There was a hissing of air as she lifted the lid, as though she had broken the seal on a vacuum. The hissing was followed by a long, drawn-out scream of pain. Her hands starting to tremble, Heather looked into the container and beheld the pale, fluorescent glow of an imprisoned spirit.

Realizing that it had been freed from its earthenware prison, the spirit slowly drifted out of the container. Ebbing up Heather's arm, the bluish glow circled her neck in a spiritual embrace. As the spirit wrapped around her, Heather's mind was flooded with visions of a little boy's life—as well as visions of his death. She shared the horrors of a young Indian boy as he was tortured, killed, and finally eaten by a dwarfish creature with a long, pointed index finger. It was the same hideous creature she had seen in the pool's reflection.

She shared the boy's pain and suffering, howling in anger at the loss of his life and the loss his parents must have felt. The spirit caressed her mind a final time and then floated up through the air, disappearing through the hole in the roof. Free.

"Thank you…"

The words drifted back to her from the opening as the boy's spirit, free at last, went to join his relatives who were already somewhere in the Umbra.

Turning, Heather snatched a second earthenware container from the shelf. She hurled the container against the wall, breaking it and releasing the spirit trapped inside. She smashed another, and another, freeing the spirits they contained. Thirty-one containers, thirty-one spirits. She smashed each and every one of them, and then looked for more to break.

Only when she was absolutely certain there were no more containers to smash, no more spirits to free, did Heather allow herself to flee from the oppressive evil which hung heavy inside the cabin. She staggered through the open doorway, venting her anger on the branches and vines that lay in her path.

Reaching the pool, she turned and stared back at the cabin. She took deep breaths as she waited for the anger to leave her, listening closely for any voices that might be heard. But all was quiet. Calm. She heard no voices. The children had all been set free, their spirits going to find the spirits of their parents, grandparents, and ancestors. Once again they would be united, this time for all eternity.

Her heart nearly breaking with emotion, tears flooding her eyes, Heather threw her head back and sang a Spirit Sending Song to pay honor to all the children whose spirits had been imprisoned in the earthenware containers. Sounding more like a series of long, mournful howls than an actual melody, the Sending Song was a Wendigo warrior's way of saying goodbye to a fallen brother or sister, wishing their spirit a safe and rapid journey into the next world.

Finished with the song, Heather wiped her eyes and lowered her head, noticing for the first time the lines of illumination that stretched across the ground like silvery threads of moonlight.

Moon paths!

Though unseen from where she stood, the Umbral moon must have risen while she was inside the cabin. The Moon Paths twinkled and shimmered like stars, a sprinkling of fairy dust in an already magical world. She counted a dozen different pathways, but knew there would be more. Some were as bright as neon tubing. Others were nothing more than broken fragments, barely visible in the darkness.

A flicker of doubt crossed Heather's mind. With so many different Moon Paths to choose from, how would she know which one was the right path to follow? On her previous journeys into the Umbra, Sam had always chosen the pathway to walk. But Sam wasn't here; she would have to make the decision on her own.

Which one? Which one? You can't stand here all night. Choose.

Surely it must be a simple matter for a Garou to choose the right Moon Path. Unfortunately, Heather had not been a Garou long enough to know how to do it. She was about to pick a path entirely at random, when she remembered the Fang hanging from her neck.

Of course, that was the answer. Rather than make the decision herself, she would ask Nee Yah Kah Tah Kee and her spirit guide for help. Clenching the Fang tightly in her right hand, Heather asked aloud: "Oh, Great Wolf Spirit. Please hear my words. Show me the Moon Path that will take me where you want me to go. If it be your will, guide me on the right path so I may find the lost Fang."

A few moments passed, then Heather noticed one of the paths beginning to shine brighter than all the others. Her prayer had been answered. Nee Yah Kah Tah Kee, or her spirit guide, had shown her which Moon Path to follow.

"Thank you," she whispered starting down the Moon Path that would hopefully lead her to the Realm of the Abyss. It was rumored that everything lost in the Umbra eventually ended up in the Abyss. If so, then all she had to do was follow the Moon Path to the great chasm, recover the missing Fang, and then sidestep back into the real world.

At least she hoped it would be that easy.

14

Joseph Swimmer had seen many things in his seventy years of life, things that most men would be hard-pressed to believe. He was a tribal shaman, a member of the Ketoowah society—in charge of keeping alive the traditional ceremonies, dances, and songs of the Cherokees—and he was Kinfolk to the Garou. He had sat in council with the spirits of his ancestors, smoked the sacred pipe with werewolf warriors, and fought against the minion of the Wyrm. Life no longer held any surprises for him, nor did death.

So when a large, gray timber wolf suddenly burst from the forest, only a few feet away from where he stood, Joseph was anything but surprised. He just turned away from the old pickup truck he had been loading with supplies, and watched with a mild indifference as Sam Nakai shapeshifted back into human form.

"I am surprised to see you, my friend. I thought you would be in Monterey by now," Joseph said, knowing of the ability of Garou to open portals in the Gauntlet and use moonbridges to move quickly from one place to another.

Sam shook his head and took a deep breath. The run had left him somewhat winded, and he was trying to find his voice. "We have a problem."

"Yes you do," Joseph grinned. "Your zipper is wide open."

"That is not the problem," Sam said.

"It can be if someone sees you," laughed the old man. "Especially if that someone is a pretty lady that you are trying to impress."

Somewhat annoyed, Sam reached down and zipped his pants. "There. Are you happy now?"

"Yes," Joseph nodded. "Much better. It's hard to talk to a man when his baby-maker is showing. Now, why have you come here?"

"Heather has disappeared," Sam replied. "She snuck off while I was packing our things at the camp."

Joseph clicked his tongue in disapproval. "This is not a good time for the Guardian of the Fang to be playing hide and seek. Have you looked for her?"

"Of course I've looked for her," Sam snapped. "She is not hiding; she's gone. I followed her trail, but I lost her scent. It stopped dead. Something has happened to her, but I'm not sure what."

"Do you think it is the Wyrm?" Joseph asked, concern showing in his voice.

Sam shook his head. "No. I would know if it was the Wyrm; I could smell it. There's no smell. Nothing. She just disappeared. You know the spirits of these mountains better that I do, maybe you can help me figure out what happened to her."

"You think a spirit is involved?"

"I'm not sure what it is." Sam shrugged. "It might be a spirit; it might be something else. All I know is that something strange is going on. Will you help me look for her?"

Joseph scowled at Sam. "The Guardian may be our only chance of sealing the Gauntlet against the Wyrm. Of course I will help." He turned and looked at his cabin. "The others are still inside. I better tell them that I am going with you."

Sam thought of the criticism he would receive for allowing something to befall the Guardian, especially from Michael Pathkiller. "Can't you just tell them when you get back?"

Joseph turned and looked at him oddly for a moment, then nodded. "Perhaps it would be best not to say anything now."

Since Joseph was not a Garou, and did not possess the ability to change into a wolf and run quickly through the forest, they were forced to take his antique pickup truck. Opening the passenger door, the old man climbed into the truck. He turned and smiled at Sam, waiting for him to get behind the wheel and drive.

"Why the hell am I driving?" Sam grumbled. "It's your truck."

Joseph grinned. "Why the hell am I going? It's your problem."

Defeated by the old Indian's argument, Sam walked around the pickup and climbed in the driver's side. Starting the engine, he shifted into gear and proceeded down the bumpy dirt road at a pace much slower than he would have liked to have gone.

There were no roads in the mountainous countryside where Heather had disappeared, not even a decent logging trail, so they were forced to leave the pickup at Sam's campsite and travel the rest of the way on foot. With Joseph's advanced years, Sam expected it would take forever to walk the remaining distance. He was surprised, however, at how quickly the old man could move through the forest, his walking pace equal to that of a much younger man.

Because of his smaller size, Joseph also had less of a problem weaving his way through areas of dense foliage, squeezing though tight places that Sam was forced to walk around. Several times the old man was forced to stop, waiting for his younger traveling companion to catch up. Finally, after only a few goodnatured jests about Sam's slowness, they arrived at their destination.

"This is where the girl disappeared?" Joseph asked as he spotted the waterfall. He stopped suddenly, taking a step back, apparently reluctant to get any closer to the pool of water.

Sam nodded. "Her trail leads up to the edge of the pool, but it doesn't come back out. Why? What do you know of this place?"

"Too much, I am afraid." Joseph answered, shaking his head. Reaching into his shirt pocket, he removed a small leather pouch. Opening the pouch, the old Indian said a prayer and sprinkled a pinch of tobacco on the ground. A second prayer was said, and a second pinch of tobacco was tossed into the air. Only then did Joseph approach the pool. Climbing up on the rocks, he stared down into the water for a few moments before turning to Sam.

"Long ago a *tsgili* lived near here. A witch," the old man said, pointing at the forest. "This was before my time, but still I have heard stories about her. The elders of my people say that she was an ugly, dwarfish creature with skin as hard as stone. Maybe she was one of the little people; I do not know. Everyone was afraid of this witch, because she had great magical powers and could change into anything she wanted."

"A shapeshifter?" Sam asked.

Joseph nodded. "She could appear as a cat, a bat, or even a squirrel, but her favorite disguise was that of an old woman. She would use this false image to trick children away from their villages. Those who went with her were never seen again."

He paused a moment to stare again at the water. "Some of the elders say that the old witch ate the children's livers, stealing it out of their bodies with a long, pointed index finger…a finger shaped like a sharp dagger. This may be true, but I think it was their spirits the old woman ate. Either way, none of the children that went with her ever returned to their village. My people called this witch *Utluhtu*, Spearfinger."

Sam looked around, horrified by the thought that Heather had been abducted by a witch. Being Navajo, he knew quite a bit about witches. In the land of the Dine', there were those who practiced evil magic. Among their more offensive habits were incest and the eating of human flesh. During the daytime the witches were indistinguishable from other Navajos, but when roaming at night they often dressed in the skins of wolves, bears, foxes or coyotes, thus becoming those animals. Sometimes these "skinwalkers" even dressed themselves in human skin, taking on the identity of the person they had killed.

"Does this witch still live around here?" Sam asked, the fingers of his right hand automatically going to the tiny medicine pouch concealed beneath his shirt. The pouch was a gift from a Navajo medicine man, a thing of magic to ward off witches and evil spirits. He rarely ever took it off.

Joseph shook his head. "No. That was long ago. She is dead now, killed by the warriors of a local village." He touched the wrist of his right hand. "They shot her with an arrow here, at the base of her long finger. It is her only weak spot. After they killed her, they cut her body into many pieces and threw the pieces away."

"Where did they throw the pieces?" Sam asked, already knowing the answer.

The old man pointed at the pool. "They threw her pieces in the water. They thought the spirits of the water would keep the old witch from coming back, but they were wrong. Utluhtu is too powerful. Her spirit still lives; it lives in the water."

He stepped closer to the pool. "At least it used to live here. I no longer feel its presence, so I think Utluhtu has crossed back over to the spirit world. And I think she has taken someone with her."

"Heather?"

Joseph nodded. "The little girl is in danger. I don't think Utluhtu has taken her spirit, not yet anyway. I think she is using Heather for something, but I don't know what it is."

Sam Nakai stepped back from the pool of water and started to shapeshift. "I've got to get to Heather before it's too late. If she's somewhere in the Umbra, I'll find her."

Joseph laid his hand on Sam's arm. "You cannot help her, my friend. If Utluhtu is threatened, she will eat the child's spirit and slip away."

"But I have to do something!" Sam argued, a feeling of frustration tugging at his heart.

"You will," Joseph nodded. "You will go with me to the sacred site of Nee Yah Kah Tah Kee. There we will prepare to face the Wyrm."

"But what about Heather?"

"She is no longer a little girl; she is a Wendigo warrior. Guardian of the Fang. You have done your job; you have taught her what she needed to learn. Her fate now rests in the hands of the spirits. Wherever her path leads, she must walk it alone."

Sam thought it over and then nodded. Joseph Swimmer was right; Heather was on her own.

15

Heather had almost forgotten how truly beautiful the Umbra really was. There were still a few lovely places back in the real world, places the Wyrm had yet to touch, but they could not compare to the majestic forests of the spirit world. The trees were basically the same—pines, evergreens, maples, and oaks—but in the Umbra they were taller, broader, healthier, their colors much more vivid. When clumped together they made a forest of ancient wonder and mystery, like those that once existed in America long before the appearance and the pollution of the white man.

Taking great delight in her surroundings, she followed the glowing Moon Path between towering pine trees with needles that glistened like rare gemstones in the moonlight. The ground at the base of the trees was thickly carpeted with a springy layer of fallen needles, mushrooms and delicate wildflowers.

She stopped and sniffed, the blended aroma of pine, flowers, and crisp, clean air creating an euphoric high too hard to describe. Had there been some way to bottle the essence of the Umbra, she would have done so. Instead she settled on picking one of the purple flowers and tucking it in the fur behind her left ear. She smiled at the thought of a werewolf wearing a flower, wishing for a mirror to see herself in.

In places where the trees thinned, she caught glimpses of rugged mountains that rose up into the night sky like granite giants wearing polished armor of ice and snow. They were the same mountains that existed back in the real world, but here they were higher and more magnificent, their rocky surfaces untouched by the erosion of time and weather, their spirits unmarred by the cruel hands of men. The mountains watched her passing with a smug indifference. After all, why should gods concern themselves with the coming and going of lesser creatures?

Twice Heather stopped to drink from gurgling streams with surfaces that looked like solid ice in the pale moonlight, her entire body shivering in delight at the coldness and the purity of the water. No wine or lover's kiss could ever taste so sweet, not that she had ever experienced either of those things. Other times she paused to wrap her arms around one of the pine trees, feeling the spirit of her wooden brother flowing just beneath the bark. She didn't linger long, however, for she had a job to do and knew that others were depending on her. There would be plenty of opportunities to enjoy the gifts of the spirit world after she had found the missing Fang and used it to seal the Gauntlet against the Wyrm.

Emerging from the forest, she found herself suddenly looking upon a field of tall grasses and weeds that stretched unbroken toward the distant mountains like a sea of the darkest green. There were no trees in the field, not a one, no rocks or bushes to interrupt the flatness of the land. And even though the Umbra was a place of constantly changing wonders, Heather was somewhat surprised by the field.

Things in the spirit world always corresponded to places back in the Realm, but she didn't remember seeing such a field in her travels around Cherokee, North Carolina. If the field was actually something else in the real world, a parking lot or a warehouse, then it would be little more than a grayish blight in the Umbra. But the open stretch of land that lay before her was not a blight. On the contrary, it was as healthy and vibrant as the forest she had just left.

No matter what it was back in the Realm; it was a field here and that's all that mattered. And since the Moon Path she followed cut directly through the middle of it, she would have to cross it. But before she did, Heather decided to change back into Homid. Being in Crinos form made travel easier and safer, but it also burned up a lot more energy. Food was something she hadn't brought along, nor did she want to go running around the Umbra looking for it. Scrounging up something to eat would be no problem for a Garou of experience, but she was still rather new at being a werewolf.

Transforming back into human form, she removed her clothes and shoes from her leather traveling bag and hurried to slip them on. She didn't mind being naked back in the Realm, but in the Umbra it felt like she was being constantly watched by the spirits. She probably was too. Once dressed, Heather tightened the strap on her bag and started across the field.

The tall grasses and weeds that grew in the field reached up to the girl's knees, forcing her to walk slower than she would have liked in order to avoid stepping into a hole, or tripping over anything that might lie hidden from sight. Lucky for her that she did walk slowly, because halfway across the field she stumbled upon, and nearly fell over, a wooden canoe all but invisible in the darkness and weeds. Though she didn't fall, she did bang her right shin painfully against the side of the small craft.

"Ow!" Heather cried, reaching down to rub her leg. She thought about kicking the canoe to vent her anger, but decided against it. No sense adding a hurt toe to go along with the bruised shin.

"Stupid people," she muttered, referring to the person who had carelessly left the canoe lying around. Raising her voice, Heather added, "Of all the places to leave a canoe…Someone could get hurt, you know!"

Giving her leg a final rub, she whispered, "Ow. Someone did get hurt. Me."

The pain starting to ebb, she straightened back up and examined the object of her displeasure. The canoe was about ten feet long and three feet wide, and appeared to be carved from the burned-out trunk of a tree. Someone had decorated the outside of the wooden craft with shapes and symbols, but it was too dark to clearly make out what they were. Not that she was really interested. However, she did wonder why someone had left a perfectly good canoe in the middle of a dry field.

Maybe there's a lake nearby.

There must have been a lake somewhere in the area, for all at once she heard the cries of ducks, geese and other waterfowl, and the flapping of wings. Hundreds of cries. Thousands of wings. Heather looked up, expecting to see a large flock of birds fly overhead, but the sky remained as empty as the field.

"I'm not hearing things," she said, puzzled by the emptiness of the sky. "I know I'm not."

The sounds grew louder. Heather turned and looked around, realizing that the noise seemed to come from everywhere. Maybe the field wasn't as empty as she thought. Perhaps the birds she heard were all shorter than the grasses and weeds; that would explain why they could be heard but not seen. She wondered if ducks and other such water birds lived in burrows, like rabbits. She didn't think they did, but she would have to ask Sam when she got back to the Realm just to be sure.

As the sounds of the invisible birds grew even louder, patches of grayish fog began to drift across the field like low-hanging clouds on a cold November morning. The wispy patches were followed by a heavy fog bank that rolled over the field at ground level, reducing visibility to only a few feet and bringing with it the unmistakable smell of fishy water.

There has to be a lake around here somewhere. Unless....

A chill danced down Heather's spine as the fog washed over her, for she realized something unexplainable was happening. Something quite magical.

Turning around, she started back across the field toward the safety of the forest. She had only taken a few steps, however, when the ground became soft, mushy and extremely wet.

"Hey!" Heather cried, cold water suddenly filling her tennis shoes. She stopped and looked down, startled to discover that the once dry field was now completely flooded. The water was already an inch or two above her ankles and rising fast.

What the heck is this?

She looked up. The forest she had just left was still too far away; she would never make it. Knowing she had to act quickly, Heather turned around and raced back toward the wooden canoe.

But it isn't easy to run in a wet, slippery field. Twice she slipped and fell, drenching herself from head to toe. The water was already past her knees by the time she splashed her way back to the dugout canoe. She reached out to grab the canoe, but the waves she made sent it floating away from her.

"Hey! Stop that!" Heather yelled, her frustration and fear rapidly mounting. Careful not to make any additional waves, she slowly inched forward and grabbed the wooden vessel.

"Ha! Got you!" Reaching across to hold onto both sides of the canoe at once, she carefully pulled herself up and in. The canoe rocked and threatened to capsize, but stayed right side up.

Careful not to make any sudden movements that might cause her to tip over, Heather sat up and looked around. A startled gasp escaped her lips as the heavy fog lifted as quickly as it came, taking everything with it. No longer was she in a field of tall grasses and weeds. On the contrary, Heather Ocoee now found herself smack dab in the middle of a very large body of water, a lake that seemed to stretch endlessly in all directions.

Covering the surface of the lake were countless waterfowl: ducks, geese, herons, and many more exotic varieties. Birds of every size, color, shape and description paddled about on the water and dove for fish, making enough noise to hurt her ears. A black and green mallard duck brushed up against the side of the canoe. Heather reached out to touch the duck, crying out in alarm when her hand passed right through it.

"Oh, my gosh. They're not real. But they've got to be real. I can see them, hear them…" She sniffed, wrinkling her nose. "I can even smell them. They've got to be real. It doesn't make any sense."

Suddenly, she remembered a story Sam Nakai had once told her about a magic lake, a place where the spirits of animals and birds went to when they died. The Wendigo called the lake Ataga'Hi, though few believed that it actually existed.

According to legend, only Garou and spirits could sail upon the magical waters of the sacred lake. To everyone else Ataga'Hi was nothing more than an empty field.

Leaning forward, Heather picked up the wooden paddle that lay in the bottom of the canoe. If the legend of Ataga'Hi was true, which it obviously was, on the other side of the lake she would find The Pure Land of the Legendary Realm. The home of her ancestors.

Her sight set on an imaginary point in the distance, Heather began to paddle slowly across the lake. Had she looked back, she would have been startled to see something watching her from the edge of the forest. It was a gnarled, dwarfish creature with a misshapen head, wrinkled gray skin, and a very long index finger on its right hand—the same creature whose reflection she had seen in a pool of ebony water. The creature watched Heather for a moment, then slipped quietly into the lake to follow her.

Her legs were sore from kneeling in the wooden canoe, and her arms were starting to fatigue by the time Heather reached the rocky shore that marked the beginning of the Legendary Realm. She felt a sense of awe wash over her as she jumped out and pulled the canoe up on dry ground, and maybe even a twinge of foreboding.

Here was the land of the Old Ones, ancestors to the Wendigo and the American Indians. It was here where the spirits of great chiefs and mighty warriors resided, living in death much as they had in life. Sitting Bull, Crazy Horse, Hiawatha, Runs On Fire, Long Tooth, the list of names read like a who's who of greatness, all of them protectors of Gaia and eternal enemies to the Wyrm.

The Legendary Realm was also a land of the Gods and Supernatural People. Here Tsul 'Kalu, Slanting Eyes, made his home high up in the mountains, watching protectively over the animal spirits in his domain. With a man's body the size of a giant redwood and the head of a great stag, the Hunting God was not someone you wanted to piss off. Not if you liked to go on living.

Sharing the mountains with Slanting Eyes were the Little People. Of an average height of two to four feet tall, the Little People were also known to protect the game animals, driving away or injuring the hunters who insulted them. Strong enough to tear up live oak trees by the roots with their bare hands, they delighted in helping lost children and playing mischievous pranks on unsuspecting adults.

Though they lived underground, in caves and tunnels that ran deep into the sides of the mountains, the Little People held all of their important ceremonies and celebrations outdoors. Because of their love of song, feasting, and dance, these ceremonies often lasted for days at a time, interrupted only with an occasional dive for cover when Tlanuwa, the great mythical hawk, soared overhead in search of an evening meal.

Heather paused, feeling very much like a trespasser. Who was she to tread upon the same earth as her living ancestors? What right did she have to ask help and guidance from such spirits? Despite being the Guardian of the Sacred Fang, the Chosen One, she was nothing when compared with those who now walked the spirit path and kept council with the gods.

And suddenly Heather knew that she was no longer alone. She was being watched, studied by the spirits which inhabited the Legendary Realm. Were they angry that someone so inexperienced had dared to enter their land? Or were they merely curious as to why she had come? Perhaps they already knew the answer and were just waiting to see what she would do next.

Heather felt that something should be done to recognize the presence of the spirits who were watching, but she wasn't sure what to do. An offering of smoke would probably be a proper gesture, but she didn't have a pipe and tobacco. Nor did she have sage or sweetgrass.

She kicked herself mentally for leaving the campsite without being prepared. She hadn't really expected to end up in the Umbra when she returned to the pool of water, but that was no excuse. Sam had taught her that Garou were always prepared for every situation; a true Wendigo warrior would never go anywhere without his pipe and tobacco.

Heather didn't have tobacco and a pipe, but maybe she could still make an offering of smoke. Gathering together a few small pieces of driftwood, she carefully stacked the wood in a small tipi-shaped pile near the water's edge. She also didn't have any matches, or a lighter, but then she didn't need any. Sam had taught her the Ceremony of the Flame, a ritual to create fire in places where there was none.

With her back to the lake, Heather sat cross-legged in front of the driftwood pile. Leaning forward, she gently caressed the sticks with the palms of her hands, feeling for the tiny spark of spirit life that still resided in each piece of wood. She said a prayer to those spirits, thanking them.

"My little brothers of the forest, thank you for the noble sacrifice you are about to make. May you live again in the heart of a great tree. May you always have plenty of good sunshine and lots of water to drink. Thank you, my brothers. Aho."

Focusing her energy, she touched the tip of her right index finger against the end of one of the sticks. A few moments passed, then a spark leaped from the tip of her finger to the driftwood. Heather leaned forward and blew on the spark, bringing the spirit of the flame slowly to life. A tiny spiral of smoke drifted up as the wood began to burn. She kept blowing until the flame had taken hold of the wood, then used the burning stick as a torch to light the rest of the pile.

With a glowing fire before her, Heather stood up and looked around. "Oh mighty spirits, hear my words. I am Heather Ocoee of the Wendigo tribe. I am also the Guardian of the Fang, keeper of the sacred medicine of Nee Yah Kah Tah Kee. Come, my ancestors, warm yourselves beside this fire. It is my gift to you."

A minute or two passed, and then she felt a cool wind caress her face. A spirit approached. "Oh great ancestors, you are the teachers and guides of my people. Please, warm yourself beside this fire. It is good. Talk of the old days, and remember the happy times. In return, I ask only for safe passage through your land so I may continue my quest. I am a servant of Gaia, the Sacred Mother, and an enemy to the darkness of the Wyrm."

The wind blew stronger, causing the flames of the fire to flicker and dance. She watched as the crackling sticks were consumed by flaming tongues, stepping back when the fire's heat became too intense.

The fire gave off a hissing sound as the wind whipped it back and forth. The hissing grew louder, becoming more of a growl. Suddenly, a flame shot out to the left, away from the fire, running across the rocky ground as though someone had ignited a trail of gasoline. Another flame shot out to the right.

Heather stood perfectly still, knowing that what she was seeing was anything but normal. The spirits of the land, and the spirit elements of the fire, were joining together to work their medicine. She was a witness to something truly magical.

The flames shot out in opposite directions for about five feet, then turned back. Circling around behind her, they joined together near the water's edge. Heather now stood in the middle of a circle of fire. She wasn't afraid, however, for she knew the fire was being controlled by the spirits of her ancestors. They had circled the flames around her as warriors would circle around women and children in times of danger to keep them safe. The spirits were telling Heather that they were there for her protection.

"Thank you," she said, her voice overcome with emotion. She halfway expected the flames to die down then, but they didn't. Instead they raced across the ground to engulf the dugout canoe. And as the wooden canoe began to burn, it slowly slipped back into the water as though pushed by unseen hands, drifting back across the lake to the opposite shore.

Heather watched the canoe make its way slowly across the magical lake, looking like a burning funeral barge of a Viking king. Illuminating the darkness around it, the canoe was about three hundred feet from the shore when she spotted something in the water. A person. A thing.

Lighted by the glow of the flaming canoe, she could clearly see the head and upper torso of something swimming across the lake. No. Not swimming. Whatever it was, it was standing perfectly still, perhaps treading water. It was also watching her, staring straight at Heather with a pair of eyes that glowed red as fire in the darkness.

A chill ran down the girl's spine. She didn't know what the creature was, for it was too far away to be seen clearly, but the thought of it being in the lake—watching her while she had her back to the water tending the fire—scared her. What if it had snuck up on her while she wasn't looking?

The Umbra was the land of ancient ancestral spirits, but it was also home to the spiritual minions of the Wyrm. These evil spirits, known as Banes, traveled freely through the Umbra, assuming countless shapes and forms. Certain Banes represented principals such as hate and disease, while others simply appeared to be random demonic entities. They were the parasites of the spirit world, attaching themselves to, and eventually possessing, the bodies of hapless humans who chanced their way.

Grabbing the leather pouch that hung from her neck, a frown tugged at the corner of Heather's mouth. The Fang should have warned her that danger was near, but it hadn't. The stone sliver remained cool to the touch. Was the Fang even working? Twice now since entering the Umbra it had failed to warn her of the Wyrm's presence. Had it not been for the burning canoe, she never would have known about the thing in the lake.

"Wa-do. Thank you," Heather said aloud, realizing the spirits had set fire to the canoe and sent it sailing across the water to show her what lay hidden in the darkness. They were definitely helping her on her journey, protecting her. As if in answer to her words, she heard the cry of an owl come from somewhere in the forest behind her.

You're welcome.

Not wanting to stay any longer by the water's edge, Heather reluctantly turned her back on the thing in the lake. The fire had died down, leaving behind only smoldering ashes. The spirits were gone, for now.

Locating the correct Moon Path, she followed it away from the shore and up a steep incline. At the top of the incline, the path plunged again through thick forests. Heather didn't hesitate to follow, wanting to hurry her journey along and anxious to leave the lake, and the mysterious creature, behind.

16

She was as old as the oldest memories of mankind, her heart blacker than a starless night. Once she had been a member of a forgotten race, known to the Indians as the "Little People," but that was long, long ago. Even back then Utluhtu had been utterly evil, her mind and spirit as twisted as the darkness she prayed to.

Afraid of her powers, and sickened by what she had become, her own people had driven her from their land. They wanted nothing to do with a witch, a shapeshifter, one who fed on the flesh and souls of children, adding decades and eons to her life for each innocent child she consumed. They had cast her out and turned their backs on her; the chiefs forbidding their people ever to speak her name in public again.

Homeless and alone, she had wandered the mountainous countryside, preying on the innocent, growing stronger with each life she claimed. The Indians living in the area had called her Spearfinger, a name she quite enjoyed. They told many stories about her, tales to frighten little children so they would never leave their villages by themselves.

But they always came to her, answering a silent call that only they could hear. Little girls with big brown eyes and slender limbs; boys with limber muscles and the hopes of one day becoming warriors. She fed those hopes and dreams, offering promises as false as an unfaithful lover's kiss.

The children who came to her never saw Spearfinger as she really was. In their minds she was not a wrinkled dwarf with a long index finger. Instead they saw a smiling, elderly woman; a grandmother that gladly combed the hair of little girls and boys, telling wonderful stories of how it was long ago. They would climb happily into her lap, never realizing that they would never again see their village, their parents, or those they loved.

She had eaten the flesh and souls of so many children, hundreds of children, each and every one a delight to the taste buds and senses. She liked their livers the best, for they melted on the tongue like the finest butter. And with each soul she consumed, Utluhtu added more years to her life. She became as ageless as the mountains, yet she always wanted more.

It was her greed that had gotten her into trouble. She had stayed in one place for too long, eating too many children from one particular village. Angered by the loss, the warriors had come hunting for her. They found her in the forest, the blood of a little girl still wet upon her lips. With painted faces and blood-curdling cries, the warriors attacked her with spears and arrows. But Utluhtu only laughed at them, for her skin was as tough as stone. She laughed until one of the men made a lucky shot; his arrow pierced her wrist, the only weak spot in her entire body.

She had died that day, her blood spilling from her wounded wrist to paint the ground red. After killing her, the warriors had cut her body into pieces and thrown the pieces into a pool of water. But they did not know that those such as she could never truly die. The warriors had succeeded in destroying her flesh, but Utluhtu's spirit continued to live on. Only fire could completely destroy her, and only then if it was hot enough.

The spirits inhabiting the Legendary Realm knew that Utluhtu's one weakness was fire, which was why they were forming a protective ring of flames around the wolf girl. Treading water, the old witch floated in the lake and watched as two rows of flames shot away from a tiny campfire and raced along the shore. The flames circled around behind Heather Ocoee, saving her from a danger she was totally unaware of.

The spirits knew Utluhtu's weakness. They also knew that the little girl's life force was strong, powerful enough to restore the flesh to the witch's body and allow her once again to enter the Realm. They knew this, so they were trying to protect the child. She was, after all, the Guardian.

But Utluhtu cared not for the stone sliver the girl carried. Nor was she concerned with the quest she was on. The Wyrm might be interested in such magical trinkets, but she was not. She was not of the Wyrm. Not really. They were both carved from the same evil blackness, but she had never bowed down in servitude to the Dark One. Not yet anyway.

Utluhtu and the Wyrm walked the same path, yet they were not one of the same. That was why the Fang of the Wolf did not grow hot when the witch came near, why the girl had no idea that she was being followed through the Umbra. And if it weren't for the untimely interference of certain spirit guides, the child's soul would already have been claimed and eaten long ago.

She watched with some annoyance as the spirits set fire to the canoe, and then pushed the burning vessel out into the lake. The canoe's flames pushed back the darkness, revealing her presence to the child on the shore. With eyes wide with fear, the girl stared at the witch for a moment and then hurried away from the water's edge. Utluhtu watched her leave, an evil smile touching the corners of her lips.

Run, little one. Run. Scurry. Scurry. Scurry. Hurry if you will, but you cannot escape me. None ever escape me. Even with the help of spirits you will not get away. I am coming, little one. Yes I am. I am coming to eat you all up.

PART III

What is Life? It is the flash of a firefly in the night.
It is the breath of a buffalo in the winter time.
It is the little shadow which runs across the grass and loses itself in sunset.
—Crowfoot, Blackfoot Confederacy

17

An ancient Cherokee legend tells of a great flood that covered the earth a long time ago, taking the lives of both people and animals, and of a dog who warned his Indian master to build a raft to escape that flood. To honor the pet that saved his life, the owner carved a large statue in the shape of a sitting dog and placed it on top of the mountain where the raft finally struck dry land.

But that legend, as colorful as it may be, is false, a story told by Indians so the white man would not know the truth of the sacred sitting stone. Nee Yah Kah Tah Kee was the statue of a wolf, not a dog. It was a monument of powerful medicine built by the old ones, a sacred guardian that stood before a doorway to the Umbra.

For centuries, Indians and Garou from as far away as the Black Hills of South Dakota came to the Great Wolf to pray and seek wisdom. Setting aside their differences, as they laid aside their weapons, the visiting members of the different tribes met in peace and became as brothers. No harsh words were ever spoken in the shadow of the Wolf. No fist was ever raised in anger. Even the animals were safe from harm, the deer and the rabbits often grazing within sight of their red brothers.

But the white man, his heart corrupted by the Wyrm's poison, dynamited the statue so he could build his railroad across the mountains. The iron horse carried coal and precious metals—gold and silver—ripped from the womb of the Sacred Mother.

All that remains today of Nee Yah Kah Tah Kee is a nondescript piece of rock. An eight-hundred-pound boulder that has been moved far away from the original site of the Sacred Sitting Wolf, its magic all but gone. There is another piece of the statue, however, in which the Wolf's spirit still lives—one tiny, magical sliver of stone. A Fang. But now that too was missing.

Sam Nakai stood on top of Monterey Mountain, only a few feet from the original site of the Great Wolf. The view of the surrounding mountains and valleys was inspiring, a poet's dream, but it did little to lift his spirit. He cared nothing for scenery at that particular moment, hardly even noticing the beauty of Gaia that lay before him. Instead he thought only of Heather Ocoee, wondering where the girl had gone. She was obviously somewhere in the spirit world. But where?

He wanted to go after the girl, but knew he would never find her in the vast expanse of the Umbra. Besides, if Heather used the Fang to step back into the Realm she would appear there, on the mountain. The Fang of the Wolf could open many doorways, but all of them led to the spot where Nee Yah Kah Tah Kee had once stood.

Knowing it would be better to let Heather find him, Sam turned his attention back to the others. Seventeen Garou and twenty-three Native American Kinfolk had journeyed to Tennessee from all parts of the country, coming in answer to Gaia's silent call. Some had been led by their particular spirit guides, others had been summoned by a few telephone calls and other more conventional means. But whether or not they had been guided by a spirit, or a long-distance operator, they were all warriors of distinction. Men and women of strong medicine.

Most of the Indians who had arrived so far were Cherokee, but there were also a couple of Creek and Catawba warriors in the group. And five of the thirteen Garou tribes were represented, including the Black Furies, Fianna, Get of Fenris, Uktena and Wendigo. The two male members of the Get of Fenris tribe, two brothers who seemed inseparable, had flown all the way from Germany to be a part of the fun and games.

Fun and games? I think not.

Stuffing his hands into the front pocket of his jeans, Sam looked up at the sky. In three days the moon would rise full and bright into the night sky. When it reached its zenith it would change color, becoming as crimson as blood. While the moon was red a rift in the Gauntlet would split open, allowing easy passage from the Umbra to the Realm. The Wyrm would try to squeeze through then, bringing darkness and despair to the sacred land of the Cherokee and Garou. No matter what the cost, no matter how many lives were lost, they had to prevent the Wyrm from entering the Realm.

A frown tugged at the corners of his mouth. Seventeen werewolves and twenty-three Indians. Not nearly enough combined medicine to take on the Wyrm and its army of darkness. It was a hopeless situation. Even with the Fang of the Wolf things would not be much better. But with the Fang there was a chance of winning; a very slim one, but a chance nonetheless.

He turned his gaze again to the mountainous scenery, feeling an ache deep inside his heart. The Fang and the Guardian were gone, and he was to blame. He had spoken sharply to Heather, treating her as a child instead of the keeper of the Sacred Fang. Despite her age, despite her inexperience in the ways of the Garou, she was still the Chosen One. The spirits had picked her to be the protector of Nee Yah Kah Tah Kee's medicine, as they had once picked him. By offending Heather, he had also offended the spirits, the Great Wolf, and Gaia.

Sam Nakai shook his head. He was supposed to be helping the Guardian, teaching her the ways of the tribe and pack. It was his job to make sure she survived the challenging transformation from "human" to Garou, seeing to it that she successfully completed the Rites of Passage. The future of the Garou depended on the Guardian and the medicine she carried. Instead, in a moment of crisis, he had seen Heather as nothing more than a little girl, a burden to be set aside until later. He had failed as a teacher, failed as a Garou. His actions could very well lead to the destruction of the pack, and to the death of one who was much more than just the Guardian.

Heather was his friend. During the few months they had traveled together she had become like a daughter to him, filling his days with laughter and happiness. He had taught her how to become Garou, true, but she had taught something much more important.

The girl had taught him how to look upon the world through the hopeful eyes of a child, instead of through the eyes of a tired old werewolf who had fought too many battles and seen far too much grief. He could not bear to think about something happening to her, especially as a result of something he had said. Sam was a Wendigo warrior, proud and fierce, but he was not without emotion. If Heather Ocoee died, a very large piece of his heart would die with her.

18

The luminous Umbral moon was already starting to set, and the Moon Path she followed was fading, when Heather stumbled upon a clearing in the forest. Within the clearing was a tiny village consisting of twenty or so small, rectangular houses. Made from upright wooden poles covered with sheets of bark and mud and topped with bark roofs, the windowless dwellings were laid out in neat rows that radiated out from an open square in the center of the village.

On the far side of the square, an earthen mound rose fifteen feet into the air. On top of the mound stood a wooden house much larger than all the others in the village. It was obviously the dwelling of someone important. A chief perhaps. Or a priest.

Heather blinked, suddenly realizing that she was looking upon a genuine Indian village. Not a copy. Not a fake. An original. The primitive community was something straight out of a history book, a product of times long past that still existed in the spirit world. Unfortunately, American history was never her best subject in school; therefore, she was unable to identify what tribe it was by the dwellings before her. What little she did know about the past had been taught to her by Sam Nakai.

A shadow of sadness crossed her heart, bringing with it a twinge of loneliness. Sam would know at a glance what kind of village it was, and who the inhabitants were. He would also be able to tell her what the tiny rounded huts that sat behind each house were used for. Constructed of bent saplings and interwoven strips of cane, covered with a thick layer of hardened mud, the huts looked like individual family sweatlodges, or places to store food. Perhaps they were primitive ovens, or containers to store grains, fresh vegetables and other foods. Sam would know what they were....

Sam's not here, damnit. And I don't need him. I can get along just fine by myself.

Stopping at the edge of the village, Heather waited to see if the inhabitants would consider her appearance an unwelcome intrusion. If so, she might be greeted with anything other than open arms. A few minutes passed, however, and no alarms were sounded. Nor did any spears or arrows come streaking her way. From the look of things, the entire village was deserted.

"Hello. Anybody home?" Heather shouted, becoming aware of just how quiet everything was. If the village was deserted, where had everybody gone? Though she was no history expert, she knew from Sam's teachings that an Indian village was never left completely unoccupied. Even during the hunting season, when most of the men went off in search of game, enough warriors stayed behind to protect the village. And if all the warriors did go off for some reason, there would still be women, children and old people—even dogs—left behind.

"Hello...yoo-hoo...." Her voice trailed off, the silence again descending like a blanket over the village. She would have called out again, but the little voice deep inside her head warned her that it might not be such a good idea to draw attention to herself. The moon was setting; Banes would soon be out in force, wandering through the Umbra in search of prey. Things were complicated enough without having to do battle with any of the Wyrm's followers.

Deciding that silence was golden, Heather entered the village. A creepy feeling came over her as she stopped at the first house and knocked on the door. She felt like a trespasser, an invader of flesh and blood in the land of ghosts. A few moments passed and she knocked again. When no one answered, she pushed open the wooden door and peeked inside.

The interior of the single-room house was every bit as primitive as the exterior. There was no furniture, no appliance of any kind. No televisions, stereos, or refrigerators. Not even a microwave. None of the modern conveniences that often made life so much more bearable. Instead a few woven cane mats, and a couple of moldy fur hides, served as both chairs and bedding.

The floor was dirt; the ground packed hard and then swept clean. A fire pit had been dug in the center of the room, a hole in the roof above it allowing the smoke from cooking fires to exit the dwelling. But even with the hole in the ceiling, the interior of the building smelled of smoke and grease. But the smells were old smells, the lingering fragrances of meals cooked long ago.

The house was deserted, and Heather didn't think the occupants had just stepped out for a minute. It had an empty feeling to it that came only with the passage of time. But no matter when the residents had left, they must have done so in one heck of a hurry. In addition to the mats and furs, they had left behind clay bowls, baskets and a variety of stone and bone tools.

Heather looked down at one of the baskets that lay at her feet. Beautifully woven from thin strips of cane, painted a vivid yellow and black, the basket must have taken days, if not weeks, to make. No one would go off and leave such a treasure behind—especially someone whose possessions were limited—not unless they had been forced to leave. Wondering what tragedy might have befallen the basket's owner, she retreated from the tiny dwelling and stepped back outside.

The second and third houses she checked were also unoccupied. And like the first, they too contained valuable items left behind by the owners. Apparently the entire village was deserted, perhaps for quite some time. Again she wondered what dire emergency could have happened to the residents to cause them to leave without taking their belongings with them.

She had just finished exploring the third house, stepping back outside, when she heard a thunderous crashing coming from the forest beyond the village. The noise came from the same direction Heather had just come, causing her to wonder if something was following her. An animal perhaps? Maybe. If so it had to be quite large, for the sounds were very loud and growing louder by the second.

Buffalo stampede!

The thought flashed through her mind, but only for an instant. Such a thing was ridiculous. The mighty bison was a creature of the open plains, not the forest. There had once been a buffalo native to the forests of the eastern United States, but it had become extinct years ago. And for some strange reason, Heather just didn't think she was going to find too many eastern buffalos running around in the Umbra.

Okay, it's not a buffalo. It's a bear. A really big bear.

Her gaze riveted on the dense forest, Heather watched with bated breath as something tore through the underbrush, snapping off and toppling small trees in its path.

The sounds drew louder, causing her to take an involuntary step backward. Without thinking, her right hand moved to the center of her chest to clutch the leather pouch that hung from the cord around her neck. Unlike before, the magical sliver of stone inside the pouch was hot to the touch. The Fang of the Wolf was warning her that danger approached.

The Wyrm's coming.

It might not be the Dark One himself who approached, but it was certainly one of his followers. The Fang of the Wolf only grew hot in the Wyrm's presence. The Enemy was coming her way, but Heather wasn't sure in what shape or form it would appear. Surely a Banth would not create such a ruckus. Even a pack of Black Spiral Dancers, known for their insanity, would be far quieter when moving through the spirit world.

But it wasn't a Banth or a pack of Black Spiral Dancers that made all the noise. Nor was it a herd of eastern buffalo that crashed through the forest. On the contrary, it was something far more terrifying that suddenly emerged from the underbrush. It was a creature that caused Heather Ocoee to doubt her own sanity, tearing a startled gasp from her throat.

The thing that finally rolled into view was a giant head, about four feet in diameter, its pockmarked skin a deep brown in color. Just a head. No body. No legs or arms. Nothing else. Not even a neck. It was a man's head, with a flat nose, heavy lips, and long black hair—bits of leaves and twigs clinging to it—looking upon the world with a pair of dark, wide-set eyes. Angry eyes.

Heather blinked, hoping her imagination was playing a trick on her. It wasn't. Never before had she seen anything as frightening as the giant head. Even a Black Spiral Dancer paled in comparison. Sam Nakai had told her that all kinds of spirits lived in the Legendary Realm, both good and bad, but she had never expected to come across anything quite like this. No wonder the village was deserted. With a giant head for a neighbor she would move too.

The giant head rolled to a stop in the clearing, a few feet beyond the edge of the village. Spotting Heather, the head shouted, "Ha. Ha. Ha. I see you standing there. You cannot get away."

Oh, shit.

Squinting his eyes, the giant head rolled toward her like an oversized beach ball—a fleshy brown beach ball with ears. Heather had no idea what the head wanted with her, and she didn't want to find out either. There are some things in the world which frighten even a warrior of the Wendigo tribe.

"Ha. Ha. Ha. I see you. Yes I do," shouted the head. "Here I come!"

Turning on her heels, Heather quickly ran back inside the tiny dwelling from which she had just emerged. She had just gotten the door closed when the giant head rammed the side of the building with a tremendous crash. The little girl yelped in surprise.

"Ha. Ha. Ha. You cannot get away!" The head shouted, crashing against the cabin a second time. A sprinkling of dust and tiny pieces of dried mud rained down on Heather's head from the ceiling above. She also heard the sound of wood splintering.

"My, my, my. I do believe he's mad. Was it something you said, or perhaps something you did?"

Startled by the voice, Heather spun around. She expected to find someone in the building with her, but no one was there. The only other occupant was a small brown rabbit that sat on the dirt floor a few feet away, twitching his ears and wiggling his nose. Looking around, she asked, "Who said that?"

The rabbit twitched his ears once again, and then spoke in a clear voice, "Are you blind, girl? Or are you just stupid. I said it."

"I don't believe it. You can talk!" Heather said, quite surprised.

"Of course I can talk, you idiot," answered the rabbit, a trace of sarcasm entering his voice. "You are in the Pure Land of the Legendary Realm, the home of the old ones. Here it is quite common for animals and people to speak to one another. It used to be common in your world too, before all of you humans got so damn stupid."

As the rabbit spoke, the giant head crashed against the wall again. The cabin shook and a section of bark siding broke free from the wall and fell to the floor. Turning back around, Heather saw the head peeking at her through the hole it had made.

"Ah ha. There you are!" the head shouted. "You cannot hide from me."

Heather watched with concern as the head rolled backwards, bracing herself for the collision that was sure to come.

"My. My. My. He does seem rather angry. Doesn't he?" the rabbit said. "I don't think this building will take much more abuse. I really don't. They just don't make them as sturdy as they used to. Of course, they never made them as strong as a rabbit hole. Nothing like a good hole to hide in when trouble comes around…"

Heather looked up at the ceiling, which was about ready to fall down on top of their heads. "You're right: this place is about to fall apart. We've got to get out of here. Do you have any suggestions?"

The rabbit looked up at the ceiling in silence for a moment, as though deep in thought. Finally, he asked, "I don't suppose you can change yourself into a bird and fly away?"

"No, I can't," Heather answered, somewhat annoyed at being asked such a silly question.

"Pity," the rabbit said, shaking his head sadly. He hopped across the room, stopping at a small hole burrowed beneath the back wall. "Can you make yourself small like me and climb down this hole?"

"I can't do that either," she replied.

"Then it's been nice knowing you," the rabbit said, disappearing down the hole.

She was about to yell something nasty at the rabbit when the giant head struck the building again, causing the roof to collapse on top of her. Pieces of wood and dried mud rained down from above, filling the air with a choking cloud of dust. Heather just managed to duck as one of the support logs came crashing down, missing her head by only a few inches.

"I can't turn into a bird and fly away," she shouted, angry. "Nor can I make myself small enough to climb down your stupid rabbit hole. But I can do this, by God. And this is more than enough."

Heather quickly removed her shirt as the Rage flowed like molten lava through her veins. Removing her tennis shoes and blue jeans, she willed the change to come over her. Because she was in the Umbra, a land of magic, the transformation happened very rapidly. In only a few seconds, she had changed from a small girl into a very large, powerful—and extremely pissed-off—werewolf.

Enough of this, Heather thought. Tossing fallen logs and pieces of wood out of her way, she grabbed the cabin's door and tore it free from its rope hinges. Outside the giant head was rolling at the cabin, expecting to smash into the wall again. But what it smashed into was much tougher than the building's wooden wall, and a whole hell of a lot meaner.

With a roar of anger, Heather slammed full force into the giant head. She meant to stop it, but the thing bowled her over without even slowing down. Grabbing hold of the head's ears, she rolled with it, biting, kicking and clawing.

"Let go of me!" the head shouted, suddenly changing directions.

"No way," Heather growled, biting and clawing even harder. "It's about time someone taught you some manners. That someone is me."

"Ow, you're hurting me!" The head cried, trying to break free from the Garou's grasp. Heather held on, her claws and fangs scratching at the head's stony skin, drawing blood in dozens of different places. The head pleaded for mercy, but she refused to listen. Rolling around the village, they crashed into buildings and toppled small trees.

The giant head was nearly dead, and the village almost completely destroyed, when she decided to be charitable and let it live—but only after it promised that it would never again come back to this part of the Umbra. Letting go, Heather stood and watched as the head rolled slowly back into the forest.

"I guess we showed him. Didn't we?"

Heather looked down. The little brown rabbit sat on the ground next to her, stretching his neck to appear even taller.

We?

Annoyed, she stepped back and placed a well-aimed kick to the boisterous rabbit's butt, sending him sailing like a furry missile through the air.

19

Since it was almost dawn in the land of the spirits when Heather defeated the giant rolling head, she decided to rest for the day in one of the few cabins left standing in the village. Garou rarely journeyed through the Umbra during the day. Instead they traveled at night, using the various Moon Paths for guidance. Those paths could not be seen when the pale light of Helios, the Umbra's sun, hung in the sky.

Transforming fully into a wolf, she sniffed out an empty, darkened corner directly opposite the door. Turning around in a circle until deciding on which way she wanted to face, Heather curled up on the dirt floor with her head resting on her tail. A few minutes later she was sound asleep.

It was already nighttime in the Umbra when Heather awoke, feeling refreshed and ready to continue her journey. Leaving the village, she again asked the spirits for guidance in choosing the right Moon Path, one that would hopefully lead her to the Abyss. She could have used a moon bridge to reach her destination, but not knowing what spirit guarded which bridge she decided to play it safe and stick with the path.

The night was cool, the wind scented with an array of exotic scents. As Heather padded quietly down the path in wolf form, she used her super-sensitive nose to search out and identify different smells, filing the information in the back of her mind for future reference. Many of the plant smells she did not know, however, for they no longer existed back in the Realm. Mankind was the great destroyer, bringing extinction to dozens of species of plants and animals each year. He destroyed without remorse or compassion, not thinking that some of the species he eliminated might possibly hold the cure to diseases such as cancer and AIDS.

Several times she came across a spot where a Garou had crossed the Moon Path she followed. The scents were faint with the passage of time, but noticeable nonetheless. Twice she picked up the unmistakable stench of Wyrm Spawn where a Banth had stepped upon the trail. Those scents were much fresher than that of her fellow Garou, reminding her of the dangers which might lie hidden in the shadowy darkness of the forest.

Heather knew she could easily defeat a Banth in a fair fight, one on one. She had done so before. But those of the Wyrm often did not fight fair, and they rarely traveled alone. Instead they preferred to travel in small groups of five or more, setting traps for the unwary. Foul, hideous creatures, the Banths had been known to torture their victims to death slowly —though they usually reserved that honor just for Garou.

In the case of humans, the Banths were more apt to leave their victim alive, taking over the mind and body to create chaos back in the real world. Many a crooked politician and corporate leader, responsible for the destruction of the environment, was nothing more than Wyrm-spawn in disguise. The imposters were sought out and destroyed by the Garou whenever possible, but many times they often weren't discovered until the damage had already been done.

Thinking of the Wyrm and Banths caused Heather to quicken her pace. It also caused her to stay alert and not allow her mind to wander or be overcome by the joys of the spirit world. Walking blindly into a trap, and being slowly, painfully, tortured to death, was something she could do without in her life.

She had traveled no more than a mile or so from the village when she came to a fork in the Moon Path. The fork was something of a rarity in the Umbra; most of the Paths traveled straight through the spirit world, with breaks only appearing when the light of the Umbral moon no longer shown. At the spot where the path forked stood a large boulder of gray granite and quartz. Upon the boulder sat an old Indian woman.

The old woman was rather small of stature, only around five feet tall. She was dressed in a long, white leather dress, and painted moccasins, her gray hair cascading loosely over her shoulders like an icy waterfall. Her face and hands were dark brown and wrinkled, looking like the skin of a sun-dried apple, but her eyes were clear and bright. Intelligent eyes that shone like the sparkling water of a mountain lake. The woman watched Heather as she approached in wolf form, studying her, showing absolutely no sign of fear.

Heather stopped, confused, sniffing the air. She knew the old woman had to be a spirit, but she couldn't tell if she was friendly or evil. She could detect no odor of the Wyrm, nor did her skin tingle as it always did when those of darkness were nearby. A moment or two passed before she recognized the old woman. Heather coughed in surprise when she did. It was the same Indian woman whose reflection she had seen in the pool of water—the woman holding the lost Fang of the Wolf. Transforming back into Homid form, she slowly approached the old woman.

"Ah, there you are," the Indian woman said, her face cracking into a smile. "I have been waiting for you, my sweet child."

Heather stopped while still a few feet away. "You've been waiting for me?"

The old woman nodded. "Of course I have. Do you not recognize me?"

"You are the lady I saw in the water," Heather answered.

"That's right, child," the old woman laughed, obviously delighted that Heather knew who she was. "I am the one whose reflection you saw. My name is Utluhtu."

Heather took a step closer. "Are you one of my spirit guides?"

"Perhaps," she nodded. "Are you searching for something?"

Heather quickly explained about her journey to the Realm of the Abyss in search of the second Fang, and about the Shaman Moon. The old woman listened carefully, nodding occasionally. When the girl finished telling her story, Utluhtu scratched her chin and said, "If the Fangs of the Wolf can seal the Gauntlet against the Wyrm, then they can also open it. Such magic would be very valuable to the Dark One. Very valuable indeed."

"That's why I have to find the other Fang before someone else does," Heather said, anxious to continue on her journey. "Will you help me?"

"Of course I will help you, silly child," the elderly woman replied with a crooked smile. "After all, that is why I am here."

Heather watched as Utluhtu jumped down off the granite boulder, moving with a grace and ease quite surprising for someone her age. But then again this was the spirit land, and spirits were supposed to be ageless. Maybe it was only the physical image that the Indian woman projected which was actually old.

"*Kawa gi, Lakodo Ki,*" Utluhtu said, speaking in a language Heather had never heard before. Turning around, she raised her right hand above her head. Pointing at the night sky, she repeated the words even louder. "*Kawa gi, Lakodo Ki!*"

Heather's mind must have played a trick on her, because she could have sworn that Utluhtu's right index finger actually grew longer as she spoke aloud the magical words, stretching to twice its normal length. But when she shook her head and blinked, the old woman's finger seemed to be its original size again. It was probably just a trick of the light and nothing else.

Maybe I should see an eye doctor. I think I need glasses.

Utluhtu had just spoken the magical words a second time when the air around her began to shimmer and dance, like heat waves rising off a cooking fire. The shimmering seemed to radiate out from the old woman's body, from the center of her chest, rising straight up into the night sky. And as they rose high into the starless sky, the shimmering waves of air mixed with the darkness to form something quite solid—like water, gravel and sand mixing together to form concrete.

Heather Ocoee jumped back with a startled cry, shocked by what she saw. Just behind Utluhtu a large bridge rose up into the night sky, where no bridge had been just moments before. It was a bridge of magic that stretched up into the darkness as far as the eyes could see. A bridge that led to some other place within the Umbra, perhaps to some other time.

She had seen magical bridges before. The Garou often used moon bridges to get from one place to another. But unlike moon bridges, which twinkle and glow with the essence of moonlight, the bridge Utluhtu had summoned was as black as a moonless night. An ugly, sinister-looking structure, it appeared to be carved from massive blocks of ebony stone and not magic.

"Do not look so afraid, my child," Utluhtu said, a mischievous smile touching the corners of her mouth. "You asked for a path to the Realm of the Abyss. Here is that path."

"Will this take us to the Abyss?" Heather asked, unable to disguise the fear in her voice. She was reluctant to set foot upon the ebony bridge, even if it did lead to the place she needed to go.

"It will take you to the Realm of the Abyss, and to places far beyond that," Utluhtu answered. "Strange places. Wonderful places. Realms and worlds within the Umbra that few have ever been to." She walked over to where the bridge began and started up its steep incline. When Heather didn't follow, she turned around and looked at her.

"Why do you hesitate, little one? Do you want to go to the Abyss or not?"

Heather nodded. "Yes, but…"

"Then come along, my child. I haven't got all night. This is the quickest way to the place you seek. The Moon Path you follow will take days to get there, if it even reaches that far."

Heather reluctantly walked forward and stepped upon the strange black bridge, feeling the structure give slightly beneath her weight. It felt like the bridge was made of flesh instead of stone, as though it were the decaying body of a giant dragon upon which she walked. Maybe the ebony bridge was indeed the rotting corpse of a scaly dragon; looking down, she saw rancid puddles of oil slowly forming in her footprints.

Not wanting her imagination to get the best of her, Heather focused her attention on a point in the distance and continued on. She didn't even realize she had passed Utluhtu, but suddenly the old woman was no longer in front of her. Confused, she stopped to turn back around.

As Heather started to turn around, she caught a glimpse of a hideous, troll-like creature out of the corner of her eye, standing just behind her. She yelled and jumped back in surprise, slipping on the bridge's oily surface and landing heavily on her butt.

Heather started to jump to her feet, but saw that it wasn't a misshapen creature but Utluhtu who had been standing behind her. The old woman looked quite surprised by the girl's actions.

"What's the matter, dear?" Utluhtu asked. "Did you slip?"

Heather shook her head. "No I saw someone. Or something…"

The old woman looked around. "Who, dear? I don't see anyone. Just us."

Heather looked around too. There was no one else on the bridge but the two of them. Her mind must have played a trick on her. "I guess it was just my imagination. I'm sorry," she said, feeling rather foolish for yelling like she had.

Utluhtu smiled. "That's all right, my child. My old mind sometimes plays tricks on me too. Here, let me help you up."

She stepped forward and held out her hand. Heather took it, surprised at the strength of the old woman's grip and the hardness of her skin. It felt like she had grabbed a hand made from a gnarled tree root instead of flesh and bone.

Utluhtu shook her head as she helped Heather to her feet. "Now look what you've gone and done: you've gotten yourself all dirty. Here, turn around, let me brush you off."

"No. That's okay. It's nothing." Heather said, not wanting to bother with cleaning herself off. "These are old clothes anyway."

"Tsk. Tsk. It will only take a minute. Now turn around."

Even long before she was a Garou, Heather had been taught to always respect her elders; therefore she did as Utluhtu asked, allowing the old woman to brush the dirt from her back and bottom.

"There. That's better," Utluhtu said, her voice a soothing whisper. "We can't have you walking around the Umbra all dirty, now, can we?"

Her hands swept up Heather's back to her shoulders. "My. My. Will you look at this. Your muscles are all tight. No wonder you're seeing things; you're all tensed up. Here, let old Utluhtu fix. Just stand still; we'll make it all better."

A warm, relaxing numbness seeped into Heather's body as the old Indian woman massaged and kneaded the muscles in her shoulders. She felt her tension slowly ebbing away, carrying with it all her worries and doubts. All her problems. It felt like she was floating on a raft, in the middle of a calm lake.

"There, that's better, darling. Just relax. Close your eyes and let grandmother Utluhtu make all of your problems go away."

"Yes ma'am," Heather said, leaning back and closing her eyes. She allowed Utluhtu's soothing voice and hands to take her someplace she had never been before, someplace warm and safe—a distant world where there wasn't any danger, or darkness, or foster parents who always wanted to hit you and hurt you. A world without loneliness, tears, suffering or sadness.

She heard the old woman singing, something soft and sweet, and felt the magic fingers caress her neck and slowly comb through her hair.

"Such pretty, pretty hair."

The voice came from far away now. Freed from her physical body, Heather floated on a sea of calm. She knew she was supposed to be doing something, but she could no longer remember exactly what that something was. Nor did she really care. Unlike before, nothing mattered to her now. Nothing at all.

The hands moved slowly down her back, touching her in places that brought more relaxation. More pleasure. As they paused on her lower back, a few inches above her right hip bone, Heather felt a sharp pinprick of pressure. A tiny spark of pain in her otherwise perfect world.

The tiny stabbing of pain was followed by a gentle tugging around the base of her spine. She didn't like the tugging, for it felt like someone was reaching inside her and yanking on her insides. The tugging was accompanied by the even more uncomfortable sensation of a burning in her chest.

Heather didn't know what the tugging was, but she recognized the painful burning in the center of her chest. It was heat—generated from a magical sliver of stone, in the leather pouch that she wore. The Fang of the Wolf was growing hot, warning her of danger.

Danger. The Wyrm.

The words entered her mind, but Heather tried to ignore them. She didn't want to give up her peaceful world so soon. But the Fang of the Wolf would not leave her alone. The magic of Nee Yah Kah Tah Kee grew hotter by the second, singeing both flesh and spirit.

Danger.

Heather's mind suddenly registered the mental warning. She tried to open her eyes, but couldn't. It was as though she were lost in the darkness and could not find her way back.

What's wrong? What's happening?

The tugging in her lower back grew stronger. The Fang of the Wolf grew even hotter. Heather again tried to open her eyes, but it was no use. It felt as though all of her strength had been stolen away; she was too weak even to wake up.

Suddenly she heard the cry of an owl. And from the darkness of her mind flew a winged messenger. It was the same owl she had seen on her vision quest; her spirit guide was coming to her aid.

Thank you.

But Heather was mistaken. The owl wasn't coming to help her after all. Instead, it was coming to hurt her. The spirit owl flew straight at her…straight at her face. Talons outstretched before it, the bird dove toward the girl's unprotected flesh.

My eyes. Not my eyes!

"Nooo!" Heather screamed, opening her eyes and covering her face with her hands. She expected to feel the razor sharpness of talons tearing into her flesh, but nothing happened. Slowly lowering her hands, she saw that the owl had existed only in her mind. It was a mental image, a vision, and nothing more.

But the heat of the Fang had been no vision; it had been real. Even though the Fang of the Wolf was already starting to cool, she could still feel its warmth through the leather pouch warning her of danger. And there was a weakness to her body that had not been there before. Confused, she slowly lowered her hands.

"What's the matter, little one?"

Heather spun around, momentarily forgetting where she was and why. Utluhtu stood a few feet behind her, watching with eyes that seemed to shine in the moonlight. The old woman was licking something off her right index finger, something that looked like blood.

Suddenly remembering the pinprick of pain she had felt, Heather reached behind her to touch the small of her back. She almost expected to find blood there, but her fingertips came away clean. She was not bleeding.

Utluhtu finished licking her finger and offered Heather a slight smile. "Come child," she said, walking past her. "Your destiny awaits."

Heather looked back toward the safety of the forest, feeling the sudden urge to run away from the old woman. The feeling passed, however, and she turned and followed Utluhtu up the bridge.

20

Only three more nights until the Shaman Moon rose high into the night sky. Three nights and Heather still had not returned. Sam Nakai wanted to go after her, but knew he would never find her. The spiritual world of the Umbra was vast, its regions many. He was better off staying where he was, waiting until she came back on her own. But waiting was never easy for a Garou, especially a warrior.

It did not help matters any that Michael Pathkiller was trying his best to stir up trouble among those who came to battle the Wyrm. Angered that the Fang of the Wolf had been passed on to a little girl and not him, Pathkiller openly accused

Sam of being in league with the Dark One. To the werewolves who would listen, he spoke of taking the Fang away from the "false Guardian" before its magic was lost forever. Heather could not possibly have picked a worse time to disappear.

To avoid a conflict that might turn Garou and Kinfolk against each other, and to get beyond the range of Pathkiller's bitter tongue, Sam decided to leave the others for a while and seek solitude in the town of Monterey. He knew by leaving that he was giving Michael Pathkiller the opportunity to talk freely in his absence, but it was better than what would happen if he stuck around. He was a patient man, but his patience was starting to wear a little thin. One more accusation about being in league with the Wyrm and someone was going to get seriously hurt.

Isolated by rugged countryside and a range of mountains, the town of Monterey, Tennessee, was small and quiet. Most of the stores had already closed for the evening by the time Sam arrived in town, leaving him a choice between Fran's Diner, Marty's Pizza, and the Sportsman's Bar. Since he didn't have much of an appetite, he chose the bar.

A bell jingled a happy tune as he pushed open the wooden door and entered the Sportsman's, stepping into an air-conditioned room that reeked of cigarette smoke, beer, urine and sweat. Wrinkling his nose in disgust, he walked past half-a-dozen tables, and a couple of booths, grabbing an empty stool at the end of a long, formica-topped bar. The place was busy, locals mostly, and it took a few minutes for the heavyset bartender to spot Sam.

"What'll it be, buddy?" the bartender asked in an unusually raspy voice. Wiping his hands off on a soiled dish towel, he placed a not-so-clean coaster in front of Sam.

The bartender's deep voice got the Garou's attention. Sniffing, Sam detected the sickly sweet stench of cancer on the man's breath. A fragrance like a mixture of sour grapes and shit. A quick look with the gift of sight showed that the bartender's aura was black. He was dying, probably from smoking too many cigarettes.

"I'll have a draught," Sam said. "A light if you've got it."

The bartender nodded and walked away to get Sam's order. He returned a few moments later with an icy mug of beer. He also set a clean ashtray and a bowl of pretzels on the bar. Sam ignored the ashtray and reached for a pretzel instead. Taking a sip of his beer, he turned to study the other customers.

Not counting the bartender, there were nineteen people in the Sportsman's: fourteen men and five women. Most of them were probably regulars, farmers and mountain folk who had dropped by to knock off a few cold ones after doing whatever it was they did all day. With their blue jeans, overalls, work boots, calloused hands and sunburned necks, they looked like something out of a Norman Rockwell painting. Hats were obviously in style in Monterey, as were beards, pickup trucks, and T-shirts with holes in them. Several of the men in the bar looked tough enough to flat put a hurting on a person if they had half a mind to. A few even looked like they would gladly welcome such an opportunity. Sam made sure not to stare in their direction in order to avoid a situation he could do without. Even some of the women looked like they could hold their own in a barroom brawl.

While most of the people in the bar looked like tried and true mountain folk, regular salt of the earth types, there were three young men that looked oddly out of place. They sat in the booth farthest from the door, watching the other customers with darting glances and expressions of contempt.

All three of the young men were dressed entirely in black, from the jeans and T-shirts that they wore to their studded leather jackets. One man was entirely bald, his head obviously shaved, ears, nose, eyebrows and lips adorned with numerous rings and studs. The other two wore their hair long and dyed a brilliant red color. Like their bald-headed companion, they too sported a collection of earrings and outlandish facial jewelry.

If Sam didn't know better, he would say that the three young men had been magically transported from a neo-punk nightclub in Los Angeles and placed in the Sportsman's Bar by mistake. They were probably just passing through town, and had stopped in for a quick beer or two to wash down the road dust. More than likely, they felt as out of place as they looked.

Still, there was something about the way the three men watched the other patrons, how they huddled together and spoke in nothing but whispers, that made them look sinister and menacing. They reminded him of weasels about to rob the chicken coop.

His curiosity aroused, Sam turned away from the three men and pretended to be studying his beer. But he wasn't interested in the mug he held. Instead he called upon his wolf power of hearing to listen in on what the young men were saying. He felt his right ear twitch as he summoned the gift, keeping himself in check to prevent that ear from actually changing into a wolf's. Suddenly sprouting a lupine ear was great for a laugh among friends, but it could be rather unsettling to strangers. There was an overload of distorted sounds as his sensory level shifted from human to animal, followed by a noticeable increase in volume.

Turning his head slowly, Sam attempted to sort out the different voices in the room. "Look here, I've been fishing that lake for twenty years, and I say if you want to catch the big ones you've got to use nightcrawlers. Those plastic worms aren't worth a flip...."

Wrong voice. He tried again. "Damnit, George, I'm your best friend. I wouldn't lie to you. I'm telling you the god's honest truth; Linda was screwing around on you while you were out of town...." It was all he could do to keep from laughing as he tried one more. "Man, I hate this fucking place. I hate this town. I hate this bar. I hate these people. What the hell are we doing here anyway?"

"Waiting," a second voice replied. "Waiting and watching."

"Watching? Watching for what?"

"For the enemy."

Sam's interest picked up. He stole a quick glance to his right and knew he was listening to the conversation of the three leather-clad punks sitting at the booth.

"Are you completely stupid? Do you think we are the only ones who have heard His calling? Others will have heard Him too. They will try to stop the Dark One from taking his rightful place in this world. They are the enemy. We are watching for them."

"What will we do when we see the enemy?"

"Destroy them."

"But how will we know who is who? They all look alike to me. How can you tell who's the enemy and who isn't?"

"Listen to His voice. He will tell you."

"I'm trying, but it's not always easy. I'm new at this…"

"You will learn in time."

"I hope so. Do you see any enemies in here now?"

"Yes."

"You do? Where?"

"That one. He's the enemy."

The words caught Sam off guard. Before he could stop himself, he turned and looked toward the booth. All three men were staring at him.

"There. That one. Him. He's the enemy. And he knows who we are."

A chill passed through Sam Nakai's body. The spawn of the Wyrm had come to Monterey, summoned by the voice of the dark lord they served. The Wyrm obviously knew that the Garou would try to stop it from entering the Realm through the rift. The Dark One had summoned its followers, calling them to war.

The chill he felt was replaced by an intense rage. He was only thirty feet away from three of the Wyrm-spawn. He wanted to attack them, rip their bodies into tiny pieces, and bathe in their blood. If he did, however, it would warn any others in the area that they had been discovered. Better to let them go untouched for now, though it was all he could do to control his anger.

Finishing his beer, Sam set the empty mug down on the bar and placed a five-dollar bill beside it. He stood up and slowly walked to the front door, keeping his eyes forward so he would not look at those he wanted to kill. He felt the stares of the three young men on his back as he opened the door and stepped out into the street.

The Wyrm's followers are in Monterey. It can only mean that the battle we all fear will surely come. When the Shaman Moon rises high in the sky, the Gauntlet will open and blood will flow.

Sam left town with the intention of starting back to where the others had gathered, but he decided to make a stop at Standing Stone Park first. In the center of the park was an eight-hundred-pound boulder, one of the few remaining pieces of Nee Yah Kah Tah Kee.

Even though the boulder's magic was not nearly as strong as the Fang's, he wanted to pay his respects to the stone anyway. But to his horror, he found that since his last visit to the park vandals had spraypainted graffiti on the boulder.

Sex, drugs and Rock N Roll. Your Momma Sucks. Eat Shit and Die.

"Who would do such a thing?" he asked, angry. "Have they no respect?" Pulling a handkerchief from his back pocket, he squatted down next to the boulder. He started to wipe at the graffiti, but as he touched the lettering Sam felt a strange tingling in his fingers and hand. The tingling surged up his right arm as he scrubbed the stone, bringing with it an instant headache and dizziness. He stopped rubbing and sat back.

What's wrong? What's going on?

Actually, he knew what was going on, because he had experienced such a sensation many times before. It was the same sick feeling he got each and every time he came in contact with the Wyrm's evil magic. There could be no source for such magic here, however, except....

Suspicious, Sam leaned forward and used his fingernails to carefully scrape at the graffiti he had been trying to clean away. Removing a small portion of the first letter, he saw that something had been painted beneath the word. It was a strange symbol that glowed with an unearthly green luminosity. Further scraping revealed the symbol to be an ancient Pictish rune, an evil magic sign used by members of the Black Spiral Dancers.

Sam was shocked. Were there Black Spiral Dancers in the area? Had they also come to take part in the fight, joining forces with other minions of the Wyrm's army? If so, he needed to warn the others. But why had they stopped here? Why the runes?

Because they know that only the magic of Nee Yah Kah Tah Kee can stop the Wyrm from entering the Realm through the rift. Damage the stone and you damage some of the Sacred Wolf's powers.

So engrossed with the mystery of the runes, he didn't know someone was behind him until he heard a twig snap. It was automatic reaction, more than anything else, that saved his life. When he heard the sound, Sam turned quickly and the iron rod swung at his head only struck him a glancing blow.

Sam dropped and rolled, escaping death by a mere fraction of an inch. He felt blood running down the back of his head and knew his scalp had been laid open, but it was only a minor wound at worst. He would live. Had he not moved when he did, however, his skull would have been crushed like an eggshell. Getting quickly to his feet, he turned to face his attackers.

Three men stood before him, the same three leather-clad punks he had seen in the bar. The bald-headed man, apparently the trio's leader, was the one who had struck him. In his right hand he held what looked like a tire tool. His two companions each held black-handled daggers, with curved blades that glowed as green as the Pictish runes in the moonlight. Sam had seen such daggers carried by Black Spiral Dancers, and knew that their blades were poisoned by magic. The daggers were obviously a gift to the men for services rendered.

As Sam looked upon the daggers and the men who held them, he again felt the Rage come over him. This time, however, he made no attempt to stop it. If the three puny humans standing before him wanted a fight, then, by Gaia, he was going to bloody well give them one.

His muscles quivering like electrical wires, he stood with legs spread and stared at his attackers. The bald-headed man with the tire tool started to step forward, but stopped when he saw the Garou's shirt start to ripple.

Now, Sam thought, feeling his body start to transform. *Now, Now, Now.*

A surge of adrenaline tore a cry from his throat as the wolf spirit inside him was released. The adrenaline surge was followed by a feeling of internal strength so powerful it gave him the intense desire to lift his leg and piss on those foolish enough to attack a Garou. Instead of pissing on them, he laughed at the three men.

"Time to party," Sam said, still laughing. "Let's dance."

The complete change from Homid to Crinos happened in the blink of an eye. One second Sam Nakai was standing before the three young punks, not posing much of a threat. The next second an eight-foot werewolf stood before them, which was something altogether different.

Sam expected the trio to fall victim to the Delirium. When they didn't, he realized that they were Kinfolk to the Black Spiral Dancers. They were afraid, yes, but they knew exactly what they saw. Pity for them.

With a roar of anger, Sam Nakai lunged. He charged straight at the bald-headed leader, who tried to stop him with the now totally ineffective tire tool. As he swung the iron tool, Sam lashed out with deadly claws and ripped the man's arm from his shoulder. The man screamed in pain as his arm went flying through the air. Sam lashed out again, seeking the source of the shrill noise. His claws sliced through the man's neck, severing flesh, muscle and bone. The scream was cut short as a bald head rolled across the ground like a bloody basketball.

Sam turned just as one of the other punks lunged at him, attempting to stab him in the back with a poisoned dagger. The point of the dagger scraped his ribs, causing a flash of fiery pain, but it was deflected before it could sink in far enough to do any serious damage.

That did it. Now I'm really mad.

Sweeping the dagger aside with his left forearm, Sam struck downward with his clawed right hand. The claws entered his opponent's abdomen and drew blood. Stepping forward, he thrust his hand deep inside the man's body. Slicing through internal organs like a hot knife through butter, he grabbed the Wyrm-spawn's spine and tore it out through the front of his body. Vertebrae snapping, the red-haired punk shrieked in agony as his body crumpled to the ground like a house of cards.

Two down and only one more to go.

Sam turned toward the last punk, smiling in delight when he heard a bubbling sound and detected the unmistakable smell of feces filling the air. The young man was in obvious need of new underwear, but that was the very least of his troubles.

His body trembling uncontrollably, the punk stood staring at Sam in wide-eyed terror. Knowing he could not possibly defeat a werewolf by himself, he started backing up. Sam followed, his pace matching that of the young man. Step by step. Inch by inch.

You can't get away. I won't let you. You have to fight me.

The Wyrm-spawn must have somehow read the Garou's thoughts, for he suddenly reversed directions and charged. With the knife raised high above his head, he dove at Sam in a suicidal attempt to stab him. Maybe he thought the

Black Spiral Dancers' dagger would somehow make him invisible. He was wrong. Dead wrong.

As the man dove toward him, Sam sidestepped and lashed out with an explosive punch. The punch caught his opponent in the center of his chest, snapping his ribs like pretzel sticks and driving the splintered bones through his heart. Spewing a frothy vomit of beer and blood, the punk flew backward through the air and struck the ground, never to move again.

Carefully picking up the two poisoned daggers, Sam dug a hole in the ground and buried them. He then dragged all three bodies and their body parts, into the woods and buried them as well. With so many new faces in town to oppose the Wyrm, it wouldn't do for the local authorities to uncover a massacre in their backyard. It also wouldn't do for them to find a werewolf in their midst, so after burying the bodies he transformed back into Homid form.

Washing off the blood at a water fountain, Sam returned to look upon what was left of the sacred standing stone. A troubling thought crossed his mind, causing his stomach to tighten with dread. Laying his hand upon an unpainted part of the boulder, he learned that his worse fears were true. The Black Spiral Dancers had painted their runes, and danced their evil dance, stealing what little power was left in the rock. The medicine of Nee Yah Kah Tah Kee was all almost gone. All that remained of the Sacred Wolf's magic was in a tiny sliver of stone. The Fang.

Raising his head, Sam stared out into the night. "Heather, where are you?"

21

It was like a great void, a giant crack in the very fabric of Gaia herself. Darker than darkness should ever be, it was an ebony so black it whispered of universes without stars, worlds without life.

Heather stood at the edge of the Abyss, mesmerized by the very sight of it. Nothing she had been taught in the past six months could have prepared her for this moment. No lesson, legend, or tale, no matter how descriptive or engrossingly told, could have accurately described the Realm of the Abyss or the feeling that came over her as she looked upon it.

Fear? Yes, that was part of the emotion that squeezed Heather's heart in its tight embrace and caused her limbs to tremble. But it was much more than just fear. Awe? That too, for she suddenly felt very small in the universe, a tiny grain of sand on an endless beach. But there was something else, something almost primordial—a feeling she could not put into proper words—that came over her as she gazed upon the darkness spreading before her. Somehow she knew, without really knowing how she knew, that the answer to every question ever pondered by mankind could be found somewhere in the canyon before her, for this truly was a place where the old gods came to die.

Giant cracks radiated out from the ebony canyon, twisting through the barren landscape like dry riverbeds through a desert. The cracks vanished from sight in the hazy distance, swallowed up by the shroud of mist that marked the border of the Realm of the Abyss. Stretching across the flat horizon like a giant curtain of gray, the mist appeared to be slowly inching away from the mysterious canyon, silently devouring all that was the Umbra as it went.

Tearing her gaze away from the Abyss, Heather was surprised to find that she was alone. Utluhtu had gone, taking her vile black bridge with her. No matter. The old woman was a spirit, and spirits rarely came into the Realm of the Abyss. To enter the Abyss, they had first to materialize, losing touch with the rest of the Umbra. And if the spirit's physical form was somehow destroyed, then that spirit would die and be forgotten. Even those spirits who acted as guides preferred to wait outside the Realm rather than enter it. Utluhtu would not be around to help as long as Heather remained in the Abyss. Like it or not, she was once again on her own.

I don't need her help anymore anyway. I don't need anyone's help.

The statement was a lie. Now, more than ever, she needed help in her search. She had reached the Abyss, but the missing Fang could be anywhere. And the thought of climbing down into the ebony canyon by herself to search for it made the girl's mouth go dry.

Placing her left hand lightly over the leather pouch that held the Fang of the Wolf, Heather whispered a prayer. She prayed for courage, strength, and protection from harm. Finally, she asked Nee Yah Kah Tah Kee to guide her in her search for the other Fang. The Sacred Wolf must have heard her, for she suddenly felt a tingling along the base of her spine. The stone she held also began to grow noticeably warmer. The missing Fang was somewhere in the Abyss; she could feel it.

Inching closer to the edge, she saw that three main trails, as well as several smaller pathways, led down into the canyon of darkness. From the teachings of the Wendigo, she knew that the Silent Striders had named the three main trails leading into the Abyss after the metals found in the rocks along the way. They were known as the Golden Path, the Iron Path, and the Silver Path.

Of the three, the Golden Path was supposed to be the most dangerous trail to follow. It was said that the bones of numerous Garou and other creatures lay scattered and broken on the glittering veins of gold and patterns of emeralds and rubies which marked the path. Many foolhardy warriors had been lured down the Golden Path, their eyes blinded by the wealth that lay scattered at their feet, only to slip and fall through one of the large gaps that marred the trail.

The Iron Path was the most commonly used trail. Solid and easily traversed along most of its route, the trail wove past numerous fissures and caverns that honeycombed the rocky walls of the Abyss. Heather thought about taking the Iron Path, but dismissed the idea on the grounds that it had been traveled by far too many already. What she was searching for would be found along a trail walked by only a few, if any.

Finally, she turned her attention to the path which started directly before her, the last of the three main trails. The Silver Path was a mystery to the Garou, a thing of legend and rumor. The Silver Fangs claimed it led to the heart of the Gathering Darkness, while the Uktena argued that it led only to a manifestation of the Wyrm called Eater-of-Souls, which supposedly lived at the very bottom of the Abyss. According to ancient tribal lore, only Klaital, legendary hero of the Stargazers, had ever taken the Silver Path safely through the Abyss. And though he'd finished his quest with few physical scars, his mind was never quite the same.

Though her heart beat wildly just to think about it, she knew that the Silver Path was the right path to follow. If the Fang of the Wolf was to be found along one of the more traveled trails, it would have already been discovered years ago. The Fang had not been discovered yet; therefore, it had to be in a place where few went.

Deciding that the strength and dexterity of a werewolf would be especially useful, Heather slipped free of her clothes and transformed into Crinos form. She thought about changing fully into a wolf, but there might be places on the trail where hands would be needed—places even a wolf could not travel. The transformation complete, she stuffed her clothes into her bag, readjusted the strap, and started down the Silver Path.

Heather had no way of knowing which trail, if any, would lead her to the item she sought. She could only trust her instincts and hope that the magic of Nee Yah Kah Tah Kee would intervene on her behalf. But even with the aid of the Sacred Wolf, she proceeded slowly down the narrow pathway, painfully aware of how close she walked to the edge and how deep the Abyss must truly be. One misplaced step, or a loose stone underfoot, and she would go plummeting down the steep sides of the canyon like a fallen rock. The thought of such a fall, and the bone-shattering crunch at the end of it, brought the metallic taste of fear to her mouth and caused her to slow her pace even more.

As she started down the path, an eerie stillness descended over her. A quietness with all the nervous energy of the calm before a storm. It was almost as if the Abyss devoured all noise that entered it, swallowing it whole as a snake swallows a mouse. There were no sounds. Nothing. All that could be heard was the soft plodding of her padded footfalls, and the rasping of her breathing, and even that sounded strangely different. A little softer than it should have been, a little quieter, as though everything she heard were muffled through cotton.

She stopped, a wave of fear washing over her. The silence that surrounded her was like a hungry beast, creeping closer on spider legs, reaching out from the darkness to snatch at her with deadly claws. She wanted to howl just to make some noise, pushing the silence back, but did not for fear her voice would be swallowed up the moment it left her lips. She was also afraid of drawing attention to herself. From her Wendigo teachings, she knew that hideous Wyrm Beasts stalked the Moon Paths around the Abyss. The last thing she wanted to do was alert them to her presence.

So Heather Ocoee remained as silent as her muffled footfalls as she continued along the trail that led deeper into the Abyss. Glancing down she saw several thin veins of silver cross her path, shining like streams of liquid mercury in the fading light.

The light.

Again she stopped and looked around, puzzled by what she saw. It was rapidly growing darker as she descended the steep pathway. But it was not the blackness of night, which would have been expected or even welcomed. Instead, the darkness that reached out to clutch her tight to its bosom was a peculiar absence of color and illumination. A great nothingness of gray, like an empty canvas yet untouched by an artist's brush. It was as if the light, like the sound, was being swallowed up and absorbed by the rocky walls of the Abyss.

Slipping the Fang of the Wolf from its pouch, Heather held the magical stone in her right hand and said a prayer of illumination. Instantly the Fang began to shine with a bluish glow, but the glow was not nearly as bright as it should have been. She shook the stone several times, even blew on it, but the Fang's glow remained unusually dim and lackluster.

"Must need new batteries," she joked, her feeble attempt at levity doing little to stop a feeling of dread from settling deep into her stomach. The Fang of the Wolf was her only protection, her only hope of finding its missing counterpart. If the magic of Nee Yah Kah Tah Kee was considerably weaker in the Abyss, then her quest might fail. She wondered if the stone still had enough power to open a doorway to the real world. If not, then she might be stuck in the Realm of the Abyss forever.

Don't think such thoughts. Don't. Don't. Don't. Heather shook her head several times in a vain attempt to clear her mind of doubts. *I will not fail. I must not fail. I am Garou. I am Wendigo. I will not give up without a fight, no matter what. Too many of my people are depending on me. My people. Mine. I am no longer an orphan...no longer an unwanted person. I have a family now, a very large family. I belong.*

Squaring her shoulders, Heather took a deep breath. Determination flowed through her veins like liquid fire, forcing a growl to her throat. Holding the Fang before her as a torch to light the way, she again started down the Silver Path.

The trail was now steep and narrow, made all the more hazardous by loose and fallen rock. Twice she slipped and almost fell as the outer edge of the Path crumbled beneath her feet. Had it not been for fast reflexes and a bit of luck, she would have plunged to her death like so many others had before her.

She had just stepped out onto a narrow rocky ledge, when she was buffeted by a strong wind that sprang up suddenly from the bottom of the Abyss. The wind whispered and moaned like a thousand tortured souls as it blew through the ebony canyon, snatching at her with invisible fingers and tossing stinging dirt into her eyes.

Shielding her eyes with her hands, she paused to wait for the wind to subside before continuing on. The trail was dangerous enough without attempting to navigate it with dirt in her eyes. But the wind refused to die down. Growing stronger, it screamed in anger and rocked her with powerful gusts.

One of the tribal gifts of the Wendigo was the ability to summon a strong wind, or even a blast of arctic air, which could be directed against enemies during times of battle. Sam had told Heather about this unique gift, and had even demonstrated it a couple of times. Unfortunately, he had never told her what to do to make the wind stop blowing. There had to be a way to do it; she just didn't know how. Luckily, the wind that blew up from the bottom of the Abyss began to die down of its own accord. Soon it stopped altogether.

"About time," she said, wiping dirt from her eyes and smoothing down her ruffled fur. The wind had died down, for now, but it could start up again without warning at any moment. She would have to be constantly on guard in case it did.

Continuing on her journey, Heather had gone no more than a quarter mile when she noticed tiny fissures and cracks in the rock wall. Most of the cracks were narrow, only an inch or so across, but some were big enough to stick her entire head into them—not that she felt inclined to do so. Water dripped black and oily from several of the cracks, making the trail slippery and that much more treacherous. In a dozen or so of the bigger fissures, she spotted the tattered remains of webs spun by Pattern Spiders. She didn't see any spiders, but that didn't mean there were none still around.

The fissures gradually widened as she continued down, forming narrow alcoves and caves in the rock wall. Heather checked each cave as she came to it, hoping to discover the missing Fang tucked away in some dark recess. The first two caves she looked into were empty. The third cave was also empty, but its walls were adorned with Pictish runes. The runes looked like those used in the hives of the Black Spiral Dancers.

Wyrm-spawn…danger.

Heather froze when she saw the runes. Sam had told her that Black Spiral Dancers often go on pilgrimages to the Abyss. They believed the Abyss was the actual form of the Consumption Wyrm, now dormant due to the Croatoan sacrifice. A chill danced down her back as she wondered about who had drawn the runes, and how long ago. Fearful that the Wyrm's magic might still reside within the cave, she quickly retreated.

Back on the ledge again, she surveyed her position. Heather had already descended nearly a half-mile into the Abyss, farther than most Garou had ever gone before—farther than many would ever wish to go. She was journeying into unknown territory now, uncharted waters. If she continued on, she could no longer rely on the teachings and legends of the Garou to guide her. Few had ever ventured so deep and lived to tell about it. In fact, there was only one werewolf who had ever gone farther, and he was never again quite right in the head, a victim of the terrifying things he had seen.

But she had no choice. Not really. If she turned back now all would be lost. The Shaman Moon would appear in the sky. The rift in the Gauntlet would open and the Wyrm would push through into the Realm. Her vision would also come to pass. Sam Nakai would die.

Heather would not allow that to happen, not if she could possibly prevent it. Sam was her teacher, her mentor, but he was also her friend. He had saved her life several times in the past six months, the least she could do was to try to return the favor.

And even though she was still terribly upset with him for calling her a child, Heather knew that she loved Sam as much as any daughter could possibly love a father. Maybe even more.

He's right. I am a child.

The thought upset Heather, but it also brought a smile to her lips. It was true; Sam was right. She was still a child in many ways. And when it came to being a werewolf she was barely out of infancy. Despite being chosen by the spirits to be the Guardian of the Fang—an honor she had tried more than once to refuse—there was an awful lot she had yet to learn.

How much time did she have? How long until the Shaman Moon rose high into the night sky? Heather looked up, but she could not see the sky from where she stood. She was too deep; all she saw was darkness. She didn't have to see the sky, however, to know that the hours and days were passing far too quickly. Her internal clock told her that, its rhythm keeping beat with the cycles of the moon. Tick. Tock. Tick. Tock. Time was slipping away, slipping through her fingers like fine grains of sand. She had to keep going, had to hurry.

Passing several smaller caves, Heather came to a place where the narrow ledge she traveled was broken by a large gap. She stopped and stood at the edge of the gap, staring down into the void, wondering how deep the Abyss really was. As she stood there staring, a wave of dizziness washed over her. With the dizziness came the sudden, insane desire to step off the ledge into space.

She shook her head. "Are you out of your mind? Get such crazy thoughts out of your head."

Crazy? Maybe. Yet the desire to step off the ledge grew even stronger, becoming an itch she just had to scratch. Along with the desire, and the dizziness, came a voice that whispered to her from the darkness below. A voice only she could hear.

Go on, take a step. You will not fall, I promise. You are Wendigo; in your heart you are one with the spirits. Go on. Your guides will protect you.

Was that true? Would her guides protect her? It would be quicker, and much safer, to fly than it would be to climb the rest of the way into the Abyss. Were her spirit guides still with her?

An icy wind blew up from the depths of the Abyss to ruffle her fur. With the wind came the whispered voice that only she could hear.

I am here with you, little one. I am one of your guides. Go ahead and jump. Take the step; I will help you. Trust your internal voice. Fly to me, little one. Fly. Fly. Fly.

Heather smiled, happiness filling her heart. Everything was going to work out for the better; one of her spirit guides had come to help. In answer to the voice of that guide, she picked up her right foot and started to step forward.

Spirits rarely enter the Realm of the Abyss.

The words bubbled up from the depths of her subconscious, causing her to pause. It was one of the lessons Sam Nakai had taught her; she knew it by heart.

If that was true, then it couldn't possibly be her spirit guide that she heard. It must be someone, or something, else.

Like a light switch being flipped off, Heather's head suddenly cleared and she found herself teetering on the edge of a gap. She stepped back quickly, frightened, her heart pounding. There was no voice of her spirit guide, never had been. There was only the wind blowing up from the bowels of the Abyss, attempting to lure her to her death as it had so many others before her.

Still shaken, she backed up a few feet, then took a running jump over the gap. Once safely across she hurried along the ledge as quickly as possible, anxious to put some distance between herself and that near-fatal spot. She wondered how many other Garou had succumbed to the voice of the Abyss, lured to their deaths by the evil that enveloped the area. But she only wondered for a moment. Putting everything else out of her mind, Heather concentrated on one thing and one thing only: finding the missing Fang.

22

Her scent was still on Utluhtu's deadly index finger. Sweet. Fresh. Delicious. The smell of a little girl's spirit. The odor of raw flesh and blood. Intoxicating as fine wine, it caused a shiver of delight to pass through the dwarf's twisted body as she inhaled the fragrance of Heather Ocoee.

She wanted more than just a sniff, however, much more than the tiny taste she had gotten. Utluhtu wanted to drink the girl's blood in great gulps, and chew on her flesh until there was nothing left to gnaw but bones. Even then she wouldn't be satisfied, for she would break open each and every bone, sucking out the tasty marrow until there was nothing left to suck.

But before she ate of Heather Ocoee's body, Utluhtu would feed on her spirit. Ah, the spirit. That was always the best part. As invigorating as the cool night wind. As enticing as the blood of a newborn baby. Unlike the spirits she had kept in earthenware containers—souls of innocent Indian children to snack on during the hungry, lonely times—Heather's spirit was very special. Very special indeed. It had an unbridled energy in it that she had never before experienced in a child's spirit. Any child.

Maybe it was because the little girl was part wolf. Maybe it was something else. Either way, Heather's spirit had enough magical energy in it to restore Utluhtu to the glory of her former self, putting the flesh back on her ancient bones. She would then be able to leave the spirit world and travel in the land of the living once again. The soul of the wolf child would set her free from her eternal prison in the Umbra.

"But not now. Not yet. You must wait. Yes, wait. You must be patient."

But it was so hard to be patient, so hard to wait. And now that she had tasted of the child's spirit it was ever harder. Just a taste was all she'd got. A lick. A whiff. Nothing more. She would have drained the girl dry, but Heather's spirit guide had protected her. It wasn't fair for a girl so young to have a protector, but she did. Special child. Very special indeed. Utluhtu knew that she would be unable to eat the girl as long as her spirit protectors were around. She would have to be patient and wait until Heather was alone.

"She's alone now."

It was true. Heather Ocoee did not have her spirit guides with her now. No spirit would willingly enter the Realm of the Abyss. She was alone, but she was still safe, for Utluhtu would not enter the Abyss either. The girl was safe as long as she stayed within the great crack, at least safe from being eaten by the witch.

"Not fair. Not fair at all."

But as soon as the girl found what she was looking for, she would come out of the Abyss. Utluhtu would eat then. First the child's spirit, then her flesh.

A shadow of doubt crossed the dwarf's mind. What if the girl didn't find what she was looking for? What if she stayed in the Abyss forever? Utluhtu would not be able to eat her then. Without the wolf girl's spirit, the witch would never get out of the Umbra.

"She will find it. The child is special. She will find it and then I will eat her. Must be patient. Must let the Guardian finish her task."

Utluhtu cared nothing about the Fangs Heather spoke of, but there were those who would. The Wyrm would care. The Fangs could close doorways between the Umbra and the Realm. Maybe they could open doorways too. The Wyrm would be interested in such magic. He would want the Fangs. Maybe the Dark One would reward the one who brought him the Fangs with gifts of magic, gifts of power. Utluhtu was not interested in the Fangs, but she was very interested in the Wyrm's gifts.

"Maybe the Dark One will give me the flesh of children. Tasty treats for Utluhtu."

The dwarf looked up, studying the barren landscape that stretched before her like the charcoal-gray remnants of a battlefield. Here the Umbra was not a place of vibrant colors and beauty. Here the songs of birds did not fill the air, nor the scent of flowers. Instead cancerous-looking trees sprang leafless from the soil, stretching gnarled corpse-like fingers toward a sickly gray sky. There was no sun, or moon, only a bleak grayness that filled the horizon with the melancholy of a graveyard.

In that dismal landscape, leprous-looking vines wrapped around the blackened trunks of the trees like a dying lover's embrace. Like the trees, the vines were also leafless, poisonous thorns taking the place of foliage. Dozens of tiny skeletons littered the ground around the base of the trees, the bones of birds and small animals, victims to the vines' lethal toxins. The corpse of one such victim, the body of a gray squirrel, still hung upside down from the branch of a tree, its rotting flesh impaled on several long thorns.

Feeding off the squirrel's body were half-a-dozen shiny black beetles; thousands more scurried across the ground, burrowing in the poisoned soil and swimming across puddles of blackish ooze. Some of the puddles lay quiet and still; others rolled and burst like blisters, releasing the odor of rotting eggs into the air.

Utluhtu looked at the bleak landscape before her with distaste, for what she saw repulsed even her. This rancid place within the Umbra was called a Calumn, a place infested with the influence of the Wyrm. It was a place of despair and poison for the soul, ruled over by Banes and sometimes by a Nexus Crawler. There were several Calumns within the Umbra, each drawing evil spirits to them like sugar attracts flies. Even the diseased forest around her cabin paled in comparison to the blight that lay before her now.

Though she too was evil, Utluhtu avoided the Calumns, preferring her own company to the company of others. This time, however, there was a reason for seeking out such a foul place. She knew that this particular Calumn held a portal to the Malfeas, a small realm within the Deep Umbra that was a base of operations for the servitors of the Wyrm. More like a giant Calumn than a true realm, the Malfeas was founded on a most powerful idea: corruption, the very essence of the Wyrm.

It didn't take her long to find the portal. The small, circular depression in the ground was a place where nothing at all grew, a place even the shiny black beetles avoided. Warm, vaporous gases rose upward from the depression, shimmering like smoke over a cooking fire, carrying with them the smell of things corrupted and evil. The stench of the Wyrm.

Utluhtu studied the depression for a moment before stepping into it. As she walked to its center, the ground beneath her feet shifted and moved as though hundreds of snakes lay just below the sandy surface. But it was not snakes that she trod upon. Instead it was the essence of the thing that guarded the portal, a servant to the Wyrm. Reaching the center of the depression, a voice suddenly entered her mind, speaking to her with words that dripped venom.

"What is it that you want, witch? Why have you come here?"

She looked around, searching for the source of the voice, but there was nothing and no one to see. The undulation beneath her feet increased, the ground rippling in waves. It was as if the invisible snakes had suddenly become excited.

"I come seeking the Dark One. I wish to speak with the Wyrm."

Wicked laughter filled her head, as evil as a hyena's cry. "Do not make me laugh. Who are you to speak with the Wyrm?"

The witch looked down, studying the squirming soil beneath her feet. She almost expected something to pop out of the ground, but nothing did. "Who am I? Who am I? I am Utluhtu. I am someone who can give the Dark One something he may want. Something he may want very badly. I have come to make a trade."

Again the laughter filled her head. "The Wyrm does not trade. He only takes. If you have something he wants, he will take it from you."

Utluhtu was getting annoyed at the arrogance of the voice that spoke to her. "Are you the Wyrm?" she asked, knowing that it was not. A moment of silence passed. "Well, are you?"

"I am his ears and eyes. If you have something to say, witch, you will say it to me."

The dwarf spit on the ground. "I will talk only to the Wyrm."

"You will talk to me or I will destroy you."

It was Utluhtu's turn to laugh. "Destroy me and the Dark One will never know of the gift I have to offer." She kicked at the ground. "I have wasted enough time here. I am leaving."

She took no more than two steps, when a second voice spoke to her. A darker voice, filled with such an evil essence that it caused her body to break out in quivering gooseflesh.

"I am here, old woman. You wish to make a trade with me? What is it you offer?"

Utluhtu stopped and chose her words carefully. The Wyrm was the all-powerful corrupter, the very essence of evil. It would not do to offend him. "I offer the Dark One the keys to the Realm. I offer the magic of the old one, the one the wolf people call Nee Yah Kah Tah Kee."

"You are wasting my time, witch. The magic of the Sitting Wolf has been destroyed. In two nights I will enter the Realm without your help."

"Not destroyed. Not yet," she said. "The Fangs of the Wolf still exist. They can close the doorway. The wolf girl knows this. She has one Fang. Maybe she will find the other."

"Go on. I am listening."

"If the magic of the Fangs can close the doorway, maybe they can open it too. If you possessed the Fangs, nothing could stop you from entering the Realm. Nothing at all. Not even the wolf people."

"You can bring me the Fangs?"

"I will bring them to you," she nodded.

There was a long pause of silence, and then the voice said, "What is it you want?"

Utluhtu smiled. "I want power, lots of power. Magical power. And I want children. Lots and lots of children. I want their bodies, and I want their souls. Young children. Sweet children. Tasty children."

"And for this you will deliver the Fangs of the Wolf to me?"

"Or destroy them if you wish."

"No. Do not destroy them. I may have a use for the Sitting Wolf's magic."

"Then I will bring them to you." Utluhtu nodded. "Do we have a deal?"

There was another long pause, and then the Wyrm's voice entered her mind like a slithering serpent. "Yes, we have a deal."

"Good," the witch said. She started to step out of the depression, but the voice stopped her.

"Wait. Where are you going?"

"I am going to get the Fangs."

"Good. Go. But first we must seal our bargain…seal it with a kiss. I never make a deal, unless it is done face to face."

Utluhtu turned to run, but it was too late. The ground beneath her feet suddenly opened up and she fell into the darkness, carried down through the portal to a place deep within the Umbra. There, in a cavern that glowed green with phosphorous poison, she beheld the Wyrm in its true form, gazing upon a nightmare beyond madness itself. She looked upon the face of the Dark One and screamed, for there are some things even a witch is frightened of.

23

Heather had gone no more than a hundred feet beyond the gap when the Silver Path took a sharp turn to the left. Here a pointed outcropping of rock jutted out from the canyon's wall like the belly of a fat man, nearly blocking the path completely. The outcropping left only an inch or two of ledge to walk upon, which meant she would have to cling to the jagged stones as she attempted to squeeze by. Not an easy matter, especially when the stones were worn smooth with the passage of time.

"Great. Just great. As if things weren't already difficult enough, now I've got to be a rock climber too." She looked down, staring into the depths of the Abyss. One miscalculation, one tiny slip, and she would fall to her death. "Why couldn't I have been born with a pair of wings? Or with a parachute?"

Unfortunately for Heather, she had neither wings nor a parachute. And since she couldn't fly like a bird, she had no other choice but to try to squeeze past the outcropping of rock.

"Here goes nothing."

Placing the Fang of the Wolf back in its leather pouch, she turned sideways and slowly edged her way up to the outcropping, feeling carefully for a hand hold. At first there didn't appear to be anything to grab hold of, but then she discovered a narrow crack about a foot or two above her head. The crack was just wide enough to slip her claws into. Jabbing the fingertips of her left hand into the crack, Heather pressed her stomach tight against the rocks and inched slowly to her right.

Even pressed flat against the rocks there wasn't much ledge to stand on. It was only wide enough for the first two inches of her feet, forcing her to stand on her tippy-toes. The unnatural stance put a tremendous strain on the back of her legs, causing the muscles in her calves to cramp and burn. Before she was even halfway around the outcropping, her legs began to tremble uncontrollably from the intense strain.

"Stop it. Stop it," she whispered, but her legs refused to listen and continued to shake. "Ow, that hurts. It really hurts."

Heather stopped and took a deep breath, trying to relax the muscles in her legs. But there was no way to rest them, not while she was still forced to stand on her toes. The burn she felt in her calves quickly ebbed up the back of her legs to her lower back, causing those muscles also to tighten in pain.

Time was now the enemy. If she didn't hurry up and get around the outcropping, her legs would tighten up to the point where she would not be able to move them. They already hurt bad enough to cause her to grit her teeth. And their violent trembling threatened to pull her toes from the ledge.

Hold on. Hold on. Only a few more feet. You can do it. Honest, I know you can. Slide your feet. That's right. First the right, now the left. Hold on to the rocks. Feel for the cracks.

She had just reached out with her right hand for a new hand hold, when the rocky ledge crumbled without warning beneath her feet.

Heather howled in terror as the ledge broke off, leaving her feet dangling in space. She held on by only the fingertips of her left hand; her right hand madly searching for something to grab onto. But there seemed to be no more cracks, no protrusions of any kind.

There has got to be a place. Another crack. A hole. Find it, damnit. Find it.

Her left arm and shoulder screamed in agony as she strained to hang on. She would have dug her toes into the rocks to take the strain off her arm, but her legs were so fatigued that she could barely move them. That left only the fingertips of her left hand to support the weight of an eight-foot werewolf while her right hand searched madly for a place to grab hold.

As the claws of her left hand began to slip, Heather realized that her werewolf form was about to be her undoing. Though she was much stronger in Crinos form, she was also a whole lot heavier. Gravity was pulling down on her, dragging her from the cliff face to her doom. The only thing saving her right then were her claws. If only there was some way she could still have the claws, but be much lighter at the same time.

Maybe there was.

On several occasions, she had witnessed Sam Nakai stop his transformation from Crinos to Homid, and Homid to Crinos, before it was complete. He had been demonstrating his ability to control the transformation in order to take advantage of the best of both worlds. Why change all the way when only strong legs were needed, or better eyesight and hearing? At the time she thought his demonstrations were nothing more than entertainment, but now she realized just how valuable those teachings actually were.

Heather had never stopped during the middle of a transformation, but knew she had to do so now if she wanted to survive. Her werewolf body was just too heavy. She had to get rid of it, at least some of it.

Closing her eyes, she willed the transformation from Crinos to Homid to take place. She really had to concentrate on what she was doing, making sure the change started in her feet and moved gradually up her body. She heard the popping of bones shifting, felt her body begin to shorten and grow smaller.

That's it. That's it. Careful now. Not too fast. Easy does it.

A tingling sensation coursed through her as the change took place. Heather waited until the tingling reached her shoulders and started down her arms before mentally willing the metamorphosis to halt.

Now. Now. Cut it off. Make it stop.

Easier said than done, for once the transformation started it was difficult to bring it to a stop. Heather concentrated even harder. Beads of sweat broke out on her forehead and upper lip; a blinding headache formed just behind her eyes. But she felt the transformation begin to slow. Stop.

There. That's it. Now.

Opening her eyes, she was delighted to see that her body was back in human form. Yet from her shoulders to her clawed fingertips, she was still very much a werewolf. It was such a comical sight that she couldn't help but laugh. Her laughter died quickly, however, for she was still dangling by one hand.

With the arm strength of a werewolf, and the diminished body weight of a human, Heather had no problem reaching up with her right hand and finding a second hand hold. Her feet now dangling above the ledge, she used just her arms to get around the outcropping of rock.

The ledge widened again on the other side of the outcropping. Extremely thankful to still be alive, Heather dropped to the ledge and sat down wearily. Feeling like she was on the verge of having a major heart attack, she pulled her knees to her chest and rested her head on her arms. Every muscle in her body seemed to quiver with fatigue. Her heart raced madly with fear.

I can't do this. I can't. I'm just not strong enough. I give up.

A few minutes passed before Heather had the strength or desire to raise her head and look around. What she saw brought the girl quickly to her feet.

The path she followed curved to the left, following a crevice in the canyon's wall. At the entrance to the crevice someone had carved a giant head from the black granite of the cliff's face. A man's head, strong and brooding, with wide cheekbones, heavy lips and a broad nose. At least ten feet tall and eight feet wide, the head watched the trail like a silent stone sentinel. It also watched Heather, staring at her with open eyes that flashed silver in the darkness, demanding to know who she was and what right she had to enter the Abyss.

Beyond the first head was another exactly like it, and another beyond that. Four heads in all, side by side, carved in such a way that all four of them were looking at Heather at the same time. Four Guardians—north, south, east, and west—like the four horsemen of the Apocalypse. Perhaps they were the images of powerful gods or kings. Perhaps not. Either way, they must have been carved centuries ago, crafted by an unknown race of people lost to the cruel eons of time.

As Heather stood staring at the four giant heads she felt a mild tingling dance along her scalp. The tingling was followed by the utterly profound feeling that something strange was about to happen, something to be savored and not feared. She wasn't sure what was coming, but she knew it was important.

She was no longer frightened by the giant statues. Instead she stood in quiet awe, waiting patiently for what was about to happen. Certainly some powerful magic was at work; she could feel it. Heather just didn't know whose magic it was. She hadn't long to wait, however, for as she stood there a tiny portion of her mind was unlocked, allowing a wave of lost and forgotten memories to bubble up to the surface from her subconscious.

Transported by memories she didn't know she had, the girl suddenly found herself in a small room, possibly a bedroom, in an unknown house. The walls were covered with wood paneling, the ceiling painted a soft white. Framed pictures decorated several of the walls, but they were too far away to see clearly. Heather was lying down, on a bed or maybe a sofa. She was not alone, for there were others in the room with her. She heard voices to her left, whispered words and soft laughter.

Heather tried to turn her head to see who was talking, but could not—or had not, since what she was seeing was actually a memory. She knew it was a memory and not a vision, for the room seemed familiar somehow, even though she could not recall what it was or where. The voices were also vaguely familiar, and she was comforted by the sound of them. The whispers she heard were like the sounds of a cool night wind rustling through autumn leaves.

A shadow fell over her as a man and a woman stepped into view. The woman was thin and of medium height, fair-skinned, with long reddish-brown hair. She was dressed in a flowery dress, with a red belt that held it snug about her waist. A pair of pink shell earrings matched the simple necklace she wore around her neck.

The woman's face was pleasant to look at. It was a face that radiated happiness, especially when she smiled. Though she did not know her, Heather could not imagine the woman ever being sad or troubled by anything at all in life.

The man who stood beside the woman was her complete opposite, in both appearance and mannerisms. He was tall and broad-shouldered, dark-skinned, with long, raven-black hair. His face appeared to be chiseled from stone, his eyes dark and piercing. A permanent frown seemed to be etched upon his face, as though he were contemplating the problems of the world. He wore a black T-shirt and a denim jacket; and when he scratched his chin, Heather noticed several tattoos on the knuckles of his right hand.

But the tattoos weren't really tattoos. Instead they were sacred symbols of power and medicine, branded into the man's flesh with a heated piece of iron. Heather had seen such brands numerous times since becoming a Garou. They were the markings that identified the warriors of the Wendigo, symbols that told of their pack, rank, military society, auspice and totem spirits. Sam Nakai had similar brands on his hands, though they had been nearly erased by his many years of constant battles.

As Heather realized that the man standing before her was a Garou, she also became aware of who he was. He was her father; the woman beside him her mother. Her parents, their images dredged up from the darkest recess of her mind and displayed before her like an old family movie. She had no real memory of either of them—at least not before now—because they had disappeared from her life when she was still quite young. But here they were, if only for a brief moment.

Tears running freely down her cheeks, Heather gazed upon the parents she had never known. Her mother was so beautiful; her father so handsome and strong. She knew nothing about them, other than that he was a Garou and she a human. What were their names? Had they loved her? Why had she been abandoned? Why had they been killed? A million questions popped into her mind, each one tearing at the heartstrings of her soul.

Do not waste this moment with tears. Look. Learn. Remember.

She blinked her eyes and stared at the image before her, setting each and every detail to memory. She studied the brands on her father's hands, struggling to remember what each one of them stood for. The brands were a clue to her father's identity, as well as being a clue to her own identity.

The diagonal slash marks on his right hand, extending from the knuckle of his index finger to his finger nail, stood for the number of enemies he had killed in battle. Heather counted twenty-one slashes, twenty-one kills in hand-to-hand combat. The spiral design on the knuckle of his middle finger meant that her father was a wind-caller, one who could summon the power of the wind to do his bidding. Those who could work such magic were highly regarded in the tribe.

There were two brands on his ring finger. The first was a complete circle. It stood for the full moon, and meant that her father was an Ahroun. A true spirit warrior, one of the fiercest fighters of all Garou. The second was a pack symbol. In this case it was the shape of a human eye. Heather didn't know what pack the eye represented, because she had never seen such a symbol before. But the pack it stood for was her father's pack. It was also her pack. Her people.

Only the little finger remained to be studied. Heather was almost hesitant to turn her attention to that final finger, afraid of what she might find there. In the Wendigo tradition, a warrior decorated his first three fingers with symbols that told of himself. The little finger, however, was adorned with symbols and runes which told about his offspring. His children. Heather turned her attention to her father's pinky finger and learned what she had not known about herself.

Only one brand adorned her father's little finger, which meant he had only one child. Heather. Unlike the other brands on his hand, the mark on his smallest finger was still rather new and not yet faded with the passage of time. It was the a symbol of a crescent moon, Theurge. Her auspice.

The auspice was the description of the moon under which a person was born, kind of like a Garou zodiac. Most Garou considered it the best way to define who and what a person was. It was so important, in fact, that when a new Garou was brought into a tribe they became the apprentice of an older Garou with the same auspice. The mentor would then instruct the young one in the ways and gifts of that particular auspice.

Heather had never known what her auspice was. The spirits had told Sam Nakai what her tribe was, but her moon sign had never been revealed until now.

Staring at the symbol on her father's hand, she finally understood exactly who and what she was. Children born under the light of a crescent moon were considered visionaries among the Garou. They were attuned to the spirit world, often acting as guides between the Realm and the Umbra. They were the seers, the shamans. Some joked that Theurges were "touched" by the spirits, both a blessing and a curse. No wonder she had been chosen by the spirits to be the Guardian of the Fang. It all made sense to her now, especially since Sam was also Theurge.

But Heather was not allowed to dwell on this newfound information, for the image before her faded as yet another memory floated to the surface from her subconscious. And while the first image was a scene of peace and happiness, the new one that replaced it was a vision of violence and death.

She was in a garbage-strewn alley, cradled tightly in the arms of her mother. Heather could hear her mother's heartbeat pounding loudly in her ears, could smell her fear. A few feet away stood her father, in full werewolf form. He was bleeding badly from several life-threatening wounds, yet he stood with his head held high and legs spread, forming a protective barrier between Heather, her mother, and two Black Spiral Dancers.

Unable to block out the memory that flooded her mind, she watched in horror as the Black Spiral Dancers rushed at her father from two different directions. He was armed only with a length of iron pipe, which he swung like a baseball bat, while the Dancers each had daggers with blades of silver.

His war cry filling the night, Heather's father fought bravely, bringing honor to his tribe and clan. Twice he struck each Dancer a terrible blow with the pipe, shattering bones and knocking them back across the alley. But each time they recovered and managed to get to their feet again. Darting in and out like buzzing flies and laughing like crazed hyenas, the Dancers stabbed and sliced with their deadly daggers.

Cuts appeared along her father's arms and legs, on the back of his hands, and across his face. His fur became matted with blood; droplets of crimson splattered the brick wall behind him.

Bleeding from a dozen different wounds, he sang his death song and charged at the Black Spiral Dancers. But he no longer had any strength left to fight with. Overpowering him, the Dancers dragged him to the ground and stabbed him over and over with their knives, ripping his flesh with their teeth and claws.

"Suntock! No!" It was her mother's voice, loud in Heather's ears, calling to the man she loved, calling his name. Her father's name.

Hearing his name called, he turned to the woman he loved and whispered but a single word. A name. Her name. He formed the name carefully with his lips, lovingly, knowing it would be the last word he ever spoke aloud. It was a gift of love eternal from a dying werewolf.

"Lydia...." Suntock whispered the name and reached out to her, hoping to touch the woman he loved one final time. But the Black Spiral Dancers drove him down, and then cut his throat. Heather's father died in a grimy back alley of a nameless city, his blood mixing with the garbage and rat droppings. She watched him die and felt her heart tearing with sorrow.

No, Daddy. No.

Suddenly they were running, the scenery flashing by in a blur as Heather's mother attempted to flee from the Black Spiral Dancers. She was fast, but not fast enough to outrun two Wyrm-spawned werewolves under the blood frenzy. Lydia wanted to save her daughter, but could not outrun the death that pursued her. Therefore, knowing what she must do and having no other choice, she tossed her infant daughter in a garbage bin and continued down the alley, drawing the Dancers after her, sacrificing her life so Heather would live.

The memory faded, leaving Heather trembling and crying. Because of the giant stone heads, and the magic connected to them, she had learned who and what she was. But she had also witnessed the death of her parents. The people at the orphanage had lied to her; she had not been abandoned. Her parents had sacrificed their lives in order to protect her. She had been loved right up until the very moment they had been killed by the Wyrm-spawn.

"Suntock. Lydia." She now knew the names of her mother and father, and what they looked like. She even knew their clan. The other members of the clan would remember her parents and be able to tell her more about them. Maybe they had relatives: brothers, sisters, aunts and uncles. They might have left behind a family. Her family.

Heather's sadness suddenly turned into anger. Rage. The Black Spiral Dancers had murdered her parents and stolen her childhood. She wanted revenge against the Dancers, revenge against the Wyrm. Not just for her loss, but for the loss of those who had truly loved her.

"Suntock. Lydia." They were much more than just the names of her parents. The words were now a battle cry. Clenching her fists tightly, her fingernails sinking into the palms of her hands and drawing blood, Heather vowed silently to herself that she would one day have her revenge against the Black Spiral Dancers. She would also find the missing Fang and deny the Wyrm the opportunity of entering the Realm, or she would die trying.

24

One more night until the Shaman Moon. Just one night. Already Sam Nakai could smell the Wyrm's presence. It hung in the air like the pollution of the white man's factories. For the past two nights he had also listened to the insane howls of Black Spiral Dancers as they prowled the surrounding countryside like bloodthirsty jackals on the hunt. Not just the howls of one or two, but the cries of many. Maybe even dozens.

It was extremely rare to see or hear so many Spiral Dancers moving around out in the open, even at night. They usually traveled underground, through an intricate web of tunnel systems that virtually crisscrossed the globe. He wasn't sure if such tunnels existed in the vicinity of Monterey, Tennessee, but they probably did. They seemed to be just about everywhere.

Since their tribe was outnumbered ten to one by the other Garou, the Black Spiral Dancers had decided years ago that staying underground was by far the safest mode of travel. There they were safe, for few Garou not touched by the Wyrm would dare enter the tunnels of the Dancers. Within the twisting, turning passageways all manner of beast and beastie could be found, each and every one of them utterly evil.

The tunnels were an important part of the Black Spiral caerns. Known as Pits, they served as a home as well as a avenue of transportation to the Wyrm-spawn. Some Pits even had modern conveniences, such as televisions and refrigerators. The power needed to operate such devices was often provided by tapping into underground power company conduits. Unlike the Wendigo, who chose a life of simplicity close to Gaia, the Dancers had embraced all that modern technology had to offer.

Staring off into the darkness, Sam listened to the demented howls that filled the night. Like he and the others, the Black Spiral Dancers also waited for the coming of the crimson moon, preparing for the battle destined to take place on top of Monterey Mountain. Only one more night. Just one.

"What will be will be."

He turned at the sound of the voice. Joseph Swimmer stood beside him, his all-too-familiar pipe clutched tightly in his left hand. The old Indian looked worried and upset. Gone was the smile that so often graced his face. Gone too was the laughter in his eyes. In their place were lines of concern that wrinkled his brow, and a frown which tugged constantly at the corners of his mouth. He too knew that the children of Gaia were facing one of their toughest tests ever. What should have been a happy occasion, a reunion with ancestor spirits, might turn out to be a victory for the Wyrm. If they could not seal the Gauntlet against the Dark One's evil forces, then Banths and other vile creatures would enter the Realm by the hundreds. Maybe even by the thousands.

"I should have gone after her when I had the chance," Sam said, turning back to face the night. "You should not have stopped me."

"The spirit world is a very big place," Joseph replied. "You would not have found her. You know that as well as I do."

"I still should have gone," Sam said, a bitter anger creeping into his voice. "I am her mentor. She is my responsibility."

"The girl has been through the Rites of Passage. She is no longer a pup."

Sam shook his head and sighed. "No. She is not a pup, but she still has a lot to learn about being a Garou, a lot to learn about being the Guardian of the Fang. I should have taught her more."

"You did what you could in the time you had to do it." Joseph sat down on the ground beside Sam. Pulling a box of kitchen matches from his shirt pocket, he lit his pipe. He smoked in silence for a few moments, the scent of cherry-flavored tobacco filling the air. Turning to Sam, he asked, "Did your mentor teach you everything you needed to know before you were weaned?"

"No, he didn't," Sam answered, remembering how it was when he first became a Wendigo warrior. "But that was different."

The smile returned to the old man's face. He cocked an eyebrow and clicked his tongue. "Oh? How was it different? Tell me."

Sam cleared his throat. "I was stronger. A lot stronger; almost a man. I also knew more about the ways of the Garou. Knew the teachings…the ceremonies… and the laws. I knew how to fight, how to protect myself from danger. I was ready to be on my own."

"Maybe Heather is stronger and smarter than you think." Joseph said, puffing on his pipe. "Maybe she too is ready to be on her own. The spirits think she is; why else would she have received both a vision and a guide?"

"But she still needed to prove herself," Sam argued. "She should have been tested."

"From what I have been told, I would say that she has already been tested."

"What do you mean?" Sam asked, confused. He turned to look at his friend, waiting for an answer. What he got instead was another question.

"Did she not kill a Black Spiral Dancer when first you met?" asked Joseph.

"Yes, but she didn't do it by herself," Sam replied. "Heather used the Fang of the Wolf. It was the power of Nee Yah Kah Tah Kee that killed the Dancer, not the power of a little girl."

"Are they not one and the same?" Joseph asked, a twinkle of humor lighting his eyes. "She is the Guardian of the Fang. The power of the Sacred Sitting Wolf now belongs to her."

The old Indian leaned over and touched Sam's right hand, tracing his fingertips down the slash-mark tattoos that adorned the Garou's right index finger. "You have killed many times in your life, Sam Nakai. But how many times did you kill by yourself, and how many times did you kill with the Sacred Wolf's help? You were also the Guardian once; did you not use the Fang's power to help you in time of battle?"

Sam nodded, realizing that his argument had just been defeated with words of wisdom. "You're right. Heather is no longer a child. She is the Guardian of the

Fang. The same magic that helped me will help her. She does not need to prove herself to anyone. She has already passed all the tests she needs to pass."

"Not all," Joseph said, patting Sam on the hand. "There will always be tests to take, challenges laid in our path by the spirits and by the Wyrm. I think Heather Ocoee is being tested now, as we speak."

Sam thought about the old man's words. What he said made sense, but it did not quench the anger or guilt that tugged at his heart. Anger at himself for speaking harshly to Heather when he should have been congratulating her for passing her Rites of Passage; guilt for not being able to help her now, when she probably needed help the most. "You're right, but I still wish I had gone after her."

"Your presence is needed here, in more ways than you think." Joseph Swimmer nodded over his shoulder. "We cannot afford to lose you now."

Sam looked beyond the Indian. Michael Pathkiller sat with four Wendigo from his pack and the two members of the Get of Fenris who had come all the way from Germany to join in the fight. They sat around a small fire, talking in whispers. Every once in a while, one of them would cast a glance in Sam's direction. There was nothing friendly in any of the looks he was receiving; they were cold and hostile. Pathkiller had done his best to turn the other Garou against Sam, filling their heads with lies, blaming him and Heather for their not having the Fang when it was needed most.

Had the Get of Fenris warriors fallen for Pathkiller's lies? Sam sincerely hoped not, for if they had then there could be trouble. The Get was a fierce tribe whose warriors believed that total war was the only means to combat the Wyrm. They also believed that other tribes were incapable of combating the Wyrm effectively, often feeling honor-bound to take the place of their "weak sisters." The Get commonly took possession of caerns and other sacred sites that were under attack or close to collapse, regardless of who was still maintaining them.

By speaking of his dislike for Sam and Heather, Michael Pathkiller had let the Get of Fenris warriors know that the Wendigo had been divided and weakened. Perhaps they saw this as a perfect opportunity to snatch the Sitting Wolf caern away from those who had a rightful claim to it. Maybe that was the main reason why they had showed up to offer their help.

You're paranoid. The Get of Fenris warriors have come to fight the Wyrm and nothing more.

Maybe so. The Get of Fenris were always on the front lines in the War against the Wyrm, urging those around them to immediate battle. They believed that Gaia rewarded bravery, and so they were more than willing to sacrifice their lives. Of all the tribes, theirs had the highest mortality rate.

Either way, he would keep an eye on them. It was not wise to turn one's back against a potential enemy. More than one Garou had thrown away his life by foolishly doing so. He would also keep an eye on Michael Pathkiller. Sam knew that sooner or later he would have to fight the young Garou, but he would not do so now. If they fought now it would force the rest of the Garou to choose sides, opening up old wounds and hatreds which existed between the different tribes and packs. Their combined powers would be weakened and they would have little chance of winning against the Wyrm.

No. There would be plenty of time to fight Pathkiller later, after the Shaman Moon. Next time they fought, however, one of them was going to lose much more than just an eye.

25

Beyond the giant stone heads, Heather came to a large vertical crack in the wall which parted the face of the cliff like a pair of granite curtains. The crack was about three feet wide, stretching upward hundreds of feet to disappear into the darkness. On both sides of the crack, dozens of meaningless runes and symbols had been scratched into the rocks by a sharp instrument, or perhaps by the claws of a Garou who possessed the gift of Silver Touch.

Heather stopped and stared at the runes, wondering who had ventured deep enough into the Abyss to carve such symbols. And why? Some of the scratches appeared to be quite new, causing her to look nervously over her shoulder. She felt a slight tingle in her hand when she ran her fingertips lightly over a couple of the designs. The tingling was caused by a lingering trace of magic, left behind by the person who had carved the symbols.

Whose magic?

According to one of the many Garou legends, a story told in whispers around the comforting light of a flickering campfire, there was only one permanent resident of the Realm of the Abyss and that was Nightmaster, a Shadow Lord Philodox and member of the Society of Nidhogg.

It was said that Nightmaster and his pack, the Dark Watchers, had followed the Golden Path deep into the Abyss. Like many before them, they sought riches and objects of magical power. Drawn by their own greed, they ignored the warnings of the elders as they set off on their ill-fated journey. Traveling mainly in Crinos form, they climbed deeper into the ebony canyon than most Garou would ever dream of going.

But foolish are those who search for riches and wealth in the Realm of the Abyss. While wonderful treasure can indeed be found in the great void, it is never free and rarely worth the sacrifice one has to make in order to receive it.

As the Dark Watchers descended ever deeper into the great void, the darkness of the Abyss weighed heavily on their minds. They were plagued by hallucinations and visions of evil, frightening glimpses of the Wyrm that left each and every one of them weak and trembling. Nothing was as it seemed. Shadows became hideous beasts lying in wait; the beating of their own hearts became the echoed footsteps of an unseen enemy.

Along with the hallucinations came paranoia. Though they were packmates, the members of the Dark Watchers soon came to distrust one another. Each believed that the other was out to steal all the riches for himself. Some of them even resorted to eating the nuggets of gold they found lying along the path, fearful that the others would take it from them. One by one, the members of the pack lost their sanity and went mad, their thoughts and spirits taken over by the darkness.

And as his fellow pack members went mad, Nightmaster tried to increase his personal power by sacrificing them to the Abyss. Gouging out their eyes and carving magical symbols on their foreheads with a silver-bladed knife, he hurled his pack brothers and sisters from the ledge. All were sacrificed; none were spared. He even took the life of his real sister, Shadow Dancer. Took the life of his own flesh and blood. Ignoring her pleas for mercy, he cut her throat and threw her dying body from the ledge. In the end, it was only Nightmaster who still lived.

Alone, his mind drifting in and out of reality, Nightmaster continued deeper into the Abyss until he was beyond the reach of sight and sound. He traveled in a world of nothingness, a great grayness that was the void. Some say he journeyed to the very end of the known universe. Others speculate that he crawled into the lair of the Wyrm to look upon the face of the great beast. The truth will never be known.

Exhausted, Nightmaster threw himself down on the Golden Path to rest. While he was lying there he had a vision. The Abyss spoke to him, asking him for yet another sacrifice. But there were no more bodies to give; all of his packmates were already dead. It was then that the darkness entered him, taking over his soul, transforming him into a child of the Abyss.

According to the legend, Nightmaster was now the greatest Shadow Lord, the most powerful of the Society of Nidhogg. Forever cursed by the darkness, he spends his life roaming aimlessly through the Realm of the Abyss. Searching through the caves, he imprisons and destroys all those he comes across in an insane effort to gain forgotten powers. The few Shadow Lords who claim to have encountered him say he appears as a shell of a Crinos, animated by the darkness of the void. Intelligent and cruel, he is driven only by a lust for consumption.

Again Heather glanced behind her. She didn't know if the story of Nightmaster was true or not, but someone had carved the symbols that lined both sides of the crack. She had been told that the Silver Path was basically unexplored, yet someone else had been here before her. That someone could still be walking around somewhere, lurking in the shadows, perhaps looking for another Garou to sacrifice to the darkness of the Abyss.

Nightmaster gouged out the eyes of his packmates, and then used a silver-bladed knife to carve magical symbols in their foreheads.

A shudder of revulsion passed through Heather. The last thing she wanted was to have an insane Garou pluck out her eyes like two ripe grapes, and then play tick-tack-toe on her forehead with a knife. It had to hurt, just *had* to hurt real bad.

Stepping closer to the crack, she studied the carved symbols in an effort to decipher their meaning. Perhaps they offered valuable clues to secrets hidden deep within the Abyss. Treasures. Items of magic. If they did, then those secrets would remain hidden because she was unable to translate any of the runes.

Turning away from the runes, Heather noticed that the crack in the wall was much deeper than she had first thought. In fact, it wasn't even a crack at all. It was a narrow passageway that formed the entrance to a cave. As she stood there, gazing into the entrance, she heard something scurrying about in the darkness. The Fang which hung from her neck also began to glow more brightly than ever before. The light spilled from the top of the leather pouch, bathing her in its brilliance. As the magic of Nee Yah Kah Tah Kee came to life, a strange tingling sensation coursed through the girl's body.

"It's here," she whispered, excited. "The other Fang is here."

She slipped into the narrow entrance, cautiously moving forward. The Fang's glow pushed back the darkness, revealing that the rock walls on each side of her were also covered with runes. The scurrying grew even louder, sounding like the rustle of dried corn stalks being blown about by the wind.

Rats. Oh, God. Please don't let it be rats. Anything but rats.

She hated rats, despised them. Nor was she overly fond of mice. But rodents were the very least of her troubles, for the Fang's glow suddenly pierced the blackness to reveal a nightmare. Heather stopped and stared, unable to believe what she saw.

Directly in front of her stood a male Black Spiral Dancer in full Crinos form. Nearly ten feet tall, his matted fur emblazoned with glowing green tattoos, he was a twisted, grotesque creature that looked more like a mutated weasel than a wolf. As frightful as he was, the Spiral Dancer made no move to attack. Instead he just stood there, eyes open and staring, drool dripping from the corners of his mouth, his muscles quivering and jerking as though volts of electricity flowed through his veins.

"What the heck?"

Lowering her gaze, Heather noticed what looked like reddish tree roots protruding from the cave's floor. The roots wrapped around the Spiral Dancer's legs and body, like vines around a tree, holding him tight and keeping him a prisoner. The tip of each root was pointed, stabbing into his flesh like a hundred tiny needles.

A sick feeling came over her as she realized that the roots were actually translucent. Their reddish color came from the blood they sucked from the body of the Black Spiral Dancer. The roots were feeding upon him, sucking him dry, like bizarre vampires of the plant world.

Something scurried above her. Heather looked up, absolutely terrified by what she saw. The cave's ceiling seemed to be alive. Thousands of roots hung from the roof, twisting and coiling like a mass of poisonous snakes. Entangled in the roots were the skeletons and rotting corpses of countless other victims. As she watched, the roots began to straighten and lower themselves, reaching out for her.

She turned to run, but couldn't move. Glancing down, she saw that several roots encircled her legs like the tentacles of some unseen beast. Dozens more shot out of the ground to grab her. She was trapped, imprisoned in a cave that was alive and hungry.

Get off of me!

The Rage came over Heather, flowing through her body like molten lava, pushing aside all other thoughts. She had no time to remove her clothes; her transformation into werewolf shredded her garments and snapped the strap of her traveling bag. She didn't care. Clothes could be replaced, but her life could not.

Roaring in anger, her razor-sharp claws sliced through the roots that encircled her body. But for every root she cut, two more shot out of the ground to take its place. More roots fell from the ceiling. They wrapped around her chest and throat, pinned her arms to her side.

Heather howled in pain as one of the roots climbed her leg and sank its pointed tip deep into her inner thigh. Piercing her flesh, the root began to twitch and shake as though it were in the throes of sexual ecstasy. Another tip buried itself in her left shoulder; a third climbed her right leg and penetrated her like a rapist. Her howl became a scream.

A dozen root tips pierced her flesh like the hypodermics of a mad scientist. She felt a numbness seep into her body as the twitching roots began to suck her blood, stealing away her life force. Heather struggled and tried to free herself, but the roots held her tight in their deadly embrace.

No. No. No. Not like this. Not this way.

Dizziness seeped into her body through every pore. Her vision blurred. Heather could no longer feel her legs, and could barely move her fingers. She knew that she was dying, yet there was nothing she could do about it. Nothing at all. She was like a fish on the end of a hook, struggling but to no avail. And like the lowly fish, she too was to end up as dinner. Food for the roots.

As unconsciousness descended upon her, she spotted a bluish glow at the other end of the cave. The glow came from the body of the Black Spiral Dancer, or rather it came from the object he wore. Heather blinked and looked again, unable to believe what she saw. But her eyes had not been mistaken. Around the Dancer's neck hung a simple leather cord. Attached to the cord was the missing Fang.

I've found it. It's here. I . . . .

She looked at the other Fang. It was so close, yet impossibly far. She couldn't move, could no longer struggle or fight back. She had failed. All was lost. She would die. Sam Nakai would die. The Wyrm had won.

Her last bit of strength being sucked from her, Heather Ocoee closed her eyes and allowed the darkness to swallow her. As her eyes closed, a single tear of sadness slid slowly down her cheek.

26

The hollow beat of a drum echoed across the mountains like a giant heartbeat, calling the Garou and Kinfolk to war. The drum sat in a clearing on top of Monterey Mountain, not far from where the statue of Nee Yah Kah Tah Kee had once stood. Several Cherokee elders and a young Kiowa man sat around the drum, pounding out the rhythm. Their voices filled the night with songs of courage and battle, songs to give hope to a hopeless situation and stir the blood of warriors to anger.

Around the singers danced two dozen Wendigo warriors in full Crinos form. Dressed in breechcloths of quilled and painted buckskin, and wearing their finest beadwork and feathers, faces adorned with war paint of brilliant hues, the werewolves danced the war dances of their individual military societies, each trying to outdo the other. They stomped the earth with each drumbeat, their taloned feet digging deep furrows into the ground. Carrying weapons of stone and bone, and instruments of magic, they rolled their mighty shoulders in time with the music, charging the sacred drum whenever an honoring beat sounded.

A dozen or so Native American Kinfolk also took part in the dancing, though they made sure to stay out of the way of their frenzied Garou counterparts. Most of the Indians were military veterans, many having seen combat in Vietnam or the Gulf War. A few of them actually wore their old uniforms, though most were content wearing the regalia of a traditional dancer.

Of those Indians who had dressed up for the dancing, most wore breechcloths, ribbon shirts, hairpieces made from dyed porcupine hair and deer tails, and feather bustles called "crows." Made from eagle, hawk, and even owl feathers, with trailers of red trade cloth, the feather bustles fastened to a belt so that they hung in the center of the dancer's lower back. The crows symbolized a battlefield after a conflict was over, the feathers representing the feathers dropped by birds fighting over the dead bodies.

The bustles made from eagle feathers were considered the most powerful, for the eagle was the bird most associated with bravery and war. The eagle also flew higher than all other birds, high enough to visit the home of the Great Spirit. Those who wore eagle feathers believed they wore something touched by the Creator…something touched by God. When going to war against the darkness of the Wyrm, such medicine was highly valued.

Earlier in the day, the warriors had spent their time in meditation and prayer, strengthening their personal medicine for the upcoming battle. Under the careful guidance of Joseph Swimmer, a sweatlodge had been erected on the eastern side of the mountain top. Since purification was an important part of the preparation for battle, all of the Wendigo and Native American Kinfolk, as well as several Garou from other tribes, had taken advantage of the situation to go through a sweat.

Joseph had also worked his medicine to lay down a magical boundary around the mountain. Though it had no effect on those of medicine, or even on the Wyrm-spawned, the barrier was like an invisible fence that kept all other humans away, closing their eyes and ears to the things that were happening on Monterey Mountain. The local residents heard not the drumming, or the fevered howls of the war dancers. Nor did they see the bonfire which burned brightly in the night. To them life went on as normal.

Normal? Things were definitely not normal, not unless you considered a werewolf and Indian dance session to be an everyday occurrence.

At the edge of the dance area an upright wooden pole had been stuck in the ground. As each warrior—both Garou and human—passed the pole, he struck it with his dance stick or war club, counting coup on the pole as he intended soon to do on his enemy. The sound of the war pole being struck blended in harmony with the beating of the drum. Boom…boom…boom…whack. Boom… boom…boom…whack.

The warriors hadn't far to look to find the real enemy, however, for in the valley below tiny campfires lit the night like the twinkling of a dozen stars. And from the darkness rose the sound of unholy music and the strange, haunting howls of the Black Spiral Dancers. Like the Wendigo and the Native American Kinfolk, the Spiral Dancers also danced war dances and prepared themselves for battle.

Sam Nakai stood at the edge of the mountain top, looking out over the valley below, listening to the frightful howls of his enemy. And though he too was in full Crinos form, he had no desire to join in the dancing taking place on Monterey Mountain. He stood alone, thinking about the battle to come, using a piece of paint rock to slowly apply the final color of his military society to face and fur. He had already colored his chest and legs yellow, his face black, and needed now only to draw the zig-zag lines that represented lightning. Red for lightning, yellow for the moon, and black for the death of those he had killed in battle. Those were the colors of the Sash Wearer Society.

Gripping the paint rock tightly between thumb and forefinger, he slowly drew a jagged line down his legs from thigh to ankle, and then down his left arm from shoulder to wrist. Two more lines were carefully drawn from forehead to chin, passing directly over his eyelids. Switching hands, he drew the final line down his right arm.

Slipping what was left of the paint rock into a leather pouch that contained his other war paints, Sam removed a small mirror from his backpack and studied his reflection. Almost a year had passed since the last time he'd painted himself for battle. He had been in many fights since then, but they had all been spur of the moment situations he had fought alone. This was different. This time he was going to war with other members of his tribe. And this time he was fully prepared to die.

Satisfied that his colors had been applied exactly as they should be, he replaced the mirror and pulled a roll of blue fabric from his bag. The fabric, which matched his dyed leather breechcloth, was the sash worn by the members of the Blue Sash Society of the Wendigo tribe; a cloth of honor that measured fifteen feet long by four inches wide. A narrow slit had been cut into one end of the material. Slipping his head through the opening, Sam wrapped the sash several times around his waist and then tucked the end into his leather belt.

Only the bravest Wendigo were ever asked to join the Blue Sash Society, only those who had proven themselves in combat. During a battle, members of the society would often unwrap the sash from around their waist and pin the end of it to the ground with a spear or knife. Once pinned, they had to stand and fight to the death, or until another member of the tribe rushed into battle to unpin them. They were never allowed to unpin themselves; to do so would be a terrible dishonor.

He sighed, a great sadness tugging at his heart as he remembered his brothers killed in combat. Only a few Blue Sash Wearers were left; most had died on the battlefield. They had gladly sacrificed their lives, their courage spurring other Wendigo warriors to fight even harder. Sam had also pinned himself to the ground on several occasions, but each time one of his fellow tribesmen had unstuck him so that he might live. Some would say he was one of the lucky ones, but he didn't feel so lucky. Sometimes it was more honorable to die than to go on living. Maybe he would be given that honor tonight.

Smoothing the sash around his waist, he reached again into his backpack and removed a large knife. The knife was a little over fourteen inches in length, its handle carved from the lower jawbone of a grizzly bear. The eleven tiny notches along the length of the handle stood for those who had been fatally bitten by the bear. Slipping the knife through his heavy leather belt, he adjusted it so he wouldn't accidently stab himself if he turned too quickly.

Sam removed the last item from his backpack: a small, unadorned leather pouch attached to a braided cord. The pouch contained gall medicine, which was used as an antidote to corpse powder. Made from the dust of dead and diseased bodies, corpse powder was often carried by Black Spiral Dancers—along with the wooden tubes used to blow the powder into the face of their enemies. The poisonous powder caused a painful sickness in only a few hours, death in a matter of days.

Slipping the braided cord over his head, Sam tucked the leather pouch containing the gall medicine under the end of his blue sash. Satisfied that everything was in place, he turned his attention to the Wendigo dancers and the night sky beyond them.

He had just turned back around when the singers suddenly stopped their song, the drum falling eerily silent. Momentarily caught off guard, the werewolf dancers were frozen like grotesque statues in the middle of their war dance. And then, as if an unseen signal passed between them, they all straightened to their full heights and turned to face the eastern sky. The time for dancing was past. The Shaman Moon had arrived.

Sam Nakai felt his chest tighten as he watched the full moon slowly rise above the mountains to the east. As the moon climbed higher into the night sky, it gradually changed color from yellow to orange, and finally to red. A deep crimson. The color of blood.

As the moon changed color the air on top of Monterey Mountain began to crackle and pop, as though it was suddenly filled with static electricity. The wind picked up and grew cold, snatching up leaves and twigs in its icy grasp as it swirled among the warriors. The wind brought with it the scent of the mountains—the fragrance of pine and black earth—as well as the odor of burning ozone. Sam took a deep breath, his nose telling him much more about what was going on than his eyes did. For he didn't need his eyes to know that the rift was starting to open. He could smell the fragrance of the Umbra long before he saw the patch of air that shimmered like steam over a cooking fire.

"It's happening!" One of the Wendigo cried in wolf speak. "The Gauntlet is opening!"

A tingle danced down Sam's spine; the skin at his temples pulled tight. What was happening was quite magical, something that wouldn't happen again for another hundred years. Despite the danger, it was a privilege to be standing where he was, seeing the things he was about to see. If he survived the battle that was sure to come, then he truly would be blessed.

The patch of shimmering air grew wider, thicker. It caught the crimson glow of the moonlight and twinkled like rubies in the night. Overcome with emotion, several of the Garou threw their heads back and howled. Sam wanted to howl too, but he restrained himself. He could not afford to allow himself to be caught up in the moment when so many things were at stake this night. A clear head was what was needed most.

Instead of howling, he watched as the shimmering patch of air slowly formed an opening to the spirit world. A doorway to the Umbra was opening, the Gauntlet that separated the two realms growing thinner and thinner until it was no more. Something moved in the opening, a willowy patch of mist that drifted through the Gauntlet like a tiny cloud of ground fog.

The patch of gray mist slipped through the Gauntlet into the Realm, slowly changing shape and growing solid as it did. Sam watched in awe as the mist, which was really the spirit of an ancestor, took on the appearance of the person it had once been in life. Suddenly a young Indian man stood before them, appearing exactly as he had during his lifetime. But this young man was no longer alive; he was but a spirit that had slipped through the Gauntlet to visit for a while with his family and friends. The flesh and blood that he wore were only temporary, a gift from the magic of the Shaman Moon.

Another patch of mist slipped through the Gauntlet. And another. And yet another. A woman. A second man. A child. Spirits coming to visit the land of the living. With each new arrival, the Garou threw back their heads and howled in delight. But their happiness did not last, for behind the ancestors came an army of Banth spirits and other vile creatures of the Wyrm. And like the Indian ancestors, they too became very real once they stepped through the Gauntlet into the Realm.

Everything instantly turned to chaos. The Garou no longer howled songs of happiness. Instead they screamed their war cries as they rushed forward to do battle with the Wyrm-spawn from the Umbra. Sam had just stepped forward to challenge one of the many Banths that were pouring through the Gauntlet when he heard the insane howl of a Black Spiral Dancer. He turned as several Dancers charged into their midst, attacking them from behind.

Sam cried a warning, but he was not heard. He watched in horror as one of the Black Spiral Dancers charged the singers at the drum, savagely attacking the elderly Cherokees who tried to protect the sacred instrument. Arms, legs, and chunks of bloody flesh flew through the air as the old men were literally ripped to pieces by the Wyrm's evil servant.

He was already racing toward the Wyrm-spawn werewolf when the Black Spiral Dancer, finished with his slaughter of the singers, turned in search of new prey. He hadn't far to look to find it. Joseph Swimmer stood about twenty feet away from the drum, frozen in place by the obscene savagery of what he had just witnessed.

"Nooo!" Sam Nakai screamed, urging his body to even greater speed. A Banth stepped in his path, sought to challenge him, but he separated the miserable creature's head from its shoulders with one mighty swipe of his clawed hand.

But the Banth had thrown him off stride, caused him to slow down. It wasn't much of a change in his speed, but it was enough to keep him from reaching Joseph in time to help him. He could only watch, his heart tight with dread, as the Black Spiral Dancer charged the elderly medicine man.

Use your magic, old man! Use your magic!

As if awakening from a trance, Joseph Swimmer looked up and saw the Spiral Dancer racing at him. His eyes suddenly wide with fright, he raised his right hand and pointed a small wooden staff at the werewolf. Wrapped in leather and adorned with feathers and beadwork, the staff was Joseph's most powerful medicine object, for it could cause confusion and chaos to cloud the mind of even the most furious fighter.

Unfortunately the mind of a Black Spiral Dancer is already clouded with confusion and chaos, for they have looked upon the Wyrm and have been rendered insane by what they have seen. Therefore, Joseph's magical staff had little, if any, effect on the werewolf that raced toward him.

Realizing he was about to die, and there was absolutely nothing he could do about it, Joseph Swimmer lowered his right arm and smiled at his enemy. The smile remained upon his face as the Black Spiral Dancer roared and slashed at him, black claws whistling through the air. The first slash caught the old Indian high on the shoulder and spun him around like a top. The second slashing attack tore through the back of Joseph's neck and severed his spine.

"Nooo....!" Sam screamed again, watching in horror as the claws of the Black Spiral Dancer took the life of his good friend. His scream became a howl as the Rage came over him.

Rage. Blessed Rage. Sam welcomed the sensation as it embraced his mind and soul in its fiery grip, pushing back all thoughts except one: to kill. That's all that mattered now. All that ever mattered. He would avenge the death of his friend with the Black Spiral Dancer's blood.

Behold Wyrm-spawn. I am Sam Nakai, proud warrior of the Wendigo. Wearer of the Blue Sash. Turn and face me, evil one, for I am your death.

With a roar of absolute rage, he launched himself through the air. The Black Spiral Dancer heard the roar and turned, but he didn't turn quickly enough. Sam crashed into the Wyrm-spawn's chest and took him to the ground. For Sam Nakai, the battle on top of Monterey Mountain had officially begun.

27

Where am I?

The question floated through Heather's mind like an echoed whisper, but she could not find an answer for it. No matter how hard she tried. She truly did not know where she was, or how she had gotten there. All she knew was that it was cold. Damn cold.

She stood ankle deep in new fallen snow, naked, silently watching as a parade of people staggered slowly past her. Hundreds of people. Maybe even thousands. Most of them were dark-skinned, Indians, but she did not know what tribe they belonged to. Like helpless cows, the Indians were being forcibly herded down a narrow dirt road by uniformed white men on horseback.

This can't be real. It just can't be. It's too terrible. I must be dreaming.

But it was real. Very real. She could feel the bitter cold seeping deep into her bones, causing her body to shiver uncontrollably. She could also feel the softness of the snowflakes as they touched her bare skin and melted. The haunting cries of despair, the stench of death. It was very real. All of it.

Turning, she saw that the parade of misery and suffering stretched for miles down the narrow, dirt road. Driven by soldiers armed with rifles and bayonets, shouted at and prodded like cattle, the Indians struggled on in the freezing cold. Only a few of them had blankets or warm clothing, protection from the harsh elements. Most wore only thin shirts and pants, or dresses of lightweight cotton. Some didn't even have shoes or moccasins to protect their feet.

As Heather stood there, apparently unnoticed, dozens of oxen-drawn carts rumbled past filled with the sick and dying. Old men and women, even children, rode in the back of the open carts, a thin layer of snow covering them like a frigid blanket. With each creak of the wagon, with each turn of the wheel, they moaned in pain and begged for mercy from the soldiers. Their pleas fell upon deaf ears, however, for the soldiers seemed unmoved by the tears and suffering of those around them. They sat upon their horses, dressed warmly in heavy winter coats, their gazes firmly fixed on an imaginary point on the western horizon.

Not all of the sick were able to ride; there just weren't enough wagons for everyone. Many were forced to trudge wearily along, their spirits and hearts as heavy as their footsteps, teardrops frozen into shiny ice crystals upon their frostbitten cheeks. Often too weak to take another step, they staggered and fell by the side of the road to die.

Her heart tight with sorrow, Heather reached out to help one little boy who had fallen in the snow at her feet. But as she attempted to touch him, her fingers passed through his body as though she was made of air and nothing else.

Oh, God. They're real, but I'm not. I'm a ghost. It was true. Heather Ocoee was no longer a person of the flesh. She was but a spirit, an invisible witness to another place and time.

"You cannot help them," spoke a voice.

Heather turned, surprised to see a young Indian warrior standing in the snow beside her. He was the same man she had seen on her vision quest so many nights before. The young warrior was her spirit guide.

"Who are they?" she asked.

The young man turned and looked at her, a great sadness in his eyes. "They are people from a time long before yours, my little one. They are my people. Ani-ya Wiya. The Cherokee."

"But what have they done to deserve this?" Heather asked. "What have they done wrong? Why are the soldiers being so mean to them?"

He shook his head. "They have done nothing wrong, my child. Nothing at all."

"I don't understand," she said, confused.

"Those that truly love Gaia—my people, your people—are a threat to the servants of the Wyrm. It has always been that way; it will always be that way." He watched the passing Indians in silence for a moment, then turned back to face her. "It is too late for my people, but it is not too late for yours. Look inside yourself, Heather Ocoee. Remember who you are. Remember what you are. You must not give up, no matter what. Your people are depending on you. If you fail, then they too will one day have their trail of tears."

With those ominous words of warning, her spirit guide reached out and ran the fingers of his left hand lightly down her cheek. His touch was as soft as a feather, carrying with it a feeling of love and caring so profound it brought tears to Heather's eyes. And as her spirit guide touched her, he transformed back into a snowy owl and flew away.

Heather slowly opened her eyes. The vision was gone, but the nightmare remained. She was still entangled in the roots, a prisoner, her blood feeding a living cave deep within the Abyss. As weak as she already was, it was only a matter of time before she died. If only there was some way to escape.

Look inside yourself, little one. Remember who you are. Remember what you are.

The words of Heather's spirit guide came back to her, but she didn't know what they meant. Who was she? What was she? She was a Garou, a member of the Wendigo tribe, strong and fierce…

Had she the strength, Heather would have laughed. She was a big, bad Garou—Guardian of the Fang of the Wolf—but she was still in werewolf form and still hopelessly entangled in the blood-sucking roots. Teeth and claws were of little help. Her spirit guide must have meant something else. But what? Other than being a werewolf, she was just a homid. A girl of only twelve.

That's it!

Suddenly, Heather knew what her spirit guide had been trying to tell her. She also knew how to escape. Even though she was a furious werewolf on the outside, she was still a girl on the inside. Deep down inside, where it counted the most.

Pushing the pain and dizziness out of her mind, she summoned up the very last of her strength and transformed from werewolf to human. As her body shrank to less than half its size, the pointed root tips pulled free from her flesh with wet, sucking sounds. Before the roots could readjust to the sudden size difference, Heather slipped free of their deadly grasp.

"Yes!"

Sprinting across the cave to the lifeless Black Spiral Dancer, she hurried to remove the missing Fang from around his neck. Roots sprang from the floor to encircle her legs. Before they could grab her, she slipped the leather cord holding the second Fang over her head and transformed into a wolf. With a howl, Heather leaped clear of the murderous roots and ran out of the cave.

She raced up the trail at full speed, stopping to change back into human form when she reached the giant head carvings. There was no need to go any farther, no need to climb all the way out of the Abyss. She had what she'd come for.Heather wondered if Utluhtu waited for her to return from the Abyss, but only for a moment. She no longer needed the old woman or her ebony bridge to get to where she was going.

Grabbing the Fang of the Wolf in her right hand, she used the magic of Nee Yah Kah Tah Kee to step sideways back into the Realm. As always, the Fang brought her back to the top of Monterey Mountain. But this time as she emerged back into the Realm, Heather found herself standing in the middle of a raging battle.

28

Sam Nakai tackled the Black Spiral Dancer at chest level and took him to the ground. Over and over they rolled, claws slashing, teeth biting, each trying to break through his opponent's defense to render a killing blow. Blood flowed and fur flew in fuzzy chunks, as Sam grappled with the evil werewolf.

Kill. Kill. Kill.

Only one thought filled Sam's mind. One desire. The Black Spiral Dancer was younger, stronger, but Sam was locked in the throes of Rage, his blood lust boiling. The Dancer had just slain Joseph Swimmer, killing one of the finest men Sam had ever known. He could smell the old Indian's blood on the Wyrm-spawn's claws and that made him even angrier.

Sam grabbed his enemy around the neck with the intention of ripping his throat out, but the Dancer broke the hold and countered with a solid punch to the head. The blow sent lightning bolts of pain shooting through Sam's body and caused him momentarily to see stars. A second punch knocked him to his knees.

Suddenly, the tide of battle had turned. Sensing his opponent was hurt, the Black Spiral Dancer redoubled his efforts to win the fight. Jumping to his feet, he lashed out with a well-placed kick that broke several of Sam's ribs. A second kick followed. And a third.

The breath knocked out of him, Sam could do little more than roll across the ground in an attempt to get clear of the Dancer's deadly kicks. He knew he was hurt, but he didn't know how badly and there wasn't time to find out. He had to get back on his feet. And fast.

Another roll to keep clear of a kick and then Sam suddenly reversed his direction, rolling straight at the Dancer. He caught his enemy off guard, crashing into his knees and knocking his legs out from under him. As the Black Spiral Dancer fell over top of him, Sam lashed upward, sinking the claws of his right hand deep into his opponent's belly. Blood spurted black in the moonlight as he ripped open the Dancer's stomach, spilling his guts upon the ground like a nest of steaming snakes.

Getting quickly to his feet, Sam watched with grim satisfaction as the Black Spiral Dancer made a feeble attempt to stand back up, only to sink slowly to his knees. Quivering in dying agony, the Wyrm-spawn tried to scoop his intestines off the ground and stuff them back into his body. He had actually gotten a handful or two back inside, when he toppled over and died with a gasping sigh.

"That's for my friend, Joseph Swimmer, you rotten son of a bitch."

Looking up from the lifeless body of the Black Spiral Dancer, Sam was shocked to see Heather Ocoee step through the rift into the Realm. The girl stood there in human form, wearing only the tattered remains of an oversized work shirt—a shirt Joseph had given her to wear after her vision quest. In each hand Heather held a pointed sliver of gray stone. The Fangs of the Wolf.

She's found it! My God, I don't believe it. She actually found the other Fang! She's not too late. The Gauntlet can be sealed against the Wyrm. Sam started toward Heather, but stopped when he heard someone yell in wolf tongue.

"You bitch!" Michael Pathkiller cried, running across the mountain top toward the girl. "I am the true Guardian. The Fangs belong to me!"

"No!" Sam yelled. He jumped over the body of the Black Spiral Dancer and raced after Pathkiller, tackling him from behind before he could reach Heather.

Pathkiller tripped and rolled, leaping quickly to his feet to face his unseen attacker. An evil grin touched the corners of his mouth when he saw who it was that had attacked him.

"You dare to challenge me, old man?" Pathkiller roared. "You obviously didn't learn your lesson when I took your eye. Think before you try me again; this time I may not be so merciful."

Sam stared at Michael Pathkiller in silence for a moment, then slowly unwrapped the blue sash from around his waist. Drawing the bear-jaw knife from his belt, he pinned the end of the sash to the ground. Words were not necessary, for Sam's action told the younger werewolf that, no matter what, he would not back up or surrender. This time it would be a fight to the death.

Sam straightened back up and smiled. "Come and get some, if you dare."

Michael Pathkiller roared his battle cry and charged. Sam stood his ground, didn't move. His legs slightly bent at the knees, he leaned his body forward and braced himself to absorb the impact of the attack. Even so, Pathkiller hit him with enough force to knock him over and steal his breath away.

Sam had forgotten about his broken ribs, but Pathkiller's attack sent a painful reminder shooting through the left side of his chest. He tasted blood and wondered if his lung had been punctured. If so, then he had to end this fight quickly, before he ran out of breath.

Getting back to his feet, Sam turned in time to duck a vicious swipe aimed at his head. Pathkiller still hit him, but it was a glancing blow that left only a few scratches across the top of his head. Sam countered the blow with a front kick to the groin that sent the younger werewolf sprawling.

"You weren't planning on using those for anything, were you?" Sam taunted, laughing as Pathkiller clutched his bruised testicles in pain. "Is that the best you can do? Pity. I was hoping to fight a warrior, but you are only a cliath."

His words were answered with a howl of rage as Michael Pathkiller got back to his feet and threw himself at Sam. They collided again and crashed to the ground, clawing, biting, each trying to end the life of the other. Pathkiller was a strong, aggressive fighter, but Sam Nakai was a master of unarmed combat. Relying on his intelligence and fighting experience, skills honed and perfected during his many years as the Guardian of the Fang, he slowly wore the younger werewolf down, easily blocking his blows, countering with kicks and strikes that drew blood and shattered bone.

"Is that all you've got?" Sam shouted, blocking a finger jab aimed for his one good eye. He countered with two short punches to the stomach that doubled Pathkiller over. "Is that the best you can do?" He yelled, driving his knee into the other werewolf's face, squashing his nose like a ripe plum.

Pathkiller went down hard, landing heavily on his back, his face a bloody mess of broken cartilage and shattered teeth. He stared up at Sam, his eyes glazed and unfocused with pain. He made no attempt to stand back up, nor did he try to crawl away to safety.

Sam stepped forward and grabbed his opponent around the throat, the claws of his right hand pressing into his flesh. He was about to send Pathkiller's spirit on a one-way trip into the Umbra, when he glanced up and saw an old woman appear in the rift behind Heather Ocoee.

Entering the Realm, the old woman transformed into an evil-looking, dwarfish creature. Before he could yell a warning, the creature stepped forward and stabbed a long, pointed index finger into Heather's back. The girl screamed in pain and staggered forward, falling to her knees and dropping the Fangs.

"No!" Sam cried, releasing his hold on Pathkiller's throat. He tried to reach Heather's side, but he tripped over his own sash and tumbled to the ground. Before he could get to his feet again, Pathkiller leaped on his back, attacking him with a rain of deadly blows.

"How do you like that, old man? And that? Who's the cliath now. Tell me...I dare you." The younger werewolf lashed out again and again, driving Sam to the ground and sending him to the brink of eternal darkness.

Sam Nakai was nearly dead when the blows finally stopped and the weight lifted off his back. He tried to rise, but could not. He could only roll over as the blackness of unconsciousness descended over him like a warm blanket. But even the darkness was not a blessing, for the last thing he saw was Michael Pathkiller racing toward Heather.

Frozen by the sight of Sam and Pathkiller fighting, Heather didn't realize someone was behind her until too late. She caught a glimpse of Utluhtu, right before the old woman transformed into the dwarfish creature she had seen in the reflection of the pool. And before she could even think of defending herself, the creature drove a spearlike finger deep into her back.

Fiery pain exploded through Heather's body, ripping a scream from her throat. She staggered forward and fell to her knees, dropping the Fangs.

Oh God. Oh God. What was that? What did she do to me? I think I've been stabbed. Dear God, it hurts. Hurts really bad....

The pain raced up the girl's spine to her brain, bringing tears to her eyes and causing her muscles to spasm. Heather tried to get to her feet, but she didn't have the strength. It felt like something from inside her had been snatched out through her back. Something very important. She was suddenly so weak that even raising her head was an effort.

Her body shaking with the strain, her vision blurring, Heather lifted her head and saw Michael Pathkiller running toward her at full speed. She also saw the little dwarf that was Utluhtu step past her and pick up the two Fangs of the Wolf.

His face a bloody mask of livid rage, his war cry a promise of a painful death, Pathkiller raced across the top of Monterey Mountain. He ran straight at Heather, but changed directions when he saw Utluhtu pick up the Fangs. Like a furry locomotive, the angry Garou crashed into the dwarf, attacking with teeth and claws, causing her to drop the magical stones.

Michael Pathkiller might have expected to defeat Utluhtu easily, but despite her small size the dwarf was incredibly strong. Her skin was also as hard as stone, much too hard for the claws and teeth of a werewolf to penetrate.

Enraged by the werewolf's attack, Utluhtu climbed Pathkiller's back like a monkey up a ladder, jabbing at his head and face with her deadly, pointed finger. The Garou roared and tried to shake Utluhtu lose, but the dwarf held on.

Heather watched the fight for a moment, but then her attention was drawn to the rift. Something huge was trying to squeeze through the Gauntlet. Something monstrous. It was a shadow blacker than darkness itself, a shapeless entity gazing out upon the Realm with eyes that glowed like fiery brimstone. A possible incarnation of the Wyrm itself, it was a demon from the depths of the Umbra that had come to do battle with those who fought for Gaia.

Close the rift. Close it. Hurry. Don't let that thing into this world. Heather tried to get to her feet, but she was still too weak even to stand up.

Move. Move. Move. I can't. Yes you can. Do it. Do it now.

Unable to walk, she slowly began to crawl across the ground to where the two Fangs lay. But even the action of crawling drained what little strength she had left, causing her head to swim with dizziness.

Don't stop. Don't stop. You can do it. Slide your hand. Now your legs. Move your butt, missy. Move.

She resisted the urge to look back over her shoulder, terrified of what she might see. Instead she focused her attention on the Fangs before her. Both stones glowed bright blue from the demon's presence.

A little more. Just a little more. There, got it.

Falling forward, Heather grabbed a Fang in each hand and pulled them tight against her body. Cradling the stones against her chest, she pushed herself back up into a kneeling position. Her body trembled from the strain, and tiny beads of sweat broke out on her forehead. For a second, she thought she was going to black out. But she didn't. Turning, she saw that the demon had not yet entered the Realm. There was still time to seal the rift.

"Party's over." Holding a Fang tightly in each hand, she tried to call upon the magic of Nee Yah Kah Tah Kee to close the Gauntlet. But the Wyrm's shadowy demon fought back, keeping the passageway open.

She could feel the energy of the creature as its foul, loathsome spirit reached out, searching to find the person who dared oppose it. The glowing red eyes slowly turned in Heather's direction as the thing focused its attention on her. As its gaze locked on her, the girl's mind was suddenly filled with a voice so evil it caused her to break out in a cold sweat.

Do not oppose me, wolf child. You cannot win against the Wyrm.

Heather tried to ignore the voice, concentrating instead on the magical stones she held. She whispered a prayer for strength and courage as she squeezed the Fangs even tighter.

You are weak, wolf child. Dying. You cannot resist my powers much longer. Why fight? It is no use. Join me instead. Bow down before me and I will reward you with gifts beyond your wildest dreams. Power. Money. Fame. They can all be yours.

"Liar!" Heather whispered, shaking her head to rid herself of the voice.

Am I? Then why don't you ask your mother and father. They are here, with me, in the darkness. Come, join them. They are waiting for you....

An image formed in Heather's mind, a mental picture of her mother and father. It was the same image she had seen while looking upon the carvings of the giant heads in the Abyss. Once again, she saw her mother and father standing side by side, gazing down upon her. As before, she was enveloped with a feeling of love, only this time she also heard their voices.

Heather, this is your mother. Please come with us. We love you, darling. Please join us. Don't fight, sweetheart. Put down the Fangs. We could be a family again. Just the three of us.

A shudder of anguish passed through Heather's body. She closed her eyes tight. "You are not my mother. This is nothing but a trick."

Oh, darling. How can you be so cruel? We love you and want to be with you. Please, Heather, put down the Fangs. Come with us...

Tears rolled freely down Heather's cheeks. She felt her willpower weakening, felt the Fangs begin to slip through her fingers.

That's right, darling. Join us. Be with us forever. In the darkness...

"No!" Heather screamed, opening her eyes. Grasping the Fangs tightly enough to make both her hands throb, she stared in defiance at the shapeless entity before her. "You are not my mother. Nor is my father with you. He was Garou. A warrior of the Wendigo. He would never join the Wyrm. Never!"

Realizing that Heather could not be swayed with words and false promises, the Wyrm's shapeless servant decided to change its tactics and go with a more direct approach.

It attacked.

Twin bolts of fire shot from the demon's eyes, searing flames that turned the darkness of night into day. Striking the ground with a sizzling crackle, the flames raced across the mountain top at Heather. Death was only inches away from the girl when Pathkiller and Utluhtu, still fighting over ownership of the Fangs, collided against her and knocked her out of the way.

The two bolts of fire struck Michael Pathkiller and Utluhtu dead on, encasing their bodies in flames. They screamed in agony as the demon's fire clung to them like a second skin, turning hair into ash and charring their flesh to the bone.

SHAMAN MOON

Heather watched in horror as Pathkiller and Utluhtu danced a fiery jig of death on top of Monterey Mountain, pieces of burning flesh floating away from their bodies like fiery snowflakes. Waving their arms and rolling across the ground, they tried desperately to put out the flames. But the fire was of evil magic and would not go out, no matter what they did. The two of them were little more than blackened skeletons when they finally collapsed and died, and even then their bodies continued to burn.

Looking away from the burning bodies, Heather saw the shadowy demon's eyes begin to shimmer and grow brighter. The next bolt of fire would be for her, and there was nothing she could do to stop it. Nothing at all. She was about to resign herself to a painful death, when a voice again entered her head. This time, however, the voice was not a trick of the Wyrm. It was her spirit guide who spoke to her.

Remember who you are, little one. Remember what you are. You are Garou.

The voice entered Heather's mind, pushing away all thoughts of evil.

You are Garou. You are the Guardian. Trust your instincts. Trust your guides. Never give up. There are no quitters among the Wendigo.

The voice of her spirit guide gave her courage and strength, causing anger to flow white hot through her veins. She threw back her head and cried out, allowing the Rage to take her in its fiery embrace, giving her body once again to the transformation.

Heather's cry became a howl as her body changed from human into werewolf. Somehow finding the strength to get to her feet, she stood ready to do battle with the Wyrm's personal demon. But even in Crinos form, she would be no match against the shadowy demon and the bolts of hell fire it could produce.

Use the Fangs. Use all of their power.

No! she thought, opening her hands and looking at the tiny stones she still held. If she did what her spirit guide asked, then the magic of Nee Yah Kah Tah Kee would be lost forever.

Use it, little one, or all will be lost. Use it, or your people will also have their trail of tears.

The Wyrm's servant turned its attention away from the charred, smoking remains of Pathkiller and Utluhtu, seeking out the Guardian of the Fangs. The glowing red eyes found her.

"No!" Heather raised the Fangs of the Wolf high above her head, one stone in each hand. She knew what must be done to seal the rift against the Wyrm, seal it forever. Focusing her rage on the demon, she slammed the two Fangs together as hard as she could.

And the heavens moved.

The night sky seemed to rip apart as a brilliant flash of blue light exploded from the Fangs—a flash bright enough to leave its image permanently etched on the back of Heather's eyes. Lightning split the darkness; thunder boomed like artillery blasts. A wind sprang up, blowing from the north, carrying with it a chill blast of arctic air. The breath of the Wendigo.

Heather stood with legs spread, bracing herself as the wind screamed across the mountain top toppling trees and knocking Garou and Banths off their feet. The roar of the wind grew louder, stronger, became the howl of a wolf. A howl of anger. A cry of rage.

As the howl filled the night, Nee Yah Kah Tah Kee suddenly appeared. The Great Wolf had returned to the world of the living, summoned by those on the mountain top, called by the pleas of a little girl, brought forth by the Fangs.

Twenty, thirty, maybe forty feet tall, Nee Yah Kah Tah Kee once again stood as Guardian before the rift. With fur of shimmering fire, and eyes brighter than the sun, the Great Wolf faced the Wyrm's servant, challenging the evil one to enter the Realm—daring him to try. And when the demon refused to accept the challenge, when it backed down before the powers of the Great Wolf, Nee Yah Kah Tah Kee threw his head back and howled, his voice sealing the rift forever.

Heather saw the rift close and watched as Black Spiral Dancers and Banths— those that were still alive—fled into the night to escape the wrath of Nee Yah Kah Tah Kee. She turned and looked at the Great Wolf, watching as his image slowly faded out to nothing.

An eerie quiet descended over the mountain top as Nee Yah Kah Tah Kee disappeared, bringing with it a terrible sadness. Opening her hands, Heather saw that all she held was dust. The Fangs had been destroyed. The magic of The Great Wolf was gone from the Realm forever.

"No," she whispered. "Dear God. No." Heather had sealed the rift against the Wyrm, but in doing so she destroyed the magic she had sworn to protect. She had failed as the Guardian.

"No. No. No."

A great dizziness came over her. Gone. Gone. All of it gone. Her fault. All her fault. Sinking slowly to her knees, she allowed the blackness to roll over her, praying that the darkness would carry her far, far away.

Opening her eyes, Heather Ocoee stared up at the night sky. She was once again in human form. She was also dying. Utluhtu had stabbed the girl in the back, stealing a piece of her spirit and replacing it with weakness and pain. She was too weak to sit up or stand; even taking a breath was a struggle.

Turning her head to the left, she saw Sam Nakai kneeling beside her. The old man was in Homid form, bleeding from a dozen different wounds.

"Lie still," he told her. "I will heal you."

She shook her head. "You can't. I broke the Fangs of the Wolf."

He smiled. "There is more than one way to work medicine."

Sam placed his hands over her stomach and began to sing in Navajo. As he did, Heather felt a warmth flow into her body, pushing the weakness away. But as the warmth flowed into her, she noticed the color start to drain from her mentor's face.

"Wait," she whispered, alarmed. "Stop. What are you doing?"

"Shhh…lie still. I am healing you."

"But you're hurt. Please, call Joseph…"

Sadness crept into Sam's face. "Joseph Swimmer cannot help you. He has already crossed over into the spirit world."

Heather was stunned. "He's dead?"

Sam nodded. "Yes, he was killed. But he died a brave man. Many songs will be sung about him."

A great sorrow squeezed her heart. Heather had only known Joseph for a short time, but she had been touched by the old man's strength, wisdom and kindness. "It's my fault that he died. I messed up. If I had closed the rift quicker, he would still be alive."

"It is no one's fault," he replied. "Especially not yours. You closed the rift; the Wyrm has been beaten. Now be quiet so I can help you."

Heather tried to sit up, but he held her down. "But not this way," she argued. "Not this way. You're hurt too; it will kill you."

Sam clicked his tongue in annoyance. "You have forgotten one of the lessons I taught you."

"What lesson?"

"That we are only in this world for a short time; therefore, it is wrong to cry about what should have been. Instead you must plan what still can be. Every day is precious. Every second. Give thanks for each and every day that you are here. Waste not a moment. That way, when your time is up, you can leave this world with a clear conscience and a happy heart."

He looked down at her and smiled. "I have walked this earth for many years. I have had a very full life; my heart is filled with happiness. My time is over, little one. It is your time now."

"Please, don't," Heather pleaded. She wanted to stop him, but she was too weak even to move. "There has to be some other way."

He shook his head. "Utluhtu has stolen part of your spirit. If it is not replaced soon you will die. There is no other way."

Tears formed in Heather's eyes and ran down her cheeks. "Please, Sam. Don't do this. Please don't leave me. I need you."

Again he shook his head. "I was wrong. You are no longer a little girl. You are a Wendigo warrior, and a warrior needs no one—only his medicine and his spirit guides."

"I need you," she pleaded. "Please, I'm sorry for being mad at you. You're the only real father I've ever known…the only one in my life I've ever loved."

Sam looked at her for a moment in silence, then nodded. "And I am sorry that I spoke harshly to you, little one. You are like the daughter I never had. I love you too." He started to sing again, but Heather interrupted him.

"Wait. Wait. If you love me, then why are you doing this?"

"It is not your time, my child. You still have much work to do. The Fangs may be broken, but the spirit of Nee Yah Kah Tah Kee walks with you. You are still the Guardian." He smiled and touched her chest with his index finger. "But do not worry, a part of me will always be with you. In here."

Raising his voice in song again, he called upon the spirits to work their magic. Heather felt the warmth in her stomach spread throughout her body, pushing back the weakness and driving away the pain. Through teary eyes she watched as the life slowly drained from Sam Nakai, knowing that he was making the ultimate sacrifice for her.

"Please, Sam. No."

The old man looked at her and smiled. A final smile. "You are the Guardian."

Epilogue

Heather Ocoee sat on a lonely mountain top, staring out over the valley below. Somewhere in the darkness Garou were making their way back home, returning to their packs, tribes and caerns. She listened to their howls and cries, feeling a sadness deep inside her heart, a longing that could not be filled.

Two nights ago she and the others had fought the Wyrm on top of Monterey Mountain. They had almost lost the battle, but with the help of Nee Yah Kah Tah Kee they had driven the Wyrm's demon back to its lair. The rift in the Gauntlet had also been sealed, but Joseph Swimmer and Sam Nakai had died.

She thought of Sam, feeling the tears again form in her eyes. Heather knew a Wendigo warrior should not cry, but she couldn't help it. Sam was her mentor, her friend, and the closest thing to a father she had ever known. Every time she thought of him pain squeezed her heart, and the tears flowed hot and burning down her face. Sam Nakai had given her the ultimate gift, sacrificing his own life so she could live.

Wiping the tears from her eyes, she stood up and turned to face the east. A full moon hung big and bright in the night sky, calling to the wolf spirit deep inside of her. The moon was golden; the night of the Shaman Moon had passed.

Other battles will come. Other challenges.

There would indeed be other challenges, other battles, for as long as the Wyrm's minions walked the earth the Garou could not rest. She was a Wendigo warrior now; her life dedicated to seeking out and destroying those of the Wyrm whenever and wherever she could. Before she looked for the Wyrm elsewhere, however, Heather planned on paying a visit to a certain San Francisco orphanage. There she would find a servant of the Dark One, a woman known as the Iron Maiden. A woman who deserved to die.

Placing a hand over her heart, Heather knew that she would not face any of her battles alone. Sam Nakai had left part of himself inside her, a tiny piece of his spirit. Together they would face the challenges that lay ahead. Together they would fight the Wyrm.

Where today is the Pequot?
Where are the Narragansetts, the Mohawks, the Pokanoket,
and many other once-powerful tribes of our people?
They have vanished before the avarice
and the oppression of the White Man,
as snow before a summer sun.
—Tecumseh, Shawnee

Lightning Under Glass

BY SCOTT CIENCIN

Prologue

The New Market, Calcutta. November 1, 1978.

Madness was all around him, but for Julian Ibiero, the only world that existed was the one within his mind, the one he desperately attempted to capture in his sketchbook. The handsome, dark-haired fifteen year-old sat alone on the high slate roof of the Victorian-styled clock tower overlooking the New Market's entrance.

The New Market was a collection of thousands of stalls and small shops all under a single roof. It was found just behind a street called Chowringhee. A bird and animal mart lay adjacent to the market. Anything one could possibly imagine was for sale here. Vendors sold expensive saris adorned with gold and spangles and meant to be worn by brides. Perfumes could be found in exotic and lavishly designed bottles and vials cast in every possible color. Pendants made of flowers laced with gold thread, baby crocodiles, liver salts, young boys and girls, men and women, exotic sculptures and art—*anything* one could desire.

Julian felt apart from it all as he sat on the tower. The tower's stone buttressed corners and Gothic lourves might have made it look out of place to an outsider, but such architecture was common in Calcutta, once the capital of British India. Below Julian was the clock's dial, behind him a lightning rod protected by a low lying iron fence. There was no chance of rain today. The sky was blue and would have been clear if not for the kites.

Hundreds of kites rippled high above the rooftops, scraps of cloth in every possible color. They were the favorite toys of most children. Seemingly attached to the brilliant dots of color lining the horizon were the children's hopes and dreams of escaping the wretched poverty and overcrowding, the disease and want that were their constant companions. The sky was littered with kites, the streets filled with children. The kites strained as would the children all their lives to find some small place in the world to call their own.

Julian understood this. His father had suffered greatly by choosing to marry and have a child by a woman whose country of origin had once enslaved all of India. Julian had also suffered. He was lighter skinned than many of his friends, and for that he had been taunted by his peers and denied many opportunities.

Julian had not allowed himself to become bitter. Instead, he worked harder to overcome the prejudice, and now he was considered a prized athlete at school, though art was his true love.

Julian's thoughts drifted to his mother. He missed her very much, though life had been much harder on him when she was alive. Marietta Townsend, born in London, had become a Hindu and had renounced all ties to her former life. That had not been enough for her husband's family. They ostracized him and ultimately forced him to move with his wife and child from their life of privilege in the towering *kothabari*, the brick and mortar settlements of the middle class, to the nearby abysmal slums of the bustee.

In the bustee, over four hundred families lived crammed together, and issues of caste, religion, and citizenship meant nothing. Julian had vague, nightmarish memories of those days, of the women who went out and worked while their husbands cooked, cleaned, and cared for their children, later emasculating their mates by calling them "Dokno" or *she-males* loud enough for all to hear. At night, the fierce neon of the city was hidden by the kothbari, plunging the bustee into near total darkness. Few ventured out at night. Sexual debaucheries, incest, partner- swapping and common prostitution for leverage among the throng of families was the average state of affairs. Friends were not there to be had, only other people with whom one could curry favor and perhaps win some rudimentary form of power. Julian had once heard the city of his birth referred to as "a monstrous, teeming, bewildering city," and he couldn't have agreed more.

But there was another side to Calcutta, one he discovered at the age of six, when his beloved mother died and his father was able to leave his literally back breaking job pulling a rickshaw.

Julian looked away from the vast covered marketplace, to the array of crowded streets reaching into the distance. Automobiles were rare. Only one in one thousand possessed a car, perhaps twice that number a motorcycle. Bicycles were popular, rickshaws and carts the most prevalent form of travel other than the train. Cows were considered sacred and allowed to roam free in the streets. Talk had come about some kind of subway system, like they had in the mythical glittering Mecca known as New York, but it was still a long ways off. For now, people simply put up with the pushing and shoving past rickshaws and cows to get from one locale to another.

Looking to the rickshaws, Julian could not help but think of his father once again. Shivraj Ibiero had built his jewelry business into an ongoing concern and had even been approached about becoming a *mahajan*, or money lender. But Julian's father had a deep loathing for the usurers. The man's brother had been driven to abject poverty, and ultimately suicide, by the demands placed on him by a mahajan. In all fairness, it had been his daughter's wedding that had led to this terrible state. The custom of the dowry had been legally abolished with Independence, but it was still in common practice. First the man had to come up with more than a thousand rupees for the dowry, then another thousand to feed all the guests and buy presents for the *Brahmin* who would perform the ceremony. After long negotiations with the mahajan, he had the money he needed, but it cost him all his worldly possessions as collateral. At the interest rate set, he would never see his belongings again, including his own wife's precious jewelry, part of her own dowry thirty years past. It drove him to first to despair, then to taking his own life.

Shivraj *despised* the moneylenders for what they had done to his brother. He would never become one of them, despite the common practice of jewelers also serving as usurers. The man had pride, and he had passed that along to his son.

Julian looked out at the marketplace. With a smile, he watched as a collection of basketeers, also called *memsahibs* or porters, converged on a family of tourists: An American, his wife, and a small blonde girl. They would follow and harass the father until he chose one of them to carry their purchases. If the family was lucky, the basketeer would not run off with their goods. The balding father was hurrying toward a water vendor. Julian could not see the vendor well, but he guessed that the man's darkened face would be splitting into a grin right about now. Americans rarely understood the true cost of anything and they tossed their money about without hesitation.

Julian's gaze drifted to the sketch sitting in his lap. It was one of his best ever. He considered that he should concentrate on it fully, but he was certain that the inspiration would not flee. Closing his eyes, Julian luxuriated in the warm comforting fingers of the sun as they caressed his face.

Yes, there were streets of ever-running shit to be found in Calcutta, bodies in the streets left there by families who had no money to bury them, preferring to let the hungry dogs complete a body's *chakra*, or wheel of destiny. But what city did *not* have it's problems? Julian reasoned. This was the city of his birth. He *loved* Calcutta.

Nowhere else in India, Julian had decided, could one engage in such heartfelt philosophical discussions long into the night. Any event of political importance that shook the world often elicited its first tremors of reaction here. More artists and men of letters could be found here than in any other city in India. This was the Mecca of art, culture, and film, its *muktangans*, or fairs, were glorious celebrations of life. Julian had been raised with a love of music and fine arts, and he excelled in both of the nation's athletic pastimes, cricket and football—or *soccer* as the Americans called it.

And there were Americans here. The tourist trade was constant, overflowing. *The Americans…*

This morning, Julian's friend, Viku, had related a particularly intriguing tale about a group of American tourists. Viku's older brother was a boatman. He and his companions were in their junk when a steamer that had been rented by a group of tourists nearing the end of their stay came riffling down the gentle waters of the Houghly. A trio of young women spotted the boatmen and decided this was the time to sunbathe. They blasted music and performed a long, enticing striptease, ending with only their brightly colored bikinis still on their pale flesh. Viku's brother hadn't had a woman in months. He knew that he might be punished, but he called to the women, invited them to do more than show themselves, and committed the most outrageous act of his life, exposing himself to them and motioning at his privates in a "do you want this?" gesture. One of the women, quite drunk at the time, had leaped from the ship. Viku's brother had leaped as well. They met on an abandoned hayboat, where they made love for hours. Tonight, the woman would return to the boat bringing her two friends. Viku's brother would bring his sibling and Julian.

The young man tried to imagine it. A red-head, a brunette, and a blonde. A little of everything. They would smoke *biri* and drink liquor and rut like animals. It was past time for Julian to engage in such activities. Though he was attractive, the parents of local girls forbade their daughters from even casting their gazes at him. He was a half-breed and his father was mad. Only a madman would turn his nose away from the most lucrative aspects of his profession.

To hell with the local girls, Julian thought. The Americans would be far better. Uninhibited. Julian had heard the tales of the "free love" Ashrams, where, once you were pronounced free of disease, you could sleep with anyone and everyone you desired. But Julian had never actually spoken with anyone who claimed to have been to an Ashram in person. It was always their friend who went there, not them.

Fantasies. Lies.

Tonight, Julian would taste sweet reality.

His ardor faded as he thought of his father and the way his peers regarded him. They would whisper, *every jeweler in the New Market was a moneylender. Did he think himself better than everyone else?*

In truth, Julian's father had done very well as a maker of fine jewelry. So well, in fact, that he did not like to see his son idly spending his time on pursuing his fanciful dreams of becoming an artist and sculptor.

"You owe it to your mother to help me make our business a success," the man would say. He refused to place Julian's sculptures in their heavily barred window for sale. Without the man's knowledge, Julian had bartered with a vendor two streets down in the labyrinth of shops to carry his work and take all but ten percent of the profits. So far, Julian had sold three sculptures of Shiva, their dreaded and beloved god, and a handful depicting heroic battles. Among his favorites was the many-armed goddess Durga the Inaccessible grappling with the demon Mahesasura; the lion-headed Vishnu slaying the demon-king Hiranyakasipu, an incarnation of Ravana, who would only be granted redemption when he died at Vishnu's hands; and Rama fending off the dual attacks of the Rakshasas king and the monkey general Hanuman to rescue his beloved wife Sita. Recently, Julian had been given his first commission, a sculpture of Vishnu saving the royal elephant. Though he was grateful for the work, he had been unable to concentrate on the piece. Another image haunted his imagination and his dreams.

Until today, that image had been elusive. Whenever Julian thought he had it, the picture in his head simply vanished. Today had been different. He woke with the image clearly imprinted on his consciousness. It had not fled, not even when he was forced to do his chores before he could slip away from his father's shop. Sitting on the rooftop, he had captured it's basic lines and was in no hurry to get it all down. He wanted to savor it. Reveal it bit by bit.

Suddenly, the image darted from his mind.

Julian drew a sharp, ragged breath. He couldn't believe this. He had been so arrogant, so stupid!

The young artist looked down at the collection of guidelines he had made. What had the image been? A figure in a cathedral of swords? Yes, he knew that much, but the image itself was gone. The drama of the moment, the figure's exact nature, its pose and armament—lost. He leaned back in frustration and looked down at the sketch in his lap, a half-hearted effort to capture a thing of impossible beauty and power.

"Julian!"

The teenager's heart skipped a beat as he heard his father's voice below. He loved his father dearly. It was only when the man drank that Julian was beaten. In recent months, when Shivraj had looked into Julian's face, he saw his lost, beloved wife. That threw Shivraj into a darkness from which there was no hope of returning unless his anger found release. Julian understood.

"Where are you, boy!" the man called.

Julian hurried away from his perch. Soon he was on the ground. He approached his father slowly. The man wore fancy dress today, a crimson turban, a shiny silver dress coat called a *sherani,* and tight pants called *churidar.* His flesh was darker than Julian's, his onyx eyes sharp and alert, his moustache and hair going to grey. He was a bit wide in the belly. His slightly jowled face, which could shift between impatience and total serenity, was lit up with unusual excitement.

"This is the day," Shivraj Ibiero said. "Good God, Julian, this day we will be rich."

His father did not explain what he meant by that. Shivraj said that Sunder, their shop's protector and his bodyguard, a bald, hulking, heavily muscled young man, was needed for an excursion and Julian would have to watch their goods.

"Today we deal with *honest* thieves!" Shivraj cried.

They hurried into the covered marketplace. Julian's father nudged his son. "Diwali night comes in two weeks. For once, we will have something to celebrate."

Julian was excited. The festival of Diwali honored Lakshima, goddess of wealth. Fireworks would light the sky and even the darkest recesses of Calcutta would be illuminated. They passed dozens of stalls, including the one selling Julian's sculptures. Julian wondered for an instant if he should tell his father about his triumphs now. The man was certainly in a good mood. No, he decided, better to wait until later, after this meeting was over.

They passed a lovely woman selling silk and cotton sarees. She smiled at Julian's father. The red dot on her forehead made him turn away. Julian's studies of Hindu legends led to an understanding of the *bindi,* or third eye. It had been known as a source of strength and wisdom, though in modern times, it was the equivalent of a wedding ring. Julian's father would not lie with a married woman, no matter how beautiful she was, or how lonely he felt.

At another stall, an old man with a long white beard called to Julian's father. "Have you heard the latest?"

"I have no time for this today!"

"There has been more fighting in the streets! Your precious Desai coalition threatens to crumble. Indira Gandhi *will* come back to power!"

Despite his hurry, Shivraj could not keep himself from stopping a moment and debating this. Julian accepted their verbal battle with casual indifference. In 1975, a no-confidence measure had been passed against Indira Gandhi, who was no actual relation to the slain spiritual leader who led India to freedom from British rule. In a desperate bid to keep her power, Indira Gandhi had refused to abdicate, and instead declared martial law. She jailed those who opposed her, especially Morarji Desai, and inflicted even worse hardships than ever against the people of India. To deal with the rising problem of overpopulation, she had enforced a policy of sterilizing men who fathered two or more children. But an Indian male's greatest goal in life was to bring a large family into the world, and he would not willingly embrace Yama, god of the dead, until he had seen all of his children healthy, happy, and well cared for. This unpopular policy, among many others, had led to Gandhi's ultimate downfall. Laughing, Shivraj walked away from the screaming merchant.

Soon they were at his shop, Sunder unlocking the heavy door. Julian was briskly shoved inside the sweltering twelve by twelve foot square, crammed with safes, work tables, molds, vats, and folding chairs. The teenager was startled as his father leaned in and gave his son a brief kiss on the lips.

"You are a *good* boy!" the man said, departing quickly as Julian triple-locked the door behind him. He was stunned. It had been *years* since he saw his father act this way. He wondered if he should gather up his meager earnings from the sales of his sculptures, find a priest, and beg the man to perform a *puja*, a ceremony of offering to the gods, as a means of ensuring that the man's mood remained like this forever.

You're being foolish, he told himself.

Suddenly, there was a rapping at one of the windows. Julian hurried toward it, removing the small sketchpad he had hidden in the waistband of his trousers. He set it on the side and saw that a line was forming outside. The windows were barred. The small fan his father had purchased barely kept the place livable, particularly when a new vat of silver was simmering, as it was now, in the corner.

"Where is your father?" a woman asked.

"He has departed on business," Julian said. "He will be back."

"But I have jewelry to sell."

"My father is not a usurer."

"That is why I came to him. He is a kind man, loved by many because he is not a vampire like the others."

"I understand, but if he did this for you, he *would* be just like them. Bleeding you with interest. Making it so you would never see your jewelry again. This kindness you feel for him would pass instantly."

The woman regarded him with a blank stare. "I have jewelry to sell."

"He is not a usurer," Julian said simply.

The woman's expression turned black. "He would do this for me. I am a good customer."

"Come back and ask him, I cannot speak for him."

"So I shall."

The procession went on. Julian could not enact any transactions. Even those who had come only to pick up orders were told to come back later.

Shivraj Ibiero may have refused to become a moneylender for the purist of reasons, but his decision had proven to be a shrewd bit of marketing. By refusing to become a usurer, Shivraj had separated himself from the pack of jewelers and had attained a healthy clientele that loathed performing even legitimate business with the other jewelers. The man was also a fine artisan, a master craftsman, and a very capable salesman.

After more than two hours of dealing with the unhappy public, a lull finally arrived. Julian looked to the flames beneath the vat of silver in the corner of the shop, near the "chamber pot" as his father laughingly referred to it, and inspiration struck like lightning. He recalled the image from his dreams in perfect detail. All he had to do was capture it before the image left him.

He hurried to his sketchbook, found a pencil, and set to his task. A few minutes later, when he was almost half finished, a rapping came at the window. He was tempted to ignore it, but he knew that his father would be cross if any of their loyal clients came to him later and said that Julian had been lax in his duties. With a growl of frustration, Julian went to the window. At first he saw no one. Then he looked down.

A small blonde American girl, no more than six, stood before one of the display windows, her gaze welded to a gold bracelet. She saw Julian and pointed at the bracelet.

Julian looked quickly up and down the street. He had seen this child with her parents. Where were they? Didn't they understand how dangerous it was to leave a child unattended in this place, with so many buyers and sellers of human flesh? A child like this would be worth a fortune.

"Where are your parents?" Julian said roughly.

The girl didn't seem to hear him. She stared in total fascination at the bracelet. It was gold, lined with fanciful etchings that looked like some kind of writing, though it was no language Julian could decipher. Light from his nearby lantern struck the bracelet and cast a soft golden haze around it.

The best thing was not to get involved. Julian understood this. Many of the flesh peddlers were protected by the Thugs, followers of Kali. Julian did not wish to end up strangled like some poor traveller. His friend Viku sometimes obsessed over what it would feel like. The assassins used handkerchiefs with a silver coin consecrated to Kali the Terrible in one corner to enhance their grip as they squeezed the life from a victim. Julian was unsure what ties the Thugs had to the actual temple of Kali, but he knew they existed and that their eyes were devoid of all but hatred and a lust for blood.

An image leaped into Julian's mind. Kali with her devilish eyes, her tongue dripping blood, snakes rippling from around her neck, wreaths of skulls hanging upon her flesh. She was the wife of Shiva the Destroyer, and together with Brahma the Creator and Vishnu the Preserver, she was one third of the triad that dominated the Hindu religion. Perhaps it was this child's *chakra* to fall into the hands of the body thieves. He shouldn't get involved.

Then, about one hundred yards away, Julian saw a thin, hawklike man wearing a white T-shirt, khaki slacks, and a kirpan, or dagger, normally used by the Sikh palace guards in their holy cities. He knew this man. Channi, a scout for one of the flesh merchants. The scout had yet to see the American child.

Julian looked to his sketch. He could feel his inspiration fading.

Go back to it, he told himself. *Go back to it and forget this other business. The child will go soon enough.*

Instead he cut another glance down the street. Channi was coming closer, moving purposefully.

Too late, Julian thought, his heart racing. *Too late.* If he intervened now, it would mean his life. He would not die for a stranger. Not for some foolish American.

He closed his eyes, considered the fate this child would have, and rushed to his door. He worked the triple locks quickly, slid into the street, and scooped the child up in his arms, one hand clamped over her mouth to prevent her from screaming. Without looking in Channi's direction, he turned and ran inside with the child, kicking the door shut behind him.

"Do not scream!" Julian hissed.

He took his hand off her mouth to lock the door. The entire time, he waited for the child's ear piercing scream, but it did not come. A second later, he saw why. Her gaze was once again fixed on the golden bracelet, which was now very close and no longer obscured by the streaky window and iron bars.

"You want to see that?" Julian whispered in desperation. He set the child down, snatched up the bracelet, and handed it to her. She took it from him and regarded it with awe. "It's pretty, yes? Look at it all you want. But don't make a sound, do you understand?"

The little girl did not even acknowledge his presence. She ran her small fingers over the odd patterns etched into the surface of the bracelet and found Sunder's sleeping roll to sit upon.

"Good," he said. "That's good."

A tapping came at his window. Julian froze. He looked around the cramped workshop. The child was near the door. She could not be seen by anyone peering in through the window. Julian flattened himself against the door, hiding himself from view as he prayed that his visitor would go away.

The tapping came again.

Julian was terrified. Why had he done such a foolish thing? What was he going to do with this child? He couldn't abandon the shop to go search for her parents. And for what he had done, dragging her into his shop by force, he might be branded a kidnapper!

Tap. Tap, tap, tap, tap.

Go away, please God, let them leave, Julian chanted in his mind.

"My father's a diplomat," the child said suddenly.

Julian looked down at her in horror. She had been so loud! Channi was *certain*

LIGHTNING UNDER GLASS

to have heard her.

Merciful God, what had he been thinking? This would be death for both of them!

"Ibiero!" someone called out.

A flood of relief passed through him. Julian recognized this voice. He went to the window.

The white-bearded merchant that his father had argued with over politics was there. The merchant demanded, "Where's your father?"

"I can't say," Julian whispered breathlessly.

"Tell your father he's an ass. Tell him the Janata party will fall by the wayside and the true government will rise again! You tell him that!"

"I will."

"Good."

The bearded man departed. Julian looked up and down the street. He saw no sign of Channi. The scout had moved on. Julian turned to the child.

She said, "My mommy wanted to be a school teacher, but my dad keeps getting moved around. I've been to twenty-eight countries. I didn't even know there were that many countries in the world, did you?"

I have to get her out of here. Back to her parents. But how?

His gaze drifted to the sketchpad. The fire he had felt over this work had nearly faded. His frustration had returned. All the details were blurred once more, and what he had captured was too vague for proper interpretation. It wasn't important, he told himself. The inspiration would return when he wasn't thinking about it. Or something better would come along.

"Why are you alone?" Julian asked. It suddenly occurred to him that perhaps her parents had met with violence. Anything was possible.

She didn't answer. An idea came to him: The British Embassy. He would wait until his father returned, then he would take the child to the embassy. All he had to do was keep her quiet and entertained. And judging by how her attention was all but consumed by the gold bracelet, he knew that he had just the means to bring that about.

The child's wrist was too small for the bracelet. She tried to put it on but it kept slipping off over her hand. So now she held it up to the light reaching down from his lantern, allowing it to sparkle and shine. Tiny diamonds were inlaid on the bracelet, making it shimmer in the light.

"I will make a deal with you," Julian said. "If you stay where you are, and do not make noise, or trouble, you may *keep* the bracelet."

She looked up. "Really?"

He nodded. What he wasn't telling her, of course, was for how long. He would take it from her the moment he had her safely inside the embassy.

"It's beautiful," she said.

"Yes, but it is still. Quiet. As you must be. Do you understand?"

She nodded.

"Good."

He went back to his seat and picked up his sketchbook. For the next hour, the girl proved to be no trouble at all. In fact, he sometimes forgot she was there. At one point she wandered over and asked what he was doing. He shooed her back to the doorway, where she would not be seen, then let her look at his drawings. Her eyes grew wide at the images he displayed. The gods and goddesses, their magics and incredible exploits drawing her in.

A few dozen people came to the window, but it was no problem to turn them away. The flesh peddler's scout did not return.

Julian tried to recapture his inspiration, the image that had entered his imagination and fled like a teasing woman, but he could not locate it again. He knew it would be best to let it come to him, but he could not drive away his desire to possess that image and bring it to life as a sculpture.

Suddenly, a cry sounded from the marketplace. A woman calling out a name, her voice laced with terror.

An American woman.

Julian looked up sharply. So did the child. He couldn't make out the name that was being called over the din of the marketplace, but the child understood and responded.

"Mommy!" the girl cried happily.

God was smiling upon him today. Yes, there might have been a reward of some kind if he had taken her to the embassy, but this was better. This way, his father would never know what had happened. Deep down, Julian knew that his father might not have taken a sympathetic view toward Julian's decision to snatch a child from the street and offer her protection.

Julian went to the door and undid each of the three locks. The child was scrambling by his feet. Laughing, he said, "Wait! Wait!" His relief and her excitement were palpable.

Finally, he was able to move her back and get the door open. She bolted past him and burrowed into the throng of people in the marketplace. Julian couldn't see the child's mother, but he had a sense that she was close, and that the girl would be united with her soon.

Then he saw a flash of gold amidst the pack of shoppers.

The bracelet!

No, it couldn't be that, he told himself. He hadn't seen it in her hands when she ran out, she must have left it behind. It had been her golden *hair* he had seen.

He looked down at where the child had been sitting. The bracelet was not there. He looked all around and realized that it was gone. Fear snaked into him. He would have to go after the child. There was no other choice.

Julian looked around for the keys. Where had he put them?

Then he remembered. His father hadn't *given him* the keys.

The man either had not trusted Julian to remain in the shop unless he had no choice, or he had simply forgotten in his excitement. If Julian ran after the child, he would have to leave the shop unattended. True, the safes could not be opened easily, but they *could* be lifted and carried away. And there were over a hundred valuable items in the window displays that any thief could snatch up.

He was trapped.

Cursing, he locked the door behind himself and crouched low, looking in the darkened corners, beneath tables, anywhere he could think of to see if the child had left the bracelet behind and it had rolled out of view. After twenty minutes of desperate searching, he knew it was gone.

Julian wondered what he had done to be punished by the gods in this way. He had performed an act of kindness, he had tried to save an innocent child—

No. Not innocent. The child was a thief. He would tell his father what happened and together they would go to the embassy. The girl said that her father was a diplomat. The family shouldn't be hard to track down. They would be found, the child would be confronted with her actions—

—and she would say that Julian promised she could *keep the bracelet*. Or worse, she would deny having taken it. Julian would be the one punished for falsely accusing an "honored guest" to "the charming city forever," and *he* would be punished.

Madness. What could he do?

Julian's gaze shifted to the window display. The vast array of gold and silver instantly arrested his fears. There were more than a hundred pieces here. If he moved them around a little, closed the obvious gap left by the bracelet's absence, it would look as if nothing at all had been taken. He would not have to say a thing.

He rearranged the jewelry, then went back to his sketchpad. He was worried about what would happen when his father arrived, but he knew that fear would only give him away. His only hope lay in concentrating on other things. Like the beautiful women he would bed this night.

Americans.

He no longer felt excited at the prospect.

The child had meant no harm, he told himself. She was such a little thing, a yellow rose in a sea of darkness and human degradation. He couldn't bring himself to hate her.

Suddenly, the inspiration came again. The image of the cathedral of swords and its guardian appeared in his mind with perfect clarity. Rushing over to his table, he set to work on finishing his sketch before the inspiration fled. Tomorrow, he would go to the merchant who lent him tools and workspace, and he would begin the sculpture.

There was magic in the act of sculpting. Taking something formless and revealing its inner mysteries, the patterns that gave it life and vitality. It was when he felt his hands working clay, or delicately chipping away at stone, that he felt most alive. He was a virgin, yes, but there had been one local girl who had let him feel around for a time. If he was forced to choose between the pleasures of caressing a woman's soft, firm breasts, the mounds of her ass, the sweet wetness of her fur and the folds of her sex, or the cold, hard feel of claw between his fingers as he worked it and shaped it and created a new reality with it, there would really be no choice at all for him.

He felt his ardor returning at the memory.

The distraction tonight was not to be missed, he decided. Even so, it would hardly matter compared to the visible results of his work with his hammer and chisel tomorrow.

He worked happily, confident that the bracelet's absence would never be noted.

Several hours later, when it was dark, his father finally arrived. His odor preceded him, the bracing smell of hard liquor mixed with a fragrance that seemed oddly familiar to Julian, like one he had smelled in his dreams of the cathedral. Shivraj closed the shutters over the windows. He was in a foul mood. Julian understood at once that his father's dealings had gone badly. The man said nothing. He teetered on his feet, then dropped to the floor, his eyes filling with tears.

Julian knew that the best thing he could do was simply ignore his father. Leave now and wait until his father sent word that it was time to return home.

The teenager had no idea in that moment that after he did leave this place tonight, he would not see his home again for another nineteen years. Though he felt touched by the gods when he created his art, he possessed no special gifts of prophecy. He had no idea that the wheel of his own chakra was turning, and that in moments it would cut him in half.

Julian went to his father's side, bent low beside him, and said, "Father, don't cry."

Shivraj looked up sharply. In his eyes was a madness Julian had never seen before, even during the worst of beatings. Before Julian could pull away, his father's meaty arm shot up and fastened around the teenager's throat.

"What do you know of it?" the man bellowed as he stood, dragging Julian to his feet. "They laughed at me. And do you know why? Over you!"

Julian was hurled several feet. He crashed into a table that bit hard into his back and sent a fierce lancing pain into him. The table was tipped over by his weight and Julian fell to the ground, heavy metal tools slamming down on him, one striking his skull with enough force to leave him dazed. The table followed, pinning his legs.

"Why have I been cursed?" Shivraj asked, teetering on his watery legs. That might have been the end of it. Shivraj's head was already beginning to clear, the fire within him easing. Then his gaze drifted to the window display case. Despite Julian's best efforts to rearrange the jewelry and disguise the bracelet's loss, Shivraj saw instantly that it was gone. In a low, gurgling voice laced with dark laughter, he cried, "Did you make a sale, boy?"

Julian was trying to climb free of the table. He thought quickly. The money he had made from selling his sculpture!

"Yes," Julian whispered hoarsely. "One sale. Wealthy Americans."

"How much?"

Julian gave the man a figure. All the teenager had earned from his side venture.

"That number sounds *familiar*," Shivraj said as he came to his son's side, tore the table off him, and kicked him hard in the ribs.

Julian felt something break within him. Pain exploded behind his eyes and suddenly he was straining to catch a breath. He tried to move, but the hurt was excruciating, and so he slid back to the floor.

"Father, please," he choked.

"You little piece of garbage!" Shivraj screamed as he picked up the display case filled with rings, bracelets, and necklaces. He hurled it at his son's head. His aim was off and the case struck Julian in the right shoulderblade. There was a high sharp crackle of shattered bone and Julian wailed as pinwheels and vibrant stars of fire and light exploded in his skull, piercing the darkened veil of his perceptions. A hailstorm of jewelry rained down on him.

On the bare table where the case had been, Julian's sketchbook now lay in plain sight. Shivraj didn't see it. Not at first.

"So you've stolen from me?" Shivraj asked. "This is how you pay me back for my taking care of you, you steal from me!"

"No," moaned Julian.

"This is—what? How you were going to pay for a whore? By stealing from me?"

"Father…"

"Oh, I heard of your little excursion tonight. Was it meant to be a present to one of the American bitches? My work? All that matters to me?"

"It was *one bracelet*," Julian pleaded, "stop hurting me and I'll tell you what happened!"

"I don't want to hear your lies! Do you know what *they* said to me?"

Julian tried to roll onto his side. There was something hot and rich boiling in his chest, a python made of acid uncurling within him. Had his ribs been broken? His shoulderblade?

"They said, 'how can we expect you to keep *our* secrets when your own child deceives you? How can we trust you?'" Shivraj spat. "That is what they said to me, the murdering bastards."

The Thugs, Julian thought. His father had been planning to make some kind of deal with the death cultists. But that made no sense. What need would the Thugs have of his father's skills?

"Do you notice that Sunder is not at my side? Would you like to know why?" Shivraj growled.

"Father—"

"They killed him. Slowly. It went on for hours and hours. They tortured him, *they pulled him apart*, but they kept him alive somehow when they were doing it. I've never seen such a thing. His blood everywhere, his innards, his bone… The murdering scum were sliding on the floor from his blood and laughing about it!"

Julian knew that the situation had escalated beyond the point of trying to reason with the man. He had to find a way to defend himself. He saw one of his father's tools within his reach. A hammer. He grabbed for it.

Shivraj stormed forward and stomped his boot on his son's hand. Julian wailed with pain as he heard bones snapping. His agony worsened. His father scooped up the hammer, removed his boot from Julian's shattered hand, and gripped his son's wrist. Though the shop was very small and cramped, Shivraj managed to drag Julian a few feet.

"This is the source of your evil," said Shivraj as he squeezed Julian's broken hand, making the teenager yelp like a whipped dog. "Your delicate, beautiful hands, uh? Like your mothers. Too good to carry on *my* works. No, you had to find your own calling, your own destiny."

Shivraj spotted the sketchpad. "Ahhh. Here it is." He dropped Julian and went to the book. "Pretty little pictures. This is how it began, yes? Pretty pictures. Let me show you what I think of your pretty pictures."

Tossing the sketchbook to the ground, Shivraj exposed himself and laughed wildly as he relieved himself on Julian's sketches, the foul smelling stream falling directly on the drawing Julian had labored over all day.

This was madness, Julian knew. It was as if the very order of the universe had changed and no one had bothered to inform *him*. As if reality had been reshaped solely to punish him.

Shivraj saw Julian watching him. He went over and kicked his son in the face, avoiding the groping hand that sought to catch his foot and topple him. The kick connected and broke several of Julian's teeth. Others tore into his cheek. Blood leaked from his mouth as Julian flipped onto his back. The pain overwhelmed him now, a white-hot searing companion that embraced every part of his body. Julian was left without any means of defending himself, though he was perfectly capable of understanding what had been done to him.

Let me die, Julian thought. *I know I deserve it. God, just let me die.*

"*The Euthanatos*," Shivraj whispered, "the Euthanatos… They could have been everything to us, but you had to shame me, you had to deceive me with the help of others *right here in this market!*"

Shivraj grabbed at his son's hands and dragged him to the other side of the room. Julian's head lolled. He mumbled something but could not be understood. Razor-sharp daggers covered in salt plunged into his wounds, or so it seemed to him. The pain was unmerciful, denying him the delirium he craved so badly, the release he needed more than anything.

His father knew about the sculptures he had sold in secret. These people, the Euthanatos, had been thorough in learning everything about the man, and that had been Julian's undoing.

"I could have forgiven your lying," said Shivraj as he breathed hard, the effort of dragging his son proving to be a strain. "But you *stole* from me. You took the bracelet. The last of it!"

That phrase would haunt Julian in later years. The last of it. The last of what?

"That you took that bracelet, that piece of all my works… that's something even *they* didn't know. How could they? It was happening while I was in their gentle company, watching a friend die. That you would steal from me means I have nothing, and if I have nothing, you shall have *less*."

Julian hissed, "Didn't—"

Suddenly, Julian felt his father's hand on the back of his head, yanking him up painfully to a sitting position.

"Watch," commanded Shivraj.

Julian saw something before him. A large metal vat sitting above a flame, bubbling with grey waters, steam rising up like angry wraiths.

The silver!

"No," Julian whispered, though the word cost him terribly. "Father—"

Then his arms were gripped from behind and his hands were thrust into the boiling vat of silver! Julian screamed as he felt the acids burning through his flesh, felt all manner of pain as if piranha were peeling his skin to the bone. Muscle and tissue dissolved. His heart seized up from shock and fright. He should have died, but something inside him would not allow this mercy. Nausea and a freezing chill ripped through him. He heard his father laughing!

Julian screamed, ignoring the pain from his lungs.

Oblivion finally closed over him.

The room was dark when Julian woke. He felt drained and every part of his body ached *except* his hands. The dark slowly lifted as Julian became aware of the low blue flames under the vat of silver. They crackled and hissed at him. The acrid smell of urine filled his lungs. From somewhere close, he heard his father snoring.

Then he remembered. It came back to him quickly, with the relentless power and fury of a runaway train closing on a victim caught on the tracks. He thought of his hands and wondered why he couldn't feel them.

Don't look at them, he told himself. *You mustn't.*

Julian did not have the strength to ignore this calming, inner voice. So long as he did not actually look at his hands, he could convince himself that they were still there, that there was more than a pair of stumps at the end of his forearms, or the twisted skeletal remains of fused bones and cauterized flesh.

Why was he alive? The shock alone should have been enough to kill him. Was God so angry at him that He would subject the teenager to even worse degradations when his father woke? Or was Julian being given a chance to seek vengeance for the injustice that had been done to him?

The thought calmed him, but only a little.

If he could somehow open the door and get outside, he could find someone, show them what his father had done, and make sure that his father paid. But that would mean standing, and such a task seemed beyond him at the moment. In any case, vengeance *wasn't* what he desired. He wanted his world to be as it had been. His gaze shifted to the slumbering form of his father.

No, he decided, this was not his father. It was a demon loose in his father's flesh. His father had been a gentle man who had suffered indignities and injustices without complaint for the sake of those he loved. This animal, this *beast*, was not the hidden face of the man who had given him life. It was a darksome thing that had to die if his father's kind soul was to have release. The people his father had gone to see must have sent this terrible duplicate, this demon in disguise.

But what could he do? He was a cripple now. Less than a man. He would be reduced to living in the streets, fending off the dogs, existing on the pitifully scarce charity awarded beggars. He didn't even have the strength to destroy the demon that had cursed him now and forever.

Buried beneath his despair, a glowing red ember of defiance still smoldered. He would not accept—could *not* accept this as his reality. He had power. There was a majesty to the works he had created, an even greater one in those yet to come. There was more to him as an artist than his hands. They were tools, exquisite tools, yes, but they were not the root of his power, merely the means to focus it. His true power resided in his mind, in his will, and in his need to shape reality in new ways.

That had not left him.

What he desired above all else was to perform his unique and personal magic right now. To shape the fabric of *his* existence, of his body. To give himself what had been taken by the cruel acts of the demon wearing his father's flesh: Strength. Dexterity. The ability to do what needed to be done.

He closed his eyes and prayed to his gods, to any and all gods, to anyone or anything that might listen.

There was a stirring.

Julian did not understand where this sensation originated. Within him? In some otherworldly palace where beings of Power played with the lives of humans for their own amusements? Upon the spiderweb-like pattern of all reality, all existence?

Your time has come, Lord Shaper.

It wasn't a voice. More like the gossamer wings of a butterfly gently brushing the contours of his mind, his will, his heart, and his soul.

Answer your calling.

A strange, silver glow rose up from the terrifying mass that had been his hands. Julian did not look down. He felt something at the end of his wrists. A tingling that was quickly replaced by a burning that was in turn overcome by a pain that defied description.

He did not scream.

Julian squeezed his eyes shut, but the silver luminescence did not go away. Nor did the pain. He kept his cries to the barest of whimpers though he desperately desired release. Liquid fire coursed through his veins, reaching up from what had been his hands, filling his limbs, his mind, his heart, changing him.

Shaping him.

Do not deny this, it is who and what you are.

He opened his eyes and saw a delirious warping of sights and sounds and colors. The room seemed to expand and close in on itself all at once. The grain of wood upon the floor changed and became runic symbols that he miraculously understood. A shrieking like a thousand dying wolves came in place of the slight flutter of the fire beside him.

All this he could embrace. *This* reality was far better than his own. He would give himself to it gladly.

"I'm yours," he whispered, and suddenly, darkness enveloped the room. The slight blue glow of the flames and their crackling returned. It was over, except for the pain. He could feel it in his hands—and yes, he had hands once more—a cold, horrible agony that did nothing to prohibit him from flexing his fingers, from using his new hands as the tools he so desperately desired.

He looked down at the strangers reaching out from his wrists. For an instant, his mind rebelled at what he saw. His hands were crimson, black, and silver. Bits of bone and vein and flesh and muscle all interweaved. The silver had hardened within him, had become a part of him. There were tiny flickers of light, intricate patterns that raced through his hands. On some instinctive level, he understood that he would be the only one to see these lights. Others would look at his hands and see only ugliness and deformity.

But they worked. Impossible as it was, they worked.

It would be enough for now.

Julian rose up. He touched his face, running his fingers over his closed mouth, pressing slightly. Information was passed to his brain, though he felt only the force of something moving against his skin. His hands were far from numb. They delivered onto him a constant ice-cold throbbing pain.

There was no pain in his mouth. The shattered teeth were whole once more.

Julian touched the floor with his silver hands. Closing his eyes, he knew when his new hands were upon the floor and when they were not, though he could feel only their pain. The nerves had been damaged in some hellish way, yet he knew all his hands had to tell him.

He tried drawing a breath. Yes, his ribs were fine. Moving his arms, rotating his shoulderblade, brought no discomfort whatsoever.

All had been restored.

You have Awakened.

Julian shuddered in fear. What did that mean? And what voice was this, that we was listening to?

Information flowed into him, calming him: Time would fill in the blanks. There were others like himself, fellow Shapers of reality. He would find them and learn from them.

Julian looked at his hands. They were no longer the hands of an artist, no longer human hands at all. He could not sculpt with these hands. He could not create the delicate and powerful works of beauty he had seen in his heart. Not with these hands.

That aside, they were far from useless.

"Wake up," Julian said as crossed the room and knelt over his father.

The man mumbled something, moaned.

Julian went back to the vat of silver. He was not afraid of touching it with his new hands. It couldn't cause him any worse pain than he already felt, and it would not damage him, either. He picked up the vat and splattered its contents on the body of his father. The man screamed and wailed in agony, writhing on the floor like a man set on fire.

Julian bent over him, ignoring the man's feeble punches and slaps, and closed his hands around his father's throat. He squeezed. As the life was slowly choked from the demon wearing Shivraj Ibiero's flesh, Julian met the creature's gaze. What he saw in his victim's eyes nearly made him stop.

His father hated him.

There was no demon. *This* was his father. It had been him all along, not a doppelganger sent back by the Euthanatos. The searing hatred had always been there for him to see, but Julian had not wished to be awakened to this aspect of reality.

Julian's grip nearly faltered. He wanted to know what he had done to deserve such anger, such venom.

If you turn back now, you will be lost.

The voice within him was right, Julian decided. If he spared his father's life, his own new existence would be forfeit. "I don't care why you hate me," Julian said. "Just die."

Shivraj squirmed in terror.

Julian squeezed even harder, maintaining an unyielding pressure until his father's struggles finally ceased.

He felt nothing. The killing had not been enough.

Screaming in rage, Julian raised one hand, hooking it into a claw, and tore it across his father's chest, leaving a fiery canal of crimson gore and shattered bone. Suddenly, Shivraj Ibiero's heart was in his hand. Julian crushed it and tossed it away.

Nothing at all. Not even a glimmer of satisfaction.

He looked down at his sketchbook, the drawing soggy, barely displaying any hint of the fantastic visions he had been granted. Julian turned from it in contempt. His right hand was covered in blood. He scrawled a message on the wall. It read:

WE HAVE TAKEN THE BOY.

Now he would no longer be a suspect in the murder. Instead, he was a fellow victim. There would be no manhunt for the "abducted teenager." Calcutta's resources were overtaxed as it was.

Julian also knew that his fingerprints would not be found on the body. How could they be? He no longer had flesh, let alone fingerprints. All he had to do now was slip away from the marketplace without being seen.

Then what? Go to meet Viku? Screw some stupid Americans? Have Viku's relative smuggle him downriver in his boat?

No. He could no longer trust Viku, or anyone for that matter. Tonight he needed to become a shadow. A living shadow that would disappear into the night.

He found a pair of his father's gloves and slipped them over his new hands.

Reach out, he told himself. *You have power now far beyond any you have ever dreamed of possessing. You know this place, you know these people. Reach out with your power and it will tell you where people are hiding, where they will stand to oppose you. You will be able to avoid them all. Do it.*

Julian extended his consciousness in a way very similar to the approach he used when peering within a of block of stone to see the masterpiece waiting to be released within it. Suddenly, he knew precisely what route to take to leave this place.

Once you're beyond the market, take the train to Darjeeling. You'll need money, but that can be found. The foolish travel at night. You can take what you need from them without killing, if that is what you desire.

Then travel on. Travel on…

But killing *was* what he desired. He could feel nothing. Not anger, betrayal—nothing except a desire to kill. Indiscriminate murder would not satisfy him for long. There was someone he wanted to find.

The girl.

If not for *her*, his life might have gone on as it had. Yes, his father had learned his secrets and the man had intended to punish him. But he had been driven to such lengths by the belief that his son had stolen from him, and that was not Julian's fault. It was the child's. Shivraj might *never* have revealed the hatred in his heart if not for the girl's thievery. And Julian might never have been forced to learn that all he believed about his life and his father's love had been a lie.

The child's callous act had damned him.

He would find her, he knew that. He had to. And it could not be too soon. He had to know that she would understand her fate, that she would see that she deserved the terrors and the punishments he would wreak upon her. The beginnings of a plan formed in his mind. He would wait until she was the age he was right now. When she knew enough of the world to see that she had a place in it, her own destiny to fulfill—*then* he would track her down. It would be a simple matter. For now, his own survival, and finding something to take the place of his shattered dreams, was all that mattered to him.

Sleep well, child of gold, he thought as he slipped out of his father's shop and into the night. *Sleep and dream and know hope. Find your future that I may take it from you.*

The thought brought him comfort as he became one with the night.

Three hours later, as he rode on the train, his thoughts began to clear. There was no getting away from it, he had gone mad. The sorcery, the Shaping—this seemed perfectly reasonable to him. But he knew that his feelings over the child—the murderous rage, the hunger for vengeance, the emptiness inside him that would only be filled with her dying screams—this was twisted. He had to fight these feelings. Somehow, he had to keep himself from becoming a demon incarnate like his father.

Fortunately, he had given her time. Given both of them time.

Nine years. He would seek her out then. Perhaps by then he would be sane, able to judge her properly.

For now, however, all he wanted was the child's blood, and therefore he knew that on this score if on no other, he had *certainly* lost his mind.

As the darkened countryside raced past him and his journey began, he wondered how long his madness would last.

I

Seattle, Washington. May 10, 1997.

"I worry about you," Freddy said gently.

Maxine looked up from the screen of her powerbook. She fixed her companion with her emerald gaze. "Well, I worry about you, too." Curling her lip slightly, Max looked away with an expression that asked *where the hell did that come from?*

Freddy picked himself up off the floor of his cluttered Seattle apartment. He was a short man in his late thirties with a barrel chest, a meaty belly, thick arms, and a shock of auburn hair he could do nothing with. His full beard and mustache gave his round face character and his dark eyes were unusually commanding, though he didn't seem to know any of that. He wore a fuzzy white robe and a pair of boxers underneath.

"I'm serious," he said, grunting as he dragged himself off the floor. His hair was still damp from the shower he took a few minutes ago. He looked over at the window and saw an angry golden fireball rising above Seattle. "Damn. We've been at this all night."

Max looked back at her computer. On the screen was an image of a small round hairy man, by his clothing and attitude a very silly mix of Fred Flintstone and Conan the Barbarian. Underneath the graphic was the logo: *"TROG. You pick the time. We take you there. He kicks your ass."*

"Shit, and here we could have been having sex," said Max. She leaned back from her computer and tried to stifle a yawn. Her breasts strained against her partially unbuttoned silver shirt as she put her hands behind her neck and moved her head in languid arcs to get the kinks out.

"You need a massage," said her companion.

She turned her gaze back to Freddy. Her eyes were wide and vulnerable. "Oh, God, would you?"

"As you wish," he said, reciting a line from one of their favorite films, "The Princess Bride." Freddy stood behind her and moved her long blonde hair away from her shoulders. He went to work on the tightest areas: her shoulders, the hollows on either side of her long sensuous neck, all along her spine, and her lower back.

Max tugged at her shirt. "Can I take this off?"

"Yes, I promise not to be overcome with lust."

"Bummer," she said as she unbuttoned her blouse, yanked it out of her tight bluejeans, and tossed it across the room. It landed on a couch piled high with close to a hundred research books on various historical eras. Her flesh was tanned and smooth, her figure hourglass perfect.

On her wrist was a gorgeous gold bracelet that she had owned since childhood. She reached back, unhooked her bra, and allowed her high, generous breasts to sway in the coolness of the apartment.

"Nippily," he said.

"Freddy!" Maxine chided, reaching forward and covering her hardened nipples.

He casually brushed her arms away and leaned her forward in her chair. "Will you relax?"

"Hold on." She flung the bra she still held toward the couch. It landed a few feet short and came to rest on three long white boxes filled with comics and topped with cook books.

"You've got goosebumps," said Freddy as he used his thick, powerful hands on his guest, eliciting a series of contented moans and pleasured cries. "Want me to make it a little warmer in here?"

"Would you?"

"Sure."

Freddy walked over to the thermostat; he reached it only after playing Twister over stacks of loose newspapers, magazines, manilla folders, and laser jet print-outs. He popped the thermostat onto heat, then returned. "All right, my willing victim, where were we?"

Maxine leaned forward in her chair, scooping her mass of blond hair to one side and spilling it down over her breasts to get it out of the way. Freddy's hands were on her, instinctively reaching all of her tightest spots. Then he curled his hands into claws and began scratching her back.

"Oh, jeez, that's *good!*" she cried.

"Just relax and enjoy."

"I am. This project's been killing me."

He nodded and said, "I appreciate your trying to help me."

"We're *gonna* make this work," she said, adding a long pur of contentment. She flung her arms up suddenly and nearly slapped her companion in the face. He jumped back just in time.

"Max!" he chided.

"Sorry. Would you?"

Sighing, he scratched her underarms.

"Ohhhh," she whispered, shivering with delight. "I know it looks silly but it feels sooooo good."

"We all have our zones. Don't be shy. I want to make you feel better."

She looked over her shoulder at him with imploring jade green eyes. Her fun, all-American, Jenny McCarthy/Playboy-model features imparted a mock sadness as she thrust out her sexy lower lip like a little kid.

"Oh, look at that *face,*" said Freddy as if he was talking to a one year-old. "Look at that face! What are we gonna do with that face?"

"I know one thing that could help. I don't know if you'd mind or not. I feel bad asking."

"Do your front?"

"Yeah. I get itchy all over. I don't know if that happens to you, or not, but when I start scratching an itch, the itch just travels. Goes up into my scalp, all the way down into my toes."

"And right now it's somewhere else."

She swallowed hard and nodded.

"Because you're going to go into the office today and make us both filthy rich, I'm not going to charge you for this."

Smiling, she leaned back in her chair and clasped her hands together behind her back. "You have any baby oil?"

"Oh, you want *everything*, don't you?" he said in mock annoyance as he stepped back and headed for the bathroom. "Hold on."

"Thank you." She tried but could not repress another long yawn.

"Stop that!" he called from his small bathroom, which was desperately in need of a cleaning. He popped the medicine cabinet open and rummaged around. "You'll have me doing it next."

Maxine succumbed to another yawn then said, "Sorry."

A light clicked off and Freddy was coming her way, climbing and leaping over piles of crap. He had a collection of Maxfield Parrish prints on one wall and a makeshift bookcase, all bricks and boards, consuming another. His entertainment section, couch, and desk took up a third wall. The fourth contained the front door and the entrance to his bedroom and bath. The kitchen and dining area, all six by ten feet of it, lay behind him. The dining room table was piled up with boxes, newspapers, ceramic dragons, and a host of assorted *kindling,* as he referred to it. Whenever Max came over, they usually ate off the carpeted floor or TV dinner tables.

"This place is a fire hazard," he said. "One match and it's all over."

"Fortunately neither of us smoke."

As he popped the baby oil's cap and smeared a generous amount of lotion on his large hands, Freddy said, "Fortunately."

Nervously, Maxine allowed Freddy to set her arms back at her sides.

"Relax," said Freddy as he started with her shoulders. "You're getting everything that's coming to you."

"Ohhhhhhhhhh."

"You like?" Freddy asked as he worked her tender flesh with even more vigor.

She moaned. It felt wonderful. The tension eased out of her as the pleasure threatened to reach up and overwhelm her.

"Oh, I *love* you," she murmured as she slowly relaxed once more.

"I love you, too, angel," he said as he kissed her on the top of the head. If any other man had kissed her that way, she might shown her appreciation by elbowing them in the solar plexus. At twenty-five, the last thing Maxine Anderson wanted was for any man to treat her like a child. But with Freddy it was all right. She had to have someone with whom she could let her guard down, and she trusted him. On the desk was a watercolor he had painted, a pair of children running through a field, laughing. Below it was written, "And we will be as children, friends and lovers, forever and a day. Amen." She shuddered, suddenly feeling as if she might cry.

"Something wrong?"

"No, it's perfect." Maxine closed her eyes and luxuriated in the feel of Freddy's hands upon her flesh. She leaned back, shaking her head to spill her hair back and over her shoulders. He rubbed the oil over her heart, barely grazing the tops of her breasts, eliciting a low deep moan from his subject. Delicately, he traced the length of her long, elegant neck.

Biting her lip, afraid of rejection, she said, "They hurt."

Freddy leaned forward and gently ran his hands over the expanse of her breasts, feeling her rock hard nipples in his palms. She gasped and sighed as he gripped them harder, squeezing them the way she had told him she liked, then easing off and tracing concentric rings around her breasts until he closed on her nipples and gave them each a little pinch.

In a dreamy, sensuous voice she asked, "If you were straight, would you want to fuck me?"

Freddy leaned in and kissed her cheek from behind. "Of course I would."

"I've got bad teeth."

"A diamond is judged by its flaws."

She rubbed her thighs together quickly enough to start a fire. "Why can't I find a guy like you who's not gay?"

"That's why I said I was worried about you. You're lonely. I can see it in your eyes."

He tilted her forward and went to her back.

"You sure you don't have a hard-on after doing that?" she asked. "I've got great tits. Guys used to pay money to see my tits. Hardly any of them got to do what you just did."

"No offense."

"Can I see for myself?"

"No!"

She laughed. "You got a hard on."

"Shut up!"

"Sorry." She jumped as he sprinkled baby oil directly onto her back. The droplets felt like ice. *"Cold!"*

"Oh, I'm *sorry.*" He wasn't, of course. He rubbed the oil all along her spine. She reached back and tried to touch the front of his robe, curious to see if she *had* made him hard.

"Stop," he said, gently swatting her hand away, "or I won't give you any more."

She put one hand to the side of her head and saluted.

"Better."

From somewhere close came a pitiful mewling. Maxine was now resting her head on the desk. She eased onto her right cheek and saw a pretty tiger-striped cat tentatively entering the room, making small leaps over the piles of clutter everywhere. "Hey, Friendly Cat."

The cat mewled again.

"Someone wants breakfast," Maxine said.

"I know."

"I guess it's a question of which pussy you're going to take care of first. That one or the one I've—"

Freddy backed away. "Okay, playtime's over."

Frowning, Maxine stood and faced her friend. She cupped her breasts and jiggled them. "Most guys would kill their grandmothers to get a shot at these."

"Most guys have IQs of about forty-two. Not that your boobs aren't very lovely, I'm sure, if you're into that sort of thing."

"You were bi when I met you. You had a girlfriend."

"Max."

"I bet you *do* have a boner."

"Child, please!" He went over to the stereo, put in a CD, and raised the volume as "Pussy Control," a song by the artist formerly known as Prince cranked. "This is what you need."

"It's fun to do it to music," she said, one foot swaying nervously, like a schoolgirl trying to get the attention of her favorite teacher. Innocent and slutty all at once.

"Oh, my *God*," Freddy said. "What do I have to do? Hose you down?"

"That sounds like fun."

"Not the way I'd do it. Ever seen the original 'Planet of the Apes'?"

Maxine crossed the room. It was hard to be sexy and flirtatious while navigating through piles of work, but she managed somehow. In a husky voice, she said, "I'd make love to you right now if you wanted me." Her fingers drifted to the zipper of her jeans. The button at her waist was already undone. "I'd let you do anything you want to me. Anything."

"I think you're a sex addict. I mean, seriously."

"Let me go down on you," she said, her chest rising and falling dramatically. There was a desperate yearning in her voice. "You don't have to do anything for me. That'd be enough. I just want to feel you in my mouth."

"Max, you're being a jerk. We both know what this behavior is, now stop it."

She came closer. Touched him. Ran her hand down the front of his robe. "Just close your eyes. It'll feel the same as if it was a guy. I'll even swallow."

"Max!"

Shuddering, she crossed her arms over her breasts and turned away from him. "I'm *horny*. I'm sorry. I always get like this when I've got to do a major presentation. Just feel like some release."

"I'm very glad you feel open enough to tell me all this. Now shut the fuck up."

Sighing, she went into the bathroom, wet a towel, and began to wash the baby oil off her chest and back. After the cat was fed, Freddy came to stand at the door. Her blouse and bra were in his hands.

"I really feel stupid," Maxine said, unable to look at her friend and partner. Her ardor had cooled and her embarrassment was matched only by her hurt that she had put her best friend in such an awkward position. Freddy would do damn near anything to validate her, to prop her up and make her feel better about herself. Lord knows, there were days she needed it, and he was always there for her, no matter what was going on in his life. This had been *wrong*.

"Well, you should feel stupid," said Freddy. "There's no reason to push me away. I'm not going anywhere. I promise."

"Really?"

"Yes."

Maxine looked down at the sink. How many times had she seen her hands against pure white porcelain, watched running water, and wondered how it would feel, how it would *really feel,* to slit her wrists and see her blood running down the rim of the sink, turning pink in the waters? "This presentation means so much to both of us, I don't want to fuck it up."

"You won't." He took another white robe from behind the door and draped it over her shoulders, giving her a hug at the same time.

"I don't deserve you."

"No, but you're stuck with me."

They had met at a Waldenbooks. He had already worked there for five years and she had taken a part-time job to help pay off old debts. Working part-time hadn't done a damn bit of good. Her creditors had been too impatient and she had ended up filing Chapter Eleven. She didn't have much and lost very little in the deal. But it was coming up on the end of her car lease and she was worried about whether the leasing company would allow her to get another car, or buy outright the one she had been driving. She hadn't missed any payments, there was no reason to worry. But lately, with so much riding on what she and Freddy had put together, she was terrified of *everything.*

Despite the "Big B" as she called it, she was still stuck with the student loans. Four years undergrad at half-rate due to a partial scholarship, four years to get her masters in Computer Engineering. Even with a degree from a top school, the best she could do was a second rate position with an up-and-coming software firm. Times weren't just tough, they were impossible.

Today might change all that.

"I really am worried about you," Freddy said. "You shouldn't be alone."

"I've got you." She saw something out of the corner of her eye that made her face break into a wide, lovely smile. "Look at this!"

They both stepped into the bedroom, where they could get a better look at the floor show going on in the living room. Friendly Cat was leaping into the air, pawing at nothingness, bounding from couch to chair and back again, all to the rhythms of the Prince CD.

"That's *funny,*" Maxine said. Her smile dropped and shattered like a mishandled pane of glass. Suddenly, she was shivering, quaking, on the brink of tears. "Jesus, I'm terrified." Her voice was a hoarse whisper.

Freddy took her into his arms. She was taller than he was and had to lean down to rest her face on his shoulder.

"You don't have to be scared," Freddy said as he stroked her long fiery hair, the color of a golden sun. "Neither of us have done anything stupid. If this doesn't work today, we've both got jobs, we're gonna be fine."

"I don't want to be *fine,*" she said. "I want to have some control."

Freddy nodded. He could still remember the night Maxine told him about her parents, how they died in a wreck when she was eleven, how she had been pinned in the car with them, hearing their screams, their begging and pleading and cursing God and each other and even Maxine for their pain until they finally died, her father first, her mother ten minutes later. It was eleven more hours before she was found. One hour for every year she had spent on Earth.

What she needed, more than anything, was some mastery over her own destiny. The shortcut she usually chose, the way she deluded herself into feeling that way quickly, was using her body, her sex, to crush men. Dominate them. It was an old, self-destructive game and she always came out the loser.

The embrace ended. Surrounding them in the bedroom was a gallery of Freddy's watercolors. TROG the Time Traveling Troglodyte, the hero of Freddy's unpublished children's book, starred in a half-dozen of the watercolors. She had scanned a good deal of his art into the presentation. Freddy handed Max her bra and blouse. She peeled off the robe and got dressed.

Freddy popped into the kitchen, shook a box of uncooked linguine, and grinned as Friendly Cat came running. Following him, Maxine raided the fridge, taking an Almond Joy and some naturally sweetened Apple Juice for breakfast.

"*That's* healthy," Freddy said as he opened the box of linguine and knelt down.

"Comfort food. If I'm not going to get fucked, I want some comfort food."

"It's just going to make you wired. You've got an empty stomach."

"Yes, mom."

Freddy shook the box near Friendly Cat. The cat slipped into predator mode and followed it from side to side. He dangled the hardened sticks of pasta before Friendly Cat, who pawed at them, feigned an attack, then dropped back and balanced himself on his back paws to take another swipe. "I was thinking. If this comes through..."

"Don't get too excited. Remember, hope is the enemy here."

"I know. But if it does, I was thinking maybe I could adopt a kid."

"You?" she asked. "You want to be a mother?"

"Hah-hah," he shot back. "I want to be a *parent*. I love kids. I can't think of anything better in life than helping some kid find his way in the world."

"You're gonna make me gag," Max said. "Jeez. That's maudlin."

"I thought you'd see it that way," Freddy said with a laugh. "Think about it, though."

"What do I have to think about it for? *I'm* not going to have a kid for you. I'd be willing to sleep with you, but I'm not going to get pregnant for anyone. That's why I'm on Depro-prevera. Four shots a year, bye-bye period. Hell, that's reason enough."

"You're my friend. I value your opinion."

Max saw that Freddy's expression had changed, growing more vulnerable. He was really serious about this. She knelt down and put her arm around him as she nuzzled her cheek against his. "Sorry, honey."

"It's all right."

"Let's talk about it after. When we go out for dinner tonight."

"Victory or condolence."

"That's right."

"And we're okay either way."

They stared at each other, the excitement, the expectation coursing through each of them.

"Fuck no, we're not," Max said.

Freddy stood up and screamed, "I REALLY, REALLY WANT THIS!"

"ME, TOO!" Max cried.

Unexpectedly, Freddy leaned in and gave her a quick kiss on the lips. She was so taken back, so stunned, that she had no idea how to react. He took it in stride and went back to the living room.

"Come on. It's time to send you packing. You've got to get home, get cleaned up, and get on the road."

"Yeah," Max said, pale, fighting off her initial instinct, which was to fall blindly into shock. *Don't think about it too much, it didn't mean anything.* But that was the weird part. It really *did* mean something to her. That's what made her heart race, her hands tremble. Jesus, she *really did* love this man.

Oh, fucked up! she thought. *Why do I do this to myself?*

Forcing a tight mask of composure upon her beautiful face, Max went into the living room to collect her things.

The offices of Infinity Software were located on the waterfront, in a building a few blocks down from the Seattle Center, facing Elliot Bay. Infinity was housed in a three story building which it shared with a bank on the first floor. Half the second floor and all of the third was taken up by the software firm.

She had changed into a black suit with eight double breasted gold and onyx buttons. The neckline plunged but did not reveal any cleavage, the skirt was mid-thigh and elastic tight. Men had been cutting looks over their shoulders at her since she arrived this morning. She wore black flats instead of pumps. Her jewelry was scarce, carefully chosen. The only true concession she had made to her jittery nerves was the gold bracelet she wore, her good luck charm which she had acquired during her childhood travels. Her dad had flitted between careers as a diplomat and an anthropologist. Max's passport was crammed with dozens of exotic ports of call, many she could no longer remember in any true detail.

The bracelet had strange designs carved into it, runes, someone had once commented at a party. Whenever she wore it, she felt a strange sort of comfort, as if she were jacking in to a direct connection with the parents she had lost when she was eleven, or perhaps her own personal guardian angel. She even knew the angel's face. It had once belonged to a young, handsome, smiling Indian boy. Nothing bad ever happened to her when she wore the bracelet.

On her way into the building, she caught her reflection in the glass door. Her boss would probably think she had a job interview somewhere.

Fuck what he thought. Let the bastard be the one to sweat for once.

As she entered her department, she saw Lauren Price standing near their only window. Lauren was in her forties, with brunette hair piled high, thick round glasses, too much makeup, and a power suit that was passé.

"It's creepy," said Lauren.

SCOTT CIENCIN

"What is?"

"The sun's out. This is *Seattle*. It's creepy." Lauren turned and stared at her. "You look *really* good. Wedding?"

"Something like that." Maxine went to her desk. Her office was a cubicle with gray dividers meant to mute the noise of the other fourteen people who worked in central development. She had a DS/2 terminal that was slower than most of the other machines in the department, despite the Pentium processor. Her printer was a cheap bubble jet, but it sufficed.

The fun creative frenzy that was evident in most software firms was notably absent at Infinity. Sometimes you could hear an employee sneaking in a game of Doom, or catch someone surfing the net for a better job, but on the whole, people worked solemnly, the tone set by their CEO, Ted Brenner.

Brenner was on Maxine's mind this morning. Her two o'clock meeting was with him and his executive staff. Brenner was a pragmatist. If he saw money in a venture, he went after it. All Maxine had to do was convince him that TROG would be the next Tick or Masked Rider. Use the right buzz words and it would be over and done in a half-hour. He wasn't deep and he wasn't particularly bright, but he went after cash the ways sharks went after blood, with relentless ferocity, and that was about all it had taken to build his rep.

When Max had been interviewed by Brenner personally, she thought that she had the fast track to finally putting her skills as a designer and programmer to work. It hadn't turned out that way. Instead, he had convinced her of the value of starting small and learning the business from the ground up.

"When you're ready to make your move, you come to me and we'll see if we can make things happen," the relatively young, handsome CEO had told her.

Eighteen months of drudgery had only strengthened her determination to impress this man.

She knew enough to stay on her guard with him. Ted Brenner was one of those people who could charm anyone, exhibiting a chameleon-like power to become anyone's best buddy. She knew that going in. Even so, she was convinced that he recognized the potential inside her, that in a way, she scared him a little, because she was just like him, she had the same fire, the same ambitions. It was possible that one day they would meet over drinks as equals. For that reason alone, she had decided that he wouldn't screw with her. She could honestly pull this off.

And she had the bracelet. Why worry?

"Maxine?"

She looked up sharply. James Willits, her supervisor, stood before her. Unlike Brenner, Willits was a consummate asshole. Five ten, his strong physique from working out every morning clothed in a Cardigan and a pair of relaxed fit jeans. His long blonde hair was pulled back in a pony tail, and he sported the smug, overconfident look of MacCaulay Culkin's Ritchie Rich all grown up and ready to piss on his peons. The problem, in Maxine's humble opinion, was that Willits had already gone as far as he would ever go in a company like Infinity and he was too butt fuck *stupid* to know it.

Standing next to Willits was a young woman, college age, wearing a practically skintight white dress that did little more than accentuate her chances of being named this year's Queen of Anorexia. She had a pleasant enough face, a few freckles, and a peroxide blonde hair job.

"This is Glynnis," Willits said. "She's a temp. She's here to help you with the filing and whatever else is behind."

"It wouldn't be behind, James, if people just put files back where they found them."

"Why should they? That's your job. Be a good girl. Explain what you do and how she can help. It's bad enough you're leaving on personal business at two." He checked his watch. "I've got a meeting."

Willits hurried away, then stopped and turned slowly, his brow furrowing. "By the way, what's with the suit? You have a funeral to go to or something?"

Yeah, she thought, *yours, asshole. The first thing I'm going to do when I get kicked upstairs is make sure you're on the unemployment line ASAP.* "A wedding."

"Ah." He departed. "Nice."

Max reined in her emotions expertly, just as she had for the past eighteen months. She hadn't mentioned the meeting with Brenner to her supervisor. The last thing she wanted was that little prick sitting in on the presentation, glaring at her when she was trying to seem calm and professional. She would be frightened enough as it was.

Glynnis pulled up a chair and sat beside her co-worker. Putting her head down, Glynnis whispered, "Did he actually say, 'be a good girl?'"

"Uh-huh."

"I don't know if I could put up with that."

"Do you need the money?"

"Yeah."

"You'll put up with it." Max smiled.

Glynnis surveyed Max in her black suit and took in the full impact of the look. "I wish I could look like that in a suit. I just don't have the figure."

You could try eating something once in a while, Max thought, then chided herself for being cruel. "Want to have lunch today?"

"No, I don't eat lunch. I have to do some errands for my husband."

Max nodded. She had tried. "I'll let you in on a little secret. My position might be coming open."

"You're quitting?"

Don't talk about this, Max warned herself, *you'll ruin everything, you'll jinx it.* Though she denied being superstitious, Max attributed the best things that had happened in her life to trusting her instincts. Something was gnawing at her today, something she couldn't quite identify.

Just nerves, she told herself. *That's it.*

"People move around a lot in a company like this," Max said. "Don't tell anyone I spoke about it."

"I won't."

Sure you will, Max thought darkly. *God, I'm an asshole.*

"All right. I'll show you around and introduce you to everyone a little later. Let's start off with an introduction to what I do. You'll be helping me later, once you've got your sea-legs."

"Pardon?"

"Once you feel more comfortable."

"Ah."

Max pointed to a stack of newspapers and magazines on her desk. "See those? It's my job to go through them. Daily Variety, Entertainment Weekly, the Times... I look for anything exciting that we might be able to acquire as a software property. Educational, pure entertainment, topical. Books, articles, comics, movies, toys, arcade games—whatever. When I'm done with that, I go to the Net or I get on the phone with the contacts I've made. There's a whole network of us development types in various companies, we trade information like they used to during the cold war. If there's something that Infinity just isn't going to acquire or can't rip off—sorry—and we've got permission to talk about it, meaning its a blue label file, not a red one, we can use it to barter."

"But if everyone's using the same sources..."

"People come to us directly. Agents, writers, people with interesting stories to tell. Homicide detectives who want to do CD-Roms based on real investigative procedure. Sports figures. Politicians. Kids just off the street. No one's really supposed to admit this, but if it's just the idea that's good, and the person who's attached to it isn't any big deal, what usually happens is they get dismissed, sometimes in such a way that they think their idea isn't worth anything, and then someone here gets an idea—or just happens to have been working on an idea for years—that has some passing similarities. On the other hand, if it's like, y'know, 'Hugh Grant's guide to the ultimate blow-job from an African American hooker on Sunset Boulevard,' well, there you go!"

Glynnis giggled. Her ribs showed through her dress. Max explained about licensing, contracts, the sludge pile of unsolicited submissions, how to handle the phone, and all the other facets of her job. When it seemed that Glynnis was about to be overwhelmed, Max got her started on the filing. It was an old tactic, but it worked beautifully. Glynnis was actually *grateful* to perform the mind-numbing task just so that she wouldn't have to delve into the complex list of responsibilities Max had outlined.

The morning passed sluggishly. Max saw a couple of properties that she might normally pursue, but she didn't see the sense, considering it would just be more competition for TROG.

Maxine knew she had a winner with TROG. There was no question in her mind. TROG had it all. Mortal Kombat-style fighting action, the whole of history (including a nicely constructed vision of the future) as a backdrop, an educational slant, *and* a very moral storyline that should keep idiots like Bob Dole from putting the property on their shit list. Best of all, it was the perfect platform for her secret weapon, which she had been developing for *years*. Now all she had to do was convince Brenner and his cronies.

The phone rang mid-morning. It was Freddy, wanting to know if the meeting was still on. She acted perfectly calm and reassured him. Neither spoke of the kiss that morning, though Maxine had thought about it often. After she got off the phone, Max went into the ladies room, had dry heaves for five minutes, then touched up her make-up and called Brenner's secretary to make sure she *was* still in the book.

Everything was fine. She knew that this meeting was really just a formality, it was a no-brainer that the CEO would jump at what she had to offer, but even so, waiting for the moment when you knew your life would change wasn't easy.

She thought about the kiss again. What would it be like? Her, Freddy, a child? What would it be like to really make love with him? Not to fuck, but to make love?

The questions tortured her all morning.

At lunchtime she went outside, found a secluded spot, and went over the presentation one last time. Everything was perfect. She couldn't miss.

On her way back inside, she saw Roger Aikland sitting on a bench with Julie Pratchett, a new executive assistant. Roger had black hair, a boyish, sympathetic face, and a well defined camp counselor body. He wore a white shirt, dark tie, pleated grey trousers, and freshly polished black shoes. Julie was younger than Max, with naturally curly chestnut brown hair, a roundish face, and a decent figure hidden beneath her poet's blouse and plaid skirt.

They were talking about Arlan, his estranged wife.

Again.

"Sure, she can be over there in Orlando," Roger said, "screwing anyone she wants, but I better not go near anyone, that's what they're telling me. Her lawyer's saying we're still married. But it was over, I'm telling you, the second she said she wanted a divorce. That was it. The only thing binding us together is a piece of paper. And I don't care. Not when I know she's off partying, having a good time."

Julie leaned in close, her eyes brimming with sympathy, a 'what a bitch' half-smile on her face, mixed with some kind of catlike triumph. She was totally drawn in. "That's terrible."

She practically purred the line.

Roger had been promoted over Max, though he was less qualified. It wasn't his fault. He just happened to have a penis, and she didn't. That whole X or Y chromosome thing rearing its ugly head, so to speak. Max didn't hold it against him personally. She tried not to, in any case.

All right, Roger, Max thought, *the weekend's coming and I'm going to do you a favor.*

Max went up to them. "Roger? Can I talk to you for a second?"

He nodded and excused himself. Max led him to the building's main double doors. They were a good hundred feet away from Julie.

"She's ready," Max said simply.

Roger looked to Max, glanced over at Julie, then back at Max again, perplexed. Max sighed. Men just never got it.

"Let me explain something to you," she said. "Women are natural predators. We take in everything when we walk into a room. What color shoes is she wearing?"

Roger started to look Julie's way.

"No, no, no," said Max. "From memory."

"I don't know."

"Was she wearing stockings or were her legs bare?"

"They were *nice.*"

The sigh would not be denied. "White shoes, Naturalizers, stockings, nude."

Roger looked back at Julie, only to find that she was cutting glances in his direction. He smiled. He nearly forgot to check the shoes and stockings. Max was right. He was impressed.

"I could go on all day. All I'm saying is, from the way she's holding herself, that little tremor in her voice you may have noticed—*did* you notice it?—the way she's looking at you, the way she's pushing her chest out at you... If you don't have any urgent plans and you want company this weekend, take her out to dinner, maybe on a floating restaurant, get back to your place really late, find a reason for it to be your place, offer to let her stay if she wants. And make sure your refrigerator's stocked up."

Roger thought about it. A wide smile broke out on his handsome face. "No!" he said, the word coming out, *nooooooo*, though what he really meant was, *you think? Really?* An idea came to him. "Did she put you up to this? Is this a gag?"

Max patted him on the arm. "Buy her roses. Just do me a favor? Don't be a jerk. If she offers to start doing your laundry, don't be a typical *guy*. Guys *suck*. Men are what we want. Offer to do *hers.*"

With that, Max turned and went back inside. Roger called after her, "Hey, you look really nice!"

Max's shoulders bunched together. Bad move. Julie would not appreciate that, but she would probably let it slide. Max didn't turn around to see what would happen. She had done her good deed for the day, and it made her feel better, especially after the scene with Freddy this morning. She hoped her friend would forgive her, though she knew deep down that he already had. The only thing for her to work out was the odd feeling she got in her gut every time she thought about him. He was a homosexual male. What kind of future was there in that? And did she even *want* to start thinking about a man she could have a future with?

More complications...

Soon she was back at her desk with another hour to go. The wait was excruciating. She was terrified that at any time, the phone would ring and she would be informed that her appointment had been cancelled.

It didn't happen. Instead, Roger and Julie passed by her desk. Julie seemed a little smug. Roger was beaming.

Well, good. Something was working right today. The laws of the universe hadn't suddenly been altered.

Then her boss came over to her, dumping a fresh load of files on her desk. "I need coverage of these materials before you leave."

Barely restraining her panic, Max saw that it was ten minutes after one. She would have fifty minutes to complete a three hour long project. "I'll do what I can."

"Get it done." He walked away.

"Bite my fucking ass," she whispered, low enough that even Willits wouldn't hear it with his super-powered, ultra-enhanced rat-fuck snitch-senses.

Just hold on, this is the end of it. Pretty soon you won't have to put up with this.

In a way, having this impossible project dumped on her was a relief. When it became clear that there was no way for her to get done in time, she went to the copy machine, made a duplicate of the materials, then stuck the duplicate in her desk drawer. She printed out as much as she had, then dumped it on Willits' desk at five minutes to two.

"You're done?" he asked, amazed.

"Fast work," she said, lying. She knew damn well that he wouldn't even open the file folder she had just handed him until the middle of next week. By then, she would either be working out of the third floor, or better, a home office—*or* she would have come back with her tail between her legs and finished the project off, replacing the file before he knew any better.

She went upstairs, feeling an odd, delirious calm washing over her. In the lobby, she went to the dial-in desk, punched in her ident code, then stood near the glass double doors to the executive branch and waited for Mrs. Lang, Brenner's personal assistant, to come get her.

As she waited, she traced the runes on her gold bracelet.

And prayed.

Secretaries and receptionists were a thing of the past, victims of automation. But executives never got tired of having someone else answer their phones, open their mail, and schedule their appointments. Mrs. Lang, Brenner's personal assistant, led Max to the conference room.

"Nice perfume," Max said as they walked down the corridor.

"It's new." Mrs. Lang would venture nothing more. She spoke with a soft, reassuring British accent.

They reached the conference room. The door was open and the group was already assembled. Max entered and was immediately aware of the strong scent of cologne that hung in the air. It wasn't a terrible smell. In fact, it was rather appealing, whatever it was. Max had never encountered this scent, either. The strangest thing was that every man in the conference room wore the same cologne.

What a bunch of kiss asses, Max thought as she took her place at the far end of the table, smiling confidently though all she wanted to do was run at lightspeed for the john. Mrs. Lang left the room and closed the door behind her.

The scent came to Max again. Max couldn't believe that a moment ago she found this smell pleasant. It reeked of ginger.

The foul odor gave her something else to focus on, and made these men seem that much less intimidating. They might all have been making the big bucks, but not one of them realized that they smelled like a garbage dump in the Asian district.

She raised her portfolio as she thanked Mr. Brenner and the other four men present for their time. They all wore dark business suits. The image of monkeys climbing trees was printed on Brenner's silk tie.

Ted Brenner looked like old money, with elegantly styled black hair and piercing, soulful eyes. His slight trace of jowls softened what might have been a powerful and angry countenance. Surrounding him were four men Max didn't recognize. The execs in charge of Marketing, Sales, Development, and Resources, she guessed. Max found that she couldn't focus on any of the Four Horsemen. They were faceless. Only Brenner captured her attention.

She launched into her presentation, distributing handouts as she said, "His name is TROG, gentlemen. This little guy is the going to be the one who puts Infinity Software on the map."

As she slipped a copy of the presentation in front of Brenner, she saw him smile. That was enough. She had him.

The rest would be easy.

She spoke for close to twenty minutes about the merchandising possibilities, the multi-media crossovers, the editors she had lined up at Random House Juvenile, and the contact at a major animation house, who was chomping at the bit to see what she had. The networks needed something new for Saturday mornings.

Then she hit them with her final round of ammo.

Calmly, though she still couldn't quite believe she was in this room, talking with these people, she fished a small black box out of her pocket. Her index finger fit snugly into it. She pulled a tiny antenna out, then opened her powerbook and logged onto the TROG mock-up. A medieval setting that she had cribbed from Doom and enhanced with her own elements appeared. Twisting narrow corridors, a medieval cathedral with swords melted into the stone walls.

A Cathedral of Swords.

The imagery had presented itself to her since childhood in a series of re-occurring dreams. Demons that she had reconfigured into armored warriors rushed at the camera.

"Watch carefully, gentlemen. You're going to see something you've never seen before."

The screen's perspective suddenly shifted. The viewer was suddenly dodging out of the warriors' path, a sword reaching up into the screen.

Max's finger, aimed at the monitor screen, didn't move.

"Well, it's a demo," one of the other execs said. "So?"

Max drew a circle in the air and the game abruptly froze. She cocked her head to one side, no longer nervous at all. "I don't think you're getting this. Mr. Brenner? Would you put this on your finger and be our Weaponsmaster, please?"

He shrugged and held out his hand.

"Right index finger," she prompted, watching as he fit the wand onto his finger. "Now here's what I want you to do. Keep your hand still and think about moving forward."

On the powerbook's screen, the perspective changed suddenly, the "camera" leaping forward.

"Oh, my God," Brenner whispered.

"*Think* about moving back. To the left. The right."

He did. The images on the screen changed.

"Look, you're being threatened! Do something about it!"

A handful of soldiers attacked. A pair of hands and a sword appeared on the viewer. It was wielded clumsily and the soldiers made short work of the player. Now all the execs were huddled around Brenner, mouths agape.

"This is right brain, left brain stuff," said Max. "I know it seems like something out of a Star Trek movie, but it's not that complicated, and it's *real*. Draw an X in the air with your finger."

Brenner did as she commanded. Max *loved* giving this man orders. The screen went back to a main menu page. Brenner stared down at the mechanism on his finger in wonder. Max produced another set of handouts from her portfolio and distributed them as Brenner's lap dogs passed the gadget around and started playing with it.

"What we have here is a prototype ready for patenting. Other designers are fooling around with similar setups, but they haven't brought it along the way I have. I call it the Point and Shoot system. It interprets electrical impulses from the brain. With this system, thinking *literally* makes it so."

Brenner grinned ear to ear. "You're a little miracle, aren't you?"

"I am if you say I am."

"I'm saying it."

"Then I am."

This was better than she could have hoped. Max's heart felt as it might explode at any moment. She was feeling lightheaded, but she was too crazed with enthusiasm to sit down. Hell, if she passed out, she passed out. Fuck it.

"The papers I've just given you contain schematics, all my work," Max said. "It's all laid out."

Brenner and one of his assistants scanned the new pages. Without looking up, Brenner murmured, "To say I'm very impressed is too grotesque an understatement, so I won't even bother. I know you're overqualified for the kind of work you've been doing. I know what it's been like for you because you're a woman. Your department's a boy's club. Hell, the western *world* is nothing but a boy's club. You get a bunch of guys in sales, they're laughing and joking about the women they've got on the side, who they've fucked, whatever, a woman walks in, they just shut up."

Max nodded. Brenner had it down. He knew exactly how it had been for her. What startled her was how bluntly he phrased it. She hadn't expected him to speak to her with this kind of openness. Not ever. She had to struggle not to get choked up with relief. It was all working out.

Brenner and his aide continued to scan her papers. "So you work your ass off to get their trust and they loosen up and suddenly you're invisible and they'll talk about anything in front of you, they don't see you, they don't think about what kind of effect any of this has on you. Now you're less than nothing."

He looked up at her. For the first time, Max noticed his eyes. A light blue-gray. Gorgeous.

"You've been looked over for three promotions since you've been here. That's a lot."

"Read, read!" Max said, gesturing with a shaky hand.

Brenner nodded and went back to the text. Someone handed him the Point and Shoot back. He put it on his finger and went into the game again.

How could he do that? she wondered. Concentrate on what he was reading while carrying on a conversation *and* playing a video game? The man wasn't human.

That's why he's earning the big bucks, Max. You're here. You've arrived. Enjoy it.

"Men don't want to work with women," Brenner was saying. "Don't want to be partnered up with them. They figure a woman's not going to carry her weight, she's going to have to be protected. No one's going to do that with you any more. You're going to be watched, and judged, and rewarded accordingly. And you're not going to have to become one of the boys, or put aside your humanity, your being a woman. You are going to be in a unique position. I'm promising you, from this point on, you're going to be afforded the same treatment as any man here, the same opportunities, the same benefits. Everything. You will have a voice that will be heard."

Maxine was stunned. She unconsciously touched the bracelet, her fingers tracing over the odd patterns.

This was amazing, she knew. She had believed in herself, believed in the project, and she had won. Her entire life really was about to change.

"Brilliant," Brenner said, unable to stop shaking his head. "Truly. So—anyone downstairs can take this apart and see how it's done?"

"Yes, I set this presentation up with that in mind," Max said. On some instinctive level, she knew that was the wrong answer to give. But it was an honest one. She was aware that they were going to want to verify her findings. Who wouldn't?

What she had done would sound like Michael Crichton territory to those who hadn't actually witnessed the mechanism at work. The potential applications of the software reached far beyond simple video games. The military, the auto industry, aviation—the possibilities were endless.

She was going to be a billionaire. All her evenings and weekends lost to this damn thing were finally going to pay off.

"It *is* all here," the development exec reading the papers beside Brenner whispered.

"Well, that's fabulous. Then we don't need her anymore." Brenner's expression never changed.

Max's heart seized up.

Looking up, Brenner smiled warmly. "You can go now. I think you have some personal hours or something coming to you."

Every muscle in Max's body seemed to tighten. Her head felt light and the room started to spin. "Is this a joke?"

"What do you mean?" asked Brenner.

"We—um, there's so much to do."

"It'll be handled. Have yourself a good afternoon."

"Waitaminute!"

Brenner's expression was totally open and innocent.

"What's going on here?" Max asked.

The CEO shrugged. "I don't know, Ms. Anderson. What do *you* think is going on here?"

"I think you're trying to screw me. This is ridiculous. Are you interested in this system I've brought to you?"

"Interested? It's fabulous."

"So—when do we start talking about terns for acquisition?"

Brenner seemed mystified.

"I'm not here as an employee of Infinity Software," Maxine said, stunned that she had to stand here and explain this so late in the game.

"But you *are* an employee," said Brenner.

"I know, but I'm on my own time right now. I designed the Point and Shoot Mech on my own time, with my own resources. I started it when I was in college. And TROG belongs to me and Fred Southby. This is something he's been working on for years."

"TROG is okay," said Brenner. "It's the Point and Shoot that I care about."

Max had to grip the back of a nearby chair. She felt as if she was going to faint. "So—when do we start negotiating?" she asked hesitantly. "I suppose under normal circumstances I should have had an attorney and an agent present, but as an employee…"

"Well, this is interesting," said Brenner. "You seem to be confused as to *when* you're an employee of this company and when you're *not*. Let me try and clarify matter for you."

Oh, Jesus, Max thought, struggling to stay on her feet. The trap she had fallen—no, willingly leaped into was coming clear. Why in God's name hadn't she patented the Point and Shoot? What she had been thinking?

"Ms. Anderson, you seem to be operating under a fundamental misconception about the nature of your work here," Brenner said calmly. "You don't *have* a private thought when you work for this company. Check your contract. Anything you develop, anything you even participate in developing, legally becomes the full property of Infinity Software. That includes work you do in unpaid hours. There's no reason for our discussing terms of acquiring the Point and Shoot system that you developed because we already own it legally."

Max felt sick.

"Also, you had a hand in the development of this TROG business. That means we own at least a fifty per-cent share of the property. How could you not have known that?"

"Everything you just said—"

"I'm treating you the same way I would any employee, Ms. Anderson. That's what I promised you. Don't worry, we'll be perfectly fair. If any of this turns a profit, we'll be sure to keep you in mind, and look favorably upon you when the next chance for a promotion comes around."

Max was speechless. She had come into this meeting more than willing to play hardball. But *this* was surreal. The odd scent these men gave off was getting even more pungent. She had to fight not to gag over the smell.

"You're serious, aren't you?" Max asked finally.

"Tell you what I'll do," said Brenner. "Have this Southby person, the one who developed the game with you, call and schedule an appointment. Does he have an agent?"

He'll get one, she thought. *I'll make sure of that. And a ton of lawyers.* "Yes."

"Have his agent call, then. I'm sure we can come to reasonable terms to buy out his interest in this."

Maxine shook her head, trembling. "This is—"

"Simple facts of life," said Brenner. "You can fight, but you can't win. If you fight, you'll be finished in this business. No one will hire you again. Ever. They'll think of you as trouble. If you try to go anywhere else with the Point and Shoot, there'll be legal ramifications. If your partner tries to sell this TROG character anywhere else we can taint it sufficiently that he'll never get a buyer."

This can't be happening, Max thought. *It just isn't possible.*

"No one wants trouble," Brenner continued evenly, *reasonably*. "If there's potential legal action involved, if there are questions of authorship, then TROG is dead. Simple facts of life. Do you really want to do that to your friend?"

Max came forward and started to collect her materials.

"I wouldn't do that, if I were you," Brenner said. "There are other factors that you have yet to consider."

But wait folks, there's more! She hesitated, feeling dizzy. "Like what?"

Brenner nodded to the gentleman two seats to his left. A prematurely greying man with deep blue eyes and a rugged face.

"This is Greg Callan," said Brenner. "I don't know if you recognize him from legal. Greg's best friend from Harvard is an expert in bankruptcy law." He turned to the legal consultant. "Now, Greg, correct me if I'm wrong, but couldn't it be argued that if Ms. Anderson really did possess even the raw concept for this Point and Shoot system at the time of declaring her Chapter Eleven bankruptcy—"

Oh, shit, she thought. *They knew. Fuck, what else did they know? Hey folks, here's some photos of our girl Max lap dancing at Paradys Lost in L.A. when she was seventeen, here's a few of her detoxing at nineteen, and a rare one, fellas, one of her turning snitch and testifying state's evidence against Phil Suello, a former boyfriend, to ensure that she would have no criminal record for her own part in his drug trafficking. And did we mention that he killed himself in prison and left a note that said, "This one's for you, Maxine"?*

Step right up!

She forced herself to focus on what Brenner was saying. She would not give this man the satisfaction of seeing her fall apart in front of him. Straightening herself out and getting her ass through college and graduate school had been a hard enough road. She wasn't going to let him destroy her.

"—so Greg, this system *would* then be regarded as an undeclared asset, correct?"

LIGHTNING UNDER GLASS   275

"Yes," said the lawyer. "When a person declares bankruptcy, they have to submit an inventory that includes all their assets, physical, intellectual, everything, as of the day they're declaring. In essence, a snapshot is taken. They're free and clear from that day forward. If they win the lottery the next day, their creditors are out of luck. In fact, that's actually happened. If they come up with the idea for, say, a revolutionary technology the next day, they're also going to be fine. But if they conceal anything and that's discovered later, they could be in dire trouble."

"And Ms. Anderson could be facing criminal charges for her glaring omission? For not mentioning the Point and Shoot?"

"Absolutely, Ted."

Brenner nodded. He looked back to Max. "Now—we're all friends here, Ms. Anderson. So long as you play fair, there's no reason why any of us would be moved to go to the courthouse, find out the name of your trustee, and send the man a letter."

Max thought about it. There had to be a backdoor out of this. There always was. Then she saw it. Forcing herself to hold her head up, she tried not to quiver as she said, "It cuts both ways, Mr. Brenner. If you do that, I might very well get into trouble. But the Point and Shoot system would then become the property of my creditors. And *you lose.*"

A long, low breath escaped Greg the lawyer. Brenner tensed a little at this. Not much.

Game over, Max thought, unwilling to feel even a microbe of relief until she was sure.

"Be that as it may, Ms. Anderson," Brenner said. "Our initial argument still holds."

"Respectfully, sir, the hell it does," said Max, feeling a little stronger.

Brenner was intrigued, and slightly off-balance. "How do you come to that conclusion?"

"Either we work this out, or I'll petition the bankruptcy court myself."

"I doubt that you'd want to go to jail."

Max shrugged and hopped up on the desk. The wide and stunning expanse of her legs, from less than two inches past her hips, caught the attention of every man in the room except Brenner. "I'll tell you how I figure it. I'm crazy. I don't care. I've worked too long and too hard to be fucked over by you or anyone else at this point in the game. You think I won't go to the trustee? His name's Phillip Meyer. It's not something I'm about to forget. If you want, I'll call him right now. No problem."

Brenner considered her. "You might go to jail."

"And your Board will find out that you had a cutting edge technology that would have made this company hundreds of billions in your hands and you blew it right out your officious backside. So what's it going to be?"

Brenner waited. "Bring her a phone."

Someone did. Max glanced at the lawyer. "You have the number handy?"

With that, everything stopped. No one moved, no one spoke.

Max was serious. She would call if she had to. She couldn't let Brenner win. Still, the situation was insane. It was as if the fabric of reality had changed around her in a heartbeat and she had been left out of the loop.

"What do you want?" Brenner said finally.

"By-line credit for the Point and Shoot system. A two per-cent gross royalty on any and all profits that come from it. Seed money to start up my own company which will assist in the development of this property at terms to be negotiated and give Infinity Software a first look at all new ideas we generate, though we will retain sole ownership and our own identity as a company. I also want approval at every stage of this product's development and approval on all licenses."

The room was dead silent.

"At least you don't want much," Brenner said. Everyone but Maxine laughed.

"Some of what you've asked for is negotiable," Brenner said. "But if we can come to terms, it will be with the understanding that we're in this solely for the rights to the Point and Shoot system. Your collaborator and his game go into turnaround. You cannot hire him, you can have no professional or personal contact with him. If it ever becomes known—and you will be watched—that you so much as gave him fifty cents for a newspaper, any and all of your personal and company assets become property of Infinity. You also sign a confidentially waver so that if the content of this deal is ever revealed to anyone besides the select group of attorneys that we mutually agree upon, your holdings are again liable for seizure."

Max slowly eased off the table. This man was the devil. Plain and simple. "That's about the scummiest thing I've ever heard in my life."

"It's the only way you'll get what you want."

"Why would you want to do this to Freddy?" she asked, cursing herself for referring to him this way.

"I don't. It cuts both ways, as you said. If you sign off on your rights to Point and Shoot, we'll put TROG into major development and your friend will receive a tidy sum—which he can share with you, if he's so inclined. I predict high six figures. So it's up to you. I'll help you, or I'll help him. This isn't a charity."

Maxine was outraged. "With all due respect, sir, I'd go so far as to say this is a business. And in business, it's always wisest to reward your employees when they do something to make you look better to the board and to make the company a shitload of money."

"Please. The language."

She was losing it. "I've been loyal. I've done everything right. This shouldn't be happening."

"It can, so it will."

Maxine hugged herself. "So either Freddy gets a piece of the action, and I have to depend on a kickback from him for my own work, or he gets screwed and I get what's rightfully entitled to me?"

"The latter can be argued."

Incredulous, she breathed out, "You *are* a motherfucker."

Brenner made a dismissive gesture with his hands. "I won't take that personally."

"I'm sure you won't. Why would you?"

"I think you're a little distraught, Maxine. May I call you that?"

"Most guys who try to fuck me up the ass usually call me by my first name, yeah. I encourage that, generally. But not with you. You're the exception."

"Take the weekend. Think it over."

She collected up her paperwork and the powerbook. "What if I just burn everything?"

"Then everybody loses. You'll be fired, then the police will be knocking on your door for industrial espionage and the willful destruction of Infinity Software property."

Maxine couldn't help but laugh. "You're really too much. How exactly would you prove any of this ever existed?"

"Well, there is the videotape record of this meeting."

One of the other men nudged him. "DAT."

"Whatever," he said sharply.

Maxine's gaze traveled over to a nearby mirror. "Son of a bitch."

Another of the advisors spoke up. "The version investigators would receive would be somewhat edited, of course. That can be done seamlessly. Or technical difficulties could be blamed for missing sections."

Maxine sat down hard and ran her hand through her hair. She had noticed one of the Four Horseman holding up the papers at an odd angle, as if he wanted to be sure they could be read by someone over his shoulder. The mirror was directly behind him. They had her work on tape. "You had no idea what I was bringing to you today."

"None," Brenner said. "You were wise enough not to work on your project on any of our computers, or when you were on-line at home."

"But you had me checked out, found all my weaknesses. You had a whole strategy worked out just on the off-chance that I was bringing you something decent."

"Standard procedure. I like to be prepared for anything," Brenner said. He was still wearing the Point and Shoot prototype. "I would call your coming to us today with such a wonderful product a happy accident. Most of the pitches we have to listen to are terrible."

Max got to her feet, walked over to him, and yanked at the Point and Shoot, twisting it up and back. Because Ted Brenner's finger was still in it at the time, there was a sharp high crackling. Brenner howled in agony, his eyes fading back in their sockets from the sudden pain. Maxine slid the Mech from his broken finger.

"I'm sorry, did that hurt?" she asked.

He looked down at his forefinger, which was bent at an impossible angle. "You fucking bitch!" he roared. "You broke my fucking finger!"

"Sure didn't mean to," she said, repressing a smile. She went to the door and hauled it open. "You're right. Let's talk Monday. If you're in Monday. Terrible thing about your hand. I guess that's *not* what you would call a happy accident, huh?"

Before anyone could respond, she was in the hall with the door closed behind her. A few minutes later, she was in the stairwell, shaking and crying. She pulled out the Point and Shoot Mech, tossed it to the ground, and raised her foot over it. In her mind, she saw herself smashing the Mech to pieces, then going home, reformatting her hard-drive, burning all hard copy records.

She nearly lost her balance from standing on one foot for too long. Feeling like the worst human who had ever walked the face of the earth, Max bent down and picked up the Point and Shoot. She couldn't just destroy it. There had to be a way to fix this. To make things all right for her *and* Freddy. She loved him, for God's sake. The question was, did she love him enough not to sell him out?

What she needed was a miracle. A backdoor. There was *always* a backdoor. She would find it. The whole weekend was in front of her. She would tell Freddy what happened, they would work through this.

First, she needed to get seriously wasted.

2

Dublin, Ireland.

"God almighty, it's like walking the plank," Neve whispered as she crossed her thin arms over her pale chest and shuddered. The fifteen year-old stood behind a pair of heavy curtains, looking out from the thin slit between them. Ahead was a long runway that looked for all the world—to her at least—like a man's *thingie* adorned with Christmas lights. Hundreds of people crowded around the runway, which was housed in an abandoned but still breathtaking church. Photographers, celebrities, and newshounds from all over the world waited in impatient silence. Attention '97, one of the premiere fashion events of the season, was nearly at an end. Moments ago, the techno-grind of some German band had played, signalling the transition to the final collection of the evening. When no one had appeared, the music faded, leaving only silence. That was replaced by murmurs. Coughing. Laughter and confusion. The music had started again and soon faded once more.

Still *nothing*.

All Neve had to do was walk out in this ridiculous outfit and the music would rise up, the curtains would part, and the Enigma Fashions presentation would be underway. She understood how important this was to the owner of Enigma, a stunningly beautiful man whom she now considered a friend. He had risked everything he owned to win the closing position in the show. If he failed here, he would be ruined. And it was all in her hands.

Neve was frozen.

Behind the attractive, auburn-haired fifteen year-old, a dozen of the world's most glamorous and beautiful women waited for the chance to earn their outrageous salaries. Some made $2,000 an hour, or ten to twenty grand per show. Sets were ready to be swung into place, a huge emblem made of papier mâché was set to drop. All Neve had to do was get her backside in motion. She reached out to the tall, slim woman beside her, grasping the other woman's hand.

"I can't. I'm terrified," Neve said, her chest rising and falling dramatically.

"Maybe later, after someone else starts."

Alisa Aleman, the model standing beside Neve, squeezed her hand. What Neve had described was not an option. Dozens of celebrities that Enigma had been courting since the Oscars had arrived, most of them anxious for a look at Neve. If the child didn't go on first and get it over with, she would never go out there at all.

"Once you're on stage, it's pretty exciting," said Alisa. She managed to conceal her impatience. *Dammit, child, you stood in front of Hollywood royalty and the entire world when you accepted your Oscar and you were calm enough then. This is just a runway with a few hundred people watching. Big hairy deal!*

Alisa instantly regretted the harsh thoughts. Neve was established as an actress, confident in her abilities. But she had gone on record saying that she didn't feel she was particularly attractive. Enigma's owner, who also happened to be Alisa's fiancé, had flown personally to Wyoming, where Alisa's family had a ranch, to talk her into opening his show.

Convincing Neve Ryan to appear had been a coup. The auburn-haired fifteen year-old actress had already won two Golden Globes before her Oscar. She had been labeled the next Winona Ryder and she had publicly countered with, "Hell I am, I'm the first Neve Ryan!" Instead of coming off haughty, she once again charmed the world. She was currently filming a movie with Meryl Streep and Robert DeNiro, and the buzz was that she was blowing both of them off the screen.

In person, she was one of the few celebrities Alisa had met who was actually more formidable, who radiated *more* raw energy and luminescence off screen than on. Despite this, the child was thoroughly intimidated by her surroundings and present company. Pictures of supermodels, Alisa's among them, had been tacked up on Neve's wall. They were the standard she judged her own beauty against. Alisa had hoped that being backstage with the other models, seeing how amazingly *ugly* some of them were without their make-up, would boost her confidence. Instead, though Neve had spooked most of the models with her unassuming grace and natural beauty, the child had regarded the models as if they were goddesses from another, better age.

She had looked at Alisa the same way. Alisa Aleman had a classical, old world look. She was European, with haunted eyes, naturally curly chestnut hair, about as much of a bust as Christy Turlington, and a perfect backside. She could do a Kate Moss pout and deliver the goods without press about anorexia. When she wore something revealing, her chest did not look like an air conditioning grill. It had been enough to make her a millionaire by age twenty-three.

Alisa made it a point of seeming perfectly relaxed, though her stomach was tightening into knots at the fifteen year-old's reticence. She had to get Neve out there. Where in hell was her loving fiancé? All they had worked for was threatening to crash down around them and he had vanished, leaving her to deal with the fallout. It wasn't the first time, but usually his reckless behavior was limited to their personal life. In business, at least, he was very responsible.

What would *he* do if he were here?

Alisa shrugged. Casually, she said, "Maybe it's just as well. I didn't want to tell you this, but I heard Mel's out there."

"No!" said Neve. "The rat bastard?"

"The same."

An icy determination lit in Neve's gorgeous eyes. "Does he have anyone with him?"

"Some blonde."

"Cheryl." Neve squeezed her friend's hand and performed an act of transformation unlike any Alisa had ever seen. The fifteen year-old straightened her back, thrust out her chin, and changed from a frightened, gawky teenager into the embodiment of Hollywood royalty. Visions were immediately conjured of Grace Kelly and Audrey Hepburn in their prime mixed with the innocence of Lillian Gish and the raw sexuality of Ingrid Bergman.

Alisa held her breath.

"Let's show the rat-fucker what he's missing, shall we now?" asked Neve. Then she boldly strutted onto the stage.

Alisa raced for the wings. The music was a few beats too late, but they could compensate. The curtains started to rise as gasps and overwhelming applause exploded from the audience.

Neve wore an outrageous costume, made almost entirely from dozens of firearms and strung together with strategically placed leather ammo belts. Unloaded Glock 19s, Intratec DC-9s, Rettingers, Smith and Wessons, and Rugers clanked against her seemingly nude flesh. She spun, revealing more of her backside than a stripper with only a g-string, then ambled down to the edge of the platform and peeled back her ammo vest to flash her tits at the stunned photographers. Later, the disappointment that she was wearing a sheer body suit would set in, but for now, the shooters were eating it up.

As a canned Joe Satriani electric guitar wail delivered "God Bless America," the papier mâché emblem gently floated down into view. It was a large round sign that said PC and had a red slash cut diagonally through the circle.

The other models started coming up as Neve turned, leaned all the way down to show off the perfect V of her long legs, and whipping one of the pistols from her costume, thrusting it out from between her legs.

Behind her, all manner of madness came up on the stage. A pair of foul-mouthed smokers strutted up behind Neve wearing real furs. Heavily muscled young men pulled handcarts upon which lay actors made up to look like the homeless. Models literally tread upon them as they reached the stage. More insanity followed: Women made up to look like trees from the rain forest, painted green with huge twisted brown limbs flowing from their bodies. Behind them, samurais following close, slicing off the fake limbs as the models shrieked with orgasmic delight. Doctors kicked the elderly down stairs. Women beat the living hell out of stuffed dogs and cats wearing the sign, "hey, we're cruel to one another, why not?"

Alisa smiled. The audience was both stunned and taken. The Maestro's instincts had been correct once again.

What most people who were not in the business failed to understand was that *this* part of the presentation was all about showmanship and competition. It was Vegas, grand theatrics, nothing more, meant to wake up a bored and tired audience. Going over the top was only the beginning. Also, it was a chance for the designers to express themselves as artists. No one on earth was really expected to wear these bizarre designs. The real clothing that people could wear on the street would be paraded before the crowd soon.

Alisa saw Neve coming back, laughing and jiggling her collection of unloaded firearms. From the young woman's bright face and triumphant expression, Alisa knew that Neve had been unable to see anything over the bright flashing lights. She had no idea that Alisa had lied, that the child's former boyfriend was not in the audience. When the lie was revealed, it would cost both women. Alisa's friendship with Neve would be ruined, and Neve's ability to trust would be in for a serious beating. After tonight, the child would have taken one more step toward becoming a hardened corporate commodity, a monster like most in Hollywood. Best of all, Alisa was to blame.

She felt like shit, but at least the show would be a success. That was all that was really mattered, now wasn't it?

Alisa turned and motioned to one of her assistants. "Get Neve in her next change."

"Where will you be?" asked the assistant.

"Finding out where my *beloved* is hiding." With that, Alisa ducked around to the stairs leading to the offices on the second floor. The small corridors were crowded. She passed models wearing Chewbacca hairstyles, others sporting orange and blue nail polish and riding crops. A girl stepped on her foot. Alisa looked down and saw a black shoe with penises rising off it. Then it was gone. All around her, models thrust themselves her way. Big hair, big feathers, big boas, and in some cases, big boobs. All the required equipment. And tall. She couldn't forget that. 5'9 was optimal. That way, designers could make a generic version of a dress and cast the right model later. Besides, tall women had smaller looking heads. The same head on a petite woman looked huge and strange in photos. So much bullshit, so little time...

Shoving past a pair of Marie Antoinettes wearing red silk bands around their throats and talking Valley speak, she managed to press herself through the door to their wing. There she discovered an oasis of quiet in the form of a small wood paneled outer office. It led to their recently converted suite where they would meet the reporters later. A banquet had been prepared for the reception.

Left to stand guard was Tommy Tuesdell. Nineteen, thin, suicide blonde close cropped hair, an earring, a touch too much mascara. His eyes were emerald and piercing, his face thin, his nose carved to a point by surgery.

"So where is he?" asked Alisa.

The young man looked away.

"Tommy?"

Still nothing.

"Tommy can you hear me?" she asked in a sing-song. "Can you feel me near you?"

The young man allowed a tortured half-smile to emerge. He had broken up with a lover several months earlier and to cheer him up, Alisa had taken him to a performance of "Tommy" in Quebec, then smuggled him backstage. It wasn't hard for her. She was known the world over. Instant, fleeting fame.

"He's in there," Tommy said, gesturing at the closed doors at the far side of the room.

Alisa heard music, voices.

As if he was making it up on the spot, Tommy blurted, "He's taping a response to the press!"

Surprised, Alisa said, "He's not going to talk to them?"

Nervous, Tommy shrugged. "I don't think you should go in there. Y-y-you know how he gets."

Alisa felt a sudden stabbing fear. She knew in that instant what was going on. A part of her knew better than to go into the main area of the suite. That's what he wanted. Better to just leave the ring with Tommy, go now, and never have anything to do with him again.

She went to the door. Opened it swiftly and darted inside, her heart racing.

Over the music, she heard the voices more clearly now. Racks and racks of clothing obscured her view, but she could identify at least one of the participants in the event taking place around the corner easily enough. She had heard those same animal sounds many times during lovemaking. Alisa walked through the narrow corridor of bagged clothing and saw the banquet table dead ahead.

Alisa turned the corner. She took it all in immediately, just as she was meant to.

Her fiancé, Julian Ibiero, was screwing a nineteen year-old Latina from behind. He had her bent over a chair. Both were facing her way. It was all carefully staged.

Without missing a stroke, he looked up and said, "Hi, honey. How's it going?"

Alisa glanced in the direction of the buffet. It was a smorgasbord of macrobiotic delights that had been specially prepared by Akasha Khalsa, Michael Jackson's personal cook. The spread had been Alisa's idea and she had made all the painstaking arrangements in person. Julian's dog, Butch, a large black fluffy mutt, was up on the long table, busily chomping away at the spread. A path of chaos and destruction lay along the entire left flank of the table, where Butch had clearly started. His mouth was caked with white and green cucumber sauce. He made obscene slurping noises as he chowed down on a souffle that was costing Enigma ninety dollars a serving.

"Aren't you feeling all right?" asked Julian.

I feel numb, Alisa thought, but no words came.

Below Julian was Gina Gala, a statuesque Latina with dark flowing hair that reached to the middle of her bare back, generous breasts, a tiny waist, perfect hips, and legs a mile long. Her lips were bulbous, naturally so, no lip implants, no reconstruction anywhere along her perfect body. Yet. She was almost twenty. Her time would come soon enough.

"He's got a really nice cock," Gina said with a laugh as she thrust herself back against Julian. She gasped and rolled her eyes, tightening her grip on the desk. "You should try this sometime."

"I'm doing fine," said Alisa, struggling to maintain her composure in the face of her fiancé's blatant display of loathing toward her.

Six years ago, Julian Ibiero had come out of nowhere and taken the fashion industry with the same reckless abandon he now displayed toward his new lover. He had no degree from Parsons, the New York school known as the Harvard of the fashion industry. What he had was style, boldness, and unerring instincts when it came to predicting and creating trends in the market. He was despised by most of his fellow designers, because unlike them, he was not in love with fashion. He left it to the Donna Karans and the Calvin Kleins of the world to proclaim that they were maniacs over fashion, that there was nothing more important in their lives.

In the eight months since they had become engaged, in the *two years* that Alisa had known Julian, she was still uncertain of what, if anything, he really did live for. Now she knew:

Pain.

He was handsome, lean, but exquisitely muscled. His rich black hair reached down past his collar and was feathered but still spiky enough to look a bit wild. His eyebrows were thick are dark, his eyes even darker than onyx, with slivers of pale blue and silver occasionally revealed in the pupils. His angular but beautifully sculpted cheekbones and jaws angled down and inward toward his strong square chin, and his nose was as straight and narrow as any of his models. Finally, it was his lips, full and sensuous, but not overlarge for his face, that had driven Alisa insane with desire the night she had met him. His skin was a bit lighter than most Indians Alisa had known, the flesh reminding her of coffee lightened by a delicious creme. He could have been an actor, she had told him often enough. If only he would take off his damned gloves once in a while.

He grinned at her, charming as always, seemingly oblivious to the act he was performing. He gripped his lover's firm ass with his trademark leather gloves. This pair was a soft brown leather. Julian wore gloves everywhere. In bed, in the shower. She had never seen his hands.

After we're married, he had told her. *Not before.*

Alisa had been intrigued. She loved mysteries, and she could wait.

"The show's going well?" Julian asked calmly as he screwed Gina.

Alisa shrugged. "I don't know if it's as entertaining as the one in here."

"Want to join in?" he asked.

Gina whined, "Julian—"

Alisa shook her head. "That's all right. I don't want to get in the way." She heard chomping noises from somewhere close and turned to see Butch going after another entree.

"I heard a lull out there. I was getting worried," said Julian as he continued to pound into the moaning girl beneath him.

Gina stared right into Alisa's eyes with a feral satisfaction. *Mine now, you bitch. He's all mine.*

Alisa was beyond tears, beyond hurt. She felt drained. Alisa took off the engagement ring and tossed it to the buffet table. "I hope this is really what you want."

Julian shrugged and went back to his "work." Turning, Alisa left without another word.

Less than a minute after Julian heard the outer door close, Julian pulled away from his partner and slapped her behind. There was no need for this to go on any longer. If Alisa was going to return and make a scene, she would have done so by now. "Get dressed," he growled.

"I didn't come yet," said Gina.

"What do I care?" Julian asked as he killed the music.

Startled by the coolness in his dark eyes, Gina found her scattered clothing. Her only satisfaction as she dressed was the knowledge that *he* hadn't come *either*. He was still rock hard, straining. She knew men. He would be after her again, the unfinished business of their lovemaking preying on him. When he did try to seduce her once more, she would make him pay. She would have a signed prenuptial agreement worth a good seven figures in her possession and a wedding ring on her finger before he was allowed to touch her again.

Gina strutted out, unaware that she was performing for an audience that had mentally left the room.

Soon, Julian was alone with Butch. He put on the rest of his clothes and looked at the dog, who had washed his muzzle off in the punch, dried himself on the tablecloth, and come over to stare accusingly at him.

"That went well," Julian said, hearing the sounds of the show reaching a crescendo downstairs. His time to do the walk with his girls was coming. He would be all smiles, naturally.

Butch simply stared.

"You don't have anything to say?" asked Julian.

The dog yawned and looked away.

"I suppose you're upset at being made a part of that."

Butch said nothing.

"What I did was for her own good. Better that she knows right now what I am." The designer hesitated. "She's in *love* with me. What in hell *else* was I going to do?"

The dog provided no guidance.

Julian held up his gloved hands. "Did you want me to show her what's under *these*? Tell her, 'gee, sorry hon, I've been meaning to get to around to clueing you in. See, reality's not at all what you think it is. There's this whole *other world* living side by side with ours. Remember Mark? That A&R guy we met a couple of weeks back? He's a vampire. They call themselves the Kindred. They hate the 'V' word. And Batista, Ben and Christopher's maid? Not only is she an illegal immigrant, she's a werewolf! A Garou! Here on clan business. And let's not forget about the wraiths and the changelings and the demons...'" He fixed the dog with his wild dark eyes. "You don't want me to forget about the *demons*, do you?"

Butch's gaze was unwavering.

"And there's more, guys." He hesitated. He was a little drunk, but nowhere *near* as inebriated as he would be after his tour of Dublin's rosiest sites after the show. Tears suddenly welled up in his eyes. He sank to the floor, crumpling in upon himself like a child seeking absolution for his sins. "I mean, shit. I *can't* bring her into my world. I was stupid and selfish to think that I could. Or to think that *I* could make it here, that I could forget what I am…"

Julian forced back the tears. He wasn't worthy of tears. Anyone's tears. Even his own. He knew that all too well.

Butch was silent for a minute. His head cocked slightly to one side, as if to ask, *are you finished yet?* When Julian said nothing else, Butch squatted down and took a dump before his master. Then he peed and sauntered away.

Running his hands through his thick hair, Julian rose and followed. The dog went around the corner, toward the door leading to the outer office and the chaos beyond.

"I'm glad you shared those feelings with me, Butch." Roughly, Julian said, "You could try talking to me once in a while, y'know. It's not like you're really a dog, or anything, you judgmental shithead! Dogs are supposed to be *loyal!*"

He turned a corner and saw that Butch had vanished. The only door leading out of the suite was still closed.

Julian wasn't quite sure how the canine—well, part canine—had pulled off this little trick. Right now, he couldn't have cared less. Not about the dog who wasn't a dog. Not about Alisa, or anything else for that matter.

Least of all, himself.

Several hours later, Julian was wandering the streets, midway through duplicating the high points of a circuit he and an acquaintance had made of fine Dublin pubs the last time he was in town. The duo's rationale for this tour had been quite simple. It seemed that in Dublin there were pubs on practically every block. They had no way of knowing which *particular* establishments would be to their liking if they wanted to come back this way and impress a guest with their knowledge of the area, and so they had lost a week to trying out each and every pub in Dublin. It was the least they could do for themselves, considering they had just murdered nine innocent people all because of what turned out to be a clerical error.

Amazingly, Julian could still remember his favorite haunts. Now, just as he had eight years ago, Julian desperately needed to lose himself for awhile. So a quest was in order.

He dug in.

The pubs playing traditional Irish music were the best, so far as he was concerned. He went to the "posh" Temple Bar district and took in some conversation with the pensioners and the retired American tourists in Auld Dubliner. He avoided the Norseman, far too attractive to the tourists who loved to rave about their Irish roots, but had a nice time in Museum's Rest across from Bargain Town. The rear of the pub was set up like a barn, complete with a roaring fire. Sitting there, alone with his Beamish, a fine stout brewed in Cork, Julian felt some semblance of peace. His desire to go running through the streets near any college hollering that he was a Bob Geldoff fan so he could have the living shit kicked out of him by strangers was quieted for a time. Because of that, he left hurriedly, taking a Budweiser with him as he combed the streets.

Budweiser in Dublin was brewed by Guinness, and was far superior to anything Julian had tasted in America. The unfortunate trade-off was the in the states, *Guinness* was brewed by *Budweiser*. It helped Julian to dwell on these useless facts. Otherwise, he might have to think about what a right bastard he had been tonight.

His hands ached. There had been a time when he was certain this meant practitioners of his former calling were somewhere close. Similar to American super-hero Spiderman's *"spidey-sense."* He had been indoctrinated to the world of comics when he was nineteen, living in Bangkok. Was there *anywhere* he hadn't lived?

He was tired. The press had been on him the moment the show ended. He was certain that he had handled them well. Even PETA would be appeased by his statement. He hoped.

Now as he walked down a cobbled street, he could no longer avoid thinking about Alisa. She was not the first woman to love him and come to a bad end. At least she had made it out of the relationship alive, unlike his precious Neelam, a teenage prostitute in Bangladesh who had given him shelter.

Julian knew that he had driven Alisa away for good. As he said to Butch, that was for the best. She didn't really know him, didn't understand what he had done, and could never be told about the forces that had shaped his life. And if she didn't know him, then she couldn't love him.

Yet she did love him and he *knew* that.

Knowing that he would be alone, and that it was no less than what he deserved for all the crimes he had committed in his lifetime, hurt even worse than the bitter cold pain that was his constant companion. He had given up on the notion that the hurt in his hands rose and fell depending on his nearness to sources of magick. It had more to do with the damned weather.

He sighed and ahead, a woman screamed.

He had already been heading in the direction of Trinity College, where the scream had originated. Good things had been said about the Buttery, yet another pub, this one residing on campus. Julian had planned to check it out. Now he considered turning and walking the other way.

If Butch was with him, he would be forced to see if the screamer was really in distress. He knew what his argument with the mutt would have been: *She could be crying out in delight for all we know, a couple of local lads showing her a fine evening. Or maybe she read the latest football scores and her team is ahead. Or she could be in therapy, trying to get in touch with her inner fucking child, who she put up for adoption. It's not our problem.*

Julian would go on to say that he was anything but a hero. When he became involved in a situation, it was because cash was on the table. Ultimately, all the arguments in the world wouldn't have done him a damn bit of good. Butch would have guilted him into seeing what was going on.

The scream came again.

Cursing his damn dog, Julian ran in the scream's direction. He performed a slight incantation on the way, drawing the alcohol from his blood stream. The gentle buzz vanished, leaving a heartless clarity in its wake. He was struck with images of Alisa's face. Her calm resignation. Her understanding.

Damn her to hell.

He passed a car that bore the sticker, *"My karma ran over my dogma."* It made him smile. The words felt absurdly apt. He had a sense all day that the wheel of his chakra was again turning, but he had assumed it was strictly due to his breakup with Alisa. Now he was no longer so certain.

He reached the gates of Trinity College. The campus was very beautiful. He had visited it twice before, once to privately examine the Book of Kells, an early ninth century illuminated Gospel kept in the old library, and again to attend a weekend game of the Museum Players, the Trinity College staff cricket team.

The front gate was unattended. No students mulled about. He cast a spell of shielding. It would cause bullets to hit everything in sight but him, even if fired from point blank range. The same with well aimed throwing knives, arrows, or any other kind of projectile. If anyone came close enough to stab him or strike him in any way, they would fall, or slip, or otherwise miss.

The spell cost him. He felt a fiery pain as one of the many fillings in his skull throbbed and made his gums ache and bleed. The fillings were made from material engorged with Quintessence, the primal stuff of all creation, the fuel that made any spell run.

The filling would have to be replaced later.

Julian entered the campus. He crossed College Street, and walked steadily ahead. He passed abandoned copies of the Harlot and the Piranha, campus newspapers. It was odd to find newspapers lying about on the beautiful greens. The grounds were normally better maintained.

Soon he found himself nearing the center of the campus's front square. Parliament lay dead ahead. On either side of him rose Roman-styled buildings with grand columns. The dome of the chapel could be seen above the Parliament buildings.

Julian stopped as he reached a pair of trees on either side of the walk. It was a perfect place for an ambush. The branches reached low to the ground. They were thick with leaves, two gigantic green spheres impaled by thick stems. Excellent cover.

So that's what this is all about, Julian decided. An ambush. He smiled. For once, he would be able to tell Butch to piss off over something without feeling guilty about it the next day.

He stood very still, waiting.

"Well, come on," he said finally. "I've been obliging, haven't I? Let's not take all night with this."

A total of four men crept out from behind the trees. Two on each side. The pair off to Julian's right had a guest. She was blonde, flat-chested, and very attractive. Her screams had drawn him. One of the men held a knife to her throat.

The brutes were just that. Two had straggly hair, another was bald with THIS END UP and an arrow tattooed on his forehead, and the last, the man with the hostage, was a powerfully built African. They were all dressed in torn jeans, dark jackets, T-shirts, and expensive leather boots.

"Not from around here, I take it?" Julian asked.

This End Up, who had stood beside the knife-wielder, surged forward. "We know who you are. We know all about you."

Julian looked to the long-hairs who were steadily closing on his left flank. "If I didn't know better, I'd say Bono and Geldof here were wearing jeans I designed." He turned to the youths and they froze. "Is that right? Are those Enigma jeans?"

The African with the knife growled, "Get on with this or I cut her!"

Julian sighed. He had a very good idea of what this was all about. This kind of thing happened all the time in the old west. Retired gunfighters called out by young thugs trying to get themselves branded *bad men* by popping some doddering old fool.

Julian was only thirty-five. He was also in the best shape of his life. And though he had held a position in normal society for six years, he had continued to hone his abilities as a *Lord Shaper*—his childhood name for weavers of magic, or—mages.

"Here's how it's going to be," This End Up said, careful to say each word slowly and clearly as he produced a very large automatic weapon that had been slung over his back. The weapon looked like a piece of artillery the colonial marines would have been happy with in Aliens. But it was entirely a Sleeper designed mechanism. At a glance, it looked a handgun fused to an AK-47 with a pump action shotgun erupting from its barrel and a clip that smoothly arced downward to a John Holmes length.

Magnificent.

Bono and Geldof produced identical guns. Held tightly by the knife wielder, the blonde was whimpering and crying, but to her credit, she managed not to scream again.

"I'm listening," Julian said, folding one hand over the other before him. "Though I am intrigued by the weaponry. Matching Heckler and Koch MP5s. The SD model. Silenced. I won't even venture a guess at the cost. You boys were saving up from those checks sent by mom and dad, weren't you? Or are you just Tom Clancy fans?"

Bono and Geldof traded confused glances.

"He used those in 'Clear and Present Danger.' Good book, for those who can actually read."

The straggly-haired gunmen did their best to look tough and pissed off. Julian couldn't quite manage to look impressed.

The expensive hardware might have worried Julian more if he hadn't been severely tempted to let his spell of shielding drop so that these idiots could kill him. There was only one problem. If he died, the girl would be next. The gunmen had taken no measures to hide their faces from her. On the other hand, there was always the chance she was in on it with them.

That, my boy, is what makes life interesting, he thought. *The uncertainty of it all.*

"One of two things will happen," said This End Up, only a little shaken.

"Who's running you boys?" asked Julian. "They have money, I can tell that, though they spend it somewhat foolishly."

This End Up became even more agitated, and concentrated harder on his elocution, though he was now beginning to slur his words and reveal an accent he was trying hard to disguise. "We *will* open *fire* and you *will* be *torn apart* by the bullets—"

"Or I'll flatten and you and the Mighty Ducks over here will shoot each other." Julian glanced at the straggly-hairs. "Look at where you're positioning yourselves. It's pathetic."

The gunmen leaned outward and saw that Julian was right. The crossfire would kill them all. They arced back and around so that the stray bullets would not hit their companions.

"Thank you," they muttered.

"At least you're polite." Julian looked to This End Up and shrugged. "You were saying?"

The bald gunman was spewing his words, spitting with each of them. *"Either you use your skills or you die!"*

"I see. You want me to design clothing to protect me from the bullets."

The African made a tiny cut in the woman's throat. Julian smelled the blood and tensed. "All right. I understand."

They wanted him to use his magic before a Sleeper. That would cause the demons of Paradox to arrive and slay him. Apparently they were unaware that the last time something like that had happened, he had ended up with a "loyal companion."

Speaking of which…

Julian sensed another presence. Nails scratched at the doorway to his consciousness. He smiled, then turned his attention to one of the street lamps above. Suddenly, the light exploded with a horrendous crackling. It flamed out unnaturally, like a dying sun, sending a blinding white radiance across campus. The gunmen opened fire with their MP5s, but they could no longer see Julian.

Bono's vision cleared first. "Son of a bitch is gone!"

The others confirmed this a few seconds later. There was no blood on the ground or in the grass, either.

From somewhere close came a low growl. Another light exploded. Then another. Soon they were losing sight of each other in the shadows.

The growling worsened. It rumbled like thunder.

"What the hell *is* that?" the African snapped.

"Kill her, Emalle!" screamed This End Up. "That'll get him moving on us."

"Oh, and we *really want that?*" asked Emalle. The African's handsome features screwed up in distaste. "I don't think so. As far as I'm concerned, *she's* the only thing keeping us alive right now. I told you we weren't ready for someone like Ibiero."

This End Up was no longer listening. He cast his gaze and his weapon around frantically as he strained to recall even one of the spells he had studied over the last few years. For some reason, his mind was blank. He reached for the talisman he kept in his pocket.

Someone leaned in close and kissed the nape of his neck. "A Betty Boop keychain. Niccccccce…"

It was Ibiero! This End Up whirled and opened fire. Windows shattered in the distance. The pair of straggly-haired wanna-be-rock-stars separated as they dove into the shadows for cover. Bono was the first to die, as the shadows manifested large black teeth that neatly bit his head off, sliced his torso in half, then dragged the remaining chunks of his savaged flesh into a nightmare black maw all in the space of under a second.

No one actually saw it happen, though they each had a sense of what had become of their companion. Each of the survivors heard the growls, the chewing sounds, and the crunching of bone.

This End Up spun and fired in the direction of the sounds. He did not strike the shadow creature with his bullets. Instead, he accidentally took out Geldof. The long-haired gunman danced and shuddered as the bullets ripped into him, taking away pieces of his skull, slicing off one hand, another arm, blowing away half of his pelvis and leaving only shining white bone. The corpse collapsed on itself and hit the ground. A fetid odor drifted toward the survivors.

"Oh shite, it's *shite*, they're dead, they're really dead!" This End Up wailed, his Cockney accent no longer disguised. His voice cracked. Twice.

Emalle dropped the knife and shoved the girl away. His own MP5 was slung over his shoulder, resting against his back. He brought it around face front in an elegant, fluid motion as he caught the grip, released the safety, and shot This End Up a half dozen times. The bald man squeaked in pain and surprise. He was flung a dozen feet, dancing in death the entire way.

Emalle heard motion at his feet. He looked down and saw the girl scrambling to her knees, the knife he had dropped in her hand. She was about to thrust the knife into the meaty part of his thigh when he kicked the weapon from her effortlessly, grabbed her by her pretty blonde hair, and jammed the long barrel of the gun against her skull. The growls came again. This time they seemed to surround Emalle.

"Now listen!" Emalle said. "Killing Benjoon was a peace offering. I was *against* going after you from the beginning. Just because you don't have a Tradition doesn't mean you're fair game. But these were my friends and I couldn't talk them out of it. Now they're gone. It's over. Let's end it here."

A voice came, one that might have been nothing more than an unseasonably hot breeze. Sharp inhalations of breath punctuated each syllable. "My dog's still hungry. You should have let it feed. It might have let you go."

"Hurt me and she dies," Emalle said.

The woman whimpered, terrified by the cold metal against her forehead.

"You kill her, I kill you," Julian whispered on the dark winds. "There's no percentage."

"That's right!" Emalle cried, exhilarated, picturing himself surviving the night. "No percentage!"

The growling came again. "But my dog's still hungry."

Emalle's heart sank. A look of grim determination played across his strong face. "Fuck it."

He pulled the trigger and the gun jammed.

Clearly, the odds of such a thing happening at so *convenient* a time were slim. Magick was involved. A form of coincidental magick that could easily be believed by desperate Sleepers, like the frightened blonde woman who thought she was about to die.

Emalle heard the shadow beast's roar at the exact instant it leaped from the shadows and tore him limb from limb.

Julian was on the ground, covering the face of the blonde. There should have been blood, of course, but it was absorbed by the shadows and the creature who ruled them. Julian whispered into the woman's ear, "Don't look. Don't think."

She collapsed in his arms, sobbing.

"Friends of mine. Helping me out," Julian improvised. He saw the beast consume the remains of the other gunmen, along with their weapons. One discharged as he chomped in it, but that didn't stop the shadow creature. "They're carrying out the bodies. Just cry if you need to. It's over…"

Suddenly, the blonde's hair came away in Julian's hands. He looked down at a shiny pink skull and drew away quickly.

A smiling Asian man leaned back on the grass and shook off the last of the blonde hair. He wore a brand new pair of Enigma jeans, a well worn Bullets Over Broadway T-shirt, most holey, and a roadies jacket from the Eagle's Hell Freezes Over tour. His feet were bare.

Butch leaped from the shadows, quickly positioning himself between Julian and the Asian man. He had resumed the form of a dog, but his eyes were crimson and smoke poured from between his jaws.

"X'an!" Julian cried. There had never been a blonde woman at all. It had been X'an using his talisman of transformation.

"You son of a bitch!"

"Now, now," said the shorter man. "Is that any way to speak to your mentor?"

An hour later, Julian and X'an were a mile off the ground in a private jet heading for a small cluster of islands south of Madagascar called the Seychelles Republic. Julian and X'an sat facing each other, as if they were in the back seat of a limousine. Dozens of other seats lined their compartment, but other than the captain and co-pilot, and two flight attendants, they were the only people onboard. Julian barely noticed the support staff.

Butch was all over X'an, licking his hands, his face, nuzzling the older man's lap. X'an was forced to set aside the laptop that had been in his hands. It was paused on a game of Doom. X'an had rich pure brown eyes and a crazed smile that did not inspire students to try to take the pebbles from his hand.

"What was the point of all that back there?" asked Julian finally. X'an had put him off on this issue long enough. He had to know why had the old man arranged the ambush and willingly sacrificed four of his students.

X'an sighed. "I had to know if the stories were true."

"What stories?" asked Julian warily.

"That you had bent a demon of paradox to your will and trapped him in an unassuming form."

Butch whined a little.

"You mean him?" Julian asked, patting Butch's flank. "He's just my dog!"

X'an raised a single eyebrow and waited.

"All right." Julian sighed. "I never could lie to you."

"Of course you could," said X'an. "And you did, many times. You simply couldn't get away with it."

Julian understood that he had only part of the answer he had requested. *Well, if I could never get away with lying to you, why didn't you just pick up the phone and ask me about Butch? Or come to the show or my office?*

X'an had clearly wanted to see how Julian would react in a crisis. If all the old reflexes were still finely honed. The reason for *that* had something to do with their strange destination. Julian didn't push. He had wanted to get away from the pressures of his work—and from Alisa. Besides, pressing the old man for information was surest way to make him take even longer to come to the point.

"Tell me about Butch," said X'an.

"Not much to tell. Butch was a Paradox demon. He came after me. He had to. I screwed up. I let a Sleeper see me shaping a new design—"

"A *clothing* design?"

Julian nodded. He flexed his hands. "These bloody things are next to worthless for detail work. I was in my workshop. The door should have been locked. I messed up. One of my assistants came in. He saw a mannequin come to life, the dress it wore changing color, form… It was all over."

X'an leaned down and rubbed noses with the dog. "You're a good dog, aren't you?"

Butch panted happily.

"He came to kill me. We fought for six days, chasing each other around Stockholm, until finally we got too tired to keep at it."

"The two of you were too evenly matched in power."

Butch barked loudly, startling X'an. The old man sat back in his chair. The penitent pup looked at X'an with wide sympathetic eyes and snuffed as he shuffled forward and put his head on X'an's leg. The old man stroked the dog's head. Drool soaked the knee of his jeans.

"To hear Butch tell it, the outcome was inevitable. He was just playing with me all that time," said Julian.

"Ah."

"A temporary truce was called. We started talking. Neither of us was thrilled at what we were doing with our lives."

"So the demon *consented* to becoming your pet?" X'an asked, astonished.

LIGHTNING UNDER GLASS   293

Butch stopped panting suddenly. His tongue, which had been lolling out of his mouth, was nowhere in sight. The dog's jaws clenched as he looked back at Julian. A silent communication passed between them.

"I know I did!" Julian wailed at the mutt. He looked up at X'an. "Truth is, he let his guard down and I blindsided him."

"Ah."

Julian looked directly at the mutt. "But we're friends now, right?"

The dog responded. X'an cocked his head slightly to one side. "I've never seen a dog shrug before. It's *freaky.*"

"That's Butch. I've tried to release him from this form, but nothing works."

"What about his shadow incarnation?"

"That's different. More like—"

"Letting him off his leash?" X'an offered as he scratched Butch behind the ears.

"I don't keep him on a leash. He picks and chooses his own battles."

Butch settled his head in X'an's lap.

Julian decided it was time to bring the conversation back around to the conflict at Trinity. Looking back on it now, he understood that he should have recognized X'an's influence immediately. The fledgling mages could never have "blacked out" the area so efficiently. All Sleepers, even those who might have seen the fight from a distance, had been banished from the battlefield. Julian was sure that each of them believed it was their own idea to leave:

Let's go to a pub. Take in a flick. Good time to do some shopping. Laundry needs to be done. Just tonight, why don't we get a hotel room? I've got the munchies, let's go!

Very few mages could cast a net of influence so expertly as X'an.

"Those *were* students of yours, I take it," said Julian as his ears popped and the roar of the engines became more noticeable. "Rejects."

"Quite so."

"You and your clearing house mentality."

X'an took exception to this. "Their parents were all great mages. These children were dishonoring their family names."

"For that, they had to die?"

"*You* were the one who decided on bloodshed. You could have caused all their weapons to jam, then disarmed them easily."

"Butch is the one who ate 'em! Gimme a break!"

The dog look back at his master and raised one leg.

"Don't even think about it," said Julian.

"He responds to your desires, whether either of you like it or not," said X'an. "It was part of the Binding."

Julian's shoulder sank in defeat. "I thought they were after me to make their bones. Just a bunch of newbies. And they were dangerous. They knew about me."

"You could have taken them prisoner, then interrogated them. You should have thought, 'how could they know about me? From whom did they learn my secrets? How many others know?'"

"I guess I'm not as sharp as I was six years ago."

X'an looked away, disinterested. "Ultimately, there are *always* alternatives to violence. That is one of my lessons you have never learned."

"True, but unlike most of your students, I lived to see thirty. And to walk away from the game."

X'an closed his eyes and waved his hand in the air, as if to dispel all unpleasantries. "We each make choices with our lives. Bickering will bring no one back from the dead."

"Agreed. So what will you tell the parents?"

"What they want to hear. That their children died with honor in a terrible skirmish with the Nephandi. The fallen will be revered."

"Come on. No one in their right minds would believe those kids could hold their own with the Nephandi."

"True. Which is why they died, yes?"

Julian knew there was no further point in pursuing this. He settled back and waited for X'an to tell him what he needed to know: *Why were they flying to the Seychelles?*

X'an picked up his laptop and went back to his game of Doom for a few minutes. After he was killed twice, he set the computer aside and reached over to pat Butch's flank. "Hey, fella. You know, Julian could have used that black guy in a show. He was very pretty. He had this whole Tony Todd thing going…"

Julian stared at X'an blankly.

"Candyman! Candyman!"

"All right," growled Julian. He had seen the posters for the second movie and read about the controversy the American press was attempting to stir up as the O.J. trial was about to begin. Images of an African male, with a knife, threatening a blonde Caucasian woman, could have been seen as prejudicing potential juries. Julian thought it was all ridiculous.

"Tony Todd is a very capable actor! Did you see him on X-Files? Or Hercules?"

"I—"

"What about Homicide? Or Star Trek: Deep Space Nine?"

His mentor was a die-hard cinephile. Julian did not even *try* to compete with the man on this level. The subject simply didn't interest him.

"What do you want?" Julian asked bluntly.

A fire came into X'an's deep brown eyes. "You liked the artillery, didn't you? Nice hardware. You should see some of the acquisitions I've made recently. I'm sure you will be delighted when we get you supplied."

"No," Julian said firmly as he rose from his chair and paced in the narrow aisle. "I'm out of that line of work. I told you that six years ago."

"But you were my best! Removals. Acquisitions. Seductions. Upheavals… There was no situation beyond your capacity."

"No more."

"You're not an artist anymore, but we both know you still dabble. Why should this be any different?"

Julian shot an angry gaze in his mentor's direction.

"Forgive me. What the Americans would call 'a cheap shot.'"

Lightning Under Glass   295

"I hated what I was doing when I worked for you. What I was becoming."

"Lies." X'an made a dismissive gesture. "And frankly, you *could* be an artist again, the kind of artist you wish to be, if you knew your own heart."

"Now you're the one who's lying," Julian thought as he looked down at his gloved hands. What was an artist without his hands? He could use his Art as a mage to craft dresses, he could chip away at a block of granite with his power. But he felt nothing. Just as if he was using his insensate hands. Without the ability to feel *physically connected* to his work, unless he could feel the touch of paper, canvas, clay, or stone, he somehow could not bring the images in his mind to reality. Something else would inevitably emerge. A piece of art that was finely crafted and even pleasing to the eye, satisfying to others, but not to Julian. *Not* the vision he desperately needed to express.

There was no force on earth that could heal his deformed hands. He had tried every spell known, with every possible variation, and his hands were unchanged. Medical science, even that of the Technocracy, was of no help either.

Julian came back and sank into his chair. "I told you, I'm out of the game."

"You have no fear of repercussions?"

"I made my peace with everyone when I left the life."

"You never leave it."

Julian shook with frustration. "My face is too well known. Whatever you have in mind—"

"So you don't wear your face. I'll give you my amulet. With it, you can look like anyone you choose."

Julian was surprised. He had *never* heard of his mentor loaning out one of his prized talismans. "What you offer is a great honor, but I am unworthy."

"That's for me to judge."

Julian looked down at his gloved hands. "Even if my body was altered, my hands would remain the same. We tried it once, remember?"

"You managed before with those hands. And very capably, I might add."

Julian knew that he could not reasonably argue the point.

In a low, cool voice, X'an asked, "It's all because of ten years ago, isn't it? Did you *know* that it was ten years ago to this day? Your Day of Blood?"

Actually, Julian *hadn't* realized it. He didn't want to think of that day.

"Let me see…" said X'an. "I lost five good soldiers in your shadow war with the Euthanatos… At least, the particular Euthanatos who shamed your father and killed his friend that night… What did you tell me? Oh, yes, I recall now." Lowering his voice to a Godfather rasp, he said, "'Barzini's dead. So is Phillip Tattaglia. Moe Greene is dead. Stracci. Cuneo. Today I settled all family business.'"

Julian smiled despite himself. He knew *that* movie, at least.

Softly, X'an said, "When I found you, wandering in Bangladesh, you were barely alive, barely sane. I helped you, did I not?"

Julian leaned across the gap dividing them and took X'an's hand. Butch lay down at their feet. "You gave me hope, made me well again."

"I made you function. I *could not* make you well. It seemed only vengeance could do that. So after nine years of faithful service, I showed my gratitude—"

"Please," said Julian, pained. He did not wish to be reminded of that day.

X'an was undeterred. His student clearly needed to be reminded of the past he tried so hard to forget. "I showed you my gratitude by giving you all the funding, all the weapons, all the operatives, all the intelligence you would need to make your dreams of blood a reality. You killed the Euthanatos who were responsible. And somehow, you settled the debt with those who sought reprisals for your actions. What more could you want? To this day, I don't know."

Julian was ashamed at the words that escaped him in a breathless whisper. *"The girl."*

"She died in an accident with her parents when she was eleven. You wanted to wait until she was fifteen, the age you were when she came into your life and damned you."

Julian looked away. "She didn't damn me. I damned myself."

Butch whined. The dog came over and licked his master's face.

"Would you have killed her?" X'an asked.

"Then?" Julian asked. "Without question. Now... I'm not so sure. Not that it matters."

"When you learned that the child had died, a part of you died as well. Do you recall your teachings at all? 'A man who lives only for vengeance lives not at all.' I asked you so many times, 'what will you do when you have killed them all?' Do you remember what you said?"

"That I'd be happy."

"I do not think it would have been as you imagined."

"Well, we're never going to know, now are we? I was cheated. Life wasn't fair." His hands ached. "It wasn't the first time."

"The girl's alive," X'an said.

Julian looked up sharply.

"Do what I require and I'll deliver her to you."

The mage studied his mentor's eyes and knew the man wasn't lying. His heart felt as if it might explode. His voice was hoarse as he said, "How long have you known?"

"A matter of hours. I came to you directly."

Julian couldn't believe this. For ten years he had wandered aimlessly, his one goal in life ripped away from him by a simple traffic accident. Now he could have it back.

Butch looked over at him. The dog's expression seemed to say, *Don't do it. Don't even think about it. I won't help you.*

"Huh!" X'an said suddenly. "It seems I will have to team you with someone else!"

Julian and the dog looked at X'an in surprise.

The old man shrugged. "I'm good with animals. Besides, I had anticipated this." X'an picked up his laptop and leaned in close to it, as if he was about to whisper to a genie in a bottle. "You can come out now."

Suddenly, the black, slimline computer leapt from X'an's hands. It spun in mid-air as a vortex of shimmering energies exploded from it. The energies quickly took on the form of a smiling nineteen year-old oriental. Long black hair, a muscular build, a squarish face with piercing blue eyes. The light show faded and he stood revealed, dressed mostly in black, except for a crimson sash around his waist. He was shirtless beneath his vest, his muscles glistening.

"So what's this?" Julian asked. "Hong Kong's answer to Fabio?"

The young Asian man's expression never changed. "My name's Jian Zhao. I'm—"

"A Virtual Adept, yes, thank you, I have eyes," said Julian. He looked back to his mentor. "Was I supposed to be impressed?"

X'an nodded. "That was the general idea, yes."

Julian growled, low and deep in his throat. "I don't need or *want* a partner."

"You haven't even heard about the mission yet!" said X'an.

"It doesn't matter."

"You're not going anywhere until we touch down. Why don't you let me tell you what I have in mind…"

Half an hour later, when X'an finished explaining about this mission, Julian leaned forward and said, "My answer is still 'no.' I'll do it on my own."

X'an sighed. "Mr. Tarantino was right. There are two types of people. Those who listen and those who wait to talk."

Tarantino? Julian was not familiar with the name. He let it pass. X'an's meaning was clear enough.

Butch let out an impatient bark. X'an reached down and petted him. "So you've always had this problem with him?"

"Great," said Julian. "He won't even talk to me any more, but you seem to know what he's thinking."

"It would appear so."

"You take my dog and you saddle me with *this*." Julian motioned in Jian Zhao's direction.

"Those are my terms. If you do not like them, I will find someone else."

Julian asked quietly, "What about the girl?"

"You won't find her. I daresay, she will not even be alive on Monday, should you wait that long."

"You have people with her?"

"No. If she dies, it will be as a result of a situation she's gotten into all on her own. Of course, she may find a protector and live a little longer. Perhaps even long enough for you to catch up to her without my help."

Julian looked away. "Shit."

"Will you do it?" asked X'an. "The risks are high, but so are the rewards. Best of all, you should be finished in twenty-four hours. Plenty of time to reach the states."

"That's where she is?"

"It's all I will say. And who knows if I'm telling the truth?"

Julian looked up at Jian Zhao. "Tell me your qualifications."

The young Asian man read off an impressive list.

The mage considered the mission in detail. Much as he hated to admit it,

X'an was right. It was a two person job.

"He'll do," said Julian. "I'm in."

"Fabulous!" cried Jian Zhao.

Julian rose and confronted the young Oriental. "But understand something before *you* agree to be a part of this: If you screw up, I will *not* put myself at risk to save you."

Jian Zhao nodded. "And if you are the one in danger—"

"I won't be."

"If you are, I will be there to rescue you, even at the cost of my own life. I have pledged this to my mentor and would do it in any event."

"Well, good for you," said Julian as he prepared himself to listen more carefully this time. "From the top, X'an. All of it. In detail."

X'an smiled and told the story again. When his mentor was finished, Julian thought of how he would address the seemingly myriad problems his mentor pointed out. Soon, as their plane touched down in a private airstrip, Julian felt the blood pounding in his skull. His every nerve was on fire. The fear and excitement that had been missing from his life for so long was back.

Julian felt *alive*.

3

The Art Bar, Seattle.

"God, you smell great," Maxine whispered to the man who had won her body, if not her heart, for the night. The man turned, squinting, and looked at Max with a bemused smile.

The opening line she had used was a little odd. Max *knew* that. On the other hand, it was true. Here was this Italian guy, sitting alone, minding his own business, looking like a thug out of Good Fellas or Reservoir Dogs—and smelling of Sandalwood. The scent wasn't overpowering. Instead, it was subtle. Gentle and sweet. It made her heart race.

She decided a half-hour ago that he would be the one. He had walked past her and his hand had accidently touched hers. There had been a fire in his touch, a power and a yearning.

No, there wasn't, you're just horny, you little bitch, she chided herself.

Nevertheless, she had noticed his scent and ever since had been unable to think about anything but what it would be like to lie beneath him, his body pressed against hers, that scent rippling through her senses. It was possible that she had become unusually aware of scents due to being crammed in the staff room with Brenner and the Four Horsemen, the entire lot wearing the single most *putrid* cologne she had ever smelled. Now to have someone who not only smelled good, but fucking *delectable*—was a little overwhelming. In a good way.

He looked over at her. The mischievous twinkle in his hooded eyes told her that she *had* him. There had been little doubt in Maxine's mind that she could take home any man here that she desired. Before hitting the Art Bar she had stopped off and put a worse strain on her sole remaining credit card by buying a slinky black low cut dress and matching high heel shoes. Then she had changed into the outfit sans underwear at the bus station, putting her crumpled business suit, the Point and Shoot, her powerbooks, and her papers in the lock-up. She left the bracelet on. As horrible as the meeting had been, she still had a chance to turn things around. The bracelet hadn't lost it's "magic," as far as she was concerned.

Not including the gangsta, as she thought of him, there were six likely candidates for a good time in the bar. Three men, one woman, a couple. She had connected with each of them, though no words had been spoken, and she knew that she could take her pick. One guy in particular hardly seemed to take his eyes off her. He was still watching her now. Brown hair, narrow face, stylish suit. Long thin hands. A runner, probably. Intense. She had been with guys like him. Laboring over her, barely noticing her unless she forced them to look down. No thanks.

This other guy, though, the one whose smell made her insane with desire, didn't seem to know she was alive. That had been the biggest turn on.

The gangsta smiled at her again, revealing tiny crinkly crow's feet at the corners of his eyes. A dark suit covered his strong physique, topped by a tie with a design inspired by Monet. His hands were large and powerful, his cheeks and jaw classically molded and framed by his short but perfectly coiffed raven black hair. There were no rings on his fingers, no telltale pink lines to show he was married and cruising anyway.

He's going to be hairy as anything, I just know it, Max told herself. *Probably his butt, too*. Somehow, she just didn't care. The scent he exuded was overwhelming her senses, making her easy prey for the taking.

No, I'm the predator, he's the prey, she told herself. *That's the game today. Let's not get confused here.*

Of course, if he got a little rough and wanted to take charge afterwards, that might be all right, too.

Max, you're a slut, she told herself. In reality, she was playing a part, disappearing into it. A part of her understood this, and she was doing her letter best to drown out what little voice of reason that still existed in her head. Drown it with booze, with sex, with drugs. Anything she could get her hands on. It was an old behavior pattern. Her therapist told her that she had these old tapes running in her head, telling her how to react to stressful situations. She needed to replace those tapes, stop listening to them.

She *knew* that. It changed nothing.

"Here's how it is," Max said, her heart thundering, her body shaking, but still under control. She only had three drinks in her. Maybe four. "I just got fucked and not in a good way. So I'm looking to fuck someone else. And this time get something for my trouble. Like a good time. You interested?"

He looked away, grinning, thinking it over. Finally, he glanced back at her and said, "I didn't know people really *talked* like that."

She giggled, putting her hand over her mouth, feeling her breasts sway with her laughter. A sudden heat rose in her as she saw him looking down at her cleavage.

This was going to be one *serious* distraction, and that was exactly what she needed right now. Oblivion. Putting her mind in another orbit entirely, filling her senses in such a way that she couldn't possibly think about what had happened this afternoon, about the frantic messages piling up from Freddy on her answering machine. It was cowardly, but she needed release and she needed it right away. And he was going to be *good*.

"You want to know anything about me?" he asked, sipping at his whiskey.

"You like girls?"

"I like *women.*"

"You're in luck."

He laughed. "I was supposed to meet some people, but screw 'em." He hesitated. "My car? My place?"

"Sure." Impulsively, she leaned in and kissed him. Their lips parted, tongues entwined. Sensations shot through her, a barrage of pleasure-scented shrapnel that made it impossible for her to think about anything other than taking this man and being possessed in return.

He broke the kiss, which made her even more excited. "You're not bad at that," he said as he fished into his wallet, dropped a twenty on the table.

Laughing, she realized that she liked this man. Hopefully, that wouldn't become a problem for her later.

As they rose from the table, Max saw Mr. Intense watching her again. He was looking at a mirror, studying her image that way, not looking right at her. She winked at him and he looked away, startled, as if he wasn't used to people realizing that he was watching.

"Do me a favor," Max said, glancing away from the mirror but still watching from the corner of her eye. "Kiss me again, and this time, grab my ass a little."

"Gee, I dunno," he said. "That's asking a lot."

She came for him, lips parted before their faces met. His hands were on her ass in seconds, casually, calmly kneading her flesh. Then he broke the kiss and slapped her behind sharp enough to make her start. Her cry drew the attention of everyone within a twenty foot radius.

Max laughed.

She looked back to the mirror. Strangely, Mr. Intense's long, narrow face hadn't changed expression. There was no disappointment, only that cool detachment. He just kept watching.

Max felt a little disappointed, but she decided not to worry about it. She had far better things to think about. Like the ride to her "suitor's" house.

They left the Art Bar. The streets were already dark.

"Name's Mitchell," he said. "Mitchell—"

"That's enough."

"Okay. You got a name?" He went to a black 1970 Mustang, a classic, perfectly maintained.

"You like some power under the hood?"

"I'm just not into designed obsolescence. Had this car since I was a teenager. It's a sweet ride."

You don't know the meaning of the words, she thought as he opened the door for her, then went around to the driver's side.

But you will.

Soon they were on I-5, heading for Edmonds. She would have preferred a more scenic route for what she had in mind, but the highway, with the greater chance of discovery, held its thrills as well. Maybe she'd cause some eighteen wheeler to tip over because the driver was too busy watching what she was doing instead of paying attention to the road.

Max ran her fingers over the runes etched into her bracelet. She thought of the tragedy associated with this piece of jewelry and recalled how she had come to think of the bracelet as her good luck charm. It was still clear in her mind, more from the story that had been told to her by her father years later, than her own recollections.

She had been a little girl when they had visited Calcutta. Somehow, she had wandered off and become lost in a vast marketplace. She had no idea of how much danger she was in from slavers, but the son of a jeweler had. He had sheltered her until her parents came.

Later, when her father found the bracelet with his daughter's things, he coaxed the full story from the girl. He went back to the jeweler's shop the next day, only to learn that the jeweler had been killed, his son kidnapped, apparently by the Thugs who enforced the will of the slavers. Everyone had concluded that the young artist had been taken in Maxine's place. True, he was far less valuable to them, but the gesture was meant as a warning to others.

Max was ten when she learned the full story. If that had been all of it, she might have given the bracelet away then and there. But since that afternoon in Calcutta, Max had been certain that she had seen the artist in her dreams, giving her guidance that later proved invaluable.

The final time she saw him in her dreams had been the day her parents died. He had warned her not to go with them to the store that day and so she put up a terrible fight and won the right to stay home. The artist's warning had saved her life.

After that, she had been angry with the visitor to her dreams. He must have known that her parents were going to die, why not tell her so that they could be saved as well?

It wasn't until many years later, when she was eighteen, that she found the bracelet again. She was now mature enough to wear the bracelet. Once it touched her flesh, she thought of the way she had been angry at the artist—her "guardian angel"—and decided that he had told her as much as he had been allowed to tell her, or as much as he knew. Considering the terrible times that she had endured since her parents died, Max then wished that the artist would appear in her dreams again. She wore the bracelet often, and though wretched things still happened to her, they were never quite as bad as they could have been. There was always a chance to turn things around.

Max looked up from the bracelet. She suddenly realized that she and the man she had picked up in the bar had not said a word to each other since getting in his Mustang. "Christ, that was wonderful."

"What?" he asked.

"Quiet. No nervous banter."

"Except yours."

She laughed again. Oddly enough, the smell he had exuded had changed since they had kissed. Or so it seemed to Max. The Sandalwood had faded, giving way to the rich scent of roses. In fact, she felt as if she could taste roses, like some kind of oil that had mysteriously found its way to her lips.

"You never told me your name," he said.

"Is that important?"

"I dunno. Always had a problem with lookin' down and sayin', 'hey you,' that's really great, but can you go a little faster? And try and suck, don't blow. Thanks.'"

She laughed.

"Just makes it a little more personal."

"Max. Like in Maxine."

"Pretty."

She settled back in the large comfortable seat. A few cars passed them. For a time, one seemed to be following them. Mitchell slowed down until the car swung around them, crossing two lanes over. A van rushed up between the cars before Max could get a look at who was driving. She had a brief fantasy of Mr. Intense coming after them, following them, watching them through the window to Mitchell's bedroom.

Mitchell drove on, doing only a few miles over the speed limit. He didn't seem to be in any great hurry.

Ten minutes later, they stopped before a set of metal gates.

She looked around. Christ, this was a rich area. She hadn't even been aware of their leaving the highway. Mitchell reached past her, popped open the glove compartment, and removed a small remote. He punched in a code and the gates swung inward. She saw him looking at her bracelet for a moment, at the odd designs, then he looked away, not commenting.

They drove through the gates, along a winding tree covered lane, until finally they reached what she could only describe as a mansion.

"It's fucking Wayne Manor," she gasped.

"Naw, that one's smaller," he said. There were three lesser-sized buildings, one adjacent, the other two in the distance. She looked at the main mansion and took in the rising Gothic architecture, the columns out front. Stunning.

"What is this place?" she asked.

"Home." he said.

"Do I get a kiss?"

"You can even have some tongue. "

"God, you pig!" she laughed.

He held her close, then fondled her breasts as he kissed her.

"Fuck me now. I can't wait."

"Nope," he said, getting out of his side.

"Who's gonna see?" she asked.

"Come on," he called.

"Shit!" she said as she slipped the straps back up, depositing her breasts in the push-up underwire cups. She followed him toward the front entrance. The odd array of scents he exuded fell away a little in the cool night air and she longed to be near him again. "Are there people who are going to see?"

"Nope. Help comes in during the day. I'm all alone here at night."

She went to one of the columns and ran her hand over its length suggestively. "Why don't you fuck me against this?"

"Maybe later."

"Mitchell, please. You're being mean."

"Don't worry. You'll get what you wanted. And a whole lot more."

What did he mean by *that?* she wondered. In a fleeting moment of clarity she wondered if this guy could be some kind of psycho. Maybe she would have been better off with Mr. Intense. Then she knew it was past time for worries like that, she had made a decision, and this was what she wanted more than anything. Besides, if he killed her, what the fuck difference would that make? She was dead already. And she wouldn't have to talk to you-know-who tomorrow, she wouldn't have to think at all.

"Want to talk about it?" he asked, looking at her with his hangdog head-cocked-to-one-side look of sympathy and understanding. Her distress was obvious.

"No," she said, her back straightening, her chest thrust out. "I *don't* want to talk about it. You know what I want."

He held out his hand. "Come on."

They were going to hold hands, she thought. They were going to *hold hands* like little *kids*. This guy was more than she could have hoped for. He held her hand with his right and unlocked the door by punching in a code on a nearby keypad with his left. Pushing it open, he drew her inside. Lights were coming on automatically.

She was struck by the simple elegance and majesty of her surroundings. The spacious foyer a half dozen times the size of her entire apartment. A stunning chandelier giving off a soft golden glow that looked like candlelight above her. A winding staircase leading to the second and third floors. Sculptures and paintings lining the foyer.

Max was struck by a series of Japanese woodcuts depicting beautiful, elegant Asian women in a variety of poses and activities.

"Utamaro," Mitchell said. "The name of the artist. This one is called 'Woman with a Pipe.' Then we have 'Fireflies'—"

So that's what the women were doing, Max realized, *catching fireflies.*

"—and 'Beauty with Hand Mirror.' Everything else in this place could burn to the ground and I wouldn't care, but I think I'd risk it all to save these three. Have you ever heard of the 'Floating City?'"

Max shook her head, completely drawn in.

"Utamaro died in 1806, defying government censorship. He became famous with scenes like these, capturing the beauty of the Yoshiwari—"

"The pleasure district," Max said, startled that she knew this. "Government sponsored. It was bombed in 1945, most of it burned to the ground."

"Paper houses."

Max had been to Japan when she was a child. She'd thought that most of what she had learned was lost, but for some reason this much was coming back.

"When it was destroyed, the grace of the Yoshiwari was gone, its spirit and beauty had fallen. It was another red-light district. But in its heyday, when Utamaro was alive, it was thought of as a paradise. A place to escape all earthly worries. The women, the courtesans, were thought of as celebrities, the way we would consider movie stars, only with respect and high honors." Mitchell gestured at a lovely Asian woman in the closest woodcut. "If you read the literature of the time, it was common to find stories about samurai who had burned through their fortunes pursuing a woman like this."

For a moment, Max almost felt as if she were there. Reality seemed to be warping around her, and—

—suddenly she was departing a boat from the Sumida River, debarking at the Dike of Japan, and traveling over a moat to enter Yoshiwari's high and intricately designed wooden gates. Soon, she was standing before the Five Streets, looking at paper lanterns and flowering cherry trees and Japanese maples with red leaves that gave a touch of melancholy to autumn nights. A crowd of celebrants pressed in around her. The tea houses and brothels lining the streets were filled with banquets sporting dancers and musicians. Some of the brothels were obscured by paper walls. The activities within others could be seen through their fine latticework. Hands were on her, touching her, lips kissed her ears and whispered obscene and wondrous promises—

Max shuddered and brought herself back to Mitchell's foyer. He was still talking. "A group of hedonists, artists and writers became obsessed with the *Ukiyo*, 'the Floating World,' and Utamaro was one of them. He illustrated verses for these writers. A 17th-century writer said that Ukiyo meant 'living only for the moment…singing songs, drinking wine, and diverting ourselves just in floating, floating, caring not a whit for the pauperism staring us in the face, refusing to be disheartened, like a gourd floating along with the river current.'" Mitchell turned and kissed Max once again. Roses bloomed all around her, filling her flesh with desire. "Upstairs. *Ukiyo* is upstairs…"

Again he held out her hand. She took it willingly. Greedily.

He understood fully the kind of release she needed, and she had no doubt whatsoever that he would be able to give it to her.

A furious pounding at the door downstairs woke them.

Mitchell heard it first and was already half dressed when Max stirred to consciousness. The noise was incessant.

"Hey," she said, her thoughts muddled. "What's that?"

"People I was supposed to meet before, is my guess."

She looked at him blankly.

"You remember, I told you. Back at the Art Bar."

Max shrugged. "I'm kinda fuzzy." About all she could recall right now was the incredible pleasure he had given her. It was all she wanted to think about. A variety of aromas hung in the air. Rose. Jasmine. Another scent came to her. Heavy and sweet. Like standing in a forest after a rain, the smells of thick bark and a rich fruity odor climbing up into her lungs.

He leaned in and kissed her. "Go back to sleep. I'll deal with these guys."

She settled back in the bed, contented. He took something from one of the dressers. A cute, brown teddy bear. She smiled, easily ignoring the unrelenting slamming at the door downstairs. He made a show of hugging it.

"Charge it up for you," he said, growling with exertion. "Loads of cuddles."

"I like that," she said as he handed her the bear. She took it with her under the covers and he stroked her hair until she started to drift off. She barely noticed the mild dampness of the stuffed animal, or the odd scent it gave off. She had smelled this before, she knew. When she had been in Mexico.

Didn't matter, she decided, and drifted off into what began as a lush sexual dream.

She had no idea that she had just been overwhelmed by a fragrance known as Damiana, which grew in the desert regions of Texas and Mexico. It contained alkaloids, which worked well as sexual stimulants and muscle relaxants. The scent was said to have the power to produce erotic dreams.

If she had known, she wouldn't have cared. She was lost to the Floating World. Here there were no difficult choices, no unpleasant moments to face, only unceasing ecstasy…

She did not notice the tiny drops of clear liquid easing from Mitchell's skin, dripping to the carpeted floor.

He left the room quietly.

4

Downstairs, Mitchell welcomed his four guests and showed them into his study. Three of the four men were dressed in elegant business suits, their hair perfectly coiffed, their nails manicured. Each was in his mid-forties. Attractive, square-jawed. The fourth was bald. He wore a long black overcoat, black gloves, and small rounded spectacles with onyx lenses. This last visitor trailed behind the others, saying little, his face pinched, his gaze firmly planted on the heels of the men he followed. Even when they all sat in the study, the last man refrained from admiring the collection of books and edged weapons that lined the walls. Twenty swords were mounted, their edges sharp and glinting. Generally, when visitors came to Mitchell, especially those who wanted something, they brought a sword or a piece of art. Some kind of offering. It was only proper, all things considered.

The little bald man stared at his hands, which were bunched together. Clenched.

"To what do I owe the pleasure?" Mitchell asked, confidently aware of the mock sincerity in his tone.

"You know damn well why we're here," said the first of the executives, a handsome, aging male model type. Marlboro Man, Mitch named him. A little stubble and the right clothes and he'd be rough and rugged. He had a bunch of Hugh Grant crinklies around the eyes and road map deep smile lines around his mouth.

"I know why you're here," repeated Mitch absently. "Oh. *Well*. That fucking answers my question."

The bald man flinched. He shifted uncomfortably in his seat.

"Language," said another executive. This one was an Aryan wonder. Blonde, blue-eyed, built like a god, his Germanic features classically sculpted, his hands those of classical pianist, long and beautifully articulate. He could have spoken only with his hands and still been understood.

The last executive leaned forward in his chair. As far as Mitch was concerned, he had a Dick Clark/Dorian Grey thing going on. A boyish face, a youthful hairstyle, still mistaken for mid-twenties though it was twenty years too late for that. Oozing sincerity the Boy Scout softly, reverently whispered, "The Technocracy will *not* be ignored."

"Surrender Dorothy." Mitch shrugged.

All three executives stared at him blankly.

Mitchell explained. "I thought we were playing movie quotes. You know, you were diggin' on Glenn Close from 'Fatal Attraction,' the 'I will not be ignored' shit, so I went with good old Marty Scorcese in 'After Hours.' Great flick. Rosanna Arquette's boyfriend has this Oz fixation in the bedroom and has to yell 'surrender Dorothy' before getting off."

"Vulgar," said the Aryan.

Mitchell turned to him. "Didn't I see you in one of John Leslie's better pornos? 'Chameleons,' not the sequel, maybe?"

"Show respect," the Aryan demanded. "We're men of power. If not for people like us, you wouldn't have any of this." He over-gesticulated by fluttering his hand around in a grand theatrical gesture to indicate the house, the grounds, the seven million Mitchell had in various bank accounts, CDs, and overseas investments.

Sighing, Mitchell looked over to the bald man. "Tell this example of Eurotrash inbreeding to shut up or I'll gut him next time he opens his mouth."

"Do it," said the nervous little bald man, looking up at the swords and knowing *exactly* how quickly Mitchell could take one of them down and behead everyone in the room. They could all be dead in the space of a single, muttered syllable.

The Aryan's mouth quivered, but did not open.

"Good," Mitchell said. He tried to get the bald man to look up, but he wouldn't. "Look, Chrome, tell me something. Who are these monkeys?"

The bald man nodded. "There was some headhunting at the firm. They're the current crop."

Mitchell sat back. "You picked these guys?"

"They are very skilled," Chrome said, adjusting his glasses. "The heads of their divisions."

"Do they understand what's been found? The risks involved? The rewards?"

Chrome shuddered and adjusted his round black shades. "They are the souls of discretion."

"You didn't answer my question."

Chrome gestured. Suddenly, all three men grabbed at their skulls and began screaming. They fell to the floor, gasping and shuddering in agony. Chrome said, "I put Truth Worms in their skulls. If they tell anything, they will die, their brains eaten away from within. It will take as little or as much time as I choose. They understand this."

"All right, all right," Mitchell said. "Enough with the demonstration. I've got company. I gave her something, but that doesn't mean these dickwads here won't wake her up."

Chrome gestured again. The executives fell upon one another in relief as their pain ended abruptly. Chrome finally looked up at Mitchell. "You've found what we needed? A Hollow One? Virtually adept?"

"An Acolyte, yeah."

"Does she know what she is?"

Mitchell shook his head. "Hasn't come around to it yet. I think that's best, overall."

"You have no intention of Awakening her?"

"Dunno. I planned on it, but now I kind of like her the way she is."

"The demons of paradox—"

"Gimme a break. Like I wouldn't have thought of that?" Mitchell looked over and saw the shaken not stirred executives climbing back into their seats.

"How do you propose to control her, then?"

"The old reliables. Sex, drugs, and rock 'n roll, topped off with a meaty helping of good old fashioned *revenge*."

Chrome seemed shocked. "That's it?"

"If she understands too much, then we're all screwed."

"I'm not sure about this."

Mitchell said, "Don't worry about it. When have I ever let you or the big boys down?"

The bald man's shoulders sank and he gestured at the three executives. "The 'big boys' are now these *children*. For all intents and purposes, *I* am the 'big boys.' At least for our branch. Pitiful, is it not?"

"No," Mitchell said is a rich, consoling voice. "You're very good at what you do. Very deserving. Who else among our kind could have found what we've all been searching for?"

"I *didn't* find it," Chrome said quickly. "A twenty-two-year-old snot in Newark, New Jersey found it. And he doesn't even know what it is. He thinks it's a video game. A neural net fantasy array. It's a miracle he's been able to keep it quiet, especially considering the corporation he works for."

"That's the beauty of it, Chrome. Our little helper works for the same company."

For the first time this evening, the bespectacled bald man seemed to relax. "Excellent."

SCOTT CIENCIN

"And I'm tellin' ya, don't run yourself down. Genius isn't always in coming up with the idea, it's in knowing what to do with it."

"You're a good friend," said Chrome, adjusting his glasses.

More than that, Mitchell thought, but he knew that Chrome wanted no one to be aware of the bond between them. Mitchell looked over at the executives. "These are the men you trust to re-invent reality?"

Chrome looked away as he said, "They all have excellent ideas. Phil over here is in charge of socialization." He nodded to the Boy Scout, who bit his lip and nodded. "Hunger, hopelessness, poverty, prejudice, and illness will all be wiped away."

"Groovy," said Mitchell.

Chrome pointed at the Aryan. "Erik will supervise the re-writing of history. He will also ensure that the society we build will last forever."

"Kind of a billion year Reich idea, huh, Erik?"

The Aryan looked away disagreeably.

Mitchell gestured at the Marlboro Man. "And who do we have here?"

"This is Paul Rogers—"

"No shit! Like in 'Bad Company' and that band with Jimmy Page? Y'know, with that 'Radioactive' song? The Firm, that's it!"

Marlboro said nothing.

"Paul will be in charge of beautification and the arts."

Mitchell sat back. "So what do these guys have to say about rap music? Alternative? Punk?"

A sour expression cracked the face of Paul the Marlboro Man. "If you tell me it's going to be the all Garth Brooks networks, I'm outta here!" said Mitchell, laughing whole-heartedly. No one else joined him.

Finally, Erik the Aryan got a little brave and said, "I don't understand why *he's* even involved in this. He's not even one of us. He's a mage who lost his Tradition. A rogue."

Mitchell frowned at this. He wasn't about to explain himself to this man. Besides, he hadn't "lost" his Tradition. He had fun during his days with the Cult of Ecstasy. He learned a lot from them, including his two particular talents. But there was no money in it, and Mitchell liked money. A lot.

"I want to hear it from your own lips," said Mitchell as he turned to the Three Wisemen. "You guys have been presented with the opportunity to do what the Technocracy has wanted to do for a century. To bring mankind forward, to Ascension. To permanently seal the Gauntlet. To sever mankind from any dangers that ran amok during the Mythic Age. To end magic once and for all, if need be. So present your cases."

All three were silent.

"Do it!" hissed Chrome.

Phil the Boy Scout went first. Soon, Erik was cutting him off, and within ten minutes, Paul was shouting at the top of his lungs. Mitchell allowed the argument to rage for another five minutes before he nodded to Chrome.

"That is enough, gentlemen," said the bald man. He sighed.

LIGHTNING UNDER GLASS   309

They ignored Chrome.

"Hot in here, isn't it?" Mitchell asked.

Chrome did not reply.

"I said—"

"I heard you," said Chrome, lowering his gaze. He didn't want to see this. "Yes, it's very hot."

"All right, then." Mitchell concentrated, and a clear oil oozed from the pores of his skin.

Erik the Aryan looked over sharply at Mitchell and cried, "Look at him! He sweats like some foul animal! All it takes is a few raised voices and he breaks into a sweat. We should kill him now!"

Mitchell wiped the sweat from his forehead. "Yeah, I guess I just can't stand the heat." Suddenly, his hand whipped sharply about, sending beads of sweat at each of the three men. They each recoiled, as if they had been spit upon.

"Insolent prick!" Erik screeched, rising from his chair and gesturing. "I'll kill you!"

Mitchell said nothing. Paul and Phil stood behind the other mage.

Erik raised his hand and called a flaming house of cards into existence. It was meant to grow into a tall prison, one capable of holding Mitchell. Then it was set to collapse, slicing him to pieces and turning him to ashes all at once.

"Good-bye," sighed Mitchell. A strange scent filled the study. It was sweet. Like licorice.

The bodies of all three men suddenly went slack. They fell to the floor, paralyzed. The cards fell smoking to the ground.

"That's called *Anise*, gentlemen," said Mitchell. "In its purest form, it's a poison for the nervous system. Muscular numbness is the first calling card, followed by total paralysis. What you assholes have spreading through you is Anise in its purest form—squared."

One by one they gasped as their hearts were stopped. It was over that quickly and efficiently.

"The good thing about this form of execution," Mitchell went on, "is that it forces the body to hold on to your waste materials for awhile instead of just spewing out piss and shit and ruining the carpet. Not to mention smelling up the place. You can never get that smell out. Not entirely. That's why I won't use my swords in here. All the blood would mess up my books. I like my books—"

"They're *dead*," Chrome said, shaking and staring at his shoes. "You can stop talking to them now."

Mitchell shrugged. Concern rippled through him suddenly. "Hey, sorry about the worms. They kind of took the big sleep, too. I'll pay you back. I know they're expensive."

"I'm not worried about the worms. I have another concern."

"Name it."

"These men will be missed."

"Naw, they won't," Mitchell said in a voice that indicated, *come on, don't worry about it, I'm not a goombah, y'know.* "I'll take DNA samples from them, spin doppelgangers complete in every way. Except their memories of tonight will be different, and they won't know a damn thing about the plan."

Chrome began to cry.

"What's the matter?" asked Mitchell. "You're tough. You're a Technomancer. No sleep. No dreams. Pure intellect. No personality. Shitty at parties, never get any pussy."

Chrome smiled, despite himself. "Stop that."

"What's bothering you?" This time, Mitchell's tone was much more compassionate. He reached over and put his hand on Chrome's shoulder. "You can talk to me, I'm your big brother."

Chrome removed his glasses and took in the full effect of the pure love he saw in his brother's smiling face. They had taken different paths, but each, in his way, had been a rogue.

"As you said, this cannot be done by committee," said Chrome. "I see that now."

Mitchell wiped his brother's tears away. "Look at what happens in Hollywood when you give people two hundred million dollars. You get crap like Waterworld. I don't care if that movie broke even or not, fish still stink, you know what I'm saying?"

Chrome nodded, smiling wistfully. His real name was Jeremy, but he had taken the moniker in school, after their parents died. It was a taunt that started when his hair fell out after one of his first spells backfired. No amount of raw magic or physical science could ever coax another hair to grow on the man's head. It was scorched earth. Jeremy learned to like the name, to wear it proudly, and to punish those who thought it anything less than regal. Those he couldn't subdue, Mitchell took care of with swift and oftentimes deadly efficiency.

"Now," Mitchell said. "Imagine handing all the money in the world to guys like the Betty Boop squad down there. All the power to shape reality in their image. What would we get?"

"It wouldn't be pretty," Chrome said.

"No, it wouldn't. I mean, these technomancy guys pay real well. Neither of us can complain on that score. But they've got less imagination than Hollywood, and that's saying something."

"You're right." Chrome's hands finally stopped shaking. His tears would not stop.

"Something else is bothering you," said Mitchell.

With trembling lips, Chrome said, "I'm *sorry* you're dying."

Mitchell gave his brother a firm hug. Then he pulled back and said, "Hey, it's not going to matter, soon. When we do what we have to do and rewrite everything, I won't have a tumor the size of a golfball in my head, and you can look like Jim Morrison if you want. You'd like that, wouldn't you? Big fuckin' head of hair, maybe an afro. What d'ya think?"

Chrome laughed. "I'd have to change my name again."

"Naw. Why bother? Just keep 'em guessing."

A sudden warmth spread through the bald man. He touched his chest, shuddering with the soothing energies. He relaxed, all at once. "My tears. My skin. You put something in me, mixing one of your oils in with my tears. What was it? What'd you use?"

"Don't worry."

"I'm not worried, what was it? I feel calmer." Chrome grinned broadly. "I like it!"

Mitchell smiled. "My own mix. Ylang Ylang, some clary sage, basil, lavender, mandarin—"

"It's the mandarin! I feel so much better now." And it was true. Even the bodies on the floor no longer worried him or upset him.

"So tell me about this guy in Newark. Tell me how you found out about him. If he's told anybody, if anyone has access."

Chrome spoke for close to a half hour. As he dispensed the vital information Mitchell needed, the older mage disposed of the bodies and crafted the trio of doppelgangers.

When he finished telling all he knew about the miraculous discovery in Newark, Chrome felt very tired.

Mitchell leaned forward and kissed his brother's forehead. "Just go to sleep."

"No…" said Chrome. "I should check the constructs for you. Test them for flaws. I knew those men."

"I don't make mistakes with this kind of thing. This is grade school stuff."

"No, let me," said Chrome, struggling to rise, slurring his words like a drunk. "Want to feel *useful.*"

Before Mitchell could stop him, Chrome reached out with his power and examined the perfect doubles of the men he had come here with—

—and *one other,* who waited outside, behind the wheel of the black Jaguar that Chrome had driven on the way here.

"No," said Chrome, horrified at the discovery.

Mitchell squeezed his eyes shut. He felt like shit. There was no reason for his little brother to have known. He should have made the poisons more fast acting. Now the damage was irreversible.

"You made one of me!" Chrome hollered. "There's a doppelganger out there ready to take my place! You're killing me!"

"I'm sorry," Mitchell said. "We'll be together again soon."

Chrome shuddered, overwhelmed by the horror of this betrayal. "Why?" he croaked in a small, piteous voice.

"Because God made the universe. God *alone.* Not God and his little brother Jeremy. It's really got to come down to one opinion, one vision. And I know you couldn't have stepped away."

"This can't be happening," Chrome wailed.

"I'm gonna make it so good for you when you come back," said Mitchell, trying desperately to sound reassuring. "You won't remember this, any of this, I swear, you are going to be the happiest man—"

Suddenly, a vortex of light leaped from Chrome's shiny skull. It formed into a wreath of fiery daggers and stabbed into Mitchell's head. The mage dispelled the attack easily.

"Come on," Mitchell said as his vision cleared and he encased himself in a sphere of protection. "Don't do this. You know you can't win."

Mitchell looked down at his brother, who didn't answer. Chrome sat in the chair, his head thrown back, his body perfectly relaxed. Mitchell knew his younger brother wasn't dead yet. What the hell was this?

Then it became clear to him. *Astral travel.* Chrome had abandoned his physical body. He was trying to find someone to warn about Mitchell and the Cathedral of Swords!

"Dammit," Mitchell said, touching the soulless body before him. Pure cinnamon oil left his hand, burning through Chrome's long coat. In seconds it dissolved the ribbed shirt beneath, raking through Chrome's flesh, until it reached his heart. The body jerked and spasmed. Mitchell had a brief sensation of his brother's soul as it died along with his body. Chrome's efforts had failed.

No one had been warned. He was still on schedule.

"I'm sorry," Mitchell whispered as death overtook his younger brother. "I love you."

He used his power to ease anise into Chrome's body, blocking the expulsion of waste.

"Dammit," Mitchell said, sitting before his brother's body. He commanded the trio of doppelgangers to get about their business. They were all glassy-eyed. None of them would have any memory of the night's events.

Mitchell wept for more than an hour. When he could cry no more, he disposed of the body. Before long, he was in the kitchen, trying to find something to eat. There was plenty of food, but he had no appetite. That didn't matter, he knew. He *had* to keep his strength up. Starving himself wasn't going to help him achieve his goals.

Then there was the other nightmare that he didn't want to think about: Any day now he might wake up and find that the tumor in his head had become all excited and decided to start screwing around with his ability to function in normal ways. His strange gift with oils and fragrances had been useless in trying to heal this particular problem.

So long as he still had his health, he had to protect it.

The lights in the kitchen were off. Mitchell hadn't bothered turning them on for some reason.

No, he thought, *you know the reason, motherfucker. Don't give me that shit. You're afraid you'll see a reflection in one of the windows, or the glass in the doors. And the one thing you don't want to do right now is confront yourself. You don't want to see your own ugly face, you don't want to see what you've become. Killing Jeremy. Christ almighty, there should have been another way.*

But he knew there wouldn't have been.

The door leading to the grounds opened suddenly and a man slithered into the room. Brown hair, an angular face, decent suit, nothing special. Mitchell had seen him in the Art Bar. He was the guy for whom they had put a little show. Max had called him Mr. Intense.

The guy had a gun in his hand. Mitchell was rarely startled by situations like this. He knew it was a part of the life he had chosen. Even so, he couldn't help but realize that if he hadn't forced himself to stay down here long enough to get some food, if he had gone upstairs to sink into Max's waiting arms, he probably wouldn't have lived until morning.

Before the gunman even noticed Mitchell standing off to one side, protected from view by the refrigerator, Mitchell surged forward, snatching the gun out of the man's hand and kicking him squarely in the balls, all in one fluid motion.

The guy squealed and sank to his knees, then fell over on his side, in a fetal position. Mitchell took advantage of the man's state and walked behind him to close the door. It was a little cool out tonight. He didn't want to catch cold.

Mr. Intense was reaching for his leg, where he clearly had a back-up piece. Mitchell kicked him in the head this time, knocking out a few teeth, making him spit blood on the tile floor. Kneeling, Mitchell stripped the gunman of his backup, then pulled up a chair. The mage sat down, casually aiming both weapons at the would-be-shooter.

"Hey, look, I'm in a John Woo movie!" Mitchell said as he gestured with both pieces at once.

Mr. Intense was turning into Mr. I Just Fucking Wet Myself With Fear.

"Here's how it is," Mitchell said. "For one thing, keep your friggin' mouth shut until I say you can speak, comprehende?"

The man nodded sharply.

"You don't want to die, I take it?"

A frantic shaking of his head.

"Good. I don't want to kill anyone else tonight."

The intruder's eyes went a little wide at this one, but he held his silence.

Mitchell glanced at the guns. "So you're a SIG Saur kind of guy, huh? Whadda we got here... A P226 as your primary, a P229 .357 high velocity as back-up. Y'know, I think this gun got a raw deal when the Army picked the Beretta 92Fs as their standard sidearm. At least the F.B.I.'s got more sense. They use these babies for their SWAT and Hostage Rescue Teams. See, I prefer swords, they're more elegant, but in our business, you gotta keep up on the hardware."

The assassin closed his eyes, realizing the extent of his situation.

Mitchell said, "open your eyes."

Shaking, the killer refused.

"I don't *want* to shoot you," Mitchell said evenly. "I've got a guest upstairs. I don't want to have to explain gunshots to her. So do me a favor and try not to be stupid here."

Mr. Intense opened his eyes.

Mitchell said, "I guess the idea was, you had seen my guests leaving, you waited a while, watched the place. No lights went on, so you figured I was upstairs with the wiggle," he shifted his voice to sound kind of generic gravely rap-starish, *"id dat right, homey?"*

The wanna-be shooter seemed confused.

"The girl," Mitchell said, annoyed.

"Oh, yeah. That's right."

"You were gonna go up, pop me right next to her so the noise would wake her up and scare the shit out of her at the same time, especially when she saw all my blood and brains all over her. Then she'd be pliable. Right?"

Mr. Intense moved his lips, but nothing came out. Finally, he chortled, "I'm sorry."

Mitchell shrugged. "It's what I would have done. Funny thing is, you might have been doing me a favor. At least I wouldn't have to worry about this fuckin' headache, know what I mean?"

Despite himself, Mr. Intense laughed a little at that. Mitchell joined him. They laughed and laughed, the tension broken.

"Can I get up?" asked Mr. Intense.

Mitchell's expression turned sour. "Whatdya think I am, friggin' stupid, you're gonna insult me like that?"

The assassin lowered his gaze. "Sorry. Had to try." He paused, then added, "You're her backer, right? They couldn't find out shit about you. Not a goddamned thing, except that you had money."

"That's comforting," Mitchell said. He put it all together instantly. Brenner sent this asshole. Mitchell thought about Maxine's partner, the gay guy who helped make the video game. "Did you do the other one?"

"He was peripheral."

Mitchell nodded.

"Who are you?" the assassin asked.

"Someone who's going to have to fuck you up real bad if you don't tell me everything you know."

They talked for an hour. The assassin worked for people with whom Brenner was only marginally involved. Bad people. Mitchell should have seen this coming. He could have replaced Brenner, as he did the members of the Technocracy and his brothers, but he didn't want take the risk. The doubles had a tendency to be kind of lifeless, making them perfect to replace Techoweasels, but not people with who had rich, active lives.

The whole doppelganger issue was causing him to imagine the 'Stepford Wives' as remade by Michael Crichton, so he stopped thinking about it. He had decided to work his influence over the CEO and his boys using his oils—what a smelly batch that turned out to be—and that was always risky. His drones were still capable of independent thought. They had no idea they were being manipulated, so they had sent a killer to bring Maxine in and take out anyone who was in the way. Unfortunately for Mitchell, he *just happened* to be the poor yahoo that was nearly in the way.

If one believed that anything "just happened."

But it was all right. He had the whole night ahead of him and so long as he didn't want to sleep or anything, he should be able to handle all of the damage control by morning.

"I want you to know, I appreciate what you've done," Mitchell said. "Now be a good boy and keep your friggin' mouth shut while you die."

The killer's eyes flashed open wide and he tried to speak, but Mitchell dropped the guns and leaped at him with such speed that there was no time for him to defend himself or even get out a decent last word. Mitchell twisted the man's head sharply. There was a nasty crackle as Mr. Intense's neck was broken and his body sank into Mitchell's arms. The mage used anise to block the normal business of a body dealing with death.

Mitchell disposed of this corpse the way he had the others. As he did so, he decided that he probably was going to have to Awaken his slumbering guest after all. This situation was just getting more and more complicated and he would need her in top form for the task he had in mind. At some point, he would explain how he had engineered so much of her recent misfortune, using his oils on Brenner and his toadies to control them. He wanted to make her understand that there really were no coincidences in life. Everything was planned by some guiding force, mortal or otherwise.

He believed in God, and he believed that God was tired and fed up and more than ready to let someone else have a shot at the job. Mitchell really wasn't looking forward to all the responsibility, all the blasted work that would be involved, but he knew it had to be done. The world had become a shithole and *someone* had to fix it. If the task hadn't been meant to fall into his hands, why then had the information about the programmer in Newark been delivered to him?

He went into his study, made some phone calls. The connection was bounced through a dozen way stations throughout the world, filtered, coded, encrypted— all that shit, as Mitchell would tell people.

When he was done with his phone, he got on his computer, picked up some information, then headed out into the night.

Exhausted, the mage arrived back at his estate as the sun was rising. He went upstairs to take his place next to Maxine. She was having some kind of nightmare, despite the magics he had used to ease her into an array of sexual fever dreams. It was a deep rooted nightmare, from what he could piece together from her whimperings and the images that spilled from her consciousness. He held her, kissing away her tears, and wondered if there was some way he could do what he needed to do without killing her in the process.

5

The mission sounded astonishingly simple, at least at first. Julian knew from experience it was the jobs *appearing* the most straightforward that generally turned out to be the most complex when all was said and done.

This was the mission: A client of X'an's wished to have a rival removed. A polite way of saying he wanted the bastard dead.

So far, so good.

Unfortunately, for the mission to be a success, the target had to die in a particular way.

The first faint tremors.

Both the client and the intended victim were mages.

Nine-point-three on the Richter scale.

They were both very old, very rich, very well protected, and very experienced mages.

California just fell into the ocean.

It seemed that the target had acquired, through very nasty means, a talisman of great importance to the client. The two mages had clashed over this object several times already and a blood feud had been declared over its ownership.

That would be the polar ice caps melting and flooding several continents.

The talisman was an object of enormous power, a great sword. All Julian had to do was break into the heart of a fortified compound, steal this grand old mage's most valued possession, replace it with a perfect duplicate that was, of course, the magickal equivalent of a package of high explosives rigged to go off the moment the target touched the duplicate weapon, and get out again without anyone noticing.

We now return to our regularly scheduled program.

The Seychelles Islands. Mid-afternoon.

Ninety per-cent of the population of the Seychelles Republic was concentrated in the thirty-two islands of the Mahé group in the north. These islands consisted of granite rock with sharp hills that rose to heights of nearly three thousand feet. The Republic's remaining eighty-three were situated in the south and known as coral islands. They were mainly uninhabited due to a lack of fresh water sources.

The mage that Julian had been sent to kill owned four of the southern islands. His compounds in each were identical. He moved his base of operations from one to another randomly, a kind of shell game in the event that any of his rivals became impatient with waiting for him to die and decided the best way to kill him was an air attack, whether technologically or magickally based. Or both. Precautions for just such an event were already in place. An enemy might be able to do some damage to one compound, and if they were lucky and the mage was present, it was possible that they could kill him. But the chances of even *finding* the right compound were one in four and the chances of the attackers surviving whether the mage lived or not were non-existent unless a nuclear strike was made.

The mage employed a staff of one thousand and ninety-seven. All were Sleepers. He solved the problem of fresh water and food by having both shipped in on a regular basis.

Julian at first believed that these supply boats would play a crucial role in his plans. Then he learned that his target could smell another mage a mile off. Besides, the next supply run was in five days.

Julian had brooded on the problem for hours. Finally, he had forced himself to get a little sleep. When he woke, the answer was before him.

Now it was mid-afternoon on an otherwise peaceful Saturday and he was in a small powerboat, navigating the choppy waters surrounding the closest of Nochuro Nabaska's four privately owned islands. A helicopter followed overhead. He had been commanded in five languages to turn back and warning shots had been fired into the waters around him.

Abruptly, the objections to his presence had ceased. Julian had predicted this. He had been recognized.

Or rather, the form his mentor's talisman *projected* had been identified. He wore the flesh of a fellow Indian, Durjaya Vikram. The name literally meant "difficult to conquer and glorious king." Julian now understood one of the reasons X'an chose him for this mission: If the illusion cast upon his flesh by the talisman was somehow dispelled during the heat of battle, he looked enough like the client to perhaps fool Nochuro.

Vikram and Nochuro had only seen each other's faces twice, though they had met dozens of times. The first time had been during an explosive battle in World War II, an encounter that somehow prompted their mutual animosity, and a confrontation five years ago, in Tel Aviv. Vikram was paranoid about allowing anyone to see his true face. His strength, he believed, lay in his paradoxical fame and anonymity. Everyone in their circles had heard of Durjaya Vikram, but few could put a face to the name. Despite the feud between the mages, Nochuro had not plastered his rival's face on the Internet. Such an act would have been beneath him, Nochuro had once explained. Only his guards knew the man's face so they might spot him if he tried to infiltrate the island when Nochuro was away and therefore unable to sense the arrival of a fellow mage.

Julian wore traditional Rajput armor, the standard of an Indian Knight of the 1700s. He wore a heavy black cloth coat covered with intricate designs, large diamonds shapes with gold studs at their center. A rectangular gold plate squeezed narrow in the middle covered his heart, a large golden circle his internal organs. A pair of gold plates shaped like fingernails went over his shins and gold plating covered his arms and legs under the beautiful cloth coat. He carried only a sword, opting to dispose of the Matchlock musket a true knight of the day would have carried. His head was shielded by an elaborate helm that seemingly covered his eyes, though he could see out through tiny slits. A large gold diamond studded with gems protected his nose. The armor was highlighted with bright crimson cloth trim.

It was hot as hell, but he could move well enough with the armor. His hands were covered by the gauntlets. That had been the whole point of the costume. The psychological benefit was an added bonus. It would appeal to Nochuro's sense of honor and hopefully assist Julian in his goal of winning a private audience—and duel—with Nochuro.

Julian felt strange wearing these traditional armors. When he had been a boy, the Hindu religion meant everything to him. He was fascinated by the history of his people and possessed a deep respect for their past. He had been visited, shortly before his Awakening, by visions of a Cathedral of Swords and a shadowy weaponsmaster who stood guard there. The weaponsmaster did not wear these armors, his garb was very different, but Julian's present wardrobe brought the figure to mind.

Julian preferred not to think of the past, despite the constant reminders that lay just beyond his pained wrists. He had become a citizen of the world, aware of everything, believing in nothing.

So much had been lost, he thought as the shore approached. *So very much...*

A figure was already on the shore, waiting. Suddenly, Julian heard a buzzing in the microcircuitry Jian Zhao had woven into his armors. The speaker inside his helm hummed.

"Did you hear the one about Carlos the Jackal?" Jian Zhao asked, his voice crackling.

Julian thought this discourse unwise, but Zhao had assured him that no technology or technology-based sorcery would be able to spy on their conversation. He had that all worked out. For some unfathomable reason—perhaps because he *wanted* to—Julian believed the young genius.

"What about Carlos?" Julian whispered. They had almost worked together, once.

"He got himself busted. You know how—or more to the point—*where* they got him?"

"Tell me."

"He was in a doctor's office, about to get fat liposuctioned from his waist."

Julian hesitated. "You're joking."

"True. Saw it in Forbes F.Y.I.."

Julian found that he was actually beginning to like his companion's company and that meant he was breaking one of his mentor's cardinal rules. Among the rules of the game, '*never think of the target or the client as human beings*' was near the very top of the list. '*Never question why*' and '*never judge*' held the top positions.

As Julian closed on the shore and identified the figure waiting for him, he found himself doing all these things. He wondered if he was going soft, if his time in the realm of the Sleepers had domesticated him, rendering him unable to return even briefly to his former profession as a sorcerous mercenary and assassin-for-hire.

"That's him," Jian Zhao whispered in Julian's ear.

"Then you'd better go." There was a sudden silence. Jian Zhao was already ensconced in his hiding place.

Julian brought his vessel as close as he could to shore, then sank into the waist deep waters to walk the rest of the distance. The island was beautiful. The coral reef was white, flaky, even a tad pink in places. Mostly, it was sand, rock, and stone. The fortress lay on a hill about 3,000 feet away. It looked like an ancient Japanese fort.

Nochuro stood waiting, a sword in his hand. Julian could feel that it wasn't the sword he had come here to retrieve. This sword was also a powerful talisman, but the mythical sword of Roland was unique and impossible to miss—at least to those who were attuned with the Art, and with swords and their history. Julian was talented with any weapon. Swords were his favorites.

The target wore a pink shirt, soft white cotton trousers, and ivory walking shoes. A golf outfit. Nochuro had plenty of time to change into appropriate garb for this battle. His attire was meant as a sign of contempt. Not good.

Julian studied Nochuro's face. The ancient mage looked about twenty five. Slimmer than Jian Zhao, with short cropped hair, but many of the same classical Asian features. He was handsome and strong.

The client and the target had used their spells to keep themselves young over the centuries. Another reason why Julian was ideal for this mission. Not only was he an Indian, he was also very youthful in appearance, like Vikram.

"You know what I want," Julian said, aware that his voice would sound like a perfect replica of Vikram's.

Julian had chosen this island at random. He had been lucky enough to find the island upon which Nochuro currently resided. That the sword would be here too was almost too much to ask. In any event, Julian had a plan for retrieving the prize.

Nochuro mercifully did not waste time with idle banter.

The battle raged for nine solid hours. Swords were drawn. The sands sprouted razor-lined tentacles. Fire spirits soared through the air, their bodies, their essences, becoming living weapons. Avatars of emotion took shape at Julian's desperate urging. People turned into snakes with acid-dripping, rapier-like tongues. They could not kill Nochuro with kindness, envy, greed—or even lust and desire.

Spiralling spheres of entropy reached out for Nochuro. Murder machines quoting lines from Jerry Seinfeld came forward, seeking to disarm with their absurdity while lightning coiled and leaped from within them. Nochuro was encased in flames, frozen solid and shattered, made into a pillar of salt.

He shrugged it off.

Music rose up around Nochuro, meant to burst his eardrums and leave him a drooling, whimpering wreck, or better yet, a corpse. He danced to the noise.

His blood boiled, aneurisms exploded within him, and the heads of murderous inhuman beasts sprang from his fingers and sought to tear out his throat. He transformed a dozen times, died and was reborn a dozen more.

Nothing stopped him.

Nochuro surged forward, gesturing with his hands, carving the air and tearing apart his enemy. Julian screamed as he was attacked. From his pleas for mercy, it was clear that he never expected to lose this battle. He was reduced to begging for his life.

Nochuro took great pleasure in the agony he caused his victim, and was careful to leave Julian wishing for death, but still horribly alive.

"You will not die until I command it," Nochuro commanded.

Nochuro was unaware that now his shadow seemed a little deeper than normal, just as his enemy's had a short time earlier. The mage drew an invisible, incapacitating prison around Julian, then took a radio the size of a comb from his back pocket and called in his helicopter. Naturally, all of his people had been sent away to prevent them from seeing the magickal duel. Nochuro was flown to the easternmost of his four islands, where he passed through a dozen rigorous physical and magickal security checkpoints before descending into a deep winding labyrinth where he came upon his beloved sword, the ultimate symbol of his triumph over Vikram.

Nochuro took the sword of Roland from its shrine and placed the weapon he had used against his enemy in its place. Then he turned and walked quickly away.

He never noticed the way his shadow lengthened and swelled behind him. A figure rose out of his shadow, a brawny Asian who quickly replaced the sword left behind with a lethal magickal construct that quickly adjusted itself into the image of the bloodied sword Nochuro had used moments before. The figure darted back into the grand mage's shadow, never quite parting from it.

Soon Nochuro was gone.

Julian Ibiero was barely alive. Technically speaking, the plan was going along perfectly. Nochuro was *supposed* to have defeated him. Julian had correctly wagered that the mage would want to finish his rival with the sword that had come to represent the animosity between them—the very item Julian had been sent to collect. Jian Zhao had hid in his shadow, then transferred to Nochuro's shadow during the battle. In this way, Nochuro would never sense the Virtual Adept's presence.

In the distance, the egg beating of helicopter blades slicing through the night air. Lights flashing down on the shore to pick a decent place to land.

According to plan, Julian would now be "murdered" by Nochuro with the powerful, mystical sword. Of course, that would be an illusion meant to lure Nochuro into a false sense of security. Zhao would transfer back to the "corpse's" shadow and the "body" would be packed up and flown back to Vikram's people. Once they were in the air, Julian would miraculously revive, take control of the craft with Zhao's help, and head out to X'an's palace in the snowy, mountainous reaches of Burma.

There was only one problem. None of this was an act. Julian was broken inside. He didn't have the strength or the will to conjure.

He was going to die.

It was ironic, Julian thought. X'an knew him better than he knew himself. The man probably had no information on the girl. And soon it wouldn't matter. He knew that Julian could not take Nochuro. This is why X'an sent him. He was expendable. Just as the four youths who had died at Trinity had been.

"Wakey wakey, rise and shine, show a leg, the morning's fine!" Nochuro called.

Julian looked up. He was so dazed that he hadn't even heard or seen the helicopter land and take off again. Had no awareness at all of the sounds of sand crunching beneath golf shoes. Must have blacked out.

Nochuro was covered in blood. Julian's blood. Strangely, Julian wasn't afraid to die. He hadn't been worried about his mortality for a long time. In fact, he welcomed an end to the torture. Struggling to a kneeling position, he positioned his head so that Nochuro could remove it with one clean sweep of his weapon.

The triumphant mage dismissed the magickal prison in which he had bound his victim. He approached with the sword held high, then he brought it down swiftly, jamming it into the sand next to Julian's face.

Nochuro sat down and conjured a small fire. "If it's any consolation, I thought the Andrew Lloyd Webber was *inspired*. If there's anything in this life that could drive a man insane—"

"I'll kill you," Julian chortled. He understood what this was. Nochuro was offering his enemy a chance at the weapon, a chance to die fighting, a warrior. He would take it.

When he could muster the strength.

"You will kill me," repeated Nochuro. "No, I doubt that. Would you like to hear Durandal's story? A bedtime story?"

Durandal was the name of the sword.

Julian nodded sharply. He had been cut in several dozen places. Blood leaked from between his chapped lips. He spat out something that might have been tissue.

There were days when he dreamed that the silver his father thrust his hands into had been rife with Quintessence. That the source of magic had fused with his body, his blood. But Quintessence was not a self-replenishing thing, not when it was cut away from the source that spawned it originally. It was orphaned primal matter.

Still… He could feel a tingling in his hands. A fire, an itch that had been absent since the day of his Awakening.

If he removed the gauntlets and proved to Nochuro that he was not Vikram, would it change anything?

Probably not.

His thoughts went to the child. She would be free of him now, free of his thirst for vengeance, his insane desire for her blood. It was still strong, pulsing within him, giving him what little strength he had.

Or was it his determination to make one final selfless act, to turn at last from the path of revenge, that spurred him on?

He would never know, he decided. And once he was mercifully dead, it would no longer matter.

His gaze drifted to the sword.

Durandal. Sword of Roland.

Dazzling.

A sparkling light was gathering around it. A light so pure that Julian could almost understand why these two mages had fought so hard to possess it.

Nochuro saw that his enemy was once again with him. The man had gone into some kind of trance for a few seconds. He told the story of the great hero Roland, wielder of Durandal. Roland's tale had been immortalized in the epic length narrative poem *Chanson de Roland*. This particular *chansonae de geste*, as such poems were called, had played somewhat with the historical facts. Roland, a young French soldier, laid down his life at Roncesvalles during Charlemagne's invasion of Spain in 778. He died at the hands of the Basques, though the *Chanson de Roland* made the villains the Saracens.

The sword had once belonged to Hector, if one believed the legends. Roland supposedly took the sword from the giant Jutmundus. An amazing fighter, Roland died as a result of betrayal by Ganelon, Count of Mayence and Paladin to Charlemagne. Ganelon had been jealous of Roland, and when Roland sent him as an ambassador to Marsillus, the pagan king of Sargoassa, the Paladin gave the route Roland's Christian army would take when returning to France. Roland was ambushed in a pass with 20,000 men. He fought with his men until 100,000 Saracens lay dead. Only Roland and fifty of his men lived through the battle.

Exhausted, they turned to see another army of Saracens advancing, this one 50,000 strong. Roland blew his enchanted horn, also taken from the giant. Though Charlemagne heard him, Ganelon convinced Charlemagne that it could not be Roland, who was supposedly on a grand and glorious hunt. The wounded Roland attempted to shatter Durandal, but the sword could not be destroyed. It was cast into a poisoned stream.

Nochuro described his efforts during WWII to find what remained of the legendary stream. "I know the sword was meant to rest there forever, that had been Roland's wish as it was unbreakable and could easily fall into the wrong hands... But over the course of years, streams are sometimes diverted, and sometimes they dry out..."

Julian blacked out from the pain he suffered. When he came to, Nochuro was still talking.

"I knew it at once. In its hilt is a thread from the cloak of the Virgin Mary, a tooth of St. Peter, a hair from St. Denys, and a drop of blood, still hot and wet and fresh, from St. Basil."

Julian could see the hilt. The blade was glorious.

Nochuro then explained how Vikram had nearly unraveled all of Nochuro's plans with a single thoughtless act. Now Julian understood the rivalry and the hatred between Nochuro and Vikram. Nochuro went on to detail what he would do with Durandal. His plans were horrifying. Julian was relieved that Nochuro would die when he brought Durandal back to its hiding place, but he worried about who would find the sword afterwards. It was a dangerous weapon, one that had to be guarded carefully. Perhaps Jian Zhao understood and would come back for it.

No. Zhao was too good a soldier. He had been given an exact criteria by X'an. The retrieval of Durandal was not a part of his job.

Of course not, Julian realized. The real Vikram would close in once his rival was dead and take the weapon. From what Julian knew of Vikram, that one was just as mad as Nochuro.

He was no longer so anxious to die.

The rules, he thought. Never question why. Never judge.

"We are not protectors of mankind. We are neutral, available to those who bid the highest..." X'an words.

Worst of all, Julian considered, the scrawny old bastard had his dog.

Gathering his strength, Julian unleashed a final magickal onslaught on Nochuro. He conjured a fantastic beast, part illusion, part flesh. It came in, low and screaming.

Nochuro set it to feed on itself and reached for the sword. The older mage was faster than Julian. Nochuro's fingers nearly touched its hilt when suddenly, the magickal construct Julian had created died in a hailstorm of light far greater than the gentle illumination cast by Durandal. Nochuro's shadow stretched forward and fell upon the sword's hilt before either mage could grab it.

The blade disappeared, swallowed by shadow.

Nochuro paused, stunned and surprised for the very first time in eight hundred years.

Julian felt energized, if only for an instant. The look on Nochuro's face was enough to invigorate even one who might as well have been dead, like him. He aimed a well placed kick at Nochuro's throat. It connected with the ancient mage's aura of protection. His throat was not crushed, but the force was great enough to send Nochuro tumbling back. He fell in an undignified heap.

Jian Zhao rose from the mage's shadow, wielding the sword. Nochuro rose to a crouch and saw his death coming an instant before it arrived. The prophecy was written in Zhao's eyes.

The sword flashed once. It sliced through Nochuro's protective magicks easily and lopped the mage's head off with the sound of sugar cane being harvested in a field. Zhao knew that sound. It made him smile, even as the mage's blood rose up at him in a torrent and the headless corpse twitched and fell to the ground.

Zhao felt a surge of energy move through the sword. Spinning, he cried, "Catch!"

Julian saw the sword gently sailing through the air toward him. He thrust out his hand and caught it by the hilt. There was a flash of lightning as strange energies coalesced inside him, easing his pain. The fire within his stomach went out and the throbbing pain in his skull vanished.

He looked down at his chest, the flesh exposed through his shredded armor, and saw a network of scars, but no wounds. The sword had healed him.

"How else do you think Roland survived as long as he did?" Jian Zhao asked as he spun in Julian's direction, kicking the sword from the mage's foot, and striking Julian's temple with the other. In the fragment of a second it took Jian Zhao to come back to earth after his assault, Julian Ibiero was flung into darkness.

The dull roar of engines came to Julian. He opened his eyes and was surprised to find himself sitting in the first class compartment of a commercial airliner. He had a window seat. No one sat next to him, though all the rest of the seats were occupied.

Looking out the window, he saw the sparkling ocean beneath him. The sun was rising. He heard movement and glanced to his right. A pretty young flight attendant, short blonde hair, deep blue eyes, too short to be a model, stood before him. Her name badge read "Christina."

"Hey, look who's back with us!" she said brightly.

Julian smiled at her. He raised his hand in her direction. It moved stiffly, shaking slightly. He was startled to see wrinkles and liver spots dotting his flesh.

SCOTT CIENCIN

His throat was dry. He managed to order a drink, though he didn't recognize the voice that left his throat.

He looked down at his hands. They were uncovered. Shriveled with age. Touching his chest, he felt for X'an's amulet. It was gone. His flesh was hot and felt alien.

What had been done to him?

The flight attendant returned with his drink. "You seem a little disoriented, Mr. Huan. Are you all right?"

He nodded. Mr. Huan?

"The facilities," he muttered.

Christina stepped back and motioned toward her right with a Vanna White flourish. "Would you like me to get Bob or one of the other flight attendants to help you?"

"No, no… Thank you, I'll be fine…" Again, that voice. Like soot being shoveled around in a furnace. Tinged with an Asian accent. Mr. Huan. That made sense.

Julian moved stiffly, unable to straighten up all the way, as he left his chair and navigated the short distance through the aisle to the lavatory. He locked himself inside and took a look at himself in the mirror.

The changes to his appearance were not so complete as he might have expected. He looked Asian, all right, and old as hell. Kind of like… X'an.

Julian grinned broadly as he understood what had happened. The make-up covering his face nearly cracked and he regained his controlled expression. He wore a dark grey suit. Julian searched the pockets. In his possession was a ticket to Seattle, Washington, an address in that city, a passport, and a wallet crammed with cash and credit cards made out in his assumed name. There was also a pair of baggage claim tickets and a slimline pocket organizer. Julian opened the organizer, about the size of two business cards laid end to end. There was a keypad and a small LED readout. Words raced across the small screen:

LISTEN CAREFULLY. THIS UNIT IS INFECTED WITH A POTENT VIRUS THAT WILL WIPE ITS MEMORY ONCE THIS MESSAGE HAS PLAYED A SINGLE TIME. GREETINGS, JULIAN. JIAN ZHAO HERE. AS YOU MIGHT HAVE GUESSED, I'M NOT NEARLY AS LOYAL TO X'AN AND OUR MERCENARY CAUSE AS ONE MIGHT HAVE THOUGHT. CLEARLY, NEITHER ARE YOU. I MUST THANK YOU. YOU COULD HAVE BETRAYED MY PRESENCE TO NOCHURO AT ANY TIME AND PERHAPS USED THE MAN'S DISTRACTION TO SAVE YOUR OWN LIFE. INSTEAD, YOU WERE PREPARED TO DIE RATHER THAN BETRAY ME. FOR THAT, YOU WILL BE REWARDED.

Julian ran his hand over the latex mask covering his features. Jian Zhao had no idea what was really going through Julian's mind at the time. If he had, he might not have been so generous.

I HAVE TAKEN THE AMULET. IT SHOULD COME IN HANDY. YOUR HAIR WAS DYED GREY, MAKE-UP ADORNS YOUR FLESH, INCLUDING LATEX GLOVES TO COVER YOUR WOUNDED HANDS. REALLY, I DON'T KNOW WHY YOU NEVER THOUGHT OF SUCH A THING YOURSELF, NOT THAT I WISH TO CRITICIZE. IF THIS MAKES YOU UNCOMFORTABLE, THERE IS A CARRYALL IN THE COMPARTMENT OVER YOUR SEAT. A PAIR OF GLOVES AND VARIOUS AND SUNDRY OTHER ITEMS YOU MAY REQUIRE ARE THERE, INCLUDING IN-STRUCTIONS ON WHERE TO PROCURE ANY WEAPONRY OR HARDWARE YOU NEED IN YOUR QUEST.

I HAVE BETRAYED X'AN AND TAKEN NOCHURO'S FORTUNE AND EMPIRE FOR MYSELF. BUT THE SWORD OF ROLAND IS YOURS. DO WITH IT AS YOU WILL. X'AN WILL NOT COME AFTER ME. I AM NOW A MAN OF STATUS. A POTENTIAL CLIENT. I DON'T KNOW HOW HE WILL RESPOND TO WHAT HE WILL SURELY REGARD AS YOUR BETRAYAL, HENCE THE SWORD, WHICH YOU CAN UTILIZE AS A PEACE OFFERING, IF YOU WILL. THE ADDRESS I GAVE YOU IS THE CURRENT LOCATION OF YOUR PERSONAL TARGET. AN ESTATE IN EDMONDS. I GIVE YOU ALL THIS AND MY ASSURANCE THAT IF YOU NEED MY HELP IN THE FUTURE, IT WILL BE GIVEN TO THE BEST OF MY ABILITY.

YOURS,

JIAN ZHAO

Julian watched as the LED's text suddenly turned to gibberish. He looked down and saw the sorcerous fires moving through his hands begin to burn through the latex gloves. He had very little time left to return to his seat and find his gloves. Bright silver mixed with crimson chunks of meat were already beginning to show through the "fake skin." This was why he did not use such flimsy materials in *his* gloves.

He returned to his seat and had his hands safely ensconced in his own gloves before the worst of the dissolution began.

Seattle, Washington, in only six hours, the captain said.

Julian nodded silently.

He sat back and enjoyed the ride.

6

Edmonds, Washington.

Maxine Anderson was awake in more than one sense of the word. It was close to noon on Sunday. Mitchell's estate was now seething with security personnel. He had revealed many truths to Max the previous day, not the least of which was that her life was in serious danger.

Mitchell had made many fantastic claims. When she found herself doubting them, she had gone upstairs to the bedroom and watched the videotape of their lovemaking Friday night. With each viewing, the bizarre truth was reinforced in

SCOTT CIENCIN

her mind. Now she no longer needed to see the tape. She had memorized the images it contained, of Mitchell warping and changing his body to please her.

Strangely, she was no longer frightened, because she now understood that she and Mitchell were of the same rare breed. He was older, and far more experienced, but *she* had a certain raw power that impressed him.

Magic existed in the world and they had the power to wield it, though in different ways. They were mages.

This is how the revelations began.

On Saturday morning, Mitchell woke Maxine. The window was open. Cool air filtered in, whipping the curtains about. Soft golden sunlight, sparkling and clear, filled the room, dispelling any air of mystery it may have held. A strange smell, fragrant and overpowering, reached into Max's lungs, bestowing upon her an astounding clarity. She normally had a terrible time getting fully awake in the morning. Breakfast usually consisted of the three "C"s: concentrated coffee, pure milk chocolate, and too much caffeine. She would get wired and her heart would race, but she would still feel a little "thick" upstairs.

Not this morning.

She had no hangover. In fact, she seemed to suffer no ill effects whatsoever of the booze and the weird drugs Mitchell had somehow gotten into her.

Christ, she thought. This is a little anti-climactic. No head or body aches, no nausea, no great punishment to let you know that you're a fucking worthless shit and you would destroy your body from the inside out by the time you were thirty. Without all that, the moral lessons taken away, the cautionary tales no longer playing on the radio inside her head, what was the point of getting wasted?

She looked at Mitchell and realized she was naked.

"Hey," she said, laying back, parting her legs a little. She remembered him, remembered coming here and everything they had done together. And she remembered why.

She was just as desperate now as she had been the previous day to put off talking with Freddy. Laughing, Max said, "You up for another helping?"

She reached out with her foot, brushing her toes against his crotch. Gently, he reached down and guided her foot away. He was already dressed. His piercing eyes held a magnificent beauty, and a strange sadness she had never seen before.

Suddenly, she understood. She broke away from his gaze and looked for her dress. "All right, I get it. I'll get the fuck out."

"What?" he asked, his genuine confusion stopping her in her tracks. "No. That's not what I want."

She resisted the urge to settle back on the bed again, though the power of his gaze seemed to be forcing her that way.

"Are you cold?" he asked her, stepping away from the bed and opening an armoire. He removed a soft green robe and draped it over her shoulders. She pulled it close and tied the sash.

Looking down at the bed, she whispered, "I really should get going. There's some things I need to take care of." She ran her hand over her forehead and kept doing it as if she was trying to sand her skin down to the bone. "I'd like to take a shower first if you don't mind, then maybe if you'd give me a ride back to the Art Bar, or get me a taxi—"

"Max," he said, immediately gaining her full attention. He swallowed hard. "I don't know how to tell you."

"Tell me what?" she asked with a taunting, resigned, and nasty edge to her voice. "That you're married? What do I care?"

He looked at her strangely.

"Sorry," she said, shuddering. "Old behavior pattern. Leave before you can be left. Strike out before anyone can hit you. My therapist says I really need to work on it."

Mitchell pulled up a chair from the corner. "Max, it's all changed, everything's changed."

She waited. What was he talking about?

"I know who you are."

She pulled the sash of the robe even tighter and tried not to be afraid. Then she thought of her purse. It was somewhere in his car. "You went through my bag."

"Didn't even occur to me."

Now she *was* getting scared, and against her better judgement, she told him so.

He nodded. "I'm sorry. Some of what's going on *is* scary. I think so, anyway." He winced and touched his head, as if he was suffering from some terrible headache. Gritting his teeth to ignore the pain, he went on, "I'm just not going to be doing you any favors if I sugarcoat things. Here's how it is: A man came here looking for you last night. He followed us from the bar."

It came to her quickly. "Mr. Intense."

Mitchell nodded. "I know how it sounds, what I'm about to say. Like something out of a movie, but it's true."

She waited.

"He had a gun. He was here to kill you."

The world seemed to close on her suddenly. She felt a little dizzy, and another fragrance exploded into the air. A calming breeze passed through her. She looked to the window.

Garden must be right outside, she thought. *That's what I'm smelling.*

"Are you some kind of psycho?" Max asked with a nervous half-laugh, refusing to look back at Mitchell. Instead, her gaze was fixed on the door. She felt that she had a good chance of reaching it before he could.

"I was lucky. I was in the kitchen when he came in. He didn't see me."

Against all reason, she looked back at Mitchell. He seemed contrite, all that he had to tell her weighing him down. The man leaned forward in his chair, resting his elbows on his knees, his hands dangling near enough to touch, but not quite touching one another. His body was relaxed, not tensed for an attack. Max had a good deal of training in recognizing the signs and countering attacks.

"So this guy came in," she prompted, "with a gun."

"I was in the army, I know how to take care of myself. Some things you don't forget."

Max silently agreed. Quietly, she asked, "Where's this guy now?"

"He told me he'd been hired by a guy named Brenner."

Max felt her heart seize up again. Then the calming fragrance drifted toward her and engulfed her, easing her tension.

"I got the whole story, Max. He followed us here, saw the way we were playing around outside, and decided we were going to be in for the night. So he doubled back to the bus station, got your lap top, your Point and Shoot." Mitchell nodded to a dresser. The items were there.

Oh, God, she thought. *Freddy!*

Mitchell looked up sharply, as if he knew what was on her mind. "Max, he already went by to see your friend."

"No," Max cried hoarsely.

"It was in the papers this morning. I always knew Brenner was a son-of-a-bitch, but I didn't think he'd resort to having people killed just so he didn't have to give them a cut of the profits from their own work. I was wrong. It was supposed to look like two unrelated killings. Different M.O., no apparent connection between the victims." Mitchell looked away. "I'm *so* sorry."

"I want to see," Max said quickly, her mind still struggling to deny what she sensed in her heart to be the truth. "The newspaper. I want to see it."

Mitchell rose then hesitated. "You sure?"

Max nodded. Mitchell left the room for a moment, then returned with the newspaper. She saw her friend's photograph, read the article. His body had been ripped apart.

Jesus, Max chanted in her mind, *Jesus, no!!!*

Then she was screaming, wailing, in Mitchell's arms, beating at him even as he helped her to the bathroom, where she threw up until she could produce no more than dry heaves. She collapsed in the corner, her eyes red and stinging. There had been no comforting fragrances this time. Just harsh, cold reality.

Her eyes widened as she regarded Mitchell. "How do I know *you're* not working for Brenner?"

"Yeah, if I had come on to *you* last night, I could see where you might of thought that," Mitchell said. "Keep in mind, I was just sitting there. You came into my life. I didn't come into yours."

Max thought about that. "I gotta get out of here."

"And go where?"

She looked at him sharply. "Well, this guy. The one who told you about me, about what's going on, we have to bring him to the police, we—"

Mitchell shook his head.

"You?" she said, her voice quavering. Was the man before her capable of killing someone?

"I got careless. He, y'know, whadda they call it? Got the drop on me. Was gonna shoot me. I had to… I didn't want to, I had to." Mitchell looked down at his hands as if they were alien creatures. "First time I ever had to… Sorry."

Max allowed Mitchell to lead her back to the bed. He sat beside her as they looked out the window together and said nothing for almost an hour.

Through the window, Max could see the garden she had envisioned. It was even more glorious than she could have imagined. Flowers of every kind, every color…

For a time, she simply shorted out. No thoughts went through her mind. Then slowly, she was aware of more than the soft blue of the sky and the walls of his estate in the distance.

She thought of Freddy. His touch, his laugh. How she would never hear his voice again. It was just as it had been with her parents.

Max felt Freddy's loss deeply. She loved him so much. Now it felt as if a part of *her* was also dead.

What tortured her the most, however, was the tiny pang of relief she had felt when she had learned of his death. There was no longer any chance that she might betray him because she was weak and selfish. That she might have sold him out. He died thinking her something better than what she was, believing her to be a decent human being.

That thought, though it had lasted only a single shattering instant, had confirmed every miserable notion she had ever had about her own self-worth. She understood now the path that she had set herself on in the stairwell of Infinity Inc., when she had been faced with the chance to destroy the Point and Shoot, to devote herself to fighting Brenner and the Four Horseman. She had made a decision in that instant. And folded. Everything that followed, buying the dress, picking up Mitchell, was a desperate attempt for consolation, a need to be shown that she had some value, that she wasn't a worthless bitch because she was going to ruin a man who had been her only real family for so many years.

Mitchell touched Max's hand. She started at first, but before he could pull away, she covered her hand in both of his.

"He had a cat," Max said.

"The guy, he—"

"All right." She had hoped that some small part of Freddy had lived on. Clearly even this was too much to ask for.

Suddenly, as she continued to look out the window, she became aware of men patrolling the grounds. Armed men.

"I think you need to know some things about me," Mitchell said. "I'm not a nice man. I have a lot of money. I made some of that money doing some pretty nasty things. Stealing, mostly. Generally, I feel bad about that, but considering the present circumstances, I don't think a nice man would be able to help you."

"Help me?"

"I killed a man last night, Max. I took his life. But what he knew, they know. This guy Brenner… My contacts tell me he's connected. That means there's going to be others."

"More killers sent to find me," Max said, trying to reconcile herself to the absurd yet terrifying concept.

"Thing is, I'm kind of connected, too. That's why those people are out there. Now, I've already talked to the son-of-a-bitch on the phone."

"Brenner?"

"Yeah. He claimed he didn't know anything about the hit, but I made it clear to him that I'm a player, too, and if he wants a war, he's got one. I suggested he and I should meet, work out some kind of settlement."

"Settlement," Max said numbly. As she spoke, her voice rose to a shattering crescendo. "They killed Freddy and almost *killed us* because of a freakin' piece of software and you're talking *settlements?*"

"Brenner said 'no' to the meet. The next move's his. And as far as why all this is happening, what you made is more than just a piece of software and you know it."

"What are you talking about?"

Mitchell got up. He collected Max's laptop, her papers, the prototype. "The first thing that happened when you left that conference yesterday? Brenner's people tried to find out who was in on this with you."

"Just Freddy," Max said automatically. "Why?"

"Because the designs on the schematics you made? Anyone could have done that. Don't get me wrong, it's brilliant work." He picked up the Point and Shoot. "But to actually *build* this thing—we'd be talking about serious breakthroughs in micro-technology. Someone would have had to have built machines to have built what you showed them. The technology doesn't exist."

Max tried to think of something to say. Instead, all she could do was caress the gold bracelet, tracing one finger over its strange runes. All this was crazy.

"There was something in your head that was conveniently skipping over these little facts. If I'm not mistaken, you've probably been skipping over similar facts all your life."

"No…" Max whispered.

"If you had confronted the facts, you would have been forced to accept that what you were doing wasn't physically possible. Not on the kind of Radio Shack shoestring budget you were describing. No way. They decided you had investors. Since I have money and you came home with me, I'm it."

Max squeezed her eyes shut. A part of her knew that when she worked on electronics, she "phased out" as she thought of it. She went into a fugue and whatever she needed to build, got built. There had been all the classes in machine-working, she could read and design schematics, but that was still no explanation for how she managed to reconnect wires without solder, or sometimes created wonders of electrical engineering with just a quick trip to Radio Shack. In all truth, her odd ability scared her and with the exception of the Point and Shoot, she hadn't applied that talent to anything in many years.

"Do you remember what we did last night?" Mitchell asked.

"Please, I'm not—"

"No, no," Mitchell said in a calm, understanding voice. "Believe me, the last thing from my mind right this minute is having sex with you. No offense."

She nodded.

"But the videotape we made might help right now. It could show you things."

A nasty little chortle escaped Max as she thought about the videotape. If she was in the mood to be aroused, and God knows, she certainly wasn't at this moment, the tape would prove to be a disappointment. In terms of photogenic stuff—and she had some experience with this—they hadn't really done that much. It would start with them sixty-nining each other, then Mitchell would lay behind her and they would do it in the spoon position. She would barely see him, and seeing him make love to her would have been the thrill.

All the tape would show was her boobs flying around and her screaming like a maniac with some guy behind her. Both sections would just drag on forever. Her finger would be itching for the scan button.

On the other hand, if it showed what she *thought* they had done, what the drugs or whatever she had been on made her *think* had happened...

"I'd like you to see a few minutes of the tape," Mitchell said. He knew this was a risk. If she accepted what he had to show her, she would be his. Otherwise, her mind would shatter and the demons of Paradox would come for him.

Fuck it, what's life without risks, he thought as he opened a cabinet, revealing a combination television monitor and VCR that was wired to the camera in the corner. The tape had already been cued up.

Holding his breath, he hit "PLAY."

Maxine stared at the flickering images, watching in bizarre fascination as the Mitchell on the video screen metamorphosized.

She knew that such special effects were possible these days. With the advances in CGI graphics, anything was possible. But there just wouldn't have been the time to doctor a videotape this way. More importantly, why would anyone go to the trouble?

Of course, if she accepted that what she was watching on the screen wasn't doctored, that meant she had to also accept that she had made love to a man who was more than human, that she had to believe in the existence of *people*—

—was he a person?—

—who were more than *human*.

The notion struck her as funny. She knew it shouldn't have, but it did. A part of her knew that she should be rolling around on the floor, frothing at the mouth, her mind unable to accept this. If Mitchell performed some of these tricks in front of her this very moment, when she was straight, she might have freaked out. Instead, she just thought it was silly.

Too bad she couldn't bring herself to laugh.

"Turn it off," she said, afraid, yet unable to look away from the image on the screen. It fascinated and repulsed her.

"Best part's coming."

"So to speak," she said, aware of what was about to happen in the video. Mitch would turn into some kind of jellyfish, covering her. No thanks.

"Max, really, I think you should—"

"I'd rather remember how that *felt*, not how it *looked*," she said, getting up and striking at the television's control panel. The tape stopped and CNN came on.

The newscaster was a blonde woman in her forties. A familiar emblem sat in the screen's upper right hand corner.

"—and this is what the owner of Enigma Fashions had to say about his controversial but well received NO PC entry to Attention '97.

A man came on the screen. She had seen his face before in magazine ads, seen him mentioned in the trades. Julian Ibiero. Midnight black hair, a panther's grace, piercing onyx eyes, and creme and coffee colored skin. He was beautiful. And though she was familiar with his face, and his odd penchance for always wearing gloves, until this moment, she had never heard his voice.

Mitchell reached for the TV, about to turn it off. Max stopped him.

"It was all in good fun," Julian said on the screen. "I respect the feelings of all these special interest groups and support many of them with my own earnings. I'm a member of PETA and a believer in what the organization does. But if one can not *occasionally* make light of one's self, then one is subject to even greater ridicule for being grandiose, judgmental, and self-serving. What we did got people talking again. And that, in the long run, should be beneficial to all these causes. The waters have been stirred. Now it is up to the people to turn their righteous indignation into something concrete and constructive…"

The sound of Julian Ibiero's voice stirred something deep within Max. She felt an odd comfort, as if she was listening to the dulcet tones of a long forgotten friend. Her fingers drifted to her gold bracelet and traced its runes.

"Enough of this," Mitchell said with a shrug, his easy-going manner once again reasserting itself as he turned off the television. "So what do you think?"

"Gee, I dunno," Max said, forcing herself not to think about Julian Ibiero and why his voice sounded so strangely familiar. Instead, she focussed on the tape she had watched. "What do I think? Hmmm. That I just had sex with Gumby? That you had *four*…"

She understood what was going on in her mind. She was being given something to focus on other than Freddy's murder. For that reason, she was accepting this madness.

"Do you believe what you saw?" Mitchell asked.

Max was silent. She looked back toward the window.

Mitchell held out his hand. "I could show you—"

"No!" she screamed, suddenly vaulting over the bed and heading for the door. He cut her off, grabbed her.

"Why would you be willing to do this for me?" she asked, breathless, fighting him, but without the strength to make her attack mean anything. She was still trying to adjust to these new circumstances, these dizzying revelations. "No one helps me, no one, *no one*—"

"LOOK," he said, loud enough to make her fall away from him, against the door, and press her hands to her ears.

He stepped back and waited for her to take her hands from her ears. "I'm sorry." Touching the side of his head, he said, "I'm *dying*. I have brain cancer. I'm only going to be a…" he swallowed hard. "A *human being* for a few more weeks, if that. Then it starts eating me alive. I won't be able to function. That's how it works. Tumors are real motherfuckers."

"Tumor?"

Mitchell restrained a smile. Max sounded as if she believed what he was saying, but she didn't want to lose him, too. She was beginning to feel that she just might need him.

"I can show you medical records," Mitchell said, "or we could go to any doctor, any hospital in the world, you pick one at random, and watch while they take their X-rays. I'm telling you the truth."

He understood from the sorrowful look in her eyes that she believed him. If you're going to lie, always tell enough of the truth along with the lie to make it sound convincing. That was one of the first things he had been taught when he decided to become a free agent, all those years ago.

"The bottom line is this," Mitchell said. "If you want to leave, you can leave at any time. I won't try to stop you. Frankly, I made that video for *myself* last night. I didn't think you were the type to hang around long, and I wanted to remember what you looked like."

Max said as she wandered around the bedroom, a little dazed.

"Why would you think I'd leave?" she asked. "You're great."

"That's usually why beautiful women leave. I can't quite get this treating them like shit thing down."

A halting series of half-laughs emerged from somewhere deep inside her. She was startled by them, but they helped.

"I've been looking for a way to make up for some of the things I've done," said Mitchell. "Getting you straight, making sure those assholes never touch you… Maybe that would balance things for me a little. Thing is, there isn't a lot of time." He tapped his head. "Because of this, I mean. I get these fucking headaches and I think, 'hey, that's it.' But it's just getting started. The pain, the falling apart. It's just gearing up, that's all."

"Why'd you show me that?" Max said, gesturing nervously at the television. "What difference does it make, even if it's real?"

"It makes a difference because I can do special things, and you're like me. You can do them, too. I can help you unlock what's inside you. I'm not saying you won't be hurt again. I don't even understand how powerful you are, or how your talents could be put to work in saving your life if someone came at you with a gun or a knife."

"Try it," Max said, feeling stronger, ready. "Try it."

Mitchell looked around, squinting in confusion. Max liked it when he squinted. "What? You want I should try and hit you or something? I outweigh you by about a hundred pounds."

That was true, Max knew, and it was all muscle. "Try it."

He came at her fast, as fast as he had ever moved in his life. He held back nothing, though he was ready to pull his punch at the last possible instant.

Max sidestepped him, grabbed his arm while tripping him with her leg, and sent him forehead first into the wall as she leaped back and kicked at the rear of his head. He froze as her foot hovered a few centimeters away from the vertebrae attaching his head to his neck. Considering her velocity, if she had allowed the kick to connect, it would have killed him easily.

"Can I get up now?" he asked, his face squished against the wall. His heart was racing. No one had ever been able to do that to him before. He sure as hell wasn't expecting it to be this woman. Instead of being pissed, he found himself smiling with approval and pride.

Goddamn it all to hell, he really *was* falling in love with her.

Or maybe it was just the tumor already effecting his behavior and good sense.

As he rose to his feet, he said, "Okay, you can defend yourself in hand-to-hand. Where'd you learn?"

"Lived overseas," Max said. "Lot of survival training when I was a kid. Kept up with it."

"Should have entered contests," he said, tensing and hoping he hadn't betrayed himself. *I should have? How do you know I didn't? How well did you check me out?*

"Never interested," she lied. She hugged herself. "I don't want to talk about what you did last night, or this tape."

"All right. But there's more to defending yourself than hand-to-hand. People use knives, guns, bombs—fire spells… What are you going to do when someone uses magick on you?"

Max considered his words. "Let's say I believed what you showed me. You can do that any time?"

He shrugged, kind of rolling his shoulders. From her weak smile, he could tell that she liked it when he did that. Finally, he said, "To be honest, only when I'm really *horny*. Strange, but true."

She laughed, despite herself.

Mitchell reached out his hand. "I just want to make it so no one can hurt you again."

Max went to him and folded herself into his arms. He made a tiny gesture and music came on. Soft, classical.

She didn't even flinch. Mitchell couldn't have been more pleased.

Late that afternoon, they were in the garden. Mitchell was going over the options he saw for ensuring Max's safety.

"It's not enough," said Max. She looked at one of the armed guards. "I want Brenner gone. I want that bastard dead."

"That could get messy. Things go back and forth, takes a lot of time, we don't have time."

She wasn't listening. "I want him to suffer, first."

Max had agreed to stay at the estate. She told Mitchell that though it was against every rule she had lived her life by, she trusted him. She knew this wasn't some movie where she was being taken in, where she would show Mitchell how she made the Point and Shoot and suddenly Brenner would step out from behind the curtain and thank Mitchell for his work.

"No," Mitchell had said. "It's not like that."

"If it was, I could imagine what you'd do. You wouldn't bother shooting me, you'd probably want to fuck me to death."

He shook his head and was unable to deny that last night had been very nice.

The thought of being with Mitchell that way again made Max blush, and excited her a little. Particularly as she now understood the possibilities in their lovemaking.

Something else excited her more. The memory of Julian Ibiero's face. The sound of his voice.

But why?

Shortly after dinner, Mitchell got a call from one of his associates. Mitchell took down some information and said to have the rest e-mailed through one of the secure lines.

It occurred to Max as she watched him in his study that he would look good with a cigarette in his mouth. It was weird that he didn't smoke. He had a face that was meant for it.

Tough and cool.

During the day, one of Mitchell's people had been sent out to get her clothes. She now wore a tight pair of jeans and a baggy sweatshirt that belonged to Mitchell. She had put in on earlier and just couldn't bring herself to take it off, though she had blouses and tees she might have worn. Wearing something of his made her feel as if his hands were on her. She liked that, and not because she wanted to lose herself in sex again.

She had other reasons.

Mitchell reported what he had learned. He talked for ten solid minutes. The entire time, Max found her smile broadening. A line from the Nine Inch Nails song came to her:

You give me reason to live.

Mitchell was doing that for her now. And that reason was vengeance.

"So tomorrow, Ted Brenner's world falls in on him," Max said. "His partners won't have any choice but to kill him."

"You bet. Best of all, you're going to be the one setting it all in motion. Not the same as pulling the trigger yourself, but—"

"But I might as well be," Max said.

Mitchell seemed saddened by this. "Yeah."

That night, she asked if she could sleep in Mitchell's bed. He went to bed in his boxers and didn't even try to touch her.

She stripped off the sweatshirt—all that was covering her at this point—and knelt on the bed before him.

"Show me," she said.

"Are you sure?" he asked, already excited and absolutely capable of transforming his flesh.

SCOTT CIENCIN

"You sure it's not going to mess up your head, seeing me—y'know. Change?" She descended on him.

It was all the encouragement he needed.

That night, for the first time since he was eight years old, Mitchell did not dream of the Cathedral of Swords and the Weaponsmaster.

Instead, he dreamed that he was on a cool, crystal lake, in a boat with Maxine, and they were on a slow, peaceful journey, one that might never end…

In the morning, after breakfast, Max played around with Mitchell's computer. She altered the Point and Shoot's hardware—in a way she didn't really comprehend—to work with Mitchell's system. Before long, she was on the Net. The line, he had assured her, was secure in every way.

Saturday night had been incredible. The amazing sexual feats she and Mitchell had performed Friday were nothing more than a prelude to their second evening of lovemaking.

At a particularly bizarre and passionate moment, Max had remembered the video camera and wished that it was running. Then she felt a tingling in her arm, a strange power that seemed to flow from the gold bracelet she wore. It reached through the walls, like invisible lightning, to the hidden wiring beyond. She felt a little dizzy, as if she was losing blood, but she was also exhilarated. A part of her was traveling through the electrical wiring, a fleeting fiery impulse that was attached to her consciousness as if by a silken thread. It reached out, found the camera, and turned it on.

Mitchell was startled, but pleased. He showed his pleasure for hours.

When she was certain that Mitchell slept, Max had repeated the experiment, reaching out with her newfound ability. No, it wasn't newfound at all. It was old and denied.

She turned lights on and off in other rooms and accidentally tripped the security system twice, sending dozens of armed men into a panic within the mansion and along its perimeter.

She apologized, but Mitchell laughed it off.

"The pussies needed a work-out," he said, laughing as he heard the men scramble outside. The soldiers burst into his room only to find Mitchell and Max laughing their asses off at something.

"False alarm," Mitchell told them. "Just a glitch."

After the crisis was over, Mitchell held Max and whispered, "They're all Sleepers, honey."

"Hmmmmm?"

"They're not mages, like us. Don't do weird stuff in front of them. If you do, things can get scary. Dangerous scary, *capice?*"

"Uh-huh," she said, but he knew she wasn't really listening. She would learn her lessons well enough.

She spent a good eight hour day on the net, figuring out how to become one with the electronic highway. By the time Mitchell returned to the study, which was awash in hidden deposits of Quintessence, most centered on his collection of swords, his guest was ready to begin.

It was a little after five in the afternoon. Max's target was Ed Hauser, an in-house software designer for Infinity Software's office in Trenton. Mitchell learned that Hauser also made some kind of breakthrough, though the details were sketchy. Whatever it was, a deal worth several hundred million dollars with various foreign concerns was already on line for the project. Max's job was to steal this man's secret project, download it into their system, then have all copies of the project, including non-linked back-ups destroyed. Hauser might be able to recreate his revolutionary work in a year or two, but not in time to save Brenner from the wrath of his associates.

Max had experimented several times today with reaching into chat groups, dragging away various parties, and constructing three dimensional "cyber villages" so that she could commune with them one-on-one. That meant manifesting links that vanished when she was done with them and creating icons, or virtual representations of herself, her surroundings, and the person she had "acquired" for study.

She had read William Gibson, Walter Jon Williams, Bruce Sterling. All she had to do was unlock her imagination and will a thing to happen. Her wild talent, her personal magic, did the rest, shaping the reality of the web according to her desires.

In one such scenario, she pulled a Star Wars follower out of a chat room and into a virtual Forest of Endor. It was a wild ride, though a bit draining. Her second encounter had centered on a sex room, and her partner was a young man from Australia. She had "performed" without much passion, but her subject didn't seem to mind.

The last encounter of this kind had been spooky as hell. Max had pulled the actual consciousness of her subject into the cyberverse she had constructed. Naturally, that had been her goal all along, but to actually accomplish such a thing was dizzying and terrifying all at once.

Now it was time for Hauser. The chat rooms were the most vulnerable. Hauser was an aspiring writer. He logged onto a virtual writer's group from five to six every Sunday without fail. Max had the location and in seconds, she was within the chat room, a text only site, no three-dimensional moldings. She hid her presence from all but Hauser. To him, she took the identity of one of the man's favorite authors and attempted to lead him away from the main room for a private chat.

From Hauser's reactions, he clearly understood how unlikely it was that Max was really the author she pretended to be. With the anonymity of screennames, it was possible to impersonate anyone on the web. Still, it was an intriguing mystery. Who was doing this and why?

And there was *always* that one in a million possibility that this really was his idol come to lift him from the ranks of low level programmer to the lofty spires of literary greatness and recognition. If he didn't pursue this opportunity, he would wonder the rest of his life.

He followed her.

Max knew that she was using the understanding of writers that she had gained from Freddy to entice this man into her trap. It felt wrong, but she couldn't allow herself to become emotional. Her complete detachment was necessary.

Once she had Hauser effectively cut off from his group, Max went into her pitch. Playing the part of the famous fantasy author Hauser worshipped, she said that she greatly admired the short stories and sample chapters he had posted in the fiction group for comment. She felt awkward approaching him this way and would have preferred to have had his publisher or agent simply call or write him—but all she had was his screen name.

Hauser stopped responding. Max knew that she was in dark territory. Hauser was now trying to decide if this was a scam to get his real name, address, and phone number.

Max quickly gave Hauser the number of a New York publisher to call in the morning. "Tricia can fill you in on what I'd like you to work on with me."

When it became clear that she would ask nothing more of Hauser, the programmer relaxed. He even became intrigued.

"Are you proposing some kind of collaboration?" Hauser typed.

Max gave away a little insider information she had learned from Freddy, who often attended science fiction and fantasy conventions, and had chatted up dozens of writers and editors. "Have you ever seen these major hardcovers written by some big famous name in publishing and someone you've never heard of?" She went on to list a few titles.

Hauser had indeed seen these books.

"What's really going on is that the big author writes a brief synopsis. A page, a paragraph… Maybe five or ten pages max. The secondary writer does the first draft of the book. The big author gives it a polish. Everyone makes a lot of money."

"They're not real collaborations?" Hauser asked.

"No. I know that may be a little disappointing to you from the point of view of a fan, but as a writer, it's something else again. This is a good way for a first timer to get in with a publisher, to make the New York Times list, which is all important, to make some serious cash, and to get the eye of an editor for your original stuff. Not to mention quotes on your original works by me and a bunch of my friends…"

Max named some more names. There was a momentary hesitation, then the moment came.

"You're the real thing, aren't you?" Hauser typed.

That's what she had been waiting for. That vulnerable instant in which all of his mental defenses would be down.

Max seized the moment. She followed the information trail directly to Hauser's computer in his small Trenton duplex. As she flowed through the information feed, a sentient bandwidth of light and sound, color, energy and clearly focussed impulses, she had to admit that the experience was intoxicating. She was still aware of her human body, sitting before a very powerful computer in

Mitchell's study, still conscious of the tingling left upon her skin by the presence of so much Quintessence, of her level breathing, of the chattering madness of swirling pixels and flowing multi-colored lines warping in on themselves then stretching outward as if for miles into unseen horizons that blazed across her computer screen—

—while this other part of her, this sentient projectile of her thoughts and her will, experienced a new reality, taking in colors that she never knew existed, feeling sensations that were wonderful and utterly alien to her experience, impossible for her to describe other than as sustained ecstasy. Suddenly, she was inside a brilliant flash of white light. The face of a total stranger rushed toward her.

Hauser. Bald, thin, with a black goatee, wearing a Rocky Horror Picture Show T-shirt, the images nearly rubbed off by wear. He sat in a cluttered workroom, his eyes wide, mouth stretched to a wide, comical "O."

Max leaped from the screen before him and pierced his skull, delving into the complex neuronet of his brain as she had the vast Internet, seizing his consciousness, and flinging it out of his body as she took residence. Hauser's mind ripped into the computer, followed the many links she had constructed, and ended up in the cage she had vacated.

He was trapped and she was inside two bodies at once, her own in Mitchell's study, and Hauser's in Trenton, New Jersey. The effect threatened to make her sick, and she so she pressed her/his eyes closed in both locations and asked for silence in both places. Mitchell heard her in Edmonds. The workroom in Trenton was already still.

She opened Ed Hauser's eyes. With only a little concentration, she was able to block the flood of sensations rushing up into her consciousness, informing her of everything this physical body experienced. She felt his sex, the strangeness of it, and quickly placed breakers around the perimeters of her consciousness, blocking all impulses except those absolutely necessary: Sight and touch. Then she limited the tactile sensation flowing from his skin, bringing down the "volume" so that she was only receiving input from the tips of his fingers. Other than that, she was numb. At least in this incarnation.

Max knew that all of this should have been weirder, more alien to her, but all her life, she had dreamed of doing things like this. Leaping out of her skin and into someone else's form. Abandoning the horrors of her life and being rewarded with a chance to begin again. Actually performing these tasks felt comfortable to her.

She went through his hard drive, piercing his security systems and double blinds easily, and found the data-clusters that matched the limited description she had been given of his project. She downloaded them to a way station she had constructed midway between the terminals in Edmonds and Trenton, then burned away all records of their existence. She went deep, ensuring that no amount of effort could ever retrieve the data from the hard drive. She checked the workroom for back-up files, then linked into Infinity Software's most secure systems. Patching in was no problem with Hauser's ID codes. Now that she had "caught the scent" of the program Hauser had created, she could use that to track down all duplicate files in her reach.

She found nothing.

Frustrated, she decided to flame everything in sight. During the day, she had encountered a patch of entropy and madness that had terrified her and soon realized that it was a free floating programming virus desperate for a host. She had avoided it easily, and took steps to shield all her various constructs and links from this virus and all others that she could imagine. Now she patched Infinity Software's systems into the virus. To spike it, she added the magickal equivalent of a molotov cocktail, a cluster of raw destructive electrical impulses that were meant to flood outward past the intraspacial links that made up the virtual community of Infinity Software and manifest like bolts of lightning in the real world, a host of mackigical guided weapons seeking out and destroying any and all physical backups of Infinity's data no matter where in the world these stores of information resided.

Desk drawers in abandoned offices exploded. The contents of safes in foreign banks were vaporized. Safety deposit boxes in tiny little Midwestern towns were melted to slag as fiery bands of angry white lightning ripped through reality. In each case, these destructive impulses would be labeled by witnesses and scientists as "freak weather phenomena." Only Max would know the truth.

That same phenomena ripped through the office surrounding Max in Edmonds. Max, residing in Hauser's flesh, gasped as lightning tore through her without harm before attacking a box of 3.5 disks, a tall cart filled with additional drives that were stacked and linked, and a baseball cap containing a handful of tape backups.

It was all gone. Max fled Hauser's mind and reached the cage where she had trapped him. All she had to do now was release him, send him back to his body, and retreat to her own.

Suddenly, she felt an odd sensation. It was her body in Edmonds. Some odd fragrance had seeped into her pores and she felt weak, unable to focus.

"Close him down," Mitchell said.

Max, her consciousness divided between her physical form in Edmonds and the sentient "projectile" that was rocketing through the information highway, rebelled against this idea.

"What?" she whispered in both places at once.

The fragrance suddenly became more potent. She was barely able to resist the command she had been given.

"He's one of the one's who killed Freddy. Do it."

Mitchell was telling her to kill Hauser! She tried to rebel against the order, but she was quickly overwhelmed.

"Now," said Mitchell. His voice was hard and cold.

Max willed it to happen and the "virtual construct" outside of Hauser's cage suddenly unleashed a torrent of arcane energies at Hauser, vaporizing his consciousness and scattering the ashes across intraspace.

She had just committed murder.

Max drifted back to the way station housing the information she had taken for Mitchell. Around her lay a universe of flashing colors, geometric patterns, waves of crashing energy. Moments ago, this new plane of existence had seemed like a paradise, the ultimate playground for her. A universe in which she could lose herself and perhaps live forever in peace.

Now it was tainted forever by the death of Ed Hauser.

"Go into the program," Mitchell commanded.

Max did as he commanded. Clearly, Mitchell could see through the monitor everything she witnessed in the virtual world. It was like a window to the sights and sounds experienced by her split consciousness. Max tried to make her physical body respond, but it just sat there in Edmonds, her fingers resting gently against the keyboard. She wanted to force her body to rip the monitor from the computer, toss it across the room. Or grab Mitchell and put his fucking head through the glass.

She was powerless.

"Execute the program, Max." Mitchell's voice.

She found herself piercing the heart of the data cluster, constructing an execute file.

In Edmonds, Mitchell tentatively raised Max's hand and dropped it on the ENTER key. Then he jumped back and away, as if expecting an explosion. Her palm mashed two other keys as it struck ENTER and the screen went blank.

"Shit," Mitchell said.

Suddenly, a single dot of light appeared at the center of the screen. Mitchell came forward as the light grew larger, brighter. He was reminded of a subway car running through a dark tunnel, a lighted passage rushing into view up ahead.

Mitchell smiled. "Oh, my."

A spiraling tunnel of light came into view, the walls crisscrossed patterns of energy that looked like a spider's web. Then the viewer was being drawn into the tunnel, which narrowed. The tunnel's walls became fog or smoke. Figures drifted out of the walls, shadowy creatures that might once have been human. They whispered softly, promising immortality, an end to pain.

"Keep going," Mitchell said steadily.

Other figures coalesced into more distinct visions of men and women, perfect physical specimens who offered undreamt of sensual delights.

Mitchell watched as Max sped down the tunnel with renewed speed. The shadows promises immortality and power beyond reckoning. Mitchell told her to ignore all of it. She followed his commands. The oils he had released into her flesh gave her no other choice.

He saw a couple detach themselves from the wall and announce themselves to Max as her mother and father.

Max hesitated.

"Don't even think about it!" Mitchell said as he placed his hands on Max's face and imparted a soothing oil into her flesh that made her even more malleable. A new fragrance filled the air. Sassafras.

She raced through the phantom figures, shuddering at their cold touch. The image on the screen came into even sharper focus. That meant Max was even more focussed on her goal. The tunnel before her wound around, making sharp, near impossible turns that she took without slowing a bit. Ahead, the tunnel branched off.

Other figures appeared, offering guidance. They told her to follow the center path.

"Bullshit," said Mitchell, "veer right."

Max did as Mitchell ordered and soon reached a dead end. Backtracking, she took the far left corridor. It led to a deadly precipice. She managed to take hold of the walls at either side of her, slowing her pace. Otherwise, she might have flown off into oblivion in the form of a pulsating black virus, sparkling with silver bands of energy—virtual piranha set to strip the flesh from her icon's bones.

Mitchell now allowed her to follow the tunnel her "helpers" indicated and take their advice at every turn.

Suddenly, a vision appeared at the end of the tunnel. A blue sky, some kind of land mass.

"Oh, man," Mitchell said, caressing Max's shoulders in the physical world. "We're almost there."

An island came into view as Max was thrust outward from the tunnel. On top of a great hillside lay a city. Incredible buildings, many made of glass or bone, rose from the earth. Max recognized Roman styling and saw a vast library in the distance. She had an impression that the library was the only real place here. Everything else was an illusion. The library seemed more solid, better defined.

Something grabbed her from below. Max was tugged downward. An image came into her mind. The swimmer at the beginning of JAWS, who is eaten by the unseen shark, yanked downward as parts of her were consumed.

Against all, reason, she looked down.

Impossibly, a doorway loomed before her. She felt as if she was inside an M.C. Escher painting, where the laws of gravity and physical reality no longer applied. A vast cathedral engulfed the doorway, its spires shaped like magnificent swords.

She had seen this place before, visited it countless times in her dreams.

Was she dreaming now?

No, she was wide awake. Some invisible force pulled her toward the blackened maw of the doorway.

"No!" cried Mitchell in the physical world.

A shadowy figure appeared. A hulking form, vaguely human, with swords and spikes driven through every inch of its flesh. It looked at Max, then beyond her.

"I'll take one of you… Take you both," the Weaponsmaster said. "Makes no difference to me."

In his study, Mitchell whispered, "Come back."

"No," said Max, an array of weapons leaping from her imagination into the virtual reality before her. She realized a pair of jagged swords and leapt at the Weaponsmaster.

In his study, Mitchell broke from Max. He reached behind his computer and grasped at the modem line. A single strand of white hot lighting coiled around the line and struck as Mitchell's fingers touched it. He was sent back across the room, flung a dozen feet into a bookcase. Tomes rained down on him, some striking him on the head and shoulders.

A sudden clarity came over Max. She looked up at the creature with whom she was about to do battle and understood that she could not win. This creature held ultimate power in this place and it amused itself by challenging those who managed the long, hazardous trek to its city. There was precious else to offer it diversion.

Max willed her weapons to vanish. The creature before her bowed its head and stepped back into the shadows. A vast door formed where the gaping darkness had been.

Realizing that time was short, Max launched herself back into the tunnel.

A line came into her mind. She had heard it while on the set of a porno film, waiting to make her adult movie debut. The lithe model having sex with a godlike stud looking around to her co-star and said the words that made Max walk away and never return to the business.

"You think you're fucking me, but I'm fucking you…"

She knew what she had to do.

Mitchell shook himself back to awareness. His first sight was of Max striking keys with an alarming ferocity as she typed and coded a series of messages into his mainframe.

The screen before her was blank.

Mitchell rose up and commanded her to stop. To turn and face him. He could tell from her smiling face that his control over her had been broken.

"You were pure," Mitchell said. "I thought they'd let you in. That's why I needed you…"

"You had me kill a man," Max said simply.

Mitchell cursed himself. "All right. Pull up the program. I've got some ideas."

"Can't," said Max. "It doesn't exist any more."

Mitchell stared at her in shock. "You downloaded it."

"Some of it. I stripped it back out and put a virus in there, after I was done infesting your programs."

Shaking his head, Mitchell refused to believe this. He could sense that she was lying. "Max, I know how this sounds, but I can explain. Really, I can. This is bigger than both of us. This guy Hauser, he had no idea what he'd found. He just thought it was a video game of some sort. A total experience VR without a helmet or gloves, direct linkage with the brain. But it's so much more..."

He was moving toward her. He said, "Now show me how to get into the goddamned program and you can go."

"Like Freddy went?"

"Max—"

"You killed him. You were behind all of this."

Mitchell didn't try to deny it.

"Did you really think that I would trust you? That I would see you as some kind of—what? Guardian angel or something? What, you think I'm fucking stupid? If you had explained about the scents, maybe I'd have gone for it. But you just went right around those. I kept wanting to ask, I kept waiting for you to explain... It was the way you smelled, this thing you do, that drew me to you in the Art Bar. Brenner and his buddies all had this terrible smell. It's what you use to control people. I smelled it just now, when you were using it on me."

Hanging his head, Mitchell reached out. One of his swords detached itself from the wall and slowly tumbled point over hilt until Mitchell snatched it from the air. "I don't want it to be like this. I know you're lying about the program. Give it to me or I won't have any choice as to what happens next."

Max looked at him coldly. She had taken a man's life and that had placed her beyond fear, at least for the moment. As far as what Mitchell wanted, the information had been scattered to the far ends of the web. Each cluster of information was infused with her power. She had arranged that only she could locate the myriad pieces of the puzzle and reassemble them. If she ran out of options, she would barter for her life with this information.

Somehow, though, she was certain it wouldn't come to that.

Mitchell raised the sword. It's point was dripping with some kind of strange oil that poured from Mitchell's flesh. He was sweating copiously. "You don't know how important this is. Not just to me, but to everyone." He waited. She was silent. "Dammit, Max, I can *make* you tell me."

"I doubt it." Max saw a figure standing in the doorway. One of Mitchell's soldiers, she assumed from the way he ignored the intruder.

He looked up at her imploringly. "You don't want to know the kinds of things I can do to you, Max. I don't want to hurt you. Please don't make me. Just give me what I need and you can leave. I've already closed down Brenner and everyone he told about your work."

"They're dead?"

He nodded. "You're free and clear to patent it, get a lawyer, an agent, and make yourself a fortune. Just tell me, then clear out. You won't ever have to see me again."

"No."

He shook with rage. "Why?"

Max smiled. "Because you want me to make it easy for you and I'm not going to. Just be aware of something before you make a move on me. This study of yours is loaded up with the stuff you told me about. Quintessence. That means we both have power here. You can hurt me…"

She touched the side of the computer. A brief electrical charge leaped from the machine and struck Mitchell. The surge raced through his body and bonded itself with the electrical charges racing to and from his brain. It settled in his neural pathways and caused his pain centers to flare in new and terrifying ways. Mitchell cast a spell that drove out the foreign energies.

"You should have killed me with that one," Mitchell said, enraged. The hand that did not contain the sword began to drip with an acid strong enough to eat through the expensive rug at his feet. "No one gets me the same way twice."

The figure in the doorway took a step into the room and said, "She won't have to."

Mitchell turned at the alien voice, surprised for the second time in his life.

Less than a dozen feet away, Max saw the intruder and was frozen in confusion. She recognized the man in an instant. Julian Ibiero, the clothing designer she had seen on television yesterday. Then he had been calm and poised, friendly—if a bit cocky. His expression was different now. He looked at her with anger, fear, and uncertainty. His gaze drifted briefly to her bracelet.

"It's been a long time," he said softly.

Without hesitation, he raised his gun and fired until it was empty.

7

Mitchell staggered back as the hailstorm of bullets tore into him. He had enacted a spell to shield himself from Max's assault and it served to keep him from being completely torn to shreds by the bullets. Only three slugs entered his body, the others were repelled.

He had no idea who this new player was. Probably just someone he had neglected to deal with when sorting out the mess with Brenner and his underworld buddies. The shooter had opted only to go after Mitchell. That meant he had to be considered Max's ally.

Under normal circumstances, Mitchell would never cut and run. Especially not in his own stronghold of power. But he was already weakened by the shockwave of energy that had assaulted him when he tried to rescue Max from the virtual world. Max's attack on his central nervous system hadn't helped, either. She learned fast.

Hey, it was a Max attack, he thought as he flooded his own body with chemicals to keep him from going into shock. I like that one.

Mitchell released a carefully woven spell that concealed the study's hidden doorway. He had been shot three times. Twice in the stomach, once in the leg. He was dripping blood, his guts were on fire, and his lungs didn't seem to want to work. His knee would barely support him. Stumbling toward the door, Mitchell noted that the gunman had tossed his automatic weapon away and produced a sword. Where the hell he had been keeping it, Mitchell had no idea. But Mitchell recognized this weapon. Swords had been his passion for many years and he had dreamed of owning this one.

The Sword of Roland faced him. The fucker looked bright and hungry, though the fire that usually surrounded it was not in evidence.

Moving faster than any human being had a right to, Mitchell stumbled through the gateway, down a flight of stone stairs, and into an all encompassing darkness.

Julian considered going after the wounded man, but he was more concerned with the woman before him. It was her. There could be no doubt. Though she had aged and looked nothing at all like the child he remembered, Julian knew it was her. The person who had destroyed his life. And she was a *mage*.

His gaze fell upon the stolen bracelet she wore. When he first saw it clamped upon her wrist, he'd been filled with rage. But he had been forced to put his feelings aside. There were greater issues at stake. All Julian understood of the magical display he had seen in the study before he made his presence known was that it had something to do with the Pattern. The shaping of all reality. He also knew that powerful forces, far beyond his ability to control, were being released. Somehow, all of it was tied to the girl. No, the woman. Maxine.

Now Maxine was looking at him with the same amount of amazement and incredulity that she might have displayed if Mighty Mouse had suddenly sprang into three-dimensional reality and saved her life. She gestured toward the sword he carried and said, "Put it down."

Julian could not help himself, he actually laughed at this. It was the wrong response. Maxine corralled her power and suddenly, electrical cords were ripping out of the walls, spewing sparks and streams of white hot power. They coiled around Julian, striking at him like rattlers.

"Put it down," Maxine repeated. Julian thought of a dozen ways he could have protected himself from Maxine's display of arcane power. She had no way of knowing that the sword he held was magical. She had no training; not even enough sense to refrain from using her powers when Sleepers were present. And that, he guessed, was what she took him for. An ordinary man.

He dropped the sword and raised his hands. A plan was forming in his mind.

"I'm the only one who can help you," Julian said, watching the writhing lightning serpents with respect and even a little fear.

"Why in the hell would I trust you?" she asked.

"I could have shot you. I didn't."

"Maybe you just ran out of bullets. Maybe a lot of things. Why the fuck should I care?"

"Because you want to get out of this."

Maxine considered his words. "Do you work for Brenner?"

He responded with a confusion that could not be manufactured.

"Are the guards still outside?" Max asked, that issue resolved.

Julian nodded, then said, "But they're not going to bother you."

His meaning quickly became evident to Max. The guards were dead. "All of them?"

"Yes."

"How many more are with you?"

"Just one. Helicopter pilot. Circling. Waiting to pick me up."

"You might be lying." Julian refused to go any further with this. The lightning snakes at his feet were easing away, becoming less fierce. He was winning her trust. Turning his gaze to the rapidly diminishing doorway Mitchell had created in the study, Julian said, "We should go after him if we want to make sure."

"Is that why you were sent here?" Max asked. "To kill him?"

Julian nodded. It was a lie, but it served the occasion.

Max edged closer to Julian. "You can tell me why, later. When we're in the helicopter."

"I didn't say anything about taking you—" "No," she said, lightning rippling within her eyes. "You didn't…"

Julian did his best to seem outraged at the idea of Maxine taking him prisoner. But as he stooped down and retrieved his sword, he couldn't have been more pleased.

"I know who you are," Max said as the helicopter left Mitchell's estate behind. She nodded to the pilot. "I recognize him, too."

"I hope so," said the pilot. "If you don't, my publicist isn't doing her job!"

Max had found it more than a little bizarre that the shooter had turned out to be a celebrity fashion designer. She supposed that there was some perverse kind of logic that the man's pilot would be Peter Jacque, a male model made famous by a series of commercials for Lucky Stiff wine coolers.

Julian said, "I gave Peter his first break."

"Yeah," said the pilot, "and he's been blackmailing me with that ever since."

"Where do you know me from?" Julian asked.

"Television," Max said quickly. She hadn't wished to betray her genuine disquiet at Julian's appearance. When she had seen him on television yesterday morning, he had seemed oddly familiar. Now that he was at her side, that feelings was stronger than ever.

But why?

"What do I call you?" Julian asked earnestly.

"You really don't know?" Max said it as more of a statement. "You weren't expecting anyone except Mitchell and his bodyguards?"

Following her lead, Julian said, "All I know is, when I got there, you were trying to flame Marazzi, just like me. That puts us on the same side. At least for now."

"Who's Marazzi?"

"Mitchell. That was his last name."

Jesus, she thought. She honestly hadn't known. "My name is Max. Maxine Anderson."

"Nice meeting you," Julian said, a bitter irony and genuine amusement edging into his tone.

They flew in silence for a time. As the helicopter sliced through the unusually rich blue sky, Julian looked down at Max's bracelet, studying the craftsmanship. He thought of his father laboring in his shop and was surprised to feel a flicker of warmth attached to the memory.

"Why were you there?" Max asked.

"It's personal," Julian said truthfully. Let her draw her own conclusions from that.

The fire came back in Max's eyes and Julian felt her power starting to build. He knew that Max was high from using magick. It happened this way sometimes with the newly Awakened.

"You know what I can do," she said in a husky voice. "I may not be pointing anything at you, but I might as well have a gun to your head. Now—"

"You mind if I mention something to you?" Julian asked. Without waiting for a reply, he said, "You seem to have this big thing going with electricity."

"I could fry your brain if I have to." Maxine didn't seem entirely sure about that. It sounded more like a question.

"I don't doubt it. Look outside, all right? If you do any of that crazy stuff up here, you're probably going to blow out our electrical system. The helicopter will drop, you'll be killed along with us. So just take it easy, all right?"

Maxine recalled her power. She seemed genuinely shaken by how close her recklessness had come to getting them all splattered. As their jaunt when on, Julian thought about the hours leading up to his assault on her captor. A drive-by had revealed that Mitchell Marazzi's estate was heavily guarded. To get a better look, he had called Peter Jacque, a former soldier and licensed pilot as well as a model. When they spotted the militia guarding the estate, he did some checking through strictly legitimate means on Marazzi. Mitchell was a wealthy man who had inherited his money from relatives in the old country. An art collector and investor.

Delving deeper, Julian saw indications of fake records. The relatives never existed. Mitchell had made his money in some other way. Considering the type of guards this man hired, he was probably a very bad man. Julian hadn't expected him to be a mage. He knew most of the freelancers, except those who worked for the Technocracy. Because so much of the Technocracy's membership came off like extras from Day of the Dead, they had to rely on freelancers who could blend in better with the outside world.

Julian decided that Maxine Anderson was a prize that Mitchell kept around as a plaything. That she had turned out to be something more, something different, had surprised him. Julian knew that he had a rather cynical view of women, but he *had* been given cause over the years.

Maxine spoke to him, lifting him out of his reverie. "What was it like for you? Shooting Mitchell, killing all those people at the estate?"

"I don't understand the question," Julian said.

"Was it easy?"

"Yes."

Max considered this for a moment, then asked, "Do you plan on killing me?"

Julian was stunned by the question. It was simple enough, and it made sense that she would ask. "Because you're a witness to what I did, you mean. And because you know that there's more to my existence than what the public knows about me."

"Pretty much."

"It crossed my mind."

"But you're not going to make a move on me because you know what I am. What I could do."

He nodded. She still had no idea that he was a mage, too. "That's not the only reason."

"Really."

Julian shrugged. "I don't like killing innocent people."

She shook her head, sensing his half-truths. "I don't buy it."

Julian shrugged. "Killing you would be bad business. I don't know what you're into. I don't even know if what you told me is your real name."

"It is."

"Whatever. I was at Marazzi's place to settle old business." That was certainly true enough. Julian knew that what he said next could make it all go to hell between him and Maxine, but he decided to take the chance anyway. "I saw some strange things. The way I figure it, I keep your secrets, you keep mine. We can put down wherever you want and then we can just get on with our lives. Just cut loose from each other. The less we know, the better."

Maxine considered this for several minutes. Finally, the airport came into view in the far distance. "You've got a lot of money."

"So?"

"You ever hear the definition of enough?"

"What's that?"

"A little more." Julian smiled.

"What are you talking about?"

"I can share something with you that's going to be worth a fortune."

"That thing Marazzi was into? What I saw in the study?"

"Something else. Something a whole lot safer."

"And what do you want?"

She said, "You know about magick."

"I know a little."

"I need someone with money, someone who can teach me things. Help me get out of the country and get all this sorted out and I'll cut you in on everything I've got going." As they closed on the airport, Max told him about the Point and Shoot and about the strange dimension to which her psychic journey had taken her.

Julian thought about this. It wouldn't be long before X'an sent people after him to retrieve the sword. His plan had been to take Maxine somewhere safe, a locale out of the country that he would choose at random. He had over a dozen residences in a variety of names that were untraceable to him.

The only problem was, he hadn't quite decided what he would do with her once he got her to a safe place. Torture her? Kill her? He had not worked out that part of the plan. All he had known from the beginning was that he had to see her.

And what he saw in Marazzi's study had to be explained. Though he belonged to no particular Tradition, Julian felt strongly that the idea of the Technocracy having some kind of direct pipeline to the Pattern was unacceptable. He had to get some kind of understanding of what Marazzi and Maxine had been involved with.

"All right," Julian said, offering his gloved hand. "I'll help you."

She took his hand as they began their descent.

Hours passed in the darkness. How many, the wounded man did not know. He heard voices above for a time. After that, all he knew was pain, and merciful oblivion.

The first thing Mitchell did when he emerged from the catacombs was check the study. His knee was bandaged and braced, and his system had been flooded with stimulants and a variety of smart drugs, including Piracetim and Deprenyl.

Mitchell's estate had formerly belonged to a paranoid arms dealer who had the catacombs installed and stocked with medical supplies, food, weaponry, and books. Mitchell had taken the catacomb's development one step further, adding magickal wards throughout. The catacombs were self-contained. They did not link to the surface world or other underground networks, providing enemies with a way in. The arms dealer had been prepared to make a final stand in his underground lair.

Mitchell never thought he would need to actually use the catacombs. His pride had been damaged a bit by being driven underground like vermin, but at least he was still alive.

In the study, Mitchell found no evidence that Maxine had been hurt. Thank God.

Strangely, there were also no clear indicators of a struggle. She was too high on her power to have been afraid of the intruder, even after he shot Mitchell. That meant either he disabled her quickly, which was very possible, or she went with him willingly.

The gun used by the intruder had been left behind. Mitchell was certain that it could be traced to some local supplier and had probably been acquired through a series of blinds. He would check it out anyway. It was always possible that the shooter had made a mistake somewhere along the line. Mitchell might just get lucky and find out the man's identity, or at least get some clues to his motives.

Mitchell tried to boot up his computer, but the system was dead. He checked the wall clock. Almost six hours had been lost. Mitchell rose slowly and painfully to his feet.

Who in the living *fuck* had shot him? He really wanted to know. That it had been another mage was incredibly troubling. Had one of the doppelgangers been discovered?

Had the secret been revealed?

No, he reasoned, if that was the case, the entire weight of the Technocracy would have been on him, not just one man. So who could it have been? One of Jeremy's friends? Had good old Chrome spoken about their venture before he died?

Again, not possible. Not to speak ill of the dead, but his brother *had* no friends. He simply wouldn't trust anyone except Mitchell.

"Shit," Mitchell whispered as he painfully made his way to the main doors leading to the grounds. Soon he stood outside, breathing in the cool night air. Leaning against one of the tall columns, he looked out at the array of bodies the intruder had left in his wake. Twenty-two men, three women. All dead. Twenty-five human lives snuffed out because Mitchell had wanted to make the illusion he presented to Max complete.

Sure, these people had been good soldiers, they knew the risks going in. But they were also Sleepers. Up against a well trained mage—particularly one in possession of the Sword of Roland—they had no chance.

Mitchell felt terrible. He wondered what kind of *animal* could do this. Looking at the slaughterhouse arrayed before him, he felt genuine concern at the idea of the woman he was growing to love being within this bastard's reach.

"All right, all right, think," he muttered. He was going to need help. That was a given. In his current condition, it would take all night to clear away and dispose of the bodies. It had been a miracle that no pilots had spotted them during the day.

If he could fix himself up, performing the task before him would be the work of a few hours, tops. But he would need help to get back into that kind of shape. It could be done, but he needed to bring in someone he could trust.

"Who to call…" he whispered. The main thing he had to worry about was time. If he hadn't blacked out from the pain when he reached the catacombs, this might not have been so great an issue. As it was, the mage who had taken Max could already be out of the country with her. If the grenade in Mitchell's skull went off before he could catch up with her, then the library and all its power to alter the Pattern could fall into her companion's grasp. Mitchell couldn't allow that.

He owed it to mankind.

The thought made him laugh, and that made him double over in pain and spit up blood. Clutching at his side, he went back to the study and made some phone calls.

Ten minutes later, he was driving out of his estate, in his 1970 Mustang. As he sped to the Sandman, a little motel twenty minutes away, he thought more about the shooter. The more he turned it over in his mind, the more he was convinced that his secret hadn't been compromised. Not yet, in any case.

There was something about this guy that screamed Rogue. If Mitchell's suspicion was true, if he and the shooter belonged to the same "fraternity," then one of the top talent agents or "procurers" would know about this guy. Mitchell had seen the son-of-a-bitch's face. The shooter had been wearing gloves, but that didn't mean anything. He wanted to avoid leaving prints. Everyone did that. But the sword this s.o.b. was carrying... That was interesting. The Sword of Roland was supposed to belong to a guy in the Seychelles Islands, last Mitchell had heard, and it wasn't the sort of item you loaned out to your underlings. The sword must have been stolen, or won in a duel. That would be a major news flash. Someone would have to know about it.

Mitchell would be able to find Maxine. He knew that. He had her scent. But he had to know everything he could about the shooter and why he had come there for Maxine. That was the only reasonable possibility left. If he hadn't come for the program, then he *must* have wanted Max.

Why?

Pulling into the parking lot of the Sandman, Mitchell cut his lights, then went around back to one of the employee entrances. He had a full set of keys. Mitchell had learned long ago to maintain a handful of safe houses within a fifty mile radius of his home. That way, if he was busted up or couldn't make it all the way back for whatever reason, he had someplace to take refuge. He also didn't like meeting some of the people he worked with—and worked for—in his home. One of the Sandman's suites was held open for him year round. Tonight, he was using it.

Mitchell smashed the hall light, then settled into the room. He tore the plug out of the single lamp in the corner, drew the curtains, and went into the small bathroom. He ran a bath and flooded the waters with the pure essences of rose, savory, cedarwood, and ylang-ylang.

His "date" arrived right on time. The credit card he had used to pay for her services in advance was not traceable. None of it was, really. She knocked and he told her to come in.

Mitchell sat in the corner, where she could barely see him. That was good. He was a fairly frightening sight right now. The blood just wouldn't stay down.

She was lit by the soft golden glow from the bathroom around the corner. A pretty red-head with a lush body.

"Dark in here," she said immediately. Not really scared. Cautious.

"Light's out in the hall, too," he said. "Hope you didn't hurt yourself. Trip or anything."

He saw her shoulders loosen. Grinning, she sniffed the air. "Nice. Smells really nice."

"I want you to take a bath."

She smiled and quickly shrugged out of her dress. "You gonna join me?"

"In a little bit."

She went into the bathroom and eased herself into the tub.

"Wow," she called. "This is great. Did you put some oils in the water or—"

She gasped suddenly as the fragrances went to work on her. In less than a minute she was thrashing around in the waters, playing with herself, screaming as she tried desperately to bring herself to orgasm.

Mitchell pictured what she must look like, and felt himself rising to the occasion. He got to his feet and made his way into the bathroom. She took one look at him and leaned back in the tub, her legs spread for him, undulating in the waters. She was unaware of his wounds, the blood, his weakness. In her eyes, he was a God.

As they made love, his flesh began to shimmer and change. A pair of bullets were expelled from the depths of his stomach and the damage they had wrought was repaired. His knee took the longest, but eventually the ligaments and muscles knitted and the shattered bone became whole.

By the time he came inside her, he *was* a God again.

Julian had lingered in one of the airport newsstands, going through Sunday newspapers, looking for reviews of his show. He found several, and seemed to be relieved by what he read.

"This is the Ibiero of old," one review read. "Exciting and playful, awash with color. The whimsical 'Down with PC' motif worked on many levels, reminding us that it is love of fashion, of creation and design, that unifies us, and that in-fighting and out of control competition hurts us all. The street collection that followed went from the practical to the outrageous. Retailers rejoiced, celebrities abounded, and Neve Ryan's appearance clinched Julian Ibiero's status as a force in fashion to be reckoned with. Bravo!"

Julian had nearly passed out with relief. He was giddy after reading the review, more like a schoolboy than the dark, brooding, and seemingly humorless adventurer who had helped Max gain her freedom.

"So you're not grumpy anymore?" Max asked later, when they were aboard the private plane he had chartered.

Julian ran his hands through his thick hair and sat back in the plush seat. "No. It's so intimidating, putting yourself out in front of the world. I was trashed one year. I was trashed so bad. Every time something good happens it's a vindication."

Max thought about her presentation to Brenner and the horsemen. She had some understanding of what he had been through.

One of the stewards brought around drinks. Max and Julian toasted to their newly formed partnership. For a single, terrifying instant, Julian pictured smashing his glass and cutting Max's throat. Telling her why in the seconds of life remaining her. The thought passed and he shuddered. When Max asked what was wrong, he blamed it on the hard liquor.

"Tell me about yourself," Julian said.

"Why should I? You're Mr. Fashion. You probably have all these great stories about Rosanne and Richard Gere and all those people."

"They're boring."

"Really?" Max sounded stunned.

Julian shrugged. "They're all right." His expression darkened suddenly.

"What is it?"

"I should check in. I don't even want to think about what my e-mail must be like right now."

He called for an inflight phone and called Marjory, his personal assistant, who was back in London. A part of him worried about revealing his location by making such a call, but he knew that X'an would give him a grace period to "come in from the cold." At least a week.

Marjory was home. She berated him for ducking out after the press conference. There were dozens of orders to be dealt with, major decisions to be made. Also, a couple of strange people had stopped by looking for him. Julian asked her to describe them. It turned out they were more of X'an disciples, ones that Julian would be sure to recognize. This was a reminder, nothing more.

"Linda was a bitch on wheels, as usual," Marjory said, referring to one of the models. "She got a little paper cut from one of the props and now she wants us to pay for cosmetic surgery."

"I don't think so. Where is it? The cut?"

Marjory told him.

"Fuck no, they're not even real."

In her seat across from Julian, Max laughed a little at that.

Julian said, "How's Naomi?"

"An angel. As usual."

His favorite model. "And Alisa?"

"She put in a letter of resignation and said that once the orders are in and everything calms down, she'll sell all her shares by proxy. A little at a time. Nothing dramatic for the press to get their teeth into. She just doesn't want to see you again, that's all."

"I don't blame her," Julian said, feeling as if he had been doubled over by a punch to the gut.

Marjory hesitated, then said, "I could talk to her for you. I bet you two could still work it out—"

Julian disconnected the line. He looked to Max. "Tell me about yourself." He *really* needed the distraction.

"My life's pretty dull."

"Doesn't look like it to me." Julian waited until his gaze was locked with that of Maxine, then he gestured to released a spell of Influence.

Max found herself talking for several hours on the flight. She told Julian of the accident that took her parents' lives, of her harrowing days in orphanages and foster homes, of the wretched mistakes she had made with her life and how she had come close to disaster so many times, only to return from the edge stronger and more prepared to cope with the next crisis. She spoke of Freddy and how she had been such a coward with him. Now that he was gone, she would never be able to make it up to him.

Julian released her from his spell. She had told him more than he had really wanted to know. Throughout his professional career, he had made a firm rule out of knowing as little as possible about his victims. The more he understood about her, the more complicated the equation became.

He tried to tell himself that the only thing keeping Maxine Anderson alive was her limited knowledge about the pathway Marazzi had found to the Pattern. Once they reached their destination and she was "debriefed," everything would change.

And yet… The only thing connecting the beautiful, vibrant young woman before him with the child who ruined his life was the bracelet she wore. A sudden violent urge rose up within him to take the bracelet from her and toss it from the plane.

As if in response to his dark impulse, a sudden flow of energy reached out from the bracelet. Max could not see the brilliant patterns of light that coalesced before the bracelet in warning. She didn't have the training.

Julian stared in horror at the construct before him, a python made of rainbow colors.

This was a bracelet his father had made. It was also, clearly, a talisman imbued with Quintessence. How was that possible?

Max saw Julian staring down at her wrist. He averted his gaze a moment too late.

"It's pretty, isn't it?" Max asked.

Julian was surprised. He hadn't looked at it quite that way before. When he glanced at it again, the serpent was gone. "It's very beautiful."

"My guardian angel gave it to me," she said absently as she looked out of the window at the clouds racing by.

Julian considered her words and felt a sudden chill as he realized that she was referring to him.

8

Seattle, Washington.

Mitchell tracked Maxine to the airport. Reconstructing where she had gone with the merc was not difficult. Mitchell booked a flight so that he could follow in person, then decided to call in favors with some fellow freelancers who were a damn shade closer to his prey than he was. He used a pay phone while his plane was being fueled. The numbers he dialed linked to a scrambler. The calls were untraceable.

On the third attempt, he actually caught someone home.

"Yeah?" a woman with a hard-edged voice said.

Mitchell burst into a falsetto and sang, *"Billie-Jean's not my lover—oooooooh!"*

"Fuck me with a chainsaw," said the woman. "Marazzi."

"Come on. It's Mitchell. You know I hate that."

"Why else would I do it? What do you want, fuckwad?"

"Mr. Fuckwad to you." He laid it out for her. What he needed from her, and what would happen if she failed to agree.

"You'd really turn me in to my ex?" she said in a surprisingly small, almost fearful voice. "After all we've been through?"

"I don't want to," Mitchell said truthfully.

"Shit," she muttered. "Give me the flight number."

After he hung up, Mitchell did a little moonwalk, then happily bounced his way back to the waiting area. He was almost to the row of seats facing the window when a sudden lancing pain ripped into his skull. The agony brought him to his knees and he clutched at the top of the closest seat to prevent himself from falling flat. He felt a terrible heat, heard a hissing, then felt his grip on the seat disappear. He fell to his side and saw how the acid dripping from his hand had eaten through the seat.

Others were noticing, too.

"Aw, shit," he said, wondering how he was going to talk himself out of this one if either airport security—or a few friendly paradox demons—arrived.

Papua, New Guinea.

The plane touched down after sixteen hours. Max had slept, but Julian felt obliged to wake her as they neared their destination. The view of the jagged, mist-enshrouded mountains below as daybreak struck was awe inspiring and not to be missed. When they reached the landing strip, the pilot had to make several runs over the airfield to scare off cattle. When it was finally cleared, they touched down. A guide met them and brought them to a small boat. The guide identified himself as Pax. He was fluent in English and wore traditional village garb. He was dark-skinned. Beautiful patterns were painted on his face. Thick painted lines followed the contours of his handsome and slightly suspicious visage. They wove about his flesh in intricate, interlocking patterns. The red and black lines were accented by dots that seemed to make them shimmer and vibrate. Hibiscus leaves were used as earrings. He wore several necklaces made of teeth, seed, and shells, and an ornate Tapa cloth skirt. He carried a long, thin drum.

Pax glanced at the long black case Julian carried, the sword safely strapped inside. "You'll make some noise, too, eh?"

Julian said nothing to that. Max was busy fending off some of the larger, nastier insects. He got her onto the boat. She cursed as she swatted at her arm. A large red lump was already ballooning up from a previous bite.

"He said you'd be coming," Pax said once they were on their way.

"He generally knows," replied Julian.

Pax nodded. "Everything. That's what he knows."

Julian looked to Max. "That's why we're here."

The journey took about another hour. They closed on the village and several men dressed as warriors hurled spears at them. Pax laughed and said, "They're just playing."

"It's their way of saying 'hello,'" explained Julian.

Max shrugged. The spears had sunk into the water well before their boat. She pointed at the beautiful patterns on their guide's face. The jagged images reminded her of lightning.

"It's like Keith Haring," she said.

Pax shook his head. "We get that a lot. I think Haring saw some Tapa."

"That's what their art is called," Julian said. "It's becoming popular in the states. Might be the coming thing."

"With money comes freedom, independence," said Pax.

Soon they were on the bank, heading toward the gates of the village. Pax beat on his drum and the rhythmic pattern was returned by those who had gathered to greet the visitors. Max and Julian were led to a sandy "village square" and surrounded by dozens of natives. A young man wearing a "Babe: The Gallant Pig" cap and a pair of khaki slacks approached. He was bare foot and bare-chested, his body adorned with elegant patterns that were perfectly symmetrical. He wore hibiscus leaves and several necklaces.

"Hero," said Julian.

The boy shook his head. "For once, it would be nice to see you when you didn't need something."

"Next time," said Julian.

"No. Never. We'll not see each other again after this. Come."

Alarmed, Julian followed Hero to a small hut. Max walked beside him. A small sun roof allowed a single shaft of light to reach down to where Hero sat, making him seem ghostlike. He popped a CD into a portable player and the soothing tones of classic Enya began to play.

Hero addressed Max. "If I didn't like you, it would have been Yanni. Or John Tesh. I keep them around to scare off the evil spirits."

Max leaned in, fascinated.

"Booga booga!" Hero cried.

When Max retreated in surprise and confusion, Hero fell to the ground laughing, clutching at his stomach. "Classic! Your face was classic."

Julian looked to Max. "He really is the Eternal Teenager. He doesn't age. Hasn't in fourteen thousand years."

"Oh."

Hero said, "I must take my pleasure somewhere. Show me what troubles you."

Max looked around. "Are you Awakened?"

"Yes," said Hero. Gently, patiently.

Frowning, Max said, "I need electricity."

"There is none. The closest phone is an hour away by dinghy."

Max looked to Julian. "Then how did he know we were coming? I thought you called."

"Your voices were heard," said Hero. "Nothing else should matter."

"Okey-doke," said Max. "But—"

Hero indicated her bracelet. "It has all the power you need. Conjure."

Max looked down at the bracelet as if it had suddenly transformed into some kind of bug. "It's magic?"

"It is. It holds the essence of magic. Quintessence. However, like anything else, it's resources are finite. Use it well. Do not use it completely."

Max nodded. She thought of the "spirit journey" she had made and willed the patterns she had seen from within the Net to bleed into this reality. Suddenly, a seething crimson shadow of the pattern she had seen sprang into existence before her. She cried out and nearly lost control of it. She had never really expected her magick to work!

Hero used his power to help her maintain control. "Just tell me. Show me."

Max did as he asked. It was slow going at first, then she was able to retrace all her steps. A cloud filled with brilliant and beautiful flashes of kaleidoscopic lightning hovered before her. She recreated her journey from Mitchell's computer into the heart of the net. She hesitated when it came time to show her murder of the man in Jersey, but she did it anyway, explaining how she had wanted to spare his life, but Mitchell had pushed her, and she didn't fight back hard enough, didn't know *how* to fight back—

Hero told her not to dwell on it. It could not be undone.

Her recreation took them through the tunnel that led to the bizarre island and its towering spires. The cathedral and the library followed. The weaponsmaster was last. Julian studied this figure as if it was someone from his past.

After the tale was told, Julian looked to Hero and said, "So what does any of it mean?"

"It's a simple thing," said Hero. "A path has been opened. Now it must be closed."

"A doorway to the Pattern?"

"Of course. You knew that already, you simply didn't wish to believe it. You came to me hoping that I would disprove what you knew in your heart."

"Waitaminute," Max asked. "What are you talking about?"

"The pathway to all life," said Hero. "To all existence. Reality has a pattern. A shape. Magick reforms that pattern in subtle ways. There is no reason why it cannot all be reshaped at once except that the path is meant never to be found. But from time to time, it is found. It's the old saying about twelve monkeys in a room with twelve typewriters. Given eternity, one of them will churn out 'War and Peace.' Humans are like those monkeys. As more and more come into existence, the chances increase. And this 'Internet' is very much like the pattern. The resonances are in place. The discovery was inevitable."

"Ascension," said Julian, thunderstruck. "We have to tell everyone."

"You won't," Hero said softly. "Your greed will get in your way. As a result, one of you will die, one will close the pathway, and one—"

"Wait," said Julian. "There's only two of us."

"There has always been three."

"Mitchell," Max said softly. "What about the third?"

"One of you will be redeemed."

Julian considered this. "So who dies?"

Hero smiled. "I haven't a clue."

Mitchell had stumbled into a nearby bathroom and locked himself in a stall. Then he braved the gauntlet and crossed over to the Near Umbra. The world suddenly became gray and lifeless. He knew that he had made it.

Mitchell considered his options. He could wait here in the john and hope none of the Doles would come after him. Okay, sure, they were really lifeless spirits made to do the Technocracy's bidding, but they sure looked like that asshole to Mitchell. baIn any event, that was one option. Wait here a few hours, then cross back into his own reality. But by that time, his flight would be gone. The next one was tomorrow. Nothing was available for charters.

His only other reasonable course of action was to venture into the gray world and try to reach the landing field. He would join the crowd, do a little more minor invisible conjuring once he was inside the plane, a scent or two to make people believe what he wanted them to, and it would all be over with.

A sudden, lancing pain made him cry out. It worsened and he whimpered, clutched at his skull and feeling as if he was going to toss at any moment.

Fuck, the headache had lessened, but it just wouldn't go away.

Mitchell decided to leave the john. Hell with it. The rest of the bathroom looked pretty much the same. The light was a little harsher, the walls a little more drab. He knew that if his entrance had been detected, there would be a welcoming committee waiting outside the bathroom. He sweated acid as a precaution. The oils his altered biochemistry emitted never effected his own body, but anyone who tried to touch his flesh right about now would have their skin seared from their bones. The hard part was clothing. He had to only manifest oils in certain parts of his body so that he didn't ruin his clothes. He also had to make sure that any beads of sweat were reassimilated back into his skin before they could drop down onto his clothes.

Frankly, it was a bitch to control.

Mitchell opened the door. Nothing waited for him. No bio-engineered freaks. No dead-eyed wraiths.

"Funky," Mitchell said. He entered the waiting area. Other than the drabness of color, the changes to the airport were subtle. Whereas before the touch of an industrial psychologist was clearly visible in the rounded corners of desks and pleasing arrangements of chairs, now all was psychotically neat and orderly. He knew that if he counted the chairs, it would come to an even number in each row, and an even number of rows. A dozen men wearing dark suits, sunglasses, and frowns were lined up before the ticket agent, presenting their papers. Mitchell had taken note of the ticket agent in the real world. A soft looking, buxom brunette, with kind of a bawdy Ashlyn Gere fuck-me-til-I-can't breathe-anymore grin. Her counterpart here was Cruella Deville. The plane waiting beyond the large perfectly square window was dark and sleek, more like a guided missile than a commercial airliner. A perfectly formed line of people waited to board the plane outside. In this part of the airport, it was still necessary to walk across some concrete and climb up stairs to get into a plane. That was how Mitchell planned to join with his fellow passengers in the real world. There would be too many questions if he had to take a flight with the Technobabblers, questions he didn't want to have to answer. Besides, he had no guarantee that *this* plane would reach the destination he had in mind.

An insubstantial figure drifted before him, scowling and shaking his head as it scooped up some lint from the otherwise perfectly maintained rug. Mitchell drew back. Wraiths *always* creeped him out. Those who disappointed or crossed the Technocracy often ended up like this.

What to do, what to do...

Well, if he went by Ilsa, She-Bitch of the SS up there at the ticket gate, she would get a good long look at him. He couldn't mask himself properly in this place. Just using magick would make him prey for security's spider-hounds. Naturally, he would have to conjure to cross the gauntlet back to his reality, but he knew no one would follow at that point...

"Fuck it," Mitchell said. He went to the window, hurled a few handfuls of acid at the glass, then took a running leap. The glass hissed and spiderweb cracks appeared just before he struck the glass, allowing him to shatter it with his weight. He plummeted to the ground, landing on a cart filled with garment bags.

One cart for hard suitcases and briefcases, another for garment bags, another for freight. A place for everything and everything in its place. What a bunch of Nazis, Mitchell thought.

He knew the drill on this side. No problem. He rolled off the cart, feeling at least one cracked rib, and started to open the door between realities.

A boot caught him below the chin. The kick sent him flying back onto the concrete. Mitchell looked up into a face that was transforming from mundane and human into something squidlike. His assailant wore a crisp gray uniform, the creases neatly ironed. Its rapidly expanding tentacles did not secrete even a drop of slime. Instead, razor like ridges were manifesting. Another rapidly transforming uniformed man came running.

Oh shit, Mitchell thought. *I'm gonna have to mix it up with the baggage handlers from hell.*

He would have preferred to make his leap back to his reality without a fight, but these guys clearly weren't about to let him explore that option. In a way, that was good. He really hated having to kill people just because they had seen his face. Innocents should never have to suffer for his fuck-ups, that was his motto. To date, he had only taken out nine people for that express reason. That wasn't bad, especially when compared with other mercs in his field.

Mitchell was traveling under a false identity buried so many layers deep that even the Technocracy wouldn't find him. What was really going to be a pain in the ass, though, was having to bail from the plane a little before it landed to make sure there was no one waiting at the other end.

Ah well, Mitchell thought as Squidd came for him, oughta get to work.

Manifesting as strong an acid as he could manage, Mitchell swept forward with his hand, slicing off most of the tentacles that made up Squidd's face. The figure collapsed, whimpering like a baby. Mitchell plunged his other fist through the back of the handler's head, then withdrew as the dying creature's body shook a little and went slack. The other handler was busy transforming into what looked like the character Pig Pen from Peanuts.

"Aw, don't do that," Mitchell said. He'd always liked that character. He could identify with him.

But the handler didn't heed Mitchell's warning. Instead, a grayish-brown cloud was enveloping. Presumably it was poison gas of some kind. Sighing, Mitchell reached over to the baggage cart and set one hand one on either end of the three foot long steel guard rail. Then came a hissing sound and a cloud of smoke rose from each of his grips as they melted steel to slag. The bar dropped loose. Mitchell snatched it up, the acids in his hands already reassimilated. He tossed it like a javelin and impaled poor old Pig Pen.

The flailing dust bunny dropped to his knees and sank back, quite dead. Mitchell heard the clatterings of the spider hounds in the distance. He turned and ran toward the crowd of onlookers boarding the plane. As he ran, he attempted to gain passage back from the Near Umbra to his favorite brand of reality. Most mages could not circumvent the Gauntlet, but he had been given special training by agents of the Technocracy. In a fleeting moment, it occurred to Mitchell that he was in a practically unique position to rebel against his employers, go back to the Tradition mages, and blow the fucking lid off a whole bunch of the Technocracy's well guarded secrets. He would probably be regarded as a hero.

Yeah, he thought, *but what was all that to solving the simple, straightforward problem of fixing a world that had gone to shit? The shortest distance between any two points is a straight line, honey pie. And Max's gonna give me back that straight line soon.*

The ache in his head got bad again. He screwed up his incantation just as the world was getting brighter and colors were returning to normal. With a curse, Mitchell was sucked back into the near Umbra. A small figure appeared before him, slamming him once in the solar plexus. If Mitchell hadn't been well padded by his suit, and if his instincts hadn't warned him to pull back at the last second, he would have been laid out by the blow. Instead, he merely stumbled, fell, and got back to his feet after a small roll. He was so pissed that instead of acids he manifested some shit that would make the little guy look like a fucking leper a second after it hit him.

"Enough," the little guy said.

Mitchell stopped—and was surprised that he had stopped. The small Asian man before him stood beside a large fluffy dog that was anything *but* a dog. Mitchell could sense a paradox demon, no matter what shape it was in.

The dog looked sick, somehow. Its eyes were a little glazed, its breath labored. Pain and anger radiated from the poor creature. Mitchell held his hands at his side. He wanted to keep them attached to his wrists. The dog looked hungry.

"My name is X'an," the small man said.

"Jesus," Mitchell said, recognizing the name. "I know about you. I was thinking of trying to get you as an agent a while back. Cool."

Suddenly, the clattering of spider-hounds came from behind Mitchell. He tensed. X'an waved his hand and the beasts retreated. The Technocracy frequent flyers were passing at a safe distance. No one else approached.

"You were making inquiries about a certain sword," X'an said. "I was in the area anyway. I couldn't help but notice your troubles."

"Yeah," Mitchell said, looking over his shoulder and spotting the retreating forms of the spider-hounds. "Thanks for your help with that."

X'an shrugged. He gestured toward Butch. "Are you available for employment? Before you answer, consider that my dog is hungry. He can feast on the living or the dead. Your answer will help him decide."

Mitchell glanced at the bodies of the two baggage handlers. The dog followed his gaze and licked its lips.

"Now why'd ya have to break up a touching moment like that for?" Mitchell asked.

"I'm impatient."

"So let's deal. I saw the guy who's got your merchandise. He's causin' problems with a ladyfriend of mine. He also shot me. You want your sword, I want to pull his spine up out of his throat. It seems are needs aren't mutually exclusive, dig?"

"I want Ibiero alive."

"That's his name? Ibiero?"

X'an told Mitchell a little about Julian. It was all Mitchell could do not to laugh his ass off.

"A fucking fashion designer," Mitchell said. "That just figures."

"Will you work with me?" X'an asked.

"Hell, yeah," Mitchell said, the pain in his head returning. "Just so long as nothing happens to Maxine."

"I have no interest in her."

"Cool." Mitchell held out his hand. "Shake on it?"

X'an did not move. Acid fell from Mitchell's fingers and hissed as it struck the concrete.

"Shit, sorry about that," Mitchell said. "Maybe we oughta leave this one at a verbal agreement, what say?"

X'an nodded.

Mitchell knelt before the dog. Butch whined. Mitchell forced away his fear as the dog surged forward and licked his face. Mitchell's hands were normal again. He stroked the dog's flanks, feeling a little odd about the ropy shapes and the odd angles that were hidden beneath Butch's fur.

"Is he gonna be all right?" Mitchell said.

"He's fine. Why do you ask?"

Mitchell looked into the dog's eyes. They were changing color. Crimson one moment, turquoise the next. Blood pooled around his eyes like tears.

"No reason…"

Port Moresby, New Guinea.

Maxine Anderson was falling in love. The language and the people of New Guinea had won her over completely. Julian had booked them a suite at the Islander Travelodge in Boroko. The wealth of department stores, banks, restaurants, and bars made Boroko one of New Guinea's most popular tourist areas.

When they had first arrived in Port Moresby, Max thought she had stepped onto the set of Escape From L.A.. High walls lined with barbed wire enclosed all the major areas. Snapping dogs and armed men were everywhere. They had gone to dinner at a nearby restaurant, passing machine gun toting security officers at the front door and the drive.

At the hotel, a fellow "tourist" lectured them on proper behavior: "For God's sake, don't hug and kiss in public. Don't go sightseeing at night. The 'rascals' are everywhere."

Max had heard about the "youth gang" problem.

"And you, miss, wear a jacket, dark clothes. You're far too attractive not to draw attention…"

In the hotel lobby, under glass, was a Queen Alexandra Birdwing, the largest butterfly in existence.

"They needed a shotgun to bring the first one down," said their overly worried tourist-friend. His wife arrived and he quickly vanished.

Max stared at the butterfly under glass. She admired its black wings, streaked with white and yellow, its crimson and black body; it was a creature of primordial beauty. She couldn't take her eyes off it.

Suddenly, the lights blinked in the lobby. A spark flew from Max's hands, and the butterfly lit up as lightning coursed through it. The creature's wings flapped a single time, tearing it from its moorings. Then it settled back into its sleep of death.

Max shuddered and turned away from the creature. She noticed a woman with dark coffee skin staring at her. The woman was young, with long black hair. She smiled, looking around and nodding, as if she was in the midst of a crowd of friendly people, though no one was near her at all.

Max had been told early on that the people of New Guinea believed that the spirits of the dead were all around them. This woman seemed to take that to heart.

Though—after what Hero and Julian had said about the dead, and the unseen world Max had never even guessed existed, she supposed that anything was possible. The woman left.

As the night had gone on, she knew that in ways, she had been brought to a nightmare city.

And yet…

There was a certain charm to New Guinea, an intermingling of art and culture in every facet of existence. Once Max heard people speaking Pidgin, she was lost. In Pidgin, a helicopter was a *Mixmaster bilong Jesus Christ*. And a piano was a *bigfella bockus, teeth alla same shark, you hittim he cry out*.

The dialect was a mix of many languages. The coastal area had another language, Moto or 'Police Moto,' spread by the local law enforcers. Hundreds of tribal languages were also heard.

In their room, Max dropped to the bed, feeling tired and achy. Her bites no longer itched, the swelling in her arm had gone down.

Julian was examining his sword.

"The airport's not too far from here," said Max. "Why didn't we just catch that flight to Tokyo you were talking about?"

"No flights until morning."

Max smiled. "Why do I have the feeling I could disprove that with a phone call?"

Julian's shoulders slumped. "Hero asked me to do him a favor. It's going to take a while."

"Can I help?"

"No. I've never been good with partners."

"I got that feeling."

He looked at her sharply. She was holding up one of the newspapers he had acquired about his show. There was a sidebar article chronicling Julian's many rocky affairs with models and celebrities.

"So what's the deal with this Alisa person?" Max asked.

"Out of my life," he said. *And she's better off that way.*

"Your choice or hers?"

Julian shrugged. "Mutual."

Max tossed the newspaper aside and picked up the novel she had bought at the airport. Neal Stephenson's Snow Crash. "Do me a favor?"

"What?" Julian was packing the sword back in its case.

"Tell me about this Edgar Case thing again. The library, all that. I'm still not getting it. Was he like us? A mage?"

Julian sat in a plush chair beside the bed. "No. Not that I'm aware. But his vision of the Pattern was influential on many of us. He saw it as a vast library that he could leave his body and travel to. If someone was sick or troubled, he helped them. Case didn't have to see them, touch them, anything. All he needed to know were some basic facts. When a person was born. Where. He would travel to the library, where each living person had his or her own book of life. To find out what was wrong with a person, if they were sick, or if they had made a wrong turn with their life that could be corrected, he read up on them. Then he came back and told them what to do. And most of the time, he was dead on."

"He didn't have any medical training, he wasn't a psychiatrist?"

"No."

"So what I saw when I was in the metaverse—"

"The what?"

Max held up the book she had been reading. "That's what they call it in here. When I was inside the web."

"Ah."

"So what I saw was the library Case found?"

"I think *it* found *him*. That's why he never met its guardian."

"And when he told people what he read in the books, told them what their future was going to be—"

"That future changed. The Pattern changed."

Max waited a long time before asking her next question. "Could those books be re-written?"

Julian seemed unnerved by the question. Max sensed that she had touched on something he had been considering, too.

"No," Julian said firmly, turning from her as he rose and collected his sword. "You can't change the past."

Max watched him leave, certain that he was lying. She thought about her parents, their screams of terror and pain that seemed to go on forever, and poor Freddy, who had been torn to pieces because of her...

She tried to read, but found it impossible. The television was clogged with Rugby matches. The national pastime. A commentator was gloating over a recent victory against Australia. Max decided to get out for a little.

The hotel was sprawling, with close to two-hundred rooms. She went downstairs, passed the *Sanmare* restaurant, and found a seat in the *Kopi Haus* coffee shop.

The woman who had been watching her earlier was there. She had been talking to a slightly overweight Brit, but when she spotted Max, she abandoned him and sat beside the blonde American.

"Call me Jean-Marie," the dark-haired woman said as she held out her hand.

"You're French?" Max asked as she shook the woman's hand.

"When I want to be." The woman laughed. She had the darkest, most piercing eyes Max had ever seen.

Max had a sudden vision of herself in bed with this woman. She dismissed it. She needed something to help her pass the time, but *that* always led to misery, one way or the other.

"What are their names?" Jean-Marie asked.

Max was taken back. "Pardon me?"

"I'll help you find them. I have a place nearby. My own *haus tambaran*. A spirit house."

It came to Max suddenly. This woman was a con-artist. A medium. A palmist probably. "Sorry, not interested."

Max rose to leave. Jean-Marie grabbed her arm. "You're adrift without a Tradition. You are cold and lost. The first step toward attainment is letting go."

"You're a mage?" Max asked.

"I'm one with the spirits. I can bring you together with those you love who never die."

Max sat back down. Slowly. "My parents?"

"Yes."

Max didn't even have to think about it. "Where...?"

Anne-Marie's house was several blocks away, close to the National Parliament building. Inside, odd statues lined the entrance hall. They looked like the elongated, mummified bodies of the dead, somehow recast in wood and stone.

Anne-Marie took her to a small room in the back. The dark-haired woman stripped off her clothing, revealing a host of scars that were almost beautiful. Patterns had been worked on her flesh with a small knife or razor. Circles reaching out from her nipples. Ridges lining her shoulders and arms. A V shape reaching up from her sex.

"This is to show you that I am what I say I am," Anne Marie said, lowering her head and holding out her arms. "Look at me if you will."

Max came closer. "Who did this to you?"

"In this country, it is forbidden for a woman to know the secrets of the spirit houses. A few villages break the taboos. I was taught and I was given the marks of the crocodile."

Max suddenly noticed the huge crocodile skull sitting on a nearby table.

"I was told the secret tales, given the responsibility of keeping the traditions, the stories, the laws of our people. But when it was found out that a woman had been so trained, my people were faced with a choice: exile me or be exterminated. They sent me away."

"I'm sorry," said Max.

Anne-Marie slipped on a black silk robe. "My spirit was *gone bagarap*. It was broken. I fell in with *dimdim*, white foreigners like yourself. They found uses for me. And I learned my true craft..."

Max hugged herself. It was cold in the darkened room. A few lit candles gave off a golden glow, but it failed to warm. "My parents."

"Yes."

The summoning took the better part of an hour, and involved stories and chants that Max found fascinating and beautiful.

Anne-Marie removed her robe once more, this time to show that the patterns up her flesh were changing. New scars manifested. Some near her eyes and throat. Her flesh rippled and its color softened. Her hair shortened and became a dirty blond. Anne-Marie covered her face with her arms, which also changed. Muscles coiled and her arms thickened. Hair sprang from her flesh. A masculine voice erupted from her throat, moaning low and deep.

She was becoming something strange and new...

Or very old.

"Dad?" Max asked.

Anne-Marie raised her head sharply and showed her new face. It wasn't Max's father.

It was the man Max had murdered in New Jersey.

"*I was hoping they'd let me make a phone call before they sent me away for good,*" said Max's victim. "*And if there's one person I'd really like to reach out and touch, well, guess what?*" Max was on her feet, backing up to the door.

The thing that had been Anne-Marie surged forward. "*It'd be you!*"

Max turned and ran, but no one alive could match the dead man's speed. Despite herself, she screamed as she felt his touch.

Julian was on his way back to the hotel when he saw a wreath of fiery bright white serpents burst from the window of the house Max had entered an hour earlier. The lightning snakes crackled as they struck the ground and dissipated. Rainbow effects were filtering into the air and the shattered window frames were buckling and fusing into art deco forms.

No one was on the street. No one saw.

Max's dumb luck.

Julian cast a spell of delirium, hoping it would persuade any Sleepers who might come along that what they were seeing could be explained in normal terms.

Pain surged through his skull. Yet another filling had been toasted with that little maneuver.

"Son of a bitch," Julian said, fingering the latch that allowed his case to spring open. He snatched up the sword, which was still covered in blood, and raced to the front door of the spirit house. He unlocked the door with a minor incantation and raced inside.

In the back room, he found Max on the floor, curled in a ball, crying. A naked man stood before her. His flesh was crimson, rippling, as if a battle was on for supremacy of his body.

"You're damned, you stupid little cunt," the man said. *"I know what comes next for ya. I know, but I'm not gonna tell. You just do me a favor and go back and tell everyone who was depending on me why I had to die like that, okay? That's all I want out of you. You just do that—"*

Julian brandished the sword in the wraith's direction.

"What took you so long?" asked the dead man. He collapsed to the floor, and the shape of Anne-Marie quickly reasserted itself.

Julian dragged Max up from the floor. He was pulling her along as she tried to walk with him, stumbling, near falling on her weakened legs. Anne-Marie called from the other room.

"The dead hate you!" she cried. "The dead hate you both!"

Julian and Max made it to their room without further incident. Max uncoiled on the bed and began crying once more.

"That's not going to do any good," Julian said, unsure of how to comfort her. He had wanted to see her tortured and in pain, but now that the moment had come, it was far from satisfying.

"You wanted to see your parents again," Julian said tonelessly.

"Y-yes," Max sobbed.

"I made that mistake once."

Max looked up at him with bright red eyes. "Your parents?"

He shook his head.

"Someone you loved?"

He nodded. "Neelam." Even after all this time, it was difficult to speak her name.

Max slowly sat up. "How'd she die?"

"It was a long time ago. I was just a boy."

Max's gaze was unflinching. She *needed* to know.

Julian didn't want to talk about this. More than anything in the world, he didn't want to. Yet he found the words leaving him, anyway. "I was like you. New to my power. New to everything." He swallowed hard. "Have you ever been to

SCOTT CIENCIN

Bangladesh?"

She shook her head. "Calcutta. Once."

Julian forced himself not to react to that. He knew all about her visit to Calcutta. His hands ached. He went on, "It's not a fun place. Especially when you're on your own. Neelam was a prostitute. She took me in. I don't know why. I've never known why. She was very young, too. Not even sixteen. And I always knew that what she did for me was different from what she did for those other men. The one's who paid her for…"

Max hung on his every word.

"I hated those men. I wanted to make money so that she wouldn't have to degrade herself… But she didn't see that she was degrading herself. She felt that she was ending the loneliness for these people. When one of her 'men-friends' became too rough, or threatened her, I fixed them. I made it so they'd never bother her again. She never knew that. She never really understood—"

"That you loved her."

Julian looked away.

"So you *are* a mage?"

"Yes," he said, wondering why he had tried to hide it from her when they first met. Perhaps it was because he didn't want her to feel on equal footing with him. Or perhaps because he didn't want to see her as anything but his victim. He didn't know…

"I made something for Neelam. A sculpture of her. I crafted it out of flames. I—I thought… I don't know what I was thinking. That we'd make love next to it on cold nights, I guess. I don't know. But she was a Sleeper. And I didn't understand the rules."

Max nodded.

"I performed real magick in front of her. I made the flame sculpture. I thought she'd be happy. Amazed, but happy. I was wrong. She got scared. Couldn't believe what she was seeing. The walls started moving. Breathing. Coming apart. And things came through."

"Julian—"

He couldn't stop now. "I can't even begin to describe them to you. I never knew things like that existed. They were like shadows, but they were hungry, and they had thousands of eyes and teeth…"

"You don't have to do this," Max said.

"They came for me. It was my fault. I was the one they should have killed. The paradox demons. But they left me alive. They thought it was so funny that I didn't know what I was. That I had these voices in my had calling me 'Lord Shaper' and that I didn't know the first thing about how the world really worked. And so they took Neelam's head off, right in front of me. A little bit at a time. Her eyes were last. They made us watch each other for hours while it was happening, they made me listen to her screams—"

Julian was shuddering. Max reached for him, her hand touching one of his gloves. "No!"

"What?" she asked, alarmed. "What'd I do?"

He backed away from her. "I just want you to understand. As bad as that was, what happened when I tried to find her spirit—that was worse. A million times worse."

Max looked away from Julian.

He said, "There's an old saying. Let the dead past bury its dead. It's true. It's true…"

Even as he spoke those words, and embraced the truth they held, he knew that he had never lived by them.

And that he would probably die because of that.

Billie Jean was a fly on the wall. She saw and heard everything that happened in Julian Ibiero's room.

In actuality, she hadn't transformed herself into an insect. Instead, she was looking out through the eyes of a fly that had wandered into the sword-wielder's room. She knew better than to use overt magick in her target's presence. And considering his companion's flare with technology, using even the most cutting edge surveillance devices was also out of the question.

So it was time for nature, and really, that was her specialty, anyway.

Billie Jean had already left messages for Mitchell, letting him know that the targets would soon be on the move. He in turn left word that they would rendezvous in Hong Kong. Hopefully, once Billie Jean had connected Mitchell with his prey, she would be allowed to go back home. She had a studio demo due in less than a week and she was going crazy trying to put the finishing touches to it when Mitchell had interrupted her.

A melody came to mind. Billie Jean divided her consciousness yet again and went to work with the small keyboard she had brought with her. She was hoping that her new demo would be strong enough to allow her to finally cut a deal with a legitimate recording house. The technocracy had approached her through several of their dummy corporations, but she had been smart enough to recognize their clumsy attempts at getting her in their debt.

Fortunately, they didn't know about Malcolm.

She and her ex-husband had a perfect relationship for a time. He was the perfect companion, a great lover, funny, charming. Then he found out what she really did for a living and it all hit the fan. Now he was the only person on the face of the earth that actually frightened her. She would do anything to avoid him, including releasing her masterpiece, "Kaleidoscope," through an assumed name. She hoped that it would establish her the way "Orinoco Flow" had Enya, with Aboriginal strains replacing Celtic folk songs.

Billie Jean sighed as the melody played itself out and she watched Julian and Maxine. She wondered if they would make love. Hopefully not. That sort of thing always made her uncomfortable, unless she was one of the participants.

She thought of Mitchell and considered how he had acted whenever they had worked together in the past. It was *possible* that he would let her go once he had his prey within reach, but not likely.

Mitchell was cute, but he was such an unmitigated bastard. Billie Jean couldn't help but wonder if the world would be better off without him.

And if maybe she should do something about that…

10

Hong Kong, China.

"Why don't you ever take these off?" Max asked, pointing at Julian's gloves. He shrugged. "Doesn't matter."

They were hurrying down a busy street. Max had been to Hong Kong before. She knew better than to allow herself to be overwhelmed by its neon glories and living, breathing history.

It was dark as they darted down a narrow alley and soon stood before the back door of a restaurant. A handful of vagrants sat around, holding bags of trash close.

Julian knocked on the door. It was opened by a short, fat man with a butcher knife and a bloody apron.

"Sarada wa do desu ka?" asked Julian.

"Densha wa itsu kimasu ka?" the cook replied.

The two men stared at each other for a moment, then broke into laughter.

"I love all this secret agent shit," the cook said.

Julian nodded. "Me, too."

Max smiled. Though they were in China, they had spoken Japanese. One had asked how the salad was, the other had responded by inquiring about the whereabouts of a bus. Silly code phrases, William Burroughs-esque non sequiturs, but effective nevertheless.

Julian and Max were led through a pair of storerooms to a hidden room with a winding downward staircase. The cook bowed, then departed. Julian and Max descended and soon came upon a wooden door braced by two more "vagrants." Max had been warned that the men and women laying in the trash outside were warriors in disguise. Guardians for the one they had come to see.

A command came over a small speaker. The guards opened the door and waited for Julian and Max to step inside. Julian was not asked to give up the case concealing his sword, nor was Max's case confiscated.

They stepped into the darkness and the door closed behind them.

At first, Max thought she had been taken to another storeroom. Electronics equipment was scattered over a host of workbenches and rickety tables. PCs were everywhere, many gutted and in the process of being cannibalized. It took Max a moment to notice the frail-looking figure in the wheelchair at the far end of the room. Objects hung in mid-air around him. Mother-boards that he was enhancing with some strange form of magick.

The man's hair was long and greasy. His head was supported by a brace. A respirator helped him breathe. A computer to Max's right flared to life. A metallic voice, synthesized by the computer, spoke to her, delivering the thoughts of the wheelchair-bound man: *"You are both very lovely. I am happy to help."*

"You're also being paid," Julian said.

"There is that."

Max looked around. She desperately did not want to stare at this man. "Where do I jack in?"

"This terminal."

She shook her head. She couldn't very well project her consciousness into a machine that already bore the thoughts of someone else. "Sorry. It seems occupied."

A cold, hollow laughter sounded from the machine. *"Hey, a guy's got to try, doesn't he?"*

Max looked at the man in the wheelchair and shook her head, smiling. He had been after a virtual *fuck*. She wanted to ask, *don't you guys think of anything else?* but she already knew the answer to that. Men were all the same. All except Julian. He didn't seem the slightest bit interested in her physically, and in a strange way, that made him somewhat desirable. A challenge for another time, perhaps.

Max opened her case and withdrew her powerbook. She ran a cable between her unit and another of the computers.

"What's your name, anyway?" Max asked as she set up the interface.

"Didn't Julian tell you? I don't have one. I wasn't deemed worthy of one at birth. I would have died, but for the mothering touch of science…"

"Okay," Max said, finishing her preparations. "I think I've heard about enough."

She sat down at her computer. Powering up her machine, she became aware of Julian and Nameless staring at her. She looked over at them. "Could you guys do me a favor and go get some ice-cream or something? I'm still pretty new to all this and I can't concentrate with people watching me."

Julian nodded and went over to the wheelchair-bound man. Their host's consciousness fled the PC he had been using as a voice box. In halting tones, struggling for breath, he said, "Got some…new…toys in the back… A game that's… a porno version… of Doom… You'll… love it…"

"Sure," said Julian with little interest. He wheeled the man off to another adjoining room, giving Max the privacy she needed.

Steeling herself, Max allowed her fingers to glide over the keyboard. On an instinctive level, she understood that she really didn't need the computer any more. All she had to do was let herself go and she could ease her consciousness directly into the metaverse, the internet—whatever one wanted to call it.

They had come to this place because it provided the most secure lines in the east, or so Julian maintained. There was also a healthy supply of Quintessence threaded into the very building blocks that were used in the construction of this underground complex.

Max went onto the net and began to pull up sites at random. Soon her vision began to blur. Her mind slowly released its hold on her body. She surrendered herself to the new electric sensations flooding through her in a way she had always tried—and failed—to surrender herself during sex.

Suddenly, she was swept forward into a cataclysmic windstorm of light and life and information and ice, precious ice...

Too many cyber-thrillers, she told herself. 'Ice' was another word for data.

The web looked more like something out of the book she had been reading than the odd, dark universe she had visited before. Information looked like crystalline chips. Knowledge leaped toward her in bands of lightning. Filling her.

Understanding followed. This environment was whatever she made of it.

A sudden clarity overtook her. She knew what she had to do. Spread a net far and wide to reclaim the scattered pieces of the puzzle she had strewn about the last time she was here. At the same time, she had to be very careful of viruses that could infect her, or other Travelers like herself—

(where in the hell had that term come from, she wondered?)

—who might collide with her or worse, merge with her.

And finally, Max also had to be careful of any virtual assassins Mitchell may have hired to be on the look out for her consciousness here in the 'Verse.

What wigged her out was how damned easy it all was.

In a few moments, she had the operation underway with a near infinite number of fail-safes installed into the "search program" she had created. She could feel tiny parts of her consciousness leaving her like reconnaissance parties. After they departed, she felt dizzy and drained, but she soon recovered.

A few moments after that, she found that she was bored. There was nothing to occupy her higher intellect. She allowed her thoughts to wander...

Images flashed before her. A recreation of the tale Julian had told of the young prostitute whose death he had caused. She saw him being held by monsters, forced to watch as a beautiful young woman screamed and screamed but could not fend off her butchers.

Suddenly, the images gave way to glinting knife-edged memories. She was eleven years old, back in the car after the accident, trapped, listening to her parents scream for mercy, for someone to save them, and finally for death.

Max forced the images away, but she couldn't avoid noting the terrible similarities between Julian's tragic story and the prolonged deaths of her own parents. Julian and Max had each known great suffering and had been forced to endure the agonies of those they loved, which was almost worse.

You have to think of something else, Max told herself. *Think about the plan...*

Julian and Max had talked about what they intended to do with the gateway to the Pattern once Max had recollected all the pieces and reassembled it. Hero had advised them to remake the bridge, then blow it up from the other side.

...one of you will die...

The only problem was, who went in to do the dirty deed? It made sense that it would be her. Julian was not a Virtual Adept. Neither was Mitchell, for that matter. But Max was no hero. She had no intention of sacrificing herself for this.

Nor had she any intention of being used the way Mitchell had used her. Julian said that he knew someone that he could trick into doing the job for them. Someone who would take Max's place when the time came. A mercenary and Virtual Adept known as Jian Zhao.

Of course, he could be lying. And where would that leave her?

Dead.

Another idea came to her suddenly. She thought about the way he had hedged in New Guinea when they had talked about changing the past and bringing the dead back to life. Was it possible they planned on attempting exactly that?

As much as she missed her parents dearly, she could not even conceive of radically altering the fabric of reality just to serve her own ends. All she wanted was get enough knowledge about the here and now out of her next jaunt to the library so that she could set herself up financially for the rest of her life. Her goal was to be comfortable and safe. Someone *else* could worry about closing the gateway.

Suddenly, her lower consciousness reported that a decent percentage of the information she had tried to retrieve had been located. Naturally, it was too immense to be stored completely in her mind and without all of its components, the formula was worthless. She would have to think about creating her own private access to wherever she would store the formula. A gateway to the gateway.

That took about five seconds. The operation to find the rest proceeded as planned.

Max knew that she couldn't simply walk away from the business with the gateway. Back in Mitchell's study, she had located a scientific formula for invoking the gateway and travelling upon it. She had broken that formula the way one might shatter a block of ice and scattered the chips throughout the 'verse— imprinted with retrieval codes that only she could recognize and employ.

She could destroy the bits of the formula that she had retrieved and the immediate danger would be resolved. But it went to follow that if one programmer in Trenton could come across the means to access the gateway, then so could others. It was the gateway itself that needed to be closed.

Still... What if she did destroy the elements of the formula she had retrieved? At least *she* would be off the hook.

Unless she was captured by Mitchell or people from this Technocracy that Julian had told her about. They would never believe that she had destroyed the formula. She could picture them binding her in some magickal way. Forcing her to try and recreate the formula. If they learned that she had destroyed it, they would kill her because she knew too much, because she was of no further use to them, or simply as payback for ruining their plans.

So the only sane course of action was to go along with Julian's plan, at least for now, and find some way to introduce a couple of changes. Her objectives would be to ensure that the gateway was destroyed, that she got what she wanted from the library, and that she would make it back to the physical world to enjoy the riches she had plundered. With wealth she could buy the protection she would need from Mitchell and the people he often worked for.

It occurred to her that she could simplify the process, at least a little. She didn't really need the library to gain information that would secure her financially for life.

That knowledge was all around her, just waiting to be had.

So what are you waiting for, Max? she asked herself.

Max considered this for almost a minute, which seemed like an eternity in this place.

Then she made her choice.

The doors swung open. Julian and Nameless entered the room. Max turned to greet them.

"I can't do it," she said, honestly enough. "There's just not enough juice in this place."

Julian slumped into a chair. "Did you bring any of it together?"

Max looked over at Nameless. "How specific do you want me to be?"

"You're right. Hold on." He regarded his business acquaintance. "Payment in the usual form?"

Nameless split his consciousness and spoke from within one of the machines. *"Of course. It has been an honor and a pleasure serving you."*

Max collected her powerbook. Within minutes, they were back on the street.

"So what really happened?" asked Julian.

"I found some of the pieces," Max said. "But not enough for it to matter. This really is an all or nothing deal."

"Did you put the pieces together? Start to build the bridge?"

"Unsafe. If the bridge was under construction, it would make it easier for Mitchell or anyone else who might be going through the 'verse to find it. Better that all the parts stay scattered, but at least now I know where to find a lot of them."

Julian nodded.

"So what do we do now?" Max asked, studying Julian's face. An idea seemed to flicker within his eyes for a moment. He turned away suddenly. Something he didn't want to share with her. Not yet, anyway.

"I don't know," said Julian. "I need time to think."

"All right," Max said. But she didn't believe it for a second. Julian had an idea of what needed to be done.

So why was he holding back?

Mitchell felt like crap after his encounter at the airport. He had journeyed to New Guinea, arriving a little too late, and was now on a plane bound for Hong Kong. Upon arrival, he would meet Billie Jean and get to the task of separating Max from Julian Ibiero, and maybe even Julian Ibiero from his fucking head—if the need arose. Screw what that little bastard X'an wanted.

Thinking about X'an made him picture the little man's companion. Shame about the dog that wasn't a dog. Mitchell hated to see animals mistreated. It was one of the problems he sought to address when he became God and reshaped all reality to his liking.

Mitchell felt a throbbing pain in his chest. The plane would land soon. In the meantime, Mitchell needed to "effect repairs." His ribs would need to mend,

LIGHTNING UNDER GLASS

along with the internal injuries he suspected that he had sustained, and his head was killing him.

He'd had opportunities for sex before getting on the plane. A pair of gorgeous nineteen-year-olds. An Egyptian-looking woman sitting alone. Just a drop of the right oil onto their flesh and they would go insane with desire for him. But for some reason, he couldn't bring himself to do that. He had never forced a woman to have sex with him, only helped to release inhibitions or heightened the experience for them. There was always a degree of interest first. Usually, a very high one.

And all he kept thinking about was Max. How her flesh had felt against his, the things she had done with him. She didn't care that he was a freak, barely human. It turned her on.

That had never happened to him before.

God help him, he really was in love with her. And for the first time in his life, he simply didn't want any of these other women.

Still… he was hurt pretty badly.

Hating himself for doing it, Mitchell took stock of his opportunities on the flight. There were two woman on the plane who had been giving him signals. One was a flight attendant, the other a college student wearing a pair of short-shorts and a tight halter. He doubted that either of them would ultimately be adventurous on their own to join the mile-high club with him, but he was certain that if he started to talking to either of them, that by the time they touched down he could have one or both of them in bed within a few hours.

He just didn't care.

Today, for the first time in twenty-three years, since he had first used sex to heal his wounds, he was going to a doctor to get himself fixed up.

He got up to go to the bathroom. On the way, he passed the college student in her little halter top. She stared at him, then flicked her gaze back to the bathroom, and fixed him with a little grin.

"Jesus Christ," he muttered as he passed her and got to the john. "You just don't make it easy on a guy, do you?"

Hey, come on, Mitchie-poo, taunted a little voice in the back of his head. *It wouldn't be temptation if it wasn't hard to resist, now would it?*

With a sigh, Mitchell put the college girl out of his mind.

Julian and Max were in the largest McDonalds either of them had ever seen. They were dressed to resemble a couple of tourists. Julian's gloves had been a problem, as always, but they coped.

In Julian's hand was a secure credit card. He swept it through a small gate. An amount appeared and he okayed it. Max was still sitting at the table.

Suddenly, a message flashed where the amount had been seconds earlier. It read:

EXCUSE YOURSELF. A BANK OF PHONES WAITS ON THE WAY TO THE MEN'S ROOM. ANSWER THE FIRST PHONE THAT RINGS.

The amount returned. Julian took his receipt and went back to the table. He told Max that they would be going in a second, he just needed to take care of something.

She nodded, barely interested.

Julian found the phones easily. Two were not in use. The moment he approached, one of them rang. He answered it.

A cold, synthesized voice said, *"You know exactly who this is."*

"What's wrong? Didn't payment clear?"

"That is not the issue. I know why your companion had need of my facilities."

Julian flinched. It was Nameless. Max must have left a trail revealing the bridge's existence, despite her efforts to remove her tracks. She was powerful but new to her power. Julian had known that this was a risk, but there had seemed no better option at the time.

"What do you want?" Julian asked.

"Pardon?"

Julian hesitated. Perhaps this wasn't the shake-down he had anticipated.

"What I want is to do you a favor. I know what your companion was doing, but I don't think that you do."

Nameless told him. Julian listened, feeling his flesh grow cold as rage slowly rose within him. By the time Nameless was done, Julian Ibiero seemed as composed as ever, but inwardly, he was fighting a losing battle with the urges that had motivated him to find Maxine Anderson in the first place.

"Here's what I want you to do," Julian said. He detailed a plan.

"Are you sure about this?" asked Nameless.

"Of course. Bill it out at the usual rate. That is why you called, isn't it?"

"You wound me."

"Fuck yourself." Julian hung up the phone.

He returned to Max.

"Let's do some sight-seeing," Julian said. "I think I'm getting an idea of what our next move should be…"

Max and Julian spent several hours wandering through Hong Kong's vast array of markets and bazaars. Poor Man's Nightclub was only open at night. It was found on Hong Kong island, near the Macau Ferry. Max found a T-shirt for an animated film she had loved in her childhood and bought it. Deciding not to wait until they got back to their hotel, Max stripped off her top, revealing her black lace bra, and put the T-shirt on. The spectacle elicited the applause of several other tourists in the area—and some locals.

Julian was understandably annoyed. They walked away quickly. "Do you understand the concept of attempting to blend in?"

Max shrugged. "I had to find some way to get your attention. You barely even seem to know that I'm alive."

Maybe that's because you won't be for too much longer, Julian thought. He smiled and said, "You're right. I've been distracted and I'm sorry. I have a lot on my mind."

"You have an idea of where we can go, don't you?" Max asked. "You just don't like it."

"Pretty much," admitted Julian. "It's where we would be expected to go. That means it would be dangerous as hell just getting in. If we could think of a way."

They didn't speak again until they reached Temple Street. They had journeyed to the Yaumati section of Kowloon. This outdoor market reminded Julian of the New Market in Calcutta. Anything and everything one could hope to buy was found in Temple Street. People crowded in from all sides, a sea of humanity swelling and writhing, people pushing at one another, ignoring curses. All too much like the home to which he had sworn never to return.

They passed a collection of vagabonds performing a heartrending rendition of a Chinese opera. Dentists pulled teeth as relatives held the victims down. Fortune tellers and street doctors argued. The buyers and sellers of flesh played mahjongg when they weren't transacting deals.

Max came to a jade merchant who was about to collect an outrageous payment from a foolish American couple for some worthless jewelry.

"This will bring luck!" cried the merchant.

Annoyed, Max snatched a knife from a nearby table and stabbed at the jade pendant. It scratched and chipped. The merchant began to curse at her.

"A knife can't hurt the real stuff," said Max to the stunned tourists. "That was just soapstone."

Julian pulled Max away from the scene she had caused. The American tourists were now all over the merchant.

They took a taxi back from Kowloon. On the way, Julian rubbed at his eyes. He was yawning by the time they reached their room.

Inside, Julian removed his shoes and socks, then stripped down to his shorts. He had never done this before in Max's presence. He knew that it would make her feel that he was truly beginning to trust her and that was exactly what he wanted.

"I'll need a few hours sleep," said Julian. "Wake me around four. We can go over our options then."

"Sure, that's fine," Max said. She held up a portable cassette player and earphone. "I found some books on tape I want to listen to. I'll keep watch."

He grunted as he lay down on his side and willed his body to sink deeply into sleep.

Max waited for two hours in the darkness, listening to the Sue Grafton mystery she had purchased. She considered whether or not she could remove at least one of Julian's gloves without waking him, but knew it wasn't worth the risk. Let him have his mysteries. She had other business to think about.

When she was certain that Julian really was asleep, she collected her powerbook, then left the hotel room.

She had no idea that Julian had left a very special pair of wake up calls. One would wake him when the job was done.

The other was for her.

Billie Jean stood in the same small room Julian and Max had visited earlier today. Nameless was before her. His guards had fled.

Twisted black claws had emerged from the torn bloody flesh at the back of her hands. Her face had become insectoid to the point of ensuring that she could never be identified, and therefore didn't have to kill unless it was truly necessary.

So far tonight, it hadn't been necessary. Two men had been gutted and a woman had had an artery severed. All three were being brought to the hospital by those who had enough sense to get the hell out of Billie Jean's way.

"I feel very uncomfortable with threatening a person in your physical condition," said Billie Jean. "So instead, I'm just gonna ask you to tell me everything you know about Julian Ibiero and Maxine Anderson. I know they were here, but all my little spies could get a look at was her sitting at one of your keyboards with a whole ton of numbers and weird symbols tearing across the screen, like."

"How much are you offering?" asked an electronic voice beside Billie Jean.

"Pardon?" she asked.

"You want information. I buy and sell information, along with services."

A pair of darksome black wings burst from Billie Jean's back, shredding what was left of her outer clothing. "I've killed people for fucking with me like this!"

The wheelchair bound man didn't even blink. "Kill... me..." he said, not using the computer. "My soul... will join... with the... machine... and I will... find you... and cast you... into... hell for harming... me..."

"You don't really believe that, do you?" Billie Jean asked.

"It is... what you... believe... that is... important..."

"Ah, fer christsake," Billie Jean muttered, realizing she was going to be stark naked when she transformed back into human form. "How much do you charge?"

Max had a meeting. She had set it up when she had been in the 'verse earlier this evening. Now she stood in a shopping complex so large that it bragged about its three miles of inner walkways along its three floors of brightly lit shops. Its full name was the Ocean Terminal-Ocean Centre-Hong Kong Hotel-Harbour City/China Hong Kong City. Somehow, it needed a name that long.

She stood across from the Amazing Grace Elephant Company, a shop that sold decorative items for the home. That she carried her powerbook was hardly unusual. She had seen hundreds of comparable machines within the sprawling, thoroughly packed shopping complex.

Her appointment was late. She would give him thirty more seconds, then she was leaving.

Suddenly, a man brushed up next to her and whispered a string of numbers in her ear.

Contact.

Billie Jean now wore a set of clothes that was too big on her, but at least she was dressed. Nameless had arranged for one of the restaurant workers to leave their casual clothing in the alley outside. Billie Jean picked it up on her way out.

Now she drove toward the Ocean-Terminal, worried that she would be too late. She had been hoping to find out what all this was really about—why Mitchell had been so intent on wresting the woman from Ibiero—but there had been no info on that score from Nameless. He had been curious himself, but the Anderson woman had managed to cover her tracks well enough on the job she had come there to do. It was the little side endeavor that she had elected to perform which Nameless had all the details about.

Billie Jean decided that she had to try to save the American. If she allowed the meeting that was scheduled to take place as planned, then Mitchell might end up so pissed that he would tell her ex how to find her. Her life would be ruined.

Shit.

She drove through the night, wondering why she couldn't catch a break just *once* in a while.

Julian woke. The call had not yet come. Instead, it was something that had been burning within him since he was a child that had shaken him back to consciousness.

Rise, Lord Shaper. Rise and see what you have wrought.

Julian looked at the clock. If he hurried, there was just enough time for him to reach the shopping complex before it was all over. He knew that Nameless had arranged for the "blessed event" to be taped for him, but that would not be enough. The permanent record might be a comfort years from now, perhaps, but he needed to see what happening, and even to look into the eyes of the little thief as she understood that everything that was about to happen to her had been her own fault.

Smiling, he dressed and ran from his room.

Max and the young Asian man exchanged powerbooks. Max went to the ladies room, sat in a stall, and turned on the computer. She half-expected it to explode in her face, but it simply powered up. She called up the root directory and found what she had been looking for. Records of deposits made in the assumed name she had created when she was in Nameless's office today.

"You're one rich bitch," she whispered, noticing the very happening numbers, eight in all, and every one of them on the correct side of the decimal point.

Forty-one million dollars.

Hot damn.

It had been nothing for her. All she had to do was crack open a few hundred "impregnable" data-bases, steal some secrets, then get a bidding war started. One choice had been harder to make than all the others. One of the people whose secrets she was selling was Julian Ibiero. She had rationalized her actions by telling herself that in ways, he was just as dangerous as Mitchell. They both wanted to reshape reality, though Mitchell had bigger plans. And Max was tired of being used.

Besides, from a strictly business related standpoint, she really didn't need Julian anymore. Despite what he had done for her, her actions seemed like a sound move. When the time came for him, she knew that he would understand, though he wouldn't like it much.

Now all she had to do was patch into a telephone line and verify that these deposits and the access code she had been given were correct. She used her power to create a kind of microwave hotlink between the powerbook's modem and the phone line buried deep in the wall behind her.

She shuddered as the connection was made and she verified the information. The deposits, as discussed, were all pending. A final confirmation would need to be made by her new "business partner."

Now it was all a matter of seconds. She had ten seconds to link with the people she had sold the information to, and give *them* an access code in return. If not, the deposits they made would be canceled.

She created the link and downloaded the code. It would lead them to a treasure trove of information that would take months to sort out, though the overall contents were easily verified.

They had ten seconds to verify her information and finalize the deposit. If not, she would taint their access to the materials she had stolen.

The seconds ticked by. Five. Six. Seven…

A message came in.

UNACCEPTABLE. FURTHER CONFIRMATION NECESSARY.

Max couldn't believe this. She reached out with her power and severed their link to the treasure trove. An instant before she broke their connection, a sliver of information penetrated her defenses.

She read the message. OURS IS A TRADITION NOT ACKNOWLEDGED BY ANY MAGES OUTSIDE OUR CIRCLE. WE WISH FOR YOU TO JOIN US. IT IS THE ONLY WAY WE CAN BE SURE THAT YOU WILL NOT BETRAY US LATER.

Max frowned. She didn't like this at all. A nice, clean deal had been set up here. But in a way, she could see their point. Betraying an organization in which she held a vested interest would be self-defeating, and considering the enterprise she had decided to undertake, she could hardly expect anyone to trust her.

She also looked at it from their point of view. What if she was setting them up to receive this information as a means of smoking them out for the intelligence agencies or their rivals?

She read the rest of the message. It gave her a time and a place. Her initiation into their ranks would be very straightforward. All she had to do was perform a minor feat of magick in a crowded store. Everyone around her would look like

Sleepers, but they would be members of her new organization. It was a show of trust. A magickal form of Russian Roulette.

"Well, all right then," Max said as she left the women's room and casually strode to her destiny.

Billie Jean spotted Max coming out of the ladies' room. She was the mistress of flies and all things of the earth. Several of her minions had been keeping watch on Max. Now all Billie Jean had to do was keep Maxine Anderson from obligingly using magick in a pack of Sleepers and getting herself and a whole lot of innocent people torn to pieces by the demons who would arrive to punish this affront.

Well, at least it wasn't anything too difficult…

Julian stood before his hotel. A line of taxis waited.

He no longer believed in the library, despite the assurances of Hero and the odd happenings he had witnessed in Mitchell's study. In fact, he was now convinced that Hero had set him on this journey because he had seen the violence and madness in Julian's heart, and he wanted to dissuade Julian from murdering Max. The library, the quest—all of it was just a distraction. Hero must have hoped that given time, Julian would see that child who had damned him had acted innocently, and that the woman she had become was nothing like the little thief he remembered.

That plan had gone to hell when Julian learned of Max's betrayal. She had performed an expert bit of industrial espionage. What she had taken had been nothing too damning. She hadn't stolen military secrets that could begin a nuclear war, for instance, or revealed the truth about J.F.K.'s assassination to the American public—wouldn't they be surprised—oh, no.

What she *had* taken had been the ideas files of several thousand corporations. Cutting edge technologies under development. Eyes only film and entertainment properties. All the upcoming work of people in the fashion industry—like himself. And literally millions of similar bits and pieces of information. The cumulative price tag that one could attach to such a treasury of information was in the nine figure range. Two, maybe three billion.

She had auctioned it all.

Julian had not considered himself an artist since his hands had been ruined by his father. He was now a designer. A creator. But hardly an artist. Still, his work had answered a need in him. It had given him some form of release and had allowed him to vent his energies toward building beauty rather than destroying it.

Maxine Anderson had elected to take that away from him tonight. To ruin him a second time.

The gateway to the pattern? A chance to reach back into the past and change the outcome of the madness that had shaped his life?

A carrot dangling at the end of a fragile stick that couldn't bear its weight.

Julian felt relieved at having been released from the burden of having to perform "heroically." That was not his nature.

What would happen tonight was Julian being true to himself.

Julian waited impatiently as a Greek couple was loaded into the taxi in the front of the line. It sped away. Julian took his place curbside, ready to hop into the next taxi the moment it pulled up into place.

Before the driver could move up into the space vacated by the cab hauling off the Greek couple, another cab circled around and jammed into the space. A flurry of angry horns sounded.

Under them, the driver called, "You're in a hurry, I'll get you there fast."

Julian didn't care about protocol right now. He liked the driver's spirit. Jumping into the cab, Julian was about to name his destination when two things happening in short order.

The cab behind his suddenly sped forward, mashing into the rear of Julian's taxi! He lurched forward in the seat and his cab, which was still in drive, rocketed a dozen feet ahead before braking.

His driver issued a curse, then stopped as his gaze fixed on the rear view mirror and his mouth fell open. Julian spun in time to see a fireball tearing through the night sky. It grew larger, brighter, as it headed in his direction.

And exploded.

"Hey, I saw you before!" said a pretty brunette. She wore a workshirt and tans slacks that were belted unnaturally tight around her thin waist. She had a page boy haircut and a friendly bounce in her walk.

Max didn't know what was going on, but she wasn't about to be stopped by this person.

"Yeah, I saw you at the Poor Man's, puttin' on that shirt. You were with that fella who was in the news. The fashion man." She held out her hands and wiggled her fingers. "Mr. Gloves."

Max didn't slow. She was hoping this person would be mowed down by the crowd that raced past as they might on a crowded city street. But the woman danced into the crowd's every pocket of low resistance and somehow kept pace.

Out of the corner of her eye, Max saw the woman's hand easing toward her back. There was something in the palm. Something like an insect's stinger.

No, it had to be a knife of some kind.

Without betraying her intent, Max swung her powerbook around, causing the woman to pierce it—instead of Max's flesh—with her weapon. Then Max thrust her elbow back into the other woman's throat. She heard a cry of surprise that was transformed into a crackling and a sick gurgling as the other woman dropped behind her, clinging to other people in the crowd on the way down. No one screamed or even paid any attention to the writhing woman on the ground, shuddering and clutching at her throat.

Not even Max, who hurried toward an elevator.

A fireball consumed the taxi. The people inside it died instantly.

Julian stared in shock. The cab that had been hit was the one that had usurped the position of Julian's cab.

Julian could smell magic. The weapon used was a mid-range missile launcher spiced up with some major hexes.

Julian burst from his cab and raced in the direction from which the missile had been launched. A crowd was gathering, but he ignored them. His attention was focused on two people who were trying to look casual as they loaded something into a rectangular case poking out the back of a van. He popped the release on his own case and had the sword of Roland in his grip a moment before his targets even saw him. With a leap, he beheaded the first and kicked the second in the ribs.

The man he had allowed to live grunted and fell to the sidewalk. Julian rolled on the ground, bounced to his feet, and placed the tip of his sword at the second man's throat.

"Who sent you?" Julian asked.

The man on the ground had auburn hair and a barrel chest. "Wassa matter? Don't recognize me, Jules?"

It was all the answer Julian needed. He realized the horrible mistake he had made tonight.

Without hesitation, Julian drove the swordpoint through the man's throat, arced it to one side, then made his escape into the night.

Undetected.

Max knew that she had waited long enough. People pressed in at her from all sides. Men, women, children. A great deception.

The time had come for her to *act*.

Julian tore through the crowd. He found Max easily. Though it should have been too late, it wasn't. He saw her raise her hands, as if to gesture and begin the weaving of a spell.

"Max, no!" he cried.

She froze and slowly looked his way.

He reached her and saw that she was simply reaching for some kind of curio. Then he looked up and saw a concave mirror from which she had been able to see his entrance.

He put the pieces together quickly. She had deduced that she had been set up and had begun to "gesture" to see what Julian would do. Had he come here to witness her destruction or try to stop it?

She had her answer.

Julian stared at her. "Maxine—"

"I don't blame you," she said. "If I had been in your position, I probably would have done the same thing."

He looked at her in open confusion. She nodded toward the exit and together they left the shop, then the sprawling complex.

They found a cheap hotel near the pier. In the room she would share with Julian tonight, Max saw a fly on the wall. She mashed it with her shoe.

While in a crowded restroom, Billie Jean winced. She examined her throat, tried to perform a few scales.

Her timbre was off. Her range limited.

Even with the best of healing magicks, her voice would never be the same.

Fuck it, she thought. Fuck Mitchell, fuck her ex-husband.

The little blonde bitch was going to pay for this.

Max turned to Julian and told him everything. What she had done, and why.

"I went back on a deal," Max said. "The deal I made with you. That was short-sighted and stupid. The only explanation I can give is that I've been sold out so many times, it seemed to make sense to do a preemptive strike."

Julian nodded.

"So it's all gone?" Max asked. "The information I copied has been erased, the deposits canceled?"

"That's right."

"We go back to the original plan? Find a place with more juice so I can recreate the gateway?"

"Yeah," Julian said. He sat in a black leather chair near the bed. Earlier tonight, two men who had been in X'an's employ had tried to kill him. They might have destroyed the Sword of Roland in the process, or at least tainted it with malignant energies. That meant X'an didn't really care about the sword any more. He was willing to betray his client. Why? Over what?

The gateway to the pattern. It had been the only possible explanation. That meant the gateway was real and no matter how much he may have wanted to see Maxine Anderson suffer for her crimes, he needed her alive.

"Um, Julian," Max said, getting her companion's attention. "Are you really just going to let this go?"

"This time," he said. "Do it again—"

"I won't."

He believed her. "I wouldn't have betrayed you with Jian Zhao."

"Okay, but one thing."

"Yeah."

"You don't want the gateway because you're worried about the fate of the world or any of that crap. It's because of Neelam. What was done to her." She nodded at his gloved hands. "And to you, too."

Julian was genuinely startled. She had guessed some, but not all of the truth. Best to let her believe this. "Go on."

"You want to change the past."

Again, a half-truth. He gestured for her to continue.

"So do I. Where do we go from here?"

A strange look passed across Julian Ibiero's handsome face. He seemed distraught, but resigned, as if his life was coming to an end and he had accepted this as an immutable fact.

His gaze shifted away from his companion as he said, "Home. We're going back to my home…"

Sanity returned to her in a dream. Maxine Anderson knew that she was dreaming, that she was lost to a half-world of wishes and quests and unfulfilled needs and desires, but she was more lucid now than she had been in many days.

In her dream, Max stood in a vast marble chamber. It was cold, freezing cold. She knew this, yet she was not affected by the elements. All she wore was a pale blue shift. There was nothing sexual about this place or her dream. The fires of unreason, of passion, had been set aside. Fear washed over her and she welcomed it. With fear came reason.

Before her was a figure she hadn't seen since she was a child. The boy from the marketplace in Calcutta. Naked, his hands at his sides, he was as beautiful as ever.

They said nothing to one another. Despite this, his very presence served to lift one veil after another from her perceptions. She thought of Freddy, who she had loved, and grief surged through her. Tears came together with racking sobs that seemed to have been torn from every part of her body. She thought of Mitchell, with whom she had willingly degraded herself in a bid for escape from heartless reality. Mitchell had opened her up, his rationale, his reason, cutting through her defenses like a surgeon's scalpel. He had made her see the unseen. Made her open herself to powers that had been at work within her all her life, forces that she had denied on some levels and embraced on other. With those forces, she had killed a man.

There would be no peace for her ever again.

And finally, she thought of Julian, the man who had seemingly saved her life. Her guardian angel. The man with whom she was now traveling to India, to Calcutta—

Home. We're going back to my home.

Max gasped as before her, the beautiful boy from the marketplace raised his hands to show her a horror she wasn't prepared to face. She screamed

and jolted awake in her seat aboard the jet taking them to India. Julian sat next to her, reading a magazine.

"Are you all right?" he asked.

Max nodded. "Just a dream."

Julian looked away. He didn't notice the way Max's gaze drifted down to his gloved hands.

Why didn't you tell me? Max thought. *All this time, why didn't you tell me?*

Something deep within her told her that she would have the answer to that question soon.

And once she had that answer, nothing would ever be the same for her again…

II

The New Market, Calcutta.

Julian's gloved hand closed round the handle of the sword case. A simple glamour kept Sleepers from being aware of what he carried. Mages who were not on their guard would also be fooled.

He felt undeserving of the honor fate had bestowed upon him. The sword of Roland was meant to be in the hands of a warrior, not a killer. The man from whom he had taken the weapon had only slightly less right to the sword than Julian.

And soon—if all went according to plan—it would be wielded against a being whose charter was of a divine nature. The Guardian at the Gate. The Weaponsmaster he had glimpsed in dreams all his life.

As he and Max approached the marketplace in full daylight, Julian chided himself for his foolish thoughts. The sword wasn't about to make a value judgement. It was enchanted steel, loyal to any who held it. A weapon, nothing more.

A weapon…

He had been something like that for the better part of his life. An unfeeling instrument of terror and death wielded by others. He had tried to change; he had cloaked himself in the garb of a businessman and tried to be a part of the Sleeper's world, but his new life had been just another illusion. A failed illusion, in the final accounting.

Julian looked up at the clock tower. When he had been a child blessed with human hands he'd sat in the tower and sketched all he saw. From his godlike vantage he had viewed a society wherein he felt perfectly at home. He knew who his god was, he knew the proper order of things; he had dreams and hopes.

Now all he had was need. An all consuming, ravenous *need.*

He had come here to play it all out again and this time to set it to right.

Or die trying.

"All right," Julian said. "They're here. All of them. I can feel them."

"Even—"

"Oh, yes," he said, unwilling to hear the name she was about to summon.

Max looked around at the swell of the crowd. "It hasn't changed," she said, hugging herself.

"No, it hasn't," said Julian. Nineteen years had come and gone and the New Market was the same as he remembered it. He felt as if he was walking into a living, breathing memory. It unsettled him.

"So this armory or whatever you called it—"

"My Chantry." He subdued a smile. Calling his fortress a Chantry was a somewhat perverse joke he had devised long ago.

"It's here? In the market?"

"No."

"So why are *we* here?" Max asked, anxiety beginning to flare within her. She knew that she might die in this foreign place and that terrified her—

The dead hate you. The dead hate you both.

But death was certain. What she feared most was the horror of never again being able to lead a normal life. Of never being able to trust anyone, love anyone— and all because of a secret that was imprinted within her brain and upon her soul.

Somehow, she had to find release.

Julian stopped short as he passed a window that he remembered fondly from his youth. Once his works had been displayed in this shop.

He gazed into the window and tensed. Beyond the glass was a collection of sculptures made with his once human hands. The display was exactly the same as it had been the day he had murdered his father.

Of course, that was impossible. The statues couldn't have been kept here like this for nineteen years. These must have been replicas created by X'an as a means of giving Julian warning. He could almost hear the old man's voice:

Give me what I want now and you can go free. Part with the woman and the sword and all will be forgiven.

But Julian needed more than forgiveness. X'an had asked him many times what he would do once he had his revenge for the act that had damned him. Today he had the means to discover an answer to that question and nothing was going to stand in his way.

"They're beautiful," Max said, staring at the statues. "I saw something like them once. Wish I could remember where."

"Come on," Julian said, roughly grabbing her arm and leading her away from the display.

They made their way through the crowd. A man slammed into Julian's arm.

"Sorry," the man said, glancing at Julian with a wicked smile. A cold lance of fear and unreason was driven through Julian's heart as he looked fully into the man's face. He was young, with hawklike features. He wore a white T-shirt, khaki slacks, and a kirpan. Julian knew him. It was Channi, the scout for the flesh merchants that Julian had hid Max from nineteen years ago.

But Channi was dead. Julian had killed him.

Channi slipped away into the crowd. Julian's heart thundered as he forced himself to go on.

All of this had been planned, Julian knew. The sight of his statues in the old shopkeeper's window. The meeting with "Channi." His hunters wished to frighten him.

He had counted on his hunters being thorough. They had not disappointed. Still, actually seeing their handiwork was disconcerting, to say the least.

When they turned a corner and came into view of the building where his father had once sold jewelry, Julian relaxed. The nasty little twelve by twelve foot square was gone, replaced by a much larger edifice. A collection of usurers had taken over. Julian knew that he should have been glad that the money lenders had taken hold here. His father would be raging in the other world over it. But all he felt was sadness mixed with his palpable relief that this building was not as he remembered it.

"Julian," Max said uneasily. "That shadow…"

He turned to see the spot that had arrested Maxine's attention. Underneath a table filled with knives, a voluminous shadow pulsed and throbbed.

Butch had come for him.

Julian told Max to run. He would find her. No matter who or what she faced in the market, he would return for her.

The moment she had gone from his side, Julian whispered, "Here, boy…"

The shadow leapt from beneath the table of knives. Blades erupted into the air, some slicing into the flesh of innocents as they sank to the ground. The table had buckled and snapped in half in the course of a heartbeat. The unnatural shadow beast merged its form with one true shadow after another. The shadow of a man carrying a basket. The shadow of a building. Of a group of people. It hid its presence wisely as it advanced on its former master.

Destruction followed in its wake. Overturned carts. Men clutching at bloody wounds or spurting sockets where limbs had been only instants before.

Julian ran. He knew that he would have to wield the sword he carried, and that it alone had the power to sear the demon's dark heart with light, but killing Butch would be the same as destroying a part of himself. He wouldn't do it unless he had to.

A shadow tinged with the paradox demon's darkness fell upon Julian's leg. He winced as the fabric of his jeans was seared and pain flared in his leg. Julian leaped over a counter, diving into the darkened recesses of a tent. He popped open the sword's case, snatched its sheath in one hand, the sword's hilt in the other. Butch entered the darkness, a wave of cold heralding his arrival.

An instant before the darkness could envelope Julian, he sliced the back of the tent open and darted into bright sunlight. Butch followed, the light forcing him to take the shape of a large black dog once more.

People ran in terror. Julian wasn't worried about the summoning of Paradox demons. This was a strange sight, yes. A man who looked like a tourist, wearing bluejeans, T-shirt, a bone colored jacket, facing off against a large, seemingly rabid dog. Strange, yes, but *not* incomprehensible. So long as overt magick was not used in the effort to subdue Butch, Julian would run no risk of summoning the demons.

Julian reached out with his mind, but he could not communicate with Butch.

The binding that had been worked upon them both so many years ago had all but been undone. Julian had been aware that X'an could perform such a severing, but he had counted on his friendship with his mentor to mean something. Now he understood his mistake.

It pained Julian to see Butch like this. His crimson eyes were filled with bloody tears and his flanks shuddered with the agonies X'an's spells of fealty had worked upon his unnatural flesh.

Julian faced the hound and considered his options.

There were incantations Julian *could* use to combat his only true friend. Protecting himself from the prying eyes of mortals whose sanity would snap if they saw those magickal works in action would be simple. He could cause a sudden wind to rise and force the tent to his left to peel from its moorings and provide cover for Butch and himself.

And there was the Sword of Roland, which could cleave Butch from this plane of existence, though not before the dog who was not a dog inflicted some grievous wounds—as X'an had planned.

Julian stood silently and lowered the sword.

With a low, inhuman growl, Butch padded toward his prey.

"I'm not going to fight you, boy," Julian said. "I trust you. I know there's enough of you still in there to keep this thing from happening."

Butch's shadow reached ahead of him. Julian could see bits of grass wither beneath it. Stones crumbled into dust.

"I need you, Butch. I've got something planned that I can't do without you. I think you'll even approve, once you're back to being your old self."

Butch barked at Julian. His maws revealed three sets of razor-sharp teeth that pulsed in and out of his pink distended gums. Julian wagered that no one around was close enough to see that little detail but him. Everything was still all right.

Julian raised his chin, exposing his throat.

Butch hesitated, a whine coming from somewhere deep inside. Then his body tensed, as if he was going to spring, and—

A shot rang out.

Julian watched in stunned silence as the side of Butch's head exploded in a shower of blood, bone, and shadow. But the spray of gore never reached the ground. It hung in the air, still attached to the dog, and slowly wove itself back into his skull.

Spinning, Julian saw a young man with a smoking gun. His hand was shaking. Julian clubbed the gun from him, but he knew it was too late. This man, and several others it seemed, had witnessed the impossible.

The air around them shimmered and rifts appeared, providing glimpses to a hellish land. Creatures beyond imagination peered out from those tears in reality. All who saw them would die, of course.

The Paradox demons had come, this time to reclaim one of their own.

"Dammit, no!" Julian said, stepping forward to stand between the shifting nightmares pulsating into the earthly plane. One looked like a collection of internal organs with eyes and teeth, another was all twitching hairs that formed amazingly graceful patterns with its body. Then each of them shifted forms, their bodies undulating into reality as they giggled and clawed at the dog who was not a dog and his protector…

Max raced hard and fast into the marketplace. Mitchell and Billie Jean surged out of the crowd and reached for her.

Changing course, her heart leaping into her throat, Max neatly avoided their hands. Then she felt something grab hold of her ankle and yank hard. She fell, striking the ground hard as she landed on her tailbone. Her gaze was riveted upon a long, green object that released her leg then slithered back under Billie Jean's skirt.

A tail.

Mitchell smashed his fist into the side of Max's face as she started to rise. She sank back down. Another blow to the kidneys kept her there. Billie Jean handcuffed her and roughly hauled her to her feet. Max was barely conscious. Her mouth was bloody slash.

A circle of spectators started to form. Mitchell raised a false ID and proclaimed himself a member of the militia. The people backed away.

"Come on," Mitchell said. They dragged Max ahead. He shoved his ID in the face of everyone who looked their way. "You want some of this? Do you?"

Before long, they were out of the marketplace, loading Max into the backseat of a car. She didn't fight them.

Billie Jean popped the trunk and nodded toward Mitchell. "Something I want you to check."

"What's that?" Mitchell asked, opening the trunk all the way and peering into its darkness.

Billie Jean transformed her hand into the razor-sharp wing of a cockroach. Without a word she thrust it through the back of Mitchell's neck, severing his head quickly and quietly. Spurting blood hit the top of the trunk as the head dropped to the floor. Billie Jean heaved the twitching torso into the back.

"Asshole!" she cried. Slamming the trunk closed, she gasped as she saw the wide-eyed balding man standing before her.

"Roger," she said with a gasp.

"Hi, honey," her ex-husband said. "Miss me?"

Billie Jean's shoulders slumped. There was no way this could be a coincidence. That bastard Marazzi did this. Now she wished that she hadn't killed the prick so fast.

"This isn't a good time, Roger," said Billie Jean. "Things are happening."

"Oh, I'm sure," said Roger eagerly. His chest heaved with excitement. His eyes were wide like those of an excited puppy dog. "I want to hear all about it."

Billie Jean sighed. She had feared this moment for so long. Not because her husband was some colossal abusive shithead. Just the opposite. He was the kindest, most gentle man she had ever known, and he loved her in ways she'd never dreamed possible.

If only she could just kill him… But there was something about that wretched perfect love of his that made her normally cutthroat instincts fade. Her fear of what he did to her drove her into hiding.

Out of the corner her eye, Billie Jean saw movement. Alarmed, she looked up to see if Anderson was trying to escape. But no, the woman was right where she had been left, her head lolling a little to one side.

"Why don't you get in the car?" she said, defeated. "We have to drop something off. Then we can play catch up."

"Hot damn!" cried Roger.

They quickly drove off, paying no attention whatsoever to the pair of shadows that crouched behind a collection of corpses lining the gutter.

"All right. Move."

Two figures emerged from the shadows. Maxine Anderson and Mitchell Marazzi.

"I don't want to hurt you," Mitchell said. "I'm not *going* to hurt you. I hope you can believe me."

Max felt as if she'd just had the shit kicked out of her. "What's going on?"

"Doppelgangers," Mitchell said. He too looked pretty wasted. "It's a trick I can't pull too often. Takes a lot out of me. Never made one of myself before."

"How'd you make one of me?" Max asked.

"When we made love," Mitchell said. "There's still bits of you—skin, hair fragments, that sort of thing—inside me from those two nights. That's how I can always find you."

"Christ. That's *gross.*"

Mitchell ignored the commentary. "Here's the deal. This guy Julian?"

"Uh-huh."

"He wants you dead."

Max looked at him strangely.

"You fucked him over when the two of you were kids." Mitchell grabbed Max's arm and brought her wrist with the bracelet up to her line of vision. "You stole this. His dear old dad went and disfigured him over it. Sweet, huh?"

Maxine's thoughts drifted to her dream. "His hands…"

"Right. The whole thing, the trauma, whatever, it woke up what was inside him. The same thing that's inside you—me, too. He killed his own father for hurting him. Can you imagine doing something like that?" Mitchell asked. He neglected to mention that he had murdered his own brother strictly out of necessity. "Tore the fucker's heart out, the way I heard the story. This is the guy you're hanging with."

"No," Max said. She didn't want to believe any of this, but she could feel, deep down, that what Mitchell was telling her was right. His damned aromas were not coming into play here. He wasn't using any of his tricks to cloud her reason.

"He was gonna kill you," said Mitchell. "He had this timetable set up. You were supposed to die when you were fifteen. The same age he was when you took the bracelet. But when he tried to find you, he was told that you were dead. That you died in a car crash when you were eleven."

"My parents died then."

"Yeah. Not you. But Julian was led to believe you were dead. Every attempt he made to find you was blocked by the one person he trusted the most. This guy, X'an. He's the real motherfucker we've all got to watch out for. He's got Billie Jean working for him now. He got the guy who was supposed to have the Sword of Roland delivered to him, some thousand-year-old mondo mage. He's even got this fucking dog that I swear is a Paradox demon, only it's bound up in the form of a mutt. This asshole X'an thought he had me, too, but I figured, shit, if this was how he treated someone who looked up at him like a father, how am I gonna do any better? I mean, you just saw B.J. take my head off, right? Well, y'know, the doppelganger she thought was me. This was not a happy sight for me to sit through, I'll tell ya. Fortunately I had old Rog keeping her distracted long enough to switch you out for your doppelganger. Sorry about the way they beat on you."

"Christ," Max said. Her head was swimming.

Mitchell held out his hand. "I'm not gonna force you to do anything. I tried that once and it was a bad mistake. Never again, all right? But I just don't think it's a good idea, your being around a guy who's had a blood debt with you from when the two of you were kids. Capice?"

Max laughed bitterly. "Like you're any better? You're a fucking thug with a God complex."

"Yeah, but I'm a good dancer. And the world needs more of that."

Max smiled, despite herself. The smile faded suddenly. "You killed Freddy."

"Yeah, I did. I'm sorry about that."

She couldn't believe this. "That's all you can say? You're *sorry?*"

"I've never been sorrier. Listen to me. X'an and his buddies want to open up your head, Max. They know what you've learned and they're determined to take the knowledge from you. The only way we can keep you safe is if we conjure up the gateway and use it to make a couple of changes in the Pattern."

"Bullshit."

"The pattern can be recreated. It's been done before. This is how. People reaching its manifestations. Like the library."

Max waited, always looking for a way out. But Mitchell was too close. She couldn't run from him. Besides, she was hurt. "Recreating the gateway's not that easy. You need Quintessence."

"Ibiero's got a place with more than enough juice. It's where he's been storing all the talismans he's collected over the years. X'an says he's never been there. Someone he trusts is running the place. No one knows who."

"What is this place?"

"Some kind of old temple. He brought the place down and killed everyone inside it."

"Sweet."

"Bunch of Euthanatos motherfuckers. Deserved it muchly from what I gather. Anyway, the temple's loaded up with one magickal trap after another. No one can get in except him. The problem is, this guy X'an figures Julian's going there.

He has people all around it. Ibiero may be the only one who can get inside, but first he's got to get *near* it and that won't happen. Not unless we help him."

"What—waitaminute. You're telling me all this stuff about Julian, then you're saying we're supposed to play along with him?"

Mitchell nodded. "Sure. I'll take care of him once we're inside."

"Let me see if I have this straight," said Max. "You expect me to trust you, right? Just to believe all this at face value?"

Mitchell nodded.

"Why?"

"Because I went and made the biggest fucking mistake of my life. I fell in love with you."

"Really."

"Pisses me off, too. But there's nothing I can do about it. I've made mistakes."

"You killed someone I loved!"

"Yeah," said Mitchell. He was thinking, *but come on. Who doesn't make mistakes?* What he said was, "Yeah. And maybe that's one of the things we can fix when we get our hands on the Pattern."

Max hated herself for it, but she found herself considering his offer anyway…

Julian fought the Paradox demons, though they warned him time and again that they had no quarrel with him. Butch had transformed to his true shape for the first time in years. He tore into a third demon who had come to join the battle.

Four Sleepers had been killed. Another was about to be slain. Julian did his best to safeguard the weeping old woman as he tried to intimidate the demons with the sword he wielded.

They didn't care.

The weapon hacked away parts of them that could never regenerate and they gave no quarter. It seared them with its light and caused them untold agonies. They ignored their wounds and the pain that would follow them for a millennium. A task needed to be performed and they were here to see it done.

Julian cast spells that he could not afford to squander. He knew that he was leaving himself weak and vulnerable for the true conflict to come, but he couldn't help himself. No matter what happened, he could not allow Butch to be taken by these monstrosities.

Could he bond himself to *another* of their kind? Bend all three to his will?

No. Not even with the power of the sword.

Suddenly, the old woman screamed. Julian turned to see Butch abandon the fight with his demon. A fourth creature had arrived and was reaching for the woman.

Butch got there first, his shadowy claws rending its flesh, his sheer weight sending it away from its intended victim.

They keep coming, Julian thought. They know this is one of their own and they just keep coming.

He looked to Butch, who seemed to sense it, too.

Suddenly, Butch abandoned the demon it had set upon and launched itself against Julian. The mage responded instinctively, his years of training causing him to raise his sword.

Butch impaled himself on it.

"No!" screamed Julian, but it was too late. He felt a fraction of Butch's power flow from him like blood. It embraced the sword, rivulets of darkness swirling and leaking down the length of the weapon, piercing Julian's flesh.

Power entered Julian. Raw, primordial power.

A gift, Julian thought, the words not really his, though they sprang up in his mind.

Two of the demons came forward and tore Butch away from Julian. Another snatched the old woman before Julian could stop them.

In seconds, they were gone.

Julian didn't bother to watch as all physical evidence of the paradox demons' presence vanished around him. Blood was everywhere, but it was human blood. He knew that he had to get out of here quickly, or else he might be blamed for what looked like a massacre. Still, he couldn't quite seem to move.

Figures approached. Forcing himself to focus, he saw Max being escorted by Mitchell Marazzi.

"Don't get freaked out," said Mitchell. "I know we got off to a bad start, you and me. You trying to kill me and all. But it doesn't mean we can't be friends."

Julian couldn't help himself. He laughed. His mind was equally divided between finding a bar and buying a drink for this guy or disemboweling him with the sword of Roland.

"You decide," he said to Max. "Alive or dead. Mitchell over there. You decide how it goes down."

Max stared at him strangely. She had never seen Julian look quite so—soulless. Empty.

It made her wonder if there could have been some truth to what Mitchell had told her.

"I want him to come in with us," said Max.

"Fine."

"That's it?" Mitchell asked. "You're not gonna—"

"Shut up," said Julian.

"I can do that."

Julian looked to the sky, wondering if they could afford to wait for the darkness. That would make the task before him easier.

Probably not. X'an would have established some link with Butch. He would know that Butch was dead and would assume that it was at Julian's hand.

"Come on," Julian said. "We're going to the temple."

"What temple?" asked Max. "You mean the fortress? Where you've stored all the talismans?" She had to pretend not to know the truth.

"It used to be a temple," Julian said. "I'll tell you the story on the way…"

12

The Euthanatos had always been fond of the Thuggees. The followers of Kali were kindred spirits. In their temple, close to fourteen thousand people had died. Most of these were at the hands of the Euthanatos and the killings had been spread out over centuries.

On Julian Ibiero's Day of Blood, one hundred and twenty three men died, along with seven women. Five of them had been soldiers provided by X'an. Julian had labored for eleven weeks to cast the spell that sealed the temple, making escape impossible. Three people who trusted him had been sacrificed in this endeavor.

At the time, it had all seemed worth it.

Julian never found the answers to the mysteries surrounding his father's relationship with the Euthanatos. He had, in fact, not even recognized several of the mysteries as such until recently, when the sight of Maxine Anderson's bracelet forced him to ask new questions about the day that had set him on the darkest path imaginable.

There had been no answers in the temple. But there had been a few surprises.

Sitting within that temple now was a patchwork quilt of a man. Only his head, with features noble and proud, was his own. He was clothed in a charcoal designer original suit that he had ordered through the web, along with a library of books.

His large hands had just taken the lives of eleven people. The twelfth cowered in the corner, his vast power rendered meaningless in this place.

In the beginning, it had been the patchwork man's custom never to speak with visitors. But over the years, the temple dweller had grown to love the sound of human voices. Even his own, though technically, he was not human any more. Or even alive by common standards. But he existed, he reasoned, he felt.

He loved to hear people's stories. It distracted him from the buzzing of fourteen thousand spirits whose torment gave him momentum if not actual life.

"Tell me another one," he said to his terrified victim.

The old man started talking. It was all quite entertaining, but the story was no substitute for what would be happening soon. Still, listening to tales helped to distract him from his impatience.

What the patchwork man needed was for Julian Ibiero to come across the threshold to his fortress. Then all would be well.

The front door had been left open.

It should only be a matter of time…

The temple had once belonged to the Buddhists. The great domed structure was constructed three hundred years before the birth of Christ. The dome itself was meant to represent the great mountain. It was enclosed by a stone outer fence with gateways known as *toranas* on each of its four sides. Worshipers circled the dome to pay their respect to Buddha. A square fence sat on top of the dome. It was called the *harika* and it represented heaven. It surrounded the yasti, a spire with three disk-shaped *chatras* that symbolized the axis of the universe.

The temple had been fashioned in the style of a structure in central India. The main difference being that the Great Stupa in Madhya Pradesh was solid like a mountain. This temple was hollow, housing a honeycomb of chambers where good, then evil—then acts beyond either limiting concept—had been conducted.

In recent years, the temple had been fitted with electricity and phone lines. A satellite dish had been installed on the property. The workman never saw the temple's lone, mysterious inhabitant. Those who were sent to deliver Julian's Ibiero's latest acquisitions always arrived at night. They were greeted at the steel door facing the west, the only way in or out of the dome itself, by a large man always draped in shadows.

Vandals were not an issue, nor thieves, squatters, or government officials. All parasites were warded off by the complex network of spells that surrounded the dome in a full three hundred and sixty degree aura of protection.

Julian Ibiero approached the temple. He had been startled by the lack of opponents standing ready to greet him. He was cautious of any traps that might have been laid for him, but he wasn't worried about the temple itself. To his mind it was little more than a depository and so he walked toward the building without fear. If he had known the truth of what waited inside, he would have abandoned all of it—his quest for answers and his chance to have his *chakra* or wheel of destiny turn one final time.

Instead, he put his hand on the stone fence and said, "Nothing. Just the wards I put in place. X'an and the others didn't leave any traps."

Max and Mitchell stood at a safe distance. They relaxed noticeably at his words.

Suddenly, from beneath a tree some thirty yards distant, came a woman's wracking sobs.

Julian found Billie Jean crumpled up in her husband's arms. She looked nothing like the hard-bitten mercenary Max had described.

"He got…inside me…" Billie Jean said finally. When she saw Mitchell, the man she had supposedly just murdered, standing above her, she seemed surprised, but not frightened.

He touched her, easing a blend of oils into her flesh, ending with a flourish of sassafras that left her calm, clear-headed, and alert.

"We never knew what you had inside there," said Billie Jean finally, staring right at Ibiero. "You're the fucking devil, you know that. Or his keeper."

Julian asked her to tell the story from the beginning. She said she would, but only after they agreed to pardon her for her role in all of this, and let her leave in peace after the tale was told.

Julian swore to this.

Nodding, Billie Jean told her story.

LIGHTNING UNDER GLASS

"On the way to meet X'an and the others, I tried to get old Rog, my ex-husband here, to wake up to reality.

"First, I transformed into something that would have given Jeff Goldblum's 'Fly' a hard-on. He wasn't the least bit upset. Then I threatened his life. Didn't work. Finally, I pulled over and asked him to take a peek at what was in the trunk. Looking down at the headless body, all he could say was, 'Just stick with the music, honey. I know you'll be able to give up your day job some time.'

"Christ."

Roger leaned over and kissed her cheek.

"X'an and the others were waiting when we got here. I had Max in the back seat and Mitchell's body in the trunk. I introduced my ex to X'an, half-hoping that he would kill him for me. But they got along well.

"The doppelganger of Maxine didn't fool X'an. He gave it to a few of his men so that they could have a more pleasant way of passing the time. Pleasant for them, anyway.

"When they were finished, they destroyed the replica.

"One of their mercs was returning from a run to the store, carrying cold drinks, when the door to the temple opened. Someone stood in the doorway."

"Sunder," whispered Julian, interrupting the tale. He saw that everyone was looking at him. "Sorry. Go on."

"X'an and the others decided to go inside. They thought it might be a trap, but they doubted that any trap had been made that they couldn't get themselves out of. They were wrong."

"Did you go in with them?" Mitchell asked.

Billie Jean looked at him strangely, eyeing his neck. "You're gonna come back on me for that, aren't you?"

"Honestly, I could give a shit right now. Answer the question."

She shook her head. "I didn't go in. But I sent some flies inside so I could watch that way. You know. Look through their eyes."

Julian seemed to be having a hard time with all of this. "Waitaminute. Are you saying that Sunder *let* them in? He opened the temple to them?"

"The big guy in the suit. Yeah."

"A suit?"

Billie Jean described it.

"One of yours?" asked Mitchell.

Julian nodded, hardly believing what he was hearing.

"Cool," said Mitchell. "Sounds like you do good work."

"Will you shut the fuck up?" asked Max.

"Hey, I was just trying to be friendly, okay?" Mitchell shrugged. "Christ. Make a couple of errors in judgement and the next thing you know, everyone's on your shit."

"Tell me the rest," said Julian.

Billie Jean went on. "It was strange inside. Thin hallways like tunnels, leading into these big glowing rooms. The thing is—I was expecting old statues, maybe skeletons, blood splattered on the walls. The kind of things you normally find in a temple. But it was all carpeted."

"What?" asked Julian.

"Carpeted, the walls scrubbed down, these nice little statues in cases along the corridors. There were some movie posters, books on shelves. Mood lights."

"You're lying."

"No, really," said Billie Jean. "I was expecting torches in braziers, spider webs, all that crap. But really, it reminded me of a condo in Palm Beach. Been down there a couple of times. Anyway, you could tell what the place used to be, no problem. No condo has those big stone chambers and stuff. But the altars were gone. No stone chairs, just leather furniture. An entertainment center. A bar."

"The Quintessence," said Julian quickly. "It was screwing with your perceptions. Making you see an environment in which you would relax."

"But they weren't my perceptions," said Billie Jean. "I was seeing what the flies saw."

Mitchell shook his head. "Okay, so your manservant or whatever remodeled when you were away. What's the big fucking—"

The sword of Roland was unsheathed and poised at Mitchell's throat before the mercenary could react. He had never seen anyone move so fast, didn't even believe it possible.

"Be quiet," cautioned Julian.

Mitchell did not show fear. He was reminded of the certainty of his own imminent death each time the pain in his skull returned. He was beyond terror now. But an odd compassion lit in his eyes, signalling that he would be silent.

"What did you see?" Julian asked.

"He killed them. One by one. Managed to separate them—I'm not sure how. Almost like the layout of the place isn't fixed. That it can be whatever he wants it to be. Turn left at a juncture one time and you're in a sauna, make the same left another time it's a dead end, or stairs leading down to the basement. I can't explain it."

"How did he kill them?"

"Strangulation," said Billie Jean. "With a cloth. And a coin."

Julian nodded. The thuggee's preferred method of execution. "What about X'an? Is he dead?"

"I don't know. Probably." She shuddered.

"What is it?" Julian asked.

"What he did. The bald man in the suit. When he looked to one of the flies that was watching him. Oh god, he went inside it, inside me..."

Julian nodded. Sunder—or whatever force now lived within the body he had constructed for the slain bodyguard—had taken advantage of the psychic link between Billie Jean and her little spies. He rode along that link and entered Billie Jean's mind, apparently savaging her in the process.

"I'm sorry," Julian said.

Billie Jean looked up sharply. "He had a message for you."

"What's that?"

"He said to tell you that your father wanted to talk with you."

LIGHTNING UNDER GLASS

Those words slammed into Julian with terrible force. He managed not to reel as their weight pressed against him.

Billie Jean glanced over at Max. "Your parents are there, too."

Max wanted to react, wanted to call Billie Jean a lying little bitch and kick her right in the face—but she refused to play into this.

"It's a trap," Max said. "X'an and his people found a way inside. Whatever controls you put in here to keep the place safe, they've found a way of undoing them. The best thing we could do right now is to get the hell out of here. There are other places with Quintessence. Mitchell's estate would probably do it."

"She's right," said Mitchell. "There's no reason why any of us should go in there."

Julian said nothing. He rose and turned his back on the small group. Then he did something he hadn't done with another human being except X'an.

He removed his gloves.

His silver hands glowed brightly in the sunlight. For once, they did not appear grotesque, though bone and muscle and silver had fused into impossible combinations. His hands were anatomically impossible, constructs that should not have been functional. Yet they were.

Max stared at his hands. The words that escaped her lips surprised even her. "They're—they're beautiful."

Julian looked down at his hands. Beautiful? No, he'd never see them that way. Those hands were responsible for so much death, so much suffering...

Shuffling those thoughts away, he started walking toward the temple. It had been fortified in such a way that no one could enter without an invitation from the patchwork man Julian had created. He still remembered the odd shock he had felt when he stormed the temple with X'an's mercenaries and found his childhood guardian among his enemies. His father had told of Sunder's horrible death, but what he had "witnessed" was simply an illusion. Sunder had been brought under the Euthanatos' control. Julian had freed him in the only way he knew how, severing his head from his body. A fire rendered the body useless, though the head was untouched. In his madness, Julian gave Sunder a new body and a task—standing watch over Julian's prizes that would be sent here over the years.

Julian had used a spell that drew upon the souls of the dead to breathe animation into Sunder's new form. It had seemed amusing to him at the time. Now he realized his horrible mistake.

"You were going to kill me, weren't you?" Max said, staring at Julian's back.

He unsheathed the sword of Roland and discarded its case. He would have no further use for it.

Finally, he said, "I hadn't decided."

Mitchell touched Max's arm. "Max, let's get out of here."

"No," she said.

He heard sobs from behind them. Turning, he nodded to Billie Jean and her ex-husband. "Go on, get the fuck out of here before I change my mind. Go!"

Billie Jean's ex-husband helped her to her feet. Together, they slowly made their way toward a dirt trail. The path led downward to a valley and a small settlement. They were quickly lost from view.

Mitchell appealed to Max one last time. "Come on. If we split now, I promise, we can play things any way you want. I'm a fucking dead man as it is with this grenade in my skull. I'll change my will, you can inherit all of it. Eight million bucks. Screw the Rock and Roll Hall of Fame. They can get along without it."

Max blinked several times, as if she was having a hard time focussing. "You were leaving your money to the Rock and Roll Hall of Fame?"

"What else was I gonna do with it? The only person I gave a shit about was my brother, and he's dead. I was gonna bring him back with the library—I was gonna fix all of it. Make a world without hate, without fear… The movies probably would have sucked… But now—"

"I'm going," said Max. "If you mean what you said, then you won't try and stop me."

Ahead, Julian was walking into the darkness of the temple's open door. Max started after him.

"All right, fuck it," said Mitchell. He walked up to Max and followed at her side. "I don't get it. This guy wanted to kill you, but now you'd follow him—"

"Into hell. Right."

"Why?"

The words that came from Max's lips were difficult, but she said them anyway. "He saved my life. I owe him."

"That's it? I owe a lot of people. Fuck 'em."

"I wouldn't expect you to understand," she said, merging with the darkness.

"Sounds like you didn't miss any of the important stuff, Mitchell," he said to himself. "Sounds like you got it just fine…"

He went ahead until he too was swallowed up by the darkness.

Julian suddenly found himself sitting across from the patchwork man. The transition had been startling. One moment he was walking through the doorway, the next he was sitting here, in a room that had been furnished in early QVC.

"Where are the others?" Julian asked.

Sunder's gaze drifted to a small form in the corner. X'an was there, curled up into a fetal position. He shuddered uncontrollably.

"What'd you do to him?" Julian asked. He rested the Sword of Roland on his lap as he crossed his legs.

"What, I don't even get a kiss?" asked Sunder. "It's been many years."

"I don't know what you are."

"Yes, you do. You just don't want to admit it to yourself." Sunder shifted position on his black leather couch. He adjusted the charcoal suit he wore. "This is very comfortable, by the way. You're a very good designer."

"Get to it."

Sunder whispered something.

Julian leaped to his feet, brandishing the sword. "What'd you do? What kind of incantation was that?"

"You're so jumpy," said Sunder, "do you want a drink? Something to eat maybe? You never eat well."

"You don't know anything about me."

Sunder sighed. "I beg to differ. Each of the talismans you sent was charged not only with magic, but with impressions from the time it was in your presence—or even lusted after by you. I've seen your attempts to grow and change as a person, your quest to get a soul, basically, and all your miserable failures. All because you can't rise above this self-hatred that drives you on."

Julian fought against the temptation to relax in the presence of his childhood guardian. "So this is how it's going to be decided? A philosophical discussion instead of a fight?"

"Must you always be such a drama queen, Julian? Lighten up. I was just talking to you in terms that I thought you would understand. You want a soul? I have a thousand or more available inside me. Pick any one you want."

Julian hesitated. "Including my father's?"

"No. Actually, his was sent to a hell beyond imagining by the Euthanatos. I'm sorry about that little deception, but I had to make sure you wouldn't leave without seeing me."

Sadness registered in Julian's eyes. "What was it you whispered before?"

"A prayer. One that was delivered in your native language. Has it been so long that you've forgotten those words?"

"Maybe."

Sunder nodded. "Let me try to put all of this in perspective for you. In 1953, a graduate student named Stanley L. Miller performed a test. Are you familiar with his work?"

"No."

"The test he performed was simple. He took two glass globes. One was filled with the gasses swirling around in Earth's atmosphere before there was life on the planet. The other was set to capture the new gasses created when he flooded the first globe with 60,000 volts of electricity. Essentially, lightning. When he was done, the second globe contained nucleotides, the building blocks that form amino acids, which in turn make life. Do you see what I'm getting at? *He made life*. And many years ago, you did, too."

Julian almost laughed. "You think you're alive?"

"I know I am. I have a soul. Likes, dislikes. Pleasures, pains. Dreams. I am alive."

"You're a fucking answering machine," Julian snarled. "I put you together to take messages and accept deliveries."

"Consider my story of life's beginnings on earth. We all come from humble backgrounds."

"Don't give me that shit. There's only one reason why you haven't attacked me yet." Julian tapped the sword. "This. You're afraid of it."

Sunder sighed heavily. "You really don't understand, do you?"

"How did you manage to kill all of X'an's people? How did you reduce him—"

Julian gestured to the quaking form in the corner "—to that?"

"Now it's you who's being ignorant. What I'm offering you, out of appreciation, out of love of the child you were—is peace."

"You mean death."

"More than that. Eternity without torment. Knowledge of the afterlife and power to circumvent its many traps and horrors. I can make you into something like a god. A lord of death."

"Gee, thanks. I think I'll pass."

"Don't be like that, Julian. Relax and try to become one with your surroundings. Understand what you're facing here."

Julian was silent. He could feel the wealth of Quintessence surrounding him. Power enough to weave spells greater than any he had ever contemplated before. There was power enough in this place to reshape parts of the world even without the library and the Pattern it cloaked.

That power had been carefully concealed from the many Traditions, from the Technocracy, from any and all who might have quested for it. Any who dared to invade this temple would have been plucked from existence by the wards surrounding it—unless they were invited inside.

Sunder, little more than a walking corpse he had animated to serve a few limited functions, was now sitting before him in a crisp new suit, acting like the lord of this place.

Julian would have to show him his place, then get on with things. Simple as that.

The mage called upon the most basic of spells to rend the flesh from Sunder's bones.

Nothing happened.

Startled, he tried casting a more complex incantation. Again, he failed.

Sunder stood. "You asked how I killed such powerful mages in a stronghold filled with Quintessence. The answer is simple: With my bare hands. You see, I've had time to prepare, Lord Shaper."

Julian looked up sharply.

"I've had years since I became—aware. Years to sift through the memories of the thousand and more whose souls gave me the power to move and speak. I've learned to do things that no other mage before me could accomplish. I have bound every talisman in this fortress to my being. No one can draw upon their power except me."

Julian stood and raised his sword as Sunder took another step forward, then cut across the room to the bar. He poured an ancient wine into a tapered glass and took a moment to appreciate its lovely qualities.

"Why did you call me Lord Shaper?" asked Julian.

"Listen to my voice, Julian. Tell me that you've never heard it before."

Julian hadn't noticed before this, but the voice leaving Sunder's lips was not the bodyguard's. It was a voice he had heard when he was a child, the voice, he'd believed, of his inner power calling to him.

"I can stretch my will back through time," said Sunder. "And I know the old argument. Just because you *can* do something doesn't mean you *should*. Still, once I understood the grand design before me, I knew that I had no choice but to complete the circle that was started the day your father came home and took your hands from you."

Julian struggled to think of a way to save himself from his creation.

"Remember the story I once told you, Julian?"

"Sunder told me stories. You're not Sunder."

"I have aspects of him. Knowledge of many. It was a Bengali folk tale about a queen whose king is dying because he rebuked the advances of a goddess. Remember?"

Julian was silent.

"The queen went to a Dakina. The witch woman told her what she could do to save her husband from his fever, then explained that it wouldn't matter. The goddess had willed his death. If he survived the fever, he would die in an accident. If that accident was prevented, some other threat would arise. No matter what the queen did, the goddess's will was not to be denied. Refusing to accept this, the queen went home and told her husband she knew how to save him from the goddess. He smiled at her—"

"And she slit his throat," said Julian, lowering the sword, but only a couple of inches.

"You see?" asked Sunder. "You can't escape your fate."

Julian's gaze flickered on his sword. "You're telling me that even though I'm holding one of the most powerful talismans ever made, a sword bound to me as these talismans are bound to you, that I can't win."

"Yes."

"That even though I have Quintessence woven into the bones of my body, it won't help me a damned bit?"

"Have you noticed the pain is lessened?" asked Sunder, gesturing at Julian's hands. "I did that for your comfort."

Julian mind rebelled against this horror. He called upon a store of Quintessence driven into his hip during a magical assault many years earlier. The pain it caused him was blinding, and the spell he attempted to cast was stillborn. Julian sank to one knee. He used the sword like a cane.

"You shattered something in your hip with that little trick," said Sunder. "Stop doing this to yourself. It pains me to see you hurt."

"Where's Max?"

"Wandering. She'll remain wandering with her companion until I have what I want."

Julian made it back to the couch.

"To answer your question about the sword, in this place, it is nothing more than steel. Powerless."

"You've woven some kind of dampening field into the temple walls," said Julian. "If we were enemies, I would find it somewhat ironic that the spoils of your many wars were now your undoing," said Sunder. "But we're not enemies."

"Then tell me something."

"Of course."

"What was my father doing with a talisman in his shop? Why was the melted silver laced with Quintessence?"

"Julian, you don't need to know that."

"Tell me."

Sunder sat down, taking another sip of his wine. "Stunning." He fixed his gaze on his visitor. "Your father was working for the Euthanatos. They were paying him to take raw Quintessence and spin it into talismans."

"The bracelet, the one Max stole—"

"No. The one you gave to her."

Julian nodded. "Why would my father have left something like that laying about in the open? He wasn't a fool."

"Yes, actually, he was. He was trying to steal from the Euthanatos. He knew they had rivals, and understood that this strange substance they gave him had worth to those rivals. The Euthanatos were very specific as to the number of talismans, their size, weight, and form. Your father melted the Quintessence and added silver to it, diminishing its power, yes, but allowing him to create more objects than just the six or seven he had been commissioned to create.

"He thought they somehow wouldn't notice," Sunder continued. "He placed profit over reason, over his life, my life, and yours. No, he wouldn't become a moneylender—but not because the vocation was beneath him, instead because of a foolish vendetta against their kind. So instead he became a thief. He placed the last of the talismans that he had created in the window display in an effort to hide it in plain sight. He believed that he knew you well enough to know that you would not defy him. And yet you did. You opened the door to a stranger in need of help. It was a kind act, and as they say, no good deed goes unpunished."

"No," said Julian, "I don't believe any of this."

"Julian, why would I lie to you?"

"Because you need something. You could have killed me any time you wanted." He fixed the dead man with his gaze. "It's the library, isn't it? The gateway to the Pattern."

Sunder smiled, then began to laugh. "Honestly? I could care less about the Pattern, except in how changes to it could affect me."

"So you want it shut down."

"Of course. And when our business is through, I will summon the woman and together she and I will achieve just that."

"Then what? Will you kill her?"

Sunder shook his head. "I'd have no reason to. Keep in mind that most of the souls whose echoes live inside me were the victims of the Euthanatos. Not the Euthanatos themselves. They are a minority whose urges are easily resisted."

"So what is it you want?" asked Julian.

"To leave here. And I can't do that without your permission."

"That's it? That's all you want?"

Sunder nodded. "You threw away your chance to live. I won't. There is much I want to experience. Such wonders in this world…"

Julian looked away. "You didn't tell me everything about my father, did you?"

"What do you mean?"

"His other clients. The ones he was selling the half silver talismans to, the Euthanatos' rivals. Who were they?"

"Oh. Sorry to have left that out." Sunder pointed back at X'an. "His people. The Tradition he belonged to before he struck out on his own. Your father sold you to X'an days before you killed him. Why else do you think X'an would have taken such great care in finding you in your mad wanderings? You were his property. It was a point of honor. He bought you, essentially, as cannon fodder. But later, when he saw what a special lad you were, well…"

Julian wanted to scream at the cowering old man in the corner. He wanted to use the Sword of Roland to disembowel him and make the bastard choke on his own innards. Instead, he said, "If you want him dead, you kill him."

Sunder applauded. "Julian, you're evolving." Sunder rose, went to X'an, and snapped his neck. The body collapsed.

It was over.

"I thought you strangled your victims."

"He was undeserving of such an honored fate."

"Saving it for me, are you?"

Sunder gazed at him pleasantly.

Julian relaxed and sat back in his chair. He bared his neck. "If it's really this simple, if my options are really this limited, then kill me. I'd be an idiot not to take your deal."

Nodding, Sunder slowly came around behind him.

"You see, Julian? Now that you know the truth, you can accept that it was never your fault. You are the victim in all of this. Guided by outside forces, by your father's foolish greed, by the voice, my voice, that whispered to you in your dreams… Your innocence, your light which was taken, can be restored. In death you can find life."

"Only God can give a gift like that."

"Then think of me as your God. One you created. It is often the way of things."

Sunder stood behind Julian now. His hands sat on either of Julian's shoulders. "Allow me to leave. Give your permission."

"You know," said Julian, "if I had a way out of this place, I would take it. I wouldn't let whatever torments you might put Max through sway me one damn bit. I would go and I would never return. You'd be trapped here, and so would she."

"But I would have a means of touching the pattern."

"You couldn't defeat the guardian at the gate. I'm beginning to see now that only one thing could." Julian closed his hand tightly around the hilt of his sword.

"Say the words and let us have an ending."

"First, a question."

"Very well."

"Do you believe in fate?"

"Most certainly."

"Not what we make for ourselves, but that there is a higher power at work in all our lives, that all that happens isn't just random happenings or events manipulated by others like us."

"I believe in God, yes, if that's what you're asking."

"Good," said Julian as he suddenly bolted from the couch and called upon the gift Butch had given him. "Tell Him I said hello."

Suddenly, a swath of darkness sliced through the air.

"Paradox magic," Sunder said hoarsely. The one force that even his defenses could not stand against. He saw Julian entering the rift he had created. A simple spell of stepping sideways in space, of folding the dimensions to allow instant travel from any one locale to another.

Sunder launched himself at Julian, who turned at the last second and drove the Sword of Roland through his chest, carving a swath where his heart beat like a triphammer.

"Ah—" Sunder began.

Julian allowed the gateway behind him to fade as he brought the sword up suddenly, tearing it through Sunder's flesh. It shattered his collar bone and ripped through his neck, half-severing his head.

Grimacing as blood pumped into his face from Sunder's wound, Julian leaned forward and said, "Who in the hell needs magic when you have a sword like this?"

Sunder sank to his knees.

"Never underestimate good old fashioned craftsmanship, you motherfucker."

Sunder's lips moved. He formed—a smile?

Julian looked down at the monster he had made and suddenly realized his mistake. For the first time, he felt the great stores of Quintessence surrounding him. The power was converging on him.

Impossibly, Sunder uttered a single phrase. "Thank you…"

It was the last thing Julian ever heard.

13

Max and Mitchell walked down yet another corridor. It seemed as if they were in an ever-changing maze, their surroundings engulfed in a psychedelic mist of strange light and color. Suddenly, the odd colors faded and the hallway before them appeared mundane and normal once again.

"So much for the Magical Mystery Tour," said Mitchell, surveying his surroundings.

They saw a room up ahead and hurried into it.

"Whoa," Mitchell said, suddenly recognizing the room in which he found himself.

It was his study in Washington. His computer was dead ahead. His collection of swords lined the wall.

"This just isn't possible," said Mitchell. "We'd have to cross the Umbra, it's, I—"

"The tour's not over," said a raspy, almost unfinished voice behind them. "My apologies."

Max and Mitchell turned to see something that both unnerved and comforted them. Mitchell moved quickly, snatching two swords down from the wall. The Daisho he brandished, a long Japanese sword and its shorter companion, had been forged in the thirteenth century by a weaponsmith at the height of his powers. Somehow he knew the weapons wouldn't do him a damn bit of good against his opponent.

"Julian?" said Max.

Standing before them was a perfect man enveloped in a shining silver radiance. The Sword of Roland was gripped in his right hand.

Mitchell raised his weapons. "You wanna play Silver Surfer, Ibiero? No problem. Just call me Galactus."

"Ibiero?" asked the shining man. He sounded confused. "I don't... have a name."

"Oh man," said Mitchell. "I just knew this fucking shit would have to get weirder before it was over. I just fucking knew it!"

The array of stars and silver clouds that clung to the swordbearer faded slightly.

"It is Julian," said Max. "I can see his face better."

"Don't let the face confuse you," said Mitchell. "You know all that weird crap I can do with oils and scents and stuff?"

"Uh-huh."

"We've never been within ten feet of whatever that thing is. I don't think it's even human."

"More human than you know," said the figure who looked like Julian. He sat down and rested the sword next to his seat. "Don't let Roland's sword worry you. It's a gift. A barter. Something we'll need."

"Are you Julian?" asked Max.

"I was him," said the man. "I was a lot of people. I'm what he wanted to become, even though he wouldn't admit it to himself."

The man held up his hands. They were flesh and blood.

Human.

"It's all very complicated," said the man. "And I'm afraid we don't have a lot of time. I'm still new at all this. I seem to have made a terrible mistake."

"What are you talking about?" asked Max.

"I thought... it would be a comfort. Returning here. There are good memories here for both of you. *Ukiyo,* 'the Floating World.' You found it here. Not once, but twice. That's rare."

"All we did was have sex here," said Max, remembering those two incredible nights with Mitchell.

"No," said the man. "You made love."

"Call it what you want—" said Max.

"You don't understand. You—*made*—love. The two of you forged a love in this place strong enough to make a man who had the power of God in his hands renounce it all rather than risk harming you. That love might be one-sided, but nevertheless, there is a power in what you did. I thought it would give you both strength and so I brought us here with the last of the Quintessence left in the temple."

"The last of it?" asked Mitchell. "What happened to the rest?"

"I… became. I was born. Reborn."

"Hey, he's born again," said Mitchell. "Now ain't that something?" He aimed the point of his long sword at the man's throat. "How about some straight fucking answers?"

"All right." The shuddered as the sword tip grazed his chin. He smiled. "Cold. I'm not used to that. It's good."

"If you were just born, you're not used to anything," said Mitchell, tapping the underside of the man's jaw with the sword. "Now come on!"

"Mitchell," Max said in warning. "Don't. I don't understand any of this either, but just—don't."

"Okay," he said, withdrawing the sword.

The man sat back. "Mitchell, you sent… doppelgangers… to the Technocracy. Do you remember?"

He nodded.

"The Technocracy has dispatched a unit of forty-seven operatives to find out why. They are crossing your lawn right now. They will be inside this building very soon. You might be able to hold them off for a time. But eventually, they will be draw upon this Quintessence that empowers you and they will break through any seals. They will drive us underground, and they will capture us. Then they will torture us until we reveal the secrets in Maxine's head. Once they're extracted—"

"Boot up the computer," Mitchell said to Max.

"Yes," said the man. "That would be our only hope…"

The Forty-Seven had been together for eleven years. Not one had ever been harmed in an incursion. They considered themselves the spiritual ancestors of the legendary forty-seven samurai who faced dishonor and death to ultimately avenge their master.

Within the next hour, forty-six would die honorably, while one would disgrace everything he ever believed in.

They raced to meet their fate.

Maxine's hands were flying over the keyboard. "How did this thing get fixed?"

"I took care of it," said the man watching over her shoulder.

"Can you people keep it down?" Mitchell said, clutching at his skull as another attack ripped through him. He fought his way through the pain and continued to conjure up their defenses. "I'm trying to concentrate here!"

"I still don't understand," whispered Max. "Who are you and what happened to Julian?"

"Julian's fate had always been to deliver me out of the darkness," said the man softly.

"Oh, that explains everything." Max leaped onto the net. She closed her eyes and allowed her consciousness to melt into that of the machine.

Alarmingly, the man beside her allowed his consciousness to melt into *her*.

"Holy shit," Max said as she entered the virtual world. It was different than the cyberpunk vistas she had envisioned before. Now she was saw a collection of limitless beings. Their bodies were the lands; their thoughts the space between them. These were creatures given form by magnificent ever-shifting starscapes, exploding suns, and a laughing, vibrant palette of colors.

She reached out for the man who had entered the virtual world with her.

She was—they were—one.

Outside, the Forty-Seven began their deployment. One of their number was distracted. His thoughts wandered, addressing his own strange, inhuman condition.

The hell of it for each of the warriors was not being able to show their faces in public. Every member of the Forty Seven looked beautiful and they knew it. Their cybernetic implants replacing flesh wherever possible, cold steel spikes jutting from torn and neatly sewed flesh, transceivers jacked into their ears, digital cameras piercing eyeballs, smart drugs and health drinks pumped into their system with a perfect one hundred per-cent recycling rate. They were more than beautiful; they were exquisite.

But the very sight of their beautiful bodies hard-wired with dark magicks and technologies far in advance of anything on the marketplace, would probably be enough to cause any Sleeper to go mad, with the usual, horrific and undesirable results. And so they lived in virtual exile. In makeshift leper colonies. And while waiting to be called into action they talked among themselves.

With longing they discussed the simple pleasures of going into a comic book store instead of doing everything mail order; of seeing movies in theaters instead of on tape. The joy of meeting a woman in a bar and taking her home. Hell, even popping into a 7-11 and getting a Frostie.

Shit, it was tough being so attractive.

That was why, when they had a chance to embark on a mission like this, bringing in a minor legend like Marazzi, facing the tiger in his lair, so to speak, so many of the Forty-Seven faced the prospect with nothing short of orgasmic bliss.

Only Joey Phillips was apathetic about the operation.

Even he wasn't sure why, exactly. This was a chance to get out, to do what he was created to do. For that, he should have been grateful.

Instead, all he could think about was the reason he had done this to himself. Why he had transformed himself from a hardworking gas station attendant in Waynesville, Nebraska, into this abomination.

It had all been over a guy. A decent guy. The first one he'd ever been willing to settle down for.

Only—he never felt good enough for Chance. That was his name. Chance. As Joey rushed into Marazzi's mansion, a mid-sized Howitzer dispatching itself from the hollow where his guts used to be, he checked his back-up memory on this.

Yep, Chance. That was it.

Chance accepted him the way he was. Chance never asked him to change. But Joey never quite felt worthy. Then he met some people who said they could help. They jammed memory cards into his brain. Did things that made him capable of absorbing raw data at what seemed like faster than light speeds. And because he could recite useless data about physics and history, because there was a little voice in his head connecting the dots in a spattering of intellectual fields for him so that he could take on Stephen fucking Hawking in a debate if he wanted to, or recite long forgotten verse from Moliere's secret unpublished work—because he could do these things and so many more, he came to believe that he was better than Chance. That he didn't need that flesh and blood loser any more.

And that was when he started allowing more and more enhancements.

Looking down at himself, he realized that he would never have the pleasure of taking a decent shit or having a real shag ever again in his life.

That was when he broke the first law and started thinking about why they were here.

That was when and where it started.

For the other members of the Forty Seven, it was when the entrance chamber became sentient and hungry, neatly slicing six of their number apart in its wood paneled maws, that they knew they were in trouble.

Mitchell's really going to honor his word, isn't he? Max asked.

Yes, said the man who had been Julian.

They were bonded in a way that brought understanding to each of them. Max grasped the totality of what Julian had become. He was both innocent and ancient. Practically all powerful, yet horribly vulnerable. A God made flesh. And flesh converted into pure energy.

In his hand was the Sword of Roland.

Max did not have to look through the eyes of her physical body in Mitchell's study to know that Julian—not Julian—was no longer standing beside her. He had fed all of his being into the machine, into the network.

Sadly, she also understood why.

I have to call you something, said Max as she went about collecting up the remnants of the Pattern bridge. *Help me out here.*

There was an acknowledgement that flooded through her being like a bold, sensual lightning, firing every nerve in both her physical and transitive bodies.

I understand. If it was not hubris, tempting fate, I would ask you to call me Agni.

The Divine Witness, Max said, suddenly aware of the significance of the name in Julian Ibiero's native religion.

I can hold nothing back from you. Nor would I wish to. The man hesitated. *You are comfortable with the name Julian? It has relevance to you? He was, in dreams, your guardian, your angel?*

It would be a comfort to call you that. Yes.

Then take comfort. Now come. We must make an offering to Ganesha.

The God of wisdom, prudence, and salvation.

It seems like the thing to do. Considering the circumstances. Do you agree?

Max could feel her physical body straining to smile. *I do.*

Mitchell registered the death agonies of two more opponents. Seventeen of the Forty-Seven had fallen. The time had come for Mitchell to finally confront them face-to-face. He knew that it would no longer matter what their orders had been. Bring him in, talk to him, torture him, whatever. They were not real samurai, as much as they boasted about their fealty to their masters. They liked to wear the costumes, they liked to play the game, but they couldn't stand up under the weight of their rhetoric. That meant they would now be out to avenge those who had fallen at their sides. Blood was all that would satisfy them.

Concentrating, he encased himself in every spell of protection that came to mind. Needing to calm himself, he thought of the night he first made love to Max and his seductive boasts about the Floating World.

Ukiyo, Ibiero had said. *You found it here. Not only once. But twice. That's rare.*

What he was doing was crazy. He had killed his own brother; he'd believed in his cause that much. Now he was willing to die and face what came after just for the sake of a woman? One who didn't even love him in return?

That about summed it up.

Mitchell went to Maxine's physical form. Somehow he wasn't surprised that Ibiero was gone.

He kissed her icy lips. No emotion registered in her eyes.

"I do, you know," he said. "I really do." He knew that he didn't have to say the word "love." It would be understood. But it pained him that he couldn't get it out.

Ukiyo. The Floating World.

"Oh my," he said, looking down at his hands, which he turned to stone with a thought. Grinning, he stripped off his clothes, allowing his flesh to run and sculpt itself into living, nerveless dark matter. Organic armor.

"Oh my, oh my," he said again, pores opening in his flesh to allow him to spill unimaginably toxic oils and the most fiery of acids.

"Now this is what I call a way of making an exit," he said, fire pouring from his charred black lips. Opening the door to the hall he cried out, "Oh sweeties! Hope I haven't kept you waiting too long!"

He launched himself into the pack of cyborg mercenaries and assassins.

The pathway opened. Max and Julian raced through it. The spirits did not try to stop them this time. The offering born by He who had been Julian was more than enough to assure their safe passage.

In as much time as it took to consider the notion, they were suddenly standing upon the sparkling shores of another continent. Julian and Max found themselves in separate bodies, their consciousnesses split once again, as they had been in the physical world.

The Weaponsmaster stood before them, prepared for any form of attack.

The mage knelt before the Guardian at the Gate and proffered the sword. "That which was yours once is yours again. Take it, Roland. And with it, protect this place from any threat."

"You know me?" asked the armored being. He shuddered as his hand closed around the sword's hilt.

"I know of you."

"And you would part with that which could, if not defeat me, occupy me long enough for your companion to tamper with the Pattern?"

Julian was unflinching. "I want nothing more than to see justice done, and to see this place stand ready, guarded from petty claims, until the true Ascension is at hand."

Roland took the sword. He nodded, whispered something, then wandered away from the doors to the library.

Julian stepped back and turned to Max. "We have a boon. We may change one thing. Only one. What will it be?"

Max was stunned. "There's nothing you want?

"I have it. I'm at peace."

She nodded. Julian Ibiero was dead. And now, as the being who had called itself Sunder had promised, he was a Lord of the Dead. He simply wasn't alone in the honor.

All this and more was known to her from the brief co-mingling of their minds and hearts.

"I know what I want," Max said. She told him what it was.

Taking her hand, he led her into the library, a facade that vanished the moment they stepped over the last boundary between all that had been and all that could be.

They became one with the Pattern.

Max's mind could not bear the brunt of such majesty alone. Julian anchored her, even as he began to change…

Joey wanted out. Simple as that. He couldn't remember how many times he had fallen on the ground laughing as he watched his tape of 'Aliens' and saw Bill Paxton whining "I'm so short! I'm so short!" even as Aliens dragged him through the floor to his death. Right now his augmented brain was short-circuiting and those same words were pouring out of his metallic throat in a perfectly synthesized and utterly panicked litany that would, in seconds, degenerate into a scream.

Degen-er-ate, he thought. Kinda sounds like de-gen-er-ite, now doesn't it, kiddies? Can you say degen-er-ite? I knew you could...

Mr. Rogers taunted Joey. A second later, Joey made the connection and knew why.

The monster that had come spewing bloody death, cutting a swatch through the survivor's ranks, was probably the most degenerate sight he had ever imagined. Joey wanted to believe this slaughterhouse around him wasn't real. That eleven more of the Forty-Seven—hey, gonna need a new name, fellas—hadn't been cut apart by this thing that giggled in the face of weapons fire.

Worst of all, the nightmare thing was coming for him.

"I'm so short!" he screamed again, wondering why in the hell he couldn't shake that line from that goddamned movie.

Suddenly, a lightning-clear burst of information penetrated his consciousness. According to his sensors, there was a hollow area beneath him.

(Paxton being pulled through the floor)

Yes! Joey thought. If he had the equipment for it, he might have cried with joy over the avenue of escape that had just been presented to him. The cybernetic portion of his brain had been trying to impart critical information to him. When he wouldn't listen, it had tried to use images that he wouldn't turn his back upon.

Training all his weaponry at the floor, Joey cut loose at full force. He would be left with no ammo when the nightmare thing reached him, but he no longer cared about that. All he wanted was a way out.

The floor disintegrated beneath him. He tumbled through it, into the underground complex that had once shielded Mitchell Marazzi after Julian Ibiero's attack.

Joey didn't care about any of that. It was dark and as he scrambled ahead, the sounds of death grew fainter.

He was going to live.

He was going to live.

Max felt herself joining with Julian for what she knew would be the last time. He had no plans of returning to the world of the living. His journey and his fight were over.

Suddenly, there was nothing. Night and day were rendered meaningless concepts. The stars and the sky had vanished.

Max felt a tremor of fear, but Julian quieted it.

Then thought and ideas and individuality were all absorbed by the void that was their form.

Breath was drawn.

From the sea of nothingness, floating, drowning, subsisting on darkness secreted away within darkness, the One willed itself to take another breath. Another.

Beings sprang from the One's mind. Creating a body from the darkness, the One expelled those beings as if they were its waste. They were the demons. Avatars of evil. Sickened, the One discarded this body, which became the night.

A new body formed, this one of goodness and light. From the One's mouth came the devas, the luminescent ones, the great shining gods of the world.

Shucking off this body, the One saw that day had been created.

One body after another was created and discarded. The ancient spirits were born. They were the twilight people and their gift would be the ability to impart wisdom to the humans who came next—but only in the hours of dusk and dawn. The moon came to be. Then ogres. Falling hairs from the One's body became snakes and other earth-crawlers. Mammals, plants, and all other life on earth came to be.

Fear suddenly rippled through the One.

Ridiculous, what was there to fear?

Loneliness.

The One split himself into two.

Max felt an infinite sadness at being separated from Julian. Some part of her consciousness grasped what was happening. Julian was raised as a Hindu. He was acting out the "Nasadiya," or There Was Not. The hymn relating to the creation of the universe. It was his way of dealing with the width and breadth of the Pattern, of placing the infinite in comfortable, conceivable terms.

History sped past them. All of human existence on the planet and so much more.

Max knew that Julian was granting her wish in the only way he knew how. He was tracing in the Pattern the events leading to the moment Max desired altered. Once he came upon that moment, the fate of the world would be subtly altered.

She knew that she should have been elated, not terrified.

But she wasn't.

Joey ran through the caverns. He had no time or interest in marveling at the weapons, drugs, and machinery he passed. All he cared about was escape. He had no idea that he went around in circles twice before he came to the stairway leading up to the study. He wanted out; this looked like an exit.

Magic pulsed through him as he mounted the stairs and passed through the gateway into the study. It made what little hair he had left after his many surgeries curl.

Then he was in the study, looking at the woman and the bizarre forms warping out of the computer screen before her. His mind could not grasp any one shape as they changed so rapidly, but he did notice that the woman's form was shimmering, flowing, dancing. To his horror, his own body was doing the same.

"Make it stop," he said, raising the butt of his empty weapon toward the back of the woman's head.

The odd phenomenon grew more intense. He felt sick and strange, his thoughts once again turning to the lover he had spurned, the terrible decision he had made to toss away his humanity.

Then a voice rang out in his skull. A voice that was painful to hear, a deafening roar that made him drop his weapon seconds before he would have crushed the woman's skull with it.

"W.Y.R.M. coming to you live from the pit of all darkness and evil, how ya doin' out there, Seattle!"

"Stop," Joey mewled piteously.

"We're gonna take a break from our usual mix of Soundgarden, Patti Smith, and Smashing Pumpkins to bring you a little sound advice. This is it, asshole. Forget the prophecies, forget the Grand Plans. The moment is at hand. If you want to be the messiah for a new age, here's all you have to do. Reach out and touch someone, Joey. There's still some flesh in you. I can smell it."

"My lips," Joey said with a groan.

"Yes, perfect," said the voice of his lord, the horror to whom he had sworn allegiance. *"Seal it with a kiss. That will be apt. And through you, I will come forth, and the land of darkness to which the Traditions wished to send us all will be the only land, the only reality. Do it!"*

"A messiah?" Joey asked.

"The guy on the cross hasn't even made it two thousand years yet," said the hissing, icy voice. *"I can guarantee you eternity!"*

"Eternity," Joey said, awestruck by the concept.

"Right. So go on. It'll be just like one of those movies you're so fond of. A single kiss. Then—fade out. Do it!"

Joey came around to the front of the shimmering woman. He leaned down, his lips parting slightly. Her face rose up before him. He could taste her breath. Sweet.

Their lips were close now. He touched the side of her face with his iron hands and saw that they were ebbing and flowing as well.

"Jesus wept," he whispered, then moved in for the kiss.

Maxine Anderson was terrified. The wonder of it all had given way to horror. She knew, beyond any doubt, that there was more to existence than the flesh. There were higher powers. God, gods… and at this moment, she was one of them.

She had asked that one event in the Pattern be altered. It had occurred to her to ask for what Mitchell had desired: A world without fear, without pain, without hunger and hatred. But it had been made clear to her that the only change she would be allowed was a subtle one. Yet—they were here. They were making the Pattern. Couldn't they make it in any image they desired? Who would stop them?

And if someone tried, what could be done to them? What in God's name *was* she right now? The co-creator of the universe? Or just some severed soul missing its flesh?

"This is wrong," she said, and she meant it. Of all the requests she could have made—I want my parents alive again, Freddy—she had chosen to return to that moment in Calcutta, when she had been a child holding a talisman that would alter the course of two lives.

Now all that child would have to do is hand back something that had been given, yes, *given* to her, and it would all be over. What Max wanted was absolution in the form of oblivion, something she had quested for all her life. She knew that the person she was now would cease to exist and Julian's trials would take a whole different course—one that she would not be responsible for in any way.

She also knew that the inherent paradoxes that would normally present themselves at a moment like this would be irrelevant. She could almost hear Freddy now: But it's time travel, it's paradoxes, like, how can you change the past if it requires the person you are now—a person who won't exist anymore—to pull it off?

The answer was before her. They were weaving a *new* Pattern. One that would supplant the old. All that was, all that had ever been, would simply pass into shadow, becoming a forgotten echo. "We have to stop," Max said. "We don't know how many lives will be affected—"

"I can tell you exactly," said the creature she had named Julian, though her guardian angel was truly dead and gone.

"I'm doing this—I'm doing it for the wrong reasons," Max added desperately. "I'm just looking to get out of being responsible for anything, it's what I'm always doing. That's got to stop. Really. Now."

"If that's what you wish."

"It is."

"Then—" he stopped. But something was terribly wrong.

Max felt the impurity the same moment as Julian. Another presence was invading this sacred place. Something dark and timeless, a primordial thing that wished nothing more than to desecrate this place of wonder with its own chattering and insane desires.

"The Wyrm," Julian whispered. "Or one of its aspects. It knows." Panic rose in Julian's voice. "Go back. You have to go back now, before it's too late!"

But each of them sensed the truth at exactly the same moment.

It was already too late.

"*One of you will die, one will close the pathway, and one—*"

"Wait," said Julian. "There's only two of us."

"There has always been three."

"Mitchell," Max said softly. "What about the third?"

"One of you will be redeemed."

Mitchell grabbed the cyborg's head and yanked him back an instant after his lips had brushed against Maxine's. It hadn't been the deep kiss that would be spoken of in legend, but the contact was enough.

Mitchell's stone form quavered as he saw the cyborg's face transform. He was now looking full into the Wyrm.

"You sure are an ugly motherfucker," Mitchell said, punching his fist through the cyborg's head.

It was as if his hand had entered a cloud of vapors. Then the soft flowing air coalesced and hardened around his hand and Mitchell screamed as the darkness tried to find a way inside him.

He drew back before it could find entry, then turned his gaze in horror to what was happening to Maxine.

She was coming apart. Her mouth was open in a scream, though no sound came out. Her body looked like a statue that was cracking and shaking apart from the inside.

He could sense her thoughts. Hers—and the man that had been Julian Ibiero. Of the Wyrm's mortal aspect, there was only an all-pervading darkness that was fighting to take control of the new Pattern being woven; its sole desire was to bring about a World of Darkness unlike any ever before conceived.

Mitchell knew instantly that something was wrong. A key element in this struggle had gone unheard from. Why? Did it have to be summoned?

"Roland," Mitchell called, having learned the Weaponsmaster's name from Julian's thoughts. "Yo, dude. This is it! This is the big one. You're needed, come on!"

Nothing. The avatar beside him laughed.

Mitchell was startled. Roland's job was to protect the Pattern. How could he forsake his duty?

Then he knew. Mitchell could feel Roland's frustration. In his hand was a weapon bound to him yet separated for so very long. One strong enough, perhaps, to cleave the Wyrm's mortal shell and shatter the gateway Maxine had created. But the Guardian at the Gate was bound by ancient covenants. It was not a matter of losing his honor if he defied the rules governing him. If he even attempted to defy his sworn oath, he would then find it impossible to access the power he would need to make good on his intent.

Catch-22.

He was trapped, powerless now that entrance to the Pattern had been granted.

Mitchell could sense Julian's attempts to force out the darkness laying claim to his new Pattern. He fought well, but what he was going up against was infinite. Or practically so.

"So you're not even bothering with me, is that it?" Mitchell said to the Wyrm's avatar. "I'm not even enough of a threat—"

"You're due for a headache," said the avatar.

Agony tore through Mitchell's skull. It seemed as if all the pain he had inflicted upon others in his lifetime was returning to him tenfold. He sank to his knees, his ardor fading, his form becoming human once more.

"I'll make it stop," said the avatar, *"if you agree to serve me."*

"Fuck off," Mitchell hissed.

"You've done it before. In the service of the Technocracy."

"I've done a lot of things I'm not proud of," Mitchell said, finding it difficult to breathe. "If I'd known you were their poster boy, I might have gone to work for the Post Office instead."

"You knew. You simply chose to ignore what you knew."

"Fair enough, shitface."

"All I want is for you to convey to your friends that their defeat is inevitable."

For a moment, Mitchell dared to hope that the Wyrm's avatar was becoming afraid. No such luck.

"I am impatient to begin my great work," said the avatar. *"You can use that impatience to your advantage. Decide quickly."*

Mitchell's agonies ceased. It took him a moment to realize that the avatar wasn't actively invading his thoughts. Mitchell sensed that it was repulsed. The idea of upholding the current Pattern, of wishing for order and light rather than its more alluring counterparts, was aberrant to it.

A wealth of possibilities opened in Mitchell's mind. He quickly considered the Weaponsmaster's plight, and thought of a way to free him.

"All right," said Mitchell. "You win." He touched Max. Suddenly, he felt the same electric connection to her that he had felt when they had made love.

Let him in, said Mitchell. *It's gone too far. Nothing can turn it back. Let the Wyrm shape the Pattern.*

Max was more dead than alive, her consciousness torn in a thousand different directions. Still, her defiance was radiant and clear. Julian's cries of what Mitchell now understood was misguided heroism merged with Max's howls of exquisite pain.

Then let me take your place, urged Mitchell. *I love you. All right? There, I said it. I don't want to see you like this. Let me in. You can go and warn the Traditions. There are still ways of keeping this from happening, but the three of us aren't powerful enough to do it on our own. You can feel that.*

Mitchell could sense Max's resolve weakening. Julian had released his hold on her. He sensed the underlying truth of what Mitchell had said.

I'm dying anyway. At least let me go doing one decent thing. Julian and I will hold this fucker off as long as we can. Please! Max let go. Mitchell felt his body and soul being dragged out of the study, down the channel, and into the Pattern. He sensed Maxine speeding the other way and tried to touch her one last time, but failed.

Suddenly, he found himself in the presence of the demi-god that had been Julian Ibiero. His body and the Pattern were linked. He could sever those ties at any moment, but to do so would mean allowing the Wyrm to take hold of the new Pattern.

Welcome to the fight, brother, said Julian.

Man, your little metamorphosis really did make you soft in the head, didn't it? asked Mitchell. Before Julian could respond, Mitchell performed a simple spell that tore Julian from the Pattern and allowed the encroaching darkness to wash over it.

Max opened her eyes. The pain had stopped. She was whole again. A massive figure lay on the floor beside her, sobbing.

"I didn't know," said Joey. "I swear, I didn't know what I was letting in, I didn't…"

This had been the Wyrm's avatar. It had abandoned him.

Max turned her gaze to the computer screen. What she saw there would haunt her the rest of her life. Laid out before her was the Wyrm—or what had Julian thought of it as? One of the Wyrm's many aspects?—and its plan for reality. She wanted to look away, but she couldn't.

It was coming. Primal matter was leaking out of the computer screen, transforming the study into an endomorphic structure. Reality was becoming the Wyrm, and soon all life would exist in the belly of the beast.

It was that simple.

The cyborg shrieked as a strange light reached for him. It engulfed him and he sank to the floor, seemingly lifeless.

Then, as suddenly as the manifestation had begun, it ended. The monstrous tentacles, the cavernous inner walls of acid-laced mucous and curling bone, all of it—was gone.

"What the fuck?" Max whispered.

The cyborg next to her sat up, shaking his head. "It's actually pretty simple, Max."

She recognized the voice. Sort of. "Mitchell?"

He nodded. "Pretty intense hardware here. Voice simulators, I guess for fooling with people's heads over the phone. Got a whole MIDI-thing going in here, I should be able to get this back to normal pretty soon."

She stared at him blankly.

"Hey, you know what they say. Any port in a storm…"

Epilogue

"All right," said Max. "Explain it again."

Mitchell was surveying his new body in a full-length mirror. "It's gonna cost a fortune to get enough of these implants out so I can show my face in public again. And man—am I gonna miss some of that wicked shit I used to be able to do. But at least this body doesn't have a goddamned tumor in its skull. Unless you wanna count all the cybercrap."

Max hugged herself. They sat in Mitchell's bedroom. The estate was a charnel house. Destroying all the evidence of the Forty-Seven's little visit was not going to be easy.

"Just tell me what happened to Julian," said Max.

"It's kind of complicated."

"Then tell me the whole thing."

Mitchell tried to shrug, but his new body felt awkward. It also wasn't particularly handsome.

Life was a bitch sometimes.

"All right," said Mitchell. "Here goes…"

The Wyrm enveloped the new Pattern and began to shape it in its own image.

Julian and Mitchell stood in a formless void apart from the Pattern. Clearly, from the manner in which the Pattern was growing, that would not be the case for long.

"Do you have any idea of what you've just done?" asked Julian.

"I hope so," said Mitchell, "I've been stabbing people in the back all my life. You would think I've gotten the hang of it by now."

Before Julian could ask what Mitchell was talking about, a Presence manifested itself around them. Once, the Presence had been a warrior. A soldier of uncommon valor and extraordinary will, but no more or less than a mortal man.

A bargain struck beyond the boundaries of the living and the dead had made him into something more, but despite his newfound power and position, Roland had felt incomplete. The unbreakable sword, Durandal, had been left in the mortal lands.

In truth, the sword had been no more or less than a symbol of his confidence and his belief in the Light. And when he died, it took a vital piece of his heart and his soul, keeping them safe for a time when they would be needed.

Roland held Durandal before him and engaged the Wyrm.

"But he was trapped," said Julian.

"Yeah," Mitchell replied. "Because permission had been given. You were told to recreate the Pattern, the hand of God or whatever was guiding you. But you were also told to make only one change. You hadn't even done that yet. I figured the Wyrm would be a greedy motherfucker. He *could* have made one change that would have brought it all crashing down over time. The slimy pus-bag could have won, no problem. But he wanted it all."

"He broke the rules," said Julian.

"Uh-huh. He wanted it all and he wanted it right now. You could see where it got him. Dumb-asses never learn to think Japanese…"

Roland had confined this aspect of the Wyrm, separating it from the greater, near-infinite mass of which it was a part. Now he was undoing the new Pattern itself, breaking its many lengths as he carved the Wyrm to pieces in the process. The fresh Pattern began to decay, just as the old one would have if it had been replaced.

The Wyrm's howls of agony were deafening roars. The only thing louder was the laughter of Roland as his Cathedral of Swords came into existence around them. The Wyrm's dying aspect was ushered into a glass jar, where it sparked like neon lightning in its now-silent attempts to free itself.

Roland, who had once again assumed the vague dimensions of a man, approached Julian and Mitchell.

"This isn't over," said Roland.

Mitchell said, "What, you want a tip? I left my wallet in my other suit." He patted his bare ass. He had been naked when he had been taken, body and soul, into the pathway.

"The pathway," said Julian. "It has to be closed before someone else finds it."

"Okay," said Mitchell, still not quite seeing the problem.

"There's only one way," said Roland, raising his sword.

Mitchell felt sick inside as he finally understood. "You have to take the life of whoever's holding the pathway open."

"That *was* Maxine," said Julian. "But you traded places with her."

"The pathway is a sacred thing," said Roland. "To sully it with blood, with murder, would desecrate it. The pathway will lose its power. It will cease to exist and no one will be able to recreate it. In time, when Ascension is at hand, a new pathway will manifest."

Sighing, Mitchell lowered himself to his knees. "Fuck, I'm dying anyway. I might as well be the sacrificial lamb or whatever." He put his hands behind his back and leaned forward, baring his neck.

Roland came forward, his sword held high.

"Waitaminute," said Mitchell, grinning. "You got anything to drink in this place? Might take the edge off a little. So to speak."

"Sadly, no," said Roland as he came to stand beside Mitchell.

"Don't," said Julian, holding out his hands for the sword. "You'll be damned if you do this."

"At least I'll be free."

"Hey, wait," said Mitchell, looking up sharply. "Is there any way I can get—"

But the sword was already falling.

"So Julian's alive?" Max asked.

"Julian Ibiero died in Calcutta," said Mitchell. "The demi-god formerly known as Julian Ibiero was still looking pretty healthy last I saw him."

"Where is he?"

"That's kind of a creepy memory for me, Max."

"Where?"

Mitchell exhaled a ragged gasp. His new cyborg body made a crackling sound along with the odd noise. "I could still see things for a couple of seconds after my head was cut off. Roland kind of like did this Shazam thing, a bolt of lightning and that was it, he was gone. Julian... He didn't look like he was going anywhere for a while. I think he was curious about the place. I'm sure that when he's ready, he'll move on. Everything went dark after that."

Max hugged herself. "Sorry."

"In terms of how the pathway was actually shut down and how or why my— whadya wanna call it, my consciousness? My soul? How that got away and came back to you, I don't have a freakin—" Mitchell backed away from the mirror and slammed into the wall. "Oh, no. Please, no."

"What is it?" Max asked, leaping off the bed where she had been sitting. "You look fine. What? I don't get it."

Mitchell looked to her sadly. "I remember now. What I was trying to ask them before they killed my ass."

"What was it?" Max asked.

Mitchell went over to a telephone. He frantically dialed a number. "Come on. Be there, be there—"

Someone picked up. "Hello?"

"Snyder, it's me."

"Mitchell?"

He put his hand over the receiver. "Something to write with. Hurry." He uncupped his hand. "It's about my will, lawyer mine. There's a young woman. She's come to mean a lot to me. She'll know what to do with the money. Her name's Maxine Anderson."

"All right…"

"I want this air tight. No one contesting it, no one trying to get their hands in where they don't belong, capice?"

"Mitchell, of course—"

"That means you, too. You know the kind of stuff I'm into. Fuck up and I will come back from the grave to fuck with your shit. Dig?"

The lawyer said, "I don't think that kind of talk is needed here, Mitchell."

Max found a notepad in one of the drawers of the entertainment center. She handed it and a pen to Mitchell. He started writing.

"And you know what else?" asked Mitchell. "I got friends who'll do the job if I find myself too busy. Still following me?"

The lawyer understood. They faxed the will Mitchell had scrawled to the lawyer and had a confirm that all would be handled appropriately before he hung up.

Mitchell seemed afraid. Max had never seen him that way.

"Oh, man," said Mitchell. "I can't believe I was so dumb I actually started believing in miracles."

"You're scaring me," said Max.

"I'm sorry about that. I really am. Look, here's the thing. I'm not real. I'm not even alive. I'm like an answering machine message, Max. Mitchell Marazzi is dead. I'm just—" he struggled for the right words. "Just an afterthought."

"Look, this is probably just the shock…"

"I wish. When we were all in each other's heads, I found out about what that Hero guy said to you two. He said that one would die, one would close the pathway, and one would be redeemed. Well, he meant all of that literally. One. Not three. One would die closing the pathway and find redemption. Me. And 'cause I was redeemed in the end, I got a little bonus. A chance to get this message to you. But really, hon, I'm over. Any second now, I'm just gonna fade and this body's gonna stop moving. Just stop, that's it. Cause it's already dead."

"Jesus," said Max.

"I've been screwing around and there's so little time," said Mitchell. "Here's the other thing I need to tell ya. The Wyrm isn't dead. Not by a long shot. But you're safe from it."

"How?"

"Well, it's not going to want word getting out about what happened with the Pattern and all. So it's going to be watching you. The second you say anything, or even try to say anything to *anyone*, you're dead. I guarantee it. But so long as you keep your mouth shut, you'll be fine. It really is over."

"Wouldn't it be better for the Wyrm just to kill me and get it over with?"

"Rules," said Mitchell. "The Wyrm violated them. It had to back down on this one point, it turns out. You leave it alone, it'll leave you alone. That's the compromise."

"So that's it?"

"I'd recommend getting out of here pretty soon. The Technocracy's going to be sending a clean-up crew out here."

They stared at each other.

"I really am sorry," said Mitchell. "I'd like to think I'm at least a slightly different person from the one who—well, your friend, a lot of other innocent people…"

"Yeah, I'd like to think so."

"One more kiss?"

She nodded and approached him. His lips were surprisingly warm and tender.

"Love you," he said, sitting down in the corner, closing his eyes.

Max took the will and left the room.

After hitching to the outskirts of Seattle, Max took a cab downtown. It wasn't until they were pulled up in front of the Art Bar that she realized she now had eight million dollars to her name and not a penny on her.

She slipped off the bracelet and held it out to the cab driver. "What do you think? It's got to be worth the cab ride, don't you think?"

He looked it over and tried to hide his obvious excitement. Then his conscience apparently kicked in. "You sure about this? You want, I could take you to a bank, an ATM, a friend's place. Someone with a little cash?"

"You keep it. I don't need it anymore," she said, getting out of the cab.

"Have a good one!" the driver said, pulling out fast, before she could change her mind. But she wouldn't.

Looking ahead to the Art Bar's front entrance, she thought about what she was about to do. A faceless stranger. Passion without love, without meaning. A few shots of oblivion to wipe it all out, to make her problems someone else's for a while.

She changed direction suddenly and walked leisurely toward the water. It was a cool, grey day.

And when it began to rain, all she could do was tilt her head back, the way she would when she was a child, letting the waters wash over her, energizing her, washing away her sins, her fears, renewing her.

Laughing, she ran to the harbor.

Except You Go Through Shadow

DAVID NIALL WILSON

1

The sky lit up like a Fourth of July gone mad. Love Constantine smiled into the brilliance, contemplating eternity. Why sweat the small stuff when the promised land was just the other side of a fragmentation grenade?

All around him he could hear the others screaming, praying, crying and rushing about madly. They disgusted him. A few short hours before they'd been soldiers, united against the mindless. Now, it seemed, they had forgotten, or never properly learned, the meaning of what was happening to them. They were letting the misplaced value of their confining, flesh-bound existence drag them down.

"There are only two things certain," Fontana had told them. "Death, and taxes. We defy the latter, but the first is our ticket out."

The words were ingrained in Love's mind. He lived and breathed them. He knew that the death and taxes line had been around long before Elliot Fontana penned it in his little book, but it had taken Fontana to find the prophecy in the words, to decipher the madness. Life was like that. There were windows and doorways to better things, different places, but sometimes you needed someone with a key to let you in, or someone with enough vision to pull aside the curtains.

The madness of the material world surrounded them. It ate at their souls and blinded their eyes, placing clues and hidden references all around for those with vision to find, but leading most into the depths of the abyss. Nothing was meaningless, and at times it was the very veneer of the mundane that held the most meaningful message.

A high-pitched screech brought Love momentarily back to his senses. Tear gas. They were firing tear-gas grenades. He reacted mechanically, letting the months of training, the hour upon grueling hour of concentrated preparation, take control of his limbs. He knew he was about to leave it behind, but not without a fight. That was part of the deal. Nothing for nothing. More prophecy.

He quickly unstrapped the military surplus gas mask from his belt, barking commands at those near him to do the same. He fitted the mask over his head, snugging the oily rubber straps and inhaling quickly, hands over the air vents to check the seal. The plastic faceplate bent inward, brushing his skin, and he removed his hands, smiling.

The AK-47 in his hands felt so natural that he often forgot it was there. He had not been firing—though the others were sending mad, half-aimed bursts across the field in front of the compound. Love Constantine was no fool. The words formed in his mind automatically: "You only get so many shots, you are judged for accuracy and control."

Fontana's personal bible for the millennium, the "Little Green Book," wound its words and its messages in and through every waking moment of Love's life. Love had painstakingly copied the volume in his own hand, adding notes and emphasis where he felt he might be weak. Fontana encouraged personalization. It was a sign of commitment. It meant you were "by God thinking about what the hell you're doing."

Many of Love's actions were purely instinct. This left his mind free; he was always thinking. Gazing out through the slotted window, he saw movement in the haze, flitting, man-sized shadows moving crab-like across the misty terrain. Smoke-screens were effectively confusing the defenders, but only because they were not paying attention.

Love would have cursed, but there was no time. He was busy sorting out his thoughts, readying himself for the journey to the next level. He took quick aim on a small group of dark figures and opened fire, using short, controlled bursts. Screams drifted through the swirling smoke and he smiled in satisfaction. Some of the figures went down. Others did not. Love was a million miles away.

Their little group was surrounded by the mindless. There would be no escape from the compound in the flesh—no other way out but to ascend to that next level and move on in a spiritual journey that could only be better than what life dished out in "real time." That was the message that Fontana had been pounding into their minds and ingraining in their souls for months. Love believed it with all his heart.

He drifted back to the moment he'd first spied Elliot Fontana, sitting on the lid of a city garbage can in the park, surrounded by the young, the lost, the homeless, spinning his prophecies with the look of madness—of *ascendence*—in his eyes.

"Music," he'd been saying. "You all know it is important. Even assholes like music, but they don't know why. Do you?

"I'll tell you why. You like it because of the words. Not the drooling, love-drip poetry, or the smash-something-quick-and-let's-die-together crazy stuff, but the *hidden* words. The prophecies."

Love had not been Love, then. He'd been Eddie. Lonely Eddie Constantine, and he'd been in search of a path, any path, that would take him permanently from his world and deposit him elsewhere. Hell, he'd been searching for someone to *lie* to him and make him believe there was such a path. He'd never counted on Elliot Fontana.

"Hank Williams, Sr.," Fontana had gone on, "was a prophet. His son, sorrowfully, missed the bus. It doesn't matter. The prophecy is there to be found, and I have the eyes that can lead you to it.

"Do you believe in the warmth of the heart? Forget it. The heart is cold. It is a cold, cold trap—a mistress who will never set you free. There is no bonding with another; there is only yourself, and the search for the next level. There is no permanence beyond the boundaries of your own mind. Hank Williams might not have known it, but he sang it. Then again, maybe he did know it. He took the hard way out, alone."

The words had droned on and on, and Eddie Constantine had found himself snared. Eddie had known all about prophecies, his mother had seen to that, but somehow this was the first set that seemed to have any real meaning. It explained so much.

If he was alone in his own universe, if everything else existed only to shield his eyes from the truth until he could ferret out the answers for himself, then the cruelty of life became a test, an intimate partner. It meant that even his mother, with her cruel, misguided lessons of faith and "holiness," had been a voice for prophecy, had he only listened.

Dimly, he wondered where Fontana was, what he was thinking in these final moments. Love's own position on the front line was an honor he'd dreamed of since first hearing of the coming "war." The war had dwindled to a single battle, but it did not matter. He would take the path of the Valkyrie. On the other side of somewhere, he and Fontana would find one another, and the next journey would begin.

The gunfire was heavy now. More of it seemed to be incoming than before, and the movements in the field blurred before his eyes.

He thought of the few others who believed, those who only hung on to belong, the new ones—not yet certain enough to be committed. They all had new names. It was the first gift Fontana gave when someone heard his message and showed signs of belief.

Love ticked them off in his mind, using the names as a word game to concentrate his thoughts. He continued to fire at the moving shadows beyond the window, shadows that grew closer with each passing moment.

There were Faith, Hope, and Charity, Love himself, the Archangels Raphael, Michael, Uriel, and Gabriel, the finest of the soldiers, and there was Fontana. The fountain, he called himself. It was his strength, his vision, that would see them through. Love believed that Fontana had wanted, in his heart, to lead the way, to sit where Love now sat and to fight as he did. It was a great sacrifice, perhaps the greatest, to wait for the reward he himself so openly offered.

Love needed no one to back him. He was finished fighting against the veil of secrecy that denied him peace. He was ready to take things into his own hands, to rip the curtains aside and dive headlong through the window of fate.

"Remember the words of Johnette, a true Concrete Blonde, and a prophetess of the new age," Fontana had told them the night before. "Love is a beast. Love," and here Fontana's grin had widened as he turned to meet his most loyal follower's eyes, "you will *be* that beast. Own it. You will lead us through into the next world. You are first of my flock, most learned in the prophecies, most able to divine the meaning behind the meaningless, after me. You are Love, and you are the beast. Rip out the heart of the world."

Even those words had held hidden prophecy, Love knew. He and the others *were* the heart of the world. He would not so much rip it out as he would irritate the world into ripping it out for him.

There was a thunderous crash to his left as something struck the wall, or blasted the damned thing into rubble. There were more screams. He could see figures running both ways. He saw Faith, her eyes lit with inner fire, rise from the smoke with a .45 and start blasting away. The return fire riddled her torso, splattering a great deal of her insides over what remained of the wall behind her. Federal justice.

Even as he spun, raising his own gun and squeezing the trigger, he glanced at that wall—at that splash of color, obscured by gas and smoke. It whirled, forming, then reforming. As the first fiery pain shot through his shoulder, he saw it coalesce into a single shape that strobed in his mind, capturing his gaze.

It was a heart, a huge dripping heart. He let the gun clatter to the floor, empty, without even trying to reload. He rose to his feet, eyes locked to the image on the wall.

Turning to the advancing, masked and body-armored mindless that stalked him through the rubble, he smiled.

"Through Faith," he said, gesturing at the splash on the wall, "we will rip out the heart of the world. Love is the Beast. I am Love…"

With that, he ripped free a grenade from his belt, pulled the pin, and dove at the wall. His leap propelled him in a graceful arc. Bullets flew, chopping bits and pieces from his flesh, but he clung to the grenade, clung to the vision. He struck the wall precisely ten seconds before the explosion transported him to Oblivion, struck it face first, smiling, with a wet thunk. The doorway to eternity was bright white and filled with glorious pain.

The authorities sifted through the rubble of Fontana Farms for days before they recovered all of the bodies. There were women, children, the four bikers who had been labeled "the Archangels."

"Funny thing about that," one of the officers smiled thinly for a news camera and tipped his hat back on his head for his moment in the limelight. "They were angels before he met them—Hell's Angels. I never seen a man could turn one of them boys from their club."

He got his wish on the second day of searching. In a small cabinet in the compound's kitchen, beneath the sink, they found a last body. It was a tall, lanky body, scorched from the fire that had ruined the walls of the room. It was tucked into a fetal position, knees supporting the thin-boned chin and face. It was the deathbed of a coward—a dried-up fountain.

Elliot Fontana had had a plan. He would survive. He would bring his "message" to a new flock, a new generation. He would see this group on, then he would turn back to the world, selflessly. He would go to the next level, but not just yet, thank you very much.

That plan had failed. He'd never believed they could hold off the feds for so long, or that so many would die. He'd thought it would be a quick skirmish, after which he'd arise miraculously from the ashes (or the sink drain), lament the dead, chastise the "mindless" and begin work on a new ministry. In the end, the next level had reached out with icy talons and claimed him.

The weapons he'd so carefully stockpiled had blown sky high, and the flames had spread quickly. He'd been wearing his mask, now melted grotesquely to his face, but that had been no good against the encroaching poison of smoke. A large cabinet, fallen across the door of his cubby-hole, had finished the job. No escape.

Elliot Fontana had moved on; his "Little Green Book" hanging from a leather thong about his neck had gone with him. Only smoke-damaged, scorched pages remained—fragments of stolen words, "found prophecy" as he'd called it—to speak of his existence. That and a pile of rotting, putrid flesh. Medium rare.

One of the officers collecting evidence for the investigation lifted the book from the body, cutting the leather strap and depositing it all in a nicely sealed, hermetically safe baggie (with the green strip for freshness). Looking down, he saw that a message had survived, after all. One line, unblemished, surrounded by scorch-marks, embedded itself in that officer's mind. Another prophecy. *Break on through to the other side…*

"Damn," he commented to no one in particular. "A Doors fan…"

The letters were sharp, as though they might have been penned very recently…maybe even in the cabinet itself, after the others had died and while the flames ate away at the cabinets. A final prophecy.

Staggering to his feet, fighting a numbing cold that gripped the very roots of his soul, Love looked about himself. He saw the land surrounding the compound, saw the bodies of the slain, though there was something odd about them, saw those not yet gone, wandering about as if he weren't even there, passing near, even through him. He shook his head.

Behind him, the searchers were headed into the compound, but he did not follow them. He wanted to. With all his will he fought the urge that drew him away from the place, the whispery Shadow voice that played at the edges of his mind. There were no clear words, but the message itself could not have reached him more fully if an AT&T operator had been reciting it in his face.

He was too weak to fight. As Elliot Fontana died in flames, Love Constantine wandered into wasted lands of shadow and pain. He followed his Shadow.

2

As Love passed from the limits of the compound, his sight began to clear. Though his mind seemed to be functioning normally, nothing looked the same. The area was alive with the trails of wisping smoke left by the attackers with their smoke screens and gas. The desolate, windswept land and the rolling dunes of sand were just as he remembered them. At the same time, it was totally warped.

Lines of federal vehicles still circled the place. Squads of men and women dressed up like refugees from some sort of television SWAT episode of the damned rushed back and forth. He stopped to watch one group, mesmerized.

There were three of them, an older woman with hints of gray in her hair, and two men. The first man was huge—at least six foot five. His shoulders were immense, nearly bulging through the sleeves of his uniform shirt, worn at least a size too small for effect. His face, though—nothing to write home about. It dripped green pus from open, running sores. His hair was wispy, falling out at the roots and trailing behind him like the straw from a poorly constructed scarecrow. Though he seemed as healthy in his movements as a bull moose in its prime, Love detected something running beneath the surface, a veneer of sickness and rot.

The woman was winking at the big guy with yellowed eyes that were veined red and bulging from their sockets. Her chest was misshapen, one breast obviously larger than the other and nothing cosmetic done to alleviate the imbalance. She hung on pus-face's arm as if he were some sort of Adonis. Love could hear them talking, laughing.

"Bunch of wacko birds, eh, Madge?" the man was saying. "Locked up in there with that long-haired nut, talking about the 'next level' and stocking up on guns like they were canned goods. You hear the crap that Fontana guy was spoutin' on the news the other night, over the phone?"

"Yeah," the woman said, drool running over her lip and staining the ratty collar of her uniform shirt. "He sure seemed to believe in it, though. All of them did. Christ, they *died* for it."

"Whatever *it* was," the man laughed.

Love slipped between two government trucks, their paint peeled and worn. The tires on one were so dry-rotted and crumbled that it was a miracle the thing wasn't sitting on its axles. What kind of feds were these, anyway?

Whatever it was, Love repeated to himself. He reached down to where the small leather book dangled from its thong around his neck. Pulling it free from his shirt, he stared at it hard, remembering, concentrating.

The book was alight with a sickly, greenish glow. The words on the slim volume's cover, *The Little Green Book* flashed brightly, flickering as ghost lights danced between the characters.

The feds continued to walk and flow around him, and he continued walking. There was no longer any need for the urging of the shadowy voice. He had to find a place where he could think. Had he turned to look at the compound, he might have changed his mind.

It stood out like an ominous, ruined castle, eerie against a dull sky. What was left of the walls had grown taller, more ominous, fronted by huge, brooding stone figures that glared after him. It was a nightmare vision, a compound from somewhere else.

There were figures moving about it. Some, like the others he'd seen, were alive. Others were not, and they picked through the ruins of the dark stone carefully, dragging free a body here and there, working methodically. There were horrible cries—cries that drove Love, finally, to move faster, though he didn't look back.

He was still wandering aimlessly when certain of the sounds behind him became clear enough to distinguish. He stopped to listen. There were voices, the snuffling, grunting sounds of beasts…booted footsteps.

"I know one of the bastards went this way," a gruff voice rolled out, far too close…far too loud. "I saw him disappear a while back. We don't quite have the full quota."

"Ah, forget him," a whiny, sniveling voice answered. "We got more than enough to handle, plenty of new stuff. No one will even know he's here. Hell, he'll probably wander right into our camp, anyway. There weren't any very strong ones."

"Not other than that woman," the louder voice returned, obviously swayed by his partner's arguments. "Now *she* will bring top dollar, you can count on that. Might even make it past the forge-fire, that one."

The two of them cackled, and Love, who had ducked into the oily shadows of an outcropping of rock, waited for them to decide his fate. If they came farther, they would find him. There was nowhere to go. Apparently they would have had him from the start if he hadn't wandered off from the compound so quickly. Silently he thanked whatever ghost voice it had been that had urged him on.

If they found him, he would fight. This he knew. He had no weapon—silently he cursed himself for dropping the rifle and wasting the grenade. Then it occurred to him that neither might be of much help in this god-forsaken situation, wherever, and whatever, it was.

He heard the beasts slavering and whining, heard the men curse as chains were tugged upon and claws scrabbled in loose earth. Then the shuffling footsteps began to recede. They were leaving. Letting himself slide down the stone to a sitting position, he dropped his head into his hands.

Eventually he lifted his eyes to the sky. It was the same pale, shadowed twilight he'd walked out into seemingly hours before. Maybe days.

He pulled the book free again, meaning to search for something familiar in the turmoil that held him fast. As he began to flip the worn, dog-eared pages, amazed at the glimmering inner luminescence that suffused them, the shadowy presence that had urged him so swiftly from the ruins of the compound returned. It bore down on his mind like a weight—confusing his fingers. He fought for control.

He felt fear growing, reaching out to grasp at the edges of his courage and fold it in upon him. As the fear grew, his remaining control of his fingers slacked, then dropped off to nothing. His hands moved on, his fingers running down verses—sayings—prophecies, searching without a thought to guide them.

Love's greatest fear was that of helplessness. The thought of confinement or subjugation drove him near to madness. Until the world had caved in on his mind, he'd had the answer to this. *He* had been in control. No matter what the risk, no matter what the cost, he'd never backed down, never released his thoughts or actions to the control of another. Not since the very earliest years of his life, when first his mother, then the older children at school, had beaten him down. Not since he'd learned to fight.

He'd let Fontana guide him, but even then had steered his own course, using the other's wisdom for wind in his sails. It was his life, his choices—they were *his* damned fingers! He lashed out with a sudden burst of mental energy, dissipating the shadowy *thing* that had so blithely wandered in and taken over. It was there, then it was gone, or retreated.

He shivered uncontrollably, feeling the release both physically and emotionally. He glanced down at the book, holding it up where he read the words that now seemed to burn so brightly from the pages that they jumped out at him.

There is strength in numbers.

Beneath this, as if in afterthought, he had scrawled his own note, *The greatest strength is in the number one.*

He stared blankly at the words. He knew why he'd written them, even remembered most of the reasons he'd believed that Fontana had included the first statement in the book. Everyone was a world unto himself, but in a world of individuals, the right to individuality was held in the hands of the masses.

He ran his finger slowly across the paper, mouthing the words, then recited them aloud, as if he could give them power. He felt a slight surge of something, something deep within his mind—half-formed. No prophecy opened to him, though, and he closed the book with a sigh, placing it back beneath his shirt.

It didn't matter. He was *one* now. Hell, he didn't know if there was anyone in this world that he knew, or that knew him, and he sure wasn't going back after the two who had been searching for him earlier. He hadn't gotten a clear look at whatever kind of beasts had been snuffling along with them, but the image that the sounds they made brought to mind was not pretty.

In the distance, he heard the plaintive sound of a train's whistle. The train station wasn't far away. He didn't know what might be waiting for him there, but it had to beat sitting alone in the desert. Christ, he'd starve before too long.

Then the realization hit him. He wasn't hungry. Not even a little. No thirst, not a twinge of the need for a ham sandwich. Nothing. It had been hours since he'd last sat down to a meal.

A bird landed on the stone above him, and he turned his gaze up to watch it. The creature had only one eye. On the other side of its face an empty, glaring socket fixed its gaze on him as if it still held sight. The bird opened its mouth and croaked at him, a dry, rasping sound. Feathers dangled at odd intervals along its flesh, and one wing was bent at a crazy angle, as if it had fallen from a great height.

He rose, moving toward the thing, but it paid no attention to him. In fact, it stared right through him. Just like the feds he'd passed. As he got close enough to touch it, it suddenly took off in a rush of wings, wings that should not have even functioned, broken as they were, swooping straight at him. He dove to the right, bracing himself for an impact that never came. He passed directly through the stone and rolled free on the other side.

The bird dove down low and scooped up what appeared to be a half-skeletal mouse from the sand, then it soared off with its dubious prize dangling from its chipped and broken beak.

Shaking his head, Love rose, dusting himself off and watching the bird until it disappeared into the twilight. There was no moon, nor was there a sun. He looked at his watch. Midnight. No way to tell. It was as bright out as it had been when he left the compound.

He had the sudden impression that he was not alone. Spinning about quickly, he searched the deeper shadows. His instincts came back to him now, his mind gratefully giving up the effort of figuring out his surroundings and turning to the more familiar topic of survival.

There were whispering voices all about him. He could make out no words, but the tones were hushed and questioning. He shifted his gaze, watching every angle in its turn, pressing against the bit of the stone that seemed solid.

At first there was nothing to concentrate on. Then she came forth, an ethereal, dark woman whose eyes were filled to the brim and beyond with tragedy. Those eyes called out to him, and Love let his arms fall to his sides, though he did not relax.

She did not speak, not at first, only watched him with a great, sorrowful curiosity. He felt her companions drawing nearer to him on both sides, but the bodies that belonged to the voices remained hidden, obscured, though there was nowhere for them to hide.

Now that they were closer, he could hear them more clearly—a jumble of words and phrases that moved sinuously through his perceptions.

"He is here."

"It is not him. How could it be him?"

"He has called, we have been summoned. It is him."

"Llanna will know. Let Llanna seek, we shall follow."

"Always we follow."

"Is it him?"

Love shut them from his mind and concentrated on the woman. She was not beautiful in any earthly way, but her appearance commanded attention, respect even. She was striking. Her features might have been carved from alabaster, smooth and pale. Her eyes drank him in, searching his soul. He tried to turn his head, but she would not release him so easily.

"You have called," she said at last. "We have waited, knowing you would come. You have called, and we have answered. The prophet has said, 'There is strength in numbers.' You have spoken, we have heeded your summons."

Not knowing what else to do, he pulled the green book from its hiding place beneath his shirt and answered her: "The greatest strength is in the number one."

A sudden, wind-like murmur surrounded him completely. The woman held her arms wide, beckoning to him.

"It is you. Come, we must hurry. Those who seek you will come back, we must return to the temple. They will take your soul. To them, the prophecy is nothing."

"Prophecy is everything," he said, not denying her position, merely asserting his own. "I will come. I have no choice. Is this the next level?"

"We will speak of levels and prophecy, but you must come now."

With no further words, the woman turned. Love followed in her wake. At their sides, materializing from the mist that surrounded them, shadowy figures appeared, marching stoically, eyes averted. Still their voices wound around him, confusing his thoughts, tossing in words and questions, answers that made no sense. He ignored them as best he could and walked, hoping that his first decision in this cold, desolate place would not turn out to be his last.

He tried for a while to count his paces, but that was impossible. He watched the landscape for familiar marks, finding a few, but they were never quite as he remembered them. Where they should have reached the road into the city, they met only stark, cobbled pavement—pavement that was slick and oily beneath his feet. Love had walked and jogged a thousand times down that stretch of road, and this was not it. Not exactly.

There were nubs and cracked pieces of whatever made up the surface sticking up at odd angles. At times they seemed to be reaching out to trip him, as if they had a mind of their own. He watched the road with amazement until, as they turned a bend, he stepped right onto what appeared to be a face—a horribly mutilated, flattened and misshapen face. It was twisted into the rictus of a scream—beyond horror—beyond pain.

He stopped, shuddering, and the woman hesitated, turning to see what was wrong. Noticing the spot in the road, she said, "You must avoid such spots. There are those who will detect the cries of the road as you pass. Quickly now."

As if her words had drawn them forth, deep, baying howls rose in the distance, and they all picked up their pace. Despite her warning to watch where he was stepping, Love did not look down at the road again. He was careful to match his steps to hers, but he was not prepared for the concept of treading on something alive, however tenuous and pathetic that life might be.

They turned off into a dense cloud of smoky fog. It had an odd, unpleasant tang to it, like some sort of incense gone bad—or rot that hadn't quite ripened to putrescence. In the mist he nearly lost her several times, hurrying to catch up. All sound was muffled, and those who had flanked him only appeared here and there, slipping in and out of his sight like phantoms.

Finally the mists cleared a bit, and Love stopped. What he saw was nothing that had ever been this close to the compound. It was, in point of fact, not possible. It was a temple—a dark, brooding tower that snaked skyward, seemingly carved from the stone of a single mountain—a mountain that did not exist...could not exist.

The doors to the place were huge, at least twenty feet in height, and there were figures gathered all around them—some reclining, some in small groups. All were shadowy with pale skin, like the woman who led him. As Love and his guide came into sight, they turned as a single entity, rising and forming into ranks.

Facing him with what might have been a smile, the woman beckoned.

"Come," she said. "They have waited for this moment a very, very long time."

"Wait." Love answered, holding back. "Who are you? What are you waiting for?"

"I am Llanna," she answered softly. "I am the priestess of this temple, and we seek Transcendence. We have read the prophecies. We have found the meanings between meanings. You have come to guide us to the next level."

"But…"

"Come. There will be time for talk later."

Unable to put the pieces into any sort of order, Love allowed himself to be led. He felt the weight of hundreds of eyes upon him, felt the weight of their pain, their hope. He felt the weight of the small green book that dangled so tantalizingly from the cord around his neck.

"Welcome, brother Love," an old man said as he passed. "We are the heart of *this* world."

Shuddering, staring blankly into the old man's eyes, he passed on into the temple. The darkness sucked him into the depths of her cold, cold heart. He whispered the words to himself, praying they would set him free:

"Why don't you free your doubtful mind?"

He repeated them like a mantra, waiting for the ice that bound him to melt.

The line of captives moved very slowly down the road, chained together at the throat and ankle. They were moving steadily and languidly through the mists of a bad dream. The world that surrounded them was warped beyond recognition, but familiar enough, all the same. It was their nightmare.

If they stumbled or fell, they were beaten. If they spoke they were beaten more severely. As they went, they were bombarded by a steady barrage of curses, insults, and laughter from the two men who drove them, uniformed men with dark, uncaring eyes and insignias the captives had never seen before.

At the head of the chain strode Elliot Fontana. His eyes took in the landscape, the rot and the swirling dust, the road beneath his feet, and yet he didn't really *see* any of it. Behind him, a number of his followers, along with a few of the feds who'd raided their compound, followed. He'd promised to lead them into the next level. Elliot Fontana was keeping his promise.

"This is a sorry lot," the larger of the two slavers snarled, flicking his whip, cracking across the backs of the last three in line. There was a sharp cry of pain, a chorus of moans. The man laughed. "Hardly worth our time to come out and drag 'em back," he added.

"They'll do for the forges, Din," the smaller, wiry man at his side answered with a wide grin. "You can't make something from nothing, as I always say. Good to know that when we go to see the paymaster, they have enough raw stuff to keep us in coin."

Both men laughed at this, but none of the prisoners gave any thought to figuring out why. They did not know how long they'd been moving, on and on without rest, without thought of food, without hope. Here there was no hunger, only the memory of it, and the hours, minutes, and days were not marked with a changing of light, or with the rising or setting of a sun. It was a world of endless twilight, and they were headed into its heart.

There was no escape. If the guards themselves hadn't been enough, the two huge beasts that stalked along at their flanks would have done the trick. The creatures could have inhabited any man's nightmares comfortably, standing the height of a pony with long, doggish snouts and the grace of huge jungle cats. Each of them had deep green eyes that shone like beacons through the murky haze. There was no intelligence in those eyes, only a hunger that swam barely beneath their surface. They were under control at the moment, but anyone who might try to break and run would be down the second he left the questionable security of the pack.

Fontana wondered, very briefly, just what that would actually mean in this place. He was no fool, and his mind, foggy as it was, had figured out quickly enough that they must all be dead. For better or for worse, this was his mythical "next level," and they'd reached it, just as he'd said they would.

The real questions were, was this an ascension they'd made, a fall, or a sidestep? Could they die again? If one of those beasts was to rip him in half, would the two parts just lie there and quiver, continuing to "live," or would it flash him to the next nightmare, wherever that might be? He was fairly certain he didn't want to know. So he walked, and he listened, trying to piece together some sort of reality from the words of his captors.

"What do you think about that one that got away, Sully?" Din's voice had gone thoughtful, questioning. "I've been at this business for a long time now, and I've never seen one so fresh that could escape me. There was something odd there, you mark my words."

"Probably those damned visionaries from that tower back there," Sully turned to gesture off into the distance. "Don't know what they want with the fresh ones, but I've heard rumors. They must have found him somehow before we were able to catch up with him. No way he got away on his own."

"Well, whatever happened, Bontempt isn't going to like it," Din muttered. "Damned Heretic bastards get bolder every day. Next thing you know they'll be trying to come and take the ones we've already got."

"That would be a mistake they wouldn't soon duplicate," Sully cackled. "Crassus and Brutus here would make short work of them even without our help, wouldn't you, fellas?"

There was no answer, no gesture of any sort that would indicate that the beasts had heard his words, but their eyes told the tale well enough. That hunger that Fontana had detected below the surface seemed to flare, just for a second, and he shuddered.

"Maybe we should just not tell him we lost one," Sully said slowly, turning to gauge his partner's reaction. "I mean, he don't know how many there were, how could he? He isn't gonna like it if we tell him we lost a fresh one; won't look good at all."

"You may have a point," Din observed, "just this once. I don't like it, though, not a bit. The way that one disappeared was downright weird, and there's been plenty of weird stuff going on lately. What happens if, say, he was stronger than we thought, and he did get away on his own? If he comes after his friends, which

I'd say is likely, not having any idea what else to do, he might not catch up with us until we reach camp. I mean, Bontempt will get him, one way or the other, but how do we explain him? It would be worse if Bontempt thought we lied than if we just lost some fresh meat."

"Well, whatever," Sully said, obviously not convinced. "If we tell him, though, you do the talking. Just looking at that eye of his gives me the willies, and if that freaking bird is there, I feel like it's staring straight into my soul, you know? It gives me the creeps."

"Yeah, that thing *is* creepy." Din agreed.

Fontana continued to survey his situation in silence. Several of his companions from the compound had made it here, as well as a few others he knew must be feds. Directly behind him, Hope and Charity were chained. Their clothing was in tatters, and under any other circumstances, the nearly naked presence of Hope's nubile young form would have gotten a real reaction from him. Now he couldn't get past her blank eyes, the dull, lifeless motions of her steps.

A few chain lengths back from the girls, all four Archangels marched. When they met his gaze, their own were empty, icy. They held their heads a bit higher than the rest, and their shoulders were bunched and tense, as if at any moment they might burst free of their bonds and begin destroying things. It made no difference. They were bound and helpless, just as he was. He let his eyes continue back down the line to Faith.

He'd heard her struggling earlier, heard her cursing at their captors and eliciting at least one grunt of pain. Next to Love, who was conspicuously missing from the chain, she had been the most faithful to his teaching, the most gullible. Next to Love, she had been the strongest. She was chained, just the same, being marched off by her pretty, pale little throat, but she still had the courage, the strength of will, to curse and to fight back.

Fontana did not curse. He did not stumble. He concentrated on his silence and his steps, getting into a measured rhythm that helped to keep him upright and balanced. He knew when his situation had gotten as bad as it could possibly get, and it wasn't there yet. He was a survivor, that was how he saw it. He needed to find out how to please these men who had bound him, how to improve his situation. He didn't know yet if he could die here, but there might be much worse fates awaiting, and he just didn't want to find out.

He was yanked to a sudden halt as a hideous scream rent the silence, startling the prisoners and sending them stumbling about blindly. The sound was unearthly and shrill, piercing to the center of his heart.

Din flashed a quick glance into the shadows beyond the road, where small twisters spun up gusts of dirt and shadowy formations rose and fell like a moonscape viewed on an acid trip. The haze had thickened about them, obscuring even more of their surroundings. "Damn," the big guard said, his hand moving instinctively to the hilt of his sword.

Moving quickly, Sully came to the end of the line and began to bully the prisoners quickly into a tighter knot, shoving them roughly and cursing as they stumbled about. Faith, who was in no mood to be pushed around again, lashed out at him with one long, muscled leg, trying to take out his knee. She missed her mark. The short man hauled back and smacked her with a backhand that sent her reeling, toppling her into the chain and nearly bringing the entire line to their knees as they were jerked by their necks and ankles. He was strong for such a small man, very strong.

"You'd better learn to do what you're told, and when, you little bitch," he snarled at Faith, who was down on one knee holding her hand to her lip, which had split. Fontana was captivated by the cut. There was no blood. Her eyes were defiant, but she did not move to attack again. "You want to see the hot end of the forge, you keep it up. You do as you're told, you might make it out of those chains some day. Otherwise," and his grin grew wider at this, "you might just *become* one of them."

"Get up here, Sully. There are Spectres out there, in case you didn't notice," Din grated. "You think they'll actually attack us on the open road?"

"I don't know," Sully answered, moving to his partner's side and gesturing to the two beasts that stalked their perimeter to move in closer, as well. "Bontempt says they've been gettin' pretty bold, lately. He lost an entire string just two weeks ago. Two of our men went down with it."

"Our men? Who?"

"Razz and Doughboy," Sully answered.

"I knew Doughboy wouldn't last," Din said slowly, "but Razz? Hell, I went out with that old coot a few times myself. He was good, real good. There must've been a bunch of them if he went down…"

Out of the corner of his left eye, Fontana saw a quick, flitting motion, but when he turned there was nothing. Then he saw another flicker to his right. He spun, tracking it, and he nearly broke his neck as the chain stopped him. He heard a sharp cry of pain as Hope was yanked after him, and several curses from down the line, but he ignored them.

The eerie cry returned, then was echoed loudly from the far side of the road. It was not *just* a sound, but more of a feeling, a summons that reached into his being and dredged up memories and fears he'd believed long forgotten. There was a sudden scuttling sound to his left and another flicker of shadow.

The two beasts were growling now, a low, throaty rumble that started somewhere deep in their huge, muscled chests and ripped upward to explode into the night like the voices of twin chainsaws. There was no fear in that sound. It brought to mind images of rending and tearing, unspeakable chaos. It dispersed the spell of the other creatures' cries as if they had never existed.

Fontana was vaguely aware that Sully had come back to twist the line into a small circle. He brought the back end forward first, then dragged Fontana around the outside. Any who made a sound, the guard cuffed violently, ignoring their struggles.

With sudden dismay, what was happening clicked in Fontana's mind. They were trying to protect those in the middle of the circle! He and the others in the outer ring were expendable. He screamed inwardly, but he did not struggle. It was pointless, and there was no need to make things worse.

Scanning the shadows fearfully, he felt a presence to his left and spun quickly about, straight into the face of death. It screamed at him through slavering jaws and row after row of razor-sharp teeth that snapped and chewed at the air madly. Those jaws were opened wide, so wide that he could look in and down, down where the thing's throat should have been, down into the whirling vortex of ever-deepening shadows that called out to his fears and his pain. He felt himself start to stumble toward it, and yanked his gaze wildly upward, only to be trapped by the creature's eyes.

They were yellow and huge, serpent's eyes with slitted pupils. As he stared at them they shifted and changed, re-formed, confusing his already weary mind. Suddenly it was his father's eyes that stared at him, burning with hatred; then it was Love's eyes, dancing with enthusiasm; only to be replaced by others, and others still. He dropped to his knees under the brutal intensity of the mental assault.

He could feel the thing's hot breath on his face, could sense the impending snap of its jaws, but he could not move to defend himself. He could only stare, offering his throat to the slaughter. His mind would not recognize the danger, not with the shifting images clouding his concentration.

Then there was a flash of darkness and another scream, more of a howl—equally loud, but different. It was a battle cry that roared its challenge to the murky skies. Fontana felt control of his limbs returning, and he pressed himself back into the bodies of those behind him, ignoring their struggles and the pummeling of their fists on his back and his head.

"No," he managed to croak, his first words in this land of horrors. "No!"

As one of the two great beasts launched itself past him, straight into the waiting jaws of the Spectre, Fontana lost control, scrabbling up and back, heedless of the pain as the chain pulled against his neck and his ankle, ignoring Hope's cries of agony. He pushed her roughly to the ground and clembed over her, trying to make his way to the questionable safety of the center of the ring of prisoners.

Behind him, inches from where he'd been cowering, he heard the Spectre scream again, and despite his fear, despite his need to escape, he turned, fascinated, to watch the battle unfold. With its spell broken, he could make out more of what the creature looked like. It was thin and skeletal with dry, dead skin pulled too tightly over bones that protruded in every direction. The thing's jaws seemed double-jointed, so widely were they opened, and it was as quick as a snake, lashing out to strike at its assailant with taloned claws.

The two creatures collided with a wet smack. They struggled for a moment, neither able to gain the hold or advantage it sought, and Fontana found himself praying, to whom or what he had no idea.

He felt the hands of the others pushing and pulling at him, beating on his head and shoulders, but he ignored them, concentrating on the battle. They were trying to drag him off Hope's prone form, but he fought them distractedly, focusing on the real danger, the real terror.

He put all his will behind the motions of the beast, gifting it with what remained of his feeble strength.

It was over in seconds. The beast dodged another lunge by the Spectre and grabbed it by the throat, giving a powerful shake of its head and tossing the remains of its opponent aside like a broken doll. Fontana wanted to cheer, to point out the victory to the others and explain how he had helped, how he had prayed, but it was at that moment the world exploded.

Faith, who had worked her way through the chain to where Fontana was floundering about on Hope's helpless form, brought down a loose brick from the road in a punishing arc and drove it into his temple. The blow flattened him, removing all strength from his limbs and replacing the nightmare images in his mind with such a twisting, confusing swirl that he couldn't focus.

Those behind him lifted him free of Hope, paying no attention to the chain that bound him to them, and tossed him in the direction of another advance of the Spectres. They remembered very little of the past hours, but they remembered one thing very clearly. They remembered who had led them here, who had taught them to seek this "other" level. They also remembered seeing the slavers drag him, kicking feebly and crying like a baby, from beneath the kitchen sink in the rubble that had once been their compound.

Paying no attention to their captives, Sully and Din were busily fighting for their own souls. Each bore a blade forged of bound souls gathered by others like themselves, infused with powers and charms stolen from the less fortunate. These were the weapons of the slavers' trade, created to ward off Spectres and worse, and both men were adept in their use. Din swung his in a great arc, cleaving one of the creatures from shoulder to waist in one smooth motion. Sully was the more agile of the two. He held a shorter, rapier-like blade, and with it he skewered first one, then another of the attacking creatures. As each was destroyed, it screamed a final time, and each such scream robbed the defenders of another small portion of strength and courage. Even in death, the single-minded hatred of the creatures found its way insidiously into their hearts.

The Spectres never really fell. As they were defeated, their bodies slumped, whirling and losing cohesion until they disappeared completely, as if pulled into some giant vortex. One moment they were there, the next, simply gone.

The voices of the creatures called to Din and Sully's Shadows, called them home to nothingness. The fears dragged forth by the Spectres' eyes from each man's heart were driven like slivers of glass into their courage and concentration, fraying it slowly, wearing them down. That was the method of the Spectres, to distract just enough for the sharpness of fang and talon to come into play.

One of them broke past the guards and leapt at the chained prisoners with a withering scream. It swung a long, muscled arm at one of the slaves, a federal agent, ripping at the man's face with incredible speed and strength.

Sully cursed, diving to the attack, but he was too late. What had once been a strong, active man, an agent of the law in another place and time, was now a faceless, flopping thing. It dragged at the chains that bound it to the others, writhing and twisting in mindless pain.

Sully ripped into the Spectre, sticking his blade deftly through its throat and stifling its cry. It fell away from him, dispersing like a dark mist, and as if on cue, the attackers melted into the shadows.

The misting twilight faced them, as completely empty as before with no evidence that it had ever been full of screaming, scrabbling forms, hideous faces. Fontana, groggy but alive, was trying to rise to his knees, shaking his head slowly from side to side.

The other man was beyond help. Where he'd had a face, nothing remained but a sort of blubbery substance. No bone, no tissue or flesh. No blood. His hands were ripping at trailing bits of his form mindlessly, scratching at the sockets that had once held his eyes. An awful, gurgling hiss passed up his throat and dispersed into the night in burps of bloody bubbles, but no real sound emerged.

"Damn," Din muttered, coming to stand at the fallen prisoner's side. "First under quota, now we'll be slowed down by at least a couple of hours."

"Hey," Sully replied, shrugging and sheathing his blade, "it could've been worse. Never saw so many of those things all at once…hope I never do again. For a minute there, I wasn't sure if we were going to make it out or not."

"Times are changing, Sully," Din said, "and they're damned sure not changing for the better."

"Cut him loose now. We need to get him bundled up and get on our way…won't do to keep Bontempt waiting. I'd like to make it there in one piece and get me some rest."

They quickly removed the man from his chains, wrapped his form to hold him immobile, and handed him to the Archangels.

"You boys help your buddy along, now," Din grinned. "He'll feel lots better when he reaches that fire."

The four big captives stared back at the slavers with ice in their eyes. They took the burden on their collective shoulders without a shrug, but the challenge remained in their eyes. For them, it was far from over.

Moments later Din and Sully yanked Fontana back to his feet and dragged him to his place at the front of the line, sending him staggering down the road with a well-placed boot to his butt. He was beyond thought now, mindless as he'd called so many others, helpless as he'd never been before. They led him like an animal, and he followed like a dog, leading the way into shadow.

4

Love was seated on a low bench in the center of a huge chamber, flanked by several others and facing Llanna, who sat directly across some sort of small, ritual fire from him. She continued to stare at him, drinking in his presence like a thirsty woman in a desert crawling toward a mirage, reaching out for something beyond her reach. For a long time they just sat there. Then she began to question him.

She spoke softly, and seldom, coaxing him to tell them what had befallen those at the compound, of the Shadow-voice that had driven him forth and saved him just before they found him, and of the bird, with its one eye and its skeletal prey. He knew it was foolish to offer so much information to someone he'd known for such a short period, but there was something in her manner that put him immediately at ease. Perhaps it was the tragedy that swam in the depths of her eyes.

"You have learned much in a very short time," she told him at last. "Most never come into the strength you already possess. Most pass into Oblivion without finding this place at all."

"I need to find the others," he told her, "if they are here. I need to find Fontana. If anyone knows the answers to another level beyond this one, it is him."

Those around him began to mumble among themselves, just softly enough that they could hear one another and he could hear none of them. It was a habit that was beginning to annoy the hell out of him. Llanna was still staring, but an even deeper sadness seemed to fill her eyes.

"You need no prophet. You are the guide—the number one. The greatest strength is in the number one, remember. Those are your own words. The others, the one you call Fontana, a woman, and several weaker ones, were taken by slavers. These slavers work for a man named Bontempt, and he works directly for the Hierarchy. The captives are bound for the forges of Stygia, unless providence steps in. They are beyond your help. You must turn your mind toward the next level. You must be our guide."

Love felt a surge of hope in his heart. "You mean they are alive? They are here, in this place, as I am here?"

"None of them is as you," she replied. "I have been in this world for countless years, searching, always, for a way to ascend, to become one with unity. Even I, after all these years, am barely your equal in strength. It burns from you like a flame. The others are nothing."

"Fontana is more than that," he insisted. "They may have him, and he may be hurt—confined in some way—but if I have strength, it came through him. I must follow them. I must find a way to help them."

The voices of those around him rose in volume. Arguments that actually threatened to reach a decibel level he could understand broke out here and there. Llanna looked troubled, but she did not lower her gaze.

"You will do as you must. We will help—will follow to the ends of the Tempest and back again. You are the guide. First, though, we must prepare. This compound you speak of…we must go there. It is there that your ties will be strongest to the man that you were. Your strength can return to you, and we shall begin another temple in your honor."

"I have no time for that. I have to catch up with the others. They already have a head start."

"You will do no good on the road alone," she told him softly. "They will take you, as well. Worse yet, there are the Spectres, and other things of shadow. You would be lost as certainly as *we* would be lost without your guidance. After so many years, I will not allow that. We will help, but you must listen to our counsel. You are strong, but you do not realize your strength."

Though the delay grated on his nerves, he knew that she was right. He knew nothing about this place, not even where it actually *was*, let alone how to survive in it.

"This man, Bontempt, he is no friend of yours, I take it?"

"No. Bontempt is friend to no one but himself. He would destroy us, our temple, and everything we believe in if he were certain he would succeed. He has harassed us for years without making an outright attempt at a raid. He would like nothing better than to chain my soul to a dance slab in his palace and sell the rest to the Stygian merchants. He does not believe in a next level. His word for us is *Heretic*."

Now they were on familiar ground. Love had faced enough prejudice and persecution over his own beliefs to understand this.

"You have encountered a part of him already," Llanna continued softly. "You have met his second eye. That bird, its name is Cyclops. It still lives in the world you have left behind. What you saw, what we all see, is its future, the certainty of its blinding in one eye and eventual death. Bontempt controls it from this side, an ability he's developed through the years. When the bird is fully linked to him, it is no longer Cyclops, but Bontempt himself. The bird flies through the Skinlands, but Bontempt can see through its eyes into the Shadowland. He will know that you are here—no more than that—but he will know you when he sees you again.

"He would have us all plying his dark trade, or as cattle. He will never change."

The little green book against his chest seemed to lurch, or to move of its own accord, and with a start Love raised his eyes to Llanna's.

"Don't go changing, to try to please them," he muttered, taking another short excerpt from the prophecies without conscious thought. Fontana had replaced the "me" in the original quote to twist it toward the mindless. Never change because of what others think, but only because of what you believe. All this flashed through his mind in a second; then he had other things to worry about.

There was an almost audible snap, a link of some sort of energy, flowing from his fingertips toward Llanna, who looked as shocked as he himself. Her image shimmered, then wavered, then stabilized again. He felt the others moving about in confusion, some advancing toward him hesitantly, others scrabbling away as if he presented some sort of threat. He ignored them.

What he felt was an exchange, of sorts. He felt pain, emotional, cloying pain that wrapped about him and sapped the strength from his soul, and yet it was not his pain. He recognized, somewhere deep inside the moment, that it was Llanna's pain he felt, the source behind the perpetual grief of her eyes. He opened himself to it, taking it within him, and in turn bits and fragments of himself leaked back across the spanning burst of energy.

He floated in a dream world. There was nothing surrounding him, no light in the sky from sun or stars, no clouds. It was a deep, murky ocean of nothingness. Words and phrases wound their way through and around him, teasing him with answers that would not quite come into focus. There were eyes, many eyes—staring at him, questioning him, adoring him. He could feel the weight of all of them at once, the emotion that drove each gaze.

There were visions to accompany the slow, undulating motion of his darkness. Birds flew screeching from the haze to dive at his eyes. All of them were missing one eye of their own, their beaks and talons glittering ebony or bone white, alternating the light and the darkness. They swooped down to fill his gaze, then away, without a sound.

For sound he heard voices—some familiar, some new. He heard Fontana's words, the prophecy of the millennium, the apocalyptic message that had driven him to this next level. He heard Faith, echoing those words, heard the war-cries of the Archangels and the roar of automatic weapons fire. He heard explosions and watched them bloom to bright, blinding brilliance against a background of dripping red in the shape of a gigantic heart.

He wanted to clear his head. He wanted to be rid of the faces and voices that were not his own. Vaguely, he recognized the woman Llanna's eyes as they took center stage in the surreal otherworld that held him captivated. He sifted through her mind, experiencing her thoughts, her fears. Images formed, coalescing, shifting, changing and rearranging, drawing him into a vortex of memory and pain that was not his own.

He saw another face—dark, feral eyes. He saw pews and an altar, a church with dark, blood-stained glass windows and dripping messiahs hanging from crosses of hewn wood. He heard chanting, felt—through Llanna—hands dropping onto her shoulders.

The man wore a clerical collar. His dark eyes had a madness to them, a shine and a glitter that were not of sane thought but of fanatical abandon. The man—priest?—gestured to the front of the church. There was a pool, surrounded by dark stone and colorful tapestries, a blood-red baptismal pool laid out in the shape of an equal-armed cross, and, floating in it, swimming and undulating through the crimson liquid, were serpents. Hundreds of serpents.

He felt Llanna shudder as the man's hand left her shoulder and traveled down to a soft breast, groping, crushing. The source of the chanting was unclear, and he could feel Llanna's fear, a tangible, acidic tang that melted to the roof of his mouth and seeped through his being.

The images shifted, the congregation and the church faded away, leaving only the altar and the pool in focus…much nearer. The pool bubbled and churned beneath her, and she brushed helplessly at the hand that still caressed her, tracing the lines of both breasts and sliding down her side. Icy fingers probed and fondled her, violating her flesh absently.

Love watched in fascination, unable to react as the man's other hand dipped down quickly, snatching one of the serpents from the bloody pool to bring it dripping and writhing into the air.

Turning to stare back into the eyes that Love had borrowed, unwillingly, the man held out the snake to Llanna, offering it fangs first, offering its bite to her soft flesh. Love felt Llanna's head shaking a helpless negation of the inevitable, felt the urgency of her fear, the quickening of heart and breath, the certainty of judgment.

The snake struck, thrusting its fangs into and through her hand, blending and blurring with the image of her flesh. She grasped it instinctively, holding it tightly and pushing away from the man with all her inadequate strength as he continued to pull her closer.

EXCEPT YOU GO THROUGH SHADOW   445

The serpent pulled free and reared back, lunging once more to dig its teeth into her wrist. He saw/felt as it turned, suddenly, from slick, writhing serpent to flaccid flesh, felt her shame, her anger, as the glittering, soulless eyes and lips that smiled without emotion drove her into depths of shame, forced her to her knees.

His senses shifted slightly, and he felt the weight of the eyes of those who stood behind them, looking on, seeing nothing as their voices rose, continuing their chant. They could not see how the priest's manhood and the serpent had merged, could not witness the shame of what Llanna was forced to endure. They saw the serpent, and they thirsted for repentance.

Above them, the face of the messiah had come to morbid life, the wooden body stiff and unmoving, the face dark and animated with accusation dripping from its eyes, boring into Llanna's soul as the man held her by the hair and manipulated her. Those eyes somehow shifted the blame to her, bearing down on her oppressively. It was she who was weak. She was to blame. Her punishment was just.

That face changed, then, too. It took on Fontana's features, glaring down first in accusation, then in anger. Then the right eye began to fade, to whirl, losing consistency and falling inward until it was a cavern, an empty, lifeless socket. Words hammered at Love's mind, pounded at Llanna's soul, and he fought beside her, trying to force the visions away, trying to focus.

"Unclean…unclean…unclean…the serpents have judged her, the power is gone from her. He is with us now. Unclean."

There was more, all too fast, too intense, for Love to grasp. He reached within himself, grappled with and ripped free a reserve of strength he hadn't even been aware of, and wrenched himself from the vision, snapping tight the doors and windows of his mind. He crashed back into reality with brain-jarring suddenness.

It had lasted only a moment—a seconds-long eternity that bound and locked them one to the other. Somehow he knew that he'd witnessed a part of her past, a part of what had brought her here. He had felt the pull of those thoughts, those visions, dragging her back toward the life she'd lost, binding her to this shadowy place. He slumped on the seat, nearly falling over backward, and feet rushed forward, strong arms materializing to support him and hold him in place.

Llanna did not speak. She only sat, shocked, staring at him across the flickering flames of the fire. Her eyes, for a few moments, were clear and bright. Her lips slipped into an expression that nearly made it to a full smile before lapsing into her natural melancholy. It was a vision, a prophecy he wanted to fulfill. In that moment, she was free.

"What happened?" Love mumbled. "That man, who…" His head was muddled, confused with invading thoughts and memories that crowded his own. He tried to rise, to pull free of the hands that supported him, but the effort robbed him of his remaining strength, and he passed into a gentle darkness.

Rising to come and stand over him, kneeling beside his body, which had been placed softly on the bench in repose, Llanna reached out gently to lay her hands on his face. There were tears in her eyes, renewed pain, but rimmed by a small ray of hope that had not been there before.

"You have come at last," she said softly. Then, turning, she gestured for the others to follow, passing orders swiftly through the halls and into the rooms and chambers beyond. There was much to do, and little time for the doing. In a silent procession, they marched back out the doors of the temple, Love carried reverently in the center of the column, and they headed for the road, returning the way they'd come—the way Love had come—returning to the compound.

All that was living, all that existed beyond the Shadowlands, had vacated the area surrounding Fontana Farms. The feds had cleared out, leaving the dust and the desert animals to bury the remains of the massacre. The ruins of the buildings rose, torn and burned, pounded by explosives and riddled by gunfire. Dust swirled around the walls; desolate, empty windows peered out upon the desert like blinded, vacant eyes. Strangely, as they marched into the field of death, Llanna's followers smiled, walked more easily. It was a place of death, and they felt the ease of it, the comfort and the strength.

Llanna's scouts had reported back soon after being dispatched. For the moment, all was clear. Bontempt's slavers had taken what they'd come for, and they were off down the road to their own camp. Nothing moved or breathed in the compound as they entered, and yet there was a presence in the air, a sensation of comfort—of belonging.

The priestess knew that this was likely a holdover from her recent experience with Love's own memories, but it was still nice to have that feeling of closeness to the past. It was renewing, invigorating. It had been a long time since she'd belonged to anything but her pain, or the memory of that pain. Too long.

They moved silently among the ruined buildings, skirting broken walls and climbing over rubble. There was a sensation that drew her onward, a magnetic attraction to her soul. Somewhere just ahead, not far in, was the place where Love had left one world and leapt headfirst into the next.

They came through the remains of a doorway, and just inside, the column stopped. All eyes were trained on the same four-foot expanse of air, for there, hovering above the ruined and broken framework of a wall that no longer existed, it hung. The heart, the heart of the world, ripped free and clear, hanging and waiting. Somehow it had escaped the sight of the slavers, or perhaps it had not reappeared until Love was close once more.

As they watched, the image whirled, faster and faster, forming into a red, pulsing funnel and snaking across the dusty floor. There was a hiss as of released pressure, and a metallic snap, and it was gone. Completely. On the ground, where they had last seen the image, was a small, egg-shaped object.

Dazedly, Llanna moved forward to reach down and claim it, turning it over and over in her hands, caressing it gently and reverently. It was a grenade. A single fragmentation grenade, complete with pin. It did not have its dull, olive-drab coloring any longer, but was a shiny, glittering black, catching at stray bits of light and shimmering as she spun it about.

EXCEPT YOU GO THROUGH SHADOW

She turned to the others, and said, "Begin." No other words were needed. They had planned long enough for this moment to perform the coming tasks in their sleep. Indeed, many of them performed them endlessly, over and over, using the monotony of their own portion of the great work as a mantra against the hopelessness. It was a focus against the lack of faith that their own Shadows worked so hard to drive into the fabric of their beings.

Love's body was placed gently near the place he had fallen, laid before the broken, crumbled wall like a sacrifice before an altar. Then they began to move stones, to carry and place them, to mix a mortar from the sand and gravel that would hold it all in place. They did not have much time, but there was no need for sleep, no lack of material. It was possible to create a temple in a very short time. It would be nothing compared to the tower, but it would hold against the creatures of the night and Shadows long enough to make their plans. It would suffice.

They would soon embark on their long-awaited journey to the next level of existence, and they believed that on the next level there would be no need for such protections as walls and towers. Their guide had arrived. It was only a matter of time.

By the time Love awakened, they had a good portion of the lower walls repaired. No one had touched the wall beside him. No one had dared. He sat up groggily, shaking his head to clear the cobwebs, and looked about himself in amazement. It was the compound, and yet it was not. The walls they'd repaired stood where the walls he remembered had stood, but they were somehow different. They were taller, deeper, formed of a type of stone he'd never seen before, one that seemed carved from the stuff of shadows.

The entire place had a forbidding atmosphere that had been lacking in his previous existence—it was on a grander scale, stark against the backdrop of murky sky. He rose shakily and staggered over to where he'd sat during the battle. The hole he'd used as a vantage point had been sealed. He turned, remembering Faith's mad charge, the splatter of blood. The heart. He knew that the wall that no longer stood before him had taken his physical form with it. He knew that, just as all that remained of the stone was dust, all that remained of his former self was a memory. He knew this, and yet it was hard to face on any level that made sense, even more difficult with this dark, warped version of his old life surrounding him and swallowing him so completely.

Llanna stood watching him; the others ignored him studiously, bustling about and continuing at their tasks as if he were still unconscious. He felt their attention, just the same. He felt the weight of their need, of the hopes they now pinned on his shoulders.

He turned to Llanna, understanding mellowing the onslaught from the pain in her eyes. He remembered clearly their shared vision. Walking over to where she stood, he placed a hand on her arm gently.

"Who was he?" He did not name the dark pastor of her nightmares in any direct way, but they were connected, and she understood.

"He was a man of God," she replied bitterly. "He was my lover. He had the gift of handling the serpents; the power of salvation was in his voice. When I told him that I loved him, that I wanted everyone to know the joy he'd brought me, he became like black ice. He brought me before them as an adulteress. He told them I'd tried to seduce him, to give the dark one purchase on his soul.

"I denied his words, and he brought me to the serpents. He brought me to them for judgment, for condemnation, and he forced me to reach into their midst, just as he had begged me only nights before that to take him in my hands, my lips, my body. The serpents took my life, he took my soul. He still walks the roads of the other world, promising the road to heaven to any who will listen."

"He stole from you what you loved most," Love breathed, moving closer and embracing her softly. "The image of what you thought he was, what he offered." She allowed him to pull her closer, pressing forward against him. "Now you seek another guide? How can you trust me?"

"Remember," she said, pulling back, "I have seen your own past. I know your heart, as you know mine."

"Then you know that it is not I who is the prophet," he said. "We must follow them, free Fontana. It is the only way to reach another level than this."

She didn't answer, but another ghost-flicker of a smile passed across her lips. He wondered what she'd seen.

"We cannot start so soon," she told him. "There are things you need to learn, and you must gather your strength. You have an object of great power in your book—another has been offered. It is a sign."

"But how will we catch up to them?" he asked her, concern edging his voice.

As if in answer, the mournful howl of a train whistle broke the silence. She smiled. "There is more than one way, for one who has the courage—for one with your strength. Do not fear, we will catch them."

With this she held forth the grenade, and his eyes grew wide. It looked just as any other grenade would, other than the color, and yet he knew it for what it was. It was the key that had unlocked the door to where he now stood. He could feel the energy trapped within it as he took it into his hands, could sense the power rippling just beneath the dimpled surface.

"We will plan, and we will prepare. You will guide us, and we cannot fail. Prophecy is on our side."

He stared into her sorrow-filled eyes, and somehow, he believed.

"I am Love," he said softly. "I am the beast. I will rip out the heart of the world."

5

The huge encampment was visible for miles as they approached, both beckoning and repelling those in the chain as they drew nearer to it. What had obviously begun as a small base camp had sprung into a hurried, makeshift city. Tents, clap-trap cabins and all manner of strange buildings had sprung up around a central annex. There, within a withered, depressing garden of stick trees and failed blossoms, stood the palace.

If the rest of the encampment spoke of the temporary and the haphazard, the antithesis of this was the palace. It was squat, geometric and hard in design like a great, ebony crystal. The sides of the massive structure gleamed as though they had been polished, lined at the top by a long string of guard towers and messenger stations. In two words: repulsive, impressive. That was how Fontana's mind summed it up.

His thoughts were a mixture of relief and dread, considering their situation. He'd known that they would not be forced to march on indefinitely, that there was a definite goal in mind. Now that this goal was in sight, he couldn't decide whether to yearn for rest or to fear imminent destruction.

He had moved for a long time in a pained daze, the throbbing of his head where Faith had brought down the brick synchronizing slowly with the forced pace of the slave chain. He remembered what had happened on the road vaguely, remembered the terror that had gripped him, remembered crawling over Hope to escape, and he remembered the quiet darkness. Of all that he remembered, it was those few moments of peace, floating free and beyond the concerns of whatever world this was, that he latched onto. He might not be able to die, but there was peace to be had—peace in Oblivion. It would not become an immediate goal, but it was nice to know that it was an option. Then he remembered the federal agent, bound and trussed, a mindless, still-heaving pile of flesh, and he wondered anew. Could he die?

The closer they got, the more depressing their predicament became. There was movement in the camp, lots of it. Smaller shadows moved through the gloom of those cast by the larger buildings, crawling over every roadway and surface like vermin. That was how they looked at first: indistinct and dark. On closer inspection, they were just as dark, though extremely varied.

There were women, children, large, armored men such as their guards, and scrawny, hollow-eyed captives, chained and led about or working at any number of mind-numbing tasks. The walls of the palace were still being finished off, and there was a huge group of slaves working at the task. There were vendors, shops, merchants peddling all sorts of unclean, filthy wares.

Here and there were hints of otherworldliness, all decayed, all crumbling and dying. These bits and pieces of what he'd left behind were the only truly familiar things they'd encountered, but Fontana tried not to think about them. He might have spent some time wondering what this place was the ruins of, but he wanted to concentrate on his own particular predicament. Saving his own ass was the priority.

The others behind him stared about themselves, lost in their own thoughts, some in apparent awe, others in a listless, hopeless stupor. He paid them no mind.

As they approached the limits of the camp, the two beasts that had saved them from the Spectres cut off at a signal from Sully, melting back into the rocks and shriveled trees. Soon after, Fontana heard the sound of their cries echoing through the murky air, and answering cries from elsewhere in the shadows. He tried to imagine a den of such creatures, a pack, and shuddered. He was only glad to be, however low on the chain, on the same side as they were, at least for the moment.

On the outskirts of the camp there were mostly tents. Their flaps hung limp in the absence of wind, even though in the distance the small whirling storms were still visible. Vacant eyes stared out from the depths of each tent, a few doorways filling with pale, wavering faces, a few flaps being pushed aside by thin, skeletal hands. Whispered voices floated through the emptiness, words that did not link up in sentences, but that filtered through his thoughts just the same.

"New meat."

"Stygia, they will go to the forge."

"The woman will hit the slabs…"

Interspersed with these fragmented sentences was laughter. Some of it was light, almost musical, some sinister. Fontana felt the weight of many eyes. Apparently he and the others had formed the first diversion these creatures, for that was what they appeared, had enjoyed in a great while—the first spectacle to relieve the boredom of the solitary, empty plains. He did not like the images their words formed in his mind…forges, flames, slave chains. He could make no more sense of the messages that might await him there than he had of the bantering comments of his captors, but the single-minded darkness of it all was beginning to wear at what remained of his courage.

Then they moved into more permanent structures. Here there were actual streets. Armed guards glanced their way, grinning and joking, calling out to Din and Sully in comfortable, familiar jocularity.

"Worthless lot, eh, Din?" one exceptionally large and ugly guard called out. "Maybe if Bontempt likes the one at the end, he'll overlook the quality of the take."

The man's leer left no doubt he was talking about Faith. Fontana risked a quick glance back, and in that instant he met her eyes. It was a mistake. He nearly stumbled at the intensity that burned there, the hatred. She had been staring at him, boring into him with her eyes. She paid no attention to those around her, though she did turn to swat at a hand that groped from the shadows toward her butt. The motion nearly sent the chain, which was mired in the steady plodding rhythm that had carried it so far, into a headlong tumble. Laughter erupted all around, and a few cheered her from the doorways of shops as they passed.

It seemed that, if Fontana's only goal was freedom and the betterment of his own position, Faith had another. He was her focus, and the thought made him cringe. He'd seen the type of enemy she could be in the compound, in the battle that had become the war.

They seemed to be headed directly for the palace, but at the last moment they turned aside. Sully continued on with the chain, directing them down a row of bleak, ramshackle buildings that had the look of barracks, or kennels. Din headed on up the steps of the palace and disappeared within. Fontana watched for a second, until the hulking form of the guard disappeared, then returned his attention to the immediate.

Sully looked somehow relieved. Though he still lashed out at his captives, both physically and verbally, there was a jocularity to his words, a spring to his step, that had not been present earlier. Fontana could only suppose that the strange, exotic smells of food and the thought of a bit of rest were the reasons for it.

They came to a halt in front of a derelict building that rose up from the dingy shadows, its dull metal sides reflecting no light. The door hung half off its hinges, and the windows were coated in the dust of the plains, blown in from the desert-like surroundings and ignored. Sully walked down the length of the chain quickly, cuffing his charges into silence and calming them into a sort of post-march daze. This was obviously their new home, at least for the moment. It didn't look very inviting, but anything, Fontana told himself, was better than more days on that road.

Two squat, evil-looking men melted from the surrounding shadows and approached Sully, their eyes gleaming.

"New meat for us, eh?" one of them gibbered. "New toys for the boys, eh?"

"You'd better keep your filthy paws off 'em," Sully growled. "Especially the one in the middle. They're here for Bontempt, as well you know, and he would take ill to your mistreatment of his property."

There were no further words from the newcomers, but their grins widened perceptibly. Fontana placed no faith in their fear of this man 'Bontempt' keeping them at bay. He decided that, at least for the moment, he would spend what little concentration his throbbing head would allow on keeping his distance from the new guards.

He was forced upon their attention for the moment, though, as the two grabbed the front of his chains and yanked hard, dragging them all toward the front of the building. Fontana stumbled forward, tripping through the doorway and into the gloomy interior. He barely managed to remain on his feet and nearly brained himself on the frame of the door, which was obviously constructed for the convenience of the squat guards and not that of the prisoners.

The interior, if anything, was even less inviting than the outside of the building had been. There were literally no furnishings. There were walls, a roof, dingy, murky windows and stagnant air. It was immediately obvious that, rather than a shelter against the weather or any sort of dangers that might have arisen, the place was a holding pen. It would have seemed ludicrous, considering the decay and disrepair of the structure itself, had it not been for the chains. Otherwise the structure would not have held a small child, let alone an adult. It was the weight of what lay outside and the memory of the road that would hold them inside. That and the cold, black rings of metal embedded in the floor—a floor which seemed to be the one point of structural soundness invested in the place.

Before he could mouth a protest, Fontana felt himself removed from the chain and thrust forcibly into the shadows, where he came up hard against one of the walls. He heard the others being treated similarly, felt the impact of flesh on the wall beside him as first Hope, then Charity slammed into it. He did not raise his head, though he could hear their moans and cries of pain and fear.

There was nothing he could do; he couldn't help them. It was best for them all to try to remain in one piece. Silence, lack of motion, these were his protection here. Any resistance would not only be futile, but might result in yet more pain, and he'd had more than enough of that.

452   DAVID NIALL WILSON

In the background he could hear a scuffle, followed by deep laughter and Faith's cursing. He didn't know if the guards had tried something with her, or she with them, but again he felt a pang of jealousy. She was so much stronger. Not particularly bright, but strong. He did not raise his head to see what might have happened, or what success she might have had. He pressed his forehead into the wall and concentrated on disappearing, becoming invisible. It was a meager protection against what might come, but it was all that he had.

Bontempt stared down at Din from his high seat—his *throne*, as he called it—with disdain.

"I will want to see the female tonight," he said somberly. "Bring her in and chain her to the central slab...we will see if we have gotten a bargain or another chain of garbage."

Din, large and powerful as he was, was sweating. He'd told his leader about the one "fresh one" that had escaped, fully expecting that he and Sully would find themselves chained to the next outgoing shipment to Stygia, but nothing had happened. Bontempt had let out a quick grunt, not even surprised, and that had been it. For several long, labored breaths, Din had waited to feel his fate smacking him in the back of the head, or skewering him from below as some secret trap was set off, but nothing was forthcoming. He described their take, much as he had a hundred times in the past, told Bontempt of the attack and the fending off the Spectres, and awaited his orders. Nothing seemed to have changed.

"I already knew of the lost one," Bontempt told him softly. There was something about the man's voice, the way he understated everything, waiting for you to fill in the rest with your imagination, that made the skin crawl. "He and Cyclops had a short meeting. Interesting specimen, that. He will come, make no mistake. He will come to free his friends, and we'll take him. It is just a matter of time.

"You did well against the Spectres. I've lost four good men now, two more while you were out, to their attacks."

"Thank you, my lord," Din said, lowering his head still further. "I will see that the woman is brought to you."

There were no further words, so he began to step backward, keeping his head lowered and his shoulders slumped. It was difficult to keep one's composure when meeting the one glaring eye their leader possessed, but it was equally difficult to avoid it without appearing disrespectful. Any action or reaction in Bontempt's presence could be a mistake.

When he had made his way out of the doors of the main chamber and into the passages of the palace, Din relaxed somewhat. Another mission, another time he would be allowed to keep his skin intact...time for a little relaxation. He would find Sully, tell him how it had gone, and get the orders to that worthless lot out at the kennel about the woman. Smiling to himself, he thought that if she was half as energetic on the slab as she'd been on the chain, it might be an interesting evening indeed.

Except You Go Through Shadow

The chains that were attached to the dancing slabs were of a different sort than those used for transport. They were just as strong, coming straight from the Stygian forges, but there were properties intertwined in their links that the lesser, utilitarian chains lacked.

Those on the slabs would sap the prisoner's free will. No matter how strongly a prisoner fought, no matter how independent their spirit, they would do as they were told while chained to the slab. Their mind might be protesting inside, screaming out for release, for their body to stop betraying the heart and mind that once guided it, but it would be to no avail.

Bontempt was ready for some entertainment. The woman would dance, and the hatred burning in her eyes would make the sight all the more enticing.

There was the upcoming journey to think of, as well—it would be good to get in some pleasant distraction before then. If it had been difficult to bring the prisoners here, the trip to the borders of Stygia, where the final bargaining would be done before they shipped their take off to the forges, would be brutal. The farther they went toward the borders of the Shadowlands, the less their control over the roads, or their own fate. If the Spectres were attacking now in the Shadowlands, they were certain to be heavily concentrated farther out.

Din and Sully were scheduled for the next trip in, along with two others and a double-length string of captives. There would be a sled of incapacitated "fresh ones" as well, like the one who'd met with the Spectre's claws out on the road. They would be slowed by the extra weight until those healed, but it would pay off if they could manage to make their way through on time and intact. Everything was a gamble—Din loved to gamble. By the time he spotted Sully on his way back from the "kennel," he was almost smiling for the first time in days.

"Got 'em all locked away?" he called out, hurrying his steps a bit.

"Tight as can be," Sully grinned. "Don't know if I trust the two watching them to keep their hands to themselves, but other than that they're safe enough. Sometimes I wonder where that lot was dug up, and why Bontempt keeps them around. What did Bontempt say?"

Din gave him a quick rundown on the meeting, adding that they needed to stop back for a moment and have the woman from the chain sent on ahead for the evening.

"I think he's got some sort of party planned," Din concluded. "There were a lot of extra tables set up, and Bontempt seemed a little distracted. Maybe if she's as good as she looks to be, we'll end up with a bonus."

"I'd settle for a couple of weeks off the road and a good bottle of Stygian whiskey," Sully muttered. "I'm in no hurry to get back to that Spectre-infested nightmare out there."

"Especially with that sorry bunch in tow," Din added. "And you can bet that Bontempt will keep the woman behind."

They walked together to the front of the kennel and called out to the guard, passing on Bontempt's instructions. The disappointment in the two men's faces was apparent. They had had their own plans, it seemed, for the saucy little captive that night, despite their orders to the contrary.

454   DAVID NIALL WILSON

Too bad, Sully thought grimly. *Don't like these guys, anyway. What kind of job is that, hanging out in a building that smells of all the souls that died in it and torturing "fresh ones" until they cart the poor sods off to their doom?*

The smelly bastards gave him the creeps almost as badly as Bontempt's damned eye.

With a shrug that said their work for the day was done, Sully and Din turned and walked off toward the tavern on the corner. The two guards, grumbling, returned to the building to fetch their master's prize, already planning how they would take their frustration out on the others.

Fontana heard them coming back, as he'd heard them leave, and he pressed himself into as small a ball as possible, rolling back against the wall and trying to will himself into invisibility. He heard them stomping about, heard their cursing, voices low and menacing as they grated through the stagnant air. He heard Faith's protest, followed by the sound of a sharp slap and more cursing. The woman was a fool.

A few moments later the door opened again, and Fontana risked a quick look. Silhouetted in the door was Faith's writhing form, held tightly between the two short, muscular guards. They held her by short lengths of chain they'd attached to the collar around her neck and the manacle on her ankle, and the restricting bonds prevented her from putting up any kind of real struggle. The three were visible for only a moment, then the door slammed shut again and the sudden loss of light blinded him momentarily.

After Din had left him, Bontempt sat for a long time, staring off at the slick, shiny walls that surrounded him and watching himself stare back with one glaring eye. He did not bother to put a patch over the empty socket where his other eye had been. He enjoyed watching others squirm, watching them do anything within their power to avoid his stare, to avoid making some gesture of disgust or expression of revulsion that would send them to their doom. He would not have taken back that eye for any amount of money—its absence had proven too valuable.

On the back of his chair, Cyclops sat. The chair was a remnant of the Skinland fortress that had stood on the same ground when Bontempt had been alive, and it was solid on the other plane as well—though no walls surrounded it, and it was rotting away. It had been his father's chair.

The bird's own gaze was restless, scanning the corners, head bobbing back and forth, never still. He could sense its thoughts. If he concentrated, he could blend the images of the bird's one good eye with that of his own and see images that evaded the sight of his subordinates, and at times, of his enemies. The bird was another asset.

This fresh one that had escaped itched at the back of his mind for some reason. There was no reason to expect that the man would cause any trouble. He hadn't been in Bontempt's world long enough to pose a real threat. It was his disappearance that worried the slaver, that and the odd glow that had arisen from the small book the man was carrying. It was some sort of Artifact, that much was certain, and it had power to spare. In untrained hands something of that sort could be more dangerous than an encampment full of Spectres. And now the guy was just gone. Disappeared.

It had to be the Heretics. That tower had spawned more problems and brought him more grief than any dozen enemies in his past. They were fanatical in their beliefs, and their beliefs were preposterous. An afterlife to the afterlife. Another level. They wanted to sail off into the Tempest in search of somewhere that did not exist. The problem was, too many of them believed.

Even a few of his own men had defected, following after that skinny little witch Llanna like she was some sort of mystical shepherdess who would lead them all away. Bontempt fully planned to take them all away, when the opportunity presented itself. He would take them away for good—all but Llanna. He had other plans for her, plans that did not involve forge fire, but chains. Plans that did not involve destruction, but bondage.

He wistfully remembered a time when such problems would not have been a factor. When Charon had been in control, the Heretics had been on the run. Things had been better. It was good to be on his own, to lead his own men, but at times he missed the security of the Legions.

Concentrating on the image of the fresh one who'd disappeared, he shrugged his shoulder slightly, and the bird took to the air. It soared up and up, passing right through the glittering ceiling of the building. Cyclops was not of this world. The restraints that bound those of Bontempt's camp, himself included, did not bind the bird. If the one he sought was still within range, Cyclops would find him.

"Find him," he sent his thoughts trailing after the bird's flight. "Find him and lead him to me."

When the bird had disappeared, Bontempt returned his gaze to the wall in front of him and let his mind wander. The evening would arrive soon, and there was much to do, much to plan. It was going to be a long night.

Love heard two sounds simultaneously, a crow's mournful cry and a train whistle heading off into the distance. He knew by now that that train was his best hope of finding Fontana, his best shot at making up the lost ground and avoiding Bontempt's agents along the way. He'd heard enough from Llanna and the others about what was to be expected by those who were captured to last him a lifetime. That was, if what he'd awakened to could in any way be likened to a lifetime.

He had decided that he do whatever they required of him, as long as it led, in the end, to wherever Fontana and the others were being held. He owed his life to these strange people, but he owed what that life meant, where it had led, and might lead beyond this point, to Fontana.

The makeshift temple had shot up around him with alarming speed. It didn't seem possible that so much could be accomplished so quickly with so little to

DAVID NIALL WILSON

work with. It was dizzying and disorienting, a constant reminder that he was not in his own world. He kept mulling this over and over to himself as the walls engulfed him, as the slight luminescence of the dingy, twilit sky disappeared in favor of a roof of slimy black stone, mulling it over and trying to find a way to come to grips with it.

He also discovered that, solid as they might look, the parts of the old compound that were still visible did not have substance for him. It was confusing at first, if he didn't pay attention. He found himself putting his hand out to steady himself and falling through doors and walls, only to come up hard against others that were new. He could stand in the middle of a brick wall and feel nothing but a slight tingle.

He hadn't asked where their building materials came from, but they'd told him anyway—part of his training. That training had actually started when he'd stepped on the stone in the road. Now he couldn't look at a single wall, a single brick, without wondering who it might have been. Had it been chained, as his friends were, or had it been dissipated in some grand, underworld war that he knew nothing about? Christ.

At least Llanna wasn't a slaver. Their material was stolen, taken in trade, bartered in the nearby cities for what was left of those of Bontempt's lot that were taken. It didn't lessen in any way his discomfort at the idea of walking on the souls of the dead, but it made dealing with his newfound "followers" a bit more bearable.

In life, Love had always had the uncomfortable feeling that he took death too lightly. Others would mourn the passing of those close to them, but Love would just go on with his life. Funerals were gatherings of the living to meet their various needs, not the tributes to the dead he believed they should be. Death was death. The body ended, the spirit went on. So he'd believed. He wondered how a few of the evangelists he'd encountered in his life would take to the idea that they might end up a cinder block on the road to heaven.

Preparations for the expedition to come had been going on pretty steadily since they'd left the tower. At first there had been some dissent among the ranks—it seemed they were in a hurry to get to the next level. From recent experience, Love could have given them an earful about that, but they wouldn't have listened.

Little Green Book, chapter two, page fourteen, verse two...*Be careful what you ask for, you just might get it.* Amen to that.

Llanna was the strength of the entire operation. It was she who convinced the others, she who made them see that, if he was their guide, they would have to follow, whether his journey led into the Tempest or the very citadels of Stygia herself. To try to tell the prophet, she'd said, what he was supposed to do, or say, was foolish. What need did they have of a guide if they already knew the answers?

Love hadn't argued with her, though he'd wanted to reiterate the fact that it was Fontana who was the prophet. He'd spent his time talking to anyone who would answer his questions, sorting it all out, and going through the prophecies. The words had always held meaning for him, but they seemed to have taken on a sort of magic in this realm, and he figured it would be good to have some control over that before they got into something he wasn't prepared, otherwise, to handle.

It was such a period of meditation that took him outside the new temple and back to the formation of rocks where he'd been headed when he first awakened to this new "life." He needed solitude to come to grips with the fact that, if he failed in what was to come, he would truly be on his own, the best shot these folks had. That was a lot to think on.

Was he leading them on? Was he just using them, twisting their belief to fit his own needs because he was too weak and inexperienced here to succeed without them?

When he left the compound, he just kept walking. He didn't really plan his route, and his feet just seemed to carry him back down a familiar path as his mind wandered. He recognized the outcropping of rocks where he'd hidden, and when he reached it, he settled himself back into place among the boulders and drifted off. It wasn't the most comfortable seat, but it was quiet.

He wasn't really worried about his safety. Llanna and the others weren't far away, and she said she hadn't detected any activity in the "real" world that would drag the slavers back. They were sent out in teams to collect when there was a site or event that brought about death on a grand scale, or destruction of any sort. That was when the greatest number of new souls would find their way into the Shadowlands, and it was the only time risking the roads was worthwhile to the slavers.

The compound, the crumbled, real-world ruins that had housed Fontana and his small band of followers, was now bleak and bare. Fontana had chosen it for his headquarters for the very reason that now rendered this a fairly safe place in this other existence. There were nearby towns, certainly, but not large ones, and not *that* near. The ruins of Fontana Farms would serve as nothing more than a haven for wild animals and a tourist attraction for the morbid. No reason Bontempt or his minions would come this far: there was no profit in it.

The loud caw of a crow and the sudden flutter of wings brought him out of his reverie and to his feet, crouching. It was the bird, what had Llanna called it, Cyclops? It was back, perched right where it had been perched the first time he'd seen it. How had the damned thing found him? How had it known he would come back, that he would find this place again?

This time it seemed aware of his presence. It was fixing him with all the intensity of its hollow, one-eyed stare, and he had the feeling that it thought of him in much the same manner that it had thought of the mouse it had killed at their previous meeting. He couldn't tell what other malevolence might be hidden behind that gaze, but he could feel another presence, an aura of hatred.

"What do you want, you bastard?" he grated, taking a menacing step toward the creature. It didn't budge an inch, just continued to stare fixedly at him. There was an intelligence swimming in the depths of that eye, a brooding aura of dark intent that sent shivers running up and down Love's back. This was no ordinary bird. In fact, he felt a different sort of presence, a probing, hungry *otherness* that reached out to him across the small space that separated him from the bird, calling to him.

"Go on," he shouted, running forward and waving his arms at the thing. It ignored him, and when he had come close enough to swing and strike at it, his hand passed on through as if there was nothing there. All he felt was a slight ripple—like a breath of icy wind—and his arm continued on, burying up to his shoulder in the ethereal Skinland stone.

He staggered back, keeping a wary eye on the bird, who strutted in a small semi-circle to keep him in sight. Love felt a tugging, as if something were scratching away at the surface of his mind, reaching within him for something—something he could remember, but that he couldn't control. Something dark, just beneath the surface. He fought to keep the probe out, to swing his own gaze to the side, or to fall to the ground—anything that would break the contact.

Then it started. Within him, he felt a presence building. A black, empty piece of his own mind had begun to answer the bird's summons, clawing its way toward the surface. Another chunk of memory snapped into place. The Shadow, that was the voice that he recognized as his own, and at the same time as wholly alien as anything else in this realm. It was whispering to him in that deep, seductive voice even now.

"You must release yourself," it said, insinuating fingers of alien thought into the widening gaps that separated his own. "You will be better off. The others are nothing. This one has power."

He felt his determination wavering, felt his strength begin to ebb. Between the continuing onslaught from the bird's one good eye and the burrowing, sinuous motion of whatever was trying to escape from within him, his defenses were crumbling.

He could sense the desire, the hunger that dripped from the darkness like rotted syrup. It wanted control. It wanted to make *him* the insignificant half-being, to disembody his spirit and take up the reins of his body. Somehow this was clear. He knew that whatever shadowy portion of his own being he might be losing control of, it did not truly want him to give in to this bird-thing. It wanted him for itself.

A heat was growing against his chest. At first it was only a glow, a slight distraction, and he cursed it—ignored it. As his struggle grew more intense, though, the heat grew as well, soaking through him, searing him, driving against his concentration and splintering it with ease. He cried out in desperation, finally managing to release the tensed muscles of his legs and collapse to knees.

He clutched at his chest, clawing at the center of the heat, the center of the pain that was robbing him of his senses. He could still feel the Shadow beating against the insides of his mind, but it was subdued, diminished by the instinct of survival that now drove his thoughts. The Shadow could not reach him. Only the pain could, and the certainty that he must end it. His clawing hands came up against leather, brushed against the sharp edges of the pages as the book flipped open.

Words leapt to the air, words he knew—words he could recite backward and forward, and yet that had not occurred to him only seconds before. *The eyes are the wells of the soul.*

EXCEPT YOU GO THROUGH SHADOW   459

The letters swirled and dipped, glittering with bright green luminescence and dancing before him. He watched, fascinated, as they began to move faster, to whirl, drawing themselves into a small funnel that emanated from the now-open pages of the book.

The bird cried again and he glanced up, startled. He'd forgotten his danger, momentarily. The creature was squawking, leaping into the air and attempting to flee, but the whirling words were surrounding it, dragging it down. His own inner battle forgotten for the moment, Love staggered to his feet, taking a step forward. He couldn't hurt the creature, but it seemed that it could be hurt all the same.

There was a terrific snap of energy as the funnel sucked itself back between the pages of the book, letters blurring to green, glowing trails as they passed from sight. The bird gave a last great flap of its wings, ripping free and careening to the side, where it plowed headlong into the stone of the rocky outcropping and veered off to the side. Love tucked the book away quickly and followed, but by the time he rounded the stone the bird was in clumsy, lopsided flight, obviously injured but alive.

Cursing, he sat back against the rock and watched until it had become a speck on the horizon. The memory of the chilly, hopeless feeling of shadows clawing their way through his mind returned to him with mind-numbing suddenness. He remembered now how that voice had led him from the compound, how it had stolen his control before and left him drained and quivering with exertion. Now it seemed that this part of him that he couldn't control would not stop at selling him out to the enemy for its own ends, whatever those might be.

He leaned back for a few more moments, catching his breath and clutching the book to his chest like the talisman it had obviously become. How it had saved him, he did not know, but he was certain that it had. When it had been words with meanings that could be ferreted out and understood, then applied rationally, prophecy had seemed a safe, protective thing. Now, seeing the strength embodied in the small green volume he carried, he wondered if he was up to the task of controlling it, if he truly had enough "vision" to know what was right and what would lead to disaster. He'd certainly come close enough to the latter this time.

Wearily, he stumbled to his feet and headed back to the new "temple," which his mind stubbornly imagined as the compound. Maybe Llanna would have some of the answers he sought. If nothing else, he could report that, though alive, Cyclops the one-eyed blackbird was on the injured reserve list. It was a start.

"What you experienced," Llanna said softly, "was your Shadow. Everyone here has a darker spirit within them, some more powerful than others. Perhaps it is time that I gave you a bit more background on your situation."

Her sorrowful eyes twisted the smile that followed her words, but Love was beginning to be able to see past the surface and read what was inside. Everything here spoke loudly of death, every scent in the air, every sight that met the eye. Even those who were "alive" here, such as it was, had a dark, brooding quality to their being. Everything was tainted by decay and pain. Everything. The hardest part to get used to, though, was how easily his new "self" accepted it.

"We call ourselves wraiths," Llanna began, beckoning for him to sit. They were in an inner court of the compound, a place where Fontana had begun a small garden. A place for meditation, he'd called it. What remained was a couple of crumbling, moss-encrusted stone benches, several withered trees, and a flooring of matted, grayish vegetation that smelled vaguely of rot, like the outskirts of a swamp on a hot, humid day. Love took the proffered seat and settled back to listen.

"This world is not so different as you might believe from the one you left behind. There are governments, laws, cities, even businesses. Bontempt is in such a business; he collects souls. He collects them and packages those he cannot use himself for shipment to Stygia, where he trades them for things he needs.

"Out here in the desert, so far from the cities, he has more control than he might elsewhere. It is the reason he puts up with seclusion. At one time he held a high office in the Legions, commanded a large portion of Stygia's forces, in fact. He was never very stable, and he slowly began to fall from grace. With his spirit of evil and his love of violence and pain, he fell naturally into the shadow trade.

"Your friends' fate might have been different had they died closer to the cities. More of them might have escaped, as you did, and it is likely that they would have fallen in with free wraiths, rather than coming to the slavers so easily and in such numbers. Most of us began our time here in chains of one sort or another; it is the way of the Shadowlands.

"My own Shadow would take me back to the depths of Stygia if I gave in to it. When I lived there, I worked my way up in the ranks until I ran a small way-station on the outskirts of Stygia. In the way of this world, I was successful, I suppose. My services, and those of my thralls, were coveted by men and women in high places...I could have had pretty much anything I wanted back then. Anything but freedom from it all. In the end, I took those who would follow, and I fled.

"We had our beliefs, but we had no direction. All we could do was to build our tower and to send our people out, send them in every imaginable direction, in search of the answers we knew must be there. Then you and your comrades built your compound, so close to our temple that from the highest of our towers you could look out, concentrate, and see it.

"We came to that place almost as soon as you did. I have walked its corridors with you, listened as the words fell into place, and seen the light of power in your eyes. We also saw what was to come, the destruction. We knew it was a sign to us, that you would be delivered at that time, so we waited.

"We could not manifest ourselves directly with the slavers already there. They had a pair of soul-snatchers with them, very powerful wraiths who have been given another shape and bound to it, feeding on those that they destroy. They have no will but Bontempt's.

"Your Shadow managed to free you. For that you should be thankful. Mine would have cast me into their arms in the confusion. We all have our battles to fight. I have seen your Shadow, and you mine, though you did not realize it. That darkness, that part of me that wanted to give in to the man that sent me here, that part of me is my Shadow."

Love sat and thought in silence for several moments before he responded. "You mean, the cities I left behind, the people that still live in the other world, they are here as well? I can see them?"

"We are separated from them by a barrier we know as the Shroud," Llanna replied, "but for the most part you can see them, or a version of them, from here. You will see them as you see this place, as you saw Bontempt's bird—you will see them as they will die. If they are close to death, you will know it. If they will die violently or in pain, it will be written on their faces.

"Some wraiths have grown so far in the power of this plane that they can visit the 'real' world—the Skinlands. I can manipulate small things there myself, and you have seen how Bontempt has managed to make his roving second eye from a living creature that he controls from this side.

"Though this looks to be a dead place, there is much of life left it in. Sometimes I believe that it is only the worst of life that remains to us, but it is a part, nonetheless, of what we have lost. You may find it harder to let go of than you think, despite your readiness to leave that place."

Love smiled back at her. "That was before I knew what my next level would be. This is not the paradise that Fontana told us to strive for, I am certain of it. Maybe you're right. Maybe we do need to strive onward, to look for the level we sought when we ended up here. Maybe this is just another crossroads."

She shrugged and continued to smile. Neither of them spoke for several long minutes, but instead they sat and just enjoyed the moment's peace the other's company could afford. There would be little peace in what was to come, that much was certain.

"So," Love said at last, "if this Bontempt knows about me now, am I in more danger, or am I still too insignificant to matter?"

"I'm afraid you have caught his attention in a way that can't be ignored," she answered. "If you truly injured Cyclops, then you have caused Bontempt himself pain. It is certain, at the very least, that he now knows about your book, and about the powers of the prophecies you carry. He will want that book for himself. It is a very powerful Artifact."

Love pulled the book free. It looked much as it had when he'd carried it through the sunlight of the Skinlands. Now, with no danger threatening and no urgent need in his mind, the flickering fire of the letters was muted. It was difficult to believe it had blazed so brightly only a few hours before.

"It was destroyed with you," she explained. "It was the one thing in your presence that meant the most to you, and you were able to bring it through with you. It is my thought that the belief of the others is manifested in its power here, as well. Kind of like using them all as a wellspring for your own power. It would explain much of the abilities you possess that one so young to the Shadowland should not.

DAVID NIALL WILSON

"There are many such items here in the Shadowlands. Some manufactured in Stygia have particular purposes that pertain to this world; others that were destroyed in the Skinlands have properties unique to that destruction, and to those who wield them. Their value is immense.

"They are linked to their original 'life' much as we are. In the case of the prophecies, I believe the book has survived because the words within it have not yet served their purpose. That is why I am so certain you can lead us to our goal. The book has come with you, so your journey is not complete."

"Bontempt's citadel," Love began. "Are we going to be able to get in and out of there to help the others without being caught ourselves?"

"We will not need to," Llanna smiled. "We know him too well. He will spend a few days gathering several chains of thralls together, then he will send them out on the road with a contingent of his men to travel the Tempest to Stygia. He has men in his command with the ability to make it there and back, if they remain on the outskirts of the city, and they will barter for what they can get from the agents of the Hierarchy for him. He does this on a regular basis, and there are only a few more days until his next shipment is due to leave.

"When they slip inside the Tempest, we will follow. Among those who believe is a man named Seth…a tracker. He knows the ways of the Tempest as well as any, its dangers and pitfalls. We must go expecting trouble—the slavers are not the worst of what roams there. We will be starting in two days' time."

Love felt a burst of relief. He hadn't known how the time spent here, idle and doing nothing, had weighed upon him. Every new story of horror and suffering that he heard only served to remind him of what Fontana and the others must be going through. The more he learned about this place, the more difficult it became to remember from whence he'd come.

He hoped Llanna was right in one respect. He hoped that whatever had happened between him and that damned bird had driven this asshole Bontempt to his knees. Somehow he felt that the confrontation between himself and the one-eyed slaver was far from over, and that was fine with him. Most of what had happened that was wrong since he'd arrived in this place could, in one way or another, be attributed to Bontempt. The slaver would have plenty to answer for when they finally came face to face. Maybe that would be the time to find out if someone in this world could die.

Bontempt's screams echoed through the entire palace, driving hands to ears and feet to pavement with staggering swiftness. When the first of his guards burst into his chamber, they found their leader stumbling about the floor, both hands pressed against the empty socket of his lost eye as if he'd been stabbed. There was no evidence of intruders or any attack, and yet Bontempt was screaming in unearthly pain, screams that nearly drove all who were near him to their knees just with the intensity of the sound.

They surrounded him warily, not getting close enough for him to flail his arms and strike them, but close enough to prevent him from running headlong into a wall, or into his "throne." There was none among them who was interested in tackling their leader physically, or in trying to restrain him. Bontempt was large, violent, and strong. If he was now crazy as well, then he was that much more dangerous.

As they waited, steering him clear of sharp objects and solid walls, his gyrations slowed, and he finally sank to his knees in the center of them, hands still pressed to the side of his face as if they were the only thing holding him together. His screams were fading, first to moans, then to curses that threatened to grow in violence and volume beyond even the heights his screams had attained.

He staggered to his feet, noticing those around him for the first time, noticing their stares and their bewildered expressions. He tensed, nearly vibrating with ill-concealed rage. It was bad enough that he'd been in such a helpless position; that his followers had *witnessed* this disgrace was more than he could stand.

"Get out!" he screamed. "Get the hell out of here! All of you! What do you think you're staring at?"

The room emptied with lightning swiftness. The last of the guards tumbled out the door, tripping over the feet and stumbling form of the man in front of him in his haste to be gone, but he wasn't fast enough. Bontempt had recovered his balance with horrifying swiftness, starting toward the fleeing guardsmen the second he'd given his order. The last man was one step too slow to avoid the pile-driver blow from behind that his leader swung down on his head.

There was a sickening crunch as the man, tumbling over the next in line ahead of him, came up face first against the frame of the door. He tried, even through his pain, to claw his way on through, but Bontempt had him by one ankle, and he was dragged back inside. The others fled down the passageway outside, cries of pain and suffering echoing, mixed with the loud, wet sounds of fists and boots contacting with plasm, and plasm with with stone.

The guard on the floor quivered a last time, then vanished, leaving Bontempt angrily stomping the stone floor. There was a snap of energy as the guard was snatched away by his own Shadow, and the lack of anything more to punish made Bontempt even angrier.

He staggered to his seat and fell heavily back into it, letting his eyes turn to the vaulted ceilings. There was an uneven fluttering, a squawk, and a ripple of pain shot through his empty socket again. He felt, rather than saw, the presence of his second eye as Cyclops limped through the wall above and plummeted toward him. The bird barely arrested its fall in time to avoid collision with the floor, veering to the back of Bontempt's chair. Dried blood was evident on the side of the bird's beak; on the bird's wing, Bontempt saw stringy bits of feather dangling from a ruined piece of flesh. He was only thankful there was no serious damage to the creature's wings, or to its good eye. It was a setback, the first such he'd ever encountered, but Cyclops would live to work another day.

And there would be work, that was certain. On all sides his enemies were closing in. If it weren't for the money—the damnably lucrative profit structure of his business—he'd have packed his men up and headed for, if not greener, at least less isolated territory.

Now there was this new one, this fresh bit of dead spirit who had not only escaped his men, but had confronted Bontempt himself, and had come out the winner. It was the book, the green, glowing book the man wore around his neck, that had made the difference. It had power, any fool could have seen it, and things of power were to be coveted. It was just one more reason to find this "Love" and destroy him. The other reasons were all personal, but that was fine. Bontempt loved to hold a grudge.

He sat back for a little bit longer, then reached down and sounded the gong that would bring back his guards. Hopefully the cowardly scum wouldn't be too terrified after his outburst to respond.

They came slinking in moments later, and, as though nothing had happened, he began giving orders. He sent one of them scurrying off to find his advisors and a Usurer. Cyclops would need some attention, and, as long as the bird needed help, as long as the pain throbbed through its head, he would feel it too. It was the price for the link. Nothing for nothing.

For some reason the words stuck in his head. They seemed, somehow, prophetic.

7

Faith fought the two muscleheaded slavers all the way, but she was weakened by the journey from the compound. There was a constant rage within her now, a rage that grew with each passing moment, threatening to overwhelm her every conscious thought. At first it had frightened her. It was not like any natural anger she'd known. It seemed sentient, separate, and yet a part of her at the same time.

The rage called out to her, taunted her, flaunted her own helplessness in her face and used the surges of shame and anger to build its own strength. Faith no longer fought it. Instead she cultivated it. She fanned the flames at every opportunity, using Fontana as a focus, like sunlight through a magnifying glass.

She knew that as the anger grew, she was growing stronger as well. She knew, also, that it still was not enough, not yet. There would come a moment when those who held her were not so watchful, a short second in time when she could move with the element of surprise as her ally. That was the moment she would wait for. If the opportunity presented itself, she would escape. Barring that, she would use her moment of freedom to rip the heart from Elliot Fontana and feed it to whatever writhing, pathetic bit of his being was left behind. From what she'd witnessed with the federal agent on the road a ways back, there might be a considerable number of pathetic bits left, and it was that image that kept her from going over the edge.

Faith, originally Cindy Lawson, had invested her soul in Elliot Fontana and his "prophecies." She'd been on the street when he found her, working for an employer with the dubious moniker of "Leroy" and taking what sustenance, and occasional pleasure, she could find on street corners to help her get by. She'd been strung out on coke, passed out on whiskey, and wiped out on life. Fontana had seen through that in an instant with his clear, icy blue eyes, and he had drawn her free of it. *Free. Right.*

His words had drawn back a part of her that had attended church as a little girl, a part of her that believed in better places and other worlds. He had promised to take her there. Of all his followers, he'd assured her, she was first in his heart. She had been first in his bed, in any case. Now she saw his shitty little prophecies for what they were: a means of getting from her what the johns on the street had at least had the courtesy to pay for.

Now, being dragged against her will through his "next level," where the promised freedom came with the price of pawing hands, leering eyes, and chains, he was finally serving a useful purpose. He was giving her a reason to live, giving her power, and for the first time in her life, she was going to take that power and do something for *herself*.

These thoughts dissipated as she drew nearer to the palace itself. It had the vague shape of a granary, or some sort of farm storage facility, but the resemblance was only cursory. The sides were shiny and black, coated with some kind of metal that resembled nothing more than it did the mud at the bottom of a riverbank.

The place was huge and brooding, like something out of a nightmare or a science-fiction movie. There were gargoyles, of a sort, mounted above the doors, and the doors themselves were massive. There were no windows, no reason for them. What would they look out over? Where would they get any light, or breeze, to improve the interior? It was like a great, slimy cathedral in the middle of the desert.

Faith vaguely remembered such a place—had it been an oil refinery?—off to the side of the road in from town. The place had been abandoned for years, though, and there was no way it had been so huge. Her memory dredged up a vague image of corrugated metal and desolate, gravel-strewn parking lots. Nothing like this place, and yet the images continued to impose themselves upon one another until the two blended, giving her a headache.

"Bontempt is gonna like this one," the shorter and wider of the two apes that led her chuckled. "Fights near as good as any I've seen. Maybe he'll let us stay when she dances, eh?"

"Not likely," the second guard grunted. "Ol' one eye will have this one to himself, don't doubt it. He'll have her on the slab in his private chambers, maybe give her a third eye or a third leg to help her dance…heh heh."

The two laughed deeply at this, and Faith renewed her struggles. She might be going where they wanted, for the moment, but no way was she going to give them the satisfaction of any fear. She reached inside, focused on an image of Fontana's terrified, mewling face as he'd crawled back over Hope like a frightened kitten, and let the rage flow through her. It washed her nerves in ice and calmed her thoughts to a slow burn of hatred.

Inside, the main hall seemed to stretch on forever. Cries of pain echoed down the stone corridor, along with deep curses and a heavy clattering. There was no evidence of life anywhere, and the two guards stopped short, looking about in consternation.

"Where is everyone?" the first wondered aloud. "Not like them to leave the door unguarded…not like them at all."

There was a flicker of motion to the side, and suddenly a man in a uniform similar to those Sully and Din had worn on the road stood at their side. The man was obviously nervous, his eyes flickering up the hall toward the screaming every couple of seconds.

"What are you doing here?" he whispered, the words echoing loudly, despite his effort to speak softly. "The old man is in a rage; something got to him. He's already taken out ol' Murph." The two guards stood in confusion, trying to take it all in and make sense of it. Bontempt? Gotten to? How was that possible, and him in his own citadel?

"We was told to bring this one to him for tonight," the second guard muttered. "Sully, he and Din said she was to dance tonight. Some sort of celebration."

The three of them stood looking at one another, none wanting to second-guess whether it was wise or unwise to take Faith into their master's chamber. The question was answered for them as the gong went off, summoning the guards.

"Hey," the shorter man said, grabbing the younger guard before he could disappear down the hall, "you want to take her in for us, since you're going in anyway?"

"Not a chance," the man said, shaking him off. "He told you to bring her, you better do it. He isn't in a mood to be trifled with, and I want all hands free if I need to get the hell out of there again."

He was gone as quickly as he'd arrived—almost magically, and Faith decided that he must have used some sort of trick to move so quickly. It was more knowledge to be filed away. Wherever this place was, the old laws of reality most certainly did not apply, and it was up to her, it seemed, to learn the new ones as quickly as possible. They certainly weren't offering any information booths or tour brochures.

Hesitantly at first, then with heavy sighs of resignation, her two captors began moving her down the hall again. The screams had faded, and a steady stream of uniformed guards had poured through large double doors at the end of the passageway ever since. They came from walls, alcoves, passageways and other rooms, and their sheer numbers weighed heavily on Faith's heart. Escape from here was going to be no easy proposition.

She was brought back to reality as one of the guards reached out and pinched her painfully on the behind.

"Let's move a bit more lively there, girl," he ordered with a nervous chuckle. "Don't want to keep him waiting, as you'll soon find out."

She tried to lash out at him with one leg, but he dodged easily. Her helplessness drove the madness closer to the surface, chipped away at the ice she was using to calm her rage.

As she was thrust forward through the door and into the arms of nightmare, Faith cast Fontana into various images of pain and torture, imagining him with ruined legs, arms, and body, imagined his eyes vacant and hollow, his tongue lolling and his nerves spasming and flopping his body about like a grounded fish. She almost smiled. Then she stumbled into the chamber, and there was no time left for pleasant visions.

Some sort of illumination, brighter than the preternatural glow that had suffused the air since her arrival in this realm, shone down from the arching, cathedral-like walls. Tapestries hung, tattered and threadbare, depicting endless scenarios of battle and war, life and death. She was surrounded by a series of raised platforms that could be mounted by steps running up their sides. On the centermost of these, seated on a large, ornate chair of the same slimy black as the outside walls, sat a huge, shaggy-headed man.

He stared down at her, pinning her to the floor like an insect with only the weight of the icy gaze of his one eye. He wore a uniform similar to that of the guards, but much more richly embellished, and a long, curving blade hung at his side, dangling nearly to the floor beside the chair.

He did not smile as he glared down at her, nor did he speak, at first. She could feel his one eye roving over her body, taking in her long, lanky form and the disheveled locks of her hair. Despite her urge to defiance, she felt herself cowering, pressing back toward guards as if for protection. Of all those she'd encountered on this far side of death, this one was the most imposing. He was obviously used to wielding power.

"Take her to the slab," the man grated at last, his inspection complete. It was as if bands of iron had been removed from her heart, and Faith nearly sobbed in relief. The guards hurried her forward, mounting one of the stone platforms near to their master's throne quickly and tossing her to the floor. She felt the rattling of chains as her own were removed and her collar was fixed to a longer, more slender set of links that wound up from a ring in the stone beneath her.

Rough hands roamed quickly over her body, and before she knew what had happened, the remaining rags that had been her clothing had been ripped from her and cast aside. With her old chains in hand, the two squat guards hurried back down the steps and bowed their way obsequiously out the doorway. Faith could almost smell their fear, and it added to her own as she tried to draw her limbs in tightly and cover her nakedness from the man on the throne and the guards standing around beneath her, gazing up in appreciation.

She tried to reach inside for the anger, for the rage that had sustained her, but the flickering lights and the sinuous, sickening touch of the silvery chains that now bound her to the stone wore away at her strength. She became suddenly aware of another set of eyes. Bird's eyes.

There was a huge crow sitting on the tip of the chair, but not like any crow she'd ever seen. It stared down at her, small strips of feathers clinging to skeletal wings, one eye as empty as that of its master, the other a black, glittering marble that flickered to mimic her every move, watching, waiting. For what?

Faith had no idea what was expected, no way to understand what was happening to her. It had been one thing to be part of the chain of slaves, to keep her thoughts and her mind to herself and worry about continuing to put one foot in front of another until she could find a way to escape. There had been only two guards then, and an entire chain of her own kind. Now it was different.

This was another world, another place entirely. This man staring at her so intensely was powerful in ways she could neither comprehend nor defend against.

She had been naked a thousand times, felt the unwanted caresses of a thousand different men, each with his own price to pay, but it had never been like this. She felt violated, and all he was doing was watching her.

"Stand," he called out. He did not scream, nor did he raise his voice, but the command was powerful still. Before she knew she had moved, her legs were beneath her, and she was rising tentatively to her feet, still twisting her knees and holding her hands in such a way that the majority of her flesh was a hidden, insubstantial knot.

For the first time since Fontana had dragged her off the streets she found herself wondering how she looked, worrying over the ragged cut of her hair and the grit and grime of the road that coated her form. Being naked in such a state was worse than showing up in rags to her, more demeaning, somehow. She imagined that it was a small lesson in how caged animals must feel when ripped from their natural habitat and put on display.

Then there was a commotion behind the throne, and a small group of guards came forward bearing a litter between them. Seated upon it was an old woman. So old, in fact, that her hair wisped about her head like fine silk, not gray, but bone white. Her features were thin, porcelain smooth, and yet there was an ancient power in her eyes that spoke of years beyond counting, of things seen and crumbled to dust before any of them had been born to their previous life, let alone this one.

"Chamelia," Bontempt said softly, rising and bowing as the crone stepped lightly from her litter. She carried a musical instrument of some sort, a bit like a flute, but longer, much longer. It glittered black and silver, and she carried it with practiced ease, despite its ungainly size, as she mounted a shorter podium near Bontempt and seated herself among a small heap of pillows.

"Darius," she answered softly. Her voice was musical and soft, like a quiet dirge heard from far away, or a lonely breeze rustling through decaying leaves.

No further words were spoken, but a respectful silence had fallen when she entered, and it held as she turned toward Faith. She brought the flute to her lips, and she played.

What sprang forth was beautiful, and horrifying, and soul-wrenching all at once. Faith could feel the notes moving around, then through her, could feel her muscles twitching with each ripple of minor chords, could feel her body responding to messages her mind could not even decode.

Yanking wildly at her chains, Faith tried to scrabble backward off the platform where she was chained. It could not end like this. She would not be a plaything, a toy. The chain held her tight, jerking her painfully to a halt, and the oily, sickening feel of it in her hands drove her to her knees once more. She was sobbing now, and hating herself for the weakness that made it so, pulling futilely at her bonds and scratching her flesh against the stone.

Bontempt was smiling down at her now. He turned and waved to Chamelia, who returned that smile, and continued to play.

"Welcome to my home," Bontempt said, rising quickly and leaning into a mocking bow with a smile. "Now we will see what kind of a student you are. Dance."

"No," Faith whispered, clutching at the chain and wrapping herself into a tight little ball. She felt the fingers of the music reaching out for her, much stronger this time, much more powerful. Her arms began to unfold, and she clutched them back, reaching for the rage, fighting to blank the sound from her mind as it slipped past her defenses and fought for control of her limbs.

"No!" She said it with more force this time, and Chamelia watched her with surprise over the top of her instrument, though she showed no signs of alarm. The musician released a swift cascade of minor notes that rapped at each of Faith's muscles in succession, releasing one and moving to the next in such a flurry of motion that she couldn't begin to fight for the control of one before the music was latching onto the next. She still fought, but it was a lost battle from the beginning, and short moments later, to the appreciation of the gathered guards and the amusement of Bontempt, who was watching her carefully, she danced.

It felt as if she were coiled in a grimy, sticky web. The strands clung to her and forced her into motion, shifting with each subtle beat, twisting with the harmonies and rippling with the melody. She sent every ounce of hatred, every bit of the rage she could latch onto, through her eyes and into the one of her captor, but it only served to widen his smile as she felt her body gyrate wildly to the musician's call.

Somewhere in the middle of the dance, Din and Sully walked in and stared, open-mouthed, but she was able to spare them only slight attention. She was tiring, losing more and more of herself to the uncanny fluidity of the musician's fingers. She felt more shame in those moments than she'd ever experienced.

The music wound into a dirge-like finale, and she preened, strutted, showed her body to them all and begged them to touch it, to mold it and use it for their own. There was no response to this, other than bright interest. Truly another world. She sank to her knees. She bowed low, her lips meeting the cool, dank stone of the floor. Her long dark hair cascaded over her shoulders to frame her head.

The music stopped, but she found that its last command remained enforced. She could not rise. She could not speak. It was maddening. There was no way to know where he was, where any of them were.

Then she felt a rough hand on the flesh of her back, and shuddered convulsively. As the fear and revulsion flashed through her, she heard the man laugh.

"She will be a good one, I think." She heard the shuffling of his feet as he descended to the level of the floor. "Bring in the drinks, the food. Let's get this evening off to a good start. Later, I think, we will watch her again."

The last words Faith heard as it all blurred to a mind-numbing roar, were, "When she is done here, have her chained in my quarters. I think I'll play with this one tonight."

The words had been directed to a single guard, and Faith found that the fear they brought was greater, even, than that of giving herself to the music. At least in the dance it had been her own hands, her own body...the thought of that one-eyed monster using her like a toy sent chills shivering through her.

Around her the party raged. The night was young—the night was everlasting—and even thoughts of revenge, and of Fontana, could not bring her the rage she needed. All she could do was play along, and hope for escape. She wanted to cry, but no tears would come. She guessed they would never come again.

8

Love had wondered how the entire entourage was going to head out into the wastelands without being noticed, but as it turned out he need not have worried. While literally all of Llanna's people accepted him as their leader, it seemed that, as in the Skinlands, such faith was not always to be taken at face value. There was a solid core of wraiths who volunteered to stay behind, to wait for word from the others. The unspoken portion of this "volunteer" effort was that they felt it was a fool's errand, or they feared it would end in disaster.

Some of them stayed behind out of fear of what might await them in the lands they'd left behind; others just didn't feel that this was the final journey. These last believed that Love, and Llanna, possibly with Fontana and the others in tow, would return to the temple before they made any final voyage into the Tempest.

Either way, it simplified things greatly. There were an even dozen of them, handpicked for the most part, and supplemented by those who would not be left for any price. A dozen against a fortress—a small group of fanatics against the odds. A pang of familiarity swept through Love's being as they all lined up before the compound. He wished that Fontana were there to share the moment.

This time they would not be defending themselves against the attacking hordes of the mindless, but would be taking the war to the field. This time there was a mission beyond self-annihilation. It was a comfortable difference, one that might have changed some things if he could only cart it back in time with him a few weeks and start this whole mess over. Having a goal, a substantial enemy who had done him a particular wrong, made it somehow more easy to concentrate his anger.

Little Green Book, chapter one, verse two: *You are what you are—you can't go back again.*

For the first time in years, he found other quotes, other prophecies beyond the ones Fontana had spouted, coming to mind. He remembered a verse his father had been fond of, a verse that had usually meant a long bout of deep-night drinking and violence: "Yeah, though I walk through the valley of darkness, I will fear no evil, for I am the baddest son of a bitch *in* this valley."

He repeated the words over and over to himself like a mantra, willing it to be so, and knowing it to be bullshit. It had never meant victory for his father, but then, his father had actually been the *drunkest* son of a bitch in the valley, so that was not surprising. Whatever victories they might win on this outing would come from their wits and their courage. All the cards were in Bontempt's hand, and he didn't seem the type of man who would hesitate to play them. Not at all.

Some of Love's old confidence was returning to him now that they were about to move. He was a doer. There were those who did things and accomplished a lot in their lives, and there were those who sat around and talked about it. Love wanted to get it on—that was how he'd come into this world, and that was how he planned to exit it, as well, if he had to carry wraiths, Spectres, crows and every other damned thing in the place on his back as he went, he aimed to go out in a blaze of glory.

Little Green Book, chapter two, verse fourteen: *The Lord helps those who help themselves.*

They took off at what served as sunset, though there was no noticeable change in the amount of light. Time was judged by what little they could discern of the Skinlands. The owls were perching on the stones, staring from scarred, skeletal faces with huge, orb-like eyes and a hunger that could be felt clear through to the Shadowlands. The creatures of night looked most appropriate from the wraith perspective…it was easy to see them as ghoulish, evil denizens of the Shadowland, much more so than the softer, gentler creatures of the day.

Love remembered tales of the owl's wisdom from his childhood. He wondered how wise they might really be, how much more they could see with their night eyes than the humans who walked about every day, oblivious to entire worlds going on about them. He wondered if they could see him now, and if so, what they would have to say.

It didn't matter. Listening to the counsel of those wiser than himself had never been a strong suit of Love's. He shouldered his share of the supplies and weapons, waved Llanna to his side, and set off. She came up to walk with him as he led them all off at an angle from the road. He knew that this was dangerous, that there were things less likely to find you on the roads, and yet it was necessary. He knew they had to reach town by midnight or be held up by another day, and the preparations hadn't been completed in time to allow them the luxury of the long way and the cleared road.

This route would cut off several miles, and Llanna assured him they could make it to the station before the train departed. Her eyes had taken on a fearful, uncertain look when she'd spoken of the trains, but now that their journey had started, her steps were firm and light. Whatever it was she feared there, she was not going to let it stop them. Love smiled. It was good to have one like her at his side. He found himself, oddly, wondering where Faith was, how she was making it in this world of darkness and shadow. After all, her death had been his gateway.

They were nearing the outskirts of San Valencez, California, when Love spotted the first flitting movements among the cactus and rocks. He thought it was his imagination, or a trick of the poor lighting, but when it repeated itself, the motion set off his internal alarms. Without slowing his steps or showing any sign that anything might be wrong, he touched Llanna's arm lightly and came up more closely beside her. She glanced up at him, curious, and he nodded his head almost imperceptibly toward an outcropping of rock.

She let her own gaze flicker over the stones and then back to his. The alarm that suffused her features was answer enough to his unasked question. They were not alone, and whatever, or whoever, was out there was not friendly. Swell.

He knew they only had until midnight to reach the station, and by his inner gauge, they had a little more than two hours left. They were only a couple of miles from the edge of town, where the train ran through—plenty of time, if there were no distractions.

"Spectres?" he whispered his question, keeping his eyes forward.

"No," Llanna answered. "We're too close to the city. These must just be bandits, probably hoping to snag a soul or two for the black-market trade. The outer city is full of them."

"Then they aren't too dangerous?" Love asked, mentally counting the movements and tallying the odds.

"Not if they don't take us by surprise," Llanna answered. "They probably hope one of us will hang a little too far back or wander off to the side, where they can be easily ambushed."

Love decided that the best way to handle things was to drag it out in the open. He stopped and called out to the others to huddle closer.

"Looks as though we have some company," he told them. "I want everyone to stay within an arm's length of the person in front of him. Keep your eyes on the shadows, and maybe they'll wait for some easier prey to happen along."

This seemed to be the case. The small entourage made their way into the first of the outlying streets without mishap. The homes that lined the street were dilapidated, rundown and dingy. Their windows glared like huge, empty eyes, and the bones of animals and humans alike lay scattered here and there among the lawns. There were rotting automobiles, toys and bikes with the rubber dried and crumbling on their rims and flaking rust eating away at the skeletal remains. A small pack of dogs trotted out of the shadows and Love hesitated, but they looked straight through him. The animals had a starved, feral gleam in their eyes. Ribs stood out from sickly, yellowed flesh, and only patches of fur remained as a poor covering against the weather. They teemed with maggots and other insects, and drool dripped to the ground from lolling tongues.

Love knew that these were living dogs, that the things that he saw were only manifestations of the death and decay to come, but it was hard to stop the initial lurch his stomach gave when the pack lunged forward, chasing a scraggly, bob-tailed cat down an alley directly across the street from where they'd first appeared. The animals leaped right through him, passing on and leaving nothing but the faintest tingle to note their passing.

Llanna and the others paid no attention whatsoever, and Love, feeling at once self-conscious and set apart in this alien landscape that they took for granted, tried to emulate their attitude. It was obviously an acquired attitude, and it would be best if he could find ways not to be distracted in what was to come. Best for himself, and best for Fontana and the others, for whom he had become the only chance.

As the dogs disappeared across an overgrown, pitted lawn, their howls turned to baying dirges by the Shroud that separated them from the Shadowlands, Llanna led them onward. A few streets up she gestured silently that they should turn.

EXCEPT YOU GO THROUGH SHADOW   473

"It's a bit quicker than the main road, and we should attract less attention," she explained. "Those who run the city are not necessarily our enemies, but neither are they friends. Each has his own agenda. If Bontempt suspects what we're up to, he might meet the price of some local official and have us bagged and delivered to his doorstep. Best to avoid them, get on the train, and get out."

Love nodded his agreement, and they slipped silently onto a street that was barely more than an alley, heading across toward the center of the city and leaving the larger roads behind. They followed as he led them away. Llanna moved closer and took his hand in her own as they went. There was an odd comfort to this gesture. Her support might prove the only thing capable of getting him through the trials to come.

The Shadow voice whispered up through his mind, dispersing his pleasant thoughts of Llanna. "I am your only way through," it hissed sibilantly. "I am your power, your key to strength. There is no way out of here except you go through shadow, and I *am* shadow."

He ignored the words, pressing on more swiftly than before.

The station was squat and gray, and it reminded him only vaguely of the place he'd arrived at before moving out to the compound. Fontana had met him at the station, grabbing one of his bags and babbling nonstop about how wonderful it was going to be, how they were going to change *their* world, if not the big one, how society would never understand, but that was the beauty of understanding.

"We will make the journey so few will ever be offered," the prophet had said. "I am the way, the truth, and the light. No one will depart this station, except they go with me…"

He hadn't been talking about the train station, but it seemed somehow appropriate now. Station Earth was beginning to look a whole hell of a lot more appealing now that he'd spent some time in the alternative.

There were shadowy figures moving in and out of the building, and when Love concentrated, he could make out the husk of the original, Skinland building. He could see a steady stream of the living moving in and out the doors like herds of cattle. He could even feel their emotions: excitement, nervousness, some fear. Then the sensation wavered, and the low-slung, moldy gray of the Shadowlands station reappeared.

There were wraiths moving in and out of the station also, but not in the numbers that they did on the other side. They were of every imaginable description, some in uniforms he could only suppose to be Legionnaires, followers of one or another of Stygia's Death Lords; others in flowing robes; still more in spiffy suits with attaché cases that had seen better days flopping at their sides. There was one common thread: all of them looked a little lost—disoriented.

"It is not like any train you've ridden before," Llanna told him softly, as though reading his mind. "It leaves every station in this realm at midnight, every night, and it can take you where you need to go, wherever that might be, but there is a price. Everything here has a price."

"Price?" he asked, spinning away from the station to meet her eyes.

"Yes. You lose a bit of your hold on where and who you were each time you ride. A small thread seems to sever in the tapestry that binds you to this place. It is a bit dizzying, and I know those who have ridden hundreds of times without noticeable change, but *you* will notice the change. Your Shadow will notice, too. It will be more at home, more in control, as long as we ride."

The building seemed to take on a darker, more subtle cast as she spoke, and Love looked it over cautiously. Tracks ran in and around the train yard, rotted wood barely supporting rusting rails, scattered bones lying among the ash and cinder gravel that ran along and beneath the rails. There were a few abandoned, dilapidated train cars along the way, some in cut-outs, others just lying on their sides.

From within the abandoned cars he could see eyes peering out, could sense others watching him as he watched them. He nodded in their direction, but Llanna shook her head quickly.

"Don't worry about them," she said. "Now that we are here, none will bother us so long as we are passengers."

Turning back to the building and squaring his shoulders, Love started forward again, pushing through the doors and into the gloomy interior of the station. There were machines and seats of all types, some vending, others for shoe-polishing, or newspapers. None of them appeared to have been operated in years, though here and there ghost-flickers of Skinlands equipment would flash in and out of sight. Shadows would move from booth to booth, ticket counters would come to dingy life, yellowed bulbs barely illuminating dusty counters as tattered pieces of paper were passed back and forth and the shadows shuffled on. Love fought to ignore them, to pay attention only to what seemed solid.

"This way," Llanna urged him. They hurried through a broken turnstile and on down a corridor that led to huge double doors. Love pushed, and they opened with an ominous creaking sound. Beyond lay the tracks, and on the first such stood the train.

It was pure black. There were no markings on its sides to indicate a company or a line, nothing but slick, oily black metal and hissing jets of steam. Against the dilapidated backdrop of the station, and seated upon the precarious remains of the tracks, it seemed out of place, totally alien. Love nearly stopped, but Llanna pushed him forward, and the others crowded in behind. Apparently he was the only one completely new to this mode of travel.

They made it to the door and up the steps just as a wheezing, sickly voice called out "All aboard!" The doors hissed shut behind them, and with a lurch, before they could even find their way to the nearest seats, the train was in motion. The mournful cry of its whistle shattered the silence, and Love fell heavily back into a padded seat that felt somehow repulsive to the touch.

It was midnight. For some reason, that bit of knowledge, that momentary connection to the world he'd left behind, seemed important. Everything seemed a bit less distant, a bit more familiar, with the reference of time temporarily returned to him. He sat back, ignoring the seat, and tried to watch through the windows as they flew out of the station and into the unknown.

EXCEPT YOU GO THROUGH SHADOW 475

There were still a million questions to ask...where did it stop? How would they know when to get off? Where would they wait to ambush Bontempt's men? Llanna didn't seem worried, so he decided he would leave that to her. Laying his head back, he rested, letting the monotonous sound and motion of the train lull him into a daze.

"Look out, Bontempt, here I come." As the darkness flashed by, he nearly laughed at the emptiness of his own words.

Fontana had managed to expand his little world about four feet in each direction over the span of his incarceration in "the kennel." Faith had never returned. He knew that the Archangels, Hope, and Charity were still with him. Two of the federal agents had been taken away, and he didn't know for certain how many that left.

He kept quiet, listened, and tried to piece together enough information to form a plan. It was hard to do this without the benefit of steady input, but he kept at it religiously. It was all that was left to him.

The others were no help. Most of them wouldn't even speak to him, and when they did the contempt in their voices, or the outright hatred, drove him away from them. The only one who'd responded otherwise had been one of the federal agents, a man named England. He'd wanted to talk about his wife and kids, and did Fontana think they'd be released soon?

The man was delusional. He believed they were political captives of some sort, prisoners bound to be released once ransom demands were met. He didn't remember Fontana, or the compound, and he had to think for quite some time to remember his own name. He remembered his wife and kids, though. Fontana thought about sliding around to where he could kick the shit out of the man, but in the end managed just to avoid him.

That left himself. The Archangels were, thankfully, chained to the far wall. He could have called out to them, but some of the others had tried talking among themselves, and the lesson had been swift and violent. Not allowed. Fontana wasn't sure if the Archangels would listen to him or kill him, given the opportunity, but they were still the strongest.

He couldn't understand how everything had turned so wrong. He had been the leader, the prophet. Granted, this wasn't much like what he'd preached, and granted as well he'd behaved badly just before passing through, and after, but he was only getting the hang of things. He was certain he could get a grasp on this world, as well. Once he knew the language, he could get others to believe in him again. If not these, then others. The guards? The slavers that had first brought him here? Someone. All he needed were some keys, keys to their minds, and he could make them believe.

The guards themselves were not very good sources of information. They muttered, never speaking clearly, and were so used to one another's company and language that they often didn't need to finish a word or sentence before the other

David Niall Wilson

began cackling, or cooing, or grumbling in response. It was maddening.

Through them, though, Fontana did learn that Faith had been taken to the main palace. She had been chained to a slab to dance for the pleasure of whoever it was that owned and ran this place.

Fontana tried to picture the fiery Faith writhing like some cheap bar-girl on a stone slab, and his imagination fell short. She might have acted that way when he met her, when the drugs and good ol' Leroy had had her jumping to a different tune, but Fontana had changed her. He couldn't see any way she could be forced to submit, not if being marched across an alien landscape with chains at her throat and attacked by spectral monstrosities couldn't break her.

So, there was a secret to be learned. There were ways here to make others listen to you, to break their spirit and control them. He had to be wary not to fall into any further restraints than he had already, and he had to find a way to gain some control of his own.

There were other things to be learned. He heard snatches of conversation about a place called "the Tempest," and others on the subject of some city named Stygia. Apparently he was to be carted off once more, all of them were. Those who were of no further use to Bontempt would be taken off to Stygia, where they would meet some fate apparently worse than slavery, though when this subject came up, only half-sentences and quick laughter were forthcoming.

Sometimes the guards would poke and prod at Hope, or one of the Archangels, trying to work some life back into them and encourage them to be lively enough to avoid "the forge." The sound of this sent chills of apprehension through Fontana's weakened frame. Forges meant heat and pain. He didn't know what work he might be asked to do in such a forge, or what might be forged there, but after the time he'd spent already in this Shadowland, he was certain that these were things he didn't want to know until after he'd managed to avoid them.

He also didn't believe that any sort of favors the girls might grant these two toadies would make a bit of difference in their fate. There seemed to be nothing sexual in any of their advances, disgusting as they might be. Fontana himself found that the sight of his two former beauties chained did nothing for him. More to be filed away. In any case, the two guards weren't high enough up the chain of command to be worth worrying over.

He couldn't spare them much concern. If the others were bound for the forges, he would have to find a way to be bound elsewhere. There had to be something he could do, something he could use to bargain with, that would make him valuable enough to avoid their fate. After all, none of them would be here without him…he had led them, however reluctantly, into this next level. He would find a way to lead them to freedom, and, if none of them managed to follow, he hoped they'd do well in the forges.

Outside the palace, preparations were nearing completion for the drive into the Tempest. Sully and Din had been kept very busy gathering supplies, putting together a small squad of men to assist them, and conferring with their guide, a grizzled old ex-Legionnaire named Cappy. There was no way to prepare for the Tempest, not in any way that would make sense or any real difference. If they could find their way in and back out again, that was as much as anyone might hope for. They were hoping for a bit more. They needed to reach their goal with their cargo intact, and it was with this in mind that they chose their "staff."

In all fairness, with Cappy at their side, their odds were better than most. He'd been in and out of Stygia more times than any other man in the camp, more than any either Din or Sully had ever known. They weren't certain that even Bontempt would be a better companion on those dark, dangerous roads.

There had been a time when one of Charon's famed Ferrymen would have seen them through, when warring factions among the Hierarchy itself would not have been one of the major dangers to avoid, but those days were so long past that neither Din nor Sully had more than passing knowledge of them. Now there were Spectres, reavers, bandits, and rogue patrols from other slavers' citadels to avoid, as well as the Tempest itself.

Rumor had it that the Ferrymen were still about. They no longer worked for the Hierarchy or the guilds, it was said, but they were there when someone truly needed a way through the Tempest. Some were thought to be aligned with the various Shadowland factions, others to have taken up residence in the very bowels of the Tempest itself.

Din had been through that hellhole three times, and each time it had seemed as if parts of his mind had faded, or that bits and pieces of whatever he was made of in this realm flaked off. Sully had only been in and out once, but he was a good man. Din wouldn't have chosen any of the others to fight at his side, despite the smaller man's sometimes whiny nature. Everyone had their faults, but Sully could put down a Spectre with the best of them.

Crassus and Brutus, of course, would accompany them, and that single factor gave Din more confidence than any ten of his fellows might have. They were an odd lot, the beasts, and they would never cease to make the short hairs at the back of his neck rise when they screamed, but they were nearly invincible warriors. Shapechanging had never appealed to Din, even in a small way. He couldn't begin to comprehend the horror of being forced to sacrifice one's own form for another so alien. But as long as they fought at his side, he didn't need to understand; it was enough to know that they were there.

Din had been working the slave routes as long as he could remember. His former life had prepared him well for such work—he'd worked with a Portugese slave ship running Africans to the islands. The local Indians had been worthless as workers, nearly as worthless as the lot he'd just brought in. The Africans had been necessary then, just to keep the sugar trade going. It had never bothered his conscience, the subjugating of his fellows. It was business, and he was very good at what he did.

He'd left no family behind, though there had been a woman once whom he might have started one with had things gone differently. He'd died on a mission, died at sea. The ship that he'd been serving aboard had gone down in a violent tropical storm, with over two hundred slaves and a crew of nearly thirty men.

When Din had awakened on the far side of the Shroud, he'd been disoriented, but he'd been quick enough to avoid capture as well. The slaves themselves, those who had come to the Shadowlands, had still been chained, and Din was the only slaver to make the passage. It didn't take him long to learn that the chains bound those men to him, still, in ways that had not been possible in his former existence.

He'd managed to drive the entire chain himself for what must have been two or three days, half-maddened by the rotting, decayed landscape around him and the lack of hunger and thirst. The slaves had reacted as though he were a demon, and they were consigned to his personal hell. Their superstitious minds told them he was their only hope, and they had not resisted.

When they'd finally come across a Legion outpost he'd been so far out of his mind that they'd left him free for the mere entertainment value, or so they said. He liked to believe that he'd been strong enough, even then, that none of them had thought the risk to be worth the possible price. Not when he came with so much else to offer.

For his chain of slaves he'd been awarded a uniform and a job. Neither had taken long to get used to. One slaving operation was much the same as another, and he'd always had the talent for it. Now he worked independently for Bontempt, hoping to move up in the Renegades' operation. The Legions had always been a bit too structured for him, and his new life afforded more possibilities. These days, with the constant slipping of the Hierarchy's authority, the Legions were little more than slaving companies themselves. At least here he had his freedom.

In any case, he would need all the experience, knowledge, and abilities at his command to make it through the Tempest to Stygia and back again. He only hoped it would be his final trip. These past months he'd been developing a certain air of fatigue, a sort of fading interest in it all. He attributed it to stagnation in his career, but maybe it was more than that. Now he was plagued by short visions—not dreams, really, but memories—visions of that woman, and those tossing seas beneath a sun forever lost to him. The scent of salt spray would hit him with sudden force, driving thought from his mind, dragging him back.

His Shadow beckoned from those long-sunken planks, called him to succumb to weakness and weariness. It was a familiar voice by now, hypnotic and subtle, but one he'd long since come to grips with. He could still control himself, and he could still drive slaves. Until the day neither of those things was true, he'd hang on, and he'd continue to do his job. There was nothing else.

He entered through the front of the palace and headed down the long hall once more. Bontempt had summoned him again, but this time he did not fear as he had on his previous visit. The issue of the lost soul was settled—at least, it seemed to be so. This visit had to be about the coming drive.

He slipped as quietly through the main door to the throne room as possible and stood at attention, waiting for his leader to acknowledge his presence. The woman was still chained in front of the throne, kneeling now in fatigue, and Din smiled. It was good to see some of that fire subdued, good to see that she had begun to come to terms with her fate. He'd not wanted to see that one go to the forges. She would make a good warrior, if she learned to obey. For a moment he wondered if he was getting soft.

Bontempt swiveled to face him at last, running his one-eyed gaze up and down the big guard's frame before speaking.

"I have seen him again, Din," Bontempt began. "Your escaped fresh one is more powerful than any so young that I've ever encountered."

Gesturing to the perch behind him where Cyclops sat, resting, he went on. "He managed to injure Cyclops. Even I could not do such a thing for many, many years after coming here. It was a book he carried that made it possible, a relic from beyond. I want that book"

"You want me to go back and look for the book?" Din asked, suddenly wary. "I leave for Stygia in two days."

"I am aware of your journey," Bontempt said steadily. "I assigned it. What I want is for you to go to the others. This one will not talk. I want you to find someone among those who remain who knows something of the one who escaped. Learn what you can, then return to me with the information. I must have that book."

Then Bontempt turned back to the slab where Faith knelt, her head resting on the stone slab. He could not see the fire blazing in her eyes, nor would he have cared. He called out to her to rise and spin for him, grinning as she complied in silent fury. Din took the dismissal for what it was and backed out the door, wondering what he'd be able to find out, and praying it would be enough to keep his hide from the forge.

Fontana recognized the voice of the slaver Din, interspersed with the noncommunicative grunts of his two guards. He could only make out a little of what was said, but he strained to get as much as possible. At first they only discussed the upcoming drive into a place called "the Tempest." This sounded no more inviting than the forge they continually mentioned, and he wanted all the information he could get on the place before they took him there.

Then the thread of the conversation turned, and he perked up considerably, sliding out until he was at the very limits of his chain and risking drawing notice to himself.

"There was one more of them," Din was saying slowly, being careful to make sure the neanderthal he was conversing with understood him clearly. "He got away right at the start, disappeared into the desert. Bontempt wants him, don't know why, but he wants him bad. We need to check through these that are still here and see what we can learn. Anything helpful will be rewarded, if you know what I mean."

The series of slobbery, grunting coos that followed left no doubt in Fontana's mind that the two idiot guards *did* understand the reward part.

Love. They had to be talking about Love. He was the only one of the truly faithful among his followers who had not been on the chain with them, the only one who might still be free.

The door opened and closed again, and the darkness wrapped itself around

DAVID NIALL WILSON

him. He scooted back to his wall as silently as possible, his mind already churning, working angles.

He briefly considered letting the others in on what he'd learned, but tossed that idea out almost immediately. Either they would ignore him or they would side against him. There was prophecy in everything. He thought back to the little green book he'd kept on the other side of the misty haze they called "the Shroud."

You've got to know when to hold them, know when to fold them, know when to walk away, and know when to run.

Too true. He could hear the two guards coming down the two sides of the room, kicking one after another of the slaves into life and questioning them quickly. A lot of those in the room were not from Fontana's group at all, but after all the time that had passed, the two morons in charge could not remember which was which, so they were questioning them all.

Fontana readied himself for the pain to come, carefully formulating the words he would use to free himself. He couldn't give away too much too quickly, or they would just take the information, beat him senseless, and go on about their business. He had to make it seem as if listening to him would benefit them in some way. Pulling such a stunt on the guards would be no big trick, but he wasn't as certain about this man Bontempt.

It took them nearly an hour to reach him. A couple of the others were aware of what was being asked of them, one—Charity, he thought—mentioned Love by name, but none of them was bright enough, or quick enough, to come up with any information that could be used to locate their missing companion.

The guards loomed above him suddenly, grabbing him by his legs and pulling him forward into the slightly brighter light, smacking his head painfully on the stone floor as he went.

The first of the guards slapped him across the face, sending sparks flying inside his brain.

"You know anything about some other guy that died with you?" guard number two asked brusquely. No wonder they weren't getting anything useful, they weren't even smart enough to word the questions properly. "Bontempt's lookin' for a guy that escaped, a new one, like you."

Shaking his head to clear the last of the cobwebs, Fontana rose to a sitting position, flinching back as the first guard motioned as if he might slap him back down. "Wait," he cried. "I know who he is, and I can help."

Neither of the guards seemed too impressed by his announcement, but the one pulled his arm back, waiting to serve up his little snack of violence until he'd heard what Fontana had to offer. It was now or never.

"I can help," he repeated slowly, his voice regaining a bit of its old force and control. "He worked for me, followed me for years. I know him better than anyone. His name is Love, Love Constantine…I gave him that name."

He could tell he was losing them a bit, confusing them, and he changed tracks quickly. "You know, Bontempt would love to hear what I have to say, I bet. If you two were to get me to him, I bet there would be a reward in it for you. It's up to you, of course," he went on, laying it thick and heavy as syrup, "but if I were you,

I wouldn't let that lout Din have the glory. I mean, I know what Bontempt needs to know, and *you* are the guys that found out…why let someone else get a reward while you sit over here in a room with a bunch of slaves?"

Unlikely as it seemed, the two were *thinking* about it. He knew then that he had them, and he let out one last hook…a bit of the old prophecy: "He who hesitates is lost," he told them. "What I know will help, but the longer it takes to start looking for him, the harder it's going to be to find him."

That was about all the input he figured the two could handle, so he waited. He could not feel his heart beating, that was a thing of his past life, but the fear was no less intense. He knew he was in the balance now, the dead zone between success and failure. They might listen, they might even take him to Bontempt, if he was incredibly lucky, but they might also just knock him back to the floor and kick him senseless. It would, as a matter of fact, be their least troublesome choice.

Greed won out. Without another word, the two lifted him to his feet, one on each arm, and one of them knelt quickly to unfasten him from the wall. He nearly keeled over from cramps and fatigue as his legs supported him for the first time since being brought in from the road. The guards shook him roughly, holding him erect until he got his bearings, and hustling him toward a side door.

Good, he thought, they'd caught the gist of what he was saying. If they were using a different exit, then they didn't plan on taking him to Din first. They must have been contemplating a way to get more of a reward for themselves before he'd spoken.

In any case, he was glad to avoid Din and Sully. Somehow he didn't think that the burly slaver would think too kindly of him after his display on the chain, and he didn't need any further obstacles between him and the goal that had suddenly materialized…freedom, or, at the very least, escape from some new form of death he could not yet comprehend.

He could see the huge, looming structure of the palace ahead, but again they turned to the side, skirting the main roads and slipping through dingy walls and buildings. Fontana ducked and cringed the first time they headed straight through one of the structures, but it only took him a few moments to begin deciphering which things were real and which were not in respect to his present state of existence.

They were gaped at by others as they passed, a few of whom followed them a few steps before melting back into the shadows, but none spoke to the two guards, and certainly not to Fontana himself. The two squat little men were intent on reaching their goal as quickly as possible, and that was fine. Fontana didn't know if he could better his situation through all of this or not, but he knew that the one person who could absolutely help him was Bontempt, and getting to see him was the first step.

They came up to the side wall of the palace, and one of the two men moved forward to the shiny surface, rapping on it insistently for a few moments until there was a grinding, sliding noise and a portal opened in the structure's side. An even *more* squat, wider version of the two guards stood silhouetted in the doorway, meaty hands on her hips. She did not look exactly pleased to see them, despite the almost familial resemblance.

"We need to go to see the boss," the first guard said quickly, trying to step through the doorway. "We got someone he wants to see."

The woman in the doorway did not budge. "You need to see the boss, why you come to this door? Why not go in the front like always, huh? You tell Beulah that."

The second guard moved slightly forward, his voice taking on a wheedling, whining tone. "Come on, Beulah, you know we wouldn't come this way unless it was important. Bontempt, he wants to know about some lost fresh one, and this guy knows something. We didn't want that asshole Din takin' all the credit, you know? I mean, *we* found him…"

"So you're sneaking around the back way, eh? Hoping ol' Beulah will put her hide on the line for you again, eh? And what's in it for me?"

The two looked at one another quickly. Obviously, they were grasping at straws that weren't there, so Fontana took a chance on another beating and spoke up quickly.

"I'm sure they'd be happy to tell Bontempt you were involved in my discovery," he said quickly. "If I get to him quickly enough to catch the one they're after, he should be pretty happy with whoever helped me get there."

The woman, Beulah, looked at him as though she'd as soon spit as listen to his words, then turned back to the others as if he'd never spoken.

"You bring him on in here, then, and you wait. I'll go on down and see if I can arrange to get you in there without too much fuss. You better remember how you got there, if anything comes of this." She turned away, then spun back quickly, a glint in her eyes that told Fontana she was no one to mess with, despite her appearance. "You better *forget* how you got in if he gets mad, too, you hear?"

Both of the men nodded quickly and stepped inside. The door snicked shut behind them, and the woman left them alone in what appeared to be some sort of kitchen.

One way or another, he was about to take the next step in his existence, and suddenly Fontana's knees weakened. Suppose he'd made a mistake? Suppose it wasn't Love they were after at all, or if they were, they already knew more than he did? What would they do with him for wasting their time?

The question quickly became moot as Beulah slipped back into the room with a grace and silence that belied her girth, motioning the three of them forward and out into a great hall that seemed to stretch on and on forever. Visions of prisoners walking the "last mile" flashed through Fontana's mind, and he felt himself beginning to tremble, but there was nowhere to go now but forward, or, more precisely, where the chains pulled him.

He nearly laughed as nervous energy flooded his system. What had he written in that green book? "Let the games begin."

10

The train was moving rapidly across the murky landscape. Trees and bushes, cracked and doubled by the onslaught of time and the skewed perspective of the Shadowlands whipped past at a dizzying rate. Love kept his eyes glued to the windows at first, uncertain of how far to trust this new means of conveyance. He'd felt the disorientation that Llanna had mentioned, felt himself slipping a bit, as if he'd come loose from his body and stepped off to one side. Nothing seemed quite the same as it had a few moments before.

His memories of the compound were fading slowly, and even the time in the temple that had grown from the ashes of his death had blurred around the edges. The present moment seemed clearer, for all that. Inside the train there was a different sort of light. It was not exactly the manmade fluorescence of a Skinland train, but it was a thousand times brighter than the steady haze of the land outside. He could make out details of his own form, of those of his companions.

The seats were worn and threadbare, springs popping up here and there and patches of duct tape crossing their upholstered surfaces like a road-map of ill-use and years. He'd had to wipe a spot on the dingy glass of the window to see beyond it. The floor of the train was littered with paper cups, bottles, wrappers and newspapers. He glanced down at one of them, then quickly away. It was not from any time he knew, or any place. It had been there a long, long time, and he did not need anything drawing his mind even further from sanity just that moment.

He turned to Llanna, and found that she was staring at him intently, watching his movements with amusement. It made him nervous, but somehow, it was comforting as well. By no fault of their own, they had shared very deeply in one another's past. They were a part of a mutual anchoring system, bound one to the other. Love had never been *in* love, that he knew of, but he imagined that this was about how it was supposed to feel.

She reached over, finally, and laid her hand across his leg. "I find that the only thing that keeps me sane on these rides is memory," she said. "I concentrate on my past, on the things that still haunt me. I guess that's funny, in a way. I mean, we're the ghosts, but it seems we can be haunted as surely and as painfully as any living person."

"You think about that church, then?" Love asked her, concern for her filling the void that his own hazy recollections had vacated.

She lowered her head. "I think about that church, and that man, all the time. Even from the other side of the Shroud, from the land of the living that he cast me out of, I feel him, and I hate him. I always believed very strongly in forgiveness, but I find that, now, I cannot practice what I would have preached."

She turned slightly, gazing out the window that he'd been watching. "We will be passing near where he lives very soon."

"We could make a detour," Love suggested. "I don't exactly know what we might accomplish, but we could go there and try...would that help?"

"I'm not certain if it would or not," she admitted. "I've always been afraid to go there, afraid that all that would happen is that he'd find a way to manipulate me even after death. In any case, it is out of the question, now. Our tickets were stamped for our destination the minute it formed in our minds…we will not be getting off anywhere along the way."

"On the way back then," Love said decisively, glad to concentrate on other worries than his own for a moment. "Just you and me. Consider it a date."

She smiled at him, and once more he saw the faintest trace of something other than sorrow flash through her eyes. Then her other words hit him, and he asked, "Tickets?"

"Check your pockets," she told him.

Complying, Love found a folded stub of paper in his left front pants pocket. He opened the ticket and stared. There was only a smudge where the name of the train line should be. If you held it one way, it seemed to say one thing, another way and it would shift yet again. It made his eyes hurt. In the destination slot it said Lavender, California. *Lavender*.

"Isn't Lavender just outside of San Valencez?" he asked her. His own knowledge of California was sketchy at best. He'd followed Fontana to the compound and the desert, but he hadn't done a lot of sightseeing on the way across country.

"Yes," Llanna replied. "There is a graveyard there, Shady Grove is its name. A lot of horrible things have happened there. There are places linked more strongly with the Tempest—links to roads known only to a few. I could take you to the Tempest, but I would have to find my way. Older ways are marked, for those who can see. Bontempt always sends his slaves through Shady Grove, and we will be there, waiting."

"But—" Love was trying to piece it all together, but every time he got a new piece of information, it all seemed to get muddier. "Why doesn't he just hook up some kind of cattle car on this train and go the same way we do? What makes you so certain we will get there first?"

"The train does not do the bidding of any, not even the Hierarchy." Llanna explained. "He might get such a party on board, but he could never get them to agree in their hearts where their destination would be. He might lose his entire string. It is simpler for him just to drive them along the road. They will get there just as surely, barring unforeseen attacks. Besides, as I told you, the train takes its price from us all. Bontempt has been here a long time. His ties to his previous life are tenuous at best, by now, especially so far from Stygia. Such a journey might be his last."

Love thought about how his own past seemed to be fading. His clearest memories were of Fontana, his most driving need to find and free his mentor. When he thought about the fact that this might be all that was holding him back from the clutches of Oblivion, he got a knotted feeling in his gut that would not go away.

He placed his own hand gently over Llanna's and scooted a little closer on the seat. There was none of the physical warmth such intimacy would have brought in his previous existence, but there was a familiarity, a bonding of spirit, that went beyond it. It was not without desire, but it was different. Whatever had happened to them that day across the fire, there was no going back from it now.

He glanced around again. All of the other seats in their car were empty, but if he looked carefully ahead he could see lights from the cars ahead. There was no usher, no ticket check, nothing.

"How will we know when we've reached Lavender?" he asked.

Almost as he spoke, the train around them faded. He nearly fell to the ground as he stumbled forward in the darkness. They were all there, grouped on a solitary platform with tracks spreading endlessly in either direction. The building was boarded up and silent. Dust coated the windows, and the door hung open and crooked, dangling by a single rusty hinge. Wind blew dust and debris through it and into the building's interior. There was no one in sight, but in the distance he could hear the mournful wail of the train sweeping off into the night.

He found that he was still holding Llanna's hand, and he turned to her, bewilderment and a touch of fear edging his voice. "What...what happened?"

"That is how it always is with the trains," she explained softly. "I didn't tell you ahead of time because I didn't want you to dwell on it."

He turned quickly back to the doorway of the train depot. "LAVENDER, CALIFORNIA," it read in faded blue lettering. Just like that. It felt as if a slice of time had just been removed. His mind would not admit to the possibility of reality just warping him into this place, or teleporting him, or any such nonsense. If he was here, he must have gotten off that train somehow, somewhere, and the knowledge of that moment had been stripped from him. He wondered how much else had gone as well, how much he would retain of what had been his mind.

His hand almost reflexively sought the book dangling about his neck. It was intact, slightly warm to the touch, but not radiating the heat that had come to mean danger. In fact, nothing seemed to have changed except that, rather than seated on a train bound for this station, he was standing at that station.

For the second time since passing through to the shadowy world that now claimed him, Love felt fear. His old fear of losing control of the moment, of *any* moment, resurfaced. He felt the darkness roiling within him, and the voice slipped insidiously up to fill his thoughts.

They did it to you, you know. They are wiping you away, bit by bit, piece by piece. They don't want another level, they just want you off this one.

He slapped his hands to his ears, knowing it was foolish to do so, but unable to fight the urge. The voice came from within. "No!" he cried, nearly falling to his knees.

The Shadow switched tracks on him, feeding the anger that he felt with a sudden surge of energy, trying to fill his mind with hatred. Again he shook his head. He felt hands falling onto his shoulder, but he brushed them off, sweeping his arms in a wide arc. He felt the satisfying connection as he hit whoever it was, and he leapt to his feet. His Shadow fought him for control, and he lashed out at everything around him, trying to find something to focus on, something that would give him an edge.

He heard voices calling his name, calling for him to stop, but he could barely make out the words, and he had no concentration to spare them. Every ounce of his soul was bent on driving the Shadow back down, burying it within himself and regaining control. He spun again, lashing out, and he heard a wail. Llanna.

The sound of her voice cracked the surface, making its way to his ears. It was a wail of pain, physical pain, and his mind began to swim clear, fighting to understand. He didn't know what might be threatening her, what might be there to hurt her. He wanted to stop it, to hurt it in return—no, that was wrong. He just wanted to stop...

With the same suddenness with which he'd been removed from the train and deposited where he stood, his mind became his own again. He shook his head slowly back and forth to clear his thoughts, staggering backward and nearly tripping over something—someone, he realized.

He snapped his eyes open and took in the scene of craziness that surrounded him. Llanna lay just to the left of him, her head held in her hands, still sobbing softly. Almost under his feet was the boy, Bobby. Bobby was not moving, even though Love had nearly tripped over him in his blind rage.

The others stood a small distance away. Seeing the clarity return to Love's eyes, a few of them moved hesitantly forward to tend to their two wounded companions. They did not meet his eyes, but skirted him warily. A few of the older ones glanced his way, and it was anything but trust that he saw in their eyes. What had he done? What had happened?

He knelt quickly at Llanna's side. One of the others moved as if to stop him, then thought better of it and stood back, waiting. He pulled her close, resting her head on his knee, and lifted her eyes to meet his. They were sorrowful, as always, but now the sorrow was mixed with pain. He felt a lurch within himself, felt the pain seeping through to him.

It was something. He clutched at it, drawing it forth. As he did so, he felt the book growing warmer, but it was not the same heat as when Cyclops had been staring him down, or when the bandits had ambushed them earlier. The heat engulfed him as well as the book, making him a part of it, and it a part of him.

Almost frantically, he clawed the book open and let his index finger drop to the page.

"No pain, no gain," he muttered.

He was engulfed. Agony shot through his face as if he'd been smacked by a sledgehammer, and he was forced over backward by the concussion. He writhed on the ground, clamping his hands to his face. He couldn't speak, nor could he rise, and the book burned at his chest all the while. He groped for sanity, clawed at it, missed, reached out again.

He tried to recite more of the prophecies, but the words would not come, would not form into coherent sentences. The pain pulsed and blossomed within him, threatening to overwhelm his senses entirely, but at the last moment it began to ebb...to fade slowly, leaving him drained and weak, but leaving him. He felt it as a physical sensation, a flow toward the center of his being, of his body. A flow toward the book.

EXCEPT YOU GO THROUGH SHADOW 487

He felt gentle hands on his shoulders, on his legs, holding him still against the earth, and this time he did not resist. There was little or no strength left to him, and his mind still whirled in the aftermath of pain and shadow. He was numb, and it took every ounce of strength he still possessed to open his eyes once more and to take in his surroundings.

The first thing that met his gaze was Llanna. She was still crying, but it was not in pain. He could tell this from her eyes, so full of sorrow, so full of love and caring. He knew then what he'd not been fully aware of before. He would give up his soul for her. He would do whatever it took to erase that sorrow and bring out that smile.

He knew that many of those around him had left their loved ones behind. Those lost loves were the ties that bound them to the Skinlands and denied them access to whatever awaited them in the next form of afterlife. Love had left nothing behind. All that he was, all that he'd built himself to be, was tied up in his interpretations of the prophecies and in the teachings of Elliot Fontana. What he'd left unfinished had been that journey to the next level. His faith bound him to his past.

For Llanna, it was not a lost love that bound her to this place, but hatred, the desire for revenge, the desire for redemption of lost faith.

Now Love had something more to bind him. He had someone to care for besides himself, and a goal beyond just reaching Oblivion. He knew now that this had been what his spirit sought. He hadn't wanted a heavenly next level. He'd wanted to fade from existence, to erase all that he hated about his life by ending it.

Faith had been abused many times over, family, friends, life—she had been ready. The others had all had commitments that they were either dodging or trying to forget.

Love had always seen this as weakness. He'd wanted them to feel as empty as he had, to hate the world that had rejected him with the same intensity that he'd hated it. Fontana had offered him a place where he was not worthless, but even that place had been in a suicide squad. All along, that was where the prophecies had been leading him. It had taken death, and the dead, to bring him to his senses. There was a certain irony in it that nearly made him smile.

He wanted Fontana to be there, to share this new revelation. He knew the man would only smile at him, whip off another quote from somewhere and set his heart at ease.

He opened his eyes farther and sat up. They were gathered around him again, and the distrust that had been growing in their collective gaze when he'd struck out at them earlier was gone, replaced by a newly bolstered confidence in his powers. Bobby was sitting off to one side, nursing a sore rib with a grimace.

"What happened?" Love asked.

"You took my pain," Llanna told him. "First your Shadow drove you half-mad, and you were trying to fight it. Your enemy was not physical, it was within you. Since you couldn't lash out at it, it was us you fought instead. We tried to hold you back, to restrain you, but it was hopeless. You nearly took my head off."

"I took that back, too, didn't I?" he asked, rubbing his head gingerly. "I'm sorry. If it helps, I can say that I definitely know *exactly* what you went through."

She smiled and reached out her hand, helping him slowly to his feet. He was weak, but not dead, and his energy seemed to be seeping back into him slowly. Whatever power resided in the book about his neck, he knew he was going to have to learn to control it better, or someone—probably himself—was going to end up seriously hurt.

"How long have we been here?" he asked. They had been on a pretty tight schedule to begin with; he didn't want anything to keep them from cutting off Fontana and the others.

"Only a few moments, actually," she said. "And the train leaves every station at midnight, remember? It was midnight when we boarded, but it was midnight when it departed this station as well."

Love didn't even ask. He didn't want to think about time warps and magic trains. He didn't feel even the itch of the shadowy presence he'd so recently battled with for possession of his body, and that was a relief. Apparently he was not the only entity tired out by the ordeal.

Without further comment they gathered their scattered supplies and set off in the direction of Shady Grove Cemetery. It wasn't a heavily traveled road, but there were signs, here and there, of those who had passed through before. As they neared their goal, the mists subsided a bit, and the barrier that separated dead from living landmarks thinned. It was as if the two merged at some point ahead, some meeting of two worlds. There was a sizzling, heavy aura of energy that permeated Love's being, drawing him forward even more quickly than he would have liked to have traveled.

"The barrier between the Shadowland and the Tempest has grown very thin here," Llanna explained.

Love remembered what she'd said about the Ferrymen. Somehow the idea that the world of ghosts had its own history was disconcerting to Love. A snatch of song returned to him, one that was not yet recorded in his book, and he whipped it out to jot some notes. The old pen he kept tucked into the front pocket of the book still worked, but the ink had an odd, greenish tint. No telling when some new "prophecy" might come in handy.

Don't pay the Ferryman, he scrawled hastily, *don't even fix a price. Don't pay the Ferryman, until he gets you to the other side.*

Llanna stopped to look askance at him, but he only smiled, slipped the book back beneath his shirt, and hurried to catch up. The spiked metal gates of the cemetery lay ahead, slightly ajar, and he could see the mists playing tag among the gravestones ahead. He'd seen a lot of boneyards in his time, but this one had all the earmarks of a Halloween special. The graves wound back and back toward a forested area, and it was obvious that they got older as you went deeper.

It was his first glimpse of such a place, and it was also the first feel he'd gotten, beyond the remains of the compound, of a place where he felt completely at ease. He fought this, knowing it was foolish to get too comfortable in strange territory. Something in the spooky, moon-like luminescence that shone from the gravestones and tombs and the stark, rotted trunks of trees that shot up here and there, leafless and skeletal, called out to him.

Such a place would have been distasteful, at best, when he'd been alive. He had only been to one funeral, his father's, and it had left a sour taste in his mouth. He remembered seeing his old man's face, pasty and silent, peaceful, and thinking it wasn't fair. The bastard was gone, he himself was still alive, and everyone around him, especially the preacher who'd droned on interminably about the saintly quality of "the deceased's soul," had forgotten what a first-class asshole the man had been.

Now, though, the peace of the graveyard was palpable to him, a restful, rejuvenating sensation. *Kind of like a hot springs spa for spooks,* he thought to himself, grinning. As they moved in through the gates, other forms became visible to them, and other eyes watched their progress. None moved to bar their way or to challenge them, but many watched. He wondered if they were only silent and stoic because they knew the party was just passing through. It seemed to Love that, if someone had such a place as this to themselves, they would want to keep it that way. It would certainly be a restful place to settle.

Llanna grabbed him by his elbow and propelled him forward. "We need to get inside the Tempest before they arrive. It will be a much easier matter to hide ourselves once we are in, and we are in no more danger there, relatively speaking, than we would be here if we were found out."

He nodded, but he did not feel the confidence he struggled to exude. Once again they were moving into unknown territory. He didn't fear for himself. It was the memory of the train ride, the sudden ending and the violent outcome of that ride, that made him wary. What if he became disoriented again? What if his Shadow wasn't as far subdued as it seemed? Once inside, if the Shadow won out, he'd be just another Spectre in the Tempest, and he doubted his Shadow-self would have much compassion for Llanna and the others, or their quest.

She saw him hesitate, and she turned to him, reading the questions in his eyes. "It is not like the train," she told him softly, "not exactly. It is not you that changes in The Tempest, but the world around you. You will be fine, but we must hurry."

He nodded once more, glanced over his shoulder at the calming expanse of graveyard behind them. Seth stepped forward and waved his arms theatrically. A bright haze grew before them, and Love plunged forward, saying a short prayer to Fontana.

"Forward," he whispered, "never straight." He'd never known just how true that could be.

In everything…prophecy.

11

Several things happened at once when Fontana was at last escorted through the two huge, cathedral-sized doors and into Bontempt's throne room. He was tossed to the floor at the foot of the throne, Bontempt turned his one dark, scowling eye full upon him, and Faith screamed. It was not a scream of fear. It was filled with venom, borne aloft by the power of her rage.

Cyclops heard, or felt, that scream from the other side of the Shroud, and he took to the air clumsily. He was not completely healed, and his flight was erratic and uneven. Bontempt rose and leaped to the floor in one swift motion, came to rest beneath the circling bird and called out to it with his mind. He assumed control of the injured form, righting it before it could strike a wall or drop to the floor, and bringing it back to the chair in an erratic flutter of wings. Once it was safely in place, he released it and turned to Faith.

"You have nearly cost me more than you could understand. I will know why."

Faith was still filled with rage, but she did not hesitate to comply with his request. She pointed at Fontana, spitting her words between her teeth in hatred. "Him," she hissed. "He is responsible. He brought us here, lied to us. We all believed in him, all of us."

"My men brought you here," Bontempt told her calmly. "You were both part of the same slave chain."

"We wouldn't have *died* if we hadn't listened to him!" she cried. "He told us he'd lead us to the next level, to heaven. We *believed* you, damn it!"

Now her eyes were turned full on Fontana again, and he cringed back into the stone where he still knelt, uncertain what his next move should be. He could boldly stand and confront his captor, but likely this would only result in his being slapped painfully back to the floor. He could remain as he was, but if he did, and if Bontempt was truly taken with Faith, then he might be silent too long and let her talk him into Oblivion. Choosing the middle road, he spoke out softly.

"I know the one you seek," he said. "She knows him too, but none as well as I. I was their teacher. His name is Love."

Faith screeched again, and this time she came to her feet, clawing her way toward the side of her stone slab. She ripped at rock and chain with her bare hands, her nails shattering painfully and small furrows actually forming in the surface. Her eyes were void of intelligence. Only her anger remained. In those eyes, Fontana saw his death, and he shuddered. The chains held.

"Be silent," Bontempt said contemptuously, and, by some odd property of the chains themselves, Faith complied. She lay there staring, and hating, but her resistance had been beaten down for the moment. Fontana felt a twinge of the old desire returning, seeing her that way, but there were much more pressing things to occupy his mind.

Bontempt had turned back to him, dismissing Faith without a second thought, and Fontana knew it was now or never. Showtime. If his silvered tongue had ever been worth a dime to him, it would have to show that worth now.

"You know this Love," Bontempt said slowly, "but you know nothing of the Shadowlands. You know his mind, but you do not know what that mind will have to deal with here. You are as young to my world as he is, but weaker, and already there are those who hate you to the point of seeking a second, more permanent death for you. Why should I trust you, and what could you possibly offer?"

Feeling the advantage he'd believed in slipping, Fontana leapt to the verbal attack. "It doesn't matter where he is, or what the circumstances. I know how he will react because he is singleminded, and there is but one goal that could be filling his mind right now. He wanted another level. He believed that I was the only road to that level, my prophecy, my teaching. If he knows I am here, that I have not been destroyed, or gone on without him, he will come after me. He will try to set us all free, myself and the others."

"He will fail," Bontempt smiled slowly. "I already have you, and there is no chance of his success, so I ask you again, what can you offer?"

Fontana took his shot, there was nothing left to lose. "If you didn't fear that there was more to it than just an easy capture, you wouldn't be looking for information," he said flatly. "I know how Love's mind works, and I know the words of his prophecy."

"The book?" Bontempt's eyes showed a quick glitter of interest, and Fontana groped for a straw, hoping his legendary luck wouldn't desert him.

"The Green Book?" he asked. "I wrote it."

"Where is *your* copy, then, prophet?" Bontempt sneered. There was a little less certainty in the man's eyes, but only a little. "Why is it that he carries your book, casting power about with its words, while you lie at my feet, chained and sniveling?"

"That is simple," Fontana said, raising his eyes to meet the other man's single orb for just an instant. "I lied. When I wrote those prophecies I was making things up. When Love read them, then made his own notes and added to them, he believed. It is his faith that brought him the book, and it is my proof that the faith is ungrounded that can bring him down. That is what I offer."

Bontempt hesitated before he went on, considering what he'd heard. Fontana could read nothing in the man's one, glaring eye, and he lowered his gaze to the floor so as not to appear rude or impertinent. It was possible that his bold speech would get him through the moment, but he was equally certain that any further show of false bravado would be called for the bluff it was, and that he would not enjoy that experience.

"Well," Bontempt said at last. "Perhaps you have a slight worth to me, after all. The telling of that tale will have to wait until you are on the road to Stygia, though. Here is my offer," and at this, he sneered, though Fontana imagined that the man considered the expression a smile. "You will help me to bring in this one you call Love. You will go with my men, a part of the slave chain, as before, but you will not be sent to the forges. If you are helpful, you will be sold into slavery.

"A resourceful man will always find his way free of slave chains, eventually. On the other hand, if you fail me, or if I get the slightest inkling that you have left something out, or worked against my best wishes, then you will be the first to go to the forges. I will personally instruct, in such a case, that your guards remain present for the smelting.

"When your soul is nothing more than molten sludge, I'll have it scooped out and molded, beaten and formed, until all that remains is a small trinket on a tiny black chain. I'll have them bring that chain to me, my friend, and I'll give it as a gift to your admirer on the slab over there," he gestured toward Faith. "I hope that I've made myself clear to you.

"Take him to a room and get him rested," Bontempt told the two guards. "I'll send Cappy and his boys around to see him later and put together their plan. I want to hear about any problems he causes, and I want to hear good news about how helpful he's been when they're through."

The guards grabbed him by his arms and lifted him to his feet. He kept his eyes low, and they spun him roughly, pointing him back at the doorway and propelling him into the hall beyond. They were rough and dangerous, but still Fontana felt relieved when it was just himself and the two idiots again. They might have him at a disadvantage, but they were now afraid to press it, considering his newfound value. He could run mental rings about them, in any case.

They pushed him down a side hall that was lined with nothing but doors, stretching off into the distance so far that the dim light couldn't illuminate the entire length of it.

"Hey," one of the guards said, as if just thinking of it, "what do you think we'll get for bringing you in, slave-meat? He seemed pretty happy to talk to you."

"I'm certain he recognized your talent and abilities," Fontana said encouragingly. "I'd wait for him to contact you, though. You don't want to seem like you're in too much of a hurry for his favor...you want him to know you are just doing your job well."

"He's right," the second guard said, pushing open one of the doors to his right. "The big man will remember who brought this guy." Turning to Fontana, he added, "You better not let us down, pal. If you do good, he'll remember. If you screw the big man, he'll remember that, too, and I wouldn't want to be you in that case. Wouldn't want to be *me* neither, you know. We'll be keepin' an eye on you."

With that, he shoved Fontana through the narrow doorway and into the room beyond. The second guard took off back down the passageway, leaving them alone. The room was not large, by any standard, nor was it all that comfortable, but it beat being chained to a stone floor in the darkness. There was a table, a single chair, and a low-slung cot for furnishings. There were no windows. The illumination seemed to seep from the walls and ceiling. There was no obvious source for the light, and yet he could see.

A large black ring was embedded in one of the walls, and from this a length of lighter, glittering chain extended. Fontana's own chains were removed, and that on the wall was attached to the manacle on his right hand. Otherwise he was free to move about. After the kennel, it was heaven.

Moments later, the door opened and the woman, Beulah, entered.

"So," she said, "you found a way to save your scrawny hide, did you? I figured a smooth talker like you would make it, somehow."

Fontana didn't know the extent of freedom his new position offered, so he kept his silence, watching her carefully. "Oh, you don't need to worry about ol' Beulah," she said, laughing. "You got enough problems. Bontempt, he may like you today, but the first time you go astray of that temper, it's done. Over. I'm happier that he barely knows I exist...makes continuing that existence much more likely.

"I don't suppose you want to tell me what it is you offered him?"

"Information," he answered, "just information."

"Better hope it's *real* useful information, then." She cracked another grin. "Everything here has a value, you know? Better that value comes from you bein' around to help out. There's other uses. The walls always need patches, the soldiers need swords, and Bontempt needs power. You could end up a lot of different ways, you don't look out, and this here is about the best of 'em.

"You get some rest," she continued. "Din and Sully will be around this evenin', maybe Cappy too. You want to be ready when they get here."

Without a further word, she left the room, and Fontana moved toward the bed.

He already felt like a new man. Even in the face of what he'd just been through, he knew that what was to come would be difficult. Din and Sully knew him from the road, knew the way he'd acted when the Spectres had attacked, knew the hatred that the others held for him, if not why. It would not be easy to win any type of trust from them. Cappy, whoever that was, might prove an even tougher nut to crack.

One thing he knew for sure. Objects here were not necessarily what they seemed. Some of them actually held the kind of power that humans had played with the notion of for centuries. Chains could compel one to do another's bidding, souls could be smelted into jewelry, even bricks for roads, and from what he'd gathered, holy objects could fulfill the wishes of their followers in ways that simple faith had never made possible in life.

He needed to find Love. He needed to possess the book. He knew the words, but here the words would not be enough. Somehow his follower's faith had endowed that little green pack of bullshit with energy and power, and it was only right that the powers, whatever they might be, should come back to Fontana. After all, *he* was the prophet.

That, he knew, was the beauty of it all. Love believed, therefore Love still believed in him. He would probably just hand over the book, if Fontana got the chance to ask him, and of all the thoughts swimming through his mind, that was foremost. He would help Bontempt in any way that he could, but he would get that book. Once he'd accomplished this, negotiations could begin anew. He might not believe in the words of prophecy, but he could use the power, and that was all that mattered.

Fontana flopped down on the cot and laid his arm across his eyes. He had no way of knowing how long it would be before his conditions worsened again, and he knew enough to take advantage of the moment's respite. He had taught the others to fight, now he had to learn himself. It was the only way out.

"You did what?" Din bellowed, grabbing the shorter guard by the shoulders and shaking him like a puppy. "You took him to Bontempt? Without seeing me first?"

"He...he knew stuff," the guard almost sniveled. "He said Bontempt would want to hear what he had to say. I thought you said the big man wanted to know about this lost one…"

"If you heard what I said," Din grated, "then you heard me say very plainly that you were to question them, then come to me and report what you found. Do you know anything about this one we lost?"

"Uh…no." the guard muttered.

"Exactly. How do you know, then, that this slave had information that was important and wasn't just trying to save his own ass from the forge? Exactly: you don't. If this turns out bad, my friend, you are getting a one-way ticket on my slave chain. Count on it."

As the big man spun away, Sully came in through the door. "What's the problem? I heard shouting…"

"This brain surgeon here took one of our slaves to Bontempt," Din told him, still shaking in anger. "Says the slave told him he had important information on our lost one."

Sully smacked himself in the forehead, shaking his head in disgust. "Christ. That's all we need, Din. Which one was it?"

Din turned back to the guard, the question obvious in his eyes, and the man merely pointed to the vacant spot along the wall where Fontana had been chained.

Sully cursed under his breath. "Not that one. First he's a coward, then they all try to beat him to death and we nearly have to drag him free of that mess, now he's to be our *help*. Maybe it's me, but it sure seems like there's something here I'm missin'."

Din was just staring at the spot on the floor, his features mottled with anger. The second of the two little squat guards had come up beside his partner, and he was fingering nervously at the handle of the cudgel he wore on his belt. Neither of them wanted any part of Din, or Sully for that matter. What had seemed a wise decision only a few short hours before was already taking on the taint of disaster.

"Look," Sully said, stepping between Din and the other two. "You made a mistake. I wouldn't make another one, if I were you. You get this chain ready to pull out two days from now. You get them rested, lined up, and chained, and you don't go near that palace. Do you understand me? We have plenty of room on our chain; two more for the forges isn't gonna bother us at all. You get this done and maybe, just maybe, I won't report to Bontempt how you disobeyed our orders."

Neither of the two shorter men spoke, but fear danced in their eyes now. They both nodded in unison, and Sully turned back to his partner, slapping him on the back and pushing him toward the door.

"Come on, Din. They aren't worth it. Let's just find Cappy and get this over with. Worst case, we slap the slave back on the chain and forget the whole thing. Maybe he *does* know something, though."

"Maybe," Din said slowly, regaining control of himself, "but if not, I sure don't want to be around when Bontempt starts looking for the ones who wasted his time, and it was me he told to question these prisoners. If this guy hasn't got anything we can use, I may smash his miserable carcass myself, just to get it out of my system."

"Let's let Cappy worry about it," Sully said, holding the door for his partner to make his way to the street. "It's his call, anyway."

The two headed off, walking briskly, and the guards watched them go, breathing a sigh of relief. In the darkness behind them, eyes gleaming with dark intelligence and a fire that lay hidden just beneath the surface, the Archangels watched. None had spoken a word since coming to this place, and yet they thought in unison. Everything that happened was recorded, filed away. Every day they grew stronger. They exchanged one quick, knowing glance, then each returned to his own solitude. They could wait. In a place like this, there was nothing but time, and as the prophet had said: "Patience is a virtue."

When the door to his room slammed open, Fontana nearly fell to the floor in his haste to sit up and shake his mind into wakefulness all at once. He managed to stagger to his feet, wild-eyed, and stare at the three men who'd entered. He recognized Din and Sully immediately, but the other man sent chills running straight through to his heart.

Cappy stood nearly six foot five inches tall, and his long, grayish hair hung to his shoulders and then some, dropping into scraggly curls across his chest. Scars crisscrossed his face, and the slit that was his mouth was as devoid of emotion as a crack in a slab of stone. Colder, if that were possible. His eyes were dark, darker even than the metal of the chains, or the walls of the palace. They were vacant holes in his face, and Fontana had to pull his own gaze free to avoid dropping into their depths and being driven, screaming, into madness.

With a smirk, Sully walked in and shoved him back onto his cot, where his head came up hard against the wall. "Meet Cappy, slave-meat. He's the one who's goin' to get you to those forges we keep telling you about. That is, unless you find a way to help us out." The expression on his face said that, not only did he not believe this likely, but that he hoped it would not happen.

Cappy took the one chair, straddling it from behind and facing Fontana once more. Din just stood by the door with a dark, brooding look to him that spoke eloquently of violence and anger. It did not take a genius to figure out that this situation had worsened.

"I...I want to help," he managed to say, fighting the urge to lower his eyes. He needed these men to trust him, or at least to believe him.

"Oh, I bet you do," Sully tossed in. "You want to help *anyone* can save your ass. We'll just have to see, though. After what you pulled on your friends back on the road, finding any worth in you isn't gonna be easy."

"Let him speak," Cappy said softly. His words slipped through Fontana like icy blasts. There was a strength in this man that could not be measured by any outward sign. He had seen things, and the mirrored, warped images of those things were trapped at the edges of his dark eyes.

Fontana plunged on. "I know the one you lost. I know him better than anyone else could know him: I taught him. His name is Love, 'the Beast.' I gave him both names, and I wrote his book of prophecy. If he wants anything in this realm, it is me. He believes that I can lead him to 'the next level,' and he will try to set me free to do so."

"That's it?" the old soldier said flatly. "We don't need to talk to you to know that. We don't need your help, either. If he tries to take you by force, he will fail."

Fontana tried to put on a brave face, not certain how successful he was being, and continued. "Bontempt must have told you more than that," he said. "Love has a book with him, a book of prophecies that followed him through to this world. He injured your master's bird with it, and from the rumors floating around, caused Bontempt himself considerable discomfort. Not to mention that he escaped these two in an open desert with nowhere to hide."

Din started forward at this, balling one large, meaty hand into a fist, but Cappy stopped him with a gesture.

"He didn't escape anyone on his own," Sully cut in angrily. "Those damned Heretics took him. There was no way to follow without leaving the chain behind."

"It doesn't matter," Cappy dismissed the entire discussion. "What does matter is how our friend here figures he can help. I haven't heard that, yet, and that's the bottom line of whether he goes straight back to the chain, or not."

"And another thing," he hissed, his voice suddenly low-pitched and sibilant. "Bontempt is not my 'master.' No man is."

"You're right, of course," Fontana continued, gaining confidence, even as he drew back. It would not do to anger this man, and yet it was obvious that he was gaining some attention now. "You already have me, and as bait, I'm certain to flush him out and bring him in. You can probably take him, too, even with his new friends. I've seen some amazing things since I got here, and I feel I've barely brushed the surface. But consider this…Even if you *do* take him, are you prepared to sustain loss in the process? If you use me for bait, he will attack. He is not without resources, so you will have to fight. Even if you win, the cost might be too great for a party getting ready to brave the Tempest."

"You know nothing of the Tempest," Cappy snapped. "You can't even begin to conceive of what lies ahead of you."

"That is also true," Fontana conceded, "but here is what I think. I think I can get him to hand over the book without a fight. If he believes he has freed me, or that he has found me alone, he will come to me. If he does, he will listen. I am his prophet."

Sully's eyes rolled, but Cappy was watching Fontana's expression intently. "I don't know if you're telling the truth, or not," he said at last, "but I know that you believe you are. Maybe that is enough. Okay, we will take you with us, in chains, but free to walk on your own. You will help us capture this 'Love' and his book of prophecy, and then we will decide what to do with you both."

Without further words he stood and turned, walking from the room. Din and Sully lingered for a long moment, staring at Fontana in disbelieving contempt, then followed their guide out. As the door closed behind them, Fontana felt himself begin to tremble uncontrollably. It was a long time before he got it under control. He could still see the man's eyes, burning into his own, could still feel the chilly breath and hear the words. He was getting in deeper and deeper, and all he could do now was wait and pray that, in the end, he'd find a way to swim back to the surface, whatever and wherever that surface might be. It was going to be one long, long night.

12

Reality skewed sharply as they slipped through the crackling, energy-filled gap into the Tempest. They held hands going through, and Love realized only seconds after plunging ahead that this was a very good thing. All around him were possibilities, changes, rippling landscapes and flickering pathways. Beneath his feet, the road seemed solid enough, not like the gliding freedom of moments before, but solid as in real-world solid. Skinlands solid. He concentrated on that, concentrated on taking each step in turn, blanking his mind to the images that assaulted his senses.

An older man named Seth, who had been quiet thus far on their journey, had gone in first, taking Llanna's hand. Love had taken her other, and offered his other behind him. He didn't know for sure who'd taken it, but he hoped everyone was still there. He also hoped it would even out soon, and that he'd be able to start trusting his senses again.

Seth seemed to know what he was doing, because they were moving steadily. Mounds and hills rolled along beside them, skies of multi-colored impossibilities roiled overhead, winds howled, and yet Love would have sworn that somewhere within that sound was a voice, calling his name. He closed his eyes, tuned out the wind, and plunged ahead. It seemed like an eternity before they slowed and he was able to look about himself again, but he knew it had probably only been a few moments.

They were on a deserted stretch of road. It wound off into the distance, between the husks of blackened trees and hills with crewcut coverings of dead, dried grass. To each side there was a patch of open ground, fading into a wall of impenetrable mist. The road seemed more a tunnel through that mist, and Love wondered just what it was that held the clouds at bay. He shivered, turning his head in a slow arc that took in every angle of his surroundings and seeing nothing he could call familiar. Finally he turned his eyes to Llanna, then to Seth, questioning.

"This is one of the byways," Seth explained. "They crisscross the Tempest like the roadways in a city, but with no rhyme or reason to their direction or destination. There are landmarks to be followed, signs for those who know how to look, but it is a dangerous place, even for the most experienced."

Love looked around once more, then asked, "But how will we hide? If they come in the same way we did, they'll come out right here. Is that right? Where can we go that they won't see us the second they arrive?"

"The mist," Seth answered softly. "We will have to hide in the mist."

All of them turned then, staring into the dark, roiling clouds that surrounded them. Little shooting lights danced through the haze. The wind, if anything, had picked up in volume. It sounded like a gale, and yet where they stood, the air was so still it was stagnant. Looking down the road, there was no variance within sight. It was all the same, empty and gloomy. It reminded Love of one of those paintings of corridors that go on and on forever.

"We must move quickly," Seth warned them. "There—" he pointed to a slightly brighter patch of haze—"there is a break in the storm. We can wait there, and we should be able still to remain aware of what happens on this byway. There may also be an escape through there to another place, should we need it…. We will have to find out when we are there."

He set off across the barren ground at a swift pace, and the others followed more slowly, less certainly. Where Seth saw safety, they saw nothing. It would take a greater act of faith than any they'd yet performed to get them through that one patch of clouds. The road, even with Bontempt's slavers at their heels, was looking more and more inviting.

Love knew that, despite his lack of experience, the others were counting on him a great deal, on his power and on his courage. He lengthened his own strides to match those of their older guide, and moments later, holding Llanna's hand, he plunged into the gray of the mist, closing his eyes and praying it wasn't the last mistake he'd ever make.

The air around him shifted from hot to cold, damp to arid in lightning-like succession. The sounds that reached his ears seemed dissociated from the world around him. He closed his eyes tightly, and yet he was still assaulted by visions, nightmares. The voices in the wind were more distinct as he and the others moved deeper into the mist, and he felt a sensation of recognition, as if they'd been spotted, or acknowledged, by something that was a part of the darkness itself. Then he burst free once more, staggered, and nearly fell to his knees as they came into a clearing.

There were two other lighter spots in the haze wall that made up their refuge, and Love assumed that they led to other byways, or places similar to the one they'd just entered. It was not so barren here. It was more like some great, dismal swamp. Black lichens hung from twisted, dying trees to trail into what appeared to be murky, ebon water. Burping bubbles reached the surface of this pond, if that was what you could call it, and noxious, foul-smelling fumes burst free each time one broke the stagnant surface of the liquid.

The trees did not end at the haze wall. Apparently whatever held these spaces open from the mist was only a veneer, a covering over the world that lay beneath. Some of the larger trees trailed off into the mist beyond, as did the far shore of the pond. For all they knew it could be one small corner of a vast, murky ocean. The group huddled closer, and Love turned back to Seth.

"How can we watch the byway from here?" he asked. "I see the ways through, but I can't make out anything on the other side."

"In this," the old man said enigmatically, "you will have to trust me. There are ways to pierce the haze that have to be learned, and I have no time at present to teach them. When the slavers enter the Tempest, I will know it, and when I know it, you will as well. We need to rest now, so that we can be ready."

They were all in agreement on that. Setting a watch, the first of which Bobby volunteered for, they found their own little niches in the clearing while avoiding the proximity of the trees and staying as far from the murky water as possible. Love and Llanna settled into a large outgrowth of roots.

The wood, if wood it was, had a rubbery, inconsistent feel to it, and Love nearly stood again before he finally settled back. It was distasteful to the touch, but he was getting used to that since his death. Most of what he'd abhorred in life felt pleasant now, and most everything else in the Shadowlands felt unclean. If he could walk on a road made of other people's souls, he could sit on a damned rubbery tree.

The sounds in the wind changed subtly soon after they'd settled in. There was more of the quality of voices to it. Love, who had thought it was only he who was hearing them, looked at Llanna inquisitively.

"There are a lot of those who have chosen to live in the Tempest," she told him. "Most of them are Spectres, completely given over to their Shadows, but there are others. It is a well-known fact that the Ferrymen still walk the byways. Sometime we'll have to ask Seth about them. He knows more of this place than all the rest of us together, but I've never asked him directly. I have not made it a practice to delve into the pasts of those who believe."

"That is a good policy," Love agreed. He remembered the sullen, empty stares of some of the "chosen" back at the compound when questioned about their lives. Their lives, before Fontana, were their own, sacred. None had wanted the others to know his weaknesses or his secrets, and the first in line for secrets had always been Love himself. Poor Eddie Constantine. Deathwish Eddie.

Now, sitting in this place, he wondered how he could have been so quick to abandon life. In surroundings so completely dead that they had life beyond that death, he felt a yearning for sunlight and laughter, for clear water and green trees. An exceptionally large spore surfaced in the pond beside them, releasing to the air with a nasty wet sound, and he was yanked back to the present.

Seth sat a few feet away from Bobby, near the hazy portal that had brought them into this place, and yet he did not face it. Instead he held his head in his hands, swayed back and forth and mumbled to himself. Love could not make out the words, but they had the rhythm of a chant, or a monotonic song of some sort. Love wondered what memories haunted Seth, and what visions he walked through as he chanted. More things he would never know. More things, in all probability, that he did not *want* to know.

Leaning back, he pulled Llanna closer to him and just held her in silence, waiting. There was little more to be said. None of them knew when the slave chain would show up, nor did they know, for certain, what they would do when it did. All they could do was sit and wait.

Love was drifting through memories of his own when he heard the scream. It was a human scream, not part of the continual voice of the storm that raged about them, and it came from his right. He was on his feet and moving almost before the echo had faded, scanning the swampy clearing and moving quickly to the side, farther from the pond.

He saw them first as blurred, sinuous shadows, rolling down and around the limbs of the trees, sliding across the bark like ebon snakes, but much larger, much darker. They were men, or they gave the impression that, at some indistinct moment in their past, they had been men, but their bodies were emaciated and worn. Those bones were not white, but black, and they were surrounded not by meat, but by sinew and tough muscle. Their eyes stared down from the branches like those of giant, predatory cats, and their elongated limbs and talons only added to the skeletal and yet somehow serpentine images they presented.

One of the women had screamed, and Love saw that the first of the creatures had crept slowly down the trunk of one of the trees and had her by the hair. The thing was tugging at her now with both hands, holding onto the tree with impossible strength, using its back feet like claws, and gibbering insanely. She was fighting valiantly, but the thing was pulling her inexorably up the tree.

Love didn't allow himself the convenience of thought. He launched himself forward, drawing the darksteel dagger that Llanna had given him, pilfered from one of Bontempt's guard patrols at some time in the past. He reached the foot of the tree and leaped upwards, directly at the side of the creature, slamming the blade home and ripping it upward in one lightning-quick motion.

Pandemonium broke loose. The creature screamed, a hideous, soulless sound that shattered the silence and nearly drove all in the vicinity to their knees with its force. The emotion of the creature's pain was palpable in the sound. It released the woman, but in that same moment it turned to face Love, clutching its side where he'd stabbed it and holding its other set of talons at the ready.

The other creatures were growing more bold, dropping to the lower branches of the trees and advancing on the small party, who had all pulled forth such weapons as they had. Love growled a war-cry and lunged again, barely avoiding a swipe from the thing's claws and slashing out toward its neck with his blade. It pulled back in time not to have its throat slit, but the knife ripped through one of its thin, bony shoulders, meeting resistance, then bulling its way through.

Collapsing, the creature fell from the tree, and Love noticed from the corner of his eye that the woman it had tried to snatch was raising a large stone over her head to crush its skull. He turned away and met the attack of the next in line face on. They were incredibly quick, and the power of their voices and their deep, glowing eyes was distracting and hypnotic. Keeping up a steady stream of curses that helped to keep his mind straight, Love tackled the thing, taking a long, deep gash down his left biceps as he managed to circle its neck with his other arm and bring the dagger across its throat. Without a thought he let it drop and leaped to the first limb of the tree. Those around him were sounding off war-cries of their own, and the creatures were backing off. This group had been chosen to fight the slavers, and they were no slouches. He waited on his perch, watching, but the things melted into the shadows as quickly as they'd appeared, leaving no trace.

He carefully watched where the branches trailed off into the mist, but there was no way to know if the things were really gone or if they were just waiting right beyond that wall of gray. He slid back down the side of the tree, taking quick stock of his surroundings, and backed away slowly. He was reluctant to take his eyes from the haze now, not trusting the slim shelter of their little node in the Tempest as he had before.

As he turned back, he looked to Seth for assistance, but the old man had never even acknowledged the attack. To Love's consternation, he sat, just as he had the last time Love had glanced his way, staring into his hands and chanting. At least he wasn't hurt.

"What were those things?" he asked no one in particular.

"Those were Spectres," Llanna replied, "very far gone to their Shadows, I should guess. That is what becomes of those who cannot keep their inner barriers tightly in place."

Love thought about it. He had fought his Shadow, but something didn't quite jibe. He had fought a dark intelligence, an insidious voice that spoke on his own level, and he had grappled with a strength nearly the equal of his own. These creatures must have been weak indeed, perhaps lowly to begin with, or very corrupt. Somehow he couldn't believe that it was only the fact they'd given in to their Shadows that had brought them to this point. There had to be something about the Tempest that ate away at them, as well.

It occurred to him for the first time that the knowledge of those who'd led him to this place was barely more complete than his own. With the exception of their elderly guide, none of them seemed to be able to get their stories straight. Maybe these creatures had been Spectres, maybe they *worked* for Spectres. Maybe they were something else altogether.

"Do you think they're gone?"

"Very likely, though they would not be the only ones in here. We hurt several of them, and the others will bide their time, either waiting to catch us off guard again, or searching out easier prey."

"The Tempest," Seth's voice came to them, though he did not look up or acknowledge them, "is like a huge entity. While we are within its boundaries, we are but another part of that entity. Those who dwell here—Spectres, Ferrymen, others—can sense movements, differences, and anomalies in the various byways and nodes. The only safe place is in the byways themselves. There they may find you, but they have to get to you by other methods. As long as we are within the haze, our presence will attract others who dwell here. There is no way to avoid it."

"Isn't this something we should have known from the start?" Love asked.

"I didn't want to alarm you." Seth answered. Love wasn't certain, but he thought he saw the whisper of a smile slide across those old lips. Christ, what kind of place, and company, was this, anyway?

Love scanned the clearing. He couldn't bring himself to sit down, not after the attack, so he decided a closer examination of their surroundings might be in order. At least it would keep him from going mad waiting.

He started with the nearest of the lighter spots in the haze, the other portals. It was tempting to stick his head through and see what was on the far side, but he resisted that temptation. The few stories he'd had time to hear about this place agreed on one thing, if nothing else, and that was that it was very easy to get lost here. Just because he could follow this portal through one way did not mean he would necessarily be able to locate it to find his way back.

He stared into the mist and concentrated, willing his eyes beyond the Shroud. At first all it did was blur his sight, putting the white mist itself out of focus, and he almost gave up. Then he saw light of a slightly different shade. It was yellow, bright—almost the sunlight of his own memory. He struggled, and images began to break free. It seemed that the mist itself did not exist anywhere except in his mind, as if his visual input had been scrambled. As he discovered the patterns he was able to shift them back to their original.

Where the twisted trees made their way through the mist into this other place, green leaves had sprouted. There was lush foliage and a stream that appeared to be a tributary of the dark pond at his back, but the water was clear. He could see small shapes flickering about in that water. Fish?

In fascination he took half a step forward. It was then that the voice slid in, locking onto his thoughts.

You would be better off over there, you know. The old man knew about the Spectres, and he knows about the sunny place over here, too. He is here for himself alone. I tried to warn you before. Step on through and see what I mean.

Love nearly did it. He felt the muscles in his legs trembling with indecision, and his own mind was falling into a cloud of doubt. Seth *had* smiled about the Spectres, and he'd made no move to help them during the attack. Could it be a setup? Could they have been led in here to their doom? Llanna herself had said that they didn't know much about the old man.

He started to move forward. No harm in checking it out.

It was at that moment that strong arms grabbed him from behind, hauling him back into the swampy clearing. He fought to free himself, wanting to feel that sun, perhaps to taste the water, though he felt no thirst. There were too many of them, and moments later someone brought a hand across his face in a sharp slap.

"Wh…?" He looked up and there was Bobby.

"We're even now, my friend," the young man smiled down at him. "I think I saved your ass. Just where did you think you were going, anyway?"

"I…" He couldn't recall the moment when his own will had lost that one small battle. This time the Shadow had been subtle, winding its way in and out quickly, planting just enough of a seed of doubt to start him forward into the mist. He wanted to turn to the others, to apologize yet again, but at that moment the haze in front of him began to shimmer, and he was forced to use all his concentration in crab-walking back away from the portal.

It was huge. The hand that slipped through that mist was golden, glowing like the sun. It was followed by the beginning of an impossibly large torso, a shoulder. Whatever it was could not make it all the way through the portal, but it was groping blindly about, sliding along the bases of the trees.

This thing, whatever it was, had been the source of the light. On the small portion of chest that was visible, what he had earlier mistaken for a stream ran in a large band downward toward whatever sort of legs and genitals the thing might have, and upward towards its face—its mouth. The claws that dug furrows in the muck were easily a foot apiece in length, and brown—tree-like. How could he have been so stupid?

He could feel a questing intelligence groping for his thoughts, trying to pinpoint him so it would know where to reach. He could tell by the expressions on the faces of the others that it was seeking them as well. Each fought his own quiet battle, and Love knew that something had to be done.

He started to reach down for the dagger, but something told him that it would be a serious mistake. A blade the size of his could not be much more than an annoyance to something that large, and there was no telling just how quick and agile the thing might be. If he lashed out at it, caused it any pain at all, it might be able to use that or his movement to locate him. There had to be another way.

Then he remembered the book. His fingers brought it eagerly from beneath his shirt, but before he could flip it open, the voice was back.

How do you know you won't wear it out? it whispered. *How do you know the power won't run out, leaving you stranded in the Tempest with no weapons?*

He shook his head. That was nonsense. The power of the prophecies was unquestionable at this point. Or was it? Did the power come from the book itself, or did it come from some quality of this realm? Would it even work in the Tempest? Would he tap into it one too many times and find that he'd placed his hope in falsehood?

Might be your last great attempt at valiance if it fails, the voice continued. *Why waste it? Let it have one of them, any of them. It will go away.*

That cut it. Love flipped the book open blindly, as usual, and stabbed at a page, beginning to read before the voice could return again and disrupt his concentration. "Knock, and the door shall be opened unto you, seek, and ye shall find."

Christ! he thought wildly. *What kind of helpful prophecy is this?*

With a roar of triumph that shook the very substance of the world surrounding them, the thing lunged. It gripped the base of the tree where the Spectres had disappeared earlier and shook it with tremendous strength. The force of its motion sent Love and the others reeling back, and the book in Love's hand was flaming, nearly blinding them all with its brilliance as it flickered, joining its light with the golden light of the creature's skin.

The air was suddenly filled with a high-pitched screech, and seconds later two of the cat-like Spectres tumbled from the branches, just outside the node. Love watched as they scrabbled frantically for purchase, trying to escape back up the trunk and into the safety of the upper levels of the tree. There was no chance. As soon as they touched down, the hand swiveled with lightning quickness, scooping them into a screaming mass and dragging them back through the second portal.

Their cries beseeched aid, soulless eyes reaching out hypnotically to try to bring those in the clearing to their aid, but there was no strength left to them. They wriggled and writhed, turned and twisted, but the grip tightened perceptibly, and all of what served as life departed them in a rush of black fluid. Seconds later the huge hand slipped back through the portal with a *snap* of energy, and all was silent.

The book no longer glowed. The spot of light that had indicated the second portal was gone completely, as though it had never been. Love collapsed against the trunk of the nearest tree and Llanna came to his side, holding him close.

"You might keep those energy waves down a bit," Seth called from his seat by the mist. "It's hard enough to concentrate through this stuff, and now you've called all of the Tempest down on our heads with your games."

That was all Love could stand. *Games?* He lunged toward the old guide, who was cackling, but he never made it that far. Seth held up a wizened hand to stop him and hissed.

"Wait…it is them. They are opening the nihil. It is a fairly large party. Larger than ours."

Love listened intently, his ire forgotten in an instant. Fontana. Did the prophet walk just the other side of this haze? Was Love about to find his old mentor and bring him to safety, or had he merely led another group of friends to join the others on the slave-chain? The moment of truth was at hand, and he did not have an easy feeling in either heart or stomach.

"I think our only hope is surprise," Seth said, all business now that the game was afoot. "We need to find a way to burst free into the byway. If we come out the way we went in, we will never get past those guards, or their barghest companions, alive. We will have to take the entire chain with us, and we will have to leap into the storm on the other side blindly."

Love's mind was churning with thoughts and images, and one popped quickly to the surface.

"I may have a prophecy for getting us through the mist in a hurry," he said quickly.

"Then here is the plan," Seth said, taking charge. No one thought to contradict him, so he continued. "We come through here low and hard. Don't bother with weapons, you won't have time. Run straight at the chain, grab it, and run like hell for the other side. You'll have to get your friends," he turned to Love as he said this, "to run as well, or we'll be a tangled mess, and there won't even be a good fight."

Love wasn't certain. As plans went, it seemed rather simplistic and dangerous. On the other hand, he had no idea what he'd *thought* they might do against an armed party. He'd heard those beasts, if not seen them, and he knew he didn't want any piece of that. Could they do it? Would they be quick enough?

He took the small green book into his hands, and he stared at it, hard. He let his mind slip back in time, let his heart open to the words once more. He sought the moments with Fontana, the power that he'd found shining in the other man's eyes. He reached back for the image of Faith, up and charging, leaving their last life without a backward glance. He wanted that feeling back, that feeling of utter abandon that had carried him through the heart of the world.

The book was warming, but he kept his eyes focused. It was not time. Over and over he repeated his father's mantra, "I am the baddest son of a bitch *in* this valley."

Tensed and bunched together, hand in hand, they waited. Seth stood at the front, eyes directly on the portal now and an odd, feral grin covering his face. The time of prophecy was at hand.

13

They were out of the palace and onto the road very quickly, once the preparations were finished. Fontana barely had a chance to settle into his slightly less subservient role before he was dragged forth again and taken through the long halls to the front of the palace. Although he was not immediately chained into the string of thralls that waited outside, he was not exactly treated deferentially.

Looking at his former companions, he knew that there was no help to be found there, either. He stood before them, his position improved, theirs the same, and the fact was not lost on them. That they had been sold out was obvious; the only question was for what. For the moment it was enough that he would not be in the chain. He had the feeling he might not have survived the journey, had this not been the case.

The two beasts, Crassus and Brutus, melted from the shadows at their sides as they left the encampment and returned to the road. They might have been standing there beside the road waiting since he'd last seen them for all the differences he could see. Somehow, though they still frightened him, the permanence of their presence was comforting. Fontana still remembered the Spectre lunging straight into his face and the way one of those creatures, no way of knowing which, had launched itself into the battle.

His own plans were still nebulous at best. He needed to get his hands on Love's copy of the Little Green Book. If it had as much power as rumor said it did, he should be able to use that power as well as Love could. He didn't have the restrictions that his old follower did. He cared about no one but himself, and he was willing to go to any length to be free again.

Sully and Din still didn't trust him. That much was clear in the way they watched him from the corners of their eyes. He knew they were hoping he'd make a mistake, do something stupid that would give them the opportunity and cause to chain him with the others and be done with him. Cappy was even worse. Even Bontempt hadn't filled him with the level of uneasiness that this man brought about by his presence alone.

Not for the first time, Fontana found himself wondering how it was that Bontempt was the one in charge. Cappy certainly didn't seem the subservient type, and in a contest of wills, the guide seemed a much more likely winner. What drew him back to the road, to the Tempest and Stygia herself, that Bontempt could use to control him? What were his secrets?

That was the best method of controlling others, Fontana knew. Learn their secrets. Find out what mattered to them, and what did not. Find out what they loved, what they hated, if they would die for a cause and what that cause might be, then find a way to make them believe that you were instrumental in seeing that cause through to completion.

His own followers had been pretty much united in the cause of escaping whatever life they'd left behind. Fontana had known all of their stories. Love, in

DAVID NIALL WILSON

particular, had been leery about revealing much of his past. Eddie Constantine. Lonely "Deathwish" Eddie.

Most of what mattered about Eddie Constantine had died long before Fontana met him in that park. Most of what made the man human had been either suppressed or destroyed by a life that just never stacked up to the dreams that surrounded it. Fontana had seen that quality, that gothic disregard for life, and he had played upon it.

It was odd that they had all ended up in chains here on this level. They had worn chains of a different sort when they'd followed him. Each was chained to his or her past by some sort of failure, either their own, or that of the world that had betrayed them. They had also been chained to Fontana, to his words, his thoughts. They'd seen in him a doorway to something better, and they'd found this. He wondered, if they really thought about it, if they'd be able to bring themselves to blame him. All they had done was to change masters.

He knew they *would* blame him, though, for everything. They would also, if they got the chance, pull him forcibly limb from limb. He supposed he deserved it, if not for bringing them here, then for lying to them and for trying to save himself by sacrificing Hope or one of the others on the road. If he hadn't before, he certainly deserved their hatred now. It didn't matter. Survival mattered, and he was a survivor.

They moved beyond the city rapidly, and he did his best to keep an equal distance between himself, the guards, and the prisoners. He didn't want one of the Archangels reaching out and grabbing him, nor did he want to raise the ire of Sully or Din, who were just waiting for him to screw something up. He didn't know the other three guards, but none of them seemed disposed to laughing or joking with the prisoners, and he knew their attitude would extend to himself.

Crassus and Brutus were another thing altogether. He found that if he strayed too much toward one side of the road or the other, they mimicked his movements. He had no intention of running, and he knew that the beasts must realize this. Still, they prowled along beside him, waiting, hungry. There was no escape for anyone under their scrutiny except the final escape, and Fontana wasn't prepared to make that jump yet.

As they moved farther away from the encampment, buildings began to appear alongside the road. Some were worm-eaten, dingy hovels, others huge, brooding factories that spewed a black miasma of soot and grime into the air. The images blended at times, superimposing upon one another oddly. Fontana gradually gained enough insight to distinguish which building actually *existed* for him here, and which he was staring at through the cloudy gulf to the Skinlands.

He could see traffic of all sorts moving on the road now. There were coaches and bikes, cars and pedestrians. Many of those he saw wore chains similar to those of the thralls he accompanied. Some were single slaves following or guarding a master, but there were a few work groups tied together for ease of labor. All of them shied away from Bontempt's chain. They ran in sheer terror if they came in too close proximity to the beasts.

Bontempt might not have anything to do with the shadow citizens of this place, but they knew him. Maybe it was just the uniforms, the mystique of Charon and the legions. Maybe it was just common sense. Cappy and the beasts alone would have commanded a wide berth from any intelligent passerby.

The living men and women they passed, often moving straight through them, paid them no attention at all. They moved about their lives, their faces worn and pitted, scarred and dangling loose flesh, pasty and unhealthy in the odd light that permeated the Shadowlands. Fontana watched them in fascination, knowing they were not even aware of his presence, watching their deaths eat away at them slowly. What a gift it would have been to see this kind of prophetic doom on a person's visage while he'd been alive!

They passed old women, rocking like animated skeletons on rotting porches. They passed packs of dogs with ribs showing and fangs yellowed and falling out. They passed through hordes of morning traffic, heading into work, the old grind. The hustle and bustle of San Valencez surrounded and suffused their path, and yet it was only a tapestry. It was nothing more than a cinematic attraction, one that he noted the guards ignored completely.

They moved through a smaller community of others living on their own plane. These slunk about the shadows or watched from the shuttered windows and doorways of their own sets of buildings, skewed, warped versions of their real-world counterparts. Many of them seemed to live in the ruined buildings, places where the original structure had burned down, barely visible through the Shroud, while in the land of death it had been rebuilt—taller, darker, leaning off at impossible angles and presenting shadows that would once have made Fontana cringe, but that now seemed somehow inviting.

If he'd been alive and watching all this in the movies, he'd have been certain that Tim Burton had a hand in it. The more they moved inward toward the center of the city, the more the other place faded and his new home kicked in. There were shops, as there had been at Bontempt's camp, but these cropped up along boulevards of dead buildings, husks of tenements and row houses, crumbled city structures. There were more people actually on the street here, and while they did not look comfortable with the beasts and the chain of slaves moving down their main street, they did not really look frightened, either.

Fontana took it all in, paying special attention to the others in different uniforms that they passed. The guards seemed a bit deferential toward these, and they wore various colors as if working for different offices of government, or possibly different governments altogether. Fontana would have liked to have questioned someone about this, to have learned more of what he would need to know if he gained the book and, after that, somehow managed his freedom, but he knew it would be unwise to speak.

As they moved on through the central streets and began to head out the other side of town, Fontana became aware of a small disturbance ahead. The guards, anxious to see what they could see, hurried their steps. Ahead the road grew hazy, as if the barriers between worlds had somehow weakened, and Fontana could just make out the figures of police, pushing back a crowd. Their faces reminded him of the creatures in the *Night of the Living Dead* zombie movies, but

DAVID NIALL WILSON

their actions were anything but those of dead people, or would have seemed so before recent revelations, anyway.

As the chain pushed forward, a small grouping of wraiths dispersed, some reluctantly. It reminded Fontana of a pack of hyenas giving up the carcass of some sort of animal to a lion. Din marched straight up to what appeared to be a city bus, turned on its side. The wheels spun at odd angles, and smoke rose from the engine compartment near the front.

An accident. There had been an accident, and now the bus was going to catch fire. Fontana cringed, but it was too late. Whatever was left of the vehicle's fuel had begun to drip from the tank toward the ground, and some of it came into contact with superheated metal from the overturned engine. There was a quick spark, then the air was filled with fire. The explosion shot metal and debris outward at an alarming rate, sending huge guttering bits of metal, upholstery, and flesh into the air and across the street.

The police he'd seen before had dived for cover moments earlier, and the crowds were following suit, dropping to the ground and covering themselves against the onslaught of debris and flame. Fontana fell to his knees, covering his ears and his eyes, but seconds later he was lifted and tossed physically to his feet. For a short instant he believed it was the force of the explosion, that he was being catapulted through the air, but the illusion was dispelled quickly. Before he could turn or protest, he felt a boot connecting painfully with his tailbone and propelling him forward.

There was no sound. There was no heat. When he finally managed a glance over his shoulder, Sully was following closely behind him, a look of pure disgust painted across his face. Nothing had happened, not on this level, and yet all but the flaming carcass of the bus was gone. Vanished. He could just make out several figures rising from the carnage, people who should be dead. Then it hit him. They were. These were "fresh ones," and Din and Sully meant to add them to the chain—a bonus for Bontempt that was certain to make him happy.

The citizens of the dead city of San Valencez, California, looked none too pleased that these slavers were going to march in and, by purest luck, harvest so many slaves and workers that by rights should have stayed in the city, but none interfered. The four slavers produced a second chain from somewhere in their packs and, under Cappy's watchful eye, efficiently pulled men, women, and children free of the bus. Not all the seats had been full, apparently, or not all of the passengers had come through to this place, but there were enough. In all, Fontana counted seven new additions to the slavers' coffers.

He felt as if, perhaps, there should be something he could do for these new ones. Just for a moment he felt a twinge of guilt. They were bound for a dark place, a place where they would either be sold as slaves or melted down and turned into money and bricks, and he was just watching. Then the guilt melted to fear and puddled into submission. There was nothing he could do. He could, maybe, look out for himself. That was all. It was a misfortune for these folks that their bus had overturned when and where it did, that was all. Not his problem.

Din and Sully were conferring with the other two slavers over the carcass of one of the newly dead. As the shock of the explosion *not* hitting him faded slowly from his numbed mind, Fontana realized that they were discussing the remaining dead. There were several that were either in some sort of catatonic shock, or unable to move for other reasons, and apparently Din didn't want to leave them behind. They already had two sleds of mutilated, inanimate corpses with them, including that of the federal agent the Spectres had gotten on the road.

Whatever was being said, it was obvious that Cappy was making the decision, because Din and Sully turned from him with a shrug, moving to the heads of the already secured chains and starting them all forward again.

"Don't worry about Bontempt," Cappy called after them. "He'll know it was the right decision. It's one thing to run a chain through the Tempest, quite another to take an army of thralls in there and expect to get out in one piece. It's enough."

Fontana began to move forward again, but he watched the two slavers who walked ahead of him closely. Din's shoulders were tense, the muscles bunched, and Fontana could tell the big man did not like being overruled on his own slave chain. It seemed that Fontana had been right in his assessment. Cappy was much more than just a guide. It was more information, more to store away and hope he got a chance to use.

Cappy stood in the middle of the road, watching as well. He didn't move, nor did he speak. His eyes bored through the backs of his companions, and his jaw was set in stern lines. His eyes glittered in the half-light of the city street, catching the ghost flickers of the fire that still burned in the other world. They were as black as obsidian, empty.

The man never even glanced Fontana's way when he passed, and that was fine. Fontana hurried his steps to put as much distance between himself and the dark leader of their mission as possible. The chains were moving off at a good pace, the newcomers struggling to keep up, stumbling along and staring wide-eyed about themselves at their new home.

Although Fontana could remember what it felt like, it was a vague memory. It seemed a long, long time since they'd dragged him from beneath the kitchen cabinets at his compound…worlds away.

Despite the best efforts of the four slavers, they did not make quite as good time as they'd originally planned. The new chain was not as agile, and they had to stop several times to whip them into submission. Fontana found that the wails and cries were getting to him, as well, and he wished they would just quit whining and live with it, such as it was. He knew these were callous thoughts, but he also knew they were attitudes he would need to cultivate if he were to stay in this world and thrive. No room here for sympathy, that much was clear.

They moved slowly but steadily to the outskirts of the city, and before long he noticed a subtle change in the air. It seemed to be pumping him full of an odd energy, and the ground around him shimmered back and forth from one world to the other. He did not see any people, and only one car passed them on the old road as they went, but he could tell that the twisted, dying trees were not a part of his current reality. There were rodents skittering about on the sides of the roads, birds flapping noisily among the trees, all with the visage and aspect of death.

Rather than ignoring the marching chains of slaves, they were spooked by their approach. Apparently every place was not the same in the ways between worlds. There was so much to learn and so little time, or opportunity, to do so before it did not matter at all.

They passed a sign that read *Shady Grove Cemetery*, and the road beneath their feet turned to gravel. The energy in the air increased steadily, and as they moved toward the gates of the old burial ground, he felt the "vibrations" of the place sinking into his bones and soothing him. It was a place of death, of pain and suffering, and yet it brought him peace. As they passed between the wrought-iron gates and into the cemetery itself, he saw others along the sides of the path.

Many of the gravestones were tenanted. Men, women, and children sat in front, leaning on the stones, or perched on top, gazing at the slave chains as they trooped past with hooded, unreadable eyes. They did not come forward to speak with the slavers, nor did they show fear or anger. They only watched. Fontana could feel some of the energy coiling about these figures, potential energy, but it never went into an active state.

It seemed that there were those who called this place home, dead people who chose the peace and solitude of the cemetery over the pseudo-life of the cities that had risen in the Shadowlands. It also appeared that, though they were not going to attack the party, they would fight for their territory if anyone tried to settle down here. Fontana didn't know exactly how he knew this, but somehow it registered in his thoughts, and he *did* know it. This was their home, and all the chains would be allowed to do was to pass through.

This became a point of interest, as well, because it was growing increasingly obvious that the energy was concentrated at some point up ahead. Little cracks seemed to run through the air and the ground, and whenever he couldn't avoid touching them, Fontana felt sparks of some sort of charge slipping through his being. The Tempest. They must be nearing this place he'd now heard so much of, and yet about which he still knew so little. If the entrance to this place involved this much energy, what must it be like inside? He shuddered, but he didn't hesitate. He had no intention of letting his fear get him strapped into one of the chains before they were inside. Things were bad enough already.

Suddenly the entire party stopped, and he heard Din, Sully, and their two companions moving down the chains, drawing everyone closer together and giving instructions to each thrall in order. As they approached him, Fontana moved in closer to the new chain, those who did not know him and thus presented the least danger. Sully watched him in disgust, but the man was all business now. It seemed that entering the Tempest was a matter to make him nervous, as well. If that were true, it would do Fontana well to pay attention.

"Keep hold of that last man on the chain," the short man told him tersely. "No matter what you see, feel, or hear, do not let go. If you get lost during the entry, we'll never find you, but someone will—understand? There are worse things than being part of our slave chain."

Fontana nodded and grabbed the chain as instructed. Whatever tension there had risen between Din and Cappy had subsided, he noted. The two were working side by side, checking the chains, checking the carts that carried the immobile carcasses, and conferring with one another softly. Whatever personal differences they might have, they shared knowledge of what was to come, as well, and that knowledge overrode all else at this particular moment.

There was an odd expression on Cappy's face as they prepared to move forward again. It was a sort of hunger, an anticipation that glittered in the ebony pits of his eyes. He wanted this. He wanted to be within the boundaries of this "Tempest" almost as badly as the beasts, Crassus and Brutus, wanted to feed. And there was one of Fontana's answers. Cappy did not challenge Bontempt because Bontempt had nothing that he wanted, other than a reason to go back, a reason to return to the Tempest. If that was so, then there must be something worth seeking within those boundaries, as well as without. A choice. Another possible path.

The preparations passed so rapidly that Fontana found, later, that he couldn't remember if they had taken an hour, or a moment. His mind was clouded by the fear and anticipation of entering yet another realm, and the certainty that, if Love and his new companions were going to make their presence known, it would happen soon.

Fontana had figured that, if they were going to make their move, that they would do so before the chains entered the Tempest. Now it was obvious that he had miscalculated. There was no sign of them, nor was there anywhere nearby that could hide them. Either they weren't coming at all, and he'd just outlived his usefulness, or they would try something once they'd entered the Tempest. What that meant about the resourcefulness of those they faced he didn't know. Apparently Love had hooked up with some folks a little more powerful than Bontempt had assumed.

Finally, making a sweeping motion with his hand that reminded Fontana of a cowboy on a wagon train, Cappy stepped into the brightest section of the light, extending his hand back to grip Din's firmly, and they all started forward. Fontana closed his eyes, gritted his teeth, and plunged ahead, following the squirming, screaming chain of slaves into the unknown. His own screams blended quickly with theirs, but to his credit, he didn't let go.

He never knew how long it took them to pass through that first part of the Tempest. There was a period wherein he was certain that they were lost, and he opened his eyes. The impossibility of his surroundings drove him back to his personal darkness, and he slammed forward, pushing at those ahead of him in his haste to be free of the madness. When they finally broke into the clear he fell to the side, finally releasing the death grip he'd held on the chain in front of him.

He opened his eyes as the walls of mist to either side of him burst open, filling the road with screaming, flashing bodies. He blinked rapidly to clear the confusion, and failed. He huddled into a ball on the ground and let the madness sweep him away as the cries of the beasts, Crassus and Brutus, blended with the curses of the slavers, the cries of some sort of intruders, and the moaning, helpless wails of the thralls. This was what it was like, he thought, at the end of the world. This was *it*. Then he thought no more.

14

The first thing that registered on Love's mind as they passed through the portal and into the byway was the second chain. He and the others burst through near the middle of the first chain of slaves, and he immediately caught sight of faces that were familiar, the broad shoulders of the Archangels, the long, silky tresses that were Hope and Charity. Where was Fontana? Where was Faith?

Sound had erupted all around him. For himself, he'd chosen the old war-cry of the compound, a sort of half rebel yell, half demon cackle that they'd developed over the weeks to galvanize their people into action. It had aspects of Love's own voice to it, but it was not complete without those of his old companions. Still, it was better than silence. He hoped that it would usher them into the presence of the chain of slaves as friends and would set the wheels in motion to get them moving.

It was impossible to tell if they'd joined him in his scream. All around him were howls, cries, wails, and curses. He saw one of the slavers, a short, wiry little man, leaping toward him with a blade drawn, but he ducked under the chain, whipping it upward so that it caught the dark, slashing blade flush, metal to metal. Putting every ounce of his strength and energy behind it, he tore at the chain.

"Michael!" he cried, "Gabriel, Uriel, the other side—now!"

They must have heard him because there was a tensing of the line, a slight hesitation, and then it moved. It moved so violently, so rapidly, that the two ends of the chain were whipped together behind them in the middle. It was as if those four, foolishly bound close to the middle of the chain, had saved every ounce of energy, every bit of hatred and carefully hoarded strength for that one moment. They exploded through the mist like human tanks, dragging Love, the chain, and one of the slavers, who cursed and scrambled along with them, trying to get his footing to use his free hand to wield his blade.

Love saw him, and he saw also that the chain was moving, that it would move whether he held on or not. He slipped in low, coming under the chain and swiping upward with his own smaller blade. The man was caught by surprise, off-balance as he was. Love's slash caught him under one arm and rendered the limb useless. The slaver released the chain, staring at his ruined arm stupidly, and the entire mess whipped into the mist on the other side.

Love leapt after it. He could hear the slavering breath of one of the beasts behind him, and he put every shred of energy remaining to him into one forward leap. He felt himself plowing into the chain as it went through, and he grabbed hold, taking hair, skin, clothing, and finally a link of the chain to pull him through.

The Archangels were dragging it all forward mindlessly now, working like a well-oiled machine, and there was nothing that Love, Fontana, or anyone could have done to bring them back under control at that moment. They had a goal, a mission, and they would fulfill it. Behind him, Love felt the byway falling away, and he chanced a glance over one shoulder. He got a fleeting glimpse of the creature, its jaws open wide and those terrible, hungering eyes boring into his soul, and beyond it…Fontana. He was not on the chain. They had failed. Then he was dragged forward and he felt himself falling, falling into a lush green meadow, then dragged back to his feet.

"This way," Seth was shouting. The old one was already moving toward another portal, and Llanna, the chain and her followers in tow, was following rapidly. Love stopped for just a moment in confusion. Go on, leave Fontana, or go back? What could he do? There were too many, and he had more responsibility now, more responsibility that he had not asked for. Cursing, he dove forward and grabbed the rear of the chain, pushing ahead to get through the opening before the slavers had a chance to follow.

He tumbled through after the others and came to a halt behind the line of thralls. Ahead he could see Seth and the others, already moving along the line and removing the chains. He saw the Archangels flexing their arms, rubbing wrists too long in restraints. He saw the look in their eyes as they glanced over their shoulders, the hunger for destruction, for revenge. He'd once admired that in them; now he felt it mirrored in his own heart. He and the others had gotten away with the chain, but the object of their search was not achieved.

Love blanked his mind to this. What mattered now was to get to a place of relative safety and regroup. He didn't know if it would be possible to find his way back through the Tempest to go after Fontana, but he knew that he *would* go back. First he had to get the others to safety. He knew the Angels would go with him, if for no other reason than that they were an awesome force with little direction. In the absence of Fontana, he could provide that direction.

Llanna and the others he wasn't so sure about. They'd followed him on his crazy, seemingly suicidal quest, but this was different. They'd pulled off a swift raid on an unsuspecting party, and the fact of the second, unexpected chain of slaves had helped as well. The slavers had been too spread out to do any real damage, and it had all happened too rapidly.

Now, though, their enemies would be wary. Now they would know that they were not the only ones making their way through the Tempest, and they would plan their defenses accordingly. There was no way to know if they would come after the lost chain. They'd already slipped through two portals from the byway...could they be followed?

Where they now stood was a long, desolate stretch of beach. A surf pounded mercilessly at the gritty sand at their feet and ebony waves flipped spray skyward to glitter against a background of milky white sky. There were mountains in the distance, but there was no sign of life anywhere. Love had come not to trust his first impressions here in the Tempest. He kept glancing uneasily at the water's edge. It was the logical place to be attacked from in this stretch. He knew that the very fact of this logic probably invalidated it, but still he watched.

"We need to get to another byway as soon as possible," Seth was saying. "We can't remain in these nodes. We will never survive. Nothing is stable here."

"We can't go back the way we came," Llanna added. "They will watch the roads, especially if they have any way of knowing what has happened. It's my guess, though, that the slavers will go on and not send any word back at all. They still have a chain of slaves to deliver, and to report failure before they've even truly begun their journey would be suicidal."

"Will they follow us?" Love asked quickly.

"Not likely," Seth answered grimly. "They had one with them who could follow, one that I know well, but I do not believe that he will consider the risk worthwhile. They still have to protect the rest of their thralls, and to do that without his guidance would not be an easy thing, even if they keep to the byways."

Love wandered among the newly freed slaves. He found Charity, Hope, and the Archangels huddled together, and he joined them quietly. They opened their circle slightly to allow him entry. Equal entry. With them, he was no prophet. With them he was Love, the Beast…nothing more. So he believed.

"We did not free Fontana," he told them grimly. "We have failed."

They stared at him numbly. He didn't know what else to tell them. His only plan in this place had been to reach Fontana and to set him free. After that, he had counted on his mentor taking the reins and leading them to whatever awaited them. At least, whatever happened, the responsibility would not be his. Now that dream had ended and reality once more had settled solidly on his shoulders.

He turned slowly to face Michael, gazing up into the big man's eyes and searching them, trying to find where he stood. "Why was Fontana not with you?" he asked finally. "Was he on the other chain?"

"He was not on any chain," Michael answered. "He had been freed to walk alongside the slavers. None of us knows how, or why, only that he no longer wore the same chains as we did."

"I have to free him," Love said, turning his head to sweep his eyes over all of his old companions. "I won't ask for any help from any of you that you do not wish to give, but I don't believe I can do this thing alone. I want Fontana here, with us, where he belongs."

The Archangels shared a dark moment of communion, their heads moving toward one another almost imperceptibly. No words were spoken. Hope started to speak up, her eyes filling with tears, but Uriel quieted her by laying a large, meaty hand on her shoulder.

"We will go. We want Fontana as badly as you do," he said.

Hope and Charity were staring at him, their mouths hanging open, but they did not speak. Something was different, wrong, about the situation, but Love could only guess at what it might be. It was obvious that, though the others were going to follow Uriel's lead, they did not all feel the same on the subject. It was not important why. It was important only that they would come with him, and that the quest was not yet at an end. All that remained was to speak with Llanna and the others.

"I don't know what the hell you all are talking about," a smallish, stout man piped up, "but I'll be damned if I'm going back to that group after *anyone* or *anything*, least of all that mealy-mouthed little traitor."

"What do you mean, *traitor*?" Love asked quickly. His temper flared quickly, and he was barely able to keep it in check. The man who'd spoken was obviously one of the federal agents who'd attacked the compound, maybe one of those he'd personally dispatched to this place. Who was he to speak like this of the prophet, the only hope Love could see of reaching anything worth having beyond where he now stood.

"You'd better watch how you answer, friend," he said, moving slowly toward the smaller man. "I've come a long way to free these people, and in particular that man...the prophet."

"Prophet, hell!" the short man blustered. Spinning quickly to Hope, he said, "The bastard almost got you killed out there on the road, tried to hide behind you when that thing attacked. If he hadn't been distracting the guards and those beast things, Jim might not be the puddle of protoplasm he got turned into during that same attack. Now the guy is walking free, like he owns the place, and your other friend, the fiery one with the pretty eyes, is gone completely. Where is she? Do you know? I bet your friend Fontana does."

Love would have grabbed the man by the throat if the Angels hadn't grabbed him first, restraining him. They did not acknowledge the man's accusations in any way. Hope looked uncomfortable, but she too remained silent. Charity was still crying, disoriented by the mad dash through the mist, and she wasn't talking either.

"You didn't understand him in the last life," Love grated at the man, "and I don't expect you to understand him here. He gave me this—" At this he held up the *Little Green Book* and waved it in the air. "I may not have had the faith or the vision to pick out the prophecies from the bullshit when I was alive, but now Fontana has given me the power to bring those words to life—to feel their power."

He turned to Llanna and her followers, who'd stood quietly by, waiting to see what would transpire. "I have to go back. I don't know if I can find them again, but I have to try. I can't just let them drag him off to Stygia and melt him into a brick. I'll understand if you don't come with me, but without your help," he turned then to Seth, "I know I'm sacrificing myself and everyone who follows me in."

He didn't ask them to come. He didn't want them to feel in any way coerced by their belief in him. He left them to discuss it among themselves and to come to their own conclusions. It felt good to have familiar faces surrounding him, to feel the comforting strength of the Archangels at his shoulders once again. He may not have been the prophet, but in war he was the leader, and when they'd left the last level, they'd gone out fighting.

Llanna didn't even turn to the others. Either she knew that they would do what she wanted, or they had conferred while he was discussing things with his own companions. She walked forward and took his hand gently in her own, gazing into his eyes.

"I still do not believe that this Fontana you seek will have the answers. I believe that *you* have them, but I will follow you until you discover this for yourself. If you say we go back, we go back, but I am as unfamiliar with this place as you. Only Seth can bring us safely through."

She turned to the old guide, and the others followed suit. Everyone in the small clearing was staring intently as Seth smoothed his hair back in a nervous gesture and glanced back the way they'd come. His dark eyes were far away, perhaps remembering something about the other man he'd seen, or about other journeys through the mist.

"I will take you where you wish to go, but I tell you now, it will be suicide. The man who guides them is as familiar with these ways as I, and between us there is no love lost."

"No fight is ever lost or won," Uriel commented, "unless the battle is joined. We cannot concede defeat without chancing victory. If they end this existence for us, what have we lost?"

Seth didn't answer, but he looked at the big man oddly. Uriel had not gotten more handsome in death. His face was creased by a long, jagged scar that stretched from just below his right eye to the point of his chin. His hair was ragged, uncombed and blowing wildly in the breeze from the demon sea at his back. He looked every bit the part of the avenging archangel, and watching him, Love felt a shiver of admiration.

The others moved to stand at Uriel's side, and each was a mirror in different color-tones and styles to the strength of his brother. Michael, tall, massive, blond hair like that of a Viking hanging limply to the middle of his back and tied with a bit of cloth he'd torn from his shirt. Gabriel, thin, taller than any in the party, and yet with a wiry strength that belied his emaciated appearance. His eyes were deep and wide, wider than any human's had the right to be, Love thought. Finally, Raphael. Raphael had not spoken a word since he was a small child. His father had seen to that; a father so mired in the bullshit of his religious fervor that he'd seen demons where a little boy's tongue had been. Raphael's eyes glowed like coals and the posture of his body, the bunched strength and fury of his muscular frame, spoke volumes that were denied to his tongue.

Seth eyed them, first one, then the other, then he turned to Love. Those black, black eyes sought something deep inside, and Love opened himself to it. He felt a probing, a warm erosion of the walls that separated him from the world. It lasted only a moment before the walls snapped back into place, but apparently it was enough.

"Perhaps I have been hasty," Seth smiled. "With such a team as this, I would scale the walls of Stygia herself, I think."

"Then we will need to start soon," Llanna chimed in as the others all gathered near, "and we will need a plan."

"Oh, the plan is not a problem," Seth assured her. "I have been saving something suitable for a long, long time now. I have some old friends I think I can count on. They aren't the safest of allies, but they may do the trick."

Love wasn't certain that he was comforted by these words, but it was good to have the old guide back on their side. He also felt the strength that the Archangels lent to the group. Only a small number of others, led and gathered together by the federal agent who'd spoken up earlier, had drawn apart. They were talking of either making their way back to the byway and out, or of waiting out the battle here, where they could remain neutral and uninvolved.

Stupidly, the man who'd spoken up seemed convinced that it was all a mistake, his being brought here. He felt that his government would be mounting some sort of counter-offensive soon, that the FBI would be coming to set them all free if they just managed to wait it out. It was best, the man told his new group of followers, not to be involved.

Love was glad to see that none of those from the compound were listening to the idiot. He truly hoped they would find their way out, but he had no real concern for their well-being. They had been trying to kill him the last time they'd met, and he felt as if he'd long since erased any possible debt he might owe them by cutting them loose from the chain.

Seth and Llanna were conferring now, and he went to sit beside them. The two of them seemed to be arguing over something, and Llanna appeared upset. She was shaking her head vigorously from side to side and slashing at the air in front of her with her hands for emphasis. Love had seldom seen her so worked up.

"It is too risky," Llanna was saying, her voice low and grating. "How will we trust them? What if they turn on us? We can't fight our way through so many."

Seth seemed unperturbed. Whatever it was that he'd proposed, he seemed set on it already.

"That is the beauty of it," Seth was explaining. "We will not fight at all. We will merely get as close as we can, send out the summoning, and when all hell breaks loose, we will slip in and try to make off with this Fontana they seek. Even if my friends prove a bit overenthusiastic, the guards will be as busy as we fighting for their lives."

"But he will know, this other," Llanna pressed him. "He will feel what it is that you intend to do; won't he try to stop you?"

"He will try to find me before I can finish the summoning. Such a call to the dark ones would be an abuse of my abilities, in his eyes. He will not want me to complete it, even though he himself will be in little danger.

"Yes, he will seek me, but I will make that part as difficult as possible. We will just not be able to stay stationary for long. Any time we do that, either he or the Spectres will home in on us like magnets to a nail. I don't have to tell you how bad that could be."

"How bad?" Love chimed in. "How much danger am I putting you all in?"

"You have sensed Oblivion," Seth said, swiveling his head so his dark, searing gaze fell full upon Love's face. "That is the price of failure. That is the *preferred* price of failure. The other possibilities are far worse."

Llanna turned to Love, and she reached into her pack at the same time. Digging about in the depths of the bag, she drew forth a small, glittering egg-shaped object.

"I've been holding this for you, waiting until it seemed the proper time. Since what is to come may be the *last* time we have a use for anything, I think it is appropriate that I pass it along now. We found this on the very spot where you passed into this world."

She held up the dark grenade and Love stared at it, fascinated. Reaching out slowly, he took it into his hands, and as he did so a charge of energy snapped between his skin and the thing's slimy surface. Llanna cried out and fell back,

DAVID NIALL WILSON

but Love was too fascinated, too caught up in the moment, to notice her dismay. He felt alive, more alive than at any moment since he'd entered the Shadowlands.

He knew what it was, as he had when she'd shown it to him at the compound. It was the dagger with which he'd sliced the heart from the last world, the grenade that had sent him over the top and through the wall. He held it reverently, studying every line, every angle. The pin was of darkest obsidian.

"What will it do?" he asked.

"I have no way of knowing," Llanna told him, "but it is obvious that whatever its purpose is, you are the one destined to pull that pin. I have the feeling that when the time comes, you will know it."

Another mystery. Another thing to follow him from his last life. The grenade was like a monument to Deathwish Eddie Constantine, to the spirit of the warrior Love Constantine. It was his only headstone.

He tucked the grenade away in his pack carefully. So here it was. They had attempted their surprise attack, and it had failed. Now they would go back. On their side was a small green book of prophecies, a black grenade whose powers were completely a mystery to them all, a dark old man with eyes of obsidian who could find his way to Hell and back, and four uprooted Archangels in search of their prophet. It sounded like some sort of cheap, dime-store fantasy novel.

"All we need is a damned elf," Love muttered.

"What?" Llanna asked, her face twisting into a frown.

"Nothing," Love answered, and for the first time since realizing his failure, he smiled. If he was going to die again, this was the group he would gift that second life to. If he was going down in flames one final time, then he would do so with a weapon in his hand and the prophecies that had served him so well and faithfully on his lips. He might be a fool, but it was good to be a fool in such company. Let the Tempest do what it could, let the beasts howl and the Spectres rend and tear. Love Constantine was going to find the heart of *this* world and rip it out by the roots.

In his pack, he could sense the grenade, silent and powerful, waiting. Pulling Llanna close, he smiled even more widely. Taking another quick verse from the prophecies, he rose and said, "Let's just do it."

15

Din was in a fury. He stormed about the byway like a man possessed. Fontana sat quietly off to one side, quivering in terror, watching and doing his best to remain invisible. He'd never seen anyone quite so out of control.

"There is nothing to be done," Cappy was saying quietly. "We can't just go tearing off across the Tempest in chase of a bunch of worthless slaves. It was a good tactic, a clean hit. They are gone. Be glad that we picked up this second chain. With a little quick talking and smooth cover up, Bontempt will never know that anything happened at all."

"No!" Din thundered. "Damn it Cappy, they took slaves from *my* chain. Don't you understand? I can't just go on and let them win, knowing they are out there, within reach, and I did nothing to stop them."

"You lost one man already," Cappy pointed out. The guard that Love had stabbed earlier was now strapped to the top of the heap of injured thralls they'd dragged in with them. "If you go off into that mess, none of you may make it back. I believe you have a very distorted view of what is 'in reach.'"

"I will be going back," Din grated.

"Oh, so you are now a Harbinger, are you?" The sarcasm in Cappy's voice was unmistakable. "You won't be needing me, then, to finish up your ridiculous vendetta? If that's the case, I think I'll just go ahead and do as *I* was hired to do and take these slaves on through to Stygia. You can explain later why you thought it better to go off on your own little revenge trip."

"This is different," Din said. "Sully, you know what Bontempt said about the one with the book, the lost one." He turned back to the old guide, changing tactics and calming himself somewhat. "Bontempt really wants this one. I don't know how, but he has power, and he hurt Cyclops. It won't matter if we carry a thousand slaves through this storm and into Stygia. If we go back without that one, we might as well sign ourselves on as thralls when we reach the city, because that's what's in store for us."

"Perhaps," Cappy said, his voice maddeningly calm. "It might be interesting, though, to see how Bontempt would carry out such a sentence on me. It might even be the most amusing thing to happen in the last millennium. It has been a long time since anything has struck me as particularly challenging."

"I suppose what we just experienced was a cakewalk," Sully spat in disgust. "If you know this damned place so well, how come you didn't see that coming? For Charon's sake, we were supposed to be *watching* for those guys. They took those slaves from us like we were a bunch of beginners, no struggle at all. Even Crassus and Brutus didn't get a clean shot at them."

There was an agreeing growl from off to the side. The two beasts were pacing back and forth, growling low in their throats and gnashing at the air. The frustration was palpable, surrounding them all like a shroud.

"I suppose this means you favor going after them, as well," Cappy sneered. "So good to know that everyone here except the one hired to know the Tempest is such an expert. What method would you use, I wonder, to track them?"

"They took that portal there," Din said quickly. "I would follow."

"And then what?" Cappy wondered aloud. "From the other side of that there are dozens, I'd guess, of different paths they might have plunged down. I doubt if they knew themselves which way they would go. Would you leap through the hole, run like hell, and hope to fall through the same holes that they did? It doesn't seem like much of a plan to me. Besides that, if you stand here long enough, that portal will not lead where it did before, either."

"I guess not," Sully said sullenly, "but then, you could track them. You may be right about us. If we followed, all we would do is get lost. Well, I think getting lost is probably a better idea than going back to tell Bontempt that we let a bunch of weaponless heretics waltz up and steal his slaves, not to mention that we failed to get the one he sent us after."

Cappy's face darkened, and it was obvious that he was going to lose his temper any second. Din stood his ground, unperturbed, but the violence that seemed ready to erupt never got its chance. Cappy's face took on a sudden stiffness, his eyes twisted to one side, then to the other, and he raised a hand toward the guards to silence any further words they might have.

Spinning toward the mist, he ran his hands lightly over the surface of the tenuous wall of the byway, then placed his cheek against the cloudy substance of the storm and listened. His eyes were far away, focused on some sound, some sensation, that was beyond the moment—watching things that the others could not see. He stood motionless, every muscle in his body taut with effort.

When he at last turned back to the confused and still angry guards, Cappy had a grim smile on his face. "You will get your wish, it seems. Whatever it was they came here for, they did not get it. The fools are coming back."

The faraway look was still in his eyes, and he seated himself quietly on one of the heaps of mutilated slaves. His ire of moments before was forgotten in the challenge of the moment, and the distant smile was beginning to slip back across his countenance. Seeing that he was lost in thought, Din asked softly, "What is it? Is there more?"

"I know the one who leads them, is all," the man said. "He and I go back more years than you could count with both your lives added together. We have walked these storms together, and yet we are no longer on the same side, it would seem."

Fontana saw a momentary flicker of uncertainty flash across Din's face, and he shivered. He understood the big man's concern. If Cappy was nervous about something, he couldn't imagine facing it. If it was going to be challenging, despite the beasts and their superior weapons, then this one they faced must be truly formidable.

Clearing his throat, knowing that the moment was almost past where he could do himself any good, Fontana said. "He is coming for me. That is why I am here. He took the chain, he took those who followed me, but he came here to free me. That is why they will return."

Sully swung around in anger, but Cappy stopped him with a gesture of one hand. He rose, looking Fontana over slowly, taking in the details, then returning to the mist.

"He speaks the truth. For their own reasons, they all return for him."

"If it were me," Din said, coming very close to Fontana and spitting the words in his face, "I'd be coming back to tear your sorry, cowardly ass limb from limb. If the others have spoken to this follower of yours, you might want to think about that. I doubt if they are coming back to ask you to be their leader, and remember this. If they come, and we take them, I am *still* going to remember. You will never escape this place without me, and I will see you in the forges."

Fontana cringed back, not quite allowing himself to come in contact with the cloying mists behind him. He remembered the passage through those mists, and he had no desire to return to them. His piece spoken, he returned to his silence, and the guards to their pacing. All there was to do was to wait.

He thought back to the things he'd done and seen since coming to this world. Somewhere in those memories there had to be an answer, a key that would unlock the mystery of how he was going to survive this. Din might well be right. If Hope, Charity, or the Archangels had talked, Love himself might have been swayed.

Somehow, though, he didn't see it that way. If the others had convinced Love that Fontana was not worth saving, they would not come back. He knew Love too well to believe that he would ever risk the entire group unless he truly believed in what he was doing. That meant the prophecies guided him, for whatever that was worth in this realm, and that would mean that he still meant to free Fontana.

What would happen afterward, with the others present, was a different thing altogether. Love might have some powers in this place that he had not had in the living world, but Fontana doubted that even Love could hold back the Archangels if they set their mind on something, and he had seen the hatred in their eyes.

Now he was in the curious position of hoping that his followers could wipe out the slavers, but at great cost to themselves, because it was beginning to look as if the only person who had no way of winning in the upcoming struggle was Fontana himself. Stygian chains seemed, at present, preferable to being ripped limb from limb, as Din had so poetically put it, so he decided to root for the guards at this juncture. Odd how things shifted when you looked at them in a different light.

"The lesser of two evils," he muttered, thinking of his book. He wished, suddenly, for the little notebook he'd carried for so long. The words might not have the meaning to him that they had to his followers, but the twisting of them, the recording of what served him as wisdom in the inanities of everyday speech and life had kept him motivated, kept him sane. He felt as if he'd lost some important edge, some courage that had seen him through previous situations, but which had abandoned him now.

You are nothing. He didn't know where the words had come from, and he spun quickly, looking at the guards, searching the fringes of the mist and moving closer to the center of the byway. *There is no hope for you. Your own people hate you. Your only hope is to throw yourself into the storm, to run and run until there is nowhere else to go.*

He looked into the mist and wondered. He was chained at his ankles, but he was not attached to anything solid that could hold him back. They had only just entered this place, making their way through one solid wall of mist. He could fling himself into that wall, force his way through to the other side—to the graveyard—lose himself among those who lived there, beg them for a space. No one would know him there, no one would care who or what he might have been previously.

Yes, the voice insinuated itself into his train of thought. *Flee. Get away while you can. The guards will chain you, flay you within an inch of unlife and melt you on the forges. I can lead you out. I can take you where you will be safe. Let me in, let me help. I am the only one left who cares.*

"No!" Fontana staggered to the middle of the pathway, nearly colliding with Din, who was still pacing, and he felt himself cuffed roughly on the side of his

DAVID NIALL WILSON

head. He reeled toward the mist, pinwheeling his arms and collapsing to avoid tripping within those swirling clouds.

"What the hell is wrong with you?" the guard snarled. "You keep down there, and you keep your ass out of my way, or they won't find much when they come here looking for you."

The voice seemed to have retreated as his head reeled from the blow, and Fontana sank to the ground in pained relief. It seemed that even the pain was better than the barrage of emotion that had struck him under the influence of that Shadow voice. He had always needed to belong, to be important to someone. Here he was not. His worst fears were of being insignificant, hated, all the things that this world seemed bent on thrusting upon him. Who was the voice, and how did it know what to say?

Around him, the tension grew. Cappy stood, facing the walls of mist into which their attackers had disappeared, his head cocked to one side as if he heard things that were beyond the others. His eyes looked right through whatever he stared at, piercing to some level that lay beyond normal sight. He was not a normal man. From the black glitter of his eyes to the deadly set of his jaw, it was obvious.

The decision to move on could not have come at a better moment, as it turned out. Love, who was going over last minute details with Seth, was distracted, suddenly, by a roaring sound that filled the air around him and echoed through his mind. What could it be? Where was it coming from?

Then the cries arose from all sides of him, and he spun toward the water in consternation. His mind did not immediately grasp what he saw. Where there had been a calm, placid beach, there was a curving wall. Where there had been pale, luminescent sky, there was darkness.

"What?"

He wasn't afforded the time or the chance to figure it out on his own. Seth had him by the arm and was herding them all toward the portal through which they'd entered.

"Tidal wave!" the old guide screamed in his ear.

It took no more words to galvanize Love into action. He grabbed the two of his followers nearest him and leaped forward, tumbling through the mists, wrestling with the images and ignoring the voices that assaulted his senses, concentrating on avoiding that huge wall of dark liquid, focusing on the other side, whatever it might be. He tumbled to soft ground, then rolled to his feet, glancing hurriedly about himself. If he'd learned no other lessons about the Tempest from his journeys, he'd learned that trouble could come from any direction at any time. He wasn't going to be taken by surprise twice in such rapid succession.

The others made it through just in time. There was a great rending roar of sound, deafening and powerful, and the ground beneath their feet trembled, but the walls between the nodes held, whatever ethereal substance they were made of. They had dodged the bullet of the great wave, but there was no time to sit on their laurels.

"There is something coming," Seth cried out. "Follow me and keep close; I'll see if I can find someplace we can regroup."

Love glanced around him. There were trees and flowers, a nearly azure sky with a few puffy clouds hanging motionless above them. It reminded him of a forest glen on a nice day. He couldn't imagine what could be troubling Seth. This seemed the perfect place to regroup. He was about to mouth these words when he saw them.

They came from the distance with a hum and rattle of sound that permeated the air. Love and the others found that they could converse only in gestures as the volume of their new attackers rose steadily. They were insects, large, flying insects that resembled nothing so much as wasps, except for their heads. Where the shoulders of the creatures joined to the thorax, a humanoid head sprouted, wide staring eyes glaring out from beneath flopping antennae. They flew in perfect unison, in formation like some kind of eerie, otherworld fighter planes, and Love pushed and prodded the others after Seth, who was working his way along the far wall.

Just as it seemed that the insect things would swarm over them, the old guide stood suddenly and, waving to Love, plunged through the portal he'd been investigating. Without thought, Love followed, dragging, pulling, and driving the others through ahead of him. As the last of them slid through the mist, he chanced a glance over his shoulder, and it almost cost him his soul. They were right there. Their inhuman eyes hovered like saucers before his face.

The closest one had drawn itself up so that its lower body was curling to meet him, so that the impact of their bodies would be on the point of a huge, dripping stinger that protruded from its rear end.

Love didn't wait to see more, or to try to defend himself. He dove headlong, hitting the portal and flying through the mist. It happened so quickly, the transition from one space to the next, that he nearly passed out from the disorienting flood of emotion and sensory overload. He felt the Shadow voice slipping upward, feeling his weakness and making a bid for control, and with the final vestiges of his strength, he pushed it back down. He never even knew it when he hit the sandy ground on the other side.

It was several long moments before he regained full consciousness, but it could have been days. He found that Llanna and Seth were leaning over him, both with worried expressions on their faces. Over their shoulders he could see the implacable countenances of the Archangels, watching, waiting, seeing if he would measure up to the task. He wanted to reassure them, to tell them that he was fine, but at that particular moment in time all his faculties were necessary for that simple act of sitting up.

He looked about himself carefully. There was nothing in sight but walls of mist and endless sand. They stretched away as continuously as the black ocean had appeared to only moments before—had it been such a short time?

"Is it safe?" he asked, directing his question at Seth. He hated the thought that his own momentary weakness might have put them all in danger as they waited for him to recover.

"It is stable enough for the moment," Seth answered hesitantly, "but there is more. It has begun. I have issued the summoning. I have no way of knowing how long it will take. This entire area of the Tempest will be swarming with every manner of creature Oblivion has to offer within the hour."

"These creatures will do your bidding?" Love asked incredulously. "If you have that kind of power, how is it that they have any chance at all?"

"They will do no man's bidding." Seth said with conviction. "They have agreed to help us, but do not trust them. They will rend and tear our people as readily as they will our enemies. I am hoping that they will be more worried about fighting for their lives than about our return.

"Cappy—that is his name—will escape. I will probably survive. This is not something I tell you to frighten you, it is merely a matter of the will to survive, and the skills to bring that end about."

"Are you saying that we will not survive this?" Llanna asked softly.

"I am saying no such thing," Seth answered crossly. "If we stick together, this will work to our advantage. We must find our way to the byway, I know that much of this plan must succeed. We must reach the byway before the true strength of the summoning wreaks its havoc. On the byways there is a relative margin of safety."

"But the slavers will be there," Love protested. "We outnumber them now, but they have blades of darksteel and those two barghests. How can we match that?"

"If our luck holds," Seth replied with a crooked grin, "and their luck does not, they will be as busy with what I have summoned as we are. I believe they will be counting on us arriving soon enough that they can take us, then retreat or forge ahead and avoid the center of the rage I have unleashed. Every creature within miles of here will have heard it, and they will rush to that spot like hungry men to the dinner bell."

"Then our best bet is to try to get close to the byway, but to hold back as long as we can keep ourselves safe," Love said thoughtfully. "We need to play tag with the Tempest."

"Exactly," Seth smiled at him. "It is exactly the type of game Cappy will enjoy the most, but I'm counting on his arrogance to lead him to the conclusion that he is winning. He was always looking for a challenge. This will be the ultimate."

"How far are we from that byway?" Love asked quickly.

"It's hard to tell, really," Seth told him seriously. "I can find the general direction of it, but the portals shift constantly. What led one place a minute ago could take you a thousand miles away, or right back where you just came from if you don't know what to look out for. I would guess that if we start moving now, it will take no more than three passages to make it to the byway."

"Three…" Llanna's face was very serious. "Then there is no way to know what we will encounter between here and there."

"None," Seth agreed. Love thought that the old man's grin might be a bit too enthusiastic.

There was something about the old guide, a feeling of antiquity beyond Love's comprehension. There was no way to know the loneliness, the boredom that such age might bring with it. If this challenge was sparking something deep inside Seth's being that brought him pleasure, even if it was a dark, dangerous pleasure, who was Love to say anything about it? He believed that if it were in the man's power, they would all make it safely through, and there was realistically nothing more he could ask.

"Everyone get any weapons you have ready," Love called out to the rest of the party. "We'll be going through here in pairs, each pair holding on to the pair in front of them. Seth and I will lead the way. Be prepared to move once we slip through each portal. There is no way to know which areas will be empty, which will be dangerous. We have to make it through three portals, and we can't do it all at once.

"If we hit that byway before the Spectres do, we will fail. They are fewer than we are, but they have the superior force. We have nothing to match those two beasts, and among us we have only a few short daggers against their swords. Are you all ready?"

They stared back at him, the strong, the weak, those who'd not wanted to accompany him at all, and the fanatics. Each had his own vision of what they faced, and each chose to face that vision in silence.

"Let's do it," Love called out, and he and Seth turned without a further word and launched themselves through the first of the chosen portals. The others followed and the storm swallowed them whole.

The first thing that assaulted Love this time was cold. He was buffeted by an icy wind that cut through the clothing he wore and into his flesh, and though he felt certain that they had come free of the mist, he was as blind as if they were fully immersed. A blizzard. The snow and ice howled around them, slicing at their limbs and numbing their muscles. It was odd to feel such sensations, feelings that had seemed lost forever in the outer reaches of the Shadowlands. Here in the Tempest, it seemed, the vision controlled the reality.

Seth didn't even try to speak with him. There was no way for sound to penetrate the raging storm, and he was too intent on the way before him. He was running his hands lightly over what Love could only suppose to be the wall of mist. He could see nothing but snow and the vague silhouette of his companion. Behind him he felt Llanna's hand gripping his belt firmly. No way to know how the others were faring, but she was there. Somehow that was very, very important suddenly. In this soundless, sightless void, being alone was the worst of his fears.

Seth seemed to find something to his liking, because he moved again suddenly, dragging Love behind. Love in turn tugged on those that followed, and they made their way slowly out of the storm and into mist once more. This time the transition seemed longer, drawn out, distracting. The voices that snatched at his thoughts seemed a bit weaker, the images that swam before his inner eye less intense, but it was deceptive.

The longer they moved through the mist, the more hypnotic those images became. He heard the voices more distinctly, more clearly, and the words distracted him. He found himself concentrating, trying to pick up their meaning, and he almost lost his grip on Seth's arm in the process.

The old guide turned, striking him roughly across the side of his head and glaring back, his eyes so close that their noses nearly brushed.

"Concentrate!" he cried over the rustling, intruding voices. "You have to pay attention. I need my strength to find the next doorway."

Love shook the cobwebs from his head and nodded. What had he been thinking? Nothing, that was what. The voices had been lulling him to a state of stupor.

He checked behind him, and Llanna gave him a firm shake on his belt, reassuring him that the others, so far as she could tell, were fine. Just ahead, Seth was on the move again, and another slightly lighter shaded spot rose in the mist ahead. With relief, Love slid through after the older man, and he felt the others dragged along in his wake. There were a couple of bad moments where the drag on his belt was stronger, pulling him back, but they overcame it. Someone had stumbled, or been pulled back to their feet, or lost. Love plowed on, and ahead there was a dim light.

They stumbled into a world of craters and mountains that rose darkly on all sides, towering over the valley where they stood. Love turned, letting Seth watch the road ahead for the moment, and counted them, one by one, as they came through. He was about to breathe a sigh of relief as it seemed they'd all made it, but as Uriel popped through with Hope and Charity in tow, the string ended abruptly. There had been four others behind them, Bobby, the federal agent, and two others.

Love started back toward the opening, but Llanna stopped him with a gentle hand on his arm. "Let them go," she said. "There is nothing you can do."

"She is right," Seth added. "I could not find them myself. Count yourself lucky we have come this far with so little loss. We are one portal away from the byway at this point, but I don't know how long the pattern will hold."

"How long before the summoning is complete?" Llanna asked quietly. "I sense powers approaching, but I cannot tell from where, or how long it will take them to arrive."

"Some will arrive more quickly," said Seth, "but they will not necessarily be the most dangerous. We should not move until we are either under attack here, or we know that they are under attack on the other side of the portal."

"So we wait again?" Love wondered aloud.

"We wait," Seth agreed, settling back on his haunches, "but not for long. Not for long at all."

Love glanced around the alien landscape that surrounded their little group, keeping a wary eye on the lips of the crater-like holes that littered the ground and watching the distance for any sign of disturbance. Others watched the cliffs above.

Little Green Book, chapter eight, verse fourteen: *My, how time flies when you don't know what's going on.*

As the skies darkened and the ground began to shake like thunder, Love clutched the book and looked at Seth.

"Hold on," the old guide told him. "They are still a few moments away. We need every second."

They huddled tight, as close to Seth's chosen portal as physically possible, waiting. There was no sign of the new threat, and yet they knew it was close at hand. The roaring, thunderous sound grew, and the longer they waited, the less they could see as all light seemed to leak from the world about them, washing the skies in deep grays and black.

At what seemed like a bit beyond the last second, when the world was about to explode around them and they were shaking so roughly that it was difficult to remain on their feet, Love heard the order to move. He leaped for the portal, felt the others surge around him, and a battle cry rose to his lips. He heard, faintly, the echoing cries of the Archangels as they burst through into the byway, cresting on a wave of sound, exploding as if shot from a cannon. The battle had begun!

16

Fontana nearly passed out from fear as the darkness descended. The air was full of roaring sounds, flashing lights, and the screams of the others. The mist roiled and tumbled about them, awash with images, faces, fangs and claws. The byway itself was still clear, but it seemed only a matter of time before that odd wall of cloud gave way completely and they were washed away in a tide of destruction and darkness.

The guards had formed the slave chain into a circle again, as they had on the road from the compound, so it was obvious that they expected an attack. This time Fontana was not included in that circle. He knew that he was being used as bait, and this knowledge was removing rational thought at an alarming rate.

He drew as near to the circle as he could. None of those on this chain knew him. He was in no danger from them, but they were all frightened and confused, having even less idea what was happening than he did. He wasn't certain if there would be safety in numbers, or if the very vulnerability of the chained captives would attract whatever it was that was coming for them, but somehow it felt better not to be standing alone in the middle of the road.

Cappy stood off to one side. Din, Sully, and the other guards gave the guide a wide berth as they prepared for what was to come.

The beasts stalked the sides of the road, snapping at images that flickered and played across the view-screen of the misty wall. There was no fear. Somehow, fear was not a part of their makeup any longer; perhaps it had been bred out as they slowly succumbed to the all-encompassing hunger that drove them. Perhaps it had been a trade-off for the humanity they'd left behind. In any case, they sensed that things were getting out of control, and the only answer they had was to destroy.

Fontana concentrated on them for a moment, using the image of their lithe forms prowling to distract him from the intensity of the nightmare that surrounded him.

Not long. The voice rose once more, taunting him. *They will fall, whining like puppies, and you will be next. No one here will care. They will not make the time or effort to save you. Your only hope is to flee.*

He wanted to scream at the voice and make it leave his head but he did not. He huddled as closely to the floor of the byway as he could physically press himself, and he waited.

Cappy was spinning slowly, scanning the walls on all sides of them. He was looking for something, concentrating.

"They are close," he said at last. The light had returned to the depths of his eyes. They were still black as the pits of hell, but animated. "Seth—that is their guide—is leading them on a course parallel to this one. They are trying to hold back until we are overrun by his—friends. He has summoned aid from the storm."

"Can they do that?" Din asked.

"I'm not certain," Cappy frowned. "I don't believe they can avoid all that have been summoned on the far sides of these walls. Without the protection of a byway, they will be under constant siege. Those Plasmics and Spectres not powerful enough to brave the byways will go after them—the easier target."

"And the other Spectres?" Sully asked.

There was no reason to answer. A whining cry, like the fall of a projectile on a battle-field, ripped through the air, and the walls were breached. It was only a small opening, like a puncture in a balloon, but they poured through it, nearly a dozen of them, before a gesture from Cappy managed to seal the breach.

Din launched himself forward with a scream of his own, as if he was relieved that the time for action had finally arrived, and he clove the first of the creatures into two pieces with a single swipe of his blade. The battle was on their own terms, this time. The Spectres, while quick, agile, and hungry, were hampered by the protections of the byway. Their hypnotic eyes and screeching voices were of little use, and in a war of claw against sword, the sword was the naturally superior weapon.

It was twelve on four, though. It was all the slavers could do to back their attackers off the slave chain, and it was obvious that it would be only moments before there were more to contend with.

"How do we get out of here once they've come through?" Sully cried, swinging his blade viciously down through the throat of one attacker and twisting it to parry a slashing set of claws that was aimed at his throat. The creatures seemed oblivious to one another's fate, using the deaths of their companions to screen their own attacks, and ignoring the fallen.

"I have a way out ready," Cappy said calmly. His own blade was a blur, and Fontana, who was cowering against the chained slaves, saw that where it touched dark flesh, all that remained afterward was more mist. The creatures he faced shied away, as if recognizing him or his weapon.

The first group of Spectres never made it within a yard of the slaves. Those that got past Crassus and Brutus were hacked quickly to bits, and it appeared that the small party might be in less danger than it had seemed. Fontana leaned forward a bit as the last of the attackers fell, Brutus' huge fangs rending the head from its body and tossing it viciously aside toward the mist.

Then Cappy spun to his rear, a flicker of alarm passing across his normally icy countenance, then gone, but not before Fontana was able to spot it. Another break in the mist had opened, and this time it was not a horde of creatures that slipped through, but a single, great hairy arm, and that arm was followed by a second. The hands, three foot across if they were an inch, actually seemed to be gripping the sides of the ripping portal and pressing it open. The skin of those arms glowed bright and yellow as the sun.

Smaller creatures were skittering through the bottom of the opening, which was widening by the second. Whatever creature owned those hands pulled and tugged at the failing fabric of the byway. It was trying to let as many through as possible, and the idea of sentient thought and an enemy of such stature was terrifying.

Cappy sprang forward, slashing at the closest of the hands with his blade and kicking out with a booted foot to send one of the smaller creatures tumbling toward Crassus. There was a great roar as his blade touched the giant's skin, and a smoking patch of darkness rose on the back of the thing's hand, but it did not dissipate as the Spectres had done and Cappy was forced to press the attack.

Meanwhile, Din was bellowing to Sully that a third rip had formed a few yards down the trail. Just as this small tide of Spectres burst through, low-slung like cats and padding on all fours toward the chain, the wall opposite Fontana seemed to open like a curtain, and a tide of people flowed through it—appearing from the mist like materializing spirits. These were no Spectres, though. These were the cavalry, such as it was.

In the lead, he saw Love, a small black dagger held high and eyes shining like the hero from some ancient saga. Beside him an older man, one with the same dark, empty eyes as Cappy, burst through and immediately turned to survey the scene before them. The Archangels and others from the first chain slid in next, and after them, a group of people that Fontana had never seen before, clustered about a slender woman.

One of the small, skittering creatures that had slipped in under the gigantic arms had found its way around the chain and spotted Fontana where he crouched. It scuttled, much like some sort of giant spider, across the ground. Three antennae twitched above its head, and a hideous row of teeth sprouted from a mouth that spanned its girth—nearly two feet. The thing's eyes were faceted, like those of an insect, and as it approached him it scampered first one way then another, as if trying to get its perception of his location straight.

Fontana rose shakily to his feet. He had no way to defend himself, and the others were far too busy defending their own lives and their property to pay any attention to him. As far as they were concerned, Elliot Fontana's usefulness had run out the second the attackers had returned to the byway, and it was now time for "the prophet" to find a way to get his own butt out of the sling he'd gotten it into.

Love saw him almost instantly upon making his way out of the mist and headed at a dead run for the creature confronting him. The others followed behind, and Fontana managed to get a glimpse of the expression on Uriel's face. It would not matter much if Love saved him unless he could save him from the Archangels as well.

Go, the voice told him. *Go now, while they are all distracted. The Spectres come from within the Tempest, not from the way that you came in. You can still escape.*

This time he did not push the voice away. He acted. The paralyzing fear that had held him immobile for so long released him suddenly, and he lurched back down the byway. They had not come far, perhaps a quarter of a mile, before Love had burst through on them and snatched the chain. If he could just make it back that far, back into that wall of mist that led to the graveyard, he might get out of this with his skin after all. The voice had been right all along, and he should have known to listen to it.

He passed Love, who ignored him, intent on the creature he now faced, and slid along the edge of the mist before the Archangels could react. The woman and her followers paid him little attention, turning toward the battle and leaping forward. The number of Spectres and impossible creatures that had made their way into the byway was growing at an alarming rate, and there was little time to consider the fate of one lone escapee.

He ran like he'd never run before, and when he saw the light growing and the mist rising at the end of the byway, he launched himself like an Olympic long-jumper into the cloudy depths. The sounds cut off behind him, and the voice rose within his head in mocking laughter as the world disappeared. He was on his way. He was going to be free.

Meanwhile, Love had made his way forward to where the crab-beast stood, wavering back and forth on its legs and twitching its antennae about. It trembled in anticipation, skittering back and forth in quick, limber rushes of too many feet.

Love lunged, but the thing moved like lightning. It slipped to one side, then scuttled back toward him as he passed, and he only avoided a claw-like mandible by fractions of an inch by diving headlong. Christ, it was fast.

He flipped over and to his feet as quickly as possible, but the thing was already moving toward him. He dove to the side, slashing at it as he passed, but catching only air with his blade.

As the thing stalked him, swaying back and forth, something clicked in his head, and he began to dance back and forth from one foot to the other. The thing hesitated, then stopped. It flicked its feelers this way, then that, as if considering, or concentrating on something.

It couldn't see him. It depended on its own motion to find objects that were stationary. By matching its side-to-side gait, he was confusing it slightly, and the creature did not want to attack in such a state. It wasn't intelligent enough to sense the danger in its hesitation.

Taking careful aim, Love drew back his arm, lunged to his right, and threw the dagger straight into the thing's maw. It took notice of the object moving toward it through the air, but it did not move. The blade caught it in the upper portion of its mouth, digging in deeply and driving it backward. Love didn't hesitate. He dove forward, taking the protruding handle of the dagger and slashing downward with it. The creature's claw whipped out, slashing his cheek, but he pulled back. He dragged his blade the other way and pulled it free, then danced away and resumed his side-to-side motion.

At that second a huge roar filled the air about him and one of the barghests dove into sight. Ignoring Love for the moment, it swung a claw at the injured crab-thing, crushing the creature's exoskeleton like an eggshell. It went flying with a high-pitched, keening sound, and the beast spun to face Love.

It looked at him with eyes from hell, scanning his face, his weapon, possibly his mind. It crouched, bunching its great muscles, and Love prepared himself to die. There was no way he could withstand the power of the thing, no way his tiny dagger was going to be a match for its claws and teeth. Then it sprang, and he dropped to his knees, watching in morbid, slow-motion fascination as the thing flew straight over his head, arching into the air.

He spun just in time to see the creature clamp its jaws over a hand the size of a small pig, wrapping itself around the appendage so that its rear claws could come into play, gouging at the flesh of the arm that was attached.

There was a roar that shook the earth, and the great beast was flung free, crashing into the slave chain with a sickening thud, then rolling free. It was limping, one front leg dragging uselessly, but its answering roar contained nothing but rage—the fury of the battle. Once more it came forward, leaping with its three good legs to grasp the hand again. This time the other hand was present as well, and the beast was gripped by the neck and lifted free. It flailed powerlessly at the mist, but it was hauled out of sight, and the portal snapped shut with a crash.

Whatever had been holding it wide had released it. The wall at that point was solid once more. As he stumbled to his feet, Love felt strong arms grabbing him from behind and helping him to stay upright. Uriel and Michael had materialized at his side, and Seth stood with them. Ahead, where the portal had been closed, a tall thin man turned toward them. He scanned the little group quickly, lifted his sword to Seth in a mock salute, and smiled.

"So," he bellowed, throwing his head back to laugh, "you have come after all."

"What I have done here will certainly close this byway forever," Seth cried in return. "We may all meet Oblivion here."

"I will not be departing this plane just yet, my friend," Cappy laughed, "and I doubt that you will, either."

He spun suddenly, dropping another of the crab things with a flick of his blade. Love hadn't even seen the thing coming, and yet this man had skewered it as if he'd known where it would be all along. What kind of an enemy did they face?

"You overestimate yourself," Seth grated. "There is a way you can meet your end here, and I am that way."

Seth launched himself forward. Still laughing, but maniacally now, Cappy spun to the side, whipping his blade in an arc that should have cloven the smaller, older guide into two separate pieces. Seth was not there. He was not moving fast; he just simply was not there.

Then he was. He'd reappeared behind Cappy, his dagger raised, and was plunging it toward the taller man's throat. Then they were both gone, and the walls bulged obscenely around them. Love gathered his group together and began to advance on the cowering slaves in the other chain. He didn't know what had happened to Fontana, but the first order of business was to get these people freed and to get out of there with all their skins intact. No small order.

Already there were more small breaches in the walls surrounding them. Din and Sully were both backing toward him, engaged by at least a dozen Spectres, and the remaining barghest roared and slashed at their side, enraged by the loss of its companion.

The third guard had fallen, and there was still no sign of Cappy or Seth. The two had vanished into their own private little battle within a battle. There would be no help forthcoming from that direction.

"We have to go back," Love cried. "If we can make it to the portal that brought us in here, maybe we can make our way out through the mist before we are overwhelmed. The byway is never going to hold."

Llanna was screaming to be heard over the screams and battle cries that surrounded them: "We need Seth to make it through!"

"We may not make it out," Love agreed, grabbing her arm and dragging her back down the byway, "but we will *certainly* not survive here. Let's go!"

They made their way along the road swiftly. The nearer they got to the portal, the stronger the walls seemed to be against the encroaching Spectres. The darkness flowed after them, overrunning the guards and spreading into a wave. It became a race. The Archangels brought up the rear, tossing aside the smaller, swifter creatures that nipped at their ankles as if they were toys, crushing them with desperate abandon.

They weren't going to make it. At the last second Love turned, and he saw that the guards stood back to back, the barghest at their side, and they were surrounded by a black tide of madness. There were nightmares walking, creatures of every description pouring through the walls, and mist flooded the byway. Whatever foundation Charon had laid to protect against this had crumbled. It was eroding behind them faster than they were moving forward, and he saw that they would be engulfed a good ten yards before they reached the final portal.

He felt the now familiar burning, but it was not coming from the book around his neck. He reached around behind himself with difficulty, and felt the side of his pack, which was heating steadily. The grenade. The damned grenade. He reached inside the bag and lifted the thing free. Without thought, he yanked out the pin, mouthed a silent prayer to any gods who might be listening, and tossed the thing over his head. He closed his eyes and dove forward toward the portal, screaming for the others to do the same, to cover up.

The snap of energy that followed was sudden, final, and deafening. It did not just shut off sound, but seemed to flood through his system, removing all form of sensation for a microsecond, then depositing him in another place altogether. It was not, as he'd hoped, the graveyard beyond the portal. It was an empty place with no vegetation, and the earth beneath his feet was a sort of empty, colorless dust. The others lay beside him, as stunned as he himself. None of them moved.

The shock of flashing from the certain doom that had faced them moments before to this new reality was overwhelming. It was a good while before Love could bring himself to move. He had to check on the others, to see who had made it. He counted, mentally ticking off the names. The Archangels were all present. Llanna lay close by his side, and beyond her the federal agent, the man who'd wanted to make his own way from the side of the black sea that seemed years in their past. Their ranks had thinned horribly. Hope was there, but Charity was nowhere to be seen. Of the dozen he'd left the compound/temple with, only seven remained. Seth was nowhere to be seen.

"Where are we?" Llanna breathed softly, sitting up and shaking her head. He reached over to lay an arm across her shoulder comfortingly.

"I have no idea. At least we seem to be alone, for the moment."

The others were moving now, most of them, checking for injuries and looking about themselves quietly. No one seemed to want to speak. No one wanted to mouth the questions or make the statements that they all feared to hear. Had they come through to another node in the Tempest itself, or had they come through to another place completely? Another level?

He vaguely remembered tossing the grenade behind him, the explosion that had followed and the silence that had engulfed him. That grenade had been formed of his journey to this level. Had it launched them another step along the way? Was this empty, lifeless place the end-all of his destiny? He suddenly wondered if he'd been right to make such a final decision for them all. At least it didn't seem to be worse than the alternative they'd faced in the byway.

He stood, and Llanna stood with him. The others rose shakily, some helping those next to them, others merely stumbling to their feet and walking in slow circles. What to do next? Love watched them all, feeling the enormous weight of responsibility that rested on his shoulders and wishing he could find someone to take it for him. He was not the leader. Eddie Constantine had never been a leader. He was a follower, the *best* follower, the number one, right-hand man to the prophet.

They weren't turning to him yet, but they would, he knew. And once again, he had set out to free Fontana, and he'd failed. Or had he? He remembered vaguely seeing his mentor running back down the passage. Had Fontana found the way out they had missed? There was no way to know now, no way to follow. Seth might have followed, but Seth was gone. Gone into the storm he'd loved, into the battle he'd led them back to. Perhaps the old man had planned it that way. What better way to go than into the heart of your greatest love?

There was a sudden commotion on the other side of his small group, and he made his way in that direction quickly. The others were dispersing quickly, parting as he made his way through, and parting as something made its way from the other side. There was a shimmering spot in the air, and it reminded Love of nothing more than it did the special effect of the transporter on a Star Trek episode. He came to stand in front of it, the others gathered at his back, two Archangels on either side of him and Llanna directly behind him, her hands on his shoulders.

They could hear something approaching, but they could not yet make it out. If he stared intently enough at the portal, it became a tunnel, another byway, but to where? No way to tell, so he waited. If death had pursued him to this faraway hole in time and space, then fine. He would meet it head on as he had the first time, and he would erase his doubts in the purity of pain and darkness. The time for running was through.

Then they heard the voice. Cursing, but with a hint of dark merriment to his words, Seth came sauntering out of the shimmering lights, dragging something behind him by a length of chain. Love's jaw dropped, and he stepped back a pace to make room as the old man looked up, waved, and yanked the chain violently forward.

Stumbling, blinking his eyes against even the dim light of the emptiness in which they all stood watching, Elliot Fontana came into view. He looked around at those gathered before him, flinching as his eyes passed over the Archangels and Hope, and finally he let his eyes come to rest on Love's face.

Love didn't know how to react. He took half a step forward, reached out a hand. He was tempted to go down on one knee and cry—though tears were beyond him now. All the thoughts, the plans he'd been forming, dispersed like so much dust in the breeze. This was it. This was the moment for which he'd worked, risked his own life and those of the others. The prophet was free at last.

"Love," Fontana croaked. "Love, it is good to see you."

Love said nothing more, but he moved forward dazedly, wrapping Fontana in a bear hug that threatened to snap the thinner man's back. He pulled back again, then, just looking.

"I found him wandering around in the mist when I went back after you all," Seth explained. "He was headed in deeper; had it in his head to make it to that graveyard outside the portal, but the byway had shifted. Pure luck I came across him."

"But," Llanna said, not taking her eyes off Love or Fontana, "where were you? We saw you and that other one—Cappy?—disappear from sight completely. Then the walls started to collapse and we ran. You never came back."

There was as much accusation as question in her words, and a great sadness grew in Seth's own eyes, mirroring her features. "There was nothing else to do," he said softly. "If I'd let him stay there and fight in the midst of the summoning, he would have been the end of us all." Seth's eyes seemed suddenly faraway— ages away.

Fontana was only vaguely aware of the conversation. His mind was numb with relief and deadened by shock.

"I am told that the prophecies followed you here," Fontana said at last, talking in a low voice that the others would not overhear. "They say my little book is quite potent in this realm. Do you still have it?"

EXCEPT YOU GO THROUGH SHADOW   535

"Of course," Love said eagerly, pulling the book from beneath his shirt hurriedly. "I have carried it like this since the first moment I woke up in this world. There was no way to follow you on the road, but with the help of these others, I was able to catch up. I hope it hasn't been *too* painful of a journey?"

"Not with freedom at hand, finally," Fontana almost whispered. "The book, though. May I see it?"

Fontana's mind was working overtime, whirling with the possibilities that the next few moments would present. He knew that the old one, Seth, knew better than to trust him. He'd been babbling about his freedom, his desire for power, working for Bontempt, all of those things and more when he'd been found in the mist. There was no way to know how much he'd given away, but he was certain it had been enough to end his chance of ever winning this group over. It was only a matter of time until the conversation shifted back to him. He had to get the book from Love *now*.

He didn't really know what he planned. He had the vague notion to make his way back to Bontempt's camp, tell the story of the attack, and try to use the power of the prophecies to make a place for himself at the palace. It was the only place he'd known in this world, and he still had a few words he'd like to have with Faith, given the proper circumstances—circumstances that could ensure her compliance and his safety.

Love was holding forth the book now. His eyes were filled with trust, innocence and hope for the future, despite all they'd been through. It was as if their deaths, the slave chain, the road and the Tempest had been swept away, and he had returned to the Love of old. All he wanted was to be told what was right, to be granted a bit of freedom to interpret and to act.

Fontana reached out, trying to shield the action from the others with his body. He could feel the heat in the air as his fingers neared the covers of the book. With a sudden lunge, he snatched the small volume, at the same time yanking on the chains that now held him, and freeing himself from Seth's momentarily slackened grip.

He felt the laughter rising from within him, felt the exhilaration of victory coursing through him. The power was flowing from the book through his fingers, his hands and arms. Love had stepped back and was watching him in shocked silence. They all were, and seconds later, when the searing pain hit him full force, he understood why.

He was on fire, burning away steadily from his arms downward in green flame. It ate at his skin like acid. His fingers became rigid, and he watched in horror as they melted away, leaving the book hovering in mid-air before him.

He staggered back, fanning his arms, then fell to the ground, trying to roll over and over and put out the flames, all to no avail. The heat spread through him, first inside, then oozing out through his skin and lapping at his hair.

Love tried to step forward again to grab the book, but he found Uriel and Michael at his sides once more, holding him back as the grim scenario continued to unfold before his eyes.

Fontana was screaming, but no sound was escaping. Love could read the agony in the man's eyes, beseeching him to put an end to it. He could not. He was held fast. In moments Fontana's face was nothing more than a grinning death's head, flame lapping at his ears and hair like so much dry timber.

With a shudder Fontana's frame gave way, and he crumbled. His features lingered for a second in the flame, then spiraled up and away as what remained of his form melted to dust, joining the surrounding nothingness as if he had never existed.

Even Seth seemed taken aback by the sudden display of power. All that remained was the book, floating in the air, its fire extinguished. Uriel and Michael released Love's arms, and he stumbled forward. He closed his own hands gingerly about the slender volume, and immediately whatever force had animated it released it. It was a book again. He tucked it quickly away, then turned to the others, first in anguish, then in growing anger.

"Why? Why wouldn't you let me stop it? I could have helped him..."

Uriel stepped forward quickly and grabbed Love by each of his shoulders, shaking him roughly. "No. You could not have stopped it, and we would not have let you if you could. You know the prophecies. They come to your aid when *you* call, and yet you cannot see what is directly before you.

"Fontana was not a prophet. He lied to us. When we were chained at the compound, while you were escaping, he had hidden himself in a cabinet. He never intended to die. He intended *us* to die, but he would have gone on, lied to others. He was not a prophet, and we were all fools."

"But..." He wanted to strike out at his old companion. He wanted to scream and rant, to cry out to the skies above them, the empty, colorless sky of the world where he'd landed them all. "You helped me to free him," he stammered at last. "You say he was no prophet, and yet you risked your life to help me free him. You said nothing."

"You would not have listened," Uriel said simply. The others nodded. "You would have gone anyway, and we would never have let you go alone. If your book had not done this," Uriel gestured to the dust where Fontana had stood only moments before, "then we would have. This is why we came. Now our revenge is complete."

"Revenge?" Love couldn't believe what he was hearing. He turned away, walking from the group quickly and holding his hands to the sides of his head in despair. Llanna followed him at a short distance. When he finally stopped, she came closer, putting her arms around him and laying her head on his shoulder.

"You have sought your answers," she said softly, "and now you have become them. I have told you from the start that your power, your prophecy, lies within you. It is thus with us all. There is only so much one can learn. Remember your own words—*the greatest power is in the number one*. How can you be so wise and so forgetful, all at once?"

He turned toward her slowly. The pain that always rode her eyes was tainted now by concern, concern for him. He thought her words through slowly, thought of what the Archangel Uriel had told him, of the greedy light that had flickered across Fontana's face when he'd reached out for the book.

"She's right, you know," Seth cut in, walking over to join them. "When I found that one, he was walking in a daze, mumbling out loud to himself as he went. He was going to take that book and sell you all out to Bontempt. He was going to go back for some revenge of his own on a woman, someone named Faith. He was going to make you his servant. That one had a lot of plans, and no backbone to bring them to reality. He is better forgotten."

"Nothing is better forgotten," Love muttered, and he took out the book, penning these words carefully in beside his last entry. He looked carefully at the words he'd written, and it dawned on him that, after all, he might have an answer that would lead them out of here. He didn't know to where, but what the hell, how much worse could it get?

Without consulting the others, without a second thought, he read from the book and smiled as the green flames rose to engulf them all in a sudden whirlwind of heat and energy. *Break on through to the other side*.

If it was good enough for Jim Morrison, he reflected, it's good enough for me. He was vaguely aware of Seth cursing and Llanna crying out as blackness grabbed them all, but he ignored them and released himself to the moment. Time to see what was next, he thought. Time to take charge.

The world around them evaporated, and moments later the empty void where they'd stood was that much more empty. Only Fontana's dust remained behind to show they'd ever existed.

17

The first thing that met Love's eyes were the softly swaying branches of trees. There were only a few crumbled, rotted leaves clinging to the branches, twig-sculpture caricatures of leaves. The trees themselves were run through with worms, their bark stripping away and great cracks running through the branches.

There was sound, as well. It was the minor harmony of a dirge, many voices lifted in the ominous, final tones of a death hymn. The ground beneath him felt good, soft and yet firm, and he rolled lazily to one side, trying to get his bearings. As he turned, gray stone filled his sight.

Anton McLean, 1802-1892 He Lost the Final Game

Love rolled to his feet in one smooth, fluid motion, memory snapping back into place, and took in his surroundings rapidly. The cobwebs were banished and instinct kicked in. Llanna lay nearby on another grave, and the others who'd been standing around him were scattered about the area. None of them had awakened yet; none of them was moving at all.

Then he saw the others. They were gathered a few yards away, hovering over graves that held none of Love's own companions, watching him and singing. The music came from this group, he saw that now. They made no move to come closer to where he stood, but he could feel an animosity in the air, a malevolent curiosity, and yet there was something more.

"Who are you?" he demanded. "Where is this place?"

At first they just continued to watch, and to sing, but after a few moments of this, one of those near the fringe of the group that faced him broke away and floated toward him. The man's feet never touched the ground, and suddenly Love remembered the graveyard, the nihil, as Seth had called it.

"This is Shady Grove," the man said solemnly. "You appeared here at the same moment that the nihil was closed. We were hoping you could explain it to us." His face was calm, placid even, and yet there was a current of emotion behind the force of his words, his manner. It would, Love thought, take an exceptional moment to get anything nearing a normal reaction from that face.

"I'm afraid my explanation will fall short of what you seek," Love explained slowly. "We were in the byway, just beyond the nihil, when it began to collapse. We escaped with our lives, it seems, but I couldn't really tell you exactly why that happened, either."

They stood, staring at one another, and around them the others began to awaken. Llanna sat up, shaking her head in bewilderment. Seth rolled quickly to his feet, as if awakened from a deep sleep into danger, taking in their surroundings quickly and efficiently. The Archangels materialized suddenly at Love's back, two at each shoulder, silent and staring ahead—ready.

"You say the byway collapsed?" the man repeated. "The byway has been open since I can remember. It was there before I came to this place, and the years between then and now are many. I don't know any who have been here in a time when the byway was not open. They have always come through here, always passed us by in silence."

"They will still come," Llanna cut in. "None knows, yet, that the pathway is closed."

"True," the man seemed to be considering the new situation carefully, "but they will not stay. Those who try to stay, we will deal with ourselves. In time, we will be left in peace."

Love didn't know what to say. He remembered the tide of darkness, the nightmare horde of Spectres that had snapped at their heels as they'd sprinted down that byway. He remembered seeing the light ahead, the shining light and energy that had marked the portal through the mists. After that, after he'd tossed his grenade into the seething mass of clouds and creatures, adding its voice and power to the chaos, his memory stopped.

So the byway had been closed, probably forever. It had been obvious that whatever power held it together was failing. Seth had done it. Small, old, and deadly—dangerous in ways none of them could fathom. He'd called all that darkness down on their heads to distract the slavers. He must have had some idea how he would have gotten them all out safely, and the arrogance, the assumed power of it made Love shudder.

"We will not attempt to stay," he said. "We will return the way we came, and we will spread the word that the portal is closed. Fewer will come, then, fewer will disturb your rest."

"For that we thank you," the old man said, "and for the shutting of the portal. I don't know how or why it has come about, but I sense that you were behind it."

"If that is true," Love told him, smiling, "then it was an accident, and I'm glad it did some good."

"You are welcome to stay," the man continued. "There is room for a few more, and the gift you have bestowed upon us is beyond price. We can make a place for any of you who would remain."

Love looked around him. Several of the others seemed to have perked up at this offer: the federal agent who remained with the group, those with no ties to Love except for death and fear, even one or two of Llanna's people. Perhaps the trip to hell and back with their "prophet" had cooled their faith. He knew his own would need some serious reconsideration.

"Any of you who feels the urge to take them up on this offer, feel free. I have things left unfinished." He turned to the Archangels, then to Llanna. "I have to go after Faith. I don't know how we'll get her out of there, but I have to try. If Fontana was a fraud, then I'm a fool, but she was special. She was the only other, besides myself, who truly believed enough to dive headlong into this next level. I can't leave her chained to a slab of stone, dancing naked for someone like Bontempt. I couldn't live with myself."

"I will help in any way that I can," Llanna assured him. "As I told you before, that slab is where Bontempt would have me, if he had his way. I wouldn't leave another to that fate if there was any way that I could help her."

The Archangels never flinched. There was no doubt that they would follow, and Seth stood his ground as well.

Hope looked a bit lost, but steady. Without Charity at her side, and with Faith held prisoner, all that remained to anchor her to sanity were the Archangels, and now Love himself. She would follow.

Love thought back over those that had been lost, remembered the belligerent federal agent who'd not wanted to return to the byway, and who had then ended up lost in the mists of the Tempest. He thought of Charity, her wide trusting eyes and the grim, tragic set of her smile. He thought of Fontana, but shifted his mind from that subject almost immediately. He wasn't ready to go that route yet. There was still too much pain.

All of them were his responsibility. In some way he had had a part in bringing them here, in the deaths of those now gone, in Faith's capture. He had been the beast who ripped out the heart of the world, and now it was time to see if he couldn't involve himself in one *hell* of a transplant.

The *Little Green Book* still hung on its thong about his neck. It was odd, but the loss of Fontana had not shaken his basic belief in the words he'd penned. There *was* something to be found in the lyrics of songs, in the verses of the poets and the ranting of politicians. There was wisdom and, if you wanted to call it that, prophecy, in the application of almost anything spoken or written.

"Those of you who are coming with me, let's get started. The longer I stay in this place, the more I want to stay longer…"

The old wraith who'd spoken for the group smiled. "That is why we love this place. Now and again we see the children come here on the other side, some to play, some to make love, and others to dream. There are still funerals in the newer parts of the graveyard, and these we welcome to our home, if they do not pass straight through to Oblivion. It is a calm place. Remember, always, that you are welcome."

Love felt his throat constrict, and though he knew that tears were no longer possible, the sensations that followed were bittersweet and familiar. He nodded to the one who had spoken, turned and waved in acknowledgment of the others who stood arrayed behind him, and started off toward the gates in the distance. The others fell in behind him, silent and solemn, like an after-the-fact funeral procession. They had their dead to mourn, and they had their thoughts to keep them busy. They passed between the graves and on toward the gravel road beyond without a word.

It wasn't until several miles later that Love chose to stop, where the gravel road met the paved freeway and headed back into the city of San Valencez. He gathered them together in a group and seated himself, facing them, on a fencepost.

"We have several things to accomplish now, I know, but there is one other thing that I need to take care of; at least, that Llanna needs to take care of. I will aid her, if I can. I have made a promise, and the way my ideals have been crumbling around me these past couple of days, I need to make good on it. The rest of you can take the road—I think that would be safest—and cut across the desert before you get too close to Bontempt and his guards. They won't be on the lookout for us yet, I don't believe, and you should be able to slip through unnoticed.

"It will be up to you to organize what efforts we can to get into that citadel and get Faith out. Stay at the perimeters and see if you can locate her, check out the defenses. I don't expect this to be easy, but maybe there's a way to get in close and see what's what."

He turned to Llanna. Her eyes were wide, and he could see that she was trembling. Her memories were catching up with her, and he'd never seen the sorrow so heavily etched on her face as it was at that moment. There was more there, though, much more. He could see a mirror of the love that was growing within him, the caring that made them both part of one whole. It was something he'd never expected to feel again, not after the compound. Even there, he had been whole within himself—the greatest power was in the number one. They had all been a team, a family, but the thing that had held them together was their respect for the fact that they would never truly be close or vulnerable. That was not the case with Llanna.

"We can be there tonight if we catch the train," he said softly.

She didn't speak, only nodding her assent.

Love turned to the others once more, held his hand out first to Seth, then to the Archangels one after the other. Finally he took Hope's hands both between his own and smiled. There were no words necessary. Stepping back and taking Llanna's hand in his own he spun away. He could feel their eyes on him as he walked away, could feel the weight of caring, and of hope. For once the burden of responsibility did not seem too heavy.

Bontempt sat in silence, watching distractedly as Faith whirled on the slab before him. The fire was still in her eyes, the hatred still burned strong, but she was learning. Already she moved more quickly to his commands, fighting less against the power of the chains that restrained her. With her friends gone and his personal promise that the other one, the one with the book, would soon join them, she had lost a bit of the wind in her sails.

Still he did not feel comfortable. He felt an itch in the back of his mind, an intuitive cry of danger that he could not wipe away, no matter how he attempted to distract himself. The slave chain had taken Fontana, the foolish one, and his friends into the Tempest several days before, but the departure did not leave him with the impression of finality that it should. Somehow he knew that there was more to come, chapters yet to be written in the story he was enmeshed in.

Cyclops sat on his shoulder, silent as always, and almost healed. With a sudden jerk of his arm, he sent the bird into the air, flapping in a circle as it sought access to the window far above. It would be a simple matter to check the road to the portal, just to be certain that all was well. If there was no trace of the slave chain, then he would assume that they had made their way into the Tempest, and once inside there was no way Cappy could lose control.

The grizzled old guide was an enigma that Bontempt had long since given up trying to figure out. There was an aura of power about the man, a strength and antiquity to his bearing. It made Bontempt nervous to have Cappy nearby, more nervous than he would have ever admitted, and the worst of it was that he was fairly certain the old guide knew it. It was much akin to the way the closest servants of the hierarchy made him feel, as if there were a greater purpose behind every moment of every day, and he, Bontempt, was only a pawn, not privy to the secrets of the real game. It was infuriating.

He'd met Cappy when they both served in the Legions, before Bontempt had taken off on his own and begun to ply the slave trade. The Hierarchy had employed all types of soldiers, guides, and those from the various outlawed Guilds. Bontempt had been in charge of a regiment, and Cappy was assigned to see them through the byways whenever travel in the Tempest was deemed necessary. The guide came to them from Stygia each time, materializing out of the shadows in his dark, unmarked uniform. Bontempt hadn't liked it then, and he liked it less now, but Cappy was an asset he couldn't survive without.

There were plenty of others, Bontempt himself included, who could navigate the byways of the Tempest. He lost several parties a year to the perpetual storm, though, and without the certainty that each chain led in by Cappy would make it to the borders of the dark city he might not have been able to sustain his holdings.

Cappy thrived on danger, especially on danger brought about by proximity to the Tempest. It was uncanny the way he could step through nihils, rarely surprised by what he found and always the quickest through to whatever goal he had set for himself. It was as though the man belonged there, as though he were part and parcel of the storm itself.

It was a life that Bontempt himself would have never chosen. He liked to be in control. In the Tempest one could control one's own mind, but the world around him was beyond any sphere of rationality. There was nothing stable there, nothing concrete that you could anchor yourself to and find your way. You had to trust instincts that were difficult even to believe in, let alone make use of.

When Bontempt had established this palace, this outpost beyond the borders of stricter Hierarchy control, Cappy had appeared. He had just walked in one day, offering his services for a high price. Bontempt had accepted at once, and the partnership had been long, comfortable, and profitable.

Now, it seemed, that comfort was threatened. No matter how he tried not to think of the one with the book and his rag-tag band of followers, he could not banish them from his mind. The girl on the slab was watching him, and he wondered if she'd somehow picked up on his nervousness. He would deal with her later. There was too much at stake to allow himself to be distracted.

He closed his eyes, concentrating, and reached out for Cyclops. He slid easily into control and, miles away and rising to coast on the desert wind, Cyclops arrowed off toward the city in the distance and the byway beyond.

He fixed his sight on the road and cruised his own course, winding toward the suggested goal slowly. He was not looking for a group of travelers, so when, hours later, he passed silently over a small band, traveling fast, that had just turned from the road, he paid them no attention whatsoever. Cyclops was hungry, and those moving below were alive—Bontempt would need to release the animal to feed, and he needed to find it something small, or dead. On second thought, he smiled inwardly, perhaps he would maintain control during that feeding. He felt the urge to rend and tear.

Ignoring the Archangels and their companions, he veered off around the edge of the city, searching for vermin and eating away at the miles between himself and the nihil.

Beyond the oldest gravestones of Shady Grove, deep in the forested area that bordered the place, the tiniest of cracks was forming in the mist. Shining brightly, glistening, it widened and spread to the height of a man. No one was near enough to notice, though the energy given off by the light was reaching outward and would soon reach the rest of the cemetery.

From the midst of the crease, a hand emerged, gripping at the sides of the hole, at the very fabric of reality, and pulling. Muscles strained, cording on thin arms and rippling with strength as the figure struggled forward, pushing free of the roiling, cloudy nothingness beyond the opening. With a grunt and a final heave that left him exhausted, lying on the ground with his face in the dust, Cappy tore himself from the Tempest.

Behind him the portal snapped shut with finality, whatever energy had held it open fizzling and dying. He did not move, at first, nor did he seem aware of his surroundings. He lay on the cool ground, soaking up the strength of the graves, letting the peaceable aura of the place seep through him and return his strength.

Finally he was able to move, to crawl forward a few feet to the nearest of the gravestones. He clawed his way up the side of the old stone until he was in a sitting position, then leaned back against it with a heavy sigh.

That had been close, he reflected, far closer than any danger he'd faced in all his years in Charon's service. He had underestimated them. Seth he'd known, and the two of them had been matched evenly enough, but he hadn't counted on the others, in particular the one with the book. That book was one of the most powerful Artifacts he'd ever seen brought over from the Skinlands. Then there was the grenade.

If he'd been turned the other way, facing the portal where Din, Sully, and Brutus had still waged their own little war instead of concentrating on Seth, he'd have seen that grenade and been able to brace against the shock. As fate would have it, he'd been swinging away from the portal, and it was his opponent who'd glimpsed what was to come, thus avoiding the worst of the blast.

The byway had closed completely. There was no way to reopen it: the power and knowledge were beyond his ken, and there was no real reason to worry over it. There were other byways. It was only Bontempt who would be affected by this.

He thought of the others, those who'd nearly ended his long run of near-impossible luck in the Tempest, and his smile was grim. They must have escaped, and that meant they would likely return to their temple. That was fine. He meant to find them and to finish what he'd begun—he had, after all, been paid.

For the moment, though, he just leaned back against the gravestone and closed his eyes. There was plenty of time, and he needed to restore his strength. As, unbeknownst to him, Cyclops winged his way toward his resting place, Cappy dropped into a deep, calming sleep.

18

Love had been prepared for almost anything except what actually met his gaze as the train slipped away into the night. His head was still a bit foggy and off-kilter from the ride, which had been no less taxing or disorienting than the first time. Now they stood at the train depot in Friendly, California, and a true realization of what he faced was setting in.

The building itself was dilapidated and worn away by wind and weather. Some of this was the effect of viewing from the Shadowlands side of existence, but there was a more deeply running decay in the place that he felt must be the real thing, an aura of age and shadow that clung to the place like a fungus.

There was no one working at the station, if you could really call it that. There were a couple of dusty old vending machines, some severe, straight-backed wooden benches, and a ticket booth that was closed and locked with a heavy chain. There was a sign designating the few hours the "Friendly Depot" was open for business, but otherwise the place might have been abandoned for years.

Behind the building the road stretched up and away, winding beneath bent, leafless trees and on up the side of a mountain. It reminded Love of a set from an old B-grade western, a stagecoach stop for someplace named Dry Gulch, or the outskirts of a ghost town.

"Not many come this way," Llanna told him softly. "It is a pretty closed community."

"I got that impression," Love replied. He stared up the road, feeling an odd chill emanating from the gravel and pitted asphalt that covered it. The trees lining the way were sinister, looming like twisted sentinels to either side of the road, which curved off out of sight less than a quarter mile away.

"It isn't as far as you might think," Llanna assured him. "It rises pretty quickly from here, and town is less than five miles away. The church is just beyond that, on the last ridge. The road ends there, and it is nearly impossible to get any higher up the mountain, even on foot."

For possibly the first time since the disastrous battle at the compound had turned his world upside down, Love felt relief at being dead. Five miles might not be too far for someone in the Shadowlands, where one could go on literally forever without rest or food, but that same five miles straight up a mountain would have taxed even the strongest living man. With a shrug, he took Llanna's hand, gazed into her eyes, and said, "Let's do it."

They made good time, walking in silence. Llanna's eyes were far away, and Love suspected that she was reliving more of her past, renewing memories that might have been repressed for years. For his own part, he was content to walk at her side, admiring her when she didn't know he was looking, and waiting for his chance to support her in whatever came next.

The roadway grew darker and more dismal as they clembed. Any vehicle that regularly navigated it would have needed four-wheel drive and truly remarkable suspension. It was obvious that most of the traffic in and out of the city was on foot, and that the only real connection they had to the world beyond their mountain was the train.

Signs of civilization began to appear along the way about two miles up, dim lights in the windows of dingy cottages and cabins, even dimmer lights from deeper in the surrounding woods, a couple of abandoned tires and the carcass of an old Ford that had been in the ditch so long the weeds had conquered it, growing up through windows and upholstery alike, eating away slowly at the floorboards with roots and rust.

There were the sounds of birds and small animals among the trees. Owls hooted, telling Love's inner clock that it was night time on both sides of the Shroud. All of this they ignored, making their way slowly toward the town.

Finally a sign loomed alongside the road, and Love stopped for a moment, pulling Llanna in close.

Welcome to Friendly, California, Population 562

"Not exactly a boom town, is it?" he asked.

Llanna didn't answer. He felt her shivering, and he held her tighter for just a moment, then released her. "Not too much longer," he promised her softly. "We'll get in there, get this over with, and get on with our…uh…lives?"

She smiled thinly, but still did not speak, and Love began to worry about her. Her face, if anything, was paler than it had been previously, and the sorrow that permeated her eyes and her soft features was so pronounced that it was

EXCEPT YOU GO THROUGH SHADOW   545

physically painful to look at her. She was trembling from head to foot, so shaky on her feet that he feared they would have to stop and rest before they even entered the town.

She trudged onward, though, keeping her eyes turned toward the ground and her thoughts to herself. Love spent the time taking in their surroundings. The city of Friendly had a rustic, down-home look to it. There was a single square in the center of town, in the middle of which the courthouse sat. Various signs and posters indicated that the post office, police station, and mayor's office were all under that same roof.

Around the square were the few businesses that kept the city going. A drugstore, saloon, department store and a bakery lined the roads, their doors locked and their windows dim. At this time of night, the city was as silent as a tomb. Nothing stirred, no stray dogs, no children sneaking around behind their parents' backs; not even the one police cruiser was out on the street, though the light from a single, dangling bulb could be seen through a barred window on the side of the courthouse.

There was nothing about the place, at first, to indicate anything odd about the community. It was behind the times, old-fashioned, and isolated, but none of those things was out of place, or even particularly unique. Still, Love could feel something, a kind of radiant "wrongness" that filled the air and slipped up through the ground beneath him and along the bones of his legs, numbing them.

There didn't seem to be anything they could do to ward themselves against the effects of this "field," so they slogged onward. It did not take long to cross the town and make their way out past the few scattered dwellings that lined the outer streets. The road ahead stretched upward, as ominous and empty as the road behind had been, and even more lonely.

There was only one reason to climb that road, one goal one could have in mind, barring an expedition to climb the sheer peaks behind the church. It was the road to worship, the Sunday street. It was the path of the righteous, and where the road below had been choppy, rutted, and full of potholes, the road beyond the city to the church was immaculate. Where the weeds below had threatened to, and in some places succeeded in, overflowing the ditches and making their way onto the chancy pavement, this trail (for it was little more than that, all things considered) was well-tended. The weeds had been hacked back several feet and the potholes had been filled in. There was the evidence of many, many hundreds of feet tramping up and down that trail regularly. Something about the sight made Love's skin crawl.

"Something is wrong," Llanna said, stopping before they'd actually set foot on the trail up the mountain. "This was a good town, a nice place to live. Sure, they were a little overboard with the religion, but they were people you could live with, that you could love. Something has changed."

Love didn't answer, just nodded his head.

"When I left here, the Reverend Forbes was the leader, both in things spiritual and in the business of the city. It wasn't that he'd been elected to office, just that his suggestions, made to god-fearing folks with no other leadership, were nearly always taken as gospel. Everybody wanted to do right by the Church, and by God.

"Now it feels like something dark and evil is seeping up through the ground. It feels rotten. I'm afraid for what has happened here, what I left behind unfinished."

"You can't blame yourself, no matter what happens," Love admonished her softly. "These folks may have been good to you when you were alive, but they were not too quick on picking up the good Reverend's failings. You can't believe you are the only one he took advantage of, especially not if his power over the town was as great as you describe it."

"But you don't understand," she said, turning to face him with the anguish alive and streaming from the depths of her deep, soulful eyes. "It was my town! These people were my friends, and when I died, though it wasn't right, it was just *me* that was affected. I lost my life, but the town went on. Now he has leaked out beyond the church, beyond the back room and the serpent pit. I can feel it. He is eating away at the heart of the people like a cancer."

Love couldn't deny feeling what she spoke of. Her words brought the sensations into a truer focus. He took her by the hand quickly and started on up the mountain.

"If what you say is true," he told her, "we can't afford to spend too much time on this road. The longer we are under the influence of this—aura—the worse things could get. You need all of your conviction and courage for what we are about to face."

He didn't really know if there was any kind of truth in what he was saying, but he kept on talking to fill the void of silence and to goad her into action. Without really understanding their situation, he understood the warning bells going off in his head well enough. They had come here to face a danger that should have been well clear of them, a danger that should have lived and breathed in a world that they had long since left behind. What they were feeling belied this and shoved the truth blatantly into their faces. For the first time since they'd left the others, Love wondered if it might not have been poor planning to try this without the others.

There was a warm glow at his chest, the green book, but he repressed the urge to pull it out and skim the pages. He knew the words well enough, but he didn't know enough about the book's power. The last thing he needed was to read some passage aloud when he didn't really need it and deplete the energy in the words before he really *did* need it.

Besides, despite the inherent discomfort of the place, there was no immediate danger presenting itself. Love felt certain, from his experiences with the volume thus far, that the green book would be burning the hell out of his chest, so to speak, were there anything truly dangerous threatening.

He noticed also that the natural luminescence he'd been existing in since his death was dimming. The closer they came to their goal, the less he was able to distinguish of his surroundings. He was beginning to worry that the light would fade completely, and that they would have to stop. There was nothing he knew of available in the way of flashlights or torches—they were stuck with whatever luminescence was provided.

Then they rounded a final curve and stopped dead in their tracks. It was no longer quite so dark—the building that loomed far above them, like a gothic castle from a dark fairy tale, glowed at every window. The light that emanated was red, blood red, interlaced with deep blues and greens and bright yellow. It took Love a moment to register that this was the effect of massive stained-glass windows, windows that portrayed scenes he'd never seen in any earthly church he'd been a part of.

There were women, dressed in the white linen robes of most biblical scenes, but kneeling, all of them, kneeling before the tall, dark image of a man who in no way resembled any image of Christ Love was familiar with. He *did* know those eyes, though. He didn't know them from his own experience, nor had he ever met this man in person, but there was no mistaking that evil. Forbes. It was the Reverend Forbes, larger than life and immortalized forever.

Love scanned the rest of the window, and he started violently. Just to the man's left, kneeling with red rivulets that had to be blood twining their way through the folds of her gown, was Llanna. The image was perfect, eerily so, and there was a dark green serpent wrapped around her forearm, poised for the strike. The image had captured all of the pain in her eyes.

Love turned swiftly, but he was too late. He turned to face empty space. Llanna was gone. Vanished, and he could sense the danger she faced as if it were his own, though he had no way to reach her, or to help.

Llanna felt the queasy, disorienting sensation of falling, and she heard the dark, compelling laughter of her Shadow as she was drawn through the nihil. Shuddering with fear, she ripped at the dark threads that drew her inward, but it was in vain. Whatever was to come, she would have to face it to be free. There was no escaping back into her mind.

She shielded her eyes from the church and its unearthly glow. She knew well enough how he would try to take her, and she wasn't going to let him get his talons into her mind before she'd even had a chance to fight him.

She headed for the front door of the church. Whatever she was going to do, she knew she needed to do it quickly. Though the church before her seemed the same, the fact that it existed in the Shadowlands, while still standing beyond the Shroud, said that there was more to the situation than met the eye. And where was Love?

As that last thought flashed through her mind, she sensed the laughter of her Shadow again, closer and more intimate than she'd sensed it in years, and she redoubled her speed.

When she stepped through the doorway into the foyer of the Church, she stopped cold. It was wrong, all wrong. It had never been so big. The place was huge, like some ancient cathedral—and dark. The church was about the size of a large two-story house with a high ceiling, ten rows of pews on each side, the altar and the snake pit/baptismal. There were no stained-glass windows—no carpet.

She stared at the floor beneath her feet. The carpet seemed to flow beneath her, liquefying more rapidly as her imagination caught hold of the image. Blood. So much blood that it ran across the floor and covered it, rising up the walls on either side and slopping across their shoes. Llanna shook her head back and forth and lifted one foot in fascination, watching as the sticky, viscous fluid trailed from the heel of her shoe to the floor.

"No," she said softly, but firmly. She concentrated on the blood, imagined the carpet that had been there only moments before, and found that the image righted itself. No blood, only an illusion, another trap. She closed her eyes, imagining the wood as it was when she'd last seen it. She visualized the foyer, filled with her friends and neighbors on a Sunday morning with light pouring in through the open doors.

When she opened her eyes, she was standing in a smaller room. The walls were of finished pine, and there was a small table in front of her that held a basket of flyers. The flyers had a picture of Christ on the cover, a very stylistic, blond, blue-eyed Christ, reaching out to her as if to beckon her inside. Across the top it said *Church of New Light* in luminescent green letters that glowed brightly.

She turned slowly, taking in the pictures on the walls, church socials and bake sales. Gray-haired matrons and austere older gentlemen in dark suits, younger women in flowered print dresses and wide white smiles, children playing games and singing in choir. These were familiar images—comfortable memories. She was about to turn to the main doorway into the chapel itself when a final portrait caught her eye.

It was of Llanna herself, her short white skirt pulled up to show tanned, muscular legs, kneeling in front of the Reverend with her head bowed. As she stared at the man's eyes, they moved, swinging from the image kneeling in supplication at his feet to meet Llanna's gaze dead on.

Llanna was nearly driven from her feet, crying out in alarm, and she turned quickly, facing away from the picture. Drawing a deep breath and fighting to rid her mind of the image of those mocking eyes, she lunged toward the main chamber of the church. As she went, laughter pealed out, strong and bright, dark and haunting.

She stumbled into the main chamber of the church and stopped. It was deceptive, this room, stretching to seemingly endless heights with lights rimming the beams that held the lofty ceiling overhead and a huge statue of Christ, his eyes the very image of the sorrow that permeated Llanna's own, hanging from a cross that overlooked the pulpit and the altar. The baptismal pool was raised behind the altar, spotlights shining down into it, and the front of the pool was made of thick glass so that all assembled could witness what went on in the water's depths.

The water swarmed with serpents, dark-green bodies writhing and twisting about one another, sliding through the water in endless circles. The motion was mesmerizing, hypnotic. Llanna tore her eyes away, sweeping them about the room in search of something she could concentrate on that would keep her thoughts in order. It was then that she noticed the throne.

Most of what she saw, she realized, was as it stood on the other side of the Shroud. The church, while still permeated with its aura of otherworldly "wrongness," was too detailed for an illusion, too bright and cheerful. Above and to the side of the baptismal pool, though, was a small balcony, and within that alcove the Reverend Forbes sat, staring out over the empty pews and watching with wild, feral eyes as Llanna turned, slowly, to face him.

"So," Forbes boomed. "You have come home, even from the realms of death, to the one you worship."

"No," Llanna whispered. The sound was weak, but her gaze remained steady.

"Oh, but I know you," he continued. "You never trusted yourself in life, why should it be different now?"

Llanna stared at Forbes, fascinated. She mouthed the word *no*, but no sound escaped.

The mocking laughter rolled out again, surrounding them, drowning out Love's words.

"You aren't dead," Llanna said accusingly. "How can you see me? How can you speak?"

"There are worlds within your mind, Llanna dearest," Forbes leered. "There are things you will never understand. I rule in the other world, but I build my castles in this one. It is the only Heaven I aspire to, and I want to make certain that it meets my needs when I make my way here on a more permanent basis."

"No." The word had force this time, and Forbes seemed a bit taken aback by the interruption. "You are evil, and you will never live in a castle, not here, not anywhere. You will be punished."

Again the laughter.

"Is it you who will punish me, little Llanna?" he asked mockingly. "Will you force my hand into the pit of serpents so that the Lord may seek his vengeance? They are mine, these snakes. They have always been mine."

"No," she said again. "They belong to a higher power. You cannot create, therefore you cannot own. They serve the same God they always did; it is you who have turned from the truth."

"Would you care to test them, then, my dear?" Forbes cooed, rising from his ornate seat and disappearing momentarily, only to reappear in front of the pool. "Would you care to take once more the test you failed so many years ago?"

"I will take the test," Llanna replied demurely, "if you will. I will sacrifice myself once more to the serpents if you have no fear in your own heart. You will be judged for your deeds; I have no fear."

"Step forward, my dear," Forbes invited, his voice like rotted silk and his hands spread wide in welcome. "I have nothing to fear from my children. You know this, and yet you will test me. I understand that. Once the test is finished, you will be mine once again."

Moving slowly, as if in a trance, Llanna made her way down the center aisle of the chapel. She did not move too quickly, but neither did she hesitate. She moved past the altar, past the pulpit, and through a dark portal in the wall beyond. Seconds later she stood on the raised platform beside Forbes, the eerie glowing light glimmering off the sinuous, rolling shapes in the pool beneath them.

Forbes grinned at her, his smile hungry and sadistic. Llanna could see, now that she was closer, the heavily etched lines of his face and the swell of a stomach too long divorced from physical activity. The aura that maintained the good reverend's image on the shadow plane was not so strong as she had thought, and his image wavered and flickered before her.

She turned to the pool beneath them and gazed into its depths, watching first one, then another serpentine body slide past. When one broke the surface, she met its eyes with implacable calm. Then she began to speak.

"It is written," she began, "that the faithful shall pick up serpents, and yet they shall not be bitten; that they shall drink poison and come to no harm. Let those without sin in their hearts step forward, let those who would repent take heart—he judges the righteous fairly, and those found unworthy shall burn in a pit of fire."

With these words, Llanna plunged her hands downward into the pool of serpents. Her eyes were closed, and a ring of golden fire rose to circle her head.

The serpents slipped in and over one another, some of them skeletal, others with skulls for heads, living, but with their deaths painted clearly across their features. Their motion split where her hands parted the water, as if they could sense her presence, but they made no move to strike.

The reverend made a gurgling sound deep in his throat, but he made no move to join her at the pool. Llanna, who had sensed that the danger from the serpents was only to her mind, now used the power of that mind to slip through the weakened curtain of the Shroud to grasp at the Reverend's mind—summoning him.

"It is your time," she said softly. "Come, Reverend…let us pray."

The room about them began to fade, and Forbes was backpedaling quickly. Llanna felt him withdrawing frantically, trying to release himself from the shadow-world he'd created, but she did not let it go. She pulled one arm free of the pool, whipping it around to grab Forbes's disappearing wrist in a tight grip. He struggled wildly, but the strength of his still-living form was no match for her, and she spun him back toward the pool.

She was too late. The room flickered, then dropped to the comfortable illumination of the Shadowlands. The rich tapestries fell to rot, the walls grew dingy and dark, and the pool dried to a pile of mildew and crumbling bones.

Llanna stumbled back, but Love was there suddenly, calling her name, and he caught her in his arms, holding her upright.

Then they heard the scream. It rose from the depths of the chapel and raced to the ceiling and beyond with incredible intensity. Love closed his eyes and clamped his hands over his ears, and he felt Llanna drawing him close. As she did, her eyes became his, and he saw what she was seeing—what she had planned and conceived.

Her effort to drag the reverend to the pool had indeed succeeded, but he'd managed to escape the Shadowlands before he reached the edge of the pool. It had not stopped his momentum. As he snapped from one world to the next, Forbes had fallen forward, stumbling against the wall of the baptismal pool. He'd flung his arms out, windmilling them helplessly, but the momentum had been too great. Gravity had done the rest.

It happened like a slow-motion movie scene, frame by frame, as Love felt Llanna savoring it, drawing strength from each expression, each cry for help to an empty church. The serpents seemed to sense Forbes' approach, several of them rearing their heads and latching onto his arms before he ever touched the water. He disappeared into the depths for a moment, then reappeared, screaming even more loudly, but helpless to drag himself free.

The serpents clung to him. They wound around his arms, his throat, latched their fangs into his skin and injected their poison, sending him to judgment. Love could watch no more, and he staggered back, dragging himself free of Llanna's embrace.

She stood for a moment longer, then returned to embrace him quickly. Pulling away, she turned resolutely back toward the road they'd followed up the mountain.

"It is done," she said softly. Love moved in front of her, stopping her with one hand and turning her face so that he could see her eyes. The sorrow had drained from her, and she was beautiful.

He let her go, slipping his arm around her back. "I guess it is." Behind them, a single candle glowed on the altar of the church…sending a soft, welcoming glow into the night.

19

Cappy rose from where he was seated within a few hours, the gleam back in his eyes and a spring in his step. He had a purpose, a challenge, and it had been a long time since he'd had either of those. He turned a last time to the grave against which he'd been sitting and offered a mock salute.

"Thanks for the hospitality, Mr. McLean," he said, smiling. He turned away then and would have left immediately, except for the damned bird.

Cyclops had appeared silently, eerily, perched precariously on the top of a crumbling gravestone and glaring at him with its one good eye. Bontempt. Somehow the bastard had known that something was wrong, or had he? Maybe he was just checking up on them. In any case, the slaver knew something was wrong now. Cappy didn't wait for questions, though he knew that the man could communicate, after a fashion, using the bird's mind as a relay. The old guide liked to take the offensive in any encounter.

"It is gone, my friend," he said quickly, sweeping his arm to the right, toward where the nihil had stood open less than a day before. "You'll have to find a new route of supply to the dark city; it is something I will look into soon."

Cyclops flapped its wings nervously, but there was no reaction. Cappy hated communicating this way. He felt idiotic talking to a bird, and the empty socket that had once housed its lost eye was a bit unnerving. Cappy did not like to feel nervous in the presence of anyone, or anything.

"They escaped through this graveyard. Din and Sully are gone. I am going after them. Expect me in a few days with a new chain of slaves, or not at all. They've made it personal now."

He turned on his heel then, and strode calmly away, ignoring the flapping sound as the bird rose from the stone to follow him. He owed nothing to the slaver, and Bontempt was beginning to grow a bit too arrogant. As he made his way through the graves the residents of the place rose to watch his progress. He ignored them, too. He needed to get out and on the road, away from it all.

With a final angry shriek, Cyclops spun off into the air and turned away, beginning the return journey to his master's side. Cappy was certain that it was not the last he would see of the creature, nor was it the last he would hear from Bontempt, but that was fine. The entire situation that comprised his existence was beginning to stagnate. It bored the hell out of him. Perhaps it was time he took matters into his own hands and set them all straight. He needed to work for no man. Bontempt had merely been a convenient excuse for him to get back to the Tempest.

With the graveyard behind him and the township of Lavender, California, visible ahead, he managed to push Bontempt and his petty concerns from the forefront of his mind. Cappy decided it was time to take a little rest. Besides the fact that there was plenty to enjoy in town, old friends to look up and a stray card game here and there, he couldn't resist stopping. He hoped that Bontempt sent his damned bird to monitor his progress. He knew his delay would wind the unstable slaver up like a top, and he hoped to be there when the string was released.

Smiling, he made his way in through the outskirts of town and disappeared into the shadowy alleys of the downtown district, whistling to himself. From far above, perched on the corner of a looming, dusty brownstone, Cyclops stared down malevolently, his eye glittering in the half-light of the swirling mists as the yellow illumination of the street lamps swallowed his quarry.

With a loud, piercing cry, he leapt to the air and banked off toward the desert beyond the city. There was no more to be seen here, and it was time to return to his master.

Bontempt had gone into a terrible rage when Cappy turned away from him, or away from the bird, anyway. The pressure of losing his only good trade route, four of his best guards, a slave chain, and then apparently the services of his best guide, all in one fell swoop, was more than his system could handle. He'd raged through the palace, throwing anything that wasn't bolted down or built in, and a few things that were.

Those in his path scurried for safety. Somehow no one was maimed or killed during his outburst. When it was over, he settled into the task of setting things straight with a cold, venomous calm that loomed more ominously, even, than the rage that had preceded it.

None of those around him had ever seen him so obsessed, so intent on a single goal. Very few of them, however, had any idea what that particular goal was, and this made it all the more mysterious. There were a few advisors, a few Legionaires who had been with him since his previous service, in on the secret. The rest of those who peopled the citadel and its surrounding camp/city had to be content with speculation, rumors, and orders.

Faith watched all the comings and goings with interest, straining to hear what they talked about whenever Bontempt brought his men into the room, trying to pierce the veil of secrecy and make sense of what was happening. She knew that the others, Hope, Charity, the Archangels, even Fontana himself, had been taken away. She'd learned, through eavesdropping, piecing together the bawdy jokes of the guards, what was to happen to the slaves in Stygia.

She dreamed of the moment she would be free to exact revenge. The only thoughts that gave her any peace were those in which she was revenging herself on Bontempt, Fontana, or both. She listened, and she waited, knowing that eventually the truth of what was happening would be revealed.

As it turned out, she didn't have all that long to wait. Bontempt had always held a contempt for his slaves, and his arrogance was second only to his vanity. When he felt that things were ready, he couldn't help gloating, and the one person who would be most affected by that gloating was Faith. After all, it was her friends he was going after.

"Well," he began one evening as she sat on her stone slab, staring up at him, "I'll be taking care of your friends once and for all in a day or so."

Faith's heart pounded, but she gave no indication of her interest. She didn't want him to withhold information just to watch her squirm. If he was still after her friends, then they were either free, or some other delay had prevented their departure for Stygia. She'd not seen the two guards nor the old guide who'd been sent with them for some time, so it seemed they must be free.

"This one you know as Love," Bontempt went on, watching her with an evil grin plastered across his face, "he has caused me a great deal of…difficulty. It will be a truly satisfying moment when I finish him off and take that book for myself."

He was obviously waiting to get a rise out of her, but she couldn't tell toward what end, so she waited.

"Just so that you don't get your hopes up," Bontempt continued at last, "know this. He may be free for the moment, and he may have freed a few of your friends. I'll let you wonder on that…free or consigned to Oblivion. It doesn't really matter. What does matter is this. I've figured your playful little friend out, and I know one thing for certain. He will come back.

"The smart thing to do, the thing I would do, or any of my men, would be to take that sorry, ragtag little bunch he's taken up with and head off in search of Heaven, or Nirvana, or whatever the flavor of the month is in paradise. Thing is, he isn't smart. Not like that. He'll come back, and *you* are the one who will lure him."

Faith half stood, then settled back down. She tried valiantly to maintain her veneer of calm, but it was cracking and falling apart rapidly. It wasn't so much the audacity of his comments, or the cool, collected way in which he pronounced the end of those she loved, but it was the *truth* of his words. The first thing that leaped to her lips was a hot denial, but it died before she could set it free. He was right. Love would never leave her here, not if he knew she was captive, and somehow she knew that Bontempt would make damn sure that he *did* know.

"You're wrong," she lied, knowing he wouldn't believe her, but unable to let it go without a shot. "He might want to come for me, but he will not lead the others here and endanger them. He wanted Fontana, not me."

"He's led those same others into almost certain doom at least twice already," Bontempt said matter-of-factly. "The fact that he is free and alive, along with a few of the others, is tribute to his phenomenal luck. He will find that he needs more than luck to deal with me. The Tempest is a random set of occurrences. I am not. I will have him here, in chains, and I will take great pleasure and a lot of time in explaining his new circumstances to him."

Faith could stand no more. She struggled violently against the chains, leaping first one way, then the other in an attempt to dislodge them from the stone. Bontempt made no move to stop her, nor did he order her to be silent, which he could have done easily enough. He merely watched, letting his smile deepen and the wild light dance in his eyes.

He was mad. That she hadn't known it for certain earlier could be chalked up to the impossibility of her situation, her inability to truly grasp the new realities that bound her. She knew her struggles were futile, and the manacles were biting deeply into the flesh of her ankles and wrists, but she could no longer contain her fury. Bontempt's smiling, leering face only made it more difficult.

"I can see why he would come for one such as you," the slaver said with grudging admiration. "You move so well in chains."

Faith was beyond thought. She lurched back and forth, screamed at the top of her lungs. None of it fazed him. She fought and cried, twisted and screeched, all to no avail. At last, beyond exhaustion, no coherent thought left to her, she collapsed on the stone, panting heavily and sobbing into the cold surface of the stone.

"Dance," Bontempt commanded, his eyes glittering in anticipation.

She looked up at him desperately. He couldn't be serious. "Dance."

Against her will, her body rose to a kneeling position, then to her feet and onto her toes. There was no music, but Bontempt began to clap his hands in a syncopated rhythm, slow and seductive, and Faith felt the power of the chains leaking through her resolve, melting her fury. First her hands, then her feet, and finally her hips began to sway, whirling slowly to the beat, forcing muscles to their limits and beyond. She had no control, no power to resist, and the anger that still flooded her mind, overpowering her common sense and driving what remained of her conscious mind deeper and deeper within her, threatened to take over once and for all. Madness beckoned.

This is what you wanted all along, the voice whispered, slipping through her defenses as her legs and arms whipped about and the pain of these motions drove into her like steel spikes. *You wanted to belong to someone strong, someone who could handle you. He will make your decisions for you, and he will take away the pain. Give him what he wants, and you can be free.*

Now there was something to concentrate on. The voice, the shadowy presence that was invading her mind, was within her power to combat. Bontempt might have her physical form tied in his chains, but within the shell of her flesh, such as it was in this place, she was still in charge.

As if sensing the inner struggle she was now engaged in, Bontempt increased the tempo of the rhythm gradually. He was still watching her with the same hungry curiosity, detached, waiting to see at what point her willpower would snap, or her body would cease to function. He wanted to control her completely, to own her body and soul, and to this end he would break her. If her Shadow drove her to madness in the process, if the anger and the fury were too great for her to contain, he would not mourn her loss. It would be entertainment beyond measure.

At some point, her mind blanked. Her body did not stop dancing. There was no limit to what it could be forced into, beyond total decimation, but her mind took the high road. Neither she nor her Shadow remained in control, only Bontempt, clapping his hands and watching as she spun and pirouetted, dipped and gyrated to the rhythm of his own inner music.

When he finally stopped, he stood and stared down at her nearly ruined form for a long, long time. It had brought no satisfaction. She had not broken, and until she drew the other to him, there would be a lack, a hole in his control that he needed desperately to fill.

Cappy's apparent defection was eating away at him slowly. He'd always known that he had no real control over the man, but outright mutiny had not seemed in the offing. Now he had to wonder if the others saw the weakness, if they would think he was going soft. That would be the worst. If they knew that Cappy was older and stronger, that would be too much. He'd worked long and hard to ensure that no one got that idea in their head, and thankfully, until now, Cappy had supported him on it. Now, as Cappy himself had put it, it was personal.

He was not going to wait for someone else to fight and win his battle. He would lure the heretics in, take the lot of them, strip that bitch Llanna down for the slabs and whisk the others off to Stygia. There would be no second reprieve, not if he had to give every one of them a private guard to see them through. Not if he had to guide them to the dark city himself.

He laid out his plans quickly as the others entered, then departed, each with his own purpose. They were puzzle pieces that formed a devious, ingenious whole. Working like this, plotting and setting the wheels of betrayal into motion, Bontempt felt almost young again. Almost.

The first group set out at once. He needed to be certain that this "Love" and his people would know what he planned. If they were to try to stop him, they would have to be aware, and it was of utmost importance that they not know that they had not discovered the information on their own. He was sacrificing good men to that end. Bontempt never underestimated his enemies, and while his men might think their small patrol, planted with information only partially true, was a match for anything they might meet on the road, Bontempt knew better. Any man who could brave the Tempest, take out seasoned veterans like Din and Sully, and piss Cappy off so royally was someone to be reckoned with.

He would make a journey. He would travel down the road to the compound where this troublesome bunch had made their transit to the Shadowlands, on the pretense of attacking the temple there. He knew that Llanna, Love, and their followers would just retreat to the larger, older temple, but that was fine. He would be out on the road, more vulnerable, in theory, than he was at present, and he would take the slave with him. He would make her dance every night at sunset. He would put her in the most demeaning positions, make demands of her that would break her or drive her to Oblivion, and he would do it openly.

Any spy coming close enough would see what he did, and report back. If he was any judge of others, and his years of leadership and success would indicate that he was, this Love could not take much of what he was about to dish out. Even if the others were wiser, even if he were warned away from Bontempt's trap, he would come. How could he not? He would not leave the woman to be tortured and ruined. That was the nature of this man, Love, and it was his weakness and his strength all at once.

Bontempt himself had never believed in anything but himself strongly enough for such faith. No philosopher or preacher had ever been able to turn his head with pretty words or promises about some other place he might or might not ever reach. What was important was this world, this life. No creator would go to such trouble to create intelligent sheep.

And yet there was a power in faith, in belief. From his experience, it didn't matter so much what that faith was centered on, but instead the depth and strength of the emotion behind it. A man who believed that if he did not jump a fence the world would end was much more likely to make it over that fence than one who merely believed he would hurt his leg. They said that faith could move mountains. No way to tell that—such faith was not available to be put to the test—but Bontempt was reasonably certain that, faith or not, a set of his chains would put an end to both belief and passion.

He watched as Faith's inert form was unchained from the stone and carried from the room. They would prepare her; she would be ready. Willing or not, preferably not, she would do her share. Her very strength, her will to fight against his control, no matter what the odds, were enough to ensure his victory. He would not give her a chance to realize what a show she was putting on...and it would be interesting to truly test her limits. Exhaustion was not half the test that humiliation and pain could be, and Bontempt was expert in the delivery of all three. It would be an interesting time, a challenge. It would be good to be back on the road.

As the doors closed behind the last of the guards and the wheels went fully into motion on his plans, Bontempt settled back into his throne. Laying his head back and closing his one eye slowly, Bontempt allowed the smile that had been itching at the corners of his mouth to take control of his face.

"Soon," he murmured to no one in particular. "Very soon."

Love and Llanna were in no hurry on their way back down that mountain, despite the horror behind them. None of it had been easy on Llanna, and Love felt that rushing back into the problems they would face soon enough, anyway, could be nothing but destructive. They chose not to take the train, not immediately, anyway, heading off across country instead. Llanna wasn't certain what they might encounter on the way, but it was likely not as dangerous as facing down Bontempt in his own citadel. Hopefully it was at least as safe as what awaited them.

It took them nearly a week to make their way to the nearest city, slipping through the shadowy desert surrounding the mountain that held Friendly, California, and back into the byways of civilization. They finally made their way to another small, backwoods train station and began the return trip. This time Love didn't feel the oppression so heavily. Llanna had found, somewhere, an ability to smile that she'd been lacking in all of her years in the Shadowlands, and it lightened Love's personal burden a bit to know he'd helped at least one person.

Now his mind was turned to Faith. He'd already led the others off on a blind mission to rescue someone who didn't deserve it; now he had to wonder if he had the power, cunning, and resources to rescue another who truly *did*. All the time he'd been rushing headlong into the Tempest after Fontana, Faith had been chained to a slab of stone, dancing for some asshole with one eye and half a brain. Just when he'd begun to feel comfortable in the position of leadership that had been thrust upon him, fate slapped him hard across the face with his own inadequacy.

He could see no way that any sort of frontal assault would work. He knew that Llanna had her own people in the camp outside the Citadel. No one in the Shadowlands, it seemed, was without their resources. Getting in and out of the camp might not be impossible, but getting into the Citadel was another thing altogether. They would be expecting him. By now Bontempt would know that the portal was closed. For all Love knew, Cappy might well have survived and made his way back to tell the entire story.

In any case, the slaver was not going to be happy, that much was certain. He'd not only lost a string of slaves, but he'd been defeated by one new to this realm. It was a humiliation that an ego that size would never be able to live with, and Love was hoping that this would prove useful. An angry man makes mistakes, and Bontempt would be furious. If they could lure him out of his citadel, there might be a chance—it might be their only chance.

Love had a vague plan to sneak into the camp after Bontempt had left and rescue Faith. He knew it was too simple for a real plan, but nothing else had yet presented itself. While he felt they would be safe enough in the temple, he had no answer to breaching the defenses of their enemy. It was a stalemate.

When they arrived back at the temple, it became a moot point. Seth met them before they even made it through the front doors, and his eyes were gleaming. Something had obviously happened while they were away, but Love, remembering other instances in which he'd seen that gleam in the old guide's eye, wasn't certain he wanted to hear the details.

"I thought you'd never get here," the old man said, taking Llanna by the arm

DAVID NIALL WILSON

and hurrying them along into the temple. "We have plans to make, and not much time left to get prepared. Bontempt went into a rage when we closed that portal, and it seems that his first thought was revenge. They march on the new temple," turning to Love, he added, "your old compound, tomorrow at dawn."

"He's attacking us?" Llanna asked, unable to take it all in at once.

"Well, he's attacking the other temple," Seth replied. "He must think we've moved our entire operation over there. Either that, or he just figures it for the easiest place to find our friend here and his book. After all the years he has left us pretty much alone, I can't imagine that he suddenly decided to come after us all on his own.

"Our people inside say he's obsessed, that he won't stop until you," he stabbed a finger pointedly into Love's chest, "are in his possession. Literally. He's sending a large force to take the temple, and, if my sources are correct, he will follow soon after on his own. There's one more thing. He's taking the girl, Faith. He must have realized, after we went to such trouble to free the others, that we would want to come back for her."

"Do you think it's a trap?" Love asked slowly. "I mean, he must know how difficult it would be for us to get into his citadel and break Faith loose. Maybe he was afraid we wouldn't go for it. Maybe he figures if he's out on the road, or even in possession of the compound, which I know better than he ever could, that we will be forced into action. If he's looking for us, and you have to believe that he is, this is going to be one tricky operation."

"You are right, my friend," Seth grinned at him. "That is the beauty of it. Of course he knows we will come, but he has no idea how, or from what direction. As long as those factors remain in our favor, we are at least fighting even."

"What about Cappy?" Love asked. He saw the old guide stiffen, but then relax immediately.

"I don't know if he made it out of there or not," Seth answered, "but I'd bet that he did. One of two things would be the case, if he did. Either he went straight to Bontempt and told him everything he knows, or he is coming after you. I have been keeping an eye on things, watching for just such a move on his part, but I can't guarantee he won't slip by me. You will need to be very, very careful in the next few days."

Great, Love thought silently. *It's not enough I've got Bontempt and that damned bird to worry about.*

Seth put an arm around his shoulder and shook him. "Don't let it eat at your mind, Love. You'll need that mind to help me figure out a plan of counter-attack."

Now Love was staring openly. "Counter-attack? Why not just get everyone out of there and into *this* temple before they arrive? Why fight them at all? If they come here, they'll never be able to breach the walls."

"But that is not the entire plan, my friend. That is just the frontal portion. Bontempt is bringing the girl so that he can draw you out. I can tell you from years of watching him that he will stop at nothing. Humiliation, torture, dismemberment, and he will do it all publicly, possibly in front of the walls of your own temple."

"It is *our* temple," Love said angrily.

"Believe what you want," Seth continued, "they built it for you. Bontempt will take that temple, and he will take your companion, as well. He will take her bit by bit. He knows you now for what you are, and he knows you won't just stand by and let him have his way with her. That means our only hope is to try, once again, to surprise him."

"So we attack," Llanna said, her brow furrowed in concentration, "after they take the temple, but before *he* reaches it. We attack him on the road, in the open. He will have the superior force, but we will have the surprise. At least we will if *this* isn't the trap."

"We have to chance that," Seth stated flatly. "We can no more take on his men inside the new temple than we could in his citadel, and locked up away from their homes they will all be ready to fight. If we don't get them before they get there, then this woman, Faith, is lost, and we may go right along with her."

Once again fate had made the decision for him. If Bontempt was expecting this attack on the road, and they would have to plan assuming that he was, then the only answer would be to outthink him. Just because an attack was expected somewhere on that stretch of road didn't mean that Bontempt would be ready for them.

So it was on Love's shoulders once more, another pile of responsibility he'd never sought. His mind drifted to the book, to the prophecies, in search of comfort.

"The Lord helps those who help themselves," he muttered. Llanna and Seth looked askance at him, but he only smiled thinly. "Let's get to work, then," he said more loudly. "We can't keep the big man waiting."

Cappy had had his fill of the soft life very quickly. As he wandered the city streets, trading stories with the oldsters on the corners and in the alleys, slipping through to catch glimpses of the living denizens of the city and to reminisce, his failure in the Tempest ate away at the back of his mind. Even as he relaxed, letting his muscles regain their strength and his thoughts level out, the pressure to move on and put it all behind him grew stronger.

He briefly considered just heading back into the Tempest and away. What difference did it make if a two-bit slaver like Bontempt lost a couple of chains of slaves? He wouldn't have minded seeing the arrogant bastard *on* one of those chains. And what difference did it make if, in the process of that loss, he'd underestimated an opponent? He was still free, and his health was returning rapidly. Why not cut loose and make his way to Stygia on his own? Someone there would need a guide; someone always needed a guide. It was an uncommon talent.

In the end he couldn't do it. His pride was too great to allow for acceptance of the situation as it stood. He would have to go after this man Love, and he would have to bring him down. Nothing else would relieve that pressure, and Cappy wasn't one to put up with minor annoyances for long.

Seth would be there, too, and the score with his old comrade was far from settled. The battle in the Tempest had brought up old memories, old accounts still past due. There were a lot of burned bridges in both their pasts, and it appeared that, at least for one of them, there had been some repair work in progress. Now his own memories were slipping back across the bridges to haunt him—an odd thought. Haunting a haunt.

So he found himself back on the road much more quickly than he'd originally planned, heading toward the temple where he knew they would be holed up, and planning how he would take his revenge. His original plan was forgotten. He owed nothing to Bontempt, and he had no intention of handing the group of heretics back over to him. He could be much more creative than that. This called for some thought and some caution. The others might forget about him, but Seth would not. If he was going to surprise them, he would have to be more clever than they were, and while he didn't believe this would be a problem, he didn't want to underestimate them again. One against so many, even one such as himself, was not the best of odds.

As he neared the edge of the city, he noticed a glittering crack in the wall of an alley, and he smiled. No sense wasting time here, or on the road. He slipped into the alley, let his essence drift toward and through the crack, and passed into the welcoming embrace of the Tempest. It was the only way to fly.

The preparations were now complete, and Bontempt found, to his surprise, that he was looking forward to being on the road again, to doing something. He'd been sitting in that throne room too long, forgetting the talents that had brought him to it in the first place. Complacency had already cost him too much. It was time to involve himself directly and take back the reins of control that had slipped in the past few weeks.

His men jumped at his commands, presented themselves more sharply, watched over their shoulders and into the shadows for his presence. They were motivated by fear, and it was a powerful motivator. The thought of going back to the Citadel to face him had been enough to force them about their tasks, but the thought that they could face him, one on one, at any moment made them efficient and alert.

Bontempt mused that, once it was all over and he had this man Love, not to mention the priestess of that damned temple, chained and groveling at his feet, he would have to spend some time away. There were plenty of missions he might have led, rather than sending others, places where his leadership and experience might have made the difference in a tidier profit or a more complete victory. He would have to thank these Heretics, once they were face to face, for returning to him the part of his existence that had always energized him, that had made him the man that he was.

The advance party was several days ahead of them, and he kept in contact through messengers. Everything seemed brighter, more full of life, now that he was on the move.

The slave, Faith, walked behind him, chained to the other servants he'd brought for amusement and labor. She had had little rest since the night he'd danced her into a stupor, and he intended to keep things that way. If she had time to consider what was happening, to think out the motives behind his actions, she would never cooperate, and though there was little she could do to resist, it was better to keep her playing right into his hands.

Every day he marched her along with the others, sometimes reaching out to trip her with the butt end of his sword, sometimes making her dance, even as she marched, and at night she was his toy. He worked her, physically and mentally, pushing her carefully toward the edges of sanity, but never quite beyond. It was important that this man Love know that there was something left to save, something left of the woman he sought across all those miles and two levels of reality.

There really was no night and day, but he insisted. The divisions of light and dark that marked the passing of time in the Skinlands were useful for scheduling rest and relaxation, for keeping the mind sharp and the wits intact. He would have driven them all the way to this compound/temple in a couple of days, but this would have given the enemy a smaller window in which to make the fatal mistake of attacking him, and he was counting on them to make that mistake.

The journey to the compound gave Bontempt time to think, to work at figuring out the ways of his enemy. He knew very little of those who'd followed the traitor, Fontana, and he knew even less of the priestess Llanna and her odd brood. He knew that they had been watching this Love for years, waiting for his arrival as if he were some sort of messiah. There seemed to be a bit of truth to their belief, as well. Bontempt wondered if it was their belief that had brought over so much power in a newcomer to the Shadowlands. In all his years, in and out of Stygia and the Tempest, Bontempt had never known one so strong, so powerful, and yet so newly dead.

Cyclops circled high above, winging off to the right at a sharp angle. Bontempt wanted to know what the enemy was planning, but he had to be cautious. If Cyclops were spotted, or if he sent in spies and they were captured, it would be an entirely new game. As long as his mission seemed to be the capture of this "compound," as the slave Fontana had termed it, then the Heretics would not worry too much.

Bontempt knew from early scouting reports that he'd been right about their first move. They had begun to evacuate the compound the second they knew he was on the approach. By the time his advance party got there, there would be no resistance left, just the empty building and the shadows. Just as he'd planned. He would take his people and move in: then the real fun would begin.

He'd seen what they had done with the place through Cyclops' one good eye, seen the brooding parapets and looming walls of the place, the half-crumbled ruins that stuck straight through the Shroud. It was a place of great death, of destruction. It would be an invigorating stop, like a home away from home. Who could say, maybe when it was all over and it was time to move on he would consider making an outpost of the place. It was certainly built along military lines, and there was no denying the power of the place, either.

DAVID NIALL WILSON

He kept a close eye on those around him, watching for the spies he knew must be among them, trying to get inside their heads. He had brought only two of the barghests with him, though he could have worked the entire pack into the ranks easily enough. There was plenty of hunting off away from the road. He wanted enough force to be safe, but too much might discourage the Heretics from coming forward.

He felt a strange kinship with the odd wraiths, their forms sculpted so far from their original humanity that almost nothing remained. He himself was a larger than life figure, his vacant, brooding eye-socket, long, straggling beard and huge, bear-like form were intimidating in the way of giants. He had never been brilliant in the ways of books or learning, nor had he been handsome, or athletic. What he had been was imposing. Never had he allowed another to rule him, not, at least, since his time in the Legions. Before that he'd listened to orders from above, but only when it suited him. He'd been on the way up, a growing power to be reckoned with. That was the past.

As they came within a good day's march from the compound, he called for a halt. This brought some odd glances from his men, who'd expected him to march them until they were out on their feet, then to flay them for their weakness. It amused him that even his own followers were confused by his actions. If he could fool them, surely he could fool a bunch of fanatics who were already fooling themselves.

There was no next level. There was no escape. He would become their new prophet, showing them the ways of darkness and chaos. They would find chains instead of peace, endless labor and pain in the place of faith. If they truly sought a god, he would become that god for them. It was the least he could do after all the amusement they had brought him.

As the others bustled about feverishly, planting the poles that would hold the tents and moving supplies into a tight, protected circle, he made his way to the slave chain and found Faith watching him through exhausted, dust-rimmed eyes. Reaching down to grab her by the hair, he lifted her back to her feet and met the hatred of her gaze head-on with his indifference.

"You will come with me," he told her with a grin, "and I will show you some new tricks. It is boring, I know, when everything is always the same, so I have saved some things to amuse you."

She kicked out at him feebly, and he let her. It was more fun to manhandle her without commanding through the chains. She was strong, fearless, and for all that, no match for his strength. He had abilities she couldn't even dream of, secrets she wouldn't understand if she saw them in front of her nose. Her trust in her comrades was commendable, but ill-placed.

Without acknowledging her protests or the pointless blows she rained down on his shoulders from behind, he took her chain in one huge hand and began walking toward where they were setting up his private tent. It was huge and dark, and nearly finished. She stumbled along in his footsteps, trying and failing to slow his progress, sobbing and cursing all in the same breath. With his face turned away, Bontempt smiled. It was only a matter of time, and for once, time was totally on his side.

Except You Go Through Shadow

20

Love's scouts reported Bontempt's stop on the road, describing the camp and the forces he'd brought along. It was almost a miracle, this chance. Why the slaver had not continued on to the compound was beyond Love's ability to comprehend.

Little Green Book, chapter fifteen, verse three: "If it seems too good to be true, it probably is."

This had proven, over the years, to be possibly the single strongest truth in the entire book of prophecies. Bontempt was arrogant, yes, but he was not stupid. He'd been around for a long time, and he held sway over a lot of different types of people. One did not rise to a position such as his by poor judgment. The only answer was that it was a trap. It was a trap, or it was a challenge from an enemy so certain of his ability to win the coming encounter that it didn't matter what the circumstances of that encounter might be. Maybe he was calling Love out.

The hell of it was, and Seth had pointed this out early on, it didn't matter if it was a trap. This was the opportunity they'd been waiting for, and they would have to take it. There was no chance of making a difference against Bontempt's forces if they allowed them the safety of the compound. Even Love's knowledge of the original structure, and that of those who'd rebuilt it, would be little help if they were continually outnumbered and outgunned. Also, there were more troops waiting. If the slaver made it all the way to his destination, he would be beyond their ability to deal with. Faith would be beyond his help.

He wanted his old belief back, the sure and certain knowledge that every answer he would ever need in life was contained somewhere in that little green book, and that nothing could stop him if he did not waver. He had thought, in those days, that the words themselves were magic. Now he knew that it wasn't just the words, it was his faith. Without that, the book was so much paper, and he had no faith in his ability to take Bontempt on in direct confrontation.

Seth found him standing just outside the walls of the temple and staring off into the distance.

"You are trying too hard," the old man told him lightly. "There is always an answer. The very nature of a question demands it."

"That doesn't mean I'll always know that answer," he replied grimly, "despite what everyone here seems to think. We are seriously outgunned here, Seth. He knows we're coming, we know we're going, and he has us hands down in any sort of battle I can picture."

"Then you have to find a type of battle you cannot picture, and trust to the prophecies," Seth said matter-of-factly. "If you can't picture the outcome of something, odds are he can't either. That at least evens up the odds a bit."

"I'm open for anything that can do that," Love sighed. "The problem is, my mind is the type that works on straight lines. I see the goal ahead of me, but I see only one route to it. It has always worked for me, but the logic that makes it work tells me it is useless to me now. We need a way to just appear in his camp, a way to cloak our movements that his scouts and that damned bird won't be able to pierce."

DAVID NIALL WILSON

"You know such a way," Seth smiled. "You know, and yet you do not see."

"The Tempest?" Love asked hesitantly. "You mean you can get there from here?"

"Well, not precisely here, but there are ways in besides the large portals, small cracks and fractures in the framework that holds the Tempest at bay. I can open these, for a time, and I can find my way to the new temple or to this camp on the road with equal ease."

"Then we can sneak right into his camp!" Love stood suddenly, elated by the news. "We can surprise them completely—how could that fail?"

"Cappy," Seth answered in a single word. "I lost him in the Tempest, but as I told you, I doubt he is far away. He is there, somwhere, either in the Tempest or in Bontempt's camp looking out for us. If we go through the Tempest, we will draw his attention all the quicker."

"That's better than letting him pull the same stunt on us," Love pointed out. "If we just wait around, trying to decide what might or might not work, he could waltz right in and cut our throats while we speak."

"I will know if he is near, but that is not enough to protect us," Seth said, agreeing. "It is best that we go where he is, where he cannot fight us without coming out of hiding. If we can get past him, we can get to Bontempt. Once we are there, we will have plenty to deal with as well, so we still need to go in with a plan."

Love stared hard at the old guide. He still couldn't quite trust him. The man just loved danger too much. He was too fond of risks that would have driven the sanity from a normal man. On the other hand, the guide had proven himself time and again to be honest and true to his word, and in this particular instance he was their only chance.

"We'll make our way through the Tempest," Love said at last, "and we'll fight the bastards on their own terms. Let's find Llanna and see if we can come up with something that will make the difference, something that will tilt the scales in our favor."

"Now you're talking," Seth grinned.

Love wished he could share Seth's enthusiasm. He had no desire to brave the Tempest again, especially not when it was most likely that the one doing the stalking this time would be Cappy, and he himself was the most likely target.

This time the group going in was large. Seth had worked 'round the clock training, instructing, and outfitting those in the temple for the journey. Although Bontempt only had a small force with him, his troops were well trained and heavily armed. It was also possible that they were lying in wait for just such an attack, and in that case Love would need all the support they could muster.

There were a few among them who had been soldiers, either in life or in the Shadowlands, as Seth had been. These were quickly separated and broken up to lead the groups of less experienced fighters. It wasn't much, but at least if they somehow got separated, each group would have someone in charge who might be able to keep their head together. Love wished that he could offer more.

Finally it was nearing dawn, and he knew they had to move out. Since they seemed to be following the rise and fall of a sun they could not even see, Bontempt's camp would be awakening and packing up, continuing on toward the compound. Love and his followers would have to catch the slaver on that road to have a chance, and they would have to choose their point of emergence from the Tempest carefully.

"I could open a nihil right in the middle of the damned road," the old guide had informed him. "But we'll need a moment to orient ourselves. We'll just have to see how it plays out."

It seemed pretty iffy. Love moved to the front of the ranks that now ran back into the temple and out of sight, three wide so as to make it through the single nihil that Seth would open. The guide had made it clear that there would be only so much time before it snapped shut, and they needed to get everyone through in an organized manner. Once they were inside and safely onto a byway, they could worry about regrouping. That was what worried Love the most. They would be jumping blindly into the Tempest. There was no way to know whether there was a byway present on the other side, or some nightmare that would engulf them all.

Love could tell that this prospect intrigued Seth, but for himself it was another weight, another burden of responsibility he did not want to shoulder. It was bad enough that they were all willing to follow him into a battle they had little chance of winning, without the necessity of battling the road on their way to war.

As the ranks moved off the main road and came to a halt near a crackling fissure in an outcropping of stone, Love gave Llanna a quick hug and leaped through the nihil on Seth's heels. The old instincts kicked in full force despite his doubts. He had only enough concentration for the moment at hand. It was too late to turn back, and they would either succeed or fail in the next few hours. For those hours he would not let the responsibility rule his thoughts.

Love Constantine the reluctant prophet had given way to Love the Beast. Training he barely remembered after all that had befallen him clicked into place with automatic precision. This was where he stood out from the crowd, in action, in control. It would not be the compound all over again, because he hadn't really been in charge then, and he hadn't expected to win, or to live through it. That had not been the object. Now he was not only fighting for his own life, but for those of his followers, and he did not intend to let them down.

He and Seth burst through the first trails of mist and Seth landed in a crouch, swinging his head quickly from side to side. There were four different lighter patches in the mist, portals, and he quickly scanned them, though how he did this Love could not tell. Their surroundings were green, deep greens and trailing vines, twisted dwarf-trees and murky pools of brown muck. The scent of moisture and growing things was in the air. No immediate danger presented itself, but Love didn't relax his guard. He'd played this game already, and it wasn't going to take him by surprise again.

With a quick gesture to their right, Seth moved off toward one of the portals, and Love motioned to those behind him to follow. He would have liked to have remained in this place as they passed through, to watch for the dangers he was certain must exist here and guard those who trailed after him, but there was no time. There was also the very real chance that the next stop would be the one with the trouble in it, and he wasn't going to leave Seth, able as he might be, to handle whatever came along on his own.

He passed through the portal right on the older man's heels and stumbled quickly through into a byway. They hadn't been too far off the byways after all, and he heaved a quick sigh of relief. Seth was grinning at him, moving down the trail to make room for those coming in behind.

"We'll make good time now," the old man said calmly. "There is somewhat less danger here. I will be able to follow the lay of the land beyond the mist easily enough. We should be able to cut down our transit time to only a couple of hours."

This was good news. It meant they would get to the road in plenty of time to await their moment for attack. For once the odds didn't loom impossibly over him. Nodding to Seth, he began to move forward. Seth fell in beside him, watching the walls of mist carefully and stopping occasionally to press his eyes, or his hands, and even once his ear, to the shifting walls. He said nothing of what he was learning, but Love trusted the man to let him know if any danger presented itself.

All of the others had made it through the portal and onto the byway without mishap. If anything had lurked in the swampy node they'd passed through, it had kept its peace, and for that Love was thankful. They were already outnumbered. He wanted to make it to the battle while he still had most of an army to command, undertrained, small and inexperienced as that army might be.

Of all the experiences he and Llanna had shared in the Tempest, this was by far the calmest. They had not gotten the opportunity to travel the byways for any length of time on that wild first visit. This was almost like walking on the road out in the Shadowlands. If it hadn't been for the sensations that bombarded their senses, the smells and colors, the roiling mist that wound its way from the walls of the byway and around their ankles, it would have been like a thousand other roads. It was not.

They passed a great number of the spots that Love had come to understand were the portals. They were indistinct, lighter patches in the mist, and he went to great lengths to give them a wide berth as he passed. He remembered the rift that had formed when Seth had summoned the darkness, the huge hand that had reached through from some other place and snatched up one of Bontempt's beasts as if it were a toy. He wanted no part of that. The dagger at his side felt wholly inadequate to the task of self-defense in this place, and yet he walked here on his way to battle.

They came around a bend and the byway branched suddenly. The trail to the left was dimmer than that on the right, but it seemed to point vaguely in the direction they needed to travel. Seth stopped, looking first one way, then the other. He waved his arms around him, closing his eyes for a moment and brushing his fingertips across the mist. Just as Love's patience was wearing thin, Seth spun on his heel and pointed down the dimmer trail.

EXCEPT YOU GO THROUGH SHADOW 567

"That is the way to our destination," he said, frowning, "but there is something there, something I can't quite make out. The byway is not clear. In the middle there is a blockage, a node."

"I thought the byways were a clear way through the Tempest," Love said, irritated. "What could cause one just to block up?"

"This from the man who blew the largest portal in this sector sky high," Seth tossed back sarcastically. "The byways *are* a clear way through. This is something that had to be placed in the path. There are any number of reasons this might have happened, most of them not good. We will still be able to get through, I believe, but it may not be as simple as just walking down this road."

"We'll do whatever we have to," Love said, heading straight off down the left-hand trail. "If this is the only way through, then we take it. Unless you have another suggestion?"

Seth thought about it for a moment, then shook his head. "This is the shortest way, even with the blockage. I might find an alternate route, but that would take time. There's no way of telling how much."

As they moved forward again, Love turned back to Llanna, who walked in the first rank of three behind them, and explained what they'd discovered.

"Pass the word back to be on the lookout for anything strange," he concluded. "We don't know what, or who, we might be facing here, and we need to be ready for the worst."

Llanna nodded, turning to the man behind her, and Love returned his concentration to the road ahead. The mists were deeper there, less contained by the borders of the path they walked upon. Seth walked softly, as if on eggshells, and he had an odd, thoughtful expression on his face. There was something bothering him, but it would do no good to pester him about it until he figured it out. Love concentrated on the road.

Ahead, a dark, shadowy mass was looming. It resembled a tent, or an awning of some sort, and it obscured the path completely. The road just ended, and the structure, whatever it was, began. As they moved cautiously forward, it became clear that the thing stretched on both sides of the byway into the mists beyond. There was no way around except by way of the nodes to either side, and there was no way to know what these might hold.

Seth stopped suddenly, as if a light had kindled in his mind to blaze out through his eyes, and he stood, staring ahead in amazement.

"It cannot be," he mumbled. "Not this place, not here."

"What is it?" Love asked quickly. "You know this place?"

"I do, or one very much like it. It is a way station, like a shelter against the storm, you might say. They were erected by Charon's servants for the Ferrymen so long ago that the names of men and places would be meaningless if I explained them. I thought the last such place had been overrun by Spectres years ago, the inhabitants slaughtered."

"How do you know that they have not?" Love asked cautiously.

"I do not," Seth answered, "but there is someone in there now, and it is not a Spectre."

"Cappy?" Love's question was hurried, belying the calm expression on his face. He'd hoped to bypass the other guide's wrath, at least until after they'd faced off with Bontempt.

"That I can't tell you," Seth answered slowly. "It could be him, or it could be any of the others. There are many travelers in the Tempest. These stations have not been used, officially, in generations of guides. Like I said, I thought the last one had been overrun years ago."

"Well, what do we do, then?" Love asked. "Is there a way through this thing?"

"That's no problem," Seth answered. "They are keyed to the auras of the Ferrymen—it will open for me."

Love started. He nearly pursued the old man's comment, but something in the guide's eyes told him it was neither the time nor the place. The Ferrymen. Seth? Love didn't want to think about the age that this indicated, or the power that had been walking so calmly at his side.

"Let's hope whoever's inside is friendly, then," Love said, moving forward again. As word passed back through the ranks of what was next, the way station loomed, solid and dark. The book at his chest had warmed slightly, but it did not burn.

Seth moved forward without a word, walking straight at the wall of the way station. Closing his eyes for a moment to collect his thoughts, Love followed.

"Let's do it," he muttered.

Cappy sat on a large, leather-covered chair and waited, his chin on one hand. The emptiness of the way station did not bother him, nor did the solitude of the Tempest. He'd been living mostly within his own mind for so long he barely noticed the world around him. Here, in the silence, he was more at home than most would be in a crowded room. He could not sit idle for an eternity, but for the moment it was comfortable.

They were coming. He'd sensed them the moment they entered the Tempest. The way station allowed him to send his senses out, to seek the byways and the nodes, but it blocked such prying activities from the outside. They would know something was here, but they would not know what. It didn't matter. He knew that the one called Love would come, in any case, and he knew that Seth would lead him. He only wished he could see his old comrade's face when he realized the nature of Cappy's temporary home. It had been lifetimes since they'd shared drinks in such a hall, years since either of them had even entered one.

The walls were hung with weapons and supplies, memorabilia of a day when Charon's hierarchy had been in its full power. There was a grand sort of decadence to this place now, the shell of a grandeur that no longer existed. It was a museum without patrons, and Cappy was beginning to feel just a little bit too much like one of the exhibits.

It hadn't taken them long to make their way to the way-station. Whatever else he might say about Seth, the man knew his way among the byways and nodes of the Tempest better than some knew their way around their own minds. He should know them well. Lifetimes had withered, civilizations crumbled, and still they walked the Tempest.

What Cappy couldn't understand was what had happened. Seth had softened, had begun, impossibly, to care about the young ones again. And he had this vision, this odd desire to move on to some other place, some level beyond Shadowlands and Tempest, beyond Stygia herself. Cappy had no desire for any of it. What he wanted was his past, and barring that, some entertaining challenges to while away the hours.

The Legions were hopelessly corrupt, and those in the Hierarchy spent more time attacking one another and erecting defenses than they did accomplishing anything. It did not seem as though the dark empire would rise again, though it had not fully crumbled. Cappy had all the time in the world, this world, anyway, and he could wait.

For now he was content that he'd found someone worthy of his time and energy, a challenge of the first order. He didn't know if he could take Seth down permanently, but he could defeat him, rob him of his companions and his purpose. That was near enough to a second death to make the millennia to come unbearable.

As the wards dropped, he reached out with his mind, reached behind and beyond himself and called into the shadows. They were waiting, those he'd prepared, those he'd chosen and called, and they answered his call eagerly. It was a shame to sacrifice this place, this comfortable bit of history, but it would be worth it in the end. He called to the Spectres, and they came. Seth was not the only one who could form a summoning, though Cappy at least had the sense to do it in a controlled fashion. He stood, facing the incoming ranks, and he smiled.

"So," he called out, his voice booming across the chamber and bringing the intruders to a shocked halt, "you are here at last. I was beginning to wonder if you'd find your way here or not."

"You knew I would come," Seth answered, moving a couple of paces ahead of the others. "You knew all along."

"Well, since you mention it, it is true," Cappy said, and he smiled. "You always were good in the byways," he added, taking a step closer. "Your problem was never one of ability, Seth, but of character. You are weak. You seek comfort from those not fit to polish your boot heels. You use skills taught you in the service of Charon himself in the service of fools. There is no level beyond this one, none other than Oblivion, and it is a shame you have given up enough of your individuality that you would seek that. Not surprising, mind you, but a shame."

Love could see that the words were finding purchase in Seth's mind, but the emotions that warred within the old guide's eyes did not include regret. There was anger, more anger than anyone could contain for long, and when the two Ferrymen's eyes met, there was a flicker of something bordering on both hatred and desire. Motioning for the others to follow his lead, Love stepped back a pace, leaving Seth to face their new adversary. He didn't relax his concentration for a moment, but neither did he wish to insult their guide by a lack of trust in his abilities.

Even as he watched, though, Seth was suddenly not there. He whipped his eyes to where Cappy stood, unperturbed, and he saw that Seth had materialized behind the other man. His dagger had somehow made its way from sheath to hand during that movement, a movement so fast that none but Cappy even noted its passing. As if in slow motion, the man turned, sliding to the side at just the right moment and reaching for Seth's arm.

Seth pivoted, avoiding the grab at his knife hand, and spun the blade back, coming in with a backhand swipe that would have taken out a lesser man's throat.

"You are still quick, despite your faults," Cappy crowed as he spun and lunged with a thrust of his own. "Too bad we don't have time to finish this, man to man. I'd have loved to see who would come out on top. Unfortunately, some friends of mine are coming, and I think you will have your hands full when they arrive. You won't recognize them, I don't think, but a couple of them served with us in the Legions. That is, they served with us before their Shadows took control, before the Tempest claimed them for its own."

The words were forced and choppy, but he showed no real signs of fatigue, nor did Seth. The two performed what might have been an elaborate ballet. There was no way to tell if one or the other had any real advantage from where Love stood, so he chose to listen to the words. At the mention of reinforcements, he moved. The book was a white-hot brand against his chest now, and he ripped at his shirt as he ran toward the two who fought at the far end of the hall, ignoring Love and the rest as if they were of no significance whatsoever.

He lunged against one of the walls, finding the handles of an ancient, black-bladed scythe and ripping it from the wall. He wasn't really familiar with this type of fighting, but any weapon was better than the tiny dagger he'd been using. The blade felt good in his hand, and he noticed with consternation that the burning of the book lessened as he gripped the smooth, black handles. There had to be something special about the scythe, something he had little or no time to learn.

Calling out to the others, who were following his lead, he charged toward Cappy, swinging the blade of the scythe up and backward in a sweeping arc. Seth heard the footsteps and turned quickly, his eyes bright. "Don't come any closer," he cried out, barely avoiding a sudden slice from Cappy's blade. "He is too fast for you, too strong. Find the exit on the far side—go after Bontempt. I will hold him!"

The point became moot when the far portal of the way station burst asunder. An avalanche of Spectres rushed through the entrance, howling like banshees and spearing toward Love's followers. The hunger and hatred in their eyes was overpowering, hypnotic, and they outnumbered the smaller group of the faithful almost two to one.

Love turned to Seth, then back to where Llanna and the others, armed now, but backed against a wall, were setting themselves to ward off the attack.

Little Green Book be damned. He grasped at his father's words, called them to his service and raised the scythe high above his head as he turned back to the center of the hall. It was too much, too much responsibility, too much pain, too much bullshit. He was calling. Cards on the table. If he was really a prophet, then it was time he prophesied.

"Yeah," he screamed, "though I walk through the valley of death, I fear no evil," he charged the first of the Spectres and slashed downward with his blade, slicing it cleanly in two and adding its shriek of pain to the force of his own words, "'cuz I'm the baddest son of a bitch *in* this valley."

Then it was a blur of motion. The scythe, which had felt unfamiliar and heavy moments before, sang through the air. His anger forced its way through him and into his arms, into his hands and the flashing movements of his blade.

The creatures fell back before him, and his success kindled hope in those who followed him. Llanna and the others were taking a heavy toll on the intruders. In this place, it seemed, even with the breaching of the wards, the Spectres were limited in what they could do. They could rend, they could bite and tear at flesh, they could feed, but they could not exert the dark power of their minds. Love waded through them as if they were standing still, slicing heads from torsos and dropping limbs away from thin, emaciated bodies with every stroke.

They swung at him in return, several of them at once charging his position to overwhelm him, but he could do no wrong. No matter what they tried, he countered, no matter what openings he left through lack of skill, they did not see them. He felt the glow of the book against his chest, but this time it didn't burn, not like before. It permeated his being with the heat, radiated into and then back out of him, using him like a lantern, burning the Spectres away like so much kindling in a forest fire.

He didn't think, nor was he really aware of what was happening beyond the figure that happened to fill his sight at any given moment, and yet they fell away at his attack. At last they turned and ran, returning through the portal with Love hot on their heels. At his back, Love could vaguely hear a voice, could make out the words—if he concentrated. His name. Someone was calling out his name.

Numbly he looked down at the blade in his hand, then at the portal through which the Spectres had fled, and then back at the blade. He turned, and he found that Llanna was at his side, reaching out to take him in her arms. He let her embrace him, but his mind was still far away, and he was chasing it, trying to bring it back.

Cappy and Seth were still at it, but now Cappy fought with a different gleam in his eye, a precision to his movements that had been lacking before. Then he had been trying to distract, not to kill. He had wanted to buy some time for the Spectres to arrive, but now that fate had foiled his plans once again, it was do or die. The two were still evenly matched, but their dance had grown grim and serious, the economy of their motions and the impossible speed breathtaking.

It happened without thought. One second Love was watching the battle, praying that Seth would be victorious, that it would end soon and that they could get back on the road, and the next he was moving again. It was as if the blade in his hand had taken on a mind of its own, as if it controlled him, not the other way around. He drew back his arm suddenly, knocking Llanna aside, and before he could think about his actions, he had whipped that arm forward, letting go of the scythe and sending it in a long, looping arc across the chamber.

Seth seemed to sense the approaching danger, and at the last second, he ducked to the side. As he did so, Cappy's face came into view. Love was across the room from him, but in that instant it was as if they were nose to nose, staring into one another's eyes. He read emotions there, hatred, confusion, arrogance— fear. At that last second, impossibly, he read that last. The blade entered Cappy's chest on a perfect trajectory, driving him backward until it had impaled him against the wall. It quivered for a moment, and Cappy's gaze dropped to it in stupefaction before rising again to meet Love's.

"I have…" Cappy forced the words out, though the life was ebbing from him rapidly, "underestimated you…again." Turning to face Seth in his final moment, he added. "Goodbye, my friend. I hope that you find what you seek, and if you do…I hope you find me there. It was…a good fight."

"It was that," Seth agreed. Cappy's head dropped to his chest, and the room was bathed in a deafening silence, a lack of sound that was eerie in its completeness.

"We have to move on," Love said at last. He reached for the scythe, but Seth stopped him.

"Take another," he said softly. "This weapon belonged, at one time, to the guardian of this way station. It aided you because you served its purpose."

Love nodded, reaching down to take the blade from Cappy's still fingers. Without a further word, he turned toward the portal that would take them to their destiny. Llanna was at his side, and Seth moved out a bit ahead of them, leading the way as always but with a different set to his shoulders. It seemed that some of the weight had been shifted, and the old guide was feeling the responsibility too…or a responsibility all his own.

They made their way swiftly down the byway, knowing it was not far to their destination, fearing and desiring the moment of truth to come almost equally. The mists rolled about their feet silently, covering any trail they might have left and cutting them off from their past.

21

The camp had been broken and Bontempt had had his men on the move for about two hours when Cyclops came wheeling through the sky from the direction of the Heretics' main temple. Nothing, really, had been learned. They had mobilized a large force beginning the evening before, but when Bontempt had sent the bird back to scout that morning, there had been no sign of them. Vanished. Either they had some alternate route to the compound that he didn't know about, or there was something he was missing. It grated on his nerves that they might be pulling a surprise of their own, not that he was worried. They still followed the one called Love, and he still wanted the woman that marched in Bontempt's chains. Tit for tat, as they say.

He briefly considered whether the smaller group of his enemies might be brash enough to attack his citadel while he was away. He had sent the majority of his troops on ahead, and most of what had remained behind marched with him. They had taken the compound/temple without resistance, as he'd anticipated, but where had all the damned Heretics gone? He smiled thinly at the thought that they might have gone after his own camp. The beasts were there, in force, prowling the outskirts of the town. He didn't need troops when they were there. It would take a damned sight more than a magic book of prophecies and a bitch priestess to breach those walls.

No, he knew they weren't that naive. They would come for him, either here or at the compound in some manner that was escaping him. He would just have to wait and see. Cyclops floated down from the sky, his eerie blank socket fixed on Bontempt in otherworldly concentration. The bird was coming in fast, faster than normal, and it appeared agitated…were the games about to begin?

He scanned the area surrounding the road, but nothing seemed to have changed. What could it be? He reached out to the bird's mind, forging the link that allowed him his second sight, but there was nothing to learn. The bird was upset, but whatever it was that was causing this was still an unknown. All he knew was what he'd already sensed; something out of the ordinary was happening. Perhaps he was about to witness a miracle, or a revelation…it would take that, at least, to impress him.

Bontempt was not one to stand below the mountain and let rocks fall on his head. He called out to those marching closest to him, and they began to circle up, gathering inward toward the center of the road. It might not be the Heretics. There were still plenty of Spectres out here, and with a disturbance in the Tempest of the magnitude capable of closing a portal, there was no telling what might have been coughed out. There could be an entire army of insane monsters out here, along *with* Spectres, and he wasn't going to take any chances on his plans being foiled by such an unexpected attack.

Everyone was moving now. They might not all know what he had in mind, but there was no doubt among them on the subject of Spectres, and many among those marching were not used to the road. All they had to judge the danger by was the stories of the slavers and guards, and these were always exaggerated. Bontempt watched them scurry about, feeling a mild contempt at the blank terror in some eyes and a satisfying glow of pride at the efficiency of the operation. Coward or hero, they were all his, all bent to his will.

He would have liked a few more moments to plan a defense, but that would have meant telling the others what he was waiting for, and there was no way to tell who might be a spy. He would have to count on superior strength and the fact that, though the element of surprise, for the moment, would be with the attackers, he was not wholly unprepared.

The attack was not immediate, and so he decided to push things a bit. He moved to the front of the crowd, and he dragged the woman, Faith, from her spot within the circled guards. She was exhausted, but still she fought against him, her eyes rimmed with fatigue and burning with hatred. He smiled at her as he pulled her into the open road.

The others stared at him as though he'd gone mad, finally, but none of them made the mistake of coming forward, or of saying anything they might regret. He ignored them. If this was the moment, then he would savor it. They would understand soon enough, and he hoped for their sake that they caught on quickly. If not, those in the front, those watching him most closely, would likely not see another day.

He took Faith by the hair, holding her up so that only her toes touched the pavement of the road. She was forced to stumble back and forth, working to keep her balance so that the tension would not increase on her hair. The pain brought tears to her eyes, but she did not cry out. She yanked her head against his pull, trying to free herself. He could feel the shivers of pain that rippled through her as the pressure increased on her hair, and he smiled.

He threw her to the dirt with a sudden shove, watching her as she knelt, panting, glaring back up at him. He did not give her the chance to speak or to make any move toward him. He began to clap his hands, starting with a slow, syncopated rhythm that built gradually in both volume and speed. She watched, her eyes betraying, just for a moment, the despair that fatigue had bred.

"Dance," he said simply.

And there, before Bontempt's gathered, wondering troops, Faith did just that. She rose slowly, and she danced. In the middle of a deserted road, no civilization in sight, no hope in existence, she danced.

Her head was flung back, her eyes to the sky, avoiding his, and her hands were thrown above her head to draw her breasts high, to twist her body just so, attempting to gain back a little of the power that he'd stolen from her. He was trapped by the vision of her, as were the others, and the only way to maintain that tiny parcel of control was to dance into their minds. She lost herself in it as the rest of those gathered in the road also began to clap, some setting up intricate backbeats, others merely echoing the clapping of their master.

It was a wild, primal sound—not music, in the strictest sense, but somehow *more* than music. It wound itself through the air, the beating of flesh on flesh beginning to blur into a chant, and a power seemed to rise from the dust beside the road.

Bontempt felt it too, and he went with it. He knew what he wanted, and what he wanted was for this to come to a head, to call the enemy to himself. The cat-and-mouse waiting game was not his style. As he drew on the energy around him, directing it to his hands and outward into the sound of the clapping, drawing together the spirits and energy of those surrounding him and weaving them into the pattern that would play the slave like an instrument, he knew his enemy would feel it. If any of the damned Heretics had any of the power they claimed, they would know, and they would come.

He did not notice the shimmering off to his left, a glimmer of misty translucent figures against a backdrop of empty air. He might have gone on with his show indefinitely, losing himself in the sound and the beautiful, writhing slave in the middle of the road, had it not been for Cyclops.

Though it was aware, the music had only a marginal effect on its senses. Restless, as always, its head twisting rapidly from side to side, blinking and staring, searching and waiting. A small part of Bontempt's thoughts remained in contact, and the urgency of these thoughts made the bird fidgety.

Suddenly, unleashing an ear-piercing cry, the bird launched itself into the air, nearly knocking the startled Bontempt from his feet. Beating his wings frantically, Cyclops fought his own panic and gravity as he struggled for altitude in the misty, dust-filled air.

Bontempt staggered, forgetting the clapping, the dancing slave, even the men surrounding him. A searing blast of pain flashed through his mind, paralyzing his limbs and ripping through his senses. As Cyclops winged higher and higher, frantically fighting against some unseen, unknown enemy, Bontempt writhed on the ground, pounding his head against the pavement in an effort to clear his thoughts, to regain control. The bird would not release their bond, and yet it was completely out of control.

He knew he had to get to his feet, to warn the others, at last, of what they faced, but he couldn't get the sound from his mind, and Cyclops' desperate battle to free himself from whatever or whoever it was that was attacking was distracting him as well. Shuddering in pain, Bontempt pulled the tattered remnant of his thoughts together for one long second, long enough to snap the cord and release Cyclops. He didn't know exactly what was wrong with the bird, but he knew he'd be better with only one eye than with a second that was driving him mad.

As he rose to his feet, shaking his head and growling like a big, hungry bear, and reaching clumsily for his sword, the world around him began to seep back in and he heard the cries of battle, the scuffling of boots. His vision snapped back into focus just in time for him to leap back, cursing, and barely avoid the thrust of a long, dark-bladed sword.

His mind latched onto that sight for a moment in confusion. It was a Ferryman's weapon, and an old one at that. It was not the sort of blade one would expect in the hands of a Heretic. He had no time to dwell on this. The man leaped forward to the attack, and once again Bontempt was barely able to avoid being skewered. With a roar, he sprang in himself, sending a crashing blow whistling through the air toward his attacker's face. The man spun easily, dodging his blade, and swung up under the cut, catching Bontempt a glancing blow across his chest that ripped through armor and skin to soak the front of his uniform in plasm.

"Cappy sends his regards," the man smiled, stepping forward nimbly to follow his advantage. Bontempt parried and attempted another thrust of his own, more cautiously this time. The man's eyes were dark, dark and deep—they reminded him of Cappy's, now that the name had come up. Who was he?

"You may not have known it," the older man went on, calmly turning aside every attempt Bontempt made to pierce his defense, "but Cappy and I go *way* back. Doubt if he ever mentioned me—haven't been on the best of terms, you know, but it's true."

At that moment one of the beasts, seeing its commander under attack, leaped at the old man who, letting out a curse of his own, jumped to the side just in time to avoid the slashing of the beast's jaws.

DAVID NIALL WILSON

Bontempt leaped away, taking in the battle scene with practiced efficiency. They were holding their own. One of the beasts was down; that left the one engaging the old Legionnaire, or whoever he was. Where was the book? He scanned the area more closely, and his eyes fixed on a younger man with long, flowing hair and deep piercing eyes. The man fought with military precision, but was obviously no swordsman, wielding his blade with more intensity and instinct than skill as he pressed his attack relentlessly.

It had to be Love. The others were rallying behind him, and now that Bontempt had the entire battle in his mind, he knew where the Heretic would be heading. He spun about quickly, spotted the slave to his left, swinging her chains viciously into the unsuspecting face of one of his men and dropping him. Bontempt let loose a smile. She was a prize truly worth fighting for. There was no time to dwell on this, however.

Running up quickly and silently behind the slave, he reached down and snatched up the loose end of the chain. He ducked as she swung back with the other.

"Stop and drop to your knees," he ordered. She fought for just a second, then dropped obediently as he reestablished his control. The chains were too powerful for her to resist. He grabbed her roughly by the hair, thrusting her directly in front of him on the road, and called out loudly.

"Love! Look what I have here, Love." He watched the young man spin to meet his gaze, and he smiled. Too easy, it was all too easy. "Come and get her," he called out.

Love saw Faith, held just off her knees, dangling and writhing in the grip of the huge, one-eyed slaver. Her eyes were dull, exhausted, and she stared right through him. He didn't know if her mind was gone, or if she was just too exhausted to register who he was. A cry of rage roared up from deep within him, dragged directly from his heart by her pain and his own outrage. Enough. It was enough. He would end this now, or die trying.

Against his chest, the book was blazing, searing into his flesh, but he ignored it. He had the blade acquired from the way station in the Tempest, and he was going to use it. No words. No prophecies. They had been the legacy of Fontana, and that legacy had proven false and misleading. He didn't want to trust it now, even though he had taken the power of the words and made it his own. He wanted to do it on his own.

Bontempt was smiling, and as Love approached on the run, he tossed Faith aside contemptuously.

"Run," Love cried out to her.

"Stay," Bontempt said calmly, sneering. Then, to Love, "I think you'll find her much more obedient than you would remember. I'm certain she'll stay put while we settle this, won't you dear?" Bontempt lashed out with one booted foot, connecting solidly with Faith's ribs. She fell face first to the pavement, grunting in pain, and she was barely able to struggle back to a sitting position to turn and glare at her captor.

It was all Love could stand. All of it hit him at once, all the anger, the frustration, the madness. It was too much. A scream of rage that rammed its way up his throat from some deep, black pit inside roared from his lips. He lunged forward, heading straight for the huge slaver who waited with his sword at the ready and a sneer planted firmly across his features. The sounds around them blended into a hum of white noise in Love's brain, and he saw nothing but the man in front of him.

Coming in close, Love feinted to one side, the side with the good eye, then spun his blade back to hack at the other. Bontempt avoided the attack easily, and Love found himself suddenly on the defensive, barely backing away from the counter-strike. The reversal in his mind was sudden and terrifying. What had he been thinking?

His training had been with a .45 caliber semi-auto and a belt of grenades, not swords. He was facing an opponent who'd walked the streets and byways of the Underworld for countless years, and who'd been trained with Charon's legions to use the weapon in his hand. The slaver's trap had snapped shut quickly and efficiently, and now all he could hope for was to find a way to escape it.

Love was backing away rapidly, instinct and reflex allowing him, barely, to keep up with the flash of his enemy's blade, but not nearly enough time for counterattacks of his own. The book burned insistently into his skin, and he knew now that he'd have to go for it. It was his only chance.

A quick glance to the left showed him that Seth was still fully engaged with the beast-thing, and the others were equally busy, though the new weapons and the shock of their entrance seemed to be leaning things in their favor. It was up to him to take Bontempt out; the only questions remaining were how, and could he pull it off?

He made his decision in an instant. It would do him no good to run from his fate. For good or for ill, Fontana's little green book had seen him through every trial thus far—it would have to aid him one last time. He continued to back away, circling toward a nearby supply wagon. He could tell from the glitter in the slaver's one eye and the arrogant tilt of the man's chin as he advanced that his opponent believed he'd already given up, that it was only a matter of time until he fell.

He reached the wagon and quickly slipped around the back corner, ripping at the cord that held the book around his neck as he went. Bontempt saw the move, and with one quick, agile thrust of his wrist, managed to twist his blade around the wagon's corner and rip at the cord. For an instant the book swung free, dangling in the air by the one end of the cord that Love held tightly in his hand. Then, as he watched in horror, it continued in an arc away from him, slipping free of the now-severed cord and sailing off to one side.

Bontempt gave a grunt of satisfaction and lunged after the book. Love could do nothing but follow, swinging wildly with his blade and letting out a banshee scream. It was all or nothing. He'd seen Fontana pick that book up and disintegrate, but he wasn't betting on the same thing happening to Bontempt. The slaver would know about such Artifacts, and he would know how to use them safely. If the book reached his hands, all was lost.

Cursing, Bontempt spun to parry his thrust, cutting back over Love's blade viciously and laying open a cut on the back of his hand. Ignoring the pain, Love countered. He prayed that his momentum, coupled with Bontempt's momentary distraction as he lunged after the book, might turn the tide a bit.

It did. His blade made contact, and bellowing in rage, Bontempt rolled to one side, coming to one knee and staring numbly down at the gaping wound that had appeared across the left side of his torso. He turned to glare at Love, and slowly began to rise to his feet. He did not wince in pain, nor did he appear particularly slowed by the wound. His movements were precise and calculated. If anything, he seemed more angry, more formidable, than before.

Then a blur of motion caught Love's attention, rounding the far edge of the wagon he'd tried to use for cover only moments before. He wasn't certain if it was a friend or an enemy, but at this point he had to take the chance. Screaming again, he thrust his blade out in front of him and charged, drawing Bontempt's contemptuous gaze to himself and praying that whoever was behind the slaver had a big, big blade.

As he drew back to send a slashing blow at his enemy's head, the blur came into focus. It was Llanna, and she held a slender, black-bladed sword high over her head. She didn't hesitate. As Bontempt swung his own blade down, she let out a scream of her own, born of rage and hatred cultivated over years of enmity. He didn't even managed to turn to meet her before her blade came down, narrowly missing his head and cleaving the flesh of his shoulder.

Bontempt wrenched the blade from her grasp as he slammed to the side, howling in pain. He dropped his own sword to rip at the hilt of the weapon protruding from his shoulder, and Love stepped in, taking a hard, solid shot at the man's midsection. Dropping to his knees, Bontempt stared at the wounds in incredulity, still tugging feebly at the sword that jutted stiffly from his shoulder. He tried to move forward, still, fixing his eye on Love in obsessive hatred. His progress was slow, and Love let him come, done with blades and prophecies and ready to finish what he'd begun with the most accurate, deadly weapons he possessed…his bare hands.

Somehow, through the pain, in the face of apparent defeat, Bontempt was still managing to smile. It was a sickly, twisted parody of a smile, but a smile nonetheless. It infuriated Love, and he moved in quickly, grasping Llanna's blade and ripping it cruelly from the wound, tearing more of the bigger man's plasm free as it came. There was no cry of pain—not this time. Not even flinching, Bontempt continued his crawling progress forward. Love tossed the blade aside without a thought.

Just as he began to move forward, to reach out for Bontempt's throat and put an end to it all, he heard the flutter of wings and the eerie, plaintive cry as Cyclops dove from the sky, making directly for his eyes with its claws extended. He dove to the side, and the animal's talons raked down the side of his face and over his shoulder. He expected to have been cut, but there was nothing. The animal had startled him, but nothing more. It couldn't reach through the Shroud.

The bird was quick, back on the attack before he fully regained his balance, and Bontempt was moving toward him more quickly now, as well. The man had been faking, buying time until his ally, his other eye, could come to his aid. Love had forgotten the bird completely. It had taken off in a squawking flash of feathers when Seth let out some sort of weird, off-key whistle from within the Tempest, and Love had assumed that it was gone for the duration, that the bond between man and puppet had been broken, at least temporarily. Another mistake.

He lurched to the side as Cyclops swung down for another distracting sweep at his face, and at that moment, Bontempt gathered what remained of his strength and will power and lunged. He aimed for Love's feet, wrapping strong arms around the smaller man's ankles and yanking backward.

Only instinct and rigorous training saved him in that instance. He went with the fall, kicking upward as he went over, and he brought both of his feet straight upward, letting the overbalance of his full weight, now unsupported, pull him free of the slaver's grasp. Both of his booted feet made solid contact with Bontempt's chin, and the big man went over backward, sprawling on the ground and lying still. Love rolled to his back, meaning to rock back to his feet, but his gaze was filled with the image of the bird. It was plummeting, dropping like a rock from above, and it was making a bee-line for his throat. It kept getting in his way, blocking his sight, and he couldn't tell if Bontempt were up and moving or still down where he'd kicked him. The bird's one good eye was fixed on him, or through him, as if it were dropping in on a fat mouse or a snake for the kill.

Tossing his arms up and closing his eyes, Love braced himself against unseen attack. It was then that he heard Faith's wavering voice, and he forced his eyes back open—forced himself to see.

She was standing over him, her legs wobbling and knocking so that she could barely support herself. The chains that held her dangled limply, weighing her down, but she ignored them. In her hands, clutched like a lifeline, was the book, and it was open as she read aloud.

"A bird in the hand," she coughed through dried, parched lips, "is worth two in the bush."

Love felt his hand move as if it were sentient, ignoring his desire that it block the bird's path. As Cyclops dropped the last foot, Love reached out and swiped his arm through the air in a lightning-quick grab. He felt a quick, feathery touch, and the bird was suddenly veering off into the sky, moving away rapidly.

Bontempt was groveling about on the road. The link had been broken, and his injuries were draining the last of his strength. Love headed straight for him. Reaching out as he passed, he gently took the book from Faith's trembling hands, pausing for a long moment to search her eyes. They were awash in pain, tortured and haunted, but in their depths he could still see the Faith he remembered, the fiery companion who had preceded him into "the heart of the world," and he smiled. There would be plenty of time when this was finished for healing, and for apology.

He turned back to Bontempt. The sounds of the battle had died down to groans and cries of pain and a steady stream of cursing. They had won. Most of Bontempt's men had been destroyed, a few others injured. Love noted that Llanna and the others were already seeing to the injuries of their remaining enemies, as well as of their own followers, talking in low tones to each. A new group of converts, he guessed, was in the making.

He walked over to stand directly beside Bontempt, who lay face down on the pavement, breathing shallowly but not moving. He reached out with the toe of one boot and pushed the big man over so that he could look into his vanquished enemy's face. The one eye was open, still sparking with hatred, but there was no reprisal to his kick.

"You...you are stronger, as a group..." Bontempt spat through ruined lips, "than I would have believed. I would have had you in chains."

Love didn't acknowledge the man's words, truthful as they might be. He flipped the little green book open and stared at the words that burned from the page. Turning to meet Bontempt's stare, he began to speak, his voice loud—carrying to the farthest edges of the battle ground.

"The eyes," he recited, "are the wells of the soul. The Lord has said, an eye for an eye. I say," he flipped the book closed and stared down at the fallen slaver, "let the blind lead the blind."

He thrust a hand down in a lightning stab, pressing the tip of one finger viciously into Bontempt's one good eye. Flicking the plasm from his finger, he turned away. He would have left it at that, but Seth appeared suddenly at his side.

"No," the old man said sharply. "It is not enough." He took his blade free one last time and, very deliberately, lopped Bontempt's head from his shoulders. Then he began to chop, piece by piece, as the slaver's body writhed helplessly on the pavement. There was a sudden flash, and it was as though Bontempt had never been there at all.

"He would have healed," Seth said softly. "He would have been back."

Love stared at Seth, looking for signs of remorse, of compassion. There was none to be seen. The eyes were the same black, emotionless, unreadable pools they had been the first moment Love had caught sight of them. Empty. Though Love knew Seth was capable of great caring, it seemed that this attitude had limits, and Bontempt had been somewhere beyond them. He turned away, tucking the book into a pocket of his pants and looking about for Faith and Llanna.

He found them together, bent over Uriel, who had a wound on his left thigh. They were working side by side, Llanna chattering away, filling the silence, and Faith just nodding her head, listening, not truly with them yet. Love was encouraged.

"Come," he said, laying a hand on Llanna's shoulder. "We need to get back to the temple and begin to plan a journey. It's about time we started off for heaven. It *has* to be a better neighborhood..."

The laughter that followed gave him hope.

pLAYING WITH FIRE

BY ESTHER M. FRIESNER

1

Tony Lee knew the truth about dreams. It wasn't the ones where you wake up screaming that were the worst: It was the ones where you tried to scream and you couldn't, where you opened your mouth to scream and you sucked in the dream-air and felt it pouring into your lungs like mud, filling them, drowning you, while all around the horrors of the dream itself clustered and gawked and dug their tentacles into your flesh until you knew that if you didn't cough the mud out of your lungs and let that one scream loose, you'd die.

That was when you woke up, if you were lucky. Tony Lee hadn't had a lucky day in his life. Now it looked like the bad joss was slipping through the seams of sleep to make sure he didn't have a lucky night either.

"Ah, God." Tony sat up in bed, head bowed over his updrawn knees, sweat pouring from his body in a thousand tiny rivers. His long, sleek horsetail of black hair was pasted to his naked back, and when he ran one hand through the carefully barbered crest of shorter hair bristling down his skull from forehead to nape, it was soaked too.

Outside it was September, still early in the month, still hot as August, most nights. What the weatherman said didn't matter: Tony was shivering. Outside a red neon sign winked on and off, letting people know that the bar four floors down was open for business. In New York, in certain parts of town, some places never seemed to close. Even this high up, you could still smell the stale beer, yeasty, sour, something to its penetrating, persistent scent that made you think of sad old men and faded women nursing faded dreams, lives that were only going through the motions day-to-day on simple momentum and wouldn't mind too much if the whole ugly world shuddered to a bloody stop.

Tony took a deep breath of the beery air, flaring his nostrils, filling his chest until there wasn't room inside him for anything but the here-and-now stink of it. Maybe it reeked, but at least this was air he could breathe. Besides, he wasn't afraid of a little stench. Bad smells were real smells, and reality was safer than the tamest dream. Somewhere he'd read how priests used fragrant incense to banish demons; he knew better. Demons liked the smell of sweet things, like incense and flowers and decaying flesh.

That was why demons loved funerals. That was how he'd met his first demon, when they went to bury his father.

He'd only been five when his father died, but he still recalled the smell of the funeral. Mama'd told him to shush when he claimed he could smell his father's body in the box, she'd even shaken him once when he insisted. She was angry with him, furious, her eyes bright red and blazing. For the life of him he couldn't understand why. Was she mad at him? Had he done something wrong? The last few weeks of his father's life, it seemed like there was nothing he could do right. Everything made her fly into a rage, rages that always ended in loud, body-racking storms of tears. He was either too loud at his play or too silent—"mopey," his mother said, and blamed him for that too. When he found her crying and tried to comfort her she shouted at him to leave her alone. When he ignored her tears she came after him, demanding to know what she'd done wrong, raising a child who didn't care about anyone but himself. Tony didn't understand; he was only five. Was it his fault his father was dead? He was afraid to ask, afraid of what she might answer, afraid of his mother and what she'd become in the weeks before the death and the funeral.

The funeral: There'd been incense then, too, lots of it. Even though it was held in a nice little white-steepled Protestant church in New Jersey, Mama'd arranged with the minister to have big joss sticks burning the whole time, rods of red-wrapped Chinese incense as long and as thick around as little Tony's arm, anchored in buckets of sand.

Funny, the things you remembered. All alone now, as grownup as seventeen years made him, miles from Jersey and Mama dead too, Tony could still see the old church, the crowd of adults thronging the pews, his mother's strained face, pale as paper. He could still feel the warmth of her hand on his arm, the itchy collar of his meticulously starched white shirt, the uncomfortable confinement of the dark gray suit she'd forced him to wear. And if Tony raised his head right now and looked into the darkest corner of his room, he knew he owned the unwanted magic to make the days and the distance between his father's funeral and today disappear, leaving him five years old again and staring into the face of the demon for the first time.

That kind of magic he didn't need. But damn it all to hell (and he pounded his knee with his fist in frustration) that was the kind of magic that he owned, free and clear and harsh. The dreams slid through the cracks, flashed into his waking mind with the blink of red neon, and held tight to the surface of his eyes. There was no escaping the dreams. There was no escaping the old demon. Tony saw him again not because he wanted to, but because he didn't have a choice.

He was very tall, that creature out of hell, tall and so thin you could pick out the bones of his hands, one by one, and see all the hollows of his skull. His eyes burned blue with a little crimson hellspark glinting in the depths. They smoldered under thick brows the color of thunderheads, and his steely hair was a monstrous lion's mane. Little Tony felt the monster's eyes on him like the kiss of a raptor's talons long before he turned to meet that awful gaze. Tony was only five: He didn't know there could be so much hate in the world, bound up in a look. He let out a small whimper of fright and clung to his mother's side.

But Mama was too shrouded in her own sorrow to have any softness to spare for her child's sudden, unreasoning terror. Eyes fixed on the casket holding her husband's body, she gritted her teeth and gave Tony's arm a hard squeeze, hissing under her breath for him to stand still, stop fussing, be silent. When he squirmed and tried to wrench his arm out of her grasp, she just held on tighter.

Later that day, after the funeral and the burial were over, after the grownups came back to the house for coffee and tea and cake, no one noticed little Tony's vanishment. He went upstairs, running as fast as he could, fleeing the soft murmurs of sympathy and the alien hands that stroked his hair, patted his shoulders, smothered him in hugs he didn't want. His fingers fumbled with the buttons as he stripped off the hateful suit, the silly little black clip-on bowtie, the white shirt with its stiff collar that threatened to strangle him. He only paused for a moment, amazed to see that his mother's fingers had left marks on his skin, aching imprints already turning an angry purplish-red. Then he needed to gasp for air and tear away the rest of his clothes.

Everything, everything had to come off, be peeled away, cast aside, even his underwear. He would have peeled off his skin if he could, anything to get rid of the feeling that someone had picked up his body and rolled it in ashes. And when he had all the terrible clothes off, he heaped them up in the center of the room and trampled them underfoot, dancing out his grief until the tears came and he tumbled into his bed, sobbing for his father.

That was how Mama found him, lying naked on top of the rumpled blanket, his face all hot and wet. "Oh, Tony!" The pain in her voice cut into his heart. Without knowing the word, he somehow understood he'd shamed her worse than if he'd peed his pants in public. But he didn't understand why his tears would make Mama say his name that way, like it was a dirty thing, something to hide.

Then the tears cleared from his eyes and he saw the demon standing behind her in the doorway, the tall, pale demon with the eyes that burned blue. The demon's thin mouth was twisted up into a smile that held neither compassion nor joy, but only mockery, and all he said was, "Well, what did you expect?" before he turned on his heel and was gone.

And she ran after him. She left little Tony lying there on his bed, naked and alone, the sunlight fading from the windows and the dark coming on. He cried and cried for her to come back, but the only ones who responded to his shrieks and sobs were some of the guests from downstairs. When they reached for him, offering soft words and open arms, he howled louder and crawled under the bed, lashing out with his feet at the few who were foolish enough to get down on the floor and try coaxing him back out again. At last they left him alone. At length he fell asleep.

That was the first night his dreams sent him plunging into the nightmare world where every breath dragged him farther into darkness, where he couldn't even hold fast to the safety of a scream. He woke up shaking like an old man. He found himself in his bed, not under it, wearing his favorite pajamas, the ones with Big Bird on them. He remembered how his father had taken him shopping and bought him those pajamas. He wondered if maybe all the bad memories were only dreams after all, if he got out of bed and went down the hall to his parents' room he'd find Dad there, sleeping quietly, his living breath making the covers rise and fall.

"Stupid kid," Tony said into the dark. Reluctantly, like a sated cat toying with a mouse too thin for the killing, the dream-memory let him go free at last. He stared at his own reflection in the window, a wavering image that flashed in and out of sight with the bar's bright red sign. He swung his feet onto the floor and stood up, stretching his arms overhead. The bedside clock flicked from 3:15 to 3:16 while he watched. "Slept in, you lazy son-of-a-bitch," Tony told himself affably. "Good thing you got today off. Joe'd have your ass." With that cheerful reflection, he went into the bathroom.

It didn't take him long to get ready; it never did. Tony liked things simple, and that included what he wore and how he looked. Jeans and a T-shirt took care of the basics for most of the year, and the shirt was plain, just one solid color, usually black or dark blue, whatever he found on sale for the cheapest price. Why bother flaunting some rock band's name when you didn't have the time or the money to go to their concerts? Why shell out extra just so you could strut around with some wise-ass catchphrase smeared across your chest? About the only time he felt tempted to go with something like that was when Phil-from-work showed up wearing I'M WITH STUPID, but even then Tony didn't know where he could find one that said YOU GOT THAT RIGHT.

When the weather turned cold, he had an old wool jacket he'd scavenged from a Salvation Army thrift shop, some other kid's basketball team castoff from Erasmus High, all the way over in Brooklyn. He wished he had a buck for every time some girl in a movie line or at one of the clubs or even in his favorite comic book shop pretended she knew him from school. He could match it with a buck for every time he told her yeah, sure, he remembered her, and they went off to have a little fun.

Fun...It had been too long. What was it, six months, seven, more? Something went wrong the last time he hooked up with a girl. Nothing he could put his finger on, exactly, just a weird feeling that got under his skin and burrowed all the way down to his bones. One minute they were tangled together in his bed, laughing, clothes already half off, and the next he was staring down at her face and seeing something so totally alien that his own laughter cut off short, choked him. She'd gone from sweet flesh and warm blood to a mask of stone, a body of ivory, cool and smooth and a million miles removed from him. Suddenly the only thought his mind could hold was *What am I doing here?*

Then he caught sight of his reflection in her eyes. Something strange looked out. It wasn't the self he knew from his mirror, with his dead father's Chinese features thinned down by his dead mother's pale Anglo blood. Something with a golden gaze and skin the burnished brown of nutshells stared out at him. Something that hid itself among a toss of silvery-green leaves and leered out at the world, a lure, a challenge.

He felt as if he could fall into the girl's eyes, plunge in after the thing he saw imprisoned there. There was a low humming in his head, a drowsy sound of honey-heavy bees. He felt himself beginning to topple into the world behind the shining lenses of the girl's eyes.

That was when she grunted and yelled and pushed him away. She called him seven kinds of weirdo, demanded to know what the fuck was wrong with him, was he drunk or stoned or just stupid? "I just dumped one crazy guy; I'm not getting involved with another one so fast. Who needs this shit? I'm gone." And she was. She left him aching inside, the way it felt when love walked away and never looked back.

But Tony knew it wasn't her he'd loved. The ghost of the golden-eyed creature he'd glimpsed in her eyes lingered for days in his memory until he went out and got drunk enough to convince himself it had all been a dream. And that was when the bad dreams really began.

Tony didn't have time for dreams, bad or good. This was New York, where dreams could get you killed if you gave them half a chance. Better to keep your eyes open, your head clear, and leave the dreams to the dead men and the past.

He finished dressing and went out, clattering down the stairs to the street. It was pretty quiet out at that hour, the between-time when the nightbirds had flown back to their caves and the daywalkers were still curled up snug and safe in their burrows. The streets were clear, with maybe one or two lone wanderers stumbling or slouching down the sidewalks. He gave them room and they took it, the wordless courtesy of the streets.

There were cars, of course. There were always cars in New York, cars at all hours. Once or twice Tony thought he saw a car crawling down the street with no one behind the wheel. He shrugged it off as a trick of the darkness and the blue-white streetlights. Once he saw a taxi like that, cruising by with no driver, only a huddle of shadows at the wheel. He stood on the curb, wondering what would happen if he'd hail it, if it would stop, if he got inside and told the shadows "Just drive." His began to raise his hand. The yellow headlights dimmed, for all the world like the glowing eyes of a lazy panther, eyelids halfway lowered to observe and consider its thoughtless prey. Tony dropped his hand, turned on his heel, and ran.

When he stopped running, he was uptown. He wasn't even running anymore. He couldn't remember when the unreasoning fear had left him, when he'd stopped running, when he'd slowed his pace back down to a walk. He stood in front of the Public Library on Fifth Avenue under the eyeless stare of the stone lions and shook his head, blinking like a man coming out of deep slumber. How had he gotten this far up into the '40s? Home was all the way down at the snout of Manhattan, where streets still had the luxury of names, if no other. His legs felt soft and achy, but his mind was blank. He'd covered more than fifty blocks on foot and it was all a blur to him.

"Ah, screw it," he muttered, and kept walking, cursing himself with every stride. "Asshole. Where the hell's your head? You know the rules: Stay alert, stay alive. One day you're gonna daydream yourself right into the business end of someone's knife." He turned west, away from the breaking dawn.

His shadow led him down forty-second street, past the sex shops and the peep shows. He kept going west, fleeing the sunrise, until at last he came to the great gateway and plunged inside.

That was Tony's name for the New York Port Authority bus terminal: the gateway. That was how he named it in his thoughts, when he had to think of it at all. He used to call it Hellgate, too, though these days he did his best to banish that image from his mind. It fit, but it brought back too much pain.

Once, a couple of years back, when he was fresh meat on the streets with no more brains than a pigeon egg, one of his tricks showed him a picture book full of stuff from the Middle Ages. Tony didn't remember the man's name—he didn't want to. What he did remember was that the man had been sort of old and pathetic, impotent and kind. He said he was a professor up at Columbia University and he showed off his books like they were his kids. Tony looked them over dutifully, even though he couldn't have cared less about things that had happened so many centuries ago. What did the plague and the serfs and the great kings have to do with him? Ever since he'd hopped that bus and come to New York City, his only concern was getting through each night without running into a crazy, getting through each day without running into evil dreams. Anything beyond that was for people who had lives to live, not just to survive.

He knew that the only reason this old guy was taking the time to talk to him, to show him all these fancy books, was because he couldn't get it up so fast, no matter how much he wanted to. Tony was just grateful that this trick wasn't like some of the others, the ones who knew they wanted him but couldn't do a damn thing about it because they felt like someone was watching them: Their parents, their wives, their kids, their bosses, anyone and everyone who didn't know or even suspect what these men really wanted, who they really were. So they blamed Tony for it, and sometimes they beat the crap out of him for it too. Or they tried. It didn't take Tony too long to wise up and learn how to fight back any way he could.

This guy was okay, though; just too old to go after what he wanted right away. So he passed the time by making conversation and sharing his books. Tony sat there, just his shirt off so far, pretending interest—what the hell, this john agreed to pay him by the hour, not the job, so what did he care how long it took?—until the man turned the page and showed him the gateway to hell.

It was a drawing done down fine, in detail. A triple-faced beast opened its middlemost mouth wide and high, fangs bared, forked tongue lolling free. Smoke gushed from the gaping nostrils of its three flat noses and at the back of its throat Tony could see the leaping fires that consumed the damned.

He'd never believed in heaven or in the image of the white-bearded, pink-faced God-the-Father that his mother tried to feed him. He'd never been able to think of the skinny, bleeding, suffering Christ as anything more than some poor, well-meaning man who'd talked too much where the wrong people could hear him. Even the devil was nothing more than a horned, red rubber Halloween mask and an arrowpoint-tipped tail you hooked to the seat of your pants with a safety pin before you went out to trick-or-treat. But for some reason, looking at this picture, Tony believed in hell. He believed so hard and so true that he could feel the heat of the eternal fires beating against his face, he could smell the pungent scent of roasting flesh and the stench of sulfur.

Except he knew it wasn't burning sinners and sulfur he smelled: It was the

PLAYING WITH FIRE   587

old cooking oil from countless fast food deep fryers and the exhaust fumes from all the buses bringing in the next crop of young meat for the city. He knew it was the place where he'd been tricked into putting one foot over the threshold to the abyss and tumbling in headfirst after.

That was the first night he told a john "I gotta go" and ran. That was the first time he tried to get free. And later that same night, before they caught him and brought him back and shoved him into the life all over again, that was the first time he went back to the gateway. He didn't believe in God or the devil, but in his own way he believed in magic, the shabby, frightened magic that was his one protection against the world. What he did that night was the start of a spell: If you walked into hell of your own free will, you could walk out again whenever you wanted.

But that was long ago. He'd made the false magic work. He was free now, and he was going to stay free or die. If he went into the Port Authority these days, these nights, he did it just to show the beast that he could walk down its throat and come out again untouched. That was what he told himself, anyhow.

He strolled into the building and got a cup of coffee from a place he knew and trusted. Even at this hour, when desperate people would pay to drink rat piss if it had enough caffeine, this place served good coffee. Tony took it black and sweet, three sugars to get him buzzing, then he walked on.

The terminal was gentrified, part of the city's ongoing attempt to tidy up the mess it had made of itself. That would've been okay, only too many people in power figured *Why go to the expense of doing a real clean-up when it's so much easier to sweep everything under the rug?* So they took out the benches and put in little jumpseats you could only lean your butt against and they did whatever else it took to make sure that the street people got the message that they weren't welcome there. Warmth and shelter for tired bones were for the folk who could afford them.

Tony strolled through the wakening building, sipping his coffee. The thing was to keep a pace going. You went too slow, the cops decided you looked like you needed to be somewhere else. You went too fast, the cops thought maybe you looked like someone who needed to be stopped dead and asked about where he'd been. The way Tony walked, he made it look like he had business being where he was.

"Ssst! Hey! Hey, Lee!"

Tony froze in his tracks, the cup of coffee almost to his lips. He knew that voice, still beautiful, even with the edges on it all broken and jagged. He turned his head slowly towards the sound, even though what he most wanted to do was run away.

"Yah, Lee, over here, man!" Scrawny body pasted tight against the shadows, a black man with a boy's voice and a face that was ten thousand years old grinned and waved and called Tony's name. "Long time, long time."

Tony closed his face, tried to force any true show of feeling safely away inside. Summoning up a false smile, he waved back and ambled over to join the man. "Hey, Skiz, how's it going?"

"*When's* it going, you mean." Skiz laughed. His teeth were the same murky yellow as the so-called whites of his eyes. Things deep in his chest rasped and rattled, like he was hiding a nest of mice down there. The smell coming off his body could've flattened a charging bull. "Any day now, if I got luck."

"Huh?" Tony's mask slipped; he let a little genuine feeling show on his face. Skiz was maybe twenty, twenty-one, just a few years older than he, but he looked like something escaped from the grave. Still, for a corpse, he did a lot of laughing.

He was laughing now, when he told Tony just about what Tony'd always expected to hear: "I got it, man. Y'know, *it?*" Before Tony could answer, Skiz clapped a finger to his lips and shook his head so violently it looked ready to snap off the thin neck. "Huh-uh, don't *you* say the name—naming things, that's what calls 'em—but *I* can say it 'cause what's there left for it to do to me, huh? Can't die twice unless you try." He drew himself up a little straighter and in that funny, formal, spell-it-out way Tony remembered, Skiz carefully enunciated, "I have got *it.* AIDS. That is what I got. Not just HIV but the whole thing, AIDS, yeah, you heard it here first, film at eleven. Still one little footstep out of the hospital but any day now, any day. Not if I can help it, though. They try to keep you going, in the hospital, and I do not want to go before I, y'know, *go*. It's like they get points for how many days they can drag you along, y'know? Fuck 'em. I'm staying out of *there* until I am out of *here* and that's all."

"Ah hell, Skiz, I'm sorry I—"

"Nah, what's sorry? Not like you give me this, huh? Say, you OK? I mean, you clean? Yet?"

Tony nodded. "I got tested. I'm OK." He felt as if he'd swallowed a lump of burning coal. When the hell was he going to learn? If you walked down the beast's throat, the beast got you. It didn't matter if the fangs didn't close on your flesh or if you could sidestep the fires, the beast got you some other way.

But Skiz didn't know about the beast. Skiz didn't know about demons. Skiz didn't know about anything except one breath following the other. Skiz was laughing again, his long fingers playing an invisible keyboard in the air. His palms and his fingernails were a cool gray against scaling skin the color of Tony's coffee.

"Oh, that's good, you sorry chink, that is real good. You got out in time and I am getting out and that is *it*, that is what matters. Timing, man; it's all in the timing." He began to hum to himself, his eyes wandering. He had a rich tenor voice, going to squeaks and shards now. Tony remembered a few years back, hearing Skiz talk about how he was only hustling until he could get a break in the music business or acting or doing voiceovers for commercials or even cartoons. "Only ways a nigger gets a chance," he'd said. "That or sports, y'know? And I can't catch a ball worth shit."

Tony swallowed hard, but the coal still burned where his heart ought to be. "Skiz...You need anything, man? I got work. I got a job at the Fulton Fish Market. I got money, and if you want a place to stay—"

"Now you tell me this," Skiz said, only he wasn't talking to Tony any more. His eyes were closed and his face was turned to the ceiling as if he had the power to make it part like the Red Sea and let a flood of daylight come pouring in. "You tell me this, baby Buddha: Why do I want to go stay with you? I mean, what for?

Been better'n a year since you been gone, two, and that was when you knew where to find me. Now? I'm a good deed you stepped in like it was dogturd and you want to scrape it offa your shoe but there's folks watching so you clap your hands and you say, 'Jesus loves me, look at what a nice surprise He give me!'"

Skiz laughed, and his laughter broke into a cough that scooped up a bloody handful of his insides and tossed them out onto the hard floor between him and Tony. Tony jumped back fast as if he'd seen a snake, then stood there rocking on his heels, looking shamed. But Skiz only wiped the red slime from his lips with the back of his hand and wiped that hand on the front of his jeans.

"OK," Tony finally managed to say. "OK, well, I guess I'll be going." He began to move away, using a funny sidestep that was only a whisper removed from backing off, the way you'd take leave of something too dangerous to turn your back on.

Skiz grinned, a blob of blood still clinging to one corner of his mouth. He looked like a refugee from a B-movie, king of the zombies, king of the vampires, lord of all the walking dead. His hand shot out and closed around Tony's forearm. "Hold it, man. You don't go. You still got dogturd on your shoe."

With that for an explanation, he sprang out of the shadows, dragging Tony along with him. Tony went, too dazed to struggle. He could take Skiz any day, even back when they'd both been strong and well. And now? No contest. But how could you fight a dead man? So Tony let Skiz take him where he would.

They hurried through the Port Authority building until, without a word of warning, Skiz stopped short. Tony bumped into him and promptly took a little jump back. His former friend gave him a knowing look but said nothing except, "There he is." A long, bony finger wrapped in dark brown skin pointed. "There he is, Mister Scoutmaster, if all you're hunting in here's a good deed."

The boy was an angel, hair the color of ripe corn, thick and wavy, smiling eyes the bright blue of May skies after rain. He looked to be about fourteen years old, but he gave the impression of being much, much younger. He sat there, leaning back against the jumpseat, smiling at all the world, indifferent to anything but joy. He wore jeans gone at the knees, black hightops with the laces undone, and a white T-shirt that had something big and blue printed on it. Tony couldn't see what it was from that distance, but the boy seemed to be very proud of it. Every so often he would stop swinging his legs, look down at his own chest, and pat the shirtfront fondly, chuckling.

"Been here one hour," Skiz said. "I saw 'im sit down, though I will swear this, that I did *not* see him come in. But he sees me. I am staring at him from number one, because you tell me now, Tony, you ever seen anything so fuckin' *beautiful*? So I know what's comin' for him. And you know too. Any minute, now. Any time."

Any minute now…

Tony forced his eyes away from the boy, scanned the area. He thought he saw a flash of navy blue, a policeman on patrol, but that was just something glimpsed out of the corner of one eye. The Port Authority was a big building, this part of it fairly peaceful at this hour of the morning. If the cops were around, they had plenty of territory to cover. Likely they'd been here when the boy first arrived, first took his place on the jumpseat. Their presence had been a stopgap, that was all, no real protection from what Tony knew would be coming, what Skiz prophesied. He could feel the dark presence all around him, even though he'd been free of it for years. You never forgot some things, no matter how much you tried. If you did forget, your dreams came to remind you.

And there it was, with its black wings mantled over the boy. It looked like a man, but Tony knew it for what it was, another of the demons that walked in human skins, wore human masks, devoured human lives. The man was tall and lean, with light brown hair and hazel eyes forever crinkled with smile lines. He looked as if he dressed himself exclusively out of the kind of menswear catalogs that catered to people who made their living off the best the city had to offer, but who did their living as far from the city stink as they could run. Fashionably rumpled khaki slacks, a nice sports shirt, an eggshell linen jacket, slip-on leather shoes without socks, everything but the weekend sailboat, that was the disguise this demon chose. Like the terminal itself, he was…gentrified.

So damn respectable-looking, Tony thought. Yeah, and faking it so he looks just a little out of place here, but still in control; not arrogant, not aggressive, but sure of himself. Wouldn't do to have him look too confident—might scare off his prey, I know how it works, goddammit, I wish I didn't. The kid's scared—I was. Trying not to show it, but it's there under that goofy smile; oh man, I know it's there, it's always there! And that bastard smells it on him, how scared he is, how alone…

The demon was coming nearer to the kid. His deeply tanned face opened up into a hesitant smile. He looked like every lost and lonesome kid imagined a *real* father should look, a *good* father, not the ones they'd run away from or the ones they'd lost, but the ideal father of their dreams. Everything about the way the demon moved seemed to say, *Don't be afraid, it's all right now, I've found you, I'll help you, you don't have to be scared any more.*

Tony could've told the kid that now was the time he really should be scared. He knew this demon. He recognized him—not just the type, but the creature itself. He'd met him once, soon after he'd come to New York himself and been "helped" by another just like him. There'd been a party, too much to drink, not enough to eat, pretty smoke and powders to send you swooping around inside your own skull and then—

"Skiz…" Tony looked around. Skiz was gone. He only wasted a moment wondering which shadow had swallowed up the lost soul, then shook it off. *Work to do.* He licked his lips, took a deep breath, and called out in a cheerful, carrying voice, "Hank! Hey, Hank, good to see you, man!" He swaggered right up to the demon and stuck out his hand. "Tony, Tony Lee, remember me? We met at Guy's place—what was it, two years ago? Time flies, huh?"

The demon was staring at him, his lips drawn back to show the keenness of his fangs. It could pass for a smile; only Tony knew it was a snarl. Yeah, Hank remembered him, all right, and he'd be willing to bet his prized Erasmus Hall jacket that Hank also remembered that Tony was one of the ones who'd clawed his way back out into the sun.

PLAYING WITH FIRE   591

No time to bait the creature now; no time for anything but what he had to do. Tony turned and looked down at the blond boy. Luminous blue eyes regarded him with an expression open and innocent as baby's. "So Nicky, what, your bus get in early? Man, I'm glad I got here ahead of time. I promised your sister I'd be waiting for you, y'know? Come on, we gotta haul ass or Ashley's gonna kill me." Tony clapped the kid on the back, talking fast. He flashed a stiff grin at the demon and added, "Small world, huh?" before snagging hold of the boy's arm and hauling him away as fast as he could without breaking into a cold sweat run. Behind him he imagined he heard the sound of great wings beating against the infernal blast, and talons clashing as they closed on empty air.

2

It was full daylight when Tony and the kid emerged from the gate. Tony had his hand on the boy's elbow, pulling him along, and for a miracle this earthbound angel wasn't kicking up any kind of a fuss over being dragged down the street like a sulky toddler. He just trotted in Tony's wake, half a stride behind him, still with that beatific smile on his face, just as if stuff like this happened to him every day.

If Tony's mind had been focused on anything except getting the kid safely away from Hank, he might have wondered about how easy it had been. Too easy. This kid wasn't a child, no matter how young he looked; what kind of teen let a total stranger take so much control? Sure, maybe at first, when the element of surprise was still working, while the kid was just as bewildered as Hank by Tony's rapidfire line of chat about his nonexistent sister. And maybe too he'd grabbed onto Tony's scam willingly, eagerly, clutching at a lifeline. Maybe he wanted to escape Hank as badly as Tony wanted to get him away, only he was still too fresh-hatched to figure out how to do it for himself. Sure, new to the city, a nice guy comes over to you, strikes up a conversation, acts like he only wants to help, you can't simply up and bolt just because he gives you a creepy feeling. Not when you're, what, fourteen, fifteen? That wouldn't be cool. That might make you look stupid. Sometimes kids cared so much about not looking stupid, not acting like a baby, that they wound up doing the demons' work for them.

But now that they'd eluded Hank, the kid was still following Tony, Mary's little lamb. If Tony hadn't been so intent on cheating all of his old demons of this new prey, a warning light might have gone on in his head. Maybe it did, and he was just too intent on putting space between the kid and the hellgate to notice it. Only when the two of them reached Times Square, retracing Tony's earlier route up Forty-second Street, did he slow, then pause, then stop.

"That was hairy," he remarked, a slow, triumphant grin spreading across his face. "Close, but hey, we won. Sorry about all that, kid. I mean, Christ, you don't know me, I don't know you, but I do know that son-of-a-bitch back there and let me tell you, I don't care how fuckin' bad you had it at home, you do not want to fall in with him. Not unless you want to—ah, shit, just take my word for it, okay?" He grinned even wider, remembering his last glimpse of Hank, relishing the look of cold frustration that twisted that well-bred, well-fed face into a mask as ugly as the soul it hid. "So...welcome to New York."

The kid stood facing him, matching smile for smile. He didn't say a word.

Tony's grin weakened, wobbled out. A frown flickered over his eyes. "You okay?"

Still the smile, still the silence.

The twin lines between Tony's brows deepened to a look of intense concern. "Uh...Can you hear me?" He touched his lips, cupped one ear, made vague gestures with his hand and felt like seven kinds of idiot for trying to fake sign language.

More silence and the smile held steady, but the beautiful head nodded. A short, crystalline peal of laughter escaped the boy's lips.

Now Tony felt a small, cold claw in the pit of his stomach. *What the hell's wrong with him? Jesus, what is he, retarded or something?* "All right, so you can hear me. Do you—can you understand what I saying? Um...You speak English?"

Again the boy nodded eagerly, but not before Tony's own thoughts slapped him down with *Dumb-ass, if he doesn't understand English, how's he gonna understand you're asking him if he does understand English?*

By now Tony was starting to panic on the inside. The kid stood with his back to a plate glass window full of tacky New York City souvenirs, hands dangling at his sides, waiting patiently. Tony had the nasty feeling that whatever he chose to say or do next, it would all be the same to this manchild. *And if I choose to leave him standing here and I just walk away, what then?* No one had to tell him the answer to that one. The kid would stay where he was now, still smiling, still beautiful, a piece of left luggage waiting for whomever noticed him next: Maybe a cop, maybe a crazy, maybe no one at all.

"Shit," Tony said between gritted teeth. "My damn luck. *Hell* of a day off." He scowled at the kid. "Okay, Einstein, you're coming with me." He started to take the boy by the arm again, then decided to try an experiment. Without laying hold of him, Tony started walking. He went about ten steps and glanced back to see what the kid was doing.

He didn't have to look behind him; the boy was at his side, keeping up, and beaming like he was on a freebie trip to Disneyworld. When Tony stopped, he stopped. He was giggling softly to himself.

"Great," Tony muttered. "Just fuckin' great. He followed me home, Mom, can I keep him?" He rubbed the side of his head in thought, then said, "I'm Tony Lee. You got a name?"

The kid tilted his head this way, then that, and hummed a tune that might have been the theme song from *Friends*. It was hard to tell: He only did the first line before he started giggling again.

Tony shook his head. "Great," he repeated. He pressed his lips together, considering his options. Right now, they seemed to be limited to two: Take the kid to the cops or take the kid to Bellevue. On second thought, both of those choices were actually one and the same. What could the cops do for someone like this except haul him down to the psych ward?

Probably the best place for him, Tony's common sense told him. *No way he's all there; he needs serious help. You can't handle this even if you wanted to. And you're too smart to want to, right?*

PLAYING WITH FIRE   593

Right?

"Kid," Tony said casually, "you like comics?"

The boy chuckled and pointed proudly at his T-shirt. For the first time, Tony noticed the design on the front. It was a picture of the Tick. The Tick was a comic book superhero, a big, over-muscled guy with a lantern jaw that made the rest of his head look absurdly tiny. He wore a skintight blue jumpsuit and a cowl mask with a couple of short, segmented antennae tacked on top. He couldn't fly, he didn't have nifty gizmos like Batman, he wasn't a mutant and there was nothing mystical or mythical or magical about him. What he was, was utterly convinced that evil was making a mess of the world and it was his job to clean it up.

He was also well-meaning, innocent, and crazy as a gin-soaked weasel.

Tony patted the kid on the shoulder. "Perfect. I know a place you're gonna love." *And so am I, 'cause once I get you there, you won't be my headache any more.* "It's kind of far from here. We could go by subway, but hell, it's a nice day. I say we take the bus. That work for you?" The kid smiled. Everything worked for him. Tony went on just as if he'd gotten a sensible answer. "Okay, so in that case we gotta catch the crosstown bus and transfer to the number fifteen, downtown, but trust me, it's worth it. C'mon." He set off again, the boy trotting beside him like a faithful hound.

It was all going so easy. It was all going so well.

It stopped going well the minute Tony tried to get the kid onto the crosstown bus. He climbed the steps all right, but while Tony dropped their fares into the coinbox, something set him off. All of a sudden he was staring goggle-eyed at the driver—some ordinary-looking middle-aged black dude with a skinny moustache and a beer gut—and he was making these weird, urgent, whimpering sounds, trying to back away. Trouble was, there were about four other people trying to crowd on behind him, all of them with that icy look in their eyes that said: *I gotta be up this early because I gotta go to a job I hate with a boss who hates me, so don't give me any problems if you know what's good for you!*

Not that any of that mattered. The kid just kept pushing back against them, all the time keeping his eyes fixed on the driver. Tony stood there yelling at him, demanding to know what was wrong, trying to get hold of his arm and haul him aboard. The people in back of him held their ground, shoving him forward or trying to. The kid began to wail like an air raid siren, head tilted back, nose pointed at the sky. Some of the old ladies on the bus shrank into themselves at the eerie sound, but most of the other passengers sat there, determined to be indifferent, working that special city magic that taught that if you ignored something well enough, you could make it go away.

Tony didn't know whether he wanted to kill the kid or die of embarrassment. He gave the bus driver a sheepish smile and shrugged. "He's a little, uh—"

To Tony's surprise, the driver smiled back. "Poor kid," he said. "He needs help. Look, I'm off shift soon. If you can get him to sit down, maybe when we hit First Avenue and my relief comes on I can help you get him down to the hospital and—"

The man's kindly offer had the effect of a lit match in an oil tank. The kid let out a shriek that made all the would-be passengers behind him jump like kangaroos, leaving him a clear path to freedom. He dashed off the bus, Tony running after him.

Tony caught up with the kid at Fifth Avenue, in sight of the Library lions again, right about the same time that his common sense started shouting *What the hell are you doing, chasing trouble? The kid's fuckin' nuts! You need this? Let him run!*

Then he got a look at the kid. The angel eyes were shimmering with tears and his entire face was transformed into the face of another boy, five years old, left alone to weep his heartbreak into a darkened room.

Tony sucked in breath, blinking rapidly. His fluttering eyelids drove away the illusion, but not the effect. He heard himself mutter, "I'm sorry. Hey, listen, don't cry, no one's gonna make you do anything you don't want to, okay? Promise. Please?" And he held out his hand.

The kid didn't take it, but at least he stopped crying. Tony motioned for him to follow and he did, though his smile was gone. Together they walked the same direction that the bus would have taken them, heading east.

It was turning into a glorious day. A fresh breeze was blowing through the streets, taking the top layer off the stench of exhaust fumes. The scent of baking bread wafted out the door of a croissant shop, making Tony's mouth water.

"You hungry, kid?"

They ate crunchy crusted French rolls and drank coffee. Then Tony bought the kid a chocolate croissant for a treat and somehow, without saying a word, the boy managed to let him know that he wanted two more. He gobbled them down as if there were wolves after him. Tony's eyes got wide just watching how fast the kid could put away groceries. *Must be starving, poor guy.*

There were sweet, sticky smears of melted chocolate rimming his mouth when he was done. For a moment Tony was afraid that the kid wouldn't know enough to wipe his own face, that Tony would have to play nanny and do it for him. But then the kid grabbed a paper napkin and cleaned himself up just fine. He even wiped the Tick's mouth for good measure.

"Talk about truth in advertising," Tony said under his breath, staring at the silkscreened superhero. The kid gave him an inquiring look and he raised his voice to add, "I was just saying how that shirt suits you. Perfect choice. You're as flaky as he is, no offense." The boy's smile was back full force; he didn't look as if he knew the meaning of jibes or digs or outright insults.

"Yeah, the Tick," Tony went on. "Good comic. I used to read him all the time. Him and his sidekick Arthur, what was he? A moth? A fat guy in a bunny suit? Those guys were nuts, but it worked for them, y'know?"

The boy's mouth turned up just a little more at the corners. His lips parted and in a voice soft and small as a mouse he said, "Knock, knock."

"Huh?" Tony cocked his head.

"Knock, knock." He looked at Tony expectantly.

"Who—who's there?"

"Arthur."

PLAYING WITH FIRE

"Arthur who?" *So he can* talk!

"Arthur any who remember?"

"Say what?"

The boy didn't respond.

"Look, I'm sorry, but I didn't get the joke," Tony said. "Arthur *what?*"

"Knock, knock," said the boy.

"Yeah, that part I got; it's the punchline I—"

"*Knock, knock.*" There was a low, insistent sound to the words.

Jesus, what the hell did I get myself into with this—Tony gave a mental shrug, and because it looked like the only thing to do he asked a second time, "Who's there?"

"Tick."

"Tick who?"

"Tick the bus, 's easier'n walking." And the kid got up, cleared the table between them, stuffed the paper coffee cups and the used napkins into the trash can, and walked out of the shop. He was humming again.

He was the one who led now, and Tony followed. He strolled happily down Forty-second Street until he found a bus stop on Second Avenue with a sign that said that the number fifteen stopped there. He lounged against the pole with an air of tranquility that a Zen master might envy and regarded Tony with calm eyes that said *I'm waiting.*

By this time, Tony was completely baffled. He gave the kid a worried look, then glanced up the street. A bus was coming. He didn't want to go through another scene like the one on the crosstown, but he didn't seem to have a choice about it. He dredged another pair of tokens out of his jeans and braced himself for the worst.

The bus pulled up, the kid got on like he owned it, and Tony was left to pay the fare and ride most of the way down to the East Village in silent confusion. It was a feeling he seldom had, these days, and hated having with his entire soul. *They want you to be confused, the demons. Confusion makes you stupid, stupidity makes you weak, weakness makes you easy. It's easier to herd a sheep than a lion.* Luckily for him, he had most of a long bus ride to recover his self-possession. By the time he stood up to ring for their stop, he was back in control, and when they stepped off the bus he led the way once more.

"Just a short walk, now," he declared.

The boy nodded, his face the same exquisite, cheerful blank it always was, except for that bad spell on the crosstown bus. Tame and totally cooperative, he followed Tony through the streets of a city now completely given up to the things of daylight.

The big sign over the storefront said *Wild Things.* The smaller sign running along the bottom of the shop window said *We Buy! Sell! Trade! New and Used Comics.* A still smaller sign to one side advertised *Jordan Avery, Prop.,* in the campy, ooze-dripping font called Crypt. The smallest sign of all clung to the store's plate glass door by four suction cups and told the world that *Wild Things* and Jordan Avery would not be open for business before noon today. Since the door itself was wide open and the steel shutters were well up, the littlest sign lied.

There was a werewolf in the doorway. Tony rubbed its snout for luck as he sidled past it. "Jordan?" he called into the interior of the shop. The place smelled a little musty with the scent of old paper and aged wood; there wasn't a soul in sight. "Hey, Jordan, you in here, man?"

Tony looked back at the kid, who was studying the freestanding cardboard cutout werewolf with unabashed delight. It was almost as tall as he. The kid cautiously extended one finger to touch the embossed fangs, only to jerk it back with a yelp of pain so convincing that Tony jumped. The kid killed himself laughing over that.

"Yeah, right, you're a real Seinfeld," Tony said to himself. He walked into the store, still calling, "Jordan? Jordan, it's me, Tony! C'mon out, I brought you a surprise."

"It better be legal." A door at the back of the shop opened and tall man with past-the-shoulders brown hair streaked with gray came out. He was carrying a pile of plastic-bagged comics. "Legal or chocolate, I'm not fussy," he added as he dropped the pile onto the counter beside the cash register.

Tony made a doubtful face. "Now *that's* kinda up for debate," he admitted.

"Tony…" There was a warning note in the older man's voice.

In a flash, Tony went on the defensive. "Hey, I'm not in any trouble, okay? I didn't come here for money, either."

"You know I don't care about stuff like that," Jordan soothed. He had deep, rumbly, bearish voice to match his body. Jordan Avery was a big man. Some people might dismiss him as fat, but they'd correct that mistake if they took the time to get a good look at him. There was no extra flesh on him at all; it was all solid power. True, he didn't carry his strength the way his comic book heroes did, in carefully sculpted arrangements of muscle and sinew, but it was still there.

He came from behind the counter to face Tony. Hazel eyes peered through pink-tinted John Lennon glasses. "What's up? What do you need?"

"Help," Tony answered. "With him."

Jordan looked at the kid, his eyes growing big as a cartoon owl's behind the wire-rimmed lenses. The kid seemed unaware of the older man's scrutiny. He still lingered in the doorway, one arm around the cardboard werewolf's shoulders, one hand cupped to his mouth, whispering secrets into the shaggy ears.

"So what's the story?" Jordan asked Tony, with a slight nod in the kid's direction.

Tony shrugged. "I was over at the Port Authority early—you know, just for somewhere to be—and there he was. Came this close to being fresh meat."

"Ah." Jordan understood. He'd known Tony in the bad old days. "Good, you did good, only—" He looked back at the kid, who was now running a cheap plastic pocket comb over the werewolf's printed fur. God alone knew where he'd gotten it. "Is he, mm, stoned or something?"

"Got me. I don't think so. I mean, his eyes look okay, he's moving pretty good, no tracks." Tony took a deep breath and let it out slow. "I kinda wish he was on drugs. That I'd know how to handle."

"What, you think he's crazy?"

"A little, yeah."

Jordan Avery rested one beefy hand on the counter behind him. "Tony, take it from me, there is no such thing as a little crazy. Not in this city. You're either sane, nuts, or working City Hall. If that boy's got mental problems, why'd you bring him to me? Do I look like Freud? Okay, maybe some." He stroked his short, pepper-and-salt beard, straightfaced.

"I thought you could tell me what I should do with him." Tony heard the pathetic, pleading note in his own voice and despised it and himself. *Listen to me, begging favors! Sure, it's only Jordan, but this isn't something I want to do. Never owe anyone anything, that's the rule. Damn! This whole thing was a mistake, a big mistake. I should've dumped this kid as soon as I got him away from Hank. When he ran off that bus I should've let him run. I should've let him get on the downtown bus and walked the other way. I should've*—the words swirled around in his head, making his temples throb. He closed his eyes tight against the pain and pinched the bridge of his nose.

"Hey, man, take it easy." Tony felt a big hand touch his shoulder, but lightly and only for a second. Jordan Avery might look like a refugee from the '60s, right down to the tie-dyed shirt and the peace symbol dangling from the rawhide cord around his neck, but looks were as far as it went. He wasn't a hugger or even a toucher, not one of those people who went around blubbering *I love, you, man!* to total strangers or even to old friends. And he sure as hell had never been stoned—not so Tony could tell, anyhow. No matter how much he seemed to be more at home in Middle Earth than in Manhattan, he had both feet planted so firmly on the ground, they cracked pavement. If you studied the front shopwindow of *Wild Things* up close and careful, you might see a tiny bit of black lettering in one corner that read *Since 1975.* You didn't stay in business in this city for better than twenty years if you really believed in elves and trolls and goblins. Jordan kept his distance; Jordan kept himself in control.

Now Jordan was saying, "—probably call Bellevue."

"*No.*" Tony's eyes snapped open, aflame. His fist slammed down on the counter, making the plastic cup full of stray pens and felt-tipped markers rattle. "Damn it, Jordan, you think I didn't think of that as soon as I figured out he wasn't just another runaway?"

"So why didn't you do it?" Jordan asked quietly.

"How could I?" Tony spread his hands, letting all other choices but one slip away through his fingers. "*Look* at him, man. Just look at him. You think he'd survive a place like that?"

"Tony, if you think Bellevue's like these hellholes from the old movies, some kind of snakepit or something—"

"I don't know what Bellevue's like. For all I know, it's a fuckin' palace with room service. But I do know that I can't put him in there. He'd die. He just flat die." The passionate conviction behind his own words took even Tony by surprise.

Jordan Avery sighed. "Okay, have it your way. Now what? What do you know about him besides the fact that he's nuts but no way he's going to see someone who could maybe do something helpful about it?"

"Not much. He talks, but—" How to explain the weird things that came out of that perfect mouth? "If he's got a name, he won't tell me."

The big man chuckled. "Everyone's got a name." He put two fingers to his mouth and blew a piercing whistle. In the doorway, the boy jerked his head up like a bird-dog. "Hey, you. Kid. Come here a sec." When the boy obeyed, Jordan pointed to the small, black, rectangular plastic nametag pinned to the front of his shirt. It was so K-Mart, it was camp, which was why he wore it. "Like it says, I'm Jordan Avery. Pleased to meet you." He stuck out his hand and added, "And you would be—?"

"Knock, knock," said the boy, shaking Jordan's hand enthusiastically.

"Huh?"

"Knock, knock! *Knock, knock*!" The boy accompanied each repetition with more vigorous pumping of Jordan's arm.

"Ask him who's there," Tony suggested when Jordan cast bewildered eyes to him.

"Errrrr...Who's there?" the big man asked uncertainly.

"Jordan."

"No, look, Jordan's *my* name." He tapped the plastic nametag with his free hand. "See? Says so right here, that makes it legal. What I want to know is—"

The boy scowled. "*Jordan*," he repeated, and jerked the man's hand back and forth furiously.

"Hey, watch it! I'm still using that thing!" Jordan's objections went unheeded, his attempts to wrench his hand free of the boy's grip came to nothing. The kid held on like a bulldog with a rat in its jaws, refusing to let go, repeating the man's name with a rising note of rage.

Finally Tony suggested, "Say 'Jordan who?'."

"What the—? Okay, fine." The man rolled his eyes, but he took Tony's advice and repeated, "Jordan who?"

It had a magical effect, that question. Immediately the boy dropped Jordan's hand, all smiles, and said, "Jordan nicest guy I know, 'spite of *that* thing what happened."

"See?" Tony said. "That's how it works with him. The only time he talks, it's always like a knock-knock joke. Doesn't make sense. '*That* thing what happened'? Huh! What's that supposed to—? Jordan? You okay?"

Jordan Avery's wide face had gone pasty white. He was staring at the kid in much the same way the kid had stared at the crosstown bus driver before he freaked out entirely. "Sure, sure, fine," he said, but his voice was unsteady. He rubbed his freed hand, never taking his eyes from the kid.

"You don't *sound* okay."

"I said I'm fine!" Jordan snapped. "Get the hell off my friggin' case!"

"Okay, okay!" Tony backed off, hands up to ward off the big man's anger. Jordan had never lit into him like that before. Matter of fact, the only time Tony could remember hearing Jordan lose it was when he caught a couple of snot-nosed kids trying to fumble their way through a crack deal on his premises. They were maybe in sixth grade; he let them off with a bellowed warning. As for the scum who was trying to sell them the shit—

It wasn't a good thing to make Jordan Avery mad.

"So, what do you think we should do about him?" Tony asked meekly.

"I know what I'm *going* to do," Jordan replied. "I'm going to finish restocking the shelves. Then I'm going to fill the cash drawer, make a couple of phone calls and after that I'm going to leave you to watch things while I go across the street for some iced tea. *That's* what I'm going to do," he concluded with the prim, satisfied air of a spinster who's just finished knitting a particularly troublesome sweater.

"But what about—?" Tony turned to the kid, only to discover that his charge had plucked a fat, felt-tipped marker from the plastic cup by the cash register and was contentedly writing something on his T-shirt. When he finished, he pointed to his work proudly, teeth sparkling a brilliant white even in the dim light of *Wild Things*.

Jordan tilted his glasses half an inch down his nose and read what the boy had block-lettered across the Tick's face. "'Nok-Nok,' huh? Very nice, son. Impressive, even. Not an easy thing, getting the letters to come out rightside up when you're writing them upside down, but you're still going to have to work on your spelling. In the meantime—" He lumbered into the back room and returned with a stack of comics which he thrust into Nok-Nok's hands "—read these and keep out of trouble."

"Good luck on that," Tony mumbled.

"Shut up and make yourself useful."

Tony worked alongside Jordan Avery while Nok-Nok found himself a corner of the store with a metal folding chair. There he holed up happily, poring over the comics he'd been given. From time to time, Tony stole a glance at the boy. *Well, it* looks *like he knows how to read*, he thought. *And he can write, and he can talk some, even if it is bizarro. What's with* him*? And why does it have to splatter all over me?*

He gave up asking himself questions without answers and got to work.

The first real customers started wandering into *Wild Things* at around eleven o'clock. Mostly they were high school kids ditching class, but some were in their twenties and thirties, the type Tony thought of as fanboys, even if they weren't all boys. Jordan knew most of them by name, and he put Tony to work helping them find the titles they were seeking with the same zeal Galahad knew when questing for the Holy Grail.

When noon struck, the store was packed. Tourists rubbed elbows with the lunch crowd, little ones fresh out of morning kindergarten tugged on their mothers' purses, demanding the newest issue of *Animaniacs* or *Tiny Toon Adventures*, pairs of devoted fans got into heated debates about whether Superman could whup Spiderman's webslinging ass. Through it all, Nok-Nok stayed put, an island of calm, reading his comics with all the application of a medieval scholar.

The crowd thinned out to nearly nothing by three. Tony counted only two customers wandering up and down the aisles at that hour. He was starting to feel

ESTHER M. FRIESNER

a little tired, and he thought that if he drank one more bottle of iced tea he'd slosh when he walked. Enough, already: Time to get Jordan Avery to make *himself* useful and hand down a decision about Nok-Nok.

Tony got his decision, all right, but it wasn't the one he'd been hoping for. "No. No, he can't stay here. This is not a hotel, motel, flophouse, or the 'Y'."

"Not *forever*, Jordan," Tony pleaded. "Just overnight, maybe two nights tops."

"I said *no*. Stop whining, it won't change anything."

"I'm not whining," Tony protested, even though he realized he was. "Look—" he lowered his voice and pointed at one of the two remaining customers in the shop, a young man who looked like he belonged in one of the upper East Side galleries, sipping designer mineral water out of a crystal champagne flute. "That's Marcus. I know him same as you, and I know you let him stay here for a whole month last winter. You put up a bed in the back room and—"

"And did you also know *why*?" Jordan replied, tight-lipped. "His lover died of AIDS in February. Marcus was clean—I made sure he got tested—but he didn't think he deserved that. He had his own place, but he couldn't be left alone there, not for a while. He needed a refuge, I gave him one, and that was all."

"Like Nok-Nok *doesn't* need a refuge?" Tony challenged.

"What Nok-Nok needs is a place to stay," Jordan countered. "There's a difference."

"Oh yeah? What?"

"It's something you can give him and I won't."

"Just one lousy day. Call it payback for all the times I help out around this place."

"You don't want to help, no one makes you."

"But how d'you expect me to—?"

"Case closed, little brother, case closed."

And it was. When Jordan Avery said those words, you could keep nagging at him but you'd have more luck pounding sand down the proverbial rat hole. Tony sighed. He knew when he was defeated, but he also liked to believe that some defeats were only temporary setbacks.

Maybe he'll change his mind tomorrow. Yeah, sure he will. Hell, he knows I don't make much money, I can't take care of the kid forever. Good old Jordan won't let them send him to Bellevue or Social Services or anything. Sure, he'll come around, I just gotta give him time.

Tony turned on his brightest smile, the one he used to flash the johns when he was angling for a bigger tip at the end of the night. "Okay, Jordan, have it your way. You know me, I'm not pushy."

Jordan snorted. "Right, and you're not stubborn either."

"Tsk-tsk. You're gonna hurt my feelings with all that sarcasm." Tony strolled over to Nok-Nok's chair and lightly flicked the comic book that the boy was reading. Shining blue eyes looked up. "C'mon, man, time to go home."

It wasn't so much of a walk from *Wild Things* to Tony's neighborhood, but it took long enough. Nok-Nok seemed to encounter something fascinating in every shop window. Tony kept finding himself walking along on his own because the

PLAYING WITH FIRE 601

kid had dropped behind to stare at something colorful or something sparkly or something as common as a discarded candy bar wrapper in the gutter.

"What is it with you?" Tony demanded, latching onto the boy's arm and dragging him along.

"Knock, knock," came the reply, accompanied by the usual grin.

"Yeah, right, knock, knock, so what else is new?" Tony sighed. "Okay, *who's there?*"

"Wanda."

"Wanda who?"

"Wanda eat!"

Tony gave the kid a searching look. "You *sure* you're nuts?"

They stopped in a small deli for sandwiches. Nok-Nok dawdled over his food so long that by the time they emerged it was dark. When they reached Tony's building, the neon sign over the bar was already a tawdry blaze of light.

Tony struck a pose, like some lord of the manor showing off the family domain, and announced, "Home, sweet home. For now." Nok-Nok giggled.

The giggle shrilled to a scream as the big dog came out of nowhere. Jaws gaping wide and red, white foam streaming back over shaggy black fur, it charged down the sidewalk, baying wildly. Claws like small black iron scimitars clattered against the pavement. Strollers and idlers in the street froze where they stood when they heard its mad howls, then ran screaming. Tony too poised to bolt, but before he took to his heels he cast one quick, instinctive glance at Nok-Nok, willing the boy already gone to safety.

No luck. Never any luck in all Tony Lee's life, so why should things be different now? Nok-Nok stood weighted to the spot, a stone angel, the terrified trembling of his lips the only sign that he was made of flesh.

"Jesus...Wake *up*, kid! Move!" Tony punched Nok-Nok roughly in the shoulder, but he wouldn't budge. Tony hooked his hand around the boy's upper arm and tried to drag him away; it was like hauling a boulder. "What's *wrong* with you?" he demanded for what seemed like the hundredth time. "*Move*, damn it! Move or—"

Tony never had the chance to finish. The black dog was there to end it for him. With a growl that set all Tony's hairs on end, the creature slowed, bunched the powerful muscles of its haunches, and launched itself right for Nok-Nok's throat.

3

Tony, you stupid son-of-a—! The thought flashed through Tony's head as he threw himself between the dog and Nok-Nok. His head filled with animal stink and he had a clear view of the beast's glittering fangs. For an instant he had the illusion of staring into a pair of glaring eyes, traffic-light green, pupils slitted into a serpent's merciless gaze. Then his whole field of vision fell into the abyss of the dog's foam-caked lips and red-ribbed throat just before he brought up his arms criss-cross before his face, warding ward off the first impact of its leap.

A hot wind blew over Tony's face. He felt warm, moist air dew his bare forearms, but the jarring sensation of the big dog's body crashing into his never came.

"What the hell—?" He lowered his arms and looked all around him, up and down the street. The dog was gone. There was only Nok-Nok, cowering in a tight ball of fear on the sidewalk behind him.

Tony looked to left and right: Nothing. Just the bar, and the entrance to his building, and the people walking along, minding their own business. No one looked frightened. No one looked *anything*. The shrieking bystanders who had fled the black dog's attack seemed to have vanished along with the beast. The passersby now on the street behaved as though there had never been the screams, or the attack, or the panic, although they had to have been within eye and earshot when it all went down. They saw Nok-Nok's huddled form and made it a point to give the boy a wide berth, but that was just good city-sense in action. It was as if the whole terrifying incident had never happened, except for poor, shuddering Nok-Nok there, and Tony's own swirling thoughts.

Tony squatted beside the boy and touched him gently. "It's okay," he said. "It's gone." Where had it gone? How? He didn't know. He didn't want to think about it. There'd be time to sift things through and maybe turn himself in to Bellevue later. For right now, it was enough that the danger had vanished. Count your blessings...

Count your blessings, Anthony. I'm surprised she never taught you that much common sense, or common courtesy. I didn't need to take you in. You could have gone into an orphanage. Still, you're at least partially my blood, and that taint—well, maybe she couldn't teach you common sense; she had so little of it to spare.

"Shut up," Tony growled under his breath to the demon-ghost. Then, a little louder he urged Nok-Nok: "Come on, it's okay now, really. You're safe. Nothing's going to happen to you now."

Slowly, fearfully, the boy raised his head and looked Tony in the eye. "Knock, knock?" It was the closest he could come to asking for reassurance.

"Right, who's there," Tony responded. "No one's there. Nothing's there. I told you, you're safe. Get up. Let's go inside."

Nok-Nok shook his head emphatically and hugged himself into a tighter ball. "Knock, knock," he repeated.

"Who's there?" By now Tony had stopped finding this little game an irritation. It was the only way he had of communicating with the kid and he knew it. Tony was a past expert in making the best of things, especially things that didn't seem like they'd ever get better. You hung in, you held on, and sometimes—just maybe, given enough time—they surprised you.

"Berry."

"Berry who?"

"Berry Thursday."

"Merry Thursday to you too." Tony relaxed a little. At least the kid was coming out of his black terror. "Only it's not Thursday, it's—oh! You mean *thirsty*? You're *very thirsty*, that it?"

Nok-Nok nodded with enthusiasm, and even gave Tony a brief round of applause.

"Well, like I said, come on upstairs. I've got some Coke in the fridge." He stood up and gestured for the boy to do likewise, but Nok-Nok held his place, knees to chin, arms and legs still knotted tight. Tony rolled his eyes. "What, you want curb service?" The boy just sat there, all innocent beauty and expectation. "All right, fine, whatever. I'll bring you down a can, but then you gotta promise me you'll quit screwing around and come up, okay?"

Nok-Nok nodded, the picture of contentment and cooperation.

Tony took the stairs up to his apartment two at a time. He wasn't even breathing hard when he reached the door, though he did give his lungs a good workout cursing the lock when it refused to open right away. *Can't leave Nok-Nok alone down there. God knows what could happen*—the door opened, yielding to key or curses or both, and Tony snatched a can of Coke from the refrigerator before clattering down the stairs so fast his feet scarcely touched the treads.

Tossing the can from one hand to the other he hit the sidewalk and announced, "Here ya go, Nok-Nok, the choice of a new—no, wait, that's Pepsi. What the hell, drink—"

Nok-Nok was no longer curled up on the pavement.

"Nok-Nok?" It had grown darker. Tony turned his face so that the neon sign painted one cheek with strange, red sigils. Then he saw him. Nok-Nok was on his feet and almost to the end of the block, whistling a pure, piercing melody, acting as if he'd never had a care in the world.

The car was waiting at the corner. It was the deep blue of summer twilight, its shiny skin aswim with reflected streetlight, whorls of silver and gold. Somehow it appeared as though whatever light rested on its surface slowly sank into the polished flanks, engulfed and devoured. Even the beams of its own headlights seemed to need to struggle to stay lit. They burned with a sullen glow, amber tinged with green.

The front door on the passenger side was open. Music trickled out, the reedy sound of piping. It kept up a perfect counterpoint to Nok-Nok's whistled tune, the two melodies rising and intertwining on the cool evening air.

"Hey! Hey, Nok-Nok! Godammit, you send me running all the way upstairs for this fuckin' soda, you damn well get your ass back here and *drink* it!"

Tony didn't know what possessed him, yelling like that; he just knew with an awful certainty that he had to keep Nok-Nok from going any closer to that car. His shout shattered the music. Nok-Nok stopped in his tracks, silent, not moving any nearer to the open door but not retreating either.

The sweet rumble of a perfectly tuned engine started up. The blue car began to move forward, gliding down the street until the open door was almost in a line with Nok-Nok.

Without thinking, Tony threw the can. It arced through the air and struck the blue car right on the hood, leaving a substantial dent that spiderwebbed into a crazy pattern of black. Nok-Nok yelped, turned on his heel, and ran back to Tony, clinging to him like a frightened child. No matter how hard Tony tried to pry the kid off him, Nok-Nok didn't let go until the open door slammed shut and the blue car pulled into traffic and drove away.

"Whew! Weirdos." Tony finally got Nok-Nok to back off, then rubbed his temples. "Look, didn't your parents ever teach you not to take rides from strangers?" Nok-Nok was smiling again. Tony just shook his head. "If you survive one week in this city, kid, I'm gonna put in for a fuckin' medal."

Tony had no sooner brought Nok-Nok into his apartment than the boy made a beeline for the Sally Army sofa, stretched out on it with his heels hanging over the armrest, and fell fast asleep. Tony spent about two minutes debating whether or not he should try to get the kid out of his clothes or just yank off his shoes. "Hell with it," he decided, and took himself off to bed. Tomorrow was a work day.

That night, despite all the strangeness of the day before, there were no bad dreams. The demons had held secret conclave and resolved to let the waking world besiege Tony for a change. That was how he felt about it, anyway. He wasn't fool enough to assume that maybe he'd cheated the demons. Absence didn't mean banishment. They were stubborn things, demons, and twice as sly as stubborn. They could wait in the dark places forever, if that was what it took to snare you. As soon as you thought they were gone for good, as soon as you laid aside the few pitiful scraps of armor you'd hammered out over the years for your soul's protection, they were back. They were back, and you were naked because you'd been stupid enough to think you were safe at last.

Not me, Tony thought in dreams that were empty of evil, empty of everything but mists and colors and chasms. *They'll never take me by surprise. I'm ready for them. I'm always ready.*

He awoke to the alarm clock's hideous, insectoid buzz and slammed it off before it could wake Nok-Nok. The boy was in deep slumber, his breathing soft and regular. Tony looked down at him by the lightspill from the bathroom. At rest, the kid looked even more like an angel.

No, not an angel, Tony thought. *Angels have swords. Angels can fight.* An image rose in his mind, a great church, and in it a pale statue glimmering in shadow. The archangel Michael trampled the dragon of Hell beneath his sandalled feet, his sword upraised for the killing blow. In memory, the carved dragon shifted shape, melted from the image every schoolchild held in mind when reading tales of wicked dragons and brave knights. Its humped body elongated beyond belief, it's paws grew longer, more articulated, ceased to grasp at the gold of worldly goods and instead held out a single, luminous pearl balanced on the tips of five yellow talons. Whiskers like streamers curled away from a lion's mouth, and its expression of mindless hate became one of wisdom, self-knowledge, and mild amusement at the angel's puny sword.

The pearl blazed up before Tony's sight in an explosion of sparks. He gasped and threw his hands up to shield his eyes. He felt a surge of heat beating against his face, his hands, but then it subsided. He lowered his hands: The room was unchanged, serene in darkness, and Nok-Nok slept on.

Tony staggered into the bathroom and ran icy cold water on the back of his head, then shook himself like a soaked dog. *Jesus!* His heart was beating rapidly, his breath shallow. He grasped the cracked porcelain lip of the sink and cast around wildly for some explanation to which he might anchor his sanity.

A dream…That's it, right, a dream. Get up, only I'm still half-asleep on my feet, right, it's happened to me before. One time when I was just getting into the routine, Joe said he caught me slinging fish in my sleep. That's what it was, just a dream…

He dressed in a hurry, then set out a box of Lucky Charms on the counter for Nok-Nok with a note taped to it. The kid could read, that was one good thing, and attaching the note to something edible would probably draw his attention once he woke. The note said to help himself to food, told him where Tony stashed his comics and magazines and books, let him in on the proper way to coax the little portable TV set on the coffee table to work, but above all, it told him to stay put until Tony came home. Muttering a prayer that the kid wouldn't freak when he woke up in the empty apartment, Tony locked his apartment door securely behind him and went to work.

Smell? What smell?

That was what Tony had said about a year ago when his then-girl showed up to surprise him at work. She'd stepped out of the shadows beside one of the big trucks that brought the fish to the Fulton Street market, wrinkled up her little nose, and asked him how he could stand the smell. At first she acted all cute and coy, claiming she couldn't tell whether the fish reeked worse than the exhaust fumes off the highway, but then she told him she'd decided: It was the fish. She asked him why he didn't try to get a different job. Her daddy was in the rag trade over on Seventh; maybe if she asked him nice he'd get Tony a job there, moving the big racks of clothing through the streets. He could work his way up from there, if he wanted. Where could he work his way up from slinging fish off trucks with the big iron hook? Nowhere. She'd ask daddy, only she wouldn't tell him she was dating Tony, just that he was a friend of a friend. Daddy would have a conniption fit if he found out his little girl was dating a Chinese guy, so she'd have to play it—

Tony told her no.

She wanted to know why, so he told her. It wasn't the reason she'd thought it was at all. It wasn't because of Daddy and his precious fits. It wasn't because Tony lacked ambition. It wasn't because he was so in love with a career of slinging fish, no, none of these.

I got this job for myself. I'll get my next job for myself, when I'm ready. I'm never going to depend on anyone else for anything in my life. Not ever again.

She told him he was stupid and she left him. He shrugged and went back to work. After that, he made it a point to avoid telling his girlfriends what he did for a living, if he could help it. Sometimes, with the ones he met while he was helping out at Wild Things, he let them believe he worked there all the time. Sometimes some of them assumed he was still in school full time, so he let them

ESTHER M. FRIESNER

believe that. Sometimes he wondered what he'd do if he ever met the girl he could tell what he really did for a living, and what he used to do, and who'd understand both.

Even after the rough day off he'd had, Tony still managed to be the first guy to show up for work that morning, except for his boss, Joe. The other guys liked to say Joe laid himself out overnight on the crushed ice with the rest of the cold fish, but they didn't say it where Joe could hear them. Joe never heard of modern management techniques. If you did your job, he let you alone. If you fucked up, he threw you out. Simple.

Tony did his job. When the first trucks pulled up for unloading, he was on them, shifting crates, moving stock. When the buyers came from the big-name midtown restaurants he was there to help steer them to the good stuff. Fish flowed off one fleet of trucks and onto another. Tony and the other guys made a human chain and made sure the flow moved fast and smooth. Even in the coldest dregs of winter nights they worked up a sweat, arms swinging, backs bending, muscles groaning with the strain. You built up a rhythm with this job, you got into the groove, you were part of the team. After awhile, you zoned out to everything but your body. Who needed to think to do a job like this?

That was one of the best parts of the job, as far as Tony was concerned, being able to work with your mind empty, nothing in your head except music from the radio.

The trouble was, today he couldn't seem to reach that point where his mind emptied itself out and gave him a little peace. All he could seem to think of was that weird kid back at his place.

What the hell am I gonna do with him? I can't keep him with me forever. I can't turn him into the cops, or Social Services, or—fuck. Maybe the church? He shook his head, tossing out that idea almost as soon as it occurred to him. What would the church do with Nok-Nok?

The main question is, what am I gonna do with him? Tony's thoughts went round and round, always coming back to the same bleak place. He became distracted, lost his concentration, fumbled a crate of smelt and almost had it smash on the sidewalk.

Joe noticed. He was a short man, squat and swarthy. "Hey Lee, you wanna wake up?" he called.

"Sorry."

"Yeah, sure. Here or on the unemployment line; your choice." He went back to his coffee and his clipboard, turning his back on Tony.

Tony bent to his job, embarrassed, mad. Joe didn't waste time on sweet talk; he was one of the fixtures at the Market, a guy who remembered the neighborhood before they yuppified the South Street Seaport area and turned it into a high-gloss tourist trap. He didn't mean anything by his caustic comments, it was just his way. But Tony still felt every sharp word; he'd had too many aimed at him in earnest for too many years to let them roll off his back.

"Hey, Ike, turn up the music!" he shouted to one of his co-workers. He didn't think of the other guys as his friends. After work, they went their separate ways.

When Tony'd first gotten this job, no one tried to make him feel welcome and he wasn't looking for any favors. They all moved together like the parts of a machine, and when the job was done, the machine came apart until it was needed again.

Ike didn't even bother acknowledging Tony's request, he just acted on it as if it'd been his idea. The music cranked up and Tony let it blast his worries about Nok-Nok clean out of his skull.

He'd just finished unloading one truck and was getting ready to shift a load of whole salmon onto a smaller delivery van for an uptown restaurant when he heard it: The music. It wasn't the rock on the radio. It was too thin, too ethereal, too soft for that. In fact, it was a miracle he heard it at all: It was only a whistle.

But it was a whistle he knew. He'd heard it before, last evening, when he'd come down from his apartment to see Nok-Nok ambling calmly up the block toward that strange blue car. He turned, following the sound around the side of the delivery van.

The fish market stood in the shadow of the FDR Drive, an elevated highway that rumbled with traffic even at this early hour. Under the highway the traffic was just as heavy, the flow made more awkward by the forest of girders that the cars and trucks had to drive between. More rumbly by the spots where old cobblestones showed through the asphalt. Across the street from the fish market were the piers and the East River and to the north the Brooklyn Bridge. In the daytime, there were plenty of people crossing the street under the highway: tourists checking out the old rigged sailing ships that were part of the South Street Seaport's lure; office workers making time for a little lunch hour shopping spree at the trendy chain stores with their approved clothing for pretty people who believed in khaki; lovers stealing away to trade plans for later over shiny glasses of crisp white wine in shiny bistros that pretended to be European.

At this hour the far shore of the highway's underside wasn't a good place to be unless you were a cop. In all the time Tony had been working at the fish market, he remembered seeing maybe four, five people over on that side of the street.

This morning, Nok-Nok made it six. He stood leaning against a lamppost, whistling his tune to the sky that was just starting to lighten. When he saw Tony, he waved happily, but he didn't stop whistling his odd, wandering tune.

"Holy sh—" Tony felt like someone had smacked him right on top of his skull with a baseball bat. *How did he find me? Did he follow me? Did I tell him where I work and forget? No I didn't, I know I didn't. So how did he get—?* "Nok-Nok!" He shouted the boy's name without thinking, out of confusion, out of anger at finding himself confused.

And Nok-Nok waved again and walked right into the street without bothering about mundane things like traffic lights or how dark it still was or how tired the driver of the bus barreling down the street right for him might be.

Tony started forward automatically, even though he knew he'd never reach the boy in time. The bus driver hit his brakes—the screech would wake the dead— but the bus kept rolling. With that unearthly sharpening of the senses that overtakes people caught in the middle of accidents unfolding around them, Tony was able to see into the bus, to make out the driver's face. He was a black man, middle-aged, and he looked scared out of his mind. He also looked—

Couldn't be. Nah, it couldn't. What the hell would the driver from the crosstown bus yesterday be doing running a bus down here on this street at this time of—?

And then, a thought that was ice between Tony's eyes: *There is no bus that runs on this street. Not now. Not ever.*

So many thoughts exploding inside his head all at once, like the petals of a bursting flower made all of flame. So many flakes of dazzling fire, all going off together, and Tony still rushing forward to try and stop what couldn't possibly be stopped in time, to try to save a boy already dead.

The girl jumped from the curb and grabbed Nok-Nok by the back of his T-shirt, jerking it like a dog's choke-chain. The bus blurred past, brakes still screeching, yet in spite of the shriek and the stink not losing any speed. It raced on down a route that didn't exist, swept along in a spate of common traffic, and became two dwindling red taillights in the dark. Tony stood in the gutter, watching until it was out of sight, his heartbeat like a runaway subway car, then forced his breathing back to normal as he looked across the street to see what had become of Nok-Nok.

He saw the boy standing tamely on the curb, holding hands with the girl who'd saved his life. She reminded Tony of his old kindergarten teacher from the way she led Nok-Nok primly to the crosswalk and made him wait for the WALK signal before letting him leave the curb. That was about as far as the resemblance went, though: Miss Hilton never wore that much black, that much leather, and her lipstick was pale pink, not the deep purple-red of crushed blackberries.

Tony watched with a kind of awe as Nok-Nok's savior approached. He didn't try to meet her halfway: Where he stood now, he was out of Joe's line of sight. He didn't want his boss to catch him slacking this way, but he knew he'd risk the worst flaying Joe could dish out if only he could get some kind of clue to what the hell was happening to his dearly salvaged life of peace.

The girl seemed to know just what she was doing, where she was going, what her purpose was. She was a little thing—only came up to Nok-Nok's chest—and her biker jacket almost swallowed her alive. Her hair was a deep garnet red, cut short so she looked like old prints of Joan of Arc. For some reason, Tony had no trouble picturing her with a sword in her hands.

She walked right up to him and said, "I'm his sister. Thanks." That was it; she turned and started to walk away.

"Hey, wait a second!" Tony called after her, taking care to keep his voice low enough so that Joe wouldn't take notice. She stopped and gave him a penetrating look out of heavily lined green eyes. "You know who he is?"

She rolled her eyes the same exasperated way Miss Hilton did when Tony screwed up making carnations out of toilet paper. "I told you: I'm his sister. My name's Sylv. Thanks a lot for looking after him. He gets lost sometimes. He's not—you know." She shrugged her shoulders.

"Yeah, I got that," Tony agreed with her unspoken assessment of Nok-Nok. "So what's his problem?"

"Huh? What do *you* think? He's a retard." Her tone as good as added *And you're another*.

Tony slouched against the side of the delivery van he was supposed to be loading, his fishhook dangling out of sight at his side. He didn't like this chick's attitude. He was liking it less by the second. For someone who was supposedly grateful to him for having saved her brother, she was acting like a real bitch.

"He's no retard," Tony told her, talking slowly, as if she lacked the brains to understand him otherwise. "He was with me most of yesterday. He can read and he can write; I saw him do both."

She made a disgusted sound. "Wow, Doctor, tell me more. Where'd you get your degree? There's plenty of retards can read and write. I oughta know what my own brother is."

"Then you wanna tell me why you let your own brother wander around like that? Or maybe you wanna tell me how you just happen to find him now? Where were you yesterday? Were you following him? Following us? Why didn't you come for him then? Why didn't you say anything? You know what I think?" He took a step towards her; she held her ground, chin raised defiantly. "I think you're as much his sister as I am, Sylvia."

Her booted foot lashed into his shin sharply. He yelped and dropped the fishhook in the street. "My name's Sylv, not *Sylvia*. Got that, asshole?" she snapped.

"Yeah, so what's *his* name, then?" Tony demanded between gritted teeth. He nodded curtly in Nok-Nok's direction while rubbing his assaulted shin.

"What is this, finals week?" Her sneer was abrasive enough to strip paint, and her laugh so condescending that it as good as said, *You're one pathetic bastard, you know that?* "His name's Charlie, okay?"

"No, it's not," Tony lied smoothly. "It's Johnny; he told me."

He watched her reaction carefully. There was a flicker of doubt in her face before she seized control again and countered, "He never did! He can't even talk right."

"Yeah, I know that, too." Tony was satisfied: If his bluff about Nok-Nok's real name worked on her, even for an instant, then his theory about Sylv was right. This city was full of all kinds of predators, all different kinds with all different plans. A coral snake was smaller and more gorgeously colored than a shark, but they both got the job done. Tony didn't know why Sylv was after Nok-Nok—he couldn't even begin to guess—but didn't need to know that, as long as he kept the kid out of her hold. *I didn't rescue him from Hank just to have this bitch get him.* "He told me the way he does, with those riddles. Jokes. You know?" He pointed at the scrawled NOK-NOK on the kid's shirtfront. Nok-Nok smiled proudly and stuck out his chest so that Sylv could get a good look at it, even in the shadow of the delivery van.

Sylv wasn't impressed or interested. "I think you're a fucking liar," she growled. "And I don't need to take this kind of shit. Come on, Joh—Charlie. We're out of here."

She grabbed Nok-Nok's wrist and started forward. Tony stepped in front of them, blocking the way. "Move it or lose it, asshole." Sylv tried to elbow Tony aside, but he eeled around her and held his ground. She lowered her head, a tiny bull about to charge. This time, when she kicked at him, he was expecting it. He dodged the flying Doc Marten with an ease and grace that cranked her anger up several levels. She dropped Nok-Nok's wrist and made fists. She was so small and so angry that Tony burst into laughter in spite of himself.

Then her eyes darted to the street and a wicked look curved her lips. Tony saw and followed her gaze. She'd spied his discarded fishhook, all cold, sharp iron. Just let her lay hands on that and there'd be a hard end to any more laughter.

She stooped for the hook, but he pounced first, shoving her back. He came up in a crouch, the keen tip glittering in every spill of streetlight. "Bad idea," he said, wagging the hook in front of him like a schoolteacher's admonishing finger. That was all he intended to do with it, just get hold of it again so that she couldn't.

That wasn't how Nok-Nok saw things. The boy's eyes fixed themselves on the hook, a mouse's helpless stare in the face of a hungry serpent. He began to shiver, then to shake in every limb. His head fell back, his mouth gaped wide, and his shrieks of mindless terror tore the dawn bloody and raw.

"What the fuck is—?" Joe came running around the corner of the van, followed by a pack of the other workers. He took in the scene in an eyeblink and reached his own conclusions. "God damn it, Lee, you crazy slant, you got shit with your old lady, you take it elsewhere. Gimme that!" His strong, hairy hand wrenched the fishhook from Tony's grasp. "Get outa here, you're fired."

Tony gave Joe a look of disbelief. "That's not—she's not—look, let me explain—"

"Explain my ass. You heard me: You're fired. Get outa here before I call a cop. Hell, I may do that anyway. He hurt you?" This last question was aimed at Sylv.

She was good, Tony had to admit it. The way she softened up that hard little nut of a face when she talked to Joe was a piece of bullshit artistry at its finest. "No, mister, I'm okay. He's just got this temper. I don't want to make any trouble. Look, I gotta go." She dodged around Tony's former boss, Nok-Nok in tow, and darted away into the streets of the city.

4

He didn't try to catch up with them. He knew that if he did, all she'd have to do was scream until a cop came. They were walking through the financial district, so finding a cop wouldn't be a problem. Somehow, where there was plenty of money, where there were plenty of slick suits and hundred dollar haircuts and real gold Rolex watches, there were plenty of cops. There were cops where Tony lived too—there had to be—but they only seemed to show up after someone was bashed or bleeding or dead. Cops in Tony's neighborhood worked the cleanup detail, cops down here worked to prevent the mess from happening in the first place. Only the rich were worth protecting.

Only the rich were worth shielding from all degrees of unpleasantness, like having to watch another ugly scene between Tony and Sylv. He'd only just met her, but already he recognized her as another like himself, streetwise, smart enough to know how the system worked, to know the system wasn't set up to take care of people like her, but sly enough to force the system to work for her anyway. If he tried to stop her, tried to force the whole Nok-Nok issue on these streets, she'd take that knowledge and use it to get him out of the way long enough for her to vanish, Nok-Nok with her.

Two could play that game, the streets and the system. So Tony trailed Sylv at a respectable distance, his face a pleasant mask, nothing at all threatening about the way he carried himself. If she tried to sic a cop on him, complaining that he was following her, she'd be the one to run afoul of the system. Sure, what'd happen if some little raggy Goth-girl said a guy was on her tail? The cop would give Tony one quick glance, Tony'd look back at him confused, blameless, very Can-I-help-you-Officer?, and Sylv would get the blue brush-off. Crazy bitch, probably on drugs or just plain nuts, you got a lot of weird shit from *that* element. Oh yeah, you didn't have to tell the cops: They knew.

Sylv knew too. She knew just what he was doing, maintaining that precise amount of distance between them. He was good at it. When she walked faster, so did he; when she slowed down on purpose, he did the same. It was pissing her off beautiful to behold. He couldn't see her face, but he could tell from the way she hunched her shoulders forward, led with her sharp little chin that she was mad and getting madder. She picked up the pace still more, hauling poor Nok-Nok behind her like a pull-toy.

Nok-Nok was being his usual self, fascinated by the strangest things, trying to make her stop or at least slow down so he could gape at the glass towers, the sudden flights of pigeons, the gutter sludge of rain-pulped paper and crumpled cardboard coffee cups. Sylv wasn't having any of that. When he tried to linger, she jerked him forward, a puppy on a choke-chain.

The day came on, sunlight melting up the sidewalks, slipping into the stone and glass canyons. The hunt continued. Block after block, Tony made sure to keep Sylv and Nok-Nok in sight. At least twice she made a wild dash across a busy avenue just as the light went from red to green. Tony plunged after her, dodging an onslaught of roaring, honking traffic, putting his neck on the line and coming within inches of being fender meat. He didn't think about what he was risking; he'd sooner be dead and damned that let her get away. Crowds grew up around them like mushrooms after rain, thickening on the sidewalks as the hour for office work came on. No crowd was thick enough to keep him from following her. He saw her hesitate at the mouth of a subway entrance, then pat her jacket pockets and make a face full of soundless curses before hurrying on.

At last they came to the streets where the cops didn't go until it was all over, the little webwork streets of Chinatown and Little Italy, the jewelry district around Canal Street. She stopped in front of a storefront covered with an old-style gateleg grill. Unlike the solid steel shutters smart businessmen pulled down to shield their shop windows, this thing left the glass vulnerable through a honeycomb of diamond-shaped gaps between the interwoven metal slats. Stars of broken glass behind the grill stood witness to the fact that plenty of people had already had their fun. The sharp-toothed holes were patched from the inside with duct tape and the grimy remains of the window were backed by slit-open cardboard boxes, making it impossible for anyone to see into the store, though the sign above the storefront claimed that this was the place if you wanted to buy top-line wholesale commercial kitchen equipment.

Sylv stood staring through the grill as if she had X-ray vision and a burning desire to equip her own hotel. She still held onto Nok-Nok, but her grip had shifted from wrist to hand and loosened. She didn't look ready to start towing him away with her again any time soon. She was tired and resigned and waiting.

Tony didn't make his move right away; he wasn't about to close in on her so fast, not until he ran through all the possible outcomes. He'd made a mistake that morning, when he'd faced her down at the fish market, and it had cost him his job. He wasn't going to screw up that way again.

This was the closest Tony had ever come to playing a game of chess. *If I move like this, what will she do? And if I move that way instead—?* The street wasn't deserted by any means—try finding an empty street in downtown Manhattan by daylight!—but there weren't too many people passing by either. If he confronted her here and now, what could she do? Scream rape? Holler that she was being mugged? Just enough witnesses to see that she was full of it, if they bothered to stick around at all.

And what if she doesn't waste time screaming? What if she's got a blade, or even a gun? She could waste me easy, then swear I was the one who—nah. If she had something like that, why'd she make a grab for my hook? She's clean. And she's waiting. Okay, man, let's see what the lady wants.

Tony took a deep breath and walked up the block to where Sylv and Nok-Nok loitered. She watched him draw near, and a thin smile twisted her blackberry mouth. "I'm not gonna bite, stupid," she said by way of greeting. "I don't do vampires."

"So what do you do? Collect stray kids for laughs? Hell of a hobby. You ever think of sticking to Barbie dolls instead?"

"Bite me," she said, still smiling. There was a smear of lipstick on her front teeth.

"I thought you didn't do vampires." By this time Tony was standing right in front of her. Nok-Nok bounced on the balls of his feet, his face shining with childlike joy, a wordless welcome for Tony. Tony ignored him, focusing all his attention on the girl. "Look, we can do this nice or nasty. Who are you really? What do you want from him?"

"Deaf *and* stupid, huh?" Her eyes taunted him. "I told you, he's my brother."

"Bullshit."

"And what's it to you if it is? Like *you're* something to him?"

"If I am, it's by accident. But that doesn't mean I'm gonna turn my back on him now, let him go off with you just because you say he's your brother. The guy I saved him from in the Port Authority could've said the same thing, and I know what that fucker really is."

"Oh, you *saved* him, huh?" The full lips writhed into an even more scornful grimace. "So when you do bring him to Jesus?"

"That's not what I do."

"Right." She dropped Nok-Nok's hand and planted her fists on her hips, defying Tony to convince her that the world was round. "Looks like you're the collector. Why don't *you* try Barbies instead?"

Tony held back his anger. Sylv was giving him grief, a hard time, and some serious ball-twisting—everything but answers. That was what she wanted, to get under his skin so bad that he'd lose his temper and forget what was important. He wouldn't give her the satisfaction.

"Truce," he told her. "And truth. Answers for answers, deal?"

"Why would I want to deal with you?" she shot back. "All you are is a fucking nuisance. Leave us alone. Go back where you belong and mind your own damn business."

"Listen," Tony said in a soft, even voice that was nowhere near a shout or a snarl. It contained its own quiet power to compel. A measure of anger leaked out of the girl's body. She stood waiting to hear, not to attack. "I didn't go looking to find Nok-Nok, but I did anyway. He was this close to a real bad situation when I met him. The only reason I saved him from it was because I've been there." Calmly, as if Sylv had every right to know, Tony told her about how it had been with him, and the Hellmouth, and the life. And while the words came so easily to his lips, a small protesting voice in the back of his mind cried out, *What the hell you telling her all this for? What's she got to know what you were? So she can use it, a weapon? You want to hear how she says it when she calls you whore?*

The voice yowled in vain. Tony answered it in his own mind with an alien serenity: *I'm asking for truth. I should be ready to offer it.* Aloud, to Sylv, he concluded, "That was my life for a year, two, eternity. That was how I survived."

"Miracle's that you survived doing that," Sylv muttered. She lowered her head, looking at him sideways out of eyes that had lost their harsh, challenging glitter. "Survived to get out of it, I mean."

"I managed to get out on my own, but you think he could?" He indicated Nok-Nok, who was using his fingertips to paint dots of his saliva on the dirty show window through the diamond gaps in the grill. "I don't. I got him out of there and took him with me because I couldn't think of anything else to do. If you really were his sister, I'd give him to you in a New York minute—I still don't know what the fuck to do with him and now you lost me my job so I don't even know what the fuck I'm gonna do to take care of *me*. But that doesn't mean I can just let him go off with someone who could turn out to be no better than chickenhawk scum."

"I see." Sylv folded her hands in front of her. Under her jacket she wore a short black jumper that made her look like a refugee from a Catholic girls' school, and the gesture stole more years from her slight body. When she finally looked directly at Tony once more, she said, "Okay. Truth. Answers. Deal. After all—" A glimmer of mirth touched her eyes "—you're my brother too."

"I'm—? Come on, quit fucking with me, you said—!"

"I said I'd give you the truth. I didn't say you'd be up for taking it. You and me and—okay, so he's decided to call himself Nok-Nok—if we weren't kin we wouldn't be standing here together now. Nok-Nok never would've found his way to you this morning, I never would've been able to track him, you never would've kept on our trail—not with the kind of distractions I was laying down between us."

"Distractions?" Tony repeated, at a loss. "Running across the street in traffic? That's no big—"

"I admit I'm not very good at it yet, not like some of the others. I'm still learning the basics of glamour, but what I've got's enough to take me shopping with the Five Finger Discount Club right under the saleslady's nose. Look!" She pointed at her thickly lipsticked mouth. "Estée Lauder from *Bloomie's* for crissake. You think I could afford to *buy* this?"

Tony didn't know what to think. All of a sudden, Sylv was opening up to him, pouring out a stream of self-styled truths that were more bewildering than the most complex tangle of lies.

"You did save Nok-Nok," she was saying now. "He told me all about it while we were trying to get away from you. And he told me it wasn't just from the creep in the bus terminal either: It was from the beast too, and the machine, and that stupid troll who almost ran him—oh wait, that was when *you* nearly got him killed and *I* saved him. Look, do me a favor, okay? Never call him by name unless he can reach you without getting himself turned into pavement pizza. When you call, he comes: The bond's *that* strong. And you fed him, too, and gave him somewhere to sleep. If you guys aren't joined at the fucking hip, I don't know—"

"For someone who doesn't talk much, Nok-Nok sure told you a lot," Tony interrupted. "And for someone who talks as much as you do, you're not telling me shit. Beasts? Trolls? Shoplifting? What are you, out of your—?"

He didn't get to say *mind*. He didn't get to ask his next question, which was going to be a wiseass crack about whether Bellevue gave family discounts. Something happened between breath and breath, something that gave him about one tenth of second to wonder whether he was going to need that Bellevue family discount himself, the tenth of a second when the dirty shopwindow burst outward in an explosion of twisting, blackening metal bars, the glitter of shattering glass, and the pungent smell of flaming cardboard. He saw the blast snake out in the slow motion vision attending all witnesses to disaster, a flower of fire opening itself to the street and pouring a shower of flashing blades from its yellow heart, every one clutched tight in the blue-black claw of a monster.

They leaped through the broken window with hell-shrieks splitting their throats. Tony saw Sylv jump between him and the window, throw herself at him, arms spread wide, crucified against a background of bright blades and brighter flames. She was stronger than she looked—the impact of her outstretched arm was enough to take him down, the other one clotheslining Nok-Nok to the ground as well. The first onslaught of metal and glass, flame and uncanny beings with their blood-streaked faces, all passed over their heads, a wave of chaos that curled too high to touch them.

But the wave came to shore. The heat from the burning storefront still pounded against Tony's face as he lay there pinned down by Sylv's arm when he tilted his head back against the pavement and saw, upside-down but clearly, the four noseless, grimacing horrors. They landed with an audible thud of heavy boots on concrete, then whirled around, grinding dust from the sidewalk with the thick nails studding their bootsoles. Flat teeth the color of rancid butter filled their mouths, and they clattered them together in a feral challenge.

Tony didn't wait for another warning; there would be none and he knew it. In one motion he shoved Sylv's arm away, rolled over, and vaulted to his feet. A glance to one side showed him Nok-Nok, the boy rolled up into his little self-shielding ball once more. For an instant, Tony imagined that the kid was glowing, but that was probably just the effect of the burning window behind them. He cast his eyes in the other direction and spied a long, sharp piece of the broken storefront grill lying on the sidewalk. He seized it and couched it like a spear, placing himself squarely in the way of the gray-skinned monsters.

The four charged at once, short knives flailing in their hands. Tony swept his makeshift spear out in a wide arc, and caught the foremost of them in the side of the head. Dark blood starred the creature's skull: Tony'd gotten lucky. There was a heavy bolt still attached to his makeshift weapon, and it worked like a spike impaled in the end of a board.

He didn't get so lucky when he scythed the shaft back the other way, hoping to take out a second creature in the same way on the backswing. He connected, but only a glancing blow. The monster staggered, regained its footing too quickly, and leaped for him, howling. Tony fell to one knee and met the nightmare with an upward stab of the metal shard. His luck was back: The wattled throat looked tough as leather, but it was only skin. The street-salvaged spear went deep, driven deeper by the force of the creature's own death-leap.

Tony dropped the metal pole. It was useless now, weighed down and bent double by the squat, gurgling body impaled on it. He thought he heard human voices above the sound of monsters shrieking for his bones and blood, the voices of ordinary people from the sane world he'd somehow lost. Someone was hollering for the cops, someone else was yelling back that the cops were coming, a woman's voice was whimpering, "My god, my God, why doesn't someone *do* something?" He heard, then he cast them far from his consciousness. There were still two nightmares attacking him, Sylv, Nok-Nok. Let the cops come; he'd rejoice to see them.

The blow came from behind. He felt it at the back of his skull, and a sweet sensation of ease and distance stole over him from the initial pain. His eyes were enveloped by a curtain of darkness, and the last thing he felt before the shadows closed around him was the roughness of sidewalk against his cheek.

5

The first sense he recovered was his sense of smell, or so it seemed to him. If he did open his eyes to reclaim vision first, it was only to a darkness as intense as the one that had overwhelmed him with that blow to the head. Wherever he was now—somewhere cool and silent and a little damp—at least it was on the right side of the grave. Tony didn't have too many beliefs about what really happened to you after you died, but he'd be willing to bet skin and bones that it didn't smell like garlic.

There were plenty of other smells surrounding him as well: The warm aroma of cinnamon, the sharp invasion of black peppercorns, the keen bite of chili, and others to which he couldn't put a name. There was one additional scent that stood apart from the rest, a scent as penetrating and pungent as chili and peppercorns combined, but no kin at all to the sharp perfume of exotic spices. Tony knew it in an instant: Gunpowder. He'd smelled it before, on the subway, in the streets, sometimes even in dreams.

"Where the hell am I?" he muttered to himself. He felt cold stone under him and at his back. He was seated against a wall, and he couldn't move his hands. They were tied behind him with a length of soft, strong cloth, a second set of silken bonds knotted securely around his ankles. Or so he assumed. It was too dark to see whether whatever tiestuff was holding his feet as helpless as his hands was of the same material.

Now that he was fully awake and aware of his situation, he was angry. He kicked his feet, trying to get them loose, nearly wrenched his shoulders from their sockets with his struggles to get free. He could have saved himself the effort: The bonds held tight and true. He tilted his head back and began to shout at the top of his lungs for help. The sound of his own voice came bounding back into his ears from the confines of the black chamber.

And then, after the last echo of his cries had faded, he heard a low, familiar, female voice say, "Hey, pipe down. If you *want* help, stop yowling like a squashed cat. No way I'm getting near enough to let you loose until you shut up, got that? I don't wanna go deaf."

"Child, don't torment him." The second voice was not familiar at all. It was a man's—old, judging by the slight crack and quaver underlying the words. "He has awakened alone in a strange place. Of course he is frightened. Of course he will cry out for help."

"I'm not afraid of you, whoever you are," Tony shot back into the dark. "So don't flatter yourself. Sylv? Sylv, that's you, isn't it? What the hell is this? Why am I all tied up this way? Were you the one who hit me? God damn it, untie me now, you dumb bitch, or—"

"Oh, like *that's* gonna get results, that kind of attitude," came Sylv's sarcastic response. "What's the magic word, Sir Galahad?"

"*Let me go!*"

This time, the silence that rushed back in the wake of Tony's enraged shout lasted so long he thought that Sylv and her unseen companion had gone off and left him alone once more. He sat there, listening to the sound of his own rasping breath for a count of fifty, before he heard a small cough coming from somewhere in the shadows.

"Okay," he said, chastened. "Okay, I'm sorry. I don't know what the hell I'm sorry for, but I am. Is that what you want? Now will you untie me?"

A spark kindled before his eyes, a little fleck of golden light that burned at the bunched tips of a man's gnarled fingers. The light was small, but it was enough to reveal the seamed face of a white-haired Chinese elder. He regarded Tony steadily, his expression both calm and kind.

"We are the ones who should be apologizing to you," he said. "An apology bound to our deepest thanks for what you have done."

"Thanks?" Tony echoed. "For what?"

The old man smiled, and it seemed to add warmth to the light still burning just above his fingertips. "For the life-gift you have preserved and brought to safety. For our return to the realm we desire with all our hearts."

His fingers slowly parted; the flame danced over his outspread palm. Tony stared into the heart of the tiny, leaping fire. It burned gold, then scarlet, then a deep green that charmed his sight with hints of shapes moving within the flame. He felt as if he stood on the edge of a high rooftop, his feet hanging halfway over the abyss, his face turned fully into a warm, entrancing wind that caressed his skin like a woman's hands. The wind carried the breath of a thousand flowers, a sweet perfume that turned to music in his ears, honey and spice under his tongue. He stretched out his arms, suddenly free of their bonds, and reached for the sound, the warmth, the sweetness as he tumbled headfirst into the void.

He fell for what felt like forever. His clothing peeled away from his plummeting body. He wore the wind for a cloak, and he knew without turning his head that he had given birth to wings. Below him, the hard, harsh, pitiless streets of the city melted into a pool of mottled gray that swirled itself around and around, drawing up rich shades of green and blue and sungold from some hidden source. He opened his mouth to nothing but joyous laughter as he plunged into the heart of so much beauty.

The trees lifted up their leafy arms to break his fall and toss him lightly from branch to branch until his bare feet touched the tender moss that grew in their shadow. All around him he heard the sounds of merrymaking, of song and artfully plucked harpstrings, the dainty notes of reed pipes, the rhythmic pulse of hand-held drums and silvery finger-cymbals, the beat of many dancing feet. A goat-flanked and cloven-hoofed creature burst from the underbrush to press a gleaming cup into his hands. It brimmed with amber wine whose fragrance sent his already bewildered senses reeling. He drank it down and knew that he was home.

Then they were all around him. Lithe and slender, small and sturdy, shaped in a hundred different molds, all somehow *right* to his eyes, even if an ordinary human would see some of the more exotic creatures among the throng as grotesques. They were not monsters to Tony; they were kin. They offered him their hands and their welcoming song and their love, drawing him into the brightness that clung to every one of them like a cloud of summer flower-dust.

He drank and danced and snatched a small painted tabor from one of them. He drummed the taut skin with his fingertips, spinning on his toes, feeling the sun's warmth as he'd never done before, sensing how his new shape could drink in heat and light, storing both in the secret places within him. The light throbbed and grew stronger, a core of power, a molten, captive sun that burned deep in his belly and only waited for his word to be set free once more. Tony felt the power, knew it, owned it, and wished he had a voice as loud as the immortal sea so that he could shout his happiness to the ends of the earth.

And in the midst of so much celebration, a voice that was the storm-haunted sea's own dull, blind, destructive power thundered out, but not from him. He heard it and froze in mid-step, his spine turned to ice. Around him, his light-souled kin too seemed turned to stone. Trolls and satyrs, long-limbed elfin lords and fair ladies of the sidhe became the statues in a ravaged garden. The trees of the wonderful woodland shed their leaves, now brown and crisped with frost, in the blast of that hideous voice.

The tree trunks themselves began to spread out like clay shapes crushed by a child's hand, turning to dully striped beige and tan wallpaper. Branches interlaced overhead and smeared into a flat, white-plastered ceiling. Flowers and moss underfoot became the sober pattern of a rug the color of gravel and old blood. Tony's eyes tried to conjure back the magic they had seen, but the sheer banality of this new place stood like a lead shield between him and his heart's lost desire.

Look at me when I'm talking to you!

Tony lifted his eyes and saw the white-haired demon. The monster towered over him, sour breath streaming over Tony's face. *When I call you, you come. Do you hear that, boy? Do you understand? You'd better. When I tell you to do something, you do it. Don't even dream of opposing me; I won't stand for it. I learned my lesson with your mother: It's doing you no favors to go easy on you. Life won't. I erred with her because she was a girl and because her mother interfered. Well, she saw what good that did the child. What a fine match the girl made, oh yes!* His laughter was hoarse and bitter, devoid of joy. *I could almost thank God that she died before she had to see where her foolishness brought our child. Too soft with her, too indulgent, too many excuses, not enough attentions paid to what was the girl's duty in life. Yes, duty! Responsibility! To herself, to us, to her own people! What a fool I raised, what a pretty fool, and another like her to distract me from the proper way to bring up my child. So that this is what I'm left with.*

The demon's contemptuous stare blazed; Tony shuddered with the chill when it set its teeth into him. The demon paced the carpet, strong hands knotted behind its back, scarcely taking its cold blue gaze from Tony's face for an instant. *This,* the demon repeated. *A mongrel brat, just as squint-eyed and ugly as your precious father, who didn't have the financial sense even to buy a decent life insurance policy. What in heaven's name was your mother thinking of, lying to me, saying she had enough money to support the two of you after he died? Idiot girl. What was she trying to prove?* The demon shook his head and kept pacing.

And what did she prove, at last? he went on, while Tony edged away until he felt the backs of his bare knees bump into the hard wooden seat of a black chair. His small fingers curled around the spindles at its back as he placed it between himself and the ranting demon.

What did she prove? the demon repeated. *That she didn't have the skills or the talent or the endurance to make it on her own in the world. I could have told her that. I did tell her precisely that more than once, for her own good. What use are fantasies? The world doesn't deal in dreams. Didn't she realize that she was too soft to put any muscle*

PLAYING WITH FIRE   619

behind her grand words? Oh, I offered her help! No one can say I don't know my duty, even if my child never knew hers. She turned it down. She said—she dared to say to my face that she'd sooner die than accept my terms. Terms! As if to accept my help meant she'd lost some sort of war. Ridiculous! It's only the purest luck that those worthless friends of hers knew where to contact me when she died or you'd be in an institution right now. I can't say that wouldn't be better for me, but it wouldn't look right. Too many people know you exist; they'd talk, the busybodies. Well, I won't give them anything to flap their jaws over. They'll never be able to say that I've neglected my only grandchild. As for you—

The demon stopped pacing and came near. Tony crouched behind the black chair, goggling out at him through the wooden bars. The demon seized the chair and flung it across the room with one hand, leaving Tony quivering, unprotected. No more of that nonsense, came the command. You're young, but you ought to realize how much I'm going to do for you. You would, if you had half a brain. Hmph. Unfortunately, you look about as intelligent as your father, which isn't saying much. Still, even a dog knows enough to be grateful for food and shelter. Hmm…

The demon pressed pale fingers to its thin lips in an attitude of deep contemplation as it squatted before the terrified child and peered at him closely. Your eyes aren't too bad after all. Not so narrow as they might be, not completely hopeless. You could almost present yourself as Mediterranean, not that that's any great improvement. Perhaps in time—well, never mind that. You might pass, but I'm not wasting my hopes on the future. For the time being, it will be enough for me if you can follow a few simple rules. Behave well, do as you're told, and we'll make the best of an unfortunate situation. All right, Anthony?

Tony opened his mouth, but nothing came out. The demon's scowl deepened. I asked you a civil question. I expect a civil answer. Now, if you please.

A—all—all ri—Tony's voice trembled. He tried to get the words out, but he couldn't Every fiber of his being, flesh and voice and spirit, only wanted to find a snug, safe, well-concealed nest into which he might crawl and hide until the demon lost interest in him and moved on to other prey.

The demon's hand slapped his cheek sharply. It was not a heavy blow, but it stung. Tears dewed Tony's eyes. The demon smiled. All right.

Tony had no idea how the dagger came into his hand. He thrust it upward without thinking. The blade shimmered silver-bright, then fountained up into a spray of sparks that flayed the skin form the demon's smirking face, burned everything away but the grinning skull and the mocking, pale blue eyes. Tony dropped the dagger and screamed.

"Quiet, please," said the old Chinese man, laying a hand on Tony's shoulder. "You will scare the child." He nodded to one side and automatically Tony's glance followed that gesture.

Under a scroll of shiny red paper painted with large gold characters, Nok-Nok sat in an elaborately carved wooden chair, munching his way through a bowl of lichee nuts. Sylv stood at his side. She was trying to take the bowl away from him, mumbling something about how too many would ruin his appetite for dinner. There was something funny about hearing that kind of Mom-talk coming out of someone like Sylv. If Tony weren't so confused, he would have laughed out loud.

Confusion was a word that didn't even come close to describing how he felt just then. The cellar where he'd been held prisoner had vanished, along with the silk bonds immobilizing him hand and foot and the vision that had surprised him there. Now he was seated on the edge of a bed covered with a dark blue satin quilt. The old man stood to his right, offering him water in a plain glass tumbler as if nothing at all extraordinary had occurred.

"Welcome back," he said. "Drink. You have been privileged with visions. We hope you will share them with us, but we don't expect you to do so with a dry throat."

Tony took the water and drank it in silence, then handed back the empty glass and said, "I'm crazy, right? That's all this can mean. The monsters, the fight, the cellar, all that weird shit I saw, I—"

"What did you see?" The old man leaned close. He looked eager, hungry, his eyes fixed on Tony's lips as they formed each word of his reply.

"I—" Tony shook his head. "I'm not sure. I was in the cellar and then—"

Sylv giggled. "Gotcha. There never was any cellar. You were here all the time, in Master Lung's bedroom."

"Huh?"

"You will forgive her," the old man said in his low, level voice. "Sylv is still very young, overly proud of every small spell she masters, as the young tend to be. Once she commands an illusion, she tends to behave as if she were the first ever to discover it. If you had had all your wits about you, I don't think she would have claimed as much success. She told me how easily you saw through her other glamours." He eyed her coolly until she looked away, sullen as a thwarted child.

"It was a good one anyhow," she mumbled.

"So it was," the old man reassured her, all forgiven. "And who knows? It might still have deceived him had I not struck him that blow."

"You?" Tony gaped at the elder. "You're the one who hit me from behind?"

"Regrettable." Brown hands spread themselves wide accepting blame. "But necessary. Sylv had sent word ahead to me that she had found the child and was bringing him back to our safekeeping."

"The child? You mean Nok-Nok?"

The old man nodded. "She also let me know that they were being followed. I did not know she meant you. I summoned certain others, then went out to meet her."

"Yeah, when I called Master Lung, I thought you were the only one on our tail," Sylv said. "Who the hell knew about those redcaps? Jeez, I hate surprises." Her teeth flashed; she had lipstick on them again.

"By the time I reached her and the child, they had attacked. I marked you at once for a fine warrior, but I had no way of telling whether you were also a discerning one. When our allies joined the fight, would you be able to tell them from our enemies? I could not know this, and I could not risk having you harm any of them. Thus I had no choice but to remove you from the battle."

"Oh." Tony rubbed the back of his head tenderly. "What did you use, a chunk of cement?"

"Fire," Master Lung replied, as if it were the most normal answer in the world to give. "Flame shaped to the seeming of…ah…I think it was a walking stick, but weighted in such a way that—"

"Yeah, right, you don't have to tell me how it was weighted." Tony called up a sheepish grin. "Man, you get a crack in the head like that, you see plenty of wild stuff. That cellar—more like a dungeon, you know?—and then I'm out of there and I'm falling into a forest. Wow! *Forest*, sure, that doesn't even come close to describing it. It was like—" His eyes grew distant, chasing the sweetsight that had escaped them. "—like the most glorious place I ever saw, something right out of my *good* dreams. And believe me, I don't have too many of those."

"Dreams, yes," the old man mused. "As you say. That place your vision brought you is the substance from which all common dreams derive. Our sleeping minds can only grasp feebly at the flimsiest images that haunt its borderlands. It is the source of the true beauty, the pure magic. It is our home, that place we call the Dreaming."

"Uh…huh." Tony's eyes shifted left and right, checking the exits. Surreptitiously he placed one hand over the other and pinched, hard. The pain made him wince.

The old man saw and smiled indulgently. "No, you are not mad. Nor are we. You are chosen. You are blessed. You are one of us." He indicated Sylv and Nok-Nok. The boy wore his usual smile of mindless contentment. Sylv's grin had more bite to it; she was enjoying seeing Tony so at sea.

"Great," Tony growled. "One of you. There's a bargain."

The old man was momentarily perplexed. "I thought you would be glad to know it. Sylv tells me that your life is hardly one of comfort. If you join us—"

"Join what?" Tony snapped. "Join who? A bunch of loony toons?" He sprang from the bed. "Look, I did you a favor with the kid, you can do me one: Just let me the hell out of here and we're even."

The old man looked deeply troubled at Tony's angry words. He turned to Sylv and asked, "You did not tell him? You did not explain?"

The girl shrugged. "When? It's kind of hard to explain stuff when you're fighting a bunch of redcaps, Master Lung. I was going to tell him how he's ours, but those bloodthirsty bastards didn't even give me the chance to get his name."

"My name is Tony." His eyes narrowed to slivers of jade. "Tony Lee, okay? And I'm not yours."

The old man gave a shallow sigh. "I'm afraid you misunderstand. Sylv means that you are ours by belonging, not by possession."

"I'm not," Tony insisted. "I don't know what you're talking about, I don't know what's been happening to me, but what I do know is that I'm no one's, not by belonging, not by possession, not by any craziness you're gonna spout at me, *no one's*, got that?"

"Tony Lee," the old man said, and his voice became a thing of power, a sound that entered into Tony's skin and placed a bridle under his tongue, compelling his silence and attention. "Tony Lee, an infant newborn into the world cries loudly, too. They say he does this because he feels cold or knows empty space around him instead of his mother's womb, but this is not so. He cries because he must accept the world, and it is strange, frightening. Still he *must* accept it, whether he wants to or not. He has no choice. Neither do you. By the vision of the Dreaming that is yours, you can not deny it. You are one of us, Tony Lee. You are a Changeling."

"A *what?*"

Sylv rolled her eyes. Taking the lichee bowl—now empty—from Nok-Nok's unresisting hands, she slipped her small body between Tony and the old man. "Let me, Master Lung," she said, then thrust the pale green dish right into Tony's face.

The porcelain hemisphere turned inside-out on itself, becoming a hideous serpent mask, fangs dripping black, smoking venom. Tony cried out and fell back onto the bed. The serpent poured itself out of the distended bowl, a never-ending stream of solidly scale-armored muscle, and slithered at will over his body, hissing. Arms sprouted from naked shoulders that humped themselves out of the serpent's body, red-tipped fingers stroked Tony's cheeks as the creature's fanged maw shrank into a milk-skinned woman's face. She kissed Tony loudly on the mouth, snickered, and vanished. He was lying on the blue satin quilt with a small green porcelain bowl balanced on his chest.

"Booga-booga," said Sylv, looking down at him. "*Not* something I learned at P.S. 269." She casually dropped a penny into the empty bowl. "So, *now* can we talk this through without you freaking every two seconds?"

"S-sure." Tony sat up slowly, holding the bowl to his chest. "Why not? Changeling, huh?" He slid the penny out of the bowl and flipped it. It came up heads. "Any money in that?"

6

"Hey, Master Lung, you maybe got a fork or something?" Tony turned on the charm bigtime, flicking the chopsticks away from his dinner plate.

The old man picked them up and put them back in one of the drawers in the tiny kitchen, then brought Tony a white plastic fork, all without saying a word.

Across the Formica tabletop, Sylv was rolling her eyes again. She seemed to give them a lot of exercise that way, especially whenever Tony opened his mouth. He was getting pretty sick and tired of it; it was no prize to be treated like everything he said was the last word in stupidity.

"Hey, I'm tired, I'm hungry, and I don't know how to use them, okay?" he rounded on her, stabbing a piece of celery. "What, you maybe think I was *born* with a pair of chopsticks in my hand?"

"No," she replied with aggravating coolness. "Up your nose, maybe. Don't be so sensitive. Did I say anything? Did I say one little word? Wow, you must think the world revolves around you. News flash: It doesn't."

"Children, please…" Master Lung brought a bowl of soft noodles to the table and resumed his own seat, between Tony and Sylv, across from Nok-Nok. "We have much to discuss. We shouldn't bicker."

"Like what?"

"Who's bickering?"

Tony and Sylv spoke in unison, then looked at each other and laughed. Nok-Nok cocked his head and joined in, though it was plain that he had no idea what was so funny.

The old man placed his hands on the tabletop. "First, we should discuss your new living arrangements, Tony."

"*New* living arrangements?"

"Sure." Sylv cut in as if it were the most obvious thing in the world. "I mean, you can't live at my place—I hardly had room for Nok-Nok—and I bet your place isn't much bigger. Nok-Nok told me how you had him sleeping on the couch, not even a fold-out couch, and if you don't think it was rough finding all that out with knock-knock jokes—"

"Wait a minute, wait a minute!" Tony put up his hands, fending off the sudden assault on his life. "Slow down, okay? First you tell me I'm a Changeling—"

"In a way, it was you who told us," said Master Lung.

"Right, right, whatever. And what *she* tells me—" he pointed the plastic fork at Sylv "—is that we don't really belong here, we don't even wanna *be* here—"

"This is New York City," Sylv said. "No one wants to be here. Except tourists."

"Funny. Ha-ha."

She smiled at him. "It's a gift. Look, what's so hard to understand? No, we don't belong here. Where we oughta be—where we need to be—is our true home, Arcadia, the Dreaming. Hey, you saw. You know what it's like there and you sure as hell know what it's like here. Where's the big problem? Try telling me you wouldn't switch this dump for all that in a heartbeat!"

"Sure, I would…if I could be sure—"

"—that it was real?" she finished for him. "Since when is reality such a bargain? Come on, Tony-boy, come off it. What kinda favors has reality done for you lately?"

"Okay, fine, I give." He took another forkful of food and chewed it moodily. "I guess if we do reach Arcadia, that'll be proof enough for me. But what I don't get is how *he's* supposed to get us there." He pointed at Nok-Nok, who had picked up a strand of lo mein and was now lowering the noodle into his mouth like a cartoon baby bird dealing with an outsized worm. "How's *he* supposed to find the way back to Arcadia? Half the time he acts like he couldn't find his own ass using both hands and a road map."

"Once more, the fact itself must prove the reality behind it," said Master Lung. "Nok-Nok is not what he appears to be—"

"Oh, *big* surprise there," Tony interrupted.

The old man merely gave him a calm look that was enough to elicit a shamefaced apology for such rudeness. "We are none of us the twins of our seemings," Master Lung continued. "But Nok-Nok's true self has been even farther removed from the shell you see here. You see, he is an eshu—"

"Gesundheit," Tony said under his breath. He thought he'd spoken too softly to be heard, but he quickly learned otherwise when Sylv slumped way down in her chair to stomp his foot under the table.

"You wanna stop being an asshole for maybe two minutes?" she inquired pleasantly. "Or are you afraid you might actually learn something?"

"Sylv, you are too harsh with him," Master Lung said. "This is all new to him, and the new is frightening, especially to the young. I myself was unable to accept my Changeling nature when it was first revealed to me because the thought of being so…other…was beyond my ability to comprehend. In time I adjusted, accepted, embraced it; so will he. We must be patient."

"As stone." Sylv's smile twisted into something nasty. "Which is what I'm gonna pick up and use on him if he doesn't learn some respect for the kithain."

"Try it," Tony said without raising his voice.

"Children, children…" The old man shook his head in bemusement. "How can he respect what he does not know? In the best of worlds, you or I would take him into keeping and teach him by slow steps all that there is for him to know of the kithain, our many peoples, and of the Sundering, the Shattering, the Concord, all the many faces and facets of Banality and the Dreaming. But this time and this necessity forbid it. So we must make do with the time we have."

He turned to Tony. "You have lived all your young life so far in a cold world, haven't you? I see its mark on you, body and spirit. Will you deny this?"

"What's to deny?" Tony lifted another forkful of food to his mouth, then set it back down on the plate, untasted. "Yeah, I guess you could say it's sucked so far. My parents are dead. My grandfather—look, I can't afford a shrink, okay? Skip the psychodrama. If there's something I need to know so Miss America over there will stop kicking the crap out of my shins, tell me already."

"And I love you, too, candyass," Sylv replied sweetly.

Master Lung overlooked the exchange of barbs. "Although your life in the world of banality has been…less than satisfactory, still it gives you the means to understand the new life which has opened to you. Just as there are many races of humanity, so there are various kiths of the fae, both here and in the Dreaming."

"Yeah, Baskin and Robbins got nothing on us," Sylv said, reaching across the table to nab Tony's half-eaten spring roll. With her mouth full she asked, "You weren't gonna eat that, were you?"

"I get it," Tony said. "I think. So you've got a lot of different kinds of Changelings and an eshu's one of them and Nok-Nok's one of the eshu."

"Very good!" The old man was clearly pleased to find such a quick pupil. "The eshu are our wanderers, our explorers, our seekers, our great tale-tellers."

"And they never ask directions," Sylv put in.

"Was that how Nok-Nok managed to find me at work after I left him shut up in my apartment?" Tony asked. "Because he can just find his way, wherever he wants to go?"

"That, in some measure," Master Lung agreed. "That and the bond which you have forged with him."

"Trust me, it wasn't my idea."

"Yours or Fate's, it no longer matters. As I said, Nok-Nok was not always as you see him. I remember the first time we met, some few years ago, when Sylv was just a fledge as you are now."

"A what?"

"New kid on the block," Sylv supplied. "Wet behind the pointed ears, if you've got 'em."

"He didn't call himself Nok-Nok then," the old man said. "If he had a name, he didn't choose to share it with me. He put me off in a most charming manner—they are all people of great charm, the eshu—and was otherwise polite. You see, he was one who had awakened to his Changeling nature quite early in his mortal life, and became a childling when he was little more than a toddler. He developed rapidly; for a time, in certain circles, the talk was all about how precocious he was. He suffered little interference form his mortal kin. Like you, he had lost his parents, and his surviving sister was not—did not—" The old man hesitated.

"She was a whore." Sylv had no trouble with hard realities. "A junkie whore. She never gave two shits about the kid. Good thing he found out who he really was so soon and joined the kithain, or who in hell knows what he'd be now." She gave Nok-Nok a once-over glance. "Not that he's anything to write home about at the moment."

"Sylv, I counsel you to practice curbing your impetuous nature," Master Lung said. "I believe you will profit from that."

Sylv bowed her head. "Yes, Master Lung."

"So Nok-Nok was a nine days' wonder, huh?" Tony rested his chin on his hand and studied the boy. "What went wrong?"

"The purpose of all Changeling life is to find again what is lost, to regain the home that is our only true refuge."

"You mean that place I saw? Arcadia?"

"Some say it is impossible," the old man said. "That at the time of the Shattering, all gateways to that paradise were irrevocably destroyed. But even this world, bound in the cold iron of banality, is greater and stranger than we can ever know. How can we claim to know its limits, or even if it has limits, when we scarcely know our own? We gather glamour to us and use its power to hold fast to the Dreaming, but where is it written that someday—somewhere we have not yet discovered—we may not find the one surviving gateway that our glamour will open wide? And what lies beyond the great gate...that is our ultimate reward."

Tony stared at the old man. As he spoke, his simple words worked their own spell of transformation. Years lifted from him, touching his face with radiance. The things he spoke of—glamour, the gateways, the Sundering—still sounded like so much gabble to Tony's practical mind and yet, listening to Master Lung, he felt his heart begin to believe.

"Of course there's a couple of folks out there who'd disagree." Sylv's flippant tone broke Master Lung's spell. "Just a redcap or two or twenty-one, and as many again of the other kithain who've thrown in their lot with the Unseelie court, just for grins. Master Lung can talk the birds out of the trees, can't he? But that doesn't work worth dick when you're trying to persuade a motley whose motto is *Screw Arcadia, Everybody Party!*" She chuckled.

"Sylv..." For the first time, Tony heard a severe note of warning creep into the old man's voice.

"Sorry," she said hastily. "But it *is* the truth. We're not gonna do him any favors by sugar-coating it, are we? If he's the guardian, he's gotta know what he's up against." She pointed one finger at Tony, the nail chewed down to the quick and covered with a dirty plastic bandage. "You've already met some of the Unseelie, but they don't all look like that. Sometimes you can't tell them from us."

"Us?" Tony repeated.

"The Seelie. The good guys. We'd all wear white hats, but it costs too much to get them fixed so they'll fit over the satyrs' horns." She gave him a searching look. "You *are* one of the good guys? You better be, or your ass is grass and *I* am the lawnmower."

"I'm shaking," Tony said dryly.

"Please, Sylv, that tongue of yours will end by undoing everything your hands have accomplished," Master Lung said. "Don't question his alliance. Hasn't he proved the mettle of his spirit before this, by how he looked after the boy? And that was before he had any knowledge of the reward awaiting him and us. Some don't need to take an oath of loyalty to the Seelie Court. Their soul already stands bondsman for their deeds. Further words are only a formality."

"Plus I look stupid in a white hat," Tony remarked.

"You don't need a white hat to—"

"*Sylv.*" The old man prevented the girl from finishing that thought.

"What'd poor little Nok-Nok do to piss off the Unseelie?" Tony asked. He remembered the black dog and the dark auto whose mysterious passengers had almost succeeded in luring the boy to who knew what fate. "Kids that smart, real teacher's pets, sometimes they show off, don't know any better, shoot their mouths off—"

"He found it." For a change, Sylv didn't make her words into a dare. "He found the way back. Now they want him dead."

At the sound of those words, Nok-Nok turned his beautiful face to her, his lower lip quivering. A small moan slipped from his mouth and there were tears ready to be shed. Master Lung pushed himself up from the table in a brusque fury so unexpected that the effect was all the more shocking.

"Before you speak your mind again, girl, make sure you have a mind to speak!" he shouted. "Don't you ever think of consequences? Do you remember nothing but your eternal revels? *This* was why he ran from us before, *this* was why we nearly lost him forever, because he overheard you speaking about him and his peril in just this way to your worthless friends."

"Don't you call them worthless!" Sylv blushed almost as red as her hair, but she thrust her shame down and turned it into a hot, self-justifying outburst instead. "Magloire and Deni know how to round up more glamour in a night than you could scrape together in a year!"

"That is because I have some scruples concerning my sources," the old man replied, composure restored.

"Anyway, how do you know that was what made him run away? Who knows *why* he does anything any more? He's nuts! Don't blame me for that, I wasn't the one who cast the fugue cantrip on him. He brought *that* on himself." She looked to Tony for justice. "You heard what Master Lung said about Nok-Nok: He was incredible, fearless, sharp as a diamond sword. He walked paths other eshu didn't dare to dream of. And one day he found the hiding place of the sluagh, Lavena Dubh."

"So?" Tony shrugged. "This is supposed to impress me?"

"Well, it would if you knew the sluagh," Sylv replied.

"The underfolk," Master Lung said, and his voice, normally soft-spoken, dropped almost to a whisper. "They live in the dark places, hidden, secretive by any measure. They dwell far from sight, far from contact with other kithain."

"And don't think we're not grateful, considering what they think of as a good time had by all," Sylv declared. An involuntary shudder ran over her small form. "Ugh! Slimy buggers. Home sweet sewer, y'know? Only the sewer's too good for some of the stuff they get up to. Just thinking about them gives me the three-night creeps."

"I share your opinion of the sluagh," said the old man. "Yet as distasteful as most of them are, there are some among them who have used their reclusive life to good purposes. They find pearls among the filth, gems of knowledge that may benefit us all. The sluagh called Lavena Dubh is rumored to be one such gatherer of wisdom. Indeed, her store of knowledge is said to be so great that we long thought she was only a legend, that she didn't exist at all. And if by some faint chance she did, that it would be impossible to find her lair and return unharmed."

"Nok-Nok didn't know the meaning of 'impossible'," Sylv said. She regarded the boy, who was presently holding one of his chopsticks between his teeth and trying to balance the other one across it. "Now he doesn't know the meaning of any damn thing."

"Did she do this to him?" Tony asked. He felt an unwarranted stirring in his gut, an unsought desire to find the sluagh himself and give her a few hard lessons on how *not* to treat an innocent guest.

"He wouldn't be here at all, if that were the case. The sluagh are thorough, when they take a dislike to someone," Master Lung answered. "I've told you that the eshu are famous for their charm, and this child possessed the power to charm eshu far older than himself...once. To charm the sluagh was not beyond his powers. He returned from his quest to the underland alive and well, and spun fine tales about his adventures before the whole royal court of the sidhe."

"No one believed him," Sylv said. "'Found Lavena Dubh?' they said. 'The Lavena Dubh? As if!' That made him mad. Never, *never* say 'Bullshit' to an eshu's face. They don't like it. If he'd been older, there would've been blood. The way it was, with his just having come to be a wilding, he got his shorts in a knot and said he'd prove that what he said was true. He announced that Lavena Dubh had given him a gift in exchange for favors rendered, a secret out of her hoard of information. He promised that he'd demonstrate it at any time and place his doubters chose, so they took him up on it." She let her chin drop into her cupped hands. "When he showed up at the place and time they picked, he was like this. I oughta know: I was one of the crowd who wanted to see his proof. Sometimes I get the feeling this was my fault."

"You are blameless, Sylv; you were not the only one to doubt his word. He was foolish to make such a promise," Master Lung said sadly. "Even the wisest among us can play the fool. Youth is full of pride and he harked more to his wounded pride than to wisdom. If he had not been provoked and doubted in open court, he might have thought better of speaking of his gift so freely. Not all ears are friendly ears, and the same words we mean for our allies alone can also reach our foes."

"What happened to him?" Tony asked. "He get ambushed? Hit in the head? Brain-damaged? Did the Unseelie steal the gift? What?"

"They could not steal this gift." The old man began to clear away the remnants of their meal. "As Sylv has told you, it was knowledge, a secret, the most priceless lore of all: The secret of our return. If ever we are to win our way back to Arcadia, it will be through our powers, and the source of those powers is glamour."

"*Not* what you're thinking." Sylv's head snapped up before Tony could open his mouth. "Glamour *is* our power. It's what lets us work magic, turn things around, shape reality to what it *oughta* be. So no cracks about supermodels or you're—"

"Right. Grass. Lawnmower," Tony said affably. Sylv just grumbled and let her head drop back into her hands.

"Think of glamour as energy, if that will make it easier for you." Master Lung stood with his back to the small chipped and pitted sink where he had stacked the dishes. He took down a box of wooden safety matches from the shelf above the drainboard, pulled one out and held it so that Tony could see the red and white-tipped head. "There is potential power here, in this tiny bud, a power that can reshape lives for good, for ill, forever. And there is power in me to summon it, to control it up to a point."

He struck the match. It flamed up, blue and yellow, until he extinguished it with a breath. "Now the power is spent, gone. My own power to summon it is useless; what is there left to summon?"

"There's always the rest of the box," Tony said.

"And when that is gone?" Master Lung waved away Tony's answer before it came. "I know, I know, then you'll tell me to buy another box of matches."

"Yeah, if I were half as stupid as *she* thinks I am." Tony pretended not to notice when Sylv stuck out her tongue at him. "My guess is, Nok-Nok's secret was something to do with how you guys could get your hands on the whole goddam match factory."

"Or better yet, it's like one day you're pumping gas and the next you're the sheik of Saudi Arabia. Ta-daaa!" Sylv jumped up, doing a lively imitation of Nixon's two-handed V-for-victory pose. Tony and Master Lung just looked at her until she subsided. "What, he's the only one can do a good analogy?" she challenged. "We don't just get glamour as easy as buying a box of matches. We gotta *work* for it; work damn hard, too! That's one thing mortals are good for: They can call it into themselves, hold it, create it, and they never know what they've got. Which leaves us to help ourselves to theirs…by strictly non-violent and benevolent means, of course." She sounded like a child reciting a well-learned lesson.

"Uh-huh." Tony tilted his chair back. "Tell me, Sylv: Are you an eshu?"

"No."

"Oh good. That means it's okay to say this to your face: Bullshit."

Master Lung's hand fell on Tony's shoulder and squeezed just enough to get his attention. His apparent age never hinted at how strong his grip could be. "You don't always need to have a barb at the end of your tongue. She's telling you the truth. This too is a gift. Show your true self to be wise enough to listen attentively. Wisdom will save your life more times than swagger."

"Yeah, I said *we* don't ravage mortals for their glamour," Sylv chimed in. "*We* as in the Seelie fae. The Unseelie do whatever it takes. Jerks."

"And as she says, it is hard work, to gather glamour from mortals." Master Lung gently took the chopsticks away from Nok-Nok and put them in the sink with the rest of the dirty dishes. "I myself find it more than difficult. I often wonder that I have enough glamour to perform some small feats of magic. But then, glamour can come from within as well, from art, from beauty, from the miracle of creation in all its guises. I am, in my humble way, master of a certain art. Perhaps it provides me with glamour enough for my wants."

"Not every Changeling's an artist," Sylv said. "Not everyone can look inside and call up their own personal source of glamour. If you can do that, it's what we call rapture. From what I hear, there's nothing like it, *nothing*. The rush, the blast, the—!" Her eyes were far away, chasing a dream of ecstasy, but she soon came back to earth. "Rapture," she repeated. "All the glamour you could ever want, all the glamour you could ever need, and all of it coming from right inside yourself. Even enough to break through the walls and reach Arcadia. Even enough for that."

Tony realized that he had become so entranced by Sylv's words that he'd almost forgotten to breathe. Revelation touched him lightly. He looked at Nok-Nok. The kid had both hands knotted to the edge of the vinyl tablecover and gave every indication that he was about to try the old yank-the-tablecloth-leave-the-stuff-standing trick. He reached over and persuaded the boy to let go before he asked, "*That's* the secret he brought back?"

Sylv nodded. "Rapture. How to master that skill so well that you'll never need to take what you can make. Freedom. And *that's* what pissed off the Unseelie."

"The Unseelie preach freedom," the old man said, "when what they mean is license. Because they've turned their backs on the Dreaming, they resent those who embrace it. They think of themselves as emperors over the rest of us, fae and mortal. What is an emperor without lesser beings to rule? What emperor would willingly allow his subjects, vassals, and chattels to escape his command?"

"So the Unseelie hit him with a cantrip that locked the secret far away, deep in his own mind," Sylv said. "It was one hell of a strong spell; it locked up any knowledge even faintly connected with the sluagh's gift. That included knowing himself, I guess." She patted Nok-Nok's hand and gave him a smile. He smiled back, seized the tablecloth, and yanked hard. The few dishes and glasses left crashed to the floor. Nok-Nok applauded his trick merrily.

"They did a good job," Tony said.

"Not good enough to satisfy them," said Master Lung. "Otherwise, why have the Unseelie taken a fresh interest in the child? They must have decided that half measures are uncertain."

"That's why they want him de—" Sylv stopped herself just in time.

"That's too bad," Tony said. He got up from the table and pushed his chair in. "No, really, it's a damn shame."

Sylv looked at him suspiciously. "Is it my imagination or do you sound just like one of those shiny, happy, uptown types, when they see some homeless dude hunched up on the sidewalk? And they do a little gasp and they say, "Oh wow, isn't just that a *pity*," and they cross the street real fast so they don't have to even touch the same air."

"I'm not—"

"You're gonna bug out on us, aren't you?" Sylv was up, knuckles on the table, sharp little chin outthrust. "You're gonna run like a bunny."

"I don't run," Tony replied. "But I don't stay for stuff that doesn't concern me either. This isn't my problem, I can't get the kid's memory back for him. What the hell do you expect me to do about it? I've got troubles of my own, mostly thanks to you. I need to find a new job, for one thing. I've got my own life to worry about: Rent to pay, groceries to buy, food to—"

Sylv's laugh was hoarse and brittle. "Says *you* it's not your problem! Haven't you been listening? You're one of *us*. You don't belong in this world any more than I do. You wanna waste your life piddling around in the dirt, pulling a nine-to-five, getting old, getting ugly, waiting for it to get better when you know it never will? That what you want when you know what you could have instead? *Magic*, Tony! All the power you need to make the world over so it suits you. Never age, never stop shining, don't just exist but really *live*!" She pressed her fists to her bosom, her eyes begging him to share her dream.

Tony brushed it all aside. "I make my own life. I get my own choices. You make it sound like I don't have any left, just because you say I'm a Changeling. I've been thinking about that: You *say* I'm one of you. You *say* my vision proves it. Then you tell me you've got magic. What's to stop you from using your magic to give me that vision? Neat trick. The number one rule of any good con game is first you let the mark think he's gonna win big, then you milk him dry. No thanks. Count me out."

"Listen, you lousy—"

Master Lung intervened before Sylv could launch into her uncensored opinion of Tony's personality. "You're right, of course," he said. "Such a thing is possible. You have only our word for it that we would never take part in such chicanery to win you over. But what is our word to you when you barely know us?"

"Ha!" Tony licked his forefinger and scored one for himself on the invisible tote board between himself and Sylv.

"Ha yourself," she countered. "Right or wrong, it doesn't change jack: You're in. You don't have a choice. You lost any choice you ever had the minute Nok-Nok took a shine to you. Don't you get it, stupid? He's *yours*. He's attached to you. That's how come he was able to track you this morning. He can track you anywhere, now, and there's not one damn thing you can do about it. Walk out of here and he walks with you, Mary and her little lamb."

"Shit." Tony turned from her, focused on Nok-Nok, tapped him on the shoulder. "Hey kid, what she said—it doesn't have to be that way. You're safe now. You're with friends, family, kith—kith—" He struggled to recall the alien word.

"Kithain," Master Lung provided.

"Right. I can't take care of you like they can. I don't *want* to. I gotta work, support myself, take care of *me*. I *don't* have anyone else like you do. Stay here. Maybe sometime I'll come back and visit, okay? See ya." He gave the boy one final pat on the back and started for the door.

He heard Nok-Nok's faithful footsteps behind him almost at once and turned so abruptly that the boy walked into him. "Knock, knock." That same bright, empty smile.

"Knock, knock, my butt. Go *back*," Tony commanded, pointing at the kitchen chair the boy had abandoned.

"*Knock, knock!*" He refused to be put off.

Tony could have insisted, but he'd learned how to recognize a losing battle. "Okay, okay, who's there?"

"Keith."

"Keith who?"

"Keith-ain and brother, hold thou fast; the champion to strive at last in flame and fire and glamour's glow, a dragon's claw of blood on snow." He hugged Tony close and whispered in his ear, "Burma-Shave," then went back to his place while Sylv rocked with laughter.

"I *said* he was nuts," she announced when she recovered herself. "Close your mouth, Tony, you'll swallow flies."

"What the hell—?"

"An augury," said Master Lung. "A sight of what will come, or may come, or perhaps it is only the product of his poor, scrambled mind. It's difficult to say."

"In other words, stay tuned," Sylv told him, draping one arm over his shoulders. "The *keith-ain* part's clear enough, anyhow. He's not about to let you go. Now you look like a practical kinda guy, Tony Lee; let's talk practicalities. You don't wanna get involved with us, not unless there's something in it for you. Am I right?"

"Yeah." Tony felt a little embarrassed to admit it.

"Okay, swell, this is New York, it's understandable. Well, there's plenty in it for you. For one thing, your life. Walk out of here and Nok-Nok follows. There's nothing you can do to stop him, unless you want to do the Unseelie's work for 'em. And speaking of the Unseelie, you know what they've got in mind for the kid. If they make their move and you're right there, you just gonna stand by and let them?"

"N—"

She didn't give him the chance to reply. "I don't think so. Not you. That's not who you are. And even if you were the kind to try to beat feet, it wouldn't help. They've seen you with him, they know there's a bond between you, but they don't know how deep it goes. If Nok-Nok can't get at his memories, who's to say you're not some bigtime seer with glamour enough to dig 'em out and tuck 'em away into your own mind?"

"That's not true! That's impossible!"

"Not true, right." Sylv ticked off Tony's objections on her fingers. "Impossible? The Unseelie don't know that, and they're not gonna waste time debating it. They don't *do* subtle. Chop off someone's head or run a knife through his guts and it takes care of *all* the possibilities. Plus, if they see you hanging with Nok-Nok, they might just whack you for grins. They're funny that way."

"I don't like this," Tony said. "No choice, that's what you keep telling me, no choice at all and I hate—"

"Save Nok-Nok's skin and you save your own; what's to choose?" Sylv shrugged, an imp in leather.

"There is strength in numbers," Master Lung said. "We two are not the only ones concerned for this child's safety. While he lives, the chance exists that the spell on him may be broken and the knowledge he possesses may be restored and shared. Many other kithain long for this, and will stand watch with you. You won't be alone. They will become your family, Tony, you'll want for nothing."

"They'll cover my rent?"

"I think that in the circumstances it might be better if you and the boy were to live here, with me," said Master Lung. "Most of our allies—our motley—have their own places nearby."

"Where's here?" Tony asked. "I wasn't exactly paying attention when you brought me in."

"We are about a block from Canal Street. I have four rooms behind my store. You will have privacy and comfort, I promise you."

"Canal Street...Chinatown?" Tony saw the old man nod. "Figures. Man, granddad would shit a brick if he could see me now. Not just owning up, *wallowing* in—ah, what the hell. The old bastard's dead too. Too bad; this would've killed him."

"Then you agree?"

It was Tony's turn to shrug. "Like Sylv said, who's got a choice? Okay."

Master Lung frowned slightly. "I hope you will join with us willingly, not solely because you see it as your only path. There is more to your new life than the duty to protect this child."

"Sure, like I'm also protecting *me*."

"Wrong." Sylv arm shifted, tightened playfully around his neck in a mock choke-hold. She had to go up on tip-toe to reach him. "Like there are also some really serious fringe benefits."

"Like what?"

"You wanna find out?" Her eyes sparkled. "Come out, Tony Lee. Come on out and play."

7

"Well, well, look what the cat dragged in," Magloire drawled, leaning back against the silver-spangled vinyl of the booth. All around him the usual Friday night crowd at Chrysalis danced and smoked and played their games, Changeling and mortal, and tried to forget that the hideous monster of banality whose name was Sunday Afternoon was coming after them in less than forty-eight hours' time.

"Didn't," said a small, sulky, black-and-white kitten at his elbow. The creature was up to its eyebrows in a dish of cream, but it reluctantly spared a moment's attention to give to the two newcomers.

"Hello, Sonnet," Tony said, sliding into the booth next to the kitten. Sonnet was one of the first Changelings to whom Sylv had introduced him when he'd first agreed to move in with Master Lung, a pooka wilding with a temper almost as sharp as her claws.

"Hiya, Mags." Sylv slipped in on the other side of the strange couple, pushing her slight body right up against the tall, hawk-faced young man.

"I told you not to call me that," he said, shoving her away. "Ugh, you're all wet."

"It's snowing out."

"Again?" His arched nostrils flared in distaste.

"Yes, *again*. It'll do that in January, if you give it half a chance," she teased. "If you don't like it, why don't you do something about it? I always thought you satyrs had Nature in your back pocket."

"When we *have* back pockets. There isn't enough glamour in this world to banish winter and you know it." Magloire adjusted the fit of his suit jacket, pure Armani, perfectly cut, fabulous. "Unless we've had a breakthrough with the boy?" His finely shaped auburn eyebrows rose.

"Status quo," Tony said.

"Status couldn't get any more quo if it tried," Sylv added. She leaned against Magloire deliberately, leaving the marks of melted snowflakes on his jacket.

He put her off again, more firmly. "*Some* people wear coats over their street clothes when it snows, Sylvia."

"*Sylv*, goddammit!" She whirled around and tried to give him an elbow-jab to the upper arm. He saw it coming, and despite being penned into the booth's semicircular seat, he was able to avoid the blow and even laugh about it to her face. She seethed, made a fist, and swung at him. His hand—large and covered with a thick coat of reddish hair—closed on it, rendering her helpless.

In his grip, her captive hand began to glow a cool green, but beyond that nothing happened. The two of them sat with eyes locked, hers full of rage, his full of mocking mirth, until the green faded and died. Only then did he let her go.

"You see, love? I'm not the only one who cares about folk taking liberties with how they pronounce my name. Do as you would be done by. A little courtesy goes a long way. I know what an effort it takes for you nockers to mind your manners, but still—"

ESTHER M. FRIESNER

"Yeah, about what it takes for you satyrs to keep it in your pants," Sylv shot back.

"Mmmm. I'm not remembering any complaints." Magloire threw his head back and bellowed with laughter. "But oh, what I *am* remembering!" He pounded on the table. A waiter dressed in skintight black and silver came hurrying over.

"Yes, sir?"

"No, nothing I—wait, on second thought, we'll have champagne, Teddy," Magloire said between gasps for breath. "Two bottles of the best. We're toasting old times."

The waiter regarded Tony, Sylv and Sonnet quizzically. "I, uh, I need to see some proof of age. For them."

The kitten arched its back and hissed. "I am Sonnet the pooka and I am three hundred and seventeen years old last Tuesday. Bring us the fucking champagne!"

The waiter acted as if Sonnet had said nothing at all out of the ordinary, as if he carded kittens all the time, and abrasive ones at that. Tony knew the truth of the situation, though: As long as the Changelings willed it so, the waiter wouldn't hear or see anything bizarre about them at all. As far as the mortal was concerned, his customers were all normal-looking young people, except for Magloire, who was teetering on the brink of his thirties. That was glamour in action, weaving delusion, tweaking the edges of reality, turning things like here and now, truth and certainty, into toys.

That's what I'll be able to do, someday, Tony thought, and he didn't know whether the pang he felt was eagerness for the power or fear of it.

The waiter reached out and took nothing from the air, then held it near his eyes under the club's wildly strobing multicolored lights. Apparently what he'd heard, instead of the pooka's angry tirade, was a polite young woman offering to cooperate fully, and what he saw was her graciously proffered ID "Thanks," he said, handing the emptiness back to Sonnet. "That's fine. Sorry I gotta be a drag about it. Club policy." He went through the same pantomime business with what were, to his eyes, Sylv's and Tony's IDs. Sylv cupped a hand over her mouth to smother an onslaught of giggles; Tony just fidgeted. "Cool," he told them at last. "Okay, well, enjoy."

"Dink," said the kitten to his retreating back.

"You really shouldn't abuse mortals so, darling." Magloire stroked the kitten's silky fur. "That one you just insulted? Teddy? He's an aspiring sculptor. I've spoken with him about the possibility of my buying one of his pieces. You should've seen how he reacted to that! Nearly wet himself, I swear. I've got an appointment to visit his apartment—poor whelp can't afford studio space—and see what he's got."

"As if I couldn't guess what you'll come away with," the kitten purred.

"You couldn't," Magloire replied. "Now if it were my sister, you *could* guess. Deni is so predictable. She'd help herself ever so gently to some of that boy's glamour and be done with it. The trouble with you pookas is you talk big, but you're really conservatives at heart."

"We are not!" Sonnet spat and lashed out at Magloire with one paw, claws bared.

The satyr only inclined his head slightly and a ribbon of white light tied itself in a fluffy bow around Sonnet's neck. The pooka in kitten form puffed out its fur, shattering the ribbon which became a very localized shower of raindrops that left the little animal bedraggled and soaked to the skin. Magloire roared his appreciation of his own jest. Sonnet growled.

Sylv reached into her small black leather shoulderbag and pulled out a funny-looking white tube. It glowed a pale red at one end, and when she brought it near Sonnet, the pooka's fur dried instantly. "Ignore him," she advised while her device did its work. "He thinks he's a real comedian."

"Don't blame me. It's the sad consequence of having one of Sonnet's fellow-pookas for my sister," Magloire said, gracious and congenial. "Dear Sonnet, you and your kith set such store by clever pranks that I find it impossible not to be drawn into the fun."

"Note the word 'clever'," Sylv said, stowing the tube back in her purse.

"I do. And what could be more clever than what I have in store for our friend Teddy? Not just a simple siphoning of glamour—the lowliest redcap could do as much—but a nurturing of his art, for future reference. I plan to go to his apartment, ooh and aah over his work, and offer to set him up in the studio he so covets. From there on, whatever glamour attends his talent will be mine."

"What if he hasn't got any talent?" Tony asked. "What if his stuff's no good?"

The satyr smiled. "My, my. I see that the months Master Lung's spent teaching you haven't been wasted. That was an *intelligent* question. If his work is good, his glamour will feed me. If his work is worthless, I'll still set him up in a studio, use my influence to hype him, turn him into an art-world *name* for all the pretty people to admire and adore. You know what will happen then?"

"As if you'd shut up if we said *yes*," Sylv muttered.

She was right; Magloire liked an audience. Whether or not they were willing to hear him out was immaterial: He simply assumed that they and the rest of the world with them were dying to hear what he had to say about any matter. "Then, my friends, he will attract others: Aspiring artists who will come trailing after him like puppies, their little pink tongues lolling from their mouths, hoping to lap up just a little of the secret of his success for themselves. They think it's contagious, you know. My toy doesn't need to have talent as long as he has fame, because his fame will be the bait to lure in more than enough mortals who *will* have the glamour I need."

Just then, the waiter returned with their order. He was a nice-looking young man, black hair in a braid down his back. Magloire favored him with an electric smile and murmured, "Next Saturday, Teddy. Don't forget." The waiter blushed. The satyr let him escape before snickering at his back.

Tony watched Magloire enjoying himself and wished he still had his old job and the iron fishhook that went with it. He knew that he'd really enjoy watching the satyr squirm at sight of that curving claw of cold iron.

Problem, smart guy, Tony's practical side prompted. *You'd squirm too.* It was true: Since his Changeling nature had manifested, even the thought of cold iron filled him with queasiness. He couldn't go back to old job at the fish market if he tried. He sipped the champagne Magloire passed him and twisted a few nasty thoughts around his mind, most of them scenarios involving the satyr.

"Do you like it?" Magloire's question took Tony off guard.

"Huh?"

"The champagne. Is it to your taste? Dry enough? Not too flinty, I hope. The proper year? I wouldn't want to offend an educated palate like yours, you know."

He was taunting him again. Tony was used to that. It was only Magloire's way, or so the others said. The satyr had a tendency to mock and tease and harry almost everyone who fell into his company, then to back off as soon as he hit a nerve. When that happened, his fulsome claims of innocence were a treat to hear. He could take phrases as simple and empty as *But you* must *excuse me, it was all in fun, I* never *meant to hurt your feelings*, and weave them into a breathtaking work of art, a snow job *par excellence*. Tony couldn't remember the last time one of Magloire's victims had refused to forgive the ingratiating fae.

Tony had made the decision to quit being anybody's victim a long time ago.

"Oh no, it's just fine." Tony's eyes sparkled over the rim of the glass. Nothing annoyed the satyr more than having a sally miss the mark. Tony had learned that lesson early on in his acquaintance with Magloire, and unlike Sylv and a lot of other Changelings in their motley he was able to field all of the satyr's verbal jabs without rising to the bait. "Good choice, Magsie," he added casually.

Correction: There *was* one thing the satyr hated more than having a sally miss the mark, and that was having a mark that shot back. Tony grinned. *Yeah, Magsie, maybe now you'll get the message to lay off of me. And you can lay off Sylv while you're at it!* The thought wasn't an iron fishhook, but it was comforting.

"That...was discourteous," Magloire said, his lips pressed so tightly together it was a wonder any sound could escape them. "I'm surprised. I expected that a man with Master Lung's reputation for wisdom would have the wit to knock the worst of the rough edges off you by now. Clearly he doesn't mean to bring you before the court any time soon. Or perhaps he's already taken your measure and reached a practical decision, in which case his reputation for wisdom's more than well-deserved. You know what they say about silk purses and pig parts."

Tony's stomach churned with resentment, but he held it down. *Don't let the bastard see he's touched you. Don't give him the satisfaction.* "Oh, I'm sorry. You mean you took that *seriously?* Just a slip of the tongue, Mag—Magloire." Tony hadn't used his phony smile for a long time, but he trotted it out now and made sure Magloire would know it was phony just by looking at it. "Gee, I sure hope you don't think I was deliberately trying to get your goat."

Sonnet laughed so hard she fell off the table and reverted to human form. Magloire rose to his feet, a scowl like a thunderhead darkening his brow.

"Okay, you've had enough," Sylv announced, latching onto Tony's arm and dragging him out of the booth. "Sorry, gangies, but someone I could mention can't hold his liquor worth shit. C'mon, Tony, time to go home." She towed him out of Chrysalis so fast that he stumbled several times trying to match her pace.

On the snowy sidewalk outside, she shoved him against a parked car just opposite the club waiting line, to the curious stares of the terminally bored wannabes hoping for admission. Even the troll who was playing bouncer that night tilted his huge head in their direction, happy for the diversion.

"You *idiot!*" Sylv shouted in his face. Someone behind the black velvet ropes cheered. The nocker glared at the crowd and gave everyone the finger, on principle, before lighting back into Tony. "Where the hell's your brain? Master Lung smother it with all that damn incense he's always burning? Jeez, didn't he teach you *anything?*"

"*Now* what did I do wrong?" Tony grumped.

"Wait, I'll make a list. You mean you don't know?"

"So I pissed off Magloire. Big deal. If he can't take it, he shouldn't—"

"—dish it out?" she finished for him. "Spoken like someone who hasn't got a clue. If you'd ever seen Magloire really dish it out, you'd be in there right now, down on your knees begging his pardon and swearing fealty to him if he promises not to kick your sorry ass into the next millennium. What, you think the only reason the rest of us let him talk trash to us is because we believe that Gosh-I-didn't-mean-it-*so*-sorry crap he spews afterwards? Ha!"

"Oh, I see," Tony said dryly. "It's because you're all scared spitless of him. *Much* more honorable."

"Who are you to talk to me of honor?" Sylv's voice dropped to the range that meant danger. "How many oaths have you sworn? How many members of our motley have you let get close enough to feel that you're their true brother and not just a goddam tourist?"

"Maybe I don't want any of them for my brothers."

"Maybe you don't deserve brothers. Maybe you don't know how to belong to a family at all."

Tony opened his mouth to reply, then shut it with a snap, thrust his hands deep in his pockets and stalked off down the street. His shoes stuck a harsh rhythm from the icy pavement as he marched along, head pulled deep into the collar of his jacket. He covered three blocks before the hurt softened enough for him slow down and hark for the sound of Sylv's footsteps following him.

Nothing.

He stopped in front of the show window of a record store and looked behind him.

Nobody. Nothing but the thin curtain of falling snow. Sylv hadn't followed him; she'd simply let him go.

The hour was late, the street nearly deserted. There were no clubs on this block of the Village to attract anyone, only shops locked up, waiting for the next day's business. Tony was alone. He could always go back to Chrysalis—the door-troll knew him and would let him jump the line with no problem. Sonnet at least would be glad to see him. He'd noticed the come-on looks that the kitten-pooka had been giving him the last few times Sylv had brought him to party at the club. Trouble was, he didn't feel the same way about her. Once upon a time, that wouldn't have stopped him. He'd have gone along for the ride, the laughs, the pleasure, letting her passion be enough to carry the two of them. Now—

Now he couldn't take a step without hearing a voice in his ear, the serene voice of Master Lung. Master Lung would never come right out and call it wrong for Tony to take what Sonnet offered and give nothing in return. Master Lung would merely let it be known that such actions were unworthy. Somehow, over the course of Tony's stay, he had come to care about Master Lung's opinion very much. Five months, and every day of those five months with its lesson. Not all the lessons had been about things as simple and as complex as right and wrong. At first the old man had limited himself to answering Tony's questions about the Changeling life, opening his eyes to the world-within-a-world that was now his place on earth.

You must learn as much as you can, Master Lung had said. *Every fool on our side is a sword in the hands of the Unseelie. Ignorance is bliss only if your idea of bliss is being run over by a subway train.*

And Tony had laughed and said that Master Lung sure didn't sound like the white folks' idea of an Oriental sage, spouting fortune cookie wisdom-bites or doing bad David Carradine imitations from old *Kung-Fu* re-runs.

But I like Kung-Fu *re-runs,* Master Lung had protested.

Lessons...Some of them sank in, some had to be pounded through Tony's skull, some kept sliding off and no amount of pounding would make them take hold.

The man who knows how to wait will live to overcome the man who merely knows how to fight. Give your enemy knowledge and you give him the battle. Keep your secrets and you keep your skin.

Tony pressed his face against the cold glass of the record store window. "What *didn't* I give that goat-assed jerk Magloire?" he whispered to the night. "Time after time, letting him know I can give as good as I get from him. What'd I accomplish? Sure, maybe he'll quit teasing me in front of Sylv and everyone, but that doesn't mean he'll leave me alone. Now he knows what *doesn't* work on me, he'll just go digging for something that *does.* I should've kept my mouth shut. I should've left it alone, pretended he could hurt me just by talking shit. He'd be happy and I'd be safe. He won't just let this go, pat me on the back and say 'Good show, old sport, well played,' like he was one of those Monty Python twits. Sylv's right. Goddam it, Sylv's *right.*" He cursed under his breath—cursed Magloire, cursed himself—and strode on until he reached the subway that took him home.

The car he got on was empty except for a trio of couples, friends who sat close together, enjoying each other's company. They spared Tony one appraising glance when he invaded their warm little kingdom—the New Yorker's patented once-over compounded of equal parts suspicion and distaste, with a pinch of fear to be added if necessary—then ignored him. He sat down as far from them as he could, hunched forward, and stared at the floor of the car as if he could read fortunes in the rivulets of melted snow swirling through the tracked-in grime.

Stupid, stupid, stupid! Every rattle of the car shook his bones with another blow of the lash he wielded against himself. *Once, just once, how about you* think *before you open your mouth? She was only trying to help you! Why'd you have to provoke her like that? Yeah, she's right: Magloire's got enough power to flay your skinny ass and you know it. Why hasn't he done it yet? Who the hell knows? Honor, maybe.*

You're still an infant, in their world. No glory for squashing a flea. But if the flea gets to be too big a pest—stupid, stupid, stupid! At least a flea's got a brain.

A bell chimed. Tony looked up just as the doors opened at his stop. He could feel the relief of the other passengers when he jumped off the car.

Chinatown on a Friday night was lively, if you knew where to look, deadly if you didn't know where to go. Tony knew both and avoided both tonight. He walked the streets with just the right air of strength, direction, and determination that sent all but the most desperate muggers looking for more vulnerable prey. When he got to Master Lung's store with its dusty display of tourist-trap crap in the barred window, he already had his door key out and ready. He let himself in by the side-door, flicked on the yellow-shaded bulb in the entryway, and sealed the door with chain and deadbolt and tumbler lock behind him.

"You're home early." Master Lung stepped out of the first doorway off the hall, taking him by surprise. The old man wore a black robe with a high collar, styled like the cheap, gaudy jackets he sold in the shop but made of rich matte silk where the others were too-shiny rayon. It was what he wore from the time he closed the shop until he retired to his bed. Every evening Tony had seen him make a ritual of it, shutting up shop, counting the day's receipts, donning the robe, making a pot of strong tea as black as the silk wrapping his slender body. When the old man turned to bend over the teapot, the kitchen light always conjured up the gleaming image of a dragon embroidered across the back of the robe. The beast, like the robe itself, was pure black silk, more a shadow than a design.

If Master Lung still wore the black dragon robe at this hour, it meant that he had not yet gone to sleep.

"You didn't have to wait up for me," Tony said, looking away from the old man as if he were a kid caught stealing candy.

"Why do you assume that that is why I am still awake?" Master Lung asked, his voice kind. "At this time of year I always have more than enough tasks to keep me up. There's no time to do them during business hours, and they must be done." He stepped into the hall and walked towards the back of the building where the kitchen was. "Come. I'd like a cup of tea. As long as you're up too, you can make it this time."

Master Lung's home consisted of four small rooms plus a bathroom and a kitchen. One entered the living quarters one of two ways: Either through the long hall that began at the street door beside the shop entrance, the way Tony had just come in, or directly through the shop itself. A door at the back of Master Lung's emporium opened onto a stockroom which doubled as the old man's pantry. The quarters themselves, including the long hallway, curved around the shop like a lover's arm embracing the beloved.

Master Lung's kitchen always smelled of good things. As Tony got down the old white teapot, its creamy sides made beautiful by painted boughs heavy with oranges, he breathed in the scents of many spices, the particular tang of smoked duck, and the lees of the joss stick that had just burned itself out in the sand pot before the Kitchen God's shrine. When the kettle on the stove began to whistle strongly, Tony poured boiling water over the carefully measured tea leaves in the pot, releasing a fresh perfume into the air.

The two men sat at one end of the kitchen table. The other end was a clutter of thin papers, red envelopes starred with gold and black Chinese characters, bamboo brushes, ink sticks and an inkstone. Master Lung took pains to put these as far out of the way as possible before pouring out the tea into two perfectly round cups.

They drank in silence, enjoying the warmth of the dark liquid trickling into their bellies, letting its heat comfort their hands through the cups' thin skins before they sipped it down. While he drank, Tony's eyes strayed over the jumble of objects at the far end of the table. Master Lung must have noted his wandering eyes, for the old man said, "You could still help me with some of them. The brush-strokes are not difficult to master if you set yourself to learn them. You'd only have to do simple ones, I promise."

Before Tony could say anything, the old man set down his teacup and bustled over to snatch up brush, paper, ink and inkstone. He ground out just a little of the chunky black stick in the inkstone's well, then added water, drop by drop, until he was satisfied with the consistency of the liquid at the tip of his brush. The bamboo danced lightly over the slip of plain white paper before him and characters bloomed like flowers.

"There," he said with some satisfaction. "Liu Lung Ming, my name, the name my father gave me and taught me how to write as soon as my hands could hold the brush. And then, when I had mastered that, he taught me to do this:" Again the bamboo brush danced, and beneath its finely pointed bristles a tiny dragon writhed across the bottom of the page. It had been birthed by only five minuscule strokes of the brush, yet it contained a wonderful lifelike quality, as if it were only waiting for the word from Master Lung to step out of myth and into reality.

The old man smiled and set aside his brush to reach for a covered porcelain dish no bigger around than a plum. He removed the lid, revealing a dab of much-used pasty red ink, then dipped his right hand into the left sleeve of his robe and withdrew a small oblong of greenish-brown soapstone surmounted at one end by a carved dragon. He dabbed the opposite end of it into the red paste rapidly. When he stamped it against the paper, it left a clean impression of stylized characters compressed into a square.

Tony studied these, then ventured: "Isn't this the same as that?" He pointed to Master Lung's own brushwork of his full, true name.

The question pleased the old man visibly. "Yes, yes, exactly. This—" He pressed the soapstone stamp into Tony's reluctant grasp "—is my chop. Very handy; I use it on most contracts and business papers. But surely you've seen such marks before?" He gestured at the scrolls that decorated the kitchen walls. Some were just red paper with gold and black characters set inside elaborately flowered borders, but some were brush-and-ink landscapes, mountains that seemed to have been pinched into existence by a playful god, rivers that dreamed through peaceful countrysides. On each of these there were also painted characters and the red mark of the artist's chop, his signature.

"Uh…I guess." Tony shrugged and handed the chop back to Master Lung.

"I would like to have one carved for you," the old man said.

"No, no thanks, don't bother. I mean, why? It's not like I'm gonna use it, and it's not like the guy's gonna be able to do it, the guy who carves 'em. There's no way he could spell Anthony Edward Lee in Chinese letters, right?" Tony tried to brush the offer aside with a winning smile.

It worked about as effectively as his phony one. Master Lung's face closed. "You know that these are called *characters*, not letters. Each carries its own meaning, not merely a single sound. You know it because I taught it to you long ago, almost on the day you first moved in, and I know that you are not a stupid man. Why do you persist in pretending that you are?"

"Hey, so I forgot, so sue me. I only remember stuff I care about. All this, it's nothing to me, no offense. I mean, I know you're getting ready for New Year's, making all these signs, taking care of business, but it's *your* New Year, not mine. I had mine two weeks ago and it's over." He made a big show of wincing and holding his head. "Except maybe the hangover part."

For a moment, Master Lung looked ready to scold him for his flippancy. But if that were so, the old man possessed more self-control than Tony had ever seen in any human being. Master Lung's scowl dissolved, swallowed up by an unreadable expression, placid as the light of the full moon.

"If no offense was intended, I take none," he said. "You will forgive me: it's plain to see that our mortal forms spring from the same culture, one for which I have an old man's fondness and pride, as well as a certain measure of admiration for the many beautiful things it has given to the world. I assumed that because you share my mortal form, you would also share my enthusiasms. Of course you're under no obligation to do so, and it is my fault alone for jumping to conclusions."

Master Lung's apology hit Tony harder than any tongue-lashing would have done. He hastened to set his teacher at ease. "Look, I'm not saying there's anything *wrong* with all this Chinese stuff, I'm just saying it's not for me. I'm not interested."

"I see." The old man inclined his head. "And your parents? Did they feel as you do?"

"Yes," Tony said quickly. Then, on reflection: "No. I don't know, maybe. My mom wasn't Chinese, just my dad, and I don't know how Chinese he was."

"You mean he too came of mixed blood?"

"Oh no, he was full Chinese. One time I overheard him and my mom talking about his family and how all of them weren't too thrilled about him marrying her because they thought he should stick with Chinese girls. They were in their room, sitting on the bed with a newspaper spread out between them. Dad was crying." Tony gazed off into that far-gone time. "That's funny: I think I was maybe only four years old, but I *remember* he was crying. Mom was holding him and saying something like 'Let it go, babe, let it go. The least you should do is call and find out if it's them or some other family,' and he had the tears rolling down his cheeks but he was saying, 'No, I won't call anyone. All these years, did any of them try to call us? Not even when the boy was born. They saw the birth notice—my brothers read the English papers even if my father likes to pretend he won't—

ESTHER M. FRIESNER

they could've made *some* effort.' And then my mom said, 'Well, it's a moot point now.' Those were her exact words. I know, because I remember wondering what a moot point was, but when I went into their room to ask them, Mom picked me up and took me out, closed the door behind her and said that Daddy needed to be alone. I could hear him crying and crying—"

"Did you ever learn why?" Master Lung asked in his gentle way.

Tony shook his head. "So anyway, no, Dad wasn't much for Chinese stuff either." *Which didn't stop Grandpa from acting like Dad spent his life sucking up rice and hauling a rickshaw,* came the bitter afterthought. *Damn, I wish I'd known Master Lung when I was still living with the old hardass in Jersey. I'd've sopped up as much of this act as I could, just to break that sarcastic bastard's stones. Always down on me, always acting like my looks were a worse shame to him than if I'd been a junkie, a thief, a killer. Hey, old man, you don't like it that your blue-eyed baby girl had a slant-eyed baby boy? Well, tough shit!* His mind howled defiance into a cavern where only ghosts dwelled.

"Interesting," Master Lung said. He finished his tea.

"I could make you another pot, if you want," Tony offered. He was feeling worse and worse for the way he'd brushed off the old man's wishes.

"Thank you, but no. However—" Master Lung stood up "—after you clear these things and put them away, we can have a lesson that you *do* like."

"Now?" Tony couldn't keep the eagerness out of his expression. If he were a puppy, his tail would have been wagging wildly. "It's not too late for—?"

"How late it will be when we begin depends on how quickly you can clean the kitchen. We must use the time we have wisely. You know very well that we'll have no chance for our studies tomorrow."

"That's right." Saturday was a heavy traffic day in Master Lung's store. Even in winter, tourists packed the streets of Chinatown thickly then, and still more thickly as the New Year celebrations came on. Stores and streets bloomed with seasonal decorations, and gawkers from Brooklyn to Berlin jostled elbows trying to get it all down in snapshot form.

Tony hadn't told the whole truth, and Master Lung knew it: there was one aspect of Chinese New Year that he loved with all his heart, and the promised lesson was part of it. He established a new land speed record for dishwashing and was ready to follow his teacher in ten minutes flat.

"Very good," said Master Lung. "And now, I just want to check and see that all is well before we go to work."

"Good idea," Tony agreed.

They walked back down the long hall where three doors waited. Master Lung silently opened the middle one and peered inside. Standing behind him, Tony looked over the old man's shoulder, straining to see into the darkness by the meager spill of the hallway light. The room itself was very small, almost a closet. It had no windows, only an old-fashioned transom over the door for ventilation. It held a bed, a chair, and a rickety old wooden filing cabinet that did double duty as nightstand and chest of drawers. A tall, slender form lay breathing peacefully under the blanket on the bed, though the pillow had been tossed out in the course of some vivid dream. Clothes littered the floor. Tony heard the old man click his tongue over the clutter.

"Tomorrow morning I will try one more time to teach him the value of putting his things away. It's not as if the boy has so much: one change of clothing and a week's supply of underwear is all I could afford to give him."

"Maybe if you tried doing it as a knock-knock joke," Tony suggested.

"Perhaps." Master Lung closed the door. He returned to the kitchen, his pupil trailing after.

They entered the pantry that also served as stockroom. A wooden panel was set into the floor midway between the shelves of groceries and the stacked boxes of paper fans and plastic chopsticks, a thick, square trapdoor right out of some old Hollywood Gothic movie, complete with the heavy metal ring to raise it and reveal the dungeon beneath.

Tony stepped in front of his teacher and pulled the trapdoor open. A gust of cold air hit him between the eyes, making his head throb with the momentary pain of eating ice cream too fast. The air smelled of black powder and burnt matches.

Master Lung flicked a switch on the storeroom wall near the open trapdoor. Light bloomed from below, illuminating a flight of clean, white, decidedly un-Gothic cement stairs complete with a handrail for safety's sake. The two men went down into Master Lung's private kingdom of wonders, shutting the trapdoor after them with a bang.

8

Lion-dogs chased each other around the ceiling, their plumy tails scattering sparks of white and gold and blue. A fisherman whose coat sizzled and spat bright red light cast a lightning-bolt line into water that erupted into a bouquet of blazing peonies. The flowers flew in a dozen different directions, spiraling down on comets' tails, and where they touched the earth, orange trees leaped up, every fruit a dazzling sun that became the face of a plump-cheeked Chinese baby.

Master Lung sat on a high, painted wooden stool, watching one miracle give birth to the next. Judging by his unruffled expression, he appeared to be attending a cherished child's first piano recital rather than standing witness to a visible litany of marvels.

The last spark faded and died. Master Lung got off the stool and crossed the basement to where Tony stood, breathing hard, his hands still aglow. Every one of the sizzling spectacles that had showered the basement room with color and light was an illusion that had sprung from his fingers.

The old man patted him on the arm. "Good, very good. They will look even finer when we translate them to full size and use real fireworks to illuminate your designs. My only criticism is that you might make the lion-dogs' eyes a little more bulbous. Think of them as demon-chasers. They must look very fierce for a job like that."

Tony blew on his hands and a cricket-sized lion-dog with goggling eyes a frog might envy scampered in circles within his cupped palms. "Like that?"

Master Lung studied his pupil's work. "Better." He stroked the miniature beast's fiery head with the tip of one forefinger. It barked furiously at him, then blew out like a match flame. "Much better."

Tony sighed happily. "Wow, my designs out there with yours. To get to see them up against the night—this is gonna be something." His eyes wandered around the basement walls. The tools of Master Lung's true trade and first love bided patiently in their heavy crates. Rockets and Roman candles, pinwheels and poppers and a dozen other kinds of fireworks awaited the day when the old man would take them out and give them the one brief, blazing burst of glory that was their purpose and their life.

His life, too. And mine, Tony thought. He recalled the first time Master Lung had brought him down into this room, about a month after he and Nok-Nok first moved in. He remembered how the old man had shown him a crystal sphere from whose depths Master Lung had called up a vision of the great fireworks displays he had created in years past.

You have talent, the old man had told him while he gazed into the sphere, enraptured by so much beauty. *What you want is an Art to give it form. This is my Art, to hang fire in the sky. It was my chosen Art long before I learned that I, like you, had faerie blood. It was my ancestors' as well, though none of them were of Changeling kind. You have shown yourself to be true to your charge, protecting the boy, attending to your lessons, becoming an accepted member of our motley. Now is the time for you to take on more. I would be honored if I could help you find an Art that you will love as much I love this.*

And Tony could never forget how hungrily he had stared into the captive display under the crystal's curve and answered: *This. This and no other.*

Above his head, Master Lung's souvenir shop with its tacky gewgaws only existed in order to support this Art—their Art—much as Magloire's tame sculptor would flourish in fame only to support the satyr's thirst for glamour. *But we're not hurting anyone to do it,* Tony thought. *We're not messing with their heads or their dreams just so we can shape our own.*

Tony lifted the lid of the nearest crate and looked inside. Safe in their protective packing, the fat white tubes looked innocent as a shipment of paper towels. He knew that elsewhere in this same basement there were other fireworks that looked like the bright red sticks of Acme brand dynamite that the cartoon coyote always employed—badly—to try to catch the roadrunner.

Beep-beep, boom-boom. Yeah, plenty of those, he mused. *Plenty of plain old firecrackers, too, single shot ones, cannon crackers, and double strings of little ones, cluster strands that'll go off like a bowl of atomic Rice Krispies. But I don't care for the noisy ones so much. The ones I love are the ones that hold the fire, hold the light. It'll be like painting the sky.* He reached out his hand to stroke the dreaming fires in their neat rows.

Master Lung's hand closed firmly on his wrist. "Unwise. Look." The old man turned Tony's hand over. A spot of hazy blue light no bigger than a poker chip still glowed in his palm.

"Jesus!" Tony jerked his hand back, away from the fireworks crate, and rubbed it rapidly against his jeans. When he looked at it again, the glow was gone. "I'm sorry, Master Lung, I forgot to turn it off. God, that could've been—"

"Unwise," the old man repeated. "Unwise and unfortunate. These devices—" he waved a hand over the stockpiled fireworks "—are the products of mortal ingenuity, but that doesn't mean they won't respond to a spark of magic as well as to an ordinary match. When you use magic to create the illusion of how your fireworks display will look, you tend to forget that the real thing as well as the illusion may be given life by the touch of glamour."

Tony bowed his head. "Yeah. I almost screwed that up bigtime. Just one spark going off the wrong way down here and—" He shuddered.

"No harm was done, unless you've learned nothing from what nearly happened." The old man patted his arm again and amiably asked, "How do you feel?"

"Dumb."

"No, I mean how are you? You must have expended a lot of energy to show me your designs."

"I guess I am a little tired," Tony admitted, and as if on cue, he yawned and stretched.

"That's to be expected. You're unaccustomed to using so much magic all at once, even though ultimately you benefit from the exercise. The effort is draining, especially for a novice."

Tony didn't like being told that he had limits. "I'm not that tired," he maintained. "And how do you know it's because I've been using magic? I used to end the night with my ass dragging back before I knew I was a Changeling. You know, from the usual mortal stuff like staying up until—say, what time is it, anyway?"

"Early morning, if you count it by the clock; late night, if you calculate it by how long you've been awake."

Tony looked at the old man's smiling face closely. "Can't be all *that* late. *You* still look pretty fresh."

"Ah! Yes, I forgot: I'm old, and so I can't possibly equal your tolerance for long hours and hard work." There was no cruel edge to Master Lung's teasing, unlike Magloire's. "Besides, I had a nap today." He consulted his wristwatch and amended this to: "Yesterday."

"Huh. Sure, that's why I'm tired, not the magic: It's late and I put in a full day's work yesterday. Man, Nok-Nok can be a handful, sometimes. We went to the zoo, did I tell you?"

Master Lung's eyes narrowed. "No, you didn't."

Tony overlooked the old man's suddenly grim expression. "Hey, I'm not surprised. By the time I got him home again, all I wanted to do was forget the day from hell. He kept trying to climb into the empty seal pool. I had to reel him back in by the belt. Then he started a scene in the monkey house. No way I could make him believe that the baboons didn't want to play knock-knock with him. He just stood there yelling 'Knock, knock! Knock, knock!' louder and louder, like tourists figure foreigners can understand English if you turn up the volume high enough." He chuckled. "So after I got him out of *there* and over to the polar bears, he broke away and I had to chase him all the way back to the seal pool again. Finally I took him over to F.A.O. Schwartz and bought him a stuffed seal so he'd calm down." Abruptly he realized that Master Lung was not sharing his amusement. "Is—is something wrong?"

"You took him to the zoo," the old man said, "and you told no one. You took him far from here, far from the range of our motley, far from safety. Did you stop to consider the wisdom of such a choice? Here, in these streets, our allies have been giving their own powers to the weaving of a shield-spell over the boy, to protect him from prying eyes. I told you, Sylv told you, she even had you walk the boundaries so you'd remember where they lie. And you took him all the way uptown, to the park, to the zoo."

"I—" Tony wanted to defend himself, but he groped in vain for any words that would better the situation. Master Lung spoke without anger, only sorrow, which made his accusation stab even deeper. Everything the old man said was true.

I forgot, Tony thought miserably. *The kid was bouncing off the walls. He didn't want to walk around Chinatown again, he knows the place by heart, it's turned into a prison. God, his eyes! Sylv told me how the eshu are wanderers. Try telling someone who's born to roam that he can't cross the street! I couldn't stand to see how he was banging his head against the bars of his cage—even if the cage was invisible—so I forgot on purpose and I let him go free. Just a little. Just so he could live.*

"So we went to the zoo, so what?" he cried. "It's the middle of winter! Who the hell saw us? The place was deserted. Suppose one of the zookeepers *was* kithain, Unseelie, and he recognized Nok-Nok? He'd've made his move right there! It was the perfect set-up for him: no witnesses. Only no one did. Nothing happened. Shit, we're in more danger here in Chinatown! With that hair and those eyes, you think maybe Nok-Nok *blends?*"

Master Lung regarded him in silence for some time after he finished his rant. Then the old man folded his hands and said, "You make a valid point. That's something we failed to consider. Perhaps we ought to look into the wisdom of moving the boy elsewhere, to another home within the motley. You'd go with him, of course." He spoke as if Tony's outburst had fallen into the same abyss of oblivion as the young man's failure of judgment.

"Go?" Tony repeated. His hands went cold. "Both of us?"

"It would have to be. You know why."

"But I don't want to go!" he blurted. "You're my teacher, my master, my—"

"What I can teach you of your Changeling heritage, another can teach as well, elsewhere," Master Lung said. "What I can teach you of this Art—" his hand swept over the hoarded fireworks surrounding them "—I have already taught. You've been a willing student. If I didn't think you were ready to command the Art on your own, I would never even have considered allowing you to add your designs to mine for the New Year's display."

Tony heard the old man's words with a sinking sensation in his belly. It was the same inflowing of forlorn despair that had washed over him in that black hour when he'd first stepped off the bus from Jersey into the hellmouth and knew that he was entirely on his own. In that moment, the fact that it was a path he had chosen willingly—even eagerly—didn't matter. Whether a man leaped from a cliff or was pushed, the void that embraced him was the same. It was the void he remembered.

"But I don't want to go," he repeated in a voice hardly louder than a whisper. "I *won't* go," he said more strongly, looking Master Lung in the eye. "There's no reason for it. No one saw us at the zoo, nothing happened. It was my fault that we left the bounds of the shield-spell, but no harm was done. Can't we let it go? Okay, so Nok-Nok doesn't look like he belongs in this neighborhood: Why don't we just get one of the motley to disguise him? It'd have to be easier than veiling a whole bunch of city blocks. If they need glamour to do it, they can have some of mine."

What there is of it, he thought. His efforts at glamour-reaping had been uneven from the first, unreliable, though he'd acquired much skill at concealing the fact from Sylv and the rest. Sometimes the precious substance seemed to flow into his body unbidden, sometimes his mightiest efforts to draw it in from a passing mortal came to nothing. *Not that I'll admit it to Master Lung.* Aloud he said, "I'll give it freely to protect the kid or I'll use it freely for myself. I'll use it to fight anything you try doing to force me out of here. I gave up everything I had to live here, to help you and the others with him. That doesn't mean you can move me around like a gaming piece. With all due respect, Master Lung, I *won't* be pushed out."

His determination seemed to please his teacher. "Well spoken, Tony. And well considered. It *would* be better to disguise the child than to shield the places where he walks, a kindness to him, an easing of the burden on the members of our motley who sustain the shielding spell. Then there would be no need for you to offer your own resources. You are young, yet. You must hold fast to your own glamour, no matter how loudly your generous spirit urges you to share. You will learn it is all too easy to have the precious stuff of dreams slip through your fingers."

"I can take care of it okay," Tony muttered.

The old man failed to hear him, lost in his own thoughts. "I should be ashamed of myself for not having thought of it earlier. A veil over the child alone, yes. What was I thinking?" He smiled at Tony. "We will go upstairs, rest, sleep, and tomorrow I'll mind the boy again and send you to Sylv. Tell her your idea and say that it has my approval. She'll see to the rest."

Tony bit his lower lip, uneasy at the mention of the nocker's name. "Ummmm, couldn't we maybe reverse that? I could mind the store and watch Nok-Nok, you could go talk to Sylv. She'll listen to you."

The old man got a canny look in his eyes. "There is trouble between you? This is new. Some trouble tonight, perhaps? I thought you came home early. What happened?"

Tony tried to act like it was nothing. "Ahhhh, I shot my mouth off at Magloire. Again. I couldn't help it; he was being an asshole. *Again.* And he was picking on her."

"You didn't think she could defend herself?"

"That's not the point!" Tony smacked his palm for emphasis. "She shouldn't have to. Okay, I'm not that dumb, I know they were lovers. Shit, maybe they still are, for all I know." The words came out steeped in bitterness. "That's all the more reason for him to lay off her. Instead he's got this—this ugly *contempt* for her, for the others, for the whole fucking world! Jeez, the way he treats her sometimes, she might as well be mortal."

Master Lung lowered his eyelids. "Magloire is the eldest living member of our motley," he said. "Not by his years of mortal existence, but old by reckoning the years since he came into his Changeling nature. He knows that he is owed respect, yet this is not the first I've heard of him scorning his mates, neglecting to give them the respect they too deserve. Not even his sister understands him."

"I think he likes being feared more than he likes being respected," Tony said. "I won't do either."

"Magloire is powerful. To defy him is—"

"I know, I know, it's *unwise.*" Tony made a dismissive gesture. "I already know I'm an idiot. Sylv told me that. She's major league pissed at me. If I show up at her place and tell her we're gonna change the game plan and use this great idea *I* had, she'll oppose it just because it came from me. That's why I think you'd better—"

"You don't fear Magloire and all his power, yet you fear Sylv?" Master Lung was puzzled.

"Well, she's got this temper—"

"Most nockers do."

"And she *kicks!*"

Master Lung chuckled. "You've mastered enough glamour to create a fireworks display, but not enough to shield your shins? I can't accept that. Go to her. Apologize for your behavior with Magloire. Promise to be wiser in future, or to avoid him if your can't vouch for your own impulses in his presence. I don't think she'll kick you for any of that." He headed for the stairs, then paused with one foot on the bottom step. "Oh! And one more thing—"

"Yeah?"

"Bring flowers."

They were halfway up the stairs when they heard the screaming. Tony's first impulse was to push Master Lung to one side and race past him, but he never got the chance. The old man could move more quickly than Tony imagined. He was nothing more than a wisp of black silk whisking out of the trapdoor before Tony could catch his breath.

Tony stumbled after him, up the stairs, out the trapdoor, through the kitchen, down the hall. The screams were louder now, screams mixed with howls and sobs and the gurgles of a person being strangled. They came from Nok-Nok's room.

By the time Tony lurched through the door of the little chamber, Master Lung was on his knees beside the bed, trying to hold the boy down. Nok-Nok's arms and legs flailed the air, thrashed against the wall. His head was jerking up and down against the mattress and the headboard indiscriminately, as though one were as soft as the other. His skull made a sickening thunk every time it hit the sharp-edged wooden slab at the head of his little bed.

"Light!" Master Lung gasped from the shadows. "Bring light!" He could do nothing, not reach for the bedside lamp, not hold a flashlight, his hands preoccupied with holding Nok-Nok as still as he could, trying to keep the boy from doing himself more harm.

Tony knew where Master Lung kept his flashlight, but he made no move to bring it. He was needed here, now, not playing scavenger hunt through the wicker baskets in the bottom of the old man's bedroom closet. He brought his hands together so that the cupped fingers formed a hollow ball and let his glamour flow into that reservoir, then tossed empty air at the ceiling.

The air caught fire as it left his hands, a smooth ball of flame that was more glow than heat. It soared to the middle of the ceiling and hung suspended there, bathing the room in light. This done, Tony hastened to Nok-Nok's bedside and threw himself across the boy's thrashing body. Master Lung fell back on his heels, panting, grateful to let Tony take over. The seizure peaked, Nok-Nok lashing out with his feet, his fists, snapping at Tony's braced forearms with foam-flecked teeth. Then he gave a hideous groan, arched his back so sharply he lifted Tony's full weight across his chest, and collapsed into unconsciousness.

Tony remained lying across Nok-Nok's limp body for just long enough to recover his breath, then pushed himself off and looked down at the boy. Nok-Nok's eyes were closed, his mouth agape, a trickle of saliva oozing down his cheek to soak the mattress. His spasms had ripped the sheet off the bed; the blanket was a crumpled lump on the floor. He'd been sleeping in underpants and his Tick T-shirt, the one he'd scrawled with his chosen name. The shirt was torn to rags, so badly shredded it was a miracle that it still clung to his body. Angry red scratch-marks crosshatched the skin beneath.

Tony rubbed his temples. "What the hell happened here?"

Master Lung shook his head. "I don't know." He took the hand Tony offered to help him to his feet, then repeated, "I don't know. I've never seen anything like this, not even when he was first stricken with the fugue cantrip of forgetfulness."

"Want me to call 911?"

"And tell them what?"

"Well, hey, that the kid had a *fit*. That he needs help."

"He does need help, but not from their world. We can't let them take him. You know what it would do to him, if he were to awaken in a hospital. So sterile, so cold, the weight of banality in those places has crushed too many our people before this."

"So what do we do?"

Master Lung took Nok-Nok's wrist gently in his hand and sought the pulse. He leaned over the boy, pulled back one eyelid, and studied what was revealed there. He laid the back of his hand against the boy's skin at several points along his body, then rested the underside of his bared forearm across Nok-Nok's brow before he gave Tony his answer: "First we will cover him. He's cold as ice, clammy.

I have brick that I heat in the stove and use for a bedwarmer, wrapped in flannel. I'll prepare it for him while you go where I tell you to bring help." He started from the room, then looked up at Tony's ball of fire, still glowing from the ceiling. "Will it last long?" he asked.

Tony spread his hands, at a loss. "Got me."

"Then perhaps you ought to move him into your room. The light is better there, and there's more space. The healer will prefer it."

Tony obeyed, scooping up Nok-Nok's insubstantial body in his arms and carrying him one door down the hall. Master Lung had ducked into his own room, leaving Tony to handle on his own the awkward business of getting the boy tucked in. At first he just let him roll on top of the blanket, then studied the situation. Carefully he pulled the ruined T-shirt off and dug up one of his own for the kid. Getting it on Nok-Nok was like playing dress-up with a rag doll, but Tony managed. He'd just pulled the covers over the boy when Master Lung returned.

"Here," the old man said, handing Tony a slip of paper. It was covered with Chinese characters.

"This a joke?"

"That is the sign you will see hanging over the doorway of the shop where you must go. I've written the street address and the cross-street on the back of the paper, but it won't do you much good: There are no numbers on any of the stores on that block. Use the address to get yourself into the vicinity, then match the characters on the paper with the signs. That, or if you should happen to run into another person on the street at this hour, ask for the Wan Sui Herb Shop."

"*Herb* shop?" Tony couldn't bar the skepticism from his voice.

Master Lung ignored it. "We can't get a better healer for the boy than you will find there. Don't worry about the hour: The proprietor is my good friend, very wise. We have both lived long enough to know that disaster doesn't respect one hour more than another. Don't waste time describing our situation—that will be obvious enough once the two of your return—just come back as quickly as you can."

Bewildered by the night's doings and by his lack of sleep, Tony stuffed the paper into his jeans' pocket without question. As he left Master Lung's home, he heard the old man's voice behind him; he was making a telephone call.

I wonder who he's—? Shit, and how come he couldn't just call this whaddyacallit herb shop while he's at it? Why send me? Unless the guy who owns it doesn't have a phone. Sure, no English sign on the place, no phone, probably doesn't even understand English, oh great! Like I'm gonna be able to make him understand what I want once I get there!

Tony strode through the narrow streets, seething. The snow had stopped falling, but there was about an inch of slippery whiteness under his feet. Dawn was coming on, a sliver of pink and gray glimpsed at the intersections of certain streets. It was colder than before. Tony's breath came out in puffs of steam and he wished he'd taken a heavier jacket instead of his old Erasmus Hall High one. The whole situation did nothing to improve his temper. The longer he walked, the more his resentment grew.

And then, on a lonesome street corner, he took a misstep and slipped on the freshly fallen snow. He fell with teeth-jarring impact, a curse on his lips, and sat there filling the new day with a thousand foul words. He got up slowly, one hand to his bruised hip, and felt a lump of spare change in the back pocket. He pulled out a quarter and stared at it, then made his own decision.

"C'mon, Jordan, you know I wouldn't call you at this hour unless it was an emergency," Tony pleaded, leaning against the pay phone. "I'm telling you, I'm not back in the life. The reason you haven't heard from me so long is—well, let me tell you the whole story when I see you. At the store, okay? I'm in Chinatown, I can get there fast. See you soon. Yeah, thanks a lot, I won't forget this. Bye."

They sat in the back room of Wild Things, the one that Jordan Avery had set aside for the gamers to use. The big man tilted his chair back on its rear legs, rested his feet on the table, and said, "Oh good. Sick elves. And here I thought that this was going to be a boring day."

"He's *not* an elf, Jordan," Tony explained for what seemed like the hundredth time. "He's—okay, so he's like an elf, but it's not like that Tolkien stuff you keep pushing on me: this is *real*."

"Let's see…" Jordan held up one big hand and ticked off two points on his fingers. "He's an *elf*, but this is *real*. Oh, come *on*, Tony, quit yanking my chain. You don't look like you're high, and I know you're not crazy. What did you really get me up at this godforsaken hour for?"

Tony clicked his tongue. "Golly, there's just no fooling you, is there, Jordan? You had it right the first time: I'm not only back in the life, this time I got wise and set myself up as a pimp. This kid's become my biggest moneymaker, only he's sick and he's scared that if I take him to the hospital they'll tell him he's HIV positive or something and as long as he doesn't know he is, he can go on pretending he's not. How's that? Now you'll help?"

Jordan brought the chair's front legs back down onto the floor with a heavy thud and leaned across the table. "Son-of-a-bitch," he remarked. "The kid really *is* an elf."

Tony smacked his forehead and rolled his eyes to heaven. "*Now* you believe it? How'd I manage to convince you?"

"It was either you claiming you'd become a pimp or you using the word 'golly' in a sentence."

"If they ever figure out how your mind works—"

"Look, Tony, let's cut the crap. I knew there was something really weird about that kid the first time you came in here with him. Elves, sure, why not? Compared to some of the stuff going down in this city…" He got up and went to make coffee. The back room of Wild Things had a tiny utility sink by the door that led to the alleyway behind the building. The coffeemaker sat on a shelf just above, along with a can of Maxwell House French Roast and several packs of filters. As Jordan went about the preparations, he asked, "When did you find out?"

"Oh, kind of the same time I found out that I was one too." And Tony told him the whole story as quickly as possible. Jordan Avery listened, the coffee pot motionless in one hand, his eyes behind the round spectacles growing wider and more owl-like by the word. Tony finally finished with: "Now I guess you do think I'm crazy, huh?"

Jordan turned away and finished setting up the coffeemaker before he found the words he wanted. "Some of the types I've got coming in here as customers, I'd be happy to have elves instead."

"Not elves: Changelings."

"Swell, whatever." He flicked the ON switch.

"And some of your customers *are*."

"Why did I know you were gonna say that?" Jordan sighed and stared as the first drops of fragrant brown liquid began to trickle into the glass pot.

"Hey, you want I should prove I'm a Changeling?" Tony challenged. "I can do it, no sweat." He brought up his hands, preparing to release a compact fireshow that would convince his old friend beyond doubt.

Jordan only waved him away. "Don't. It's too damn early for this. I've got a new rule: No magic before I've had at least two cups of coffee."

"You're making fun of me."

"I'm not. I'm a businessman. I'm just being practical. The way I see it, there's one of two things happening here: Either you're crazy as a shithouse rat and you'll wave your hands around and swear you made a castle appear, then you'll try to kill me when I say I can't see it, or else you really can do magic and when you show me it's going to make a mess in my store."

"My magic does *not* make a—"

"Hey, Tony, cool down. I'm on your side. You're an elf, you can do magic, I'm gonna take your word for all of it. I'll help you. Only thing I ask is that you answer one question for me."

"Shoot."

"The kid's an elf too, and he's sick, so why come to me? What do I know from sick elves?"

Tony closed his eyes tight, trying to summon up a vision of Master Lung's serene face. If he didn't, he knew he was going to blow up in Jordan's face screaming *Not elves! How the hell many times do I have to tell you?* Changelings, *dammit! Changelings!* Fortunately, he was able to retain self-control, and in a perfectly calm voice he replied, "I came here because I trust you. I thought maybe you'd know someone—a med student, even a failed med student, a nurse, anyone like that—who'd come take a look at the kid and do something for him, no questions asked. We can't take him to the hospital. Master Lung says it'd kill him."

"What does Master Lung say about bringing in some failed med student?" Jordan asked.

"Master Lung doesn't know I'm here. He's thinks I'm bringing back this other old guy who runs a herb shop in Chinatown. Yeah, right: the kid needs medicine, not a salad bar! I figure that if I come back with you and a real doctor, we'll get Nok-Nok taken care of. Master Lung can't argue with results." He grinned, already picturing how well it was all going to turn out.

Jordan Avery shook his head. "Tony, if the old guy sent you after a herbalist, he must know what he's doing. You just told me, the kid's not human, he's—"

"*Meat!*" The back door burst open and crashed into the wall. The first troll strode in, club raised high.

9

"What the hell are you punks doing in my store?" Jordan Avery shouted. "Get out of here!"

The troll only showed its fangs, large and yellow. "Take us to him," it demanded. "Do it and you'll live—" It raised its club high over its horned head "—if you're quick."

Jordan snatched the coffee pot, now full, from the burner and flung the contents in the troll's face. The monster shrieked and dropped his club. Jordan pounced on it before the hulking creature could draw a second breath and brought it down on the back of its neck. The troll went sprawling into the table leg, knocking it on its side. "How's that for quick, you snot-nosed bastard?"

Tony leaped to his feet, sending his chair skidding away behind him. He stared at the stricken troll, then at Jordan, but he didn't have time to utter a word of congratulations. The rear doorway was jammed, full of trolls and redcaps, all shouldering one another roughly as each tried to be the first one in. It would have been comical if not for the fact that it turned horrific each time one of them managed to bull his way into the back room.

"Goddam punks, what is it with you?" Jordan was breathing hard, the downed troll's club raised to meet the next one in.

"Where is he?" a redcap howled, slithering through the press, twin blood-blackened daggers in its hands. "The thrice-cursed eshu, the filthy sluagh's consort, *where*? Your lives for his!"

"What the—?" Jordan didn't—couldn't—comprehend the redcap's demands. Tony realized that his friend wasn't seeing the invasion of the Unseelie as they were, but in their mortal seemings. Otherwise, Jordan couldn't stand there so calmly, ready to fend off monsters. *Punks*, he'd called them; that was probably what he saw. By another kind of magic—a mortal alchemy—Jordan's brain performed a subtle spell on his sense of hearing, translating what the redcap actually said into words that sounded logical. *Eshu* and *sluagh* were gibberish to him, and had no business coming out of the mouth of street trash. What *did* make sense for him to hear was something that would make him reply:

"What, you think I'm stupid? All the cash from yesterday went to the night depository, *hours* ago!"

"Fair warned, then, fool!" The redcap leaped, screaming for blood. The big man caught him right under the jaw, slammed him into the others. "What, I'm fat, so I can't handle a baseball bat? Get out of here while you still got legs!"

Baseball bat—? Tony stared. If the knobbly, spiked length of hardwood Jordan Avery was swinging was a baseball bat, then the World Series would be a lot more interesting this year. *But that's how he sees it,* Tony recalled, gazing at Jordan with a new sense of admiration. Then his mouth went dry as he contemplated the sold wall of writhing, red-eyed minions of the Unseelie court about to surge into *Wild Things.* If he forced himself, he could see them the way Jordan did, make them dwindle in size, becoming a leather-clad mob of gangbangers, scary but human. His eyes ached; he let the vision go.

"Jordan, back off!" he hollered. "There's too many of them. Run, call the cops!"

"Ha!" Jordan took another swing with what he thought was a Louisville slugger. This time he just missed taking off the top of a redcap's head. The thing cackled; a curved knife flashed in its talons. Its gloating was cut off brutally short as the big man brought the bat up in mid-backswing and hammered it straight down on the redcap's forearm. The bones went *crack* and the hideous creature folded in on itself with agony beyond anything even its famed battle-lust could overcome. A tap on the side of the head from Jordan with the butt end of the club and the redcap was out of pain.

"The day I can't clean these cockroaches out of my store—" he was saying, taking his stance for the next comer.

"Jordan, please—"

"You run if you want, kid. But this is *my* turf and I'll be damned if I let these little shits take it over without a fight!"

Tony didn't run, wouldn't run, couldn't. The spectacle of Jordan Avery standing up to a troop of the Unseelie virtually alone held him in place. Even if the big man didn't see them as they were, what he was seeing would have spooked a fainter heart.

Or a smarter one. Run, Jordan! Oh damn it, run! Crazy man, does he want to die? For a fucking comic book store? They've got steel, there's too many of them, and the trolls, so big—jeez, what does he see when he looks at that *one?*

Tony's eyes froze on one troll, so tall and broad-shouldered that the doorway could never accommodate him even had he come alone. Size wasn't his only attribute: he was also deadly practical. He took charge of the squabbling, shoving Unseelie who, up to this point, had been their own worst enemy. A gigantic, ice-blue hand reached out, and by yank and tug and the occasional thump on the head he managed to clear the doorway so that it was no longer a bottleneck, but a breach through which his mates might charge unhindered.

They poured in like the sea. Three trolls assaulted Jordan Avery at once. They jerked the baseball bat from his hands and held him pinioned for a snarling, sneering redcap who held a wave-edged sword. The creature's gaping nasal cavities seemed to flare as its rubbery mouth distended in horrible amusement. It was in the mood for fun; this wouldn't be a quick kill.

Tony took a deep breath and filled his hands with power.

Darts of fire sprang from his fingerbones, serrated shafts that he flung against the trolls holding Jordan helpless. Three pairs of darts found the soft, vulnerable target of eyes, two more dug deep into the redcap's neck. The trolls went down, clawing and their faces, making gurgling sounds of pain that almost moved Tony to pity them.

No. No pity. No mercy. This is war. He felt the fire rising within him, turning his bones molten. Dimly he saw Jordan Avery recover himself and grab his fallen baseball bat back just in time to take advantage of the wounded redcap. This time it was a skullbone that made the sharp cracking sound on impact.

A sister-shape to Jordan's bat molded itself out of the raw fire spouting from Tony's palms. His hands closed around it, a living blaze that now took on an edge, a sword instead of a club. He waded into the thick of battle, where Jordan stood carving out a shallow safety zone around himself with the bat. Tony had never used a sword, but this was not a mortal weapon made of cold, unthinking steel. This was his creation, as much a part of his body and his will as arm or leg, hand or foot. That and more: it held its own intelligence. His hands guided the sword's stroke less often than the sword itself guided his hands.

The fireblade scythed through the ranks of redcaps, filling the air with screams that choked themselves silent on blood. It stabbed at the trolls, opening bellies into gaping red valleys, slashing through boiled leather armor like paper, filling the air with the stench of burning flesh.

And still the monsters came on. From the corner of one eye, Tony saw Jordan knock the coffeemaker into the filled sink, then swat a redcap in after it. Electricity crackled and jolted, harmonizing with yelps of anguish and the weird ululation of battle-cries. Trolls toppled like felled trees and redcaps slashed at the backs of their own comrades in their lust to reach the troublesome mortal and his Changeling friend. A blade snickered in under Tony's guard, scoring his jacket. Another came up just outside his line of sight and left a slash along his cheek. His sword answered both offenses, but they'd served their purpose: two redcaps tumbled, but others saw that there was a way to cheat the firesword and reach its champion. The renewed their attack.

Too many, too many, too many! Tony's heart hammered out a chant of despair even while he fought on, his mind on nothing but saving himself, saving Jordan. The big man was cornered now, a wedge of trolls hiding him from Tony's view. The middlemost one raised its club high, the steel spike at its end glittering.

"Jordan!" Tony's cry was made of pain, loss he couldn't hope to avoid, desperate farewell. He tried to reach the big man, but there were at least four redcaps ranged between them, teeth grinding in anticipation of what must come.

And then a word leaped into the air from somewhere at Tony's back, a word he didn't know, didn't recognize, but that he welcomed with all his heart when he saw how it exploded over the Unseelie with the force of a starburst, fire and power and light. Thunder boomed after it, shaking the walls. The trolls hemming Jordan in turned, trembling, shielding their pale green eyes from the pure, blinding white brilliance that flooded the shabby back room of *Wild Things*. Redcaps hissed and cursed and cringed, dropping their weapons with a clatter as if they had suddenly gone red-hot in their hands. The Unseelie fled, keening, dragging their wounded after them as flakes of flame descended like countless tiny bullwhips across their burning backs.

Tony too dropped his sword, threw up his arms to shield his face from the brightness. The firesword consumed itself to a streak of scorch across the floorboards. As though from far away, he heard Jordan utter one grunt of amazement before he dropped to the ground. The pattering feet of trolls and redcaps retreating up the alley behind *Wild Things* were the only sound left to be heard.

Slowly Tony lowered his arms. A winged blue shadow lay across his sight, the fading after-image of whatever shape the rescuing fire had taken within these walls. He blinked rapidly to clear his vision and the shadow leached away. At his feet the heaped bodies of the redcaps and the trolls that he and Jordan had taken down all resolved themselves into mortal seemings, a pack of gang members who'd bitten off more than they could chew. He knelt in wonder beside the nearest one, a hand resting on the fallen creature's chest.

"Yes, he is still breathing," came a sweet, lilting voice behind him.

Tony looked over one shoulder and saw a delicately made old woman, Chinese, her diminutive body sheathed in a golden, floor-length *cheongsam*, her dark gray hair braided and criss-crossed into a crown. She stood in the doorway between the back room and the main section of *Wild Things*, long, elegant hands resting on the jambs. For an instant, an impossibility flitted through Tony's mind, the thought that this lady looked as if she were another Samson, poised to push the pillars of the doorway apart and bring the whole building down on their heads. The oddest part of it was, he had no doubt that she could do it.

She came forward on silk-slippered feet like little flowers. Her gait was graceful and demure, but not hesitant or shy. Tony found himself rising to his feet unbidden as she neared him. Her face was the wrinkled gold of a dried apricot and her eyes shone when they met his. "None of them are dead," she said. "Does this surprise you?"

"Lady, believe me, I don't think I know the meaning of *surprise* any more." The words flew from Tony's mouth without reflection and he blushed to hear himself speak so forthrightly to this stranger. *Who* she was didn't signify; *what* she was...that was a different story. It would take a fool among fools to deny that the glorious phenomenon that had overthrown the small army of Unseelie troops had come from her. The single word of power still echoed in Tony's mind, her voice behind it. He didn't dare to ask her name—awe held him captive—no more than he dared to offer her anything less than full and total honesty.

She gazed down at the battered creatures. "The weapons which you and your friend used against them were chimera, the creations of magic. Chimera can not kill them."

"But—" Unthinking, Tony sucked in his wounded cheek and winced at the pain. "But I tore them open, one of them I whacked his head clean off, I—"

The old woman caressed the bleeding slash and her touch stole away the hurting. "Chimera can do damage, yes, but only cold iron can take their lives. Your life as well, child. The wounds you gave them, even the worst, have sent them into trance. They will return to the waking world in time; a very long time, for some." She looked into his eyes steadily. "You sought to kill; your kills were taken from you. Do you feel cheated?"

"No," Tony answered at once, shaking his head briskly. "Shit, I didn't *want* to kill anyone. Not even them. But when it's them or me—"

"That is well," the old woman interrupted. She cupped her hands together so that the steepled fingers resembled the closed bud of a lily and inclined her head ever so slightly to him. "I am Xia Xiao. I own the Wan Sui Herb Shop. I regret that we did not meet sooner, Tony Lee, but that was your doing more than mine. Master Lung sent you to fetch me for the child; you came here instead. You see what good it did."

To his credit, Tony didn't gape at her words. He'd voiced nothing but the truth when he'd spoken of how he no longer knew the meaning of surprise. Over the past months, under Master Lung's tutelage, in Sylv's company, he'd come to live comfortably with wonders. Why should it startle him to learn that this woman—just another granny like the dozens he saw daily on the streets on Chinatown—knew his name and his abandoned errand? She also knew how to call up a weapon potent enough to rout an Unseelie pack. Compared to that, what was a little mindreading?

"I'm—uh—I'm really sorry," he stammered.

"For what? Your disobedience of Master Lung's request or your scorn for his judgment?" The dark eyes glowed with indignation. Tony cringed in spite of the fact that he could pick up this woman with one hand. *If she didn't burn your hand right off at the wrist for trying it*, he reminded himself.

"Both," he answered. "I guess."

"You guess too much. Only certainties can save you. It was very good that Master Lung called to alert me about your errand. He has told me much about you, how you think you own the fire, how you walk with disdain among the true treasures of our people. Such a one, I told him, will never learn the lessons that matter. He imagines that his way is the only way, and the haughty spirit he carries like a dragon's wisdom-pearl is only a filthy scrap of cloth that blinds his eyes. Yes, it is very good that he informed me of your coming, for I knew that left to yourself, you would not come. So I came seeking you, and lucky for you that I did."

"You can keep your luck," Tony snapped. His awe and fear both vanished under the lash of the old woman's tongue. "We were doing fine on our own."

"Oh, were you?" Xia Xiao's eyes slewed to where Jordan Avery still sat slumped unconscious against the sink pipes.

Tony made an impatient sound. "He's just fainted. I'll take care of him." He went to his friend's side, picking his way over and around the bodies of the Unseelie. He jerked a dishrag from the little towel rack beside the sink, dampened it, and wiped the big man's face until Jordan's eyelids fluttered and he came to himself.

"What—?"

"It's okay, Jordan. Everything's okay."

"This you call okay?" The owner of *Wild Things* laid one hand to his head as he surveyed the sprawled bodies littering the floor around him.

"They're not dead. Is that okay enough for you?"

"Yeah, but—" He tallied the number of the fallen on his fingers and whistled. "All these? That wasn't me. That wasn't you either, it was that big light that—" He looked up to meet Xia Xiao's serene gaze. "You mean that *you*—?" he began to ask her. She bowed to him slightly, smiling. "Oh wow. Oh man. Elves. Shit."

Tony just shook his head and silently gave up trying to make Jordan Avery understand.

10

"You said *what* to her?" Sylv sat up straight in one of Master Lung's kitchen chairs, eyes wide.

If Tony had searched for the perfect way to make an impression on Sylv, he couldn't have done better than this. The only trouble was, it was anything but a good impression. Sylv was acting like he'd introduced himself to Xia Xiao by offering the old woman a slice of freshly roasted dog-doo, when in reality—

"Hey, all I told her was she could keep her luck!" He pushed his own chair a little ways back from the table where the tea things waited, untouched.

"You don't say things like that to *her*! Oh hell, when will you ever learn?" Sylv asked the ceiling. "First you rag on Magloire, then you talk like that to Xia Xiao. She's one of the oldest, wisest, most respected grumps in this whole flaming *city*. She could pick Magloire up by the scruff of his hairy neck and throw him all the way to Newark without breaking a sweat!"

"You think she'd—she'd do that to me?" A flicker of apprehension touched Tony's eyes. "She's got a temper that bad?" It wasn't that he was *afraid* of Xia Xiao—not exactly—it was just that the old woman's presence gave him a distinctly uncanny feeling.

Sylv's mouth hardened. "I wish she did. Maybe then you'd get it: you're nothing, Tony. Not yet, not with us. Yeah, you can gather glamour, you can do tricks, but next to the real Changelings—"

"Who are you calling *nothing*?" Tony shouted. "And who are you to decide who's a real Changeling and who's not? 'Tricks', huh? If you'd been in Jordan's shop when those Unseelie busted in, if you could've seen what I did—"

"Oh, big whoop." Sylv yawned theatrically, deliberately. "I could throw ouchy things when I was just a childing. Tony, don't you *see*?" To his surprise, her expression gentled; he was looking into the face of a caring girl, not a no-nonsense nocker. "Being a Changeling is more than grabbing glamour and flinging fireballs. We're bound to each other—our motleys, our oathcircles, our kith. It's not just us against Banality or the Unseelie, it's us *for* each other! Who we can count on, who we can *trust*, like Master Lung trusted you to bring Xia Xiao. It's like—like *family*. And for some of us, it's the only real family we've ever had."

Family… Tony's eyes clouded over. *Family, sure. Family that leaves you. Family that scorns you. Family that dies and doesn't care that you've still got to go on living, abandons you to demons and the dark. Family…And now she's telling me I flunked some kind of test to see if they can trust me? So what! So I don't get into their precious family. I've had a bellyful of family.*

"Look, I *said* I was sorry for second-guessing Master Lung!" he snapped in her face.

"Is *that* all you think this is about?" Sylv's eyes lost their warmth, frosted over. The nocker was back, and she was angry. "It's like talking to a fuckin' brick wall with you!"

Tony forged on, ignoring the jibe: "What I said to the old woman wasn't so bad. Yeah, nobody had to tell me she's a grump, the way she came down on me that hard. I was *trying* to apologize!"

"You were trying to apologize?" Sylv's lip curled. "Oh, I'm so sure."

"Huh! Like you've ever done it," Tony sneered right back at her. "Like you've ever even *tried.*"

"You want to hear *me* apologize? What for?"

Tony smirked. "Whatever. Make something up. As if you could. Nockers don't know how to say they're sorry; even I know that."

Sylv whammed both fists on the kitchen table, making the lid of the teapot rattle. "Oh yeah? I'll show you. *I'm sorry I ever thought you had a brain in your head.* There! How's *that* for an apology?"

"Leaves something to be desired," said Jordan, coming into the kitchen. "You're a nice chick, but you're one rude elf." Sylv gritted her teeth, but before she could blow up at the big man, he laid a hand on Tony's shoulder and said, "They want you in there now."

Tony stood up. "You sure? Master Lung told me to make tea." He gestured vaguely at the cups, still empty, and the teapot, now cold.

"That was an hour ago," Jordan said. "And you know it."

"Like I know how come he told me to do it," Tony mumbled. "He doesn't trust me any more. He's mad at me because of how I acted, not bringing the old lady here right away, going against him behind his back. He doesn't want me any nearer the kid than I absolutely need to be. He doesn't want me in the way."

"That's what we call the wisdom of the Orient," Sylv said with a nasty smile. Tony glared at her and she added, "Hey, you screwed up. What'd you expect? The medal of honor?"

Jordan ignored her. "He sent me for you," he told Tony. "Don't make me go back in there and say 'He didn't believe me when I said you wanted him.' They'll just make me come back after you again. I don't *like* looking like a horse's ass. Not when I've got a choice."

Tony shrugged, jamming his hands in his pockets. "He said he wanted me to make tea, too, and he never came out to drink it."

Jordan snorted. "You are too damn much sometimes, you know that?" He stiff-armed Tony aside, stalked to the table, and guzzled the teapot dry, straight from the spout. "There. Now the tea's all gone. Come with me and ask him if he wants you to make any more."

Tony gave the big man a long look. "You're a mental case, Jordan, y'know?"

"Look who's talking. Dances-with-Elves."

660   **ESTHER M. FRIESNER**

"*Changelings!*" Sylv shouted. "What the hell is so fucking hard to remember about that? *Changelings*, dammit! Changelings, Changelings, Changel—"

Her wrath was wasted. Jordan had left the kitchen, taking Tony with him.

Master Lung was waiting for them in the hallway outside Tony's bedroom. "Thank you, Mr. Avery," he said softly. "You have been a great help to us in a trying time. You're a good man."

"Don't mention it, Mr. Liu; it was nothing. I just stood there is all." Jordan didn't handle even the mildest of compliments well. He looked ready to squirm out of his skin at Master Lung's words of appreciation.

"You were an extra pair of hands where we needed them," Master Lung insisted. "As you say, you just stood there, but you stood there patiently, carefully, and silently, holding Xia Xiao's healer's box while she worked. It must have been very boring for you, and yet—"

Jordan blushed. "No biggie. Glad to. Tony's a friend, and that lady in there—what's it, Mrs. Xia? Miss? Ms.?—anyhow, she's worth doing favors for. I'd like to keep her on my side." He grinned shyly.

"Ah yes." Master Lung's eyes twinkled. "A formidable woman."

"Don't you mean a formidable elllll…Changeling?"

"Finally," Tony mumbled under his breath.

"Yes, Tony?" Master Lung tilted his head in the young man's direction. "Did you say something?"

"Nothing. I said I'm here." He sounded inexcusably sullen, even to his own ears, but he couldn't help it. Shame always turned him defensive, a hedgehog rolled up into a bristling ball. "You sent for me, remember?"

"I did." Master Lung was untroubled by Tony's spines. "I'm sorry; my error. I thought I heard you ask how Nok-Nok is feeling."

Tony's face blazed. He averted his eyes. "Um. Yeah. He better?"

"That is why I sent for you, to see for yourself." The old man pushed open the bedroom door behind him and motioned Tony inside.

Xia Xiao sat on a chair at the head of the bed, her knees, ankles, and feet together, elbows tight at her sides, hands resting flat on her thighs. She might have been an ancient mandarin's chief wife, posing for a formal portrait. The old woman's expression gave nothing away.

In the bed, Nok-Nok lay on his back, blond hair plastered to his brow with sweat. His eyes were closed, his face pasty, colorless. If not for the measured rise and fall of the covers over him, he might as well have been lying in his coffin.

"He's sleeping?" Master Lung inquired in the hushed tones of heartfelt concern reserved for sickrooms everywhere. He went nearer and leaned over the boy, trying to read the riddle of that bloodless face.

Xia Xiao shook her head. "This is no healthy sleep. Our foes have grown tired of waiting to destroy this child face-to-face. You hid him well, my old friend, yet only from the eyes of the body. I cannot tell for certain, but I would say that the Unseelie have contrived to find a Soothsayer mighty enough to strike down this helpless one from a distance with a curse beyond the first which they laid on him. In the hands of one with enough power, a curse needs no eyes. Hidden or in plain sight, it is all one to such a dark sending."

"Ai-ya." Master Lung's face fell. "And is there no hope? No way to lift this evil?"

"For the present? No. When I think of how once, this healing would have been nothing to me—" The old woman sucked in a hissing breath. "This banal world drinks our strength, saps what we once were, what we might be. Unbelief has crushed more roses than a thousand armies."

"But he lives." Master Lung clung to hope. "If not for you, the curse would have killed him."

"I have done what I can," the old woman said. Without warning, her gaze shot to Tony. "With my herbs, yes, and that is *all* that can be done for him now."

Tony's first impulse was to meet her accusation with his own. He wanted to shout back at her, to demand *How do you know? How can you be so damn sure about that? If I'd brought a real doctor like I wanted*—he smothered the words before they reached his lips. He'd seen the power this woman commanded. What could be more real than that terrible might, contained in a single word? If she said that she'd done all that could be done for Nok-Nok, it was so.

Instead of giving her a sharp reply, he bowed awkwardly before her and simply said, "Thank you."

Xia Xiao was taken aback by this. She exchanged a look with Master Lung across Nok-Nok's body, then said, "So! You were right about this one after all: He does learn."

"Not always willingly," Master Lung admitted. "But he learns."

"He has at least learned how to make worthy friends." Now the bright black eyes were studying Jordan Avery, who stood in the doorway. The big man's face turned redder still, and he tried to edge his way out of the room.

"Hey, watch it! I'm walking here!" Sylv slapped at Jordan's arm, only a little smaller around than her waist. "What's going on? How come the fledge gets to know everything and I'm left out back with the dirty dishes?"

"More to the point," drawled a second voice from out in the hallway, "why are *we?*" Magloire smoothly but firmly put Sylv to one side and entered the bedroom as if he owned it. The satyr was comfortably dressed against the winter's cold in what appeared to be a black Merino wool, knee-length designer overcoat with a mink collar. Then the collar chittered and sat up on Magloire's shoulder, red eyes glittering. The mink scampered down the length of his sleeve and sprang to the floor where it transformed into a beautiful young woman, as sleek and self-satisfied as her erstwhile bearer.

"Hello, darlings!" the pooka cried, throwing her arms wide as if to embrace the world. They dripped copious lace sleeves the color of Spanish moss, and the dress entire looked more suited to an English garden party than to a small back bedroom in Chinatown. When she caught sight of Nok-Nok's body, she gave a little gasp and thrust her jeweled knuckles to her mouth. "Oh, how awful! He looks to be positively at death's door. Magloire, you didn't tell me he'd look *this* bad! You know I can't bear seeing such things. They upset me so!"

"I didn't want to scare you off, dear sister," the satyr soothed, kneading her shoulders. "I have a horror of making social calls of this nature unaccompanied."

"But Magloire, he's so—so—ohhhhh!" She shuddered, as she did everything, elegantly.

"Oh, for the love of—!" Sylv was exasperated with the pooka's squeamish posturings. "Look, Deni, if you don't want to be here, the door works just fine."

Deni's lips parted, revealing tiny, sharp teeth. "Are you telling me I'm not welcome here, Sylv?"

"You were just acting like you didn't want to be here, welcome or not. Make up your tiny mind!"

"Oh, I know *my* mind, right enough. But as for you, my dear…" Deni lifted one exquisitely waxed eyebrow as she gave Tony a long, purposeful examination. "You *are* the mercurial one. To think that this is the same young man you spoke to me about so—oh dear, *what* is the word I want? Not *warmly*, to be precise, but still with a certain…fondness? Of course one can be quite fond of a pet, though still—" She shrugged it all away. "Yet what did I overhear not one hour ago but you positively shrieking in his face like a fishwife! *Not* what I expec—"

"How the hell did you overhear anything?" Sylv's color rose, but she kept her voice to a low growl, careful not to disturb Nok-Nok.

Deni tittered. "This is New York. Few doors are closed to you when you wear mink with real style." And the pooka flickered back into her animal shape only long enough for Sylv to understand that a mink's lithe body could slip through passageways no human and few other beasts could use.

"Stinking sneak," Sylv muttered.

"What does she mean?" Tony demanded. "What did you tell her about me?"

"None of your damn—"

"Pay Deni no mind, my friend," Magloire told him, throwing one arm around his sister's shoulders. "My sister's charming, as you already know, but she does babble."

"Hmph! When *you* babble, you call it scintillating repartee." Deni wrinkled up her nose at her brother.

"And so it is," the satyr said, surprised that anyone would think otherwise. He gave all present one of his most ingratiating smiles. "We won't impose our company on you long. We are the duly appointed representatives of the motley, and we'll leave as soon as we have some solid news to bring back to the others. They're all rather worried about the boy, small wonder. Well? How is he?" He cast a cool eye over Nok-Nok. "Not well, I can tell that much, but what is your prognosis, esteemed lady?" He bowed to Xia Xiao with a flourish.

The old woman rose from her chair and stood beside the bed, stretching out her hands over the stricken boy. Her palms glowed gold, and an answering radiance arose from the fragile form under the covers. It was a very faint light, more glimmer than glow, soon extinguished. A labored gust of breath shook her small body.

"What would you have me tell you, Magloire? That I can heal him completely? I would have done so already. That I can accomplish the task eventually? I can not say."

"Well then, let's try the fuzzy end of the lollipop," the satyr said grimly. "If there's no hope at all of bringing him back, why keep him hanging between worlds this way? It's not kind."

"I did not say there was no hope at all." Xia Xiao had a hawk's stare, proud, yet pride easily justified. "Do you think I would hesitate to release his spirit if that were so?"

"Never for a moment." The satyr made her another courtly bow. "Your wisdom is only exceeded by—"

"I have little need for the empty air of your fine words. Tell the motley this: that each member must turn to the gathering of glamour with renewed effort and give me as much of it as they dare to spare. I will turn it to the child's healing and we will continue to hope that it will be enough."

"Hope?" Deni echoed. "You mean you can't promise you'll succeed?"

"I make no promises."

"Oh!" The pooka looked flustered. "Well, my gracious, you can't expect us to go back to the others with *that*! Not seriously."

"Why not?" Xia Xiao's stare held Deni like a netted butterfly. "It is the truth."

"And you're a perfect darling to come right out and tell it to *us*, of course, but we're going to have to have something better to tell the others."

The old woman's expression neither changed nor faltered. A creature less flighty than the mink-pooka would have felt its weight like a stone hammer to the heart. Deni, however, shared her brother's native insouciance. How could anyone be displeased with *her*? To her mind, it simply wasn't a possibility.

"You *will* heal him," she continued decisively. "That's all there is to it. As far as what we tell the others, I mean. Once he's brought out of this—this coma, or trance, or whatever it is—you'll have no trouble casting off the curse that's blocking his memories. And once that's been seen to, he can teach all of us the secret he learned from Lavena Dubh and we can make all the glamour we could ever need and find our way back to Arcadia and have just the most *delicious* time. Happily ever after, as they say. Now you see, *that* is something I can tell Sonnet and Prinx and Camellia and Rupert, *that* is something they'll listen to. Otherwise, well, you can't expect sensible folk to give up their hard-earned glamour without some hope of return, can you?" Her laughter was like clear water cascading over diamonds. "So it's settled." She whirled on tiptoe and started from the bedroom.

Magloire caught her by the nape of the neck and yanked her back. "*Nothing* is settled, dear sister," he stage-whispered in her ear while she whined and twisted helplessly in his grasp. "Now the *first* thing you'll do is apologize to the lady Xia Xiao for so much as hinting at linking her august name to such a tissue of lies. Stupid lies, what's worse. I'm shocked you'd even consider trucking such a load of patent hogwash back to our companions. You'd be hooted out of the motley. Even Prinx knows when a tale's too good to be true, and Prinx couldn't outsmart a can of sardines."

"Sorry, sorry, *sorry*." Deni jerked her body left and right, but her brother held her fast. "Ohhhhh, let me go before I make *you* sorry, you—!" Reality shifted, and a mink slithered out of Magloire's fist to scuttle up his arm. It paused just long enough to nip his ear before leaping to the floor. The little animal scampered

ESTHER M. FRIESNER

out of the room, pursued by Sylv's mocking laughter.

Magloire scowled, pressing a neatly folded Irish linen handkerchief to his bleeding ear. "How right they are when they say you can choose your friends but not your relatives." He turned to Xia Xiao again, his eyes brimming with sincerity. "My deepest apologies for Deni's presumption. Naturally I shall deliver your message to the rest of our motley exactly as you gave it." He stood there, as if waiting for something.

"Well?" the old woman inquired curtly. "If you have a message to take, there is no better time than now to take it." With that, she turned her back on him and busied herself with repacking the square red lacquer box on the bedside table. Its many small drawers and compartments held her herbal remedies and other healer's gear. She only paused in her preoccupation long enough to thrust a clay pot the size of a quarter into Magloire's hands with a terse, "Here. Twice daily, for the bite."

"What'd you expect, Mags?" Sylv teased. "Maybe she'd bake you a cake?"

The satyr regarded Sylv with perfect disdain. "Hardly." He anointed his injured ear with some of the salve from the clay pot. "A cup of tea, perhaps, to soothe my feelings before I venture back out into this atrocious weather. It's cold outside, and unlike Deni, I refuse to wear fur."

"Your pardon, sir." Master Lung came up to him, bowing low. "I've been remiss in my hospitality. It would do me an undeserved honor if you would share a cup of my unworthy brewing."

"Thank you, Master Lung. *Your* manners are, as always, impeccable." The satyr gave Sylv a sideways look of victory.

"We will all have tea," Xia Xiao announced, picking up her lacquer box by its thick carrying strap and slipping this over her head. "If Master Lung will permit, I will prepare it."

Tony was following a darkly muttering Sylv out of the bedroom when Master Lung stopped him. "Someone must keep watch," was all the old man said.

"It's okay, Tony, I'll stay with you," Jordan said.

"You don't have to," Tony grumbled, drawing a chair up to Nok-Nok's bedside and trying to pretend indifference.

"No biggie," Jordan said again. A half-smile touched his lips. "Remember: I already had my tea."

It was impossible for Tony to make Jordan leave. For one thing, he owed the big man too much, too many past favors to deny him something so simple as the wish to stay. For another, Tony was honestly glad of the company. Ever since he'd come back to Master Lung's from his ill-starred errand, he'd felt the full weight of blame and exclusion. *But I was* trying *to do what was right, what I thought was best for Nok-Nok, getting him a real doctor! How was I to know anything about Xia Xiao's power? I thought Master Lung was sending me after some quack, just because it was a Chinese quack. Like if something's Chinese it's automatically better, in his book. Try to make me believe that crap. Now they're treating me like I'm a moron who can't even be trusted to go buy a newspaper, or be in on whatever it is they're discussing out there in the kitchen right now. It's not my fault, goddammit! It's not!* The hard, proud voice inside him cried out against the injustice of it all, never pausing to ask whether the sense of blame and exclusion alike truly came from Master Lung and Xia Xiao, or only from himself.

Silence settled over the room. Tony could hear the faint sounds of tea preparation and conversation from the kitchen. He sat hunched forward, looking at his linked hands instead of at the form in the bed. From the corner of one eye he saw that Jordan had made no move to fetch himself a chair. The big man stood in the bedroom doorway like a soldier in a guard box.

"If you want to keep me company, you're doing a crummy job of it," Tony remarked.

Jordan shifted his shoulders, part stretch, part shrug. "I'm not much good with small talk, and anyway, I don't know what you can talk about in a sickroom." He looked into Nok-Nok's unconscious face. "Poor kid. Poor, poor kid. I wish there was something I could do."

"No, you don't. That's a lie and you know it." The words were bitten off short and sharp, keen as Deni's teeth. In his self-inflicted misery, Tony lashed out at the handiest available target. Anything to take his mind off himself. "If you did want to help him, why didn't you do it when you had the chance? When I first brought him into *Wild Things*, why didn't you let him stay there?"

"What am I running, an elf hostel?" Jordan spread his hands, but the grin on his face was shaky, a clown mask made of eggshell.

"Bullshit, Jordan." Tony felt his face settle into steely, unforgiving lines. He hated what he was doing to the man who'd helped him get out of the life, but he couldn't hold back the words. "You didn't know he was a Changeling then any more than I did. He was just a kid to you. You've been there for others kids. You were there for me. Why couldn't you be there for him?"

Jordan lowered his eyes. "I've never given anyone a place to stay, Tony. Not on my own turf. All I did for you was I gave you some information, where to find a decent place to live, a rec to get yourself another job. I wouldn't have let you stay in the back of the store or in my place, even if you'd asked. That's my rule. I don't break it for anyone."

"Stupid rule," Tony sneered, feeling the fires leaping up inside him, unable to turn their all-destroying flame into healing light. "Who do you think you are, Greta Garbo? You vant to be aloooone? You think maybe if you give someone a place to stay, he's gonna get a look at you in your underwear? Is that the big problem?" If he didn't continue to strike at Jordan—and never mind the injustice of it!—he would have the fires eating at his own soul. And when that same soul cried out at the unfairness of his attack against this man he called friend, his street-hardened survival instinct gritted back *It's the world that's unfair, not me!* "What, you think if Nok-Nok caught a peek at you like that he'd fall in love with you or something? Oh yeah, right, I'll just—"

"I was taking care of a kid one time, and he died," Jordan said in a low, strange, uninflected voice. The tone alone brought Tony's runaway mouth to a dead stop, and the words that followed scooped his breathing shallow as he listened. "It was summer, the year I turned fourteen, up at this place in Vermont, a lot of cottages on a lake. Everyone knew everyone else, all the kids grew up together, it was like having another family besides your own, bigger than your own, always someone you could go to when your parents wouldn't listen or understand or just let you down the way they do." A deep sigh shook Jordan's large frame.

"His name was Nicky; he was eight years old," he went on. "His parents were going out that night to the local summer stock theater, so they asked me to take care of him. He really liked me, Tony; I was like a big brother to him. About eight-thirty I told him it was bedtime, but he knew he could get around me, so he asked for one more game of hide-and-seek. Sure, I said yes. Why not? I figured he'd hide in a closet, maybe, or under one of the beds. I'd find him easy, put him to bed, read him the next chapter of *The Hobbit*—he loved that book so much— and that'd be that. No problems. I covered my eyes and started counting to a hundred. I was in the kitchen, at the very back of the cottage. I never knew that he could move so quietly. I never even heard the screen door close when he slipped outside. By the time I finished searching the house for him, it was full dark. I ran outside, looked everywhere, couldn't find him. I was scared to holler for him to come out and show himself. What if someone else heard? What'd they think of me, letting a kid get away on me like that? I was crying, but I didn't make a sound. Even today, when I cry, I do it quietly. No sobs. No nothing. Just the tears come down."

"What happened?" Tony asked, his voice barely more than a whisper. Even though there were three of them in the darkened bedroom, two of them speaking, it felt very still. "Did you find him?"

Jordan shook his head. "Two days later they did. He'd taken one of those chintzy inflatable pool rafts some other kid left by the lake shore. He must've thought it'd be so cool, slipping out onto the water, me not being able to find him. He didn't care about getting his pajamas wet or anything; the *adventure*, that was counted. Like Bilbo Baggins having his adventures in Middle Earth."

"It wasn't your fault, Jordan," Tony said softly. "You were just a kid yourself. How could you know what he'd do?"

"That's what the told me, my folks, everyone," Jordan replied. "Everyone except Nicky's parents. They left without saying a word to me; nothing. Next summer, they didn't come back."

"Yeah, well, did you expect they—?"

"No one said anything about that. Everyone was so eager to let me know that it wasn't my fault, that everything was okay. But no one ever asked me to mind their kids again." He was staring off into the shadows, into a lost time. "New people came to the lake that year. They took the cottage Nicky's family used to take. They had a couple of children, and my parents told them I was a pretty good babysitter, for a boy, so they hired me. They had two kids, a boy and a girl. The boy was just about Nicky's age."

He stopped speaking. Tony gazed at him, feeling the weight of all the empty seconds, feeling his throat grow raw and tight though he hadn't been the one talking. "Go on, Jordan," he said, the words coming out hoarsely. "Did something happen to that boy too?"

Jordan made as if to nod his head, then shook it instead, then shrugged. "He was a handful, that one. A real brat. He didn't give me a break the whole evening, wouldn't eat his dinner, pitched fits like a two-year-old, beat on his sister, you name it. Then it was time to put the little son-of-a-bitch to bed. He wouldn't go. When I tried to talk him into it, he jumped on the livingroom sofa and shouted at me, 'What'll you do if I won't, huh? Kill me too?'"

"How'd he—?"

"The other kids told him, they must've. The other kids, the little ones I used to sit for, maybe even some of the big kids, the ones I thought were my friends." Jordan closed his eyes, pain lancing across his face. "I hit him, Tony. I grabbed him off the sofa by the scruff of the neck and I smacked him across the face." His eyes opened; they were filled with tears. "His sister saw it. She was younger, five years old was all, and she started screaming and he squirmed out of my grip and went running out of the cottage to the place next door, screaming too, his nose bloody, and then there were people, people all around me, my parents, and someone called the police, and—and—and—"

He was breathing hard, raspy breaths. "I don't know what the little girl said about what happened. The police took me into town with my parents following after in our car. The kid's parents showed up. The town doctor was there and I heard what he told them, all right. Up to then, until he spoke up, I didn't even imagine what they must've been thinking I'd done to their son, but when he said that I'd only slapped him—"

Another shudder of air rushed into his lungs. "Okay. Not 'only' slapped him. I know I should never have raised my hand to that kid no matter what he said, but I wasn't much more than a kid myself. Like kids don't lash out when you make them mad! Like grown-ups don't! But slapping his face, that was *it*, that was *all* I did to him, that was what the doctor himself told them and still—*still* the things his parents yelled at me—! Like nothing mattered to them but what they'd decided to believe."

Tony moved swiftly, rising from his chair, reaching out to offer the big man one touch of human comfort, but Jordan pulled away. "No. Please, no." His lips were trembling, and he held up his hands in a warding gesture, as if Tony were a nightmare closing in on him. "It's only safe for me if I keep my distance. It's only safe for you if I don't get close."

"Jordan, man, that's *such* bullshit." Tony held up his hands, filled with nothing but frustration. "*You* knew you didn't do anything, your *family* knew the truth, there was *evidence* in your favor right there, right away, so what the hell did you care what anyone else—?"

"We never went back to the lake," Jordan said. His eyes were vacant again. "That fall, my parents put me in a different school, a place for kids with…problems. I tried to tell them I didn't need to go, didn't want to, but they were firm about it. They said they'd been wrong not to do it the year before. They said it was what I needed, even if I couldn't see it that way, that it would be better if things didn't get any more out of hand for me. Out of control. Control." He put acid into the word. "I wanted to be a teacher, Tony. I always liked helping kids. My parents knew—from the time I was old enough to tell them what I wanted to be when I grew up, that's what I told them: a teacher." One final sigh, little more than a wistful ghost.

"You'd be a good teacher, Jordan," Tony said gently, trying again to draw near the big man.

"That's what my parents used to tell me. But when I went to college, they started saying that maybe I shouldn't go in with just one goal in mind. Maybe teaching wasn't the right choice for me. Maybe I'd be happier doing something with less…pressure. Kids could be a real pain, sometimes, they said. Kids could push you pretty far, give them half a chance. Why walk into all that aggravation willingly? Maybe I could find something else to do."

His smile was rueful, bitter. "I sure did. Drink. Drugs. I managed to hang in there until sophomore year before I flunked out totally. Pretty amazing, huh? You wanna talk pressure, you try taking your freshman finals stoned out of your skull."

"But—but you're okay now." Tony's worried expression added the unspoken afterword *Aren't you?*

"I came back, if that's what you mean. It took a long time, but I did. And I can take care of myself. But if I take care of anyone else, it's on my terms, by the limits I set, the distances. Distance keeps it safe. That includes everyone. Even you." He nodded in Nok-Nok's direction. "Even him."

"Distance," said a well-known voice from the hallway. "Distance sounds like an excellent idea." Magloire pushed Jordan aside as if the big man weighed less than a cloud of dandelion fluff. "Why don't we put some distance between this creature and our prize, the sooner the better?" He looked back over one shoulder to where Sylv and Deni still bided in the hall, gazing at Jordan Avery wide-eyed. "Or do we want to risk losing Arcadia forever?"

11

"What is all this noise?" Master Lung demanded, striding into the middle of the row. Everyone in the bedroom was shouting at once—Tony and Magloire and Sylv and even Deni, who had returned—everyone except Jordan and Nok-Nok. "Have you all lost your minds? Do you think such an uproar will help the boy? You above all, Magloire! You were there in the kitchen when Xia Xiao left. You heard what she said about his care: He needs *peace*."

"Whatever she said he does need, I can tell you what he *doesn't*." Magloire's teeth flashed in the semi-darkness, his eyes sparkling with a cold, golden light. "He doesn't need the risk of being left alone with *that*." He jabbed one elegant finger at Jordan.

"I was going," Jordan mumbled, his back pressing hard against the plastered wall. "I have to go now, I have to leave."

"You stay where you are!" Tony grabbed the big man's arm, in spite of Jordan's best attempts to wrench it away. "Master Lung, you've got to listen: Magloire's lying about Jordan, he's making trouble, he's—"

"My brother is within his rights!" Deni was back, wearing her human form, all past spats with her satyr sibling pushed aside, if not forgotten. "The boy belongs to all of us, all our motley, and it's our first duty to protect him, to guard him against any harm! Anything happens to him could affect the knowledge locked up inside him, jar it out of him, lose it to us forever!"

"Nothing's gonna happen to him," Tony shot back in Deni's face. "Not from Jordan, anyway, you stupid weasel!"

Deni gasped at the insult. Her brother stepped gracefully back into the fray with: "Which shows what a great judge you are of the situation, when you can't even tell a mink from a weasel, or a ghoul from a guardian." He was looking hard and steadily at Jordan again. "This one doesn't do well with boys. I heard him say so himself. Not that he dislikes them—quite the contrary—and there, you see, is where we have our problem."

"In the first place, that's a fucking lie," Tony gritted. "And in the second, what the hell do you think he'd do to Nok-Nok when the kid's like *this?*" He gestured dramatically at the pale-faced form on the bed.

"You'd like to have us risk finding out?" Magloire's voice was honey laced with venom. "Educational, but not wise."

"Tony, come on, let me go, please," Jordan begged, trying to work his arm free, to edge away. "I shouldn't be here anyhow. I don't belong. This isn't my—"

"Listen to your friend, Tony," Magloire said. "Whatever else he is, he's at least smart enough to realize that he has no business being here, in our company. A willing departure saves him the inconvenience of one that is enforced." The satyr deftly stepped between the bed and the others. The silvery-gray twists of his horns showed themselves for an instant, a space of time so fleeting that it seemed a trick of the light, an illusion, the work of an overactive imagination. Yet the memory of those sharp points remained behind, impressed on the memory, a threat made visible.

"That will be enough, Magloire," Master Lung said without raising his voice. "This is *my* home. Remember that."

"I meant you no offense, Master Lung," the satyr replied indifferently. "We're civilized; we all observe the proprieties. *This* is your home, yes, and your word must be supreme under this roof because it belongs to you. However, *that*—" he nodded at Nok-Nok "—does not."

"Like he's yours?" Tony challenged. Jordan made another try at jerking his arm free. Tony whipped his head around to shout in the big man's face, "Damn it, you stop that, Jordan! He's got no right treat you this way! He's twisting everything around—bad enough he was eavesdropping on us like some cheap keyhole-peeper, but he's taking half-truths and warping them into lies, nothing but a lot of stinking lies! We don't let him get away with that. We can't. You have to stay, you have to fight, you—"

"*No!*" Jordan shouted back, tears streaming down his face. "I don't have to take any more of this, Tony. He's right: I *don't* belong here, I don't have to let you use me to win some fight you've got going with him, I don't have to do *anything!*" And he gave Tony a stiff-armed shot to the chest that sent him stumbling backwards into Magloire. Jordan didn't stay to see where Tony landed; he bolted out the door.

"You bastard." Tony pulled himself away from Magloire as if the satyr's touch had the power to contaminate. "Why did you do that? Why?"

Master Lung sucked in his breath, scowling at them both. "You've shamed me," was all he said before he too left. The sound of a door slamming reached them from the end of the hallway.

"Well!" Deni planted her hands on her hips. "Where's he off to?"

"Probably gone after that guy," Sylv provided. "Like he wants to apologize for your brother being such a jerk to him. It's a courtesy thing; you wouldn't understand."

Deni sniffed disdainfully. "The day I need to get a lesson in manners from a nocker—! That'll be the day I take beauty hints from a redcap."

"It could only help," Sylv purred.

"Courtesy," Tony repeated bitterly, looking at Sylv. "Like you can talk about courtesy. You were barking just as loud as these two about how Jordan should get out of here."

"Yeah, well, he *should!*" Sylv maintained, thrusting her sharp little chin up at him. "Magloire said—"

"You're dumb enough to believe everything he tells you, no questions asked? If Magloire told you your ass was made of cream cheese you'd go buy a sack of bagels!" Tony yelled at her. "I'm telling you he's lying about Jordan!"

"Oh, like I should believe everything *you* tell me? How do I know *you're* not lying? I've known him a hell of a lot longer than I've known you!"

In the bed, Nok-Nok moaned and twisted, a look of agony contorting the delicate features of his face. Deni gave a little sob and wrung her slender hands.

"Ohhhh, *now* what's wrong with him? Why did he do that, why did he make that sound? What should we do for him? I'll get him some water." She started for the door, then stopped in her tracks. "No, wait, how could he drink it? He'd choke on it. Oh, God!" She dithered back and forth, a mouse caught under a belljar. "Oh God, why'd Xia Xiao have to leave? He's *awful*, he's just getting worse and worse, I know he is. And Master Lung's gone too! God, what if he *dies* on us? What do we do? What *should* we do?"

"We could do worse than give him some peace and quiet," Magloire remarked, looking meaningfully at Tony and Sylv. "At least until Master Lung returns."

"So who's not being peaceful?" Sylv demanded. "All I'm doing is telling this yo-yo he's a real horse's—"

Another groan came from the bed, echoed by the distraught Deni. That was enough for Tony. With an impatient sound he grabbed Sylv's hand and yanked her out of the bedroom and down the hall to the kitchen. It took almost no effort to fling the outraged nocker into a chair. "*Now* you can call me any part of a horse you want," he told her dryly.

"Who died and made you king turd?" she snarled at him, back on her feet in a heartbeat. "How dare you treat me like that?"

"Shhhh!" came the shrill hiss from the bedroom, followed by Deni's stage-whispered: "Put a *sock* in it, Sylv, we can still hear you in here!"

"You wanna *hear* something?" Sylv hollered back. "You want me to give you something to hear, you bloody *ferret?*" She would have lunged out of the kitchen, back to the bedroom, but Tony put himself in her way.

"As much as I hate to say it, Magloire got one thing right: Nok-Nok needs it quiet."

"So I'll be quiet." She gave him a look that could flay a rhino raw, but she lowered her voice surprisingly. "Now move it or lose it."

Tony shook his head. "They're so concerned about keeping Nok-Nok safe, let *them* watch him for awhile. You and I have to get this settled between us."

"Get what settled?" Sylv countered. "Says who? *You?* Oh, pardon me while I leap to obey your royal whim, Your Exalted Snotness!" She tried to elbow her way past him. When that didn't work, she took a swing at him with her foot.

It was just as Master Iung had told Xia Xiao: Tony could learn. He'd learned what to expect from Sylv when she got angry. All nockers had ugly tempers, and when Sylv's got riled up—as it inevitably did whenever they were together for any length of time—she'd always wind up trying to chip his shins with her Doc Martins.

Tony sidestepped the kick, sighed briefly, and before Sylv could take another swing at him he grabbed her around the waist, slung her over his shoulder, and carried her into the pantry. While she jerked and flailed in his grasp, he stooped over the trapdoor, hooked his shoe through the ringpull, kicked it open, and trundled her down the stairs. At the bottom he planted her on the steps and took a pace back, hands on hips, an artist contemplating a finished composition.

"There," he said, satisfied. "Now we really can talk with no one to complain they can hear us. Or you can run away back upstairs to your boyfriend. Your choice. What's it gonna be?"

Sylv leaped to her feet from the step, looking ready to take him up on the second option, but then she relaxed, sinking back down onto the concrete slab, rubbing her behind. "That stings," she growled. "Anyone ever teach you that's no way to treat a lady?"

Tony opened his mouth to make the obvious rejoinder, but like Sylv, thought better of his first impulse. The feisty nocker was already mad at him. There was no sense in trying to extinguish a burning match with a bucket of kerosene. "Sorry," he said.

"That's it?" Sylv rose to her feet, giving him a quizzical look. "'Sorry'? No wisecracks about how I'm no lady?" Her hard little face softened just a bit. "I bet you were thinking it, though."

Tony smiled. "I cannot tell a lie."

"Uh-huh." It came out dripping irony, but she was smiling too. "But Magloire can. That what you wanted to tell me?"

"Yeah. Unless maybe you already knew it."

"Oh sure. He lies like a rug, when it suits him, but only about stuff that doesn't matter. Which is one reason he is not my—jeez, did you actually call him my *boyfriend?*"

"What stuff?" Tony asked, ignoring her sarcasm.

Sylv shrugged. "You know, stupid stuff: love." She looked at her feet, and suddenly she seemed to lose the nocker's hard shell of cynicism. She was very young.

Tony took a step closer to her, reached out to touch her cheek. She jerked her head away at his touch. No tears streaked her face, but he could see old hurts cupped in the depths of her eyes. "You love him?" It was a rough thing to ask.

"No." She didn't hesitate at all with that reply, and her voice didn't tremble when she gave it. "I used to, I guess. He could be so damn *good* at it, such a moonlight-and-roses romantic. And I was always saying about how I didn't give a rat's ass about stuff like that—wine and poetry and all that long-walks-in-the-rain bullshit you read in the Personals. But he knew. He could read me like a book—like that candyass ever bothered to pick *up* a book. God, was *I* an idiot."

"For what? For believing in love?"

"For believing a satyr could love anyone but himself. Man, someone really beat me upside the head with the stupid stick when I was born, you know?" She offered him one of her rare, genuine smiles. "I wish I knew what you're gonna be, Tony, what kith. I can't tell yet. It'd be a damn shame if you turned out to be a satyr too. I fuckin' *hate* making the same mistake twice."

And she kissed him.

When at last she released him to catch his breath she added, "That's in case you're *not* a satyr. On account. But if you are, it never happened, okay?"

"A...downpayment?" he ventured, fingers brushing his lips as if he'd just discovered their presence.

Now she was grinning. "That's it. Hey, don't read too much into it. You're a good-looking guy. I've had my eye on you a while. I had to warn the others off you—that's what Deni was going on about before—but who the hell could get near you until now? Without you making me mad enough to spit in your eye instead of kiss you, I mean. You can be the world's most *aggravating* son-of-a—"

"That's it?" he cut her off, suspicious. "Just my looks?"

She shrugged. "You want *me* to lie too? Bad enough that you and Magloire—"

"*He's* the liar, not me!" Tony snapped.

"Whatever."

"No, *not* 'whatever'! Look, Sylv, you want me? Fine. Great. I want you, too. I've been wanting you for—oh shit, never mind that now. But what Magloire did, what he said about Jordan, I can't let it go. I can't let you go on believing it no matter how much I want you. It's just not true. I know. There's only four kinds of people in this world that I've ever met: There's victims and predators and friends and nothings. Jordan's a friend. Jordan's a victim, too. He's the one who saved me from staying a victim all my life, who gave me a hand up out of the dark, who—"

"Where do we send the medal?" Sylv quipped. "Why is it so important that I buy into what you say's the truth about him, huh? How's that gonna affect how we are together?"

"Because I know the difference," he said, without even the wisp of a jest in his voice. "Because I've had too many times with someone's body alone, and I won't have any more. Because the way I want you, Sylv, isn't just wanting your body. It's not enough for me. It shouldn't be for you."

"Oh," she replied. One eyebrow rose. "Well, that's too bad, 'cause it is. Enough for me. If you can't handle it—" She drew in a deep breath, as if to let loose a sigh, but it caught in her throat and instead she wrinkled up her nose and asked, "What stinks down here?" She looked around at the stockpiled armory of Master Lung's profession and art. There was a screened air duct in one corner of the basement, up near the ceiling, but it was only about a foot square and the breeze it admitted was far too scanty to disperse the accumulated tang of so much gunpowder. "Wow. I guess it's not a good time to ask if you mind if I smoke, huh?"

Tony refused to buy into her light words. "Sylv…" He reached out his hands to her, pleading.

Shed shook her head and turned away deliberately. "Nuh-uh. Don't put me through this. I can't do what you want, not the way you want it."

"You could *try*."

She whirled around wearing a Fury's face. "Why the hell *should* I, damn it? Because you say so? Well, I say *no*. That's gotta count for something, too, what I want. Come on, Tony, why do you have to be like this? We could have fun, it'd be good, it could even be great. I know things, ways to use our powers together that'll take us so far beyond anything you ever had with mortals—! And once Nok-Nok's well and we learn his secrets, there won't be any limits left for us, for you and me together. What do you need with love when you could have all that? And we could have it, Tony." She threw her arms around his neck.

"Because if I could have you to love, I could live without all that. That's all." He surprised himself by how gently he reached up and disentangled himself from her embrace. *Now I'm in for it,* he thought, expecting her to burst into a fresh rage. Instead, for one magical instant, he thought he saw the impossible: Her eyes softened. She was looking at him with wonder, with tenderness, with the first seeds of trust, and with—

The trapdoor overhead slammed shut with a report like thunder. Tony and Sylv looked up at once. The rhythmic thud of running feet made the ceiling rumble. Something fell over with a crash, and the bone-chilling sound of a muffled shriek made Tony's hair stand on end.

Then he felt it, the electrical charge like a ripple of fear over his skin. He prickled in a thousand places, every nerve humming, every sense coming into sharpest focus. The cellar room took on a dull red glow, the boxes surrounding him and Sylv began to shake, the rockets and crackers and Roman candles inside rattling fast, then faster.

Sylv cursed and dug her hand into her jacket pocket, pulling out what looked like a Swiss Army knife. It glowed with the swiftly forming image of a sword, but no sword like any he'd ever seen in books or movies. This sword looked like every gadget-geek's wet dream, a blade whose weighty hilt was studded with a tight array of controls, gauges, and LED displays. Sylv used both hands to wield it—for the moment only on guard—but her hard, back-the-hell-off-whatever-you-are look made him move away from her even though his first instinct was to step in and shield her.

Maybe she doesn't need shielding, he thought as the dryness of fear climbed up his throat and the rattling from the fireworks boxes grew louder. His palms burned, and his skin felt like it belonged to someone else, someone who'd shrunk it down two sizes and poured it full of acid before giving it back to its rightful owner. He was alternately gasping for breath and panting like a woman in labor.

"*Stop* that, dammit!" Sylv gritted. "What the fuck's wrong with you? You got claustrophobia or what?" She was turning around slowly, with small, pivoting steps, sweeping the room with her blade the way a cop might cover an alleyway with his gun. The hum of the glowing sword blended with the low thrumming that seemed to come from the stone walls themselves. Even with space between them, Tony could sense how taut, how tightly pulled Sylv's every nerve was. One touch and she'd snap, and when she did, someone was going to die.

"What's—what's happening?" he rasped.

"You tell me," she shot back, her voice a low, feral growl. "Only later. Let's get the fuck outa here." She bolted for the steps and lowered her blade to shove at the trapdoor. It wouldn't budge. She cursed and put her shoulder to it, with as little luck, then backed down a couple of steps and motioned for Tony to give it a try. He edged past her nervously while she protected his back, ready to take on whatever in the name of all hell was making the boxes of captive lightning shiver like wet dogs.

Tony pushed at the trapdoor with all his strength. It didn't so much as give a fraction of an inch. *Not bolted shut*, he thought. *Not blocked, either. Even if you moved a heavy chunk of furniture over it, to keep it down, there'd be* some *give. And what was there upstairs to hold it down like this? Nothing that heavy in the pantry, nothing in the kitchen unless someone shoved the fridge on top of it. But who, how—?* He gave another try, grunting with the effort. It was as if the trapdoor had become somehow welded into one piece with the rest of the pantry floor. He turned to Sylv, spreading his hands helplessly. "I can't—"

She wasn't in the market for excuses. "Get outa my way." She shoved past him, holding her blade bolt upright in both hands. With a guttural cry she thrust it straight up into the trapdoor. The sword penetrated the heavy panel halfway to the hilt, green and orange sparks flying, then stuck. Push or pull with all her might, Sylv couldn't move it one way or the other. Her string of obscenities rose to a crescendo as she hooked her hands over the hilt's crosspiece and let her full weight hang from it: No use.

She dropped away panting while tiny threads of fire crept lazily around the place where the sword had gone in.

"Fuck," she remarked almost calmly, giving the trapped sword a hard stare.

"Let me try," Tony said, reaching over her head for the blade. He laid hold of it with both hands and closed his eyes. Against the dark backdrop of his lowered lids he visualized the sudden, harsh blossom of an exploding rocket and sent that measure of power shooting up from his heart, through his arms, into the core of the blade. The sword moaned and whined, the green and orange sparks spurting in whole fountains of fire now, as a tiny border of char formed around the place where the blade was in contact with the trapdoor.

"Tony, stop!" Sylv's voice seemed to come from very far away. Rapt in the discharge of power, Tony heard it only as a distant breeze that had somehow learned his name. He delved deeper into himself, painting entire orchards of blazing fireworks shooting up out of the dark soil, trees of flame whose captive glamour leaped free in fresh eruptions of fire.

"Tony, no! Stop! Stop, before you kill us! You goddam stubborn asshole, don't you see? You'll set all this stuff on fire and blow us to hell if you... don't...stop...*now*!"

Something was pounding on his back. Then something hard and heavy swept in at him from the right. He felt it thud into his gut just below the ribcage, knocking the wind out of him and sending him tumbling backwards down the cellar stairs. He hit a second object on his way down, smaller and softer but much louder. Coming slowly up out of the trance that had possessed him, he blinked off the last afterimages of his conjured fireworks and looked around.

"Get off me, you jerk," said Sylv.

"Huh?" He looked down. He was sitting on top of the nocker, who still clutched a sturdy length of board lumber in her hand. "Oh! Oh God, sorry." He scrambled up and yanked her to her feet. For a second he wasn't sure whether she was going to hit him with the board again, just for the hell of it, to relieve her feelings. For another second it looked like she was thinking over exactly the same thing, but she ended by letting the slat drop. The sound of it hitting the floor was swallowed up by the continuing rattle of all the wooden packing cases walling them in.

"Jeez, what's *with* you? You were *out* there, man. Thought I was gonna have to whack you upside the head with that thing to make you let go." She sounded angry, but with a definite undertone of envy and admiration. "*Damn*, you've got it!"

"Hell with what I've got," Tony said, his jaw tight. "Only thing we both need to get is out, fast." He stared up at the sword, still wedged into the trapdoor. The rim of char around it was wider, but not by much. "Damn it. Damn it, what more can we do?"

"Let me in! Let me in!"

Sylv and Tony jerked their heads around as one at the sound of Deni's high, panic-stricken call. A harsh, scrabbling sound echoed out of the screened air duct before either one of them could ask aloud where the pooka's voice was coming from. Behind the mesh, a lithe, furry body writhed in an agony of impatience and fear, claws raking the wire. "Hurry! He has him! Oh, please!"

Tony picked up the board Sylv had dropped and raced to the air duct. The resourceful nocker had wrenched it from one of the still-rumbling crates of fireworks, and its jagged edge slid easily under the rim of the screen keeping the mink captive. As soon as Tony pried it off, Deni jumped right into his arms and took back her human form. For one disconcerting instant Tony was holding a gigantic mink with a woman's face before the transformation was complete. He gave an involuntary exclamation of startlement and threw her from his arms. She staggered backward on paws that became feet and lurched into one of the crates, gasping.

"Sorry, sorry," Tony said for what felt like the thousandth time. He offered her a hand up, but pulled a little too hard and wound up holding her tight against him. This time she was the one to break the embrace.

"Get out of here!" she cried. "Oh God, get out before it happens!"

"Like we want to stay?" Sylv shouted at her. "Your fuckin' brother locked us in down here, you go shimmy your hairy little butt back up and unlock the trapdoor now, got it?"

"I can't, I can't!" Deni went into a frenzy of moaning and hand-wringing. "He's the stronger of us, you know that! I don't have the power to lift his spells." She rolled her eyes at the growing rumble coming from the crates. "Three minutes left, that's all. Oh God, you've *got* to find a way out of here!"

"Like we're staying here for our health," Sylv sneered. "*Three* minutes?"

For an answer, Deni only groaned louder and began to shift back into her animal shape. Tony seized hold of her shoulders while she still had shoulders and shook her roughly. The transformation reversed itself and she stared in his face as he demanded, "What's Magloire done? Where is he? Don't just snivel; talk!"

Deni took in a long, gasping gulp of breath, then spoke rapidly. "We were watching Nok-Nok when I started to get sleepy, just like that, for no reason. It had to be a spell; it hit me so suddenly I couldn't fight it. I nodded off, but something woke me, a loud noise—a door slamming, I think—and I woke up in time to see Magloire going out the door with Nok-Nok in his arms. *Trying* to go out. *He* was back; Jordan."

"Back?" Tony echoed. "Why?"

Deni ignored the question, all her consciousness focused on getting her story told as quickly as possible. "I heard them yelling at each other while I was coming out of the last of the sleep spell my brother laid on me. Then I saw Magloire drop Nok-Nok, sort of shove him into a wall so he was propped up against it, and draw a silver claw-hook on your friend. He cut him and cut him and cut him and—" She was going hysterical again. This time Sylv was the one who stepped in and brought the pooka back with a sharp slap across the face.

"Three minutes, remember?" she snarled.

Deni was breathing shallowly, her eyes glazing over with terror, but she nodded and said, "He never looked back. He must've thought I was still asleep. He paused just long enough to sing the words that would make all this—" she gestured at the stockpiled fireworks "—blow up as soon as he had Nok-Nok well away. I started after him, to stop him, but—but—" She began to weep.

"You did the right thing, Deni," Tony said calmly. In one of the boxes, a string of firecrackers began to pop—not a full-fledged explosion, but the sulky, reluctant sound of the last few kernels of microwave popcorn. "If you know your brother's too strong for you to fight alone, you did right. Now get out the way you came, save yourself, try to carry Jordan out too. Go on, go!" He pushed her in the direction of the air duct.

She stumbled towards it, still sobbing. Sylv grabbed Tony's arm. "That's *it?*" she snapped. "That's all you're gonna do? Let her get away and let us stay here and burn like a couple of—?"

"Shut up." Tony wasn't listening to her; not really. Tony wasn't looking at her. He turned his back on the still-ranting nocker and fixed his gaze on the nearest crate of fireworks.

The label said it held a dozen bottle rockets. The rumbling was louder than ever; the cellar walls seemed to be shaking with the vibrations from the crates under Magloire's spell. Tony closed off all his outer senses one by one, leaving only the path of sight open. He filled his eyes with the bright green and gold logo on the crate's label, a writhing dragon with outspread claws, trailing whiskers, scarlet eyes. He held the dragon's painted stare, drawing in the power of the beast. As he felt himself sliding into the dragon's eyes of fire, rogue thoughts began to leap and cavort wildly through his head, a last distraction to what he knew he must do, and yet a distraction he was incapable of fighting…just yet:

Jordan's hurt, Nok-Nok's gone, stolen, still sick and maybe dying somewhere out there, Sylv, Sylv, Sylv, trapped, trapped, trapped, the fire inside and the fire outside burning towards the blast unless I—unless I—but Magloire's spell's too strong, he's too strong, and I don't know how to counteract a spell, and definitely not how to counter one of his, trapped, trapped, Sylv, Jordan, Nok-Nok—and Master Lung, where's he? Maybe hurt too, up there, Magloire might've crossed his path as well, and the old man tried to stop him, and the silver claw-hook, whatever the hell that is, maybe he cut him with it too, and he's lying helpless up there, bleeding, and the fire, the fire, the fire—!

He threw back his head and screamed, a scream so loud that for an instant it seemed to blot out the ominous shuddering of the crates, to beat back the heat that was now swelling into the room from all sides. Tony drove his thoughts into stillness with that scream, then forced his consciousness into a single burning pinpoint of power, and called in every shred and shard and fiber of glamour in his keeping into one twisting, spinning, blazing core just as the first crate of fireworks exploded.

One last thought went through Tony's mind as the roar and the ghastly, gorgeous light came rolling towards him in a wave of devastation: *I can't undo his spell, but what I can do—*

And then he was no longer thinking; he could only act. The fire rushed out to meet him and his glamour rushed ahead to meet it halfway. Shining, prismatic globes of air streamed from his hands, a hundred, a thousand, ten thousand spheres of clearest ice that clasped themselves around the fire. Wondrous bursts of Roman candles filled the safety of enclosed places, the report of stuttering firecrackers came through the glimmering bubbles as little more than the chitter of crickets, and all the rockets—fire and thunder and searing death and beauty wrapped up in a single skin—all these were captured and held fast in the spheres of Tony's making. Captured in airy prisons, the fires flared out all their heart-stopping splendor in safety, every globe a sky against which the young master of spark and blaze and riotous color painted his dreams.

And then it was over. Tony's vision cleared to behold a landscape of fast-dispersing smoke, of broken and blackened wooden crates, of shattered, shining globes like broken ornaments from a giant's Christmas tree. His head filling with the stench of burned gunpowder. "Sylv?" he choked into the haze.

ESTHER M. FRIESNER

"Here." The nocker's voice came to him through an attack of coughing. The smoke was gone, sucked down into the last few gleaming fragments of the fire-spheres at Tony's feet. Sylv stood there, seemingly untouched, rubbing her eyes ferociously. "*Shit*, that smarts."

"You okay?" He went to her, forced her to drop the fist that was still knuckling her left eye, and lifted up her chin to gaze into her face.

She returned his look of concern with an awful grimace, left eye squinched up tight. "*Some* people could manage to hold back a blast that big before some *other* people got a goddam splinter in their eye. My eye. Ow. Fuck. How bad does it look?"

"I can't tell. Open up and I'll see."

She tried to open her eye; she failed. There was a long, red scratch streaking her left temple. When Tony tried to trace its path, she squealed and slugged his shoulder. "Stop! It hurts! Oh God, it hurts!" she wailed.

"Sylv, please—" He tried again to examine her injury, and again she rebuffed him, pain filling her mouth with unholy names. He felt a pang in his belly. He couldn't stand to see her suffer so. Her hurt was his. He carried the full guilt of it, though reason cried out that this was Magloire's doing. Reason didn't count.

"Oh, Sylv—!" His voice ached with as much pain as hers. She moaned and pulled away form him, but his left hand closed firmly on her arm, keeping her near, and his right crept up almost by its own will to shield her wounded face from further harm. He held his hand a little distance away from her temple, her eye, and saw the ghost of rainbow flames glow in his palm. A miniature blossom of fireworks leaped from the curve of flesh. Sylv yelped as it lanced between her eyelids.

And then she gasped with wonder. Her body, twisted tight, relaxed. She opened her eyes wide, both of them, and looked at Tony as if she were seeing him for the first time.

"Even the scar," he breathed. This time when his fingers traced the path where the angry red mark had marred Sylv's temple, she didn't jerk away. "What happened? What'd I do? How—?"

Before she could find the power to reply, there was a resounding crash and a clatter as Sylv's sword dropped free of the trapdoor and tumbled down the stairs. The nocker whirled away to grab it up just as the trapdoor was pulled back. Deni stuck her face through the opening.

"Holy shit," the pooka remarked, taking in the scene. "You're all right? What the hell happ—?"

Sylv didn't give her a chance to finish. The nocker was up the stairs and out of the cellar before Deni could get out of the way. By the time Tony emerged into the pantry, Deni was just managing to get back on her feet. Her stockings were a memory and her elegant legs were already purpling with bruises. Sylv believed that the shortest distance between two points was a straight line, even if *some* people chose to stand right in the middle of it.

She turned to the door that the nocker had obviously used to rush out and shouted, "The word you're looking for is *Excuse me*, you stupid bitch!"

Sylv's head popped back into the doorframe. "Okay, you stupid bitch, you're excused," she replied. "Now get outa the way and let Tony through. Jordan needs him."

"Jordan? What can he do for—?"

"He's a *healer*, you idiot. He healed *me*. He's got the Primal art in him the same as breath and blood. So move it or—"

Deni didn't need to be told twice. She made a wild grab for Tony and hustled him out of the pantry into Sylv's waiting arms. "A healer," she repeated in awe as she thrust him through the door. "Who knew?"

12

"Why isn't it working? Damn it, *why won't it work?*" Tony cried. He sat on a chair by Jordan's bedside, holding his hands over the big man's bleeding body as if warming them at a fire, only this time there were no healing flames cupped in his palms, only shadows. Sylv stood just behind his right shoulder, Deni at a more judicious distance. The females Changelings watched over Tony's futile efforts, their faces both rapt and strained.

Jordan Avery lay stretched out on Nok-Nok's abandoned bed, his eyes closed, his breath a shallow rasping sound in his throat. "It worked on *you*, why won't it work on *him?*" Tony turned to plead with Sylv as if the nocker had the ability to set everything to rights.

She didn't, and it made her even more prickly than normal. "How the fuck should *I* know?" she snapped at him. "Like it's *my* fault? Like I'm hiding something, just for kicks? Oh yeah, there's nothing I get off on more than watching someone die...*not*. Treat *me* like a stinkin' redcap and I'll—"

"What has happened here?" Master Lung's voice made them all whirl around. The old Chinese man stood staring at the scene in Nok-Nok's bedroom with a face gone the color of spilled wax. "Where is the child?"

They answered him all at once:

"We don't know."

"Magloire's got him."

"Look, about the cellar—"

"The cellar?" Master Lung repeated. Tony nodded miserably. The old man scurried off, only to return shortly and say, "His doing too. I am thankful you escaped. Now tell me: what is this?" He indicated Jordan. "I went after this man, I found him, I sent him back here ahead of me. I wanted to—" He paused as if he were a boy about to be caught in a shameful deed. "I wanted to bring a common doctor here to examine the child." He looked at Tony. "That is what you wanted, wasn't it?"

Tony only shook his head dumbly. Doctor or herbalist or magical healer, what did any of that matter now? Nok-Nok was gone and Jordan would soon be dead. Whatever a claw-hook was, it cut deep: Jordan's body was a roadmap carved in red. He had lost a lot of blood, and despite their best efforts to staunch the flow with strips of torn-up sheets, he was losing more. The bed was gummy with it.

"*Try*, Tony," Sylv urged in his ear. "Try again, the way you did for me."

Tony wanted to explain to her that he hadn't *tried* when he'd healed her; he'd simply done it. It was like the old kid's poem about the bug that could walk on water right up until the moment that it *thought* about how it could do that, and then it sank.

Deni was talking with Master Lung, telling him everything that had happened. The old man's eyes shone with pity and grief. "And I could not even find a doctor who would come here," he murmured. "They all told me to bring the patient to them, or to call 911 and have him taken to a hospital." He blinked. "What am I thinking? I'll call for an ambulance for *him*, at least." He started from the room.

Red silk shot with gold flashed in the doorway. A wizened brown hand held itself up before Master Lung's face. "Stay," said Xia Xiao. She was as tiny and fragile-looking as before, except now she came before them dressed in strangely regal robes which she wore with a queen's haughty grace. "We do not want outsiders meddling in any of this."

Master Lung stood aside as the healer slipped past him and came to stand over the bed where Jordan Avery lay bleeding. To Tony's horror she dipped one fingertip into the blood welling up out of the dozen cuts across the big man's chest and put it to her lips. "Silver," she pronounced. Dark eyes darted birdlike over the damage done. "A claw-hook's work, no doubt of it." She looked long and hard at Deni. "For this, there can be no further forgiveness for your brother. Do not waste the Court's time with more of your begging for his pardon."

Deni's answered look was as hard and cold as Xia Xiao's. "Not this time," she said, her voice flint. "Not now and nevermore." Her face looked as if someone had sucked it down to skin and bone. "I didn't want to think of it, about how maybe he was telling me the truth, but he bragged and—"

"Bragged?" The old woman looked at her steadily. "What truth is this?"

"He said that we were unappreciated among the Seelie, and that his talents, at least, deserved better." Deni tried to maintain an emotionless expression as she recounted her kinsman's shameful words, but her voice shook at the edge of tears. "He said he was sick of playing by any rules but his own and that—" She almost lost control then, but recovered to finish quickly: "—that there were some Changelings out there who'd understand and welcome him for it."

"The Unseelie." Sylv mouthed the word as if tasting filth on her tongue. "That *fucker*. That lousy, treacherous, bloodless *bastard*." She glowered at Deni, her fury wanting someone to blame.

The pooka's spirit shattered under Sylv's poisonous stare. "I thought—I thought he was joking." The tears came down her face silently, like water flowing over stone.

"Some joke."

"Let Magloire go where he will," Xia Xiao pronounced. "For now, he is not our concern." She looked at the bleeding man on the bed.

"Xia Xiao, can you help me?" Tony implored, looking up at the formidable old woman. "Just before, down in the cellar, Sylv got hurt and I—I did something or other, and she healed, only now I can't do it for Jordan, and I—"

"Hush." Again the brown hand came up, the staying gesture like a dancer's. "If you could, I would be afraid that all your arts are only mirror-glims—petty tricks of glamour loaned out by the true faerie to common mortals, deceits to let them believe they are of our kind." Here she looked meaningfully at Sylv.

"Hey! The hell I did! *You're* a fine one to talk," the nocker shot back. "Anything he's got, he came by naturally, okay? Like *I* would've waited 'til the last fuckin' second down there to dump cold water on the big blowout if it was *my* power? Nuh-uh, lady, it's all his."

"Give me your chair, Tony," Xia Xiao said, turning from Sylv as if the nocker hadn't spoken at all. Tony did as he was told, sparing a single, confused glance in Sylv's direction as he did so. From what he knew, the nocker didn't care for being ignored, or even overlooked. If anyone gave her a silver less than all the respect she thought she deserved, fireworks went off, and not the kind that Tony could control. Yet there she stood, placid as a carved wooden saint. She was even smiling at the old woman.

Not that Xia Xiao was aware of it. She had slipped into Tony's seat and was running her hands over Jordan's body, long, sweeping, stroking motions from the crown of his head to the soles of his feet. Tony leaned in nearer to watch, then whispered, "If—if you want, I could go get your herb box."

Xia Xiao treated his words the same as she had treated Sylv's. He might as well have been standing on a distant star, whispering into the void. But a strong hand closed above his elbow and pulled him back. Master Lung regarded him solemnly and said, "The box is not necessary. The true healing lies there." He nodded towards the old woman's hands, now flying over Jordan's body faster and faster, until they became a golden blur. The bloody clothing covering the big man began to shimmer, then to melt before Tony's eyes until it vanished completely, leaving only the bare skin exposed to the air. Xia Xiao folded her hands in her lap and bowed her head.

"First, give the hurt to the light," she said, sounding like a schoolteacher presenting her first grade class with A-is-for-apple. She looked up at Tony, and suddenly he realized that she was teaching him. "Next—" She pulled back her left sleeve with the fingertips of her right hand "—read the path of the blood in its proper channels." She clenched her left hand into a small, brown fist, then flung the fingers wide. A burst of crimson light exploded from the palm, cast itself into ribbons that writhed over Jordan's skin in a network that showed all the myriad pathways of the heart. Under the touch of the glowing map of veins and arteries and even the tiniest of capillaries, Jordan's wounds seemed to freeze the escaping blood in place. The slashes left by Magloire's savage attack still gleamed moist and red, but at least no more blood was lost. Xia Xiao pressed her hands together firmly as if in prayer, then let them drop to her knees and turned her face to Tony. "This will hold a little while. We can talk."

"I—I never knew you had that kind of magic in you." Tony stood awestruck. Now that he really looked at the old woman, he could feel the power that lay over her entire body like a cloud. The force of her magic was so great, so demanding of attention, that all his senses screamed out to call him an idiot for never having noticed it before.

"Do not be ashamed for your ignorance." She spoke as if his thoughts were spelled out in the air between them. "You are very new to this, very young, untrained in almost all things belonging to your Arts, and I am very old and good at concealing things. It was my hand that hid the lost tripod of Zhou from the grasping claws of Shi Huang Di, the First Emperor, the ungodly burner of books. It was my Art that lifted up the great wind that turned the fireships at the Battle of Red Bluff and remade the face of the Middle Kingdom. It was my spirit that danced before Xuang-tzu's eyes as a butterfly and gave him a glimpse of the Dreaming."

She rose from the chair, but she did not stand. The tiny body floated up, turning gently in midair, Xia Xiao's dark eyes bright with tender laughter. They all gazed at her, seeing from moment to moment how face seemed to soften, then re-form itself. Her flesh became wet clay under an invisible potter's touch, age and youth flickering in and out of sight like moth wings glimpsed by the light of a wind-tossed paper lantern.

"Xia Xiao!" Master Lung exclaimed as if in pain. He took a step towards her, arms outstretched, ready to rescue her whether or not she was if any peril.

"No, old friend," she said gently, her face settling back into its familiar guise. She made a wide gesture of wiping away and Master Lung folded over in sleep.

Tony cried out and dropped to the floor beside the old man, drawing his teacher across his knees and cradling him like an infant. "Let him go!" he yelled at Xia Xiao.

"In a little. For now, it is better so," she said. Her eyes brimmed with regret as she gazed on Master Lung's peaceful face. "He has always been a faithful servant. I will not reward him with a hard truth until I must."

"What hard truth? What are you talking about?"

Xia Xiao spared a moment to glance at Jordan's body. Only when she was satisfied that her net of holding was still well in place, preventing further loss of blood, did she say, "That he can never be the one to teach you the true mastery of your given Arts."

"That's impossible!" Tony cried. "What about all he taught me about controlling the fireworks, forming them, loosing them, holding them back? What he taught me saved my life and Sylv's just now!"

"What saved your life was your own power to master glamour. What he taught you was how to use the same tools he has used all his life." She lowered her voice and somewhat sadly added: "One who teaches an infant to read and write can not claim he has made the child into an immortal poet. That comes from within the child himself."

Sylv squatted down beside Tony and rested her hand on his shoulder. Her sharp little chin jerked at the sleeping Master Lung as she murmured, "I guess it's time you knew: he's not one of us. He's only a mortal."

Tony stared—first at Sylv, then at Master Lung—with such a look of horror on his face that the old man might as well have sprouted the fangs and deer antlers

PLAYING WITH FIRE   683

of a dragon. "But—but—" He turned his eyes to Xia Xiao. "He thinks he's a Changeling."

"Because it suits us that he think so," the old woman replied calmly. "It is a deception of convenience. I have loaned him a certain measure of power and allowed him to think that the minor enchantments he wrought from it were all of his own making. The delusion does him no harm and gives us free access to a source of glamour of great potency."

"A source…Him?" Tony asked.

Xia Xiao inclined her head in agreement. "A source that will remain open to us for as long as he fancies himself one of us. Surely, child, you know this much of the way of the world? Mortals tend to give of themselves more freely when they believe that they are helping their own kind. Oh yes, a great source of glamour indeed. Master Lung is, in his chosen field, an artist. For him, fireworks are more than mere toys and trifles to amuse his customers, noisemakers to make children laugh and pretend to be afraid. He uses fire to give form to the visions of his mind, the songs of his soul. He masters thunder, bends lightning to his will, and makes the night sky bloom with a thousand flowers. He is a master of his art in more than name." Her eyes glowed warmly at Tony. "As are you."

It was a compliment of the highest, but Tony brushed it aside like a fall of dead leaves. "He's a fool. A dupe. Not that it's any fault of his. Damn it, I thought you were *different*." He made a fist and tensed as if to spring for the old woman. Then he recalled the burden in his lap. He gazed at Master Lung's face, serene in spell-sent sleep. He could read the lines and creases in the flesh like an archaic script that traced a tale of many woes, but many joys as well.

He went to get a doctor because that was what I thought would be best for Nok-Nok. He cares about what I think. He cares about me, Tony realized.

He lifted his eyes to Xia Xiao's and they were cold with a terrible judgment. "You're no better than Magloire."

"Hey!" Sylv gave him a shot in the back with her knuckles. "Watch your mouth, flamer! She's, like, only the oldest, sharpest, most respected grump in this whole goat-sucking city! Shit, even the sidhe take the time to please-and-thank-you her, and those piss-sniffing prettyboys don't bother about any of us unless they step in something and need their boots cleaned."

"Like none of *you* bother about mortals unless you can use them!" he sniped. "I know users. I hate them. If that's what being a Changeling means, then I don't want any part of it."

For a second, he thought he saw a look of deep hurt in Sylv's eyes. It was just as suddenly gone, buried deep behind the nocker's preferred facade of pugnacity. "You don't like us? Fine, who's keeping you here? Don't let the doorknob hit you in the ass on the way out!"

Enough!

The word was not spoken or shouted or uttered in any way that Tony's earthly senses could perceive. It was not even spoken in his mind, but rather seemed to blast its way out of every long bone in his body, sending splinters of chalky white tearing outward through the flesh. Yet when he looked, he was unharmed. Only then did he glance up to see that Sylv and Deni too were staring open-mouthed at their own limbs as if startled to see them still attached to their bodies.

"Better," Xia Xiao said, her lips snapping shut over a word actually spoken aloud. Her body slowly returned to the chair beside Jordan's bed. Like a fussy housewife plucking lint from her child's sweater, she reached out over the crimson net of blood encasing the big man and daintily tweaked a strand here into place, shifted the position of a strand there.

When she was once more satisfied, she said to Tony, "You condemn as quickly as they once condemned you who never knew you. *Whore!*"

He jerked his head back and his cheeks reddened as if he had been slapped. The old woman folded the fingers of one hand inward, then cast it open at Tony. Crumpled dollar bills fluttered around his head like bats before blowing away to sprinklings of ash. The clean anger in Tony's eyes was now beaten back before a helpless look of fear and wonder.

Xia Xiao shook her head. "I do not call you by that name, Tony," she said, and there was love enough in her voice to heal every hurt he had ever known in the bad times. "I only seek to help you understand. Go. Leave Master Lung here, in our care, and go into his bedroom. Open the bottom drawer of his chest and look for an old book, a photo album. Open it, but take care! Open it only to the last page."

"Why? What's wrong if I look through all of—?"

"Only the last page holds the information you need, the facts that will let you understand why we have done what we have done with Master Lung. To look elsewhere—well, I can not stop you from doing that, but I would rather you did not. A book may hold words, or pictures, or both, and sometimes these are only smears of ink and blots of color on paper. Yet sometimes these are all the record of a man's life when he has lost everything else. They are his treasure, to be stolen from him or to be shared out by his own hand, if you give him that choice."

"Like the choice you gave him?" Tony muttered. But he gently eased the sleeping man from his lap and left the room to do as Xia Xiao had instructed him.

He found the photo album exactly where Xia Xiao had told him it would be. It was as old and brown and wrinkled as the grump herself, with a little gold scrolling running around the edge of the front cover. He sat on a chair in the old man's room with the book across his knees and dutifully turned it over so that he would open it to the last page.

It was a terrible fire. The newspaper clipping pasted to the album's endpage reported that the engines of three separate fire departments in the area had been called out to stop it. The owner of the old two-family house up in Yonkers—a bachelor schoolteacher—had died in the blaze, along with the married brother who live in the other half of the building, the brother's wife and two children, and the aged grandmother who shared the bachelor brother's quarters. The fire had begun in the middle of the night and spread rapidly. When questioned, the fire chief had been unable to give a conclusive answer as to the cause of the blaze, but said that he was pretty sure it had spread so rapidly because of flammable substances improperly stored in the property's basement.

There was a photograph of the one survivor, an old man whose face was a smear of soot and singe. The reporter covering the tragedy recorded how this man—husband, father, father-in-law and grandfather to the victims—had come back from a trip into the city to see his home ablaze, and how he had dashed past the firefighters like a madman, into the heart of the flames, trying to save lives already lost. All he had been able to do before the firefighters dragged him back out again was find the body of the family cat, and that poor creature too was dead, killed by the smoke. He stood there holding the stiffening bit of fur to his chest, his eyes already taking on the glaze of madness.

"Master Lung…"

"Yeah." A shadow fell over the clipping. Tony jerked his eyes from the page to see Sylv standing before him. "It happened a long time ago, maybe fifteen years, maybe twenty, I dunno."

Tony checked the clipping for its date and said, "Fifteen."

"Whatever. All I know is, it was before *my* time. My time in the motley, I mean. Hell, from what Xia Xiao told me, I wouldn't know one face of the kithain in it then. They're all gone now, dead or moved on. We used to have a sidhe in with us in those days, can you see it? Jeez. Thank God he's gone on to serve King David's household. A sidhe…" She gagged theatrically. "Anyhow, the only reason Master Lung didn't die that night was he'd been in town, talking with some of his old buddies, planning out the fireworks displays for Chinese New Year. Planning and drinking and laughing about how his old woman nagged him to move the stuff the hell out of their daughter's house, 'cause the grandkids were getting into it and if they got hold of some matches there'd be hell to pay."

"So that's where the fire came from," Tony mused.

Sylv shook her head, then shrugged. "Maybe, maybe not. See, that was another reason he'd gone into the city: to move the stuff out. There wasn't even the teensiest little firecracker left behind."

"How would you know?"

"Same way I know any of this: Xia Xiao told me, told us all. She was here in those days. She's *always* been here. And she knew Master Lung then, only he didn't know who she really was, if you follow."

Tony nodded. "He thought she was just a herbalist."

"And he still thinks so. Or he did, until tonight, when she showed him." Sylv gave a dry little chuckle. "Women! I guess we can't keep secrets after all."

"But how did she know that he wasn't to blame for the fire? Is she a—a Soothsayer?"

"Huh! Nah. She says she was there at the New Year's planning meeting when Master Lung and this other pal of his showed up toting the boxes. Master Lung was going on about how his old lady wanted the stuff out of the house and how his buddy Jiang made real sure to pick up every last piece of it."

"Then why did he—?"

"Every last *whole* piece. After it happened, when Xia Xiao found him

ESTHER M. FRIESNER

wandering the streets weeks later, he was babbling something about how maybe he and Jiang weren't careful enough, how they probably overlooked a cracker or a rocket that got broken open and scattered powder down in the basement of his son's house, how when the first spark of the fire hit that—" She puffed out her cheeks to make the sound of a major explosion, then shook her head again. "And there was no telling him anything else. Poor crazy old man."

"But he wasn't to blame," Tony insisted, as if he had the evidence to prove it. "He couldn't have been! You see how he works, how much attention he pays to details. He wouldn't have overlooked *anything* when he cleaned the stuff out of the cellar there. It's just not the way he is."

"He had to blame someone. There had to be a reason for what happened. If there wasn't, it was somehow worse than thinking it was all his own fault."

"I don't see how."

"You don't have to. Anyway, after it happened, he wandered off. Like I said, Xia Xiao found him in Chinatown a couple of weeks later. Poor guy was still holding onto that cat. He had it all wrapped up in a piece of silk—god knows where he found *that*—and he was talking to it like it was one of his grandkids. Must've been pretty ripe by then." Her laugh over that was short, and held no joy.

"So first thing Xia Xiao does is get him cleaned up and she takes the cat's body away from him and she lets him live with her awhile, but it's no good: He's crazy. The quiet kind of crazy where they just sit there, looking at the wall all the time, and only eating when there's food put right up to their mouths. I don't even wanna think about how he must've smelled. Hell, at least while he was carrying that dead cat around with him he was moving and talking. Xia Xiao took it from him and the last light blew out."

"So how'd he come here? How come he's got the clipping, the album, all this, a life again?"

"You *sure* you want me to tell you?" Sylv said, her voice hard with sarcasm. "I remember how pissed off you got when she admitted she tricked him into thinking he was a Changeling. I wouldn't want to offend your high morals by telling you the details of how she screwed with head, even if now you can probably guess why."

"That's how she brought him out of it?" Tony asked, hardly able to believe it. "By telling him he was—?"

"Shit, she couldn't *tell* him anything, the way he was. She had to *show* him. She rigged it good, but like I said, Xia Xiao's one of the oldest, the smartest, the best."

"How?"

"It was the Feast of the Hungry Ghosts." Xia Xiao herself came into the room. There was a slight hesitation to her steps, as if she were suddenly very tired, though her face was unchanged. "It is all right," she said in answer to the question in Tony's eyes. "I have finished with your friend. He will recover quickly now. The healing of the wounds themselves was the easy part. What silver opens, silver closes." She pulled a jade-tipped hairpin from her carefully anchored gray tresses, let them both see the gleam of the moon-metal shaft, then replaced it. "I had to wait until the lifestream had replenished itself before I could seal up the vessel."

"Sylv's been telling me how you saved Master Lung's sanity," Tony said, abashed. "If that's why you lied to him about being a Changeling, I'm sorry for what I said to you before."

"'If'?" Xia Xiao echoed.

"No, I mean—oh damn, now I'm sorry for that, too. I don't know what to say any more; I keep tripping over my own tongue."

"Promises, promises," Sylv purred, a hint of the old deviltry back in her voice.

"No need for apologies from either of us," Xia Xiao said. "I have profited as much from Master Lung's recovery as has he. It was, as I said, the Feast of the Hungry Ghosts, the time when the gates of Hell are opened and the unrevered dead stream back up to earth to claim their due. Those who died by violence, those who died without descendants to perform the proper sacrifices, those whose descendants have turned away from the old ways of worship, all of these return. Plague rides with them, and a host of other ills, unless the living do what they can to placate the unsatisfied dead.

"I took Master Lung with me into a temple. I used my Arts to weave the proper spells of shielding so that to the casual eye, we were not there. Large joss sticks were burning, each almost as thick around as a boy's body. Offerings of food and drink were arranged in the proper manner. Braziers stood ready to receive the offerings of hell money and other gifts—houses, cars, servants, every luxury— all crafted of paper. By burning these we send them on to where our beloved ancestors have need of them. I gave him a thin pasteboard box filled with slips of paper shaped like children's toys and told him, 'For your grandchildren.' He looked at the papers, then at me, and let them fall from his hand top the temple floor." Xia Xiao's mouth tightened. "That was when I called forth the dragon."

"*Damn.*" Sylv stamped her foot. "The cool stuff you miss out on seeing just 'cause you're not born early enough to be there. Rats."

"It was nothing to regret so dreadfully, child," Xia Xiao told her. "It was not a real dragon; it was the thinnest of illusions, an infant chimera, one that even you could summon up without a second thought. His mind was badly weakened by grief and guilt, the doors between his mortal reality and fantasy all but melted away. He did not need to see much to be convinced. The dragon stooped before him, took him up on its shoulder, and gave him the great pearl of power and wisdom that was in its keeping. When he gazed into the pearl, he thought he saw his true nature, his true blood, his true calling. So he told me when he recovered from the illusion. It was the baldest of deceits, the crudest of lies—I admit it, but I do not regret it. Banality stole all that made his life something more than just a tally of days and seasons and years. We have given him back a reason to live, and he has given us the means to thrust back the dread autumn for a little while longer. No, I can never regret any of this."

Tony stood, laying the open album down on top of Master Lung's chest of drawers. Without knowing why, he found himself bowing to Xia Xiao, hands pressed together in a gesture of reverence.

Sylv peeped at the clipping. "You give him this, too?" she asked.

"I? No. That was always his. After the dragon blew away into the smoke that had spawned it, Master Lung was himself again. He looked down at his soiled clothes, then he looked for me. I was not there. Instead, the first person he saw was Popo, an old boggan grump who belonged to our motley in those days. I had contrived it so. Popo did exactly what I had instructed him to do: first he welcomed him into the ranks of our kind, then he introduced him to the rest of our motley, and finally he took Master Lung back to his friend Jiang's place, so that he might reestablish a foothold in the mortal world. Jiang hadn't seen him since the night of the fire; he'd thought him dead."

"So what'd that make him think of Popo?" Sylv asked.

"Popo's mortal name and seeming was George Ricci, a member of the New York City police force. He was killed in the line of duty ten years ago. It did not look strange for a policeman to bring Master Lung to his friend's home. Master Lung fell into Jiang's arms, both men weeping tears of gratitude for this reunion. By the time they parted, Popo was gone."

"But—the album?"

"That was in Jiang's keeping, along with all of Master Lung's earthly goods that had been rescued from the fire. Even then Master Lung was a member of great respect in the community; ways were found to ensure that his unclaimed property did not vanish into the city bureaucracy. As for the clipping itself, I put it there."

"You?" Tony was incredulous. "Even knowing that the fire was what drove him insane? Why—?"

"A man who keeps his demon close at hand is that demon's master. A man who banishes his demon to the shadows, afraid to face it, lets that demon master him. That is what I told Master Lung when he first came to this place to live and work, after he had reclaimed his life among mortals and taken his place among Changelings. That is when I gave him the clipping. He was free to burn it or to keep it." She nodded towards the album. "You see the choice he has made."

"Speaking of choices, is there any Diet Coke in this house? If not, I'll drink regular, I guess." Jordan Avery's voice boomed through the doorway, followed an instant later by the man himself. He stood leaning against the jamb, holding a blood-spattered sheet around his shoulders, a shaky grin on his face. "Caffeine free, though. Okay?"

Tony rushed over to embrace his friend, smiling so broadly he thought his face would split. "Okay!"

"Hey, hey, cool it, all I wanted was a Coke!" Jordan pushed Tony back, laughing. "And a shirt. And maybe a change of pants while I'm at it. The next blood gets spilled on *me* belongs to Magloire."

13

Xia Xiao looked down at the oranges that Tony had poured into her lap. "What is this for, child?" the healer asked wearily.

"Happy new year." Tony did his best to brighten his half-hearted smile. It still wasn't his new year and from the way things had been going, it would be anything but happy.

In the days since Nok-Nok's vanishment, he and the rest of the motley had combed the city, but turned up nothing—no sign of either the boy nor his kidnapper. Magloire was sharp and Magloire knew New York. There were only so many places the motley could search in any given span of twenty-four hours, whereas there were tens of thousands of places their quarry could be. Sometimes one of them stumbled across a sign of Magloire's presence, but it was strictly that-was-then. The sign was always old, the trail leading off from it invariably cold, the satyr's ghostly laughter harsh in everyone's mind.

As Sylv so succinctly put it: "Aw, *fuck.*"

Xia Xiao leaned back in her carved rosewood chair, winter sunlight streaming in through narrow show-window fronting the Wan Sui Herb Shop. The shadows of the characters painted on the glass fell on the floor between herself and Tony, dust motes dancing in the light, the smell of many herbs and other medicinal compounds sharp and sweet on the air. No matter what the calendar said, winter was hanging on. Outside it was very cold, with piles of dirty snow hugging the sidewalks, but inside the shop it was cozy and warm. She picked up one of the oranges and turned it slowly around in her hand. "Did Master Lung send you here with these?"

"Nope. Strictly my own idea. That is, he told me about the tradition and all. Just by-the-way, not like he actually expected me to *do* anything about it."

"Why did you?"

Tony shrugged. "I dunno. It sounded kind of cool. And it's a sign of respect for your elders. On the way back, I'm gonna make another stop at the fruit stand and buy some more to give to him."

"That is good of you." Xia Xiao's approval fell on Tony like the comfort of a warm blanket on a cold night. "How is he? Does he recall anything of being put under a sleep spell?"

"Didn't you hear this from Sylv or someone else before now? He woke up in his own bed the next morning and he didn't remember a thing about it, only that you'd come to his house to heal Jordan."

"Sometimes enchantments, like walls, have cracks in them so small that one does not perceive them at first. I wove most of that spell's strength into the deepness of the sleep that overcame him, not into the forgetfulness I wished to cover the entire incident. If there was a weakness in that portion of the spell, it might not show itself immediately."

"Well, I guess you can stop worrying about that now. If he does remember anything about it, he hasn't said a word to me or the rest of the motley. Either he doesn't remember or he's just been too busy to talk about it. He's been working 'round the clock lately, not even stopping for meals, almost. I bet when I give him the oranges *that*'ll stop him." Tony grinned. "I can't wait to see the look on his face when I do it."

The grump's face warmed with a smile. "If you really wish to surprise him, greet him properly: *Gong xi fa cai*."

"*Gong xi*...what?"

Patiently Xia Xiao coached Tony through the correct pronunciation of the traditional Chinese new year greeting.

"And make certain that you give him an even number of oranges, too," she said when he was finally able to say it to her satisfaction.

"Huh?"

"Even numbers are auspicious. See here what I have for you." She dipped one hand into the belled sleeve of her jacket and pulled out a pair of paper packets the same bright red as the silk garment itself.

Tony looked at the Chinese characters printed in gold foil on the red packets, puzzled. "Um...thanks."

Xia Xiao cackled with laughter. "Do not stand on ceremony. Open them!" He did, and found two crisp ten dollar bills in each one. "*Hong bao*," the old woman explained. "Another new year's tradition. They are gifts of good luck, but only if the amount inside is an even number. I have given you a pair of them, which should double your good fortune."

"I don't know a lot of people who'd be too fussy about getting an odd amount of money," Tony joked, folding up the bills and putting them away.

"If you still turn your back on what is a part of you, at least have the wisdom not to mock good fortune. That is the one thing of which we all have need, from a well-omened birth to an auspicious death."

"I don't know if that's the way I'd describe any kind of death, Xia Xiao," Tony said, "but as far as needing good fortune, I'm with you. The motley could sure use a better kind of luck than what we've been having lately. Poor Nok-Nok. I guess I really let him down."

"Not yet," Xia Xiao said. "There is still time. Magloire has gone to ground. He has not yet brought the child before the lords of the Unseelie Court."

"How do you know? You're no Soothsayer."

"No, I am not. Nor is Tirall. He is something more useful: A sluagh. He goes— in the flesh but unseen—to places which a Soothsayer merely glimpses."

Tony's skin rippled over his bones with distaste. In his dealings with his fellow Changelings he had yet to encounter a sluagh face to face, but Sylv and Deni and Sonnet had filled his ears with enough overly descriptive tales of the underdwellers and their clammy ways for him to be glad of it. Guardians of great secrets they might be, but there was something inherently repulsive about them. Or so he'd concluded from what he'd been told.

"You...*know* a sluagh?"

"As should you. Tirall is of our motley, after all, even though he does not choose to frequent our gatherings."

Thank God, thought Tony.

"Solitary as he is, he has thrown himself into the search for Magloire as diligently as the rest of you, once I informed him of the situation," Xia Xiao continued. "He walks where none of you know the way...or would care to. He is the one who brought me word that the Unseelie Court has yet to claim a triumph over us. Magloire has not shown his face there either, and there is not even a whisper of the boy. The recaps and trolls still seek him, not knowing that he is already in the keeping of one of their own allies."

"Like Magloire could be on anyone's side but his own," Tony said bitterly.

"All the better reason to renew your search," the old one counseled.

"Everyone else," Tony said. "Not me. I've got to take a couple of days off the hunt. You know…"

"Ah. Yes, I do." Xia Xiao nodded. "The celebrations begin. Master Lung must have a great display planned to usher in the new year for us, greater than any before. And you too will have a hand in that."

"If the cops don't stop us."

Xia Xiao smiled indulgently. "If there is a law against fireworks but the only ones with the power to enforce that law can not *see* the fireworks, is the law broken? Our motley is not the only one to admire Master Lung's craft. Even the sidhe of the High King's court have a fondness for his spectacular artistry. We cooperate, pooling our glamour to cast a warding that shields the eyes and ears of any who believe that such displays are foolish, frivolous, dangerous, and we unite our powers also to ensure that there is never anything truly dangerous about it. Only those who seek to see the dragon will behold him. Those who disbelieve may gaze into the truth of his golden eye and see no more than a paper lantern."

"So that's how we get away with it? I was wondering." Tony pulled his jacket collar up around his ears. "Well, I guess I'll be going home now."

"Do not forget the oranges," Xia Xiang called out as the door closed after him.

"Oranges?" Sylv was seated at the kitchen table with Master Lung when Tony came in and set down his new year's gift before his teacher. She looked around the room where bowls and baskets were already brimming with the golden fruit. "I think you guys have got a serious overstock problem going here."

"*Gong xi fa cai*, Master Lung," Tony said proudly, ignoring Sylv's comments.

The old man's face lit up with joy to hear those words. "Thank you, my son," he said. If Tony had mispronounced the greeting in any way, one could not tell from Master Lung's delighted reaction. He got up and went over to the counter where a row of blue and white ceramic canisters stood. Taking the lid off the second largest, he pulled out a red envelope and handed it to Tony.

Tony was about to open it when Sylv began clamoring, "What's that? What's in it? C'mon, open it up! No secrets."

Before Tony could open his mouth, Master Lung gently chided the nocker: "Sylv, it would be impolite for Tony to open his *hong bao* in front of the giver unless I request him to do so."

Sylv's eyes narrowed to suspicious slits. "Open his *what*?"

"This." Tony wiggled the red envelope in front of her. "How many years you been hanging around Master Lung and you don't know what *this* is?"

"Oh, like *you're* Mr. Cultural Literacy all of a sudden," she shot back. "You can't fool *me*, Lee: You were just over visiting Xia Xiao. She's the one gave you the *Cliff's Notes* crash course in Chinese New Year 101."

Master Lung sighed. "A woman's tongue has slain more men than a thousand executioners. Open the *hong bao*, Tony, so that we may have some peace."

Tony obeyed, making a long, slow, deliberately provoking job of it. But even he couldn't stretch out the opening of a single envelope by much, and soon Sylv's eyes were fixed hungrily on the stack of bills he revealed.

"Now *that's* what I call getting a good price for your oranges," she said.

"Here, child, I have not forgotten you." Chuckling, Master Lung went back to the blue and white canister and withdrew two of the red envelopes. Sylv all but snatched them from his hand, then stood there holding them with the expression of a four-year-old who has been shown her Christmas gifts and has been told that she must wait another day before she can have them.

"So what are you waiting for?" Tony prodded.

"I got just as many manners as you," she replied haughtily.

"Please, you would honor me if you would open them here and now," Master Lung said, eager to keep the peace so recently won.

He didn't have to tell her twice. She almost ripped the money in half in her hurry to get it out of the envelopes.

A little slip of white paper no bigger than the printed strips tucked into fortune cookies fluttered to the floor. Sylv was too busy counting her money to notice, but Tony did. He stooped to pick it up. "You forgot your fortune, Sylv. It says you're going to learn that money isn't everything," he kidded her.

"Fortune?" Master Lung's brows met. "I put nothing inside my *hong baos* but the gift itself. Let me see—"

He stretched out his hand for the little slip of paper. He might as well have been invisible. Tony was looking at it closely, reading the neatly lettered message, every word a snake's track. Sylv watched his face darken. Nockers hated being kept out of the loop. She slammed her money down on the kitchen table and gave him a shove.

"*What?*" she barked.

Tony looked up at her. "What do you think? It's a message from Magloire. We can stop looking for Nok-Nok."

"Oh no!" Sylv's fist flew to her mouth. "You mean he's—?"

"Alive. Still alive, barely alive, but alive enough to interest the Unseelie...or us, if we can meet Magloire's price."

"His...price?"

"Here." Tony handed the slip of paper to Sylv. Soon the little kitchen was filled with the racket of a nocker giving her vocabulary a good, strong workout.

"At least there's enough oranges to go around," said Telamon, picking up three from the basket in the center of the gaming table in the back room of *Wild Things* and juggling them. Like Magloire, he was a satyr, though little more than a childling. He was still mostly rough edges, but there was good substance underneath and no one better in all the motley for carrying out orders.

"Tony brought them," Sylv grumbled. "He's got a thing for oranges, this time of year."

"Hey, vitamin C's even good for elves," Jordan Avery said, knowing exactly what he was saying and what effect it would have on Sylv. The nocker snagged a fruit from the basket and pitched it fastball style at Jordan, who ducked. It splatted against a poster on the wall behind him, streaking sticky juice all over the slick picture of a raging werewolf.

"Gi' us one," said Prinx. The troll lunged his huge paw out and scooped one of Telamon's flying oranges out of midair, then popped it into his mouth whole and made a face. "Oooogh. Nasty."

"You numbskull, you're s'posed to *peel* 'em first." A second troll, a female named Varna sat beside Prinx the better to give him an elbow to the ribs when the occasion demanded it. She reminded Tony a lot of Sylv, only built on an epic scale.

"Arh?" Prinx helped himself to a second orange, tore off the peel in huge, ragged pieces that took out dripping chunks of the fruit along with them. By the time he had all the peel off, there was nothing left in his hand but a puddle of juice. "Don't work," he announced.

Varna sighed with gusty regret. "If only you were a plain old mortal bucketbrain," she said. "You could've had a future in politics."

"Where is Xia Xiao?" Sonnet asked, pacing the length of the table on velvet paws. The little black-and-white cat's tail was switching angrily, her fur fluffed up high, her eyes shooting sparks.

"She'll be here," Tony soothed. "It's hard for her to get out of Chinatown at this time of year, just like it is for Master Lung. Too much to do."

"We shouldn't have told her about this," Deni said, her voice skirling up the way it always did lately. The mink-pooka had dwindled to a shadow of her svelte and fashionable self since her brother's treachery came to light. Say what her motley mates would to allay her fears that Magloire's dirty doings soiled her as well, Deni still persisted in acting as if she were guilty of some unnamed crime. It had stolen the sparkle from her eyes and the mischief from her heart. She had become a tangled skein of nerves; little things sent her off into a panic and she had become prey to unexpected attacks of stammering. Tony couldn't remember the last time he'd seen her take her animal form or trade verbal barbs with Sylv or taste any form of joy. There was a dreadful *something* that seemed to hang about her—he would call it a *grayness*, if anyone had asked him to name it. It was nothing he could see, but he could sense it, right enough, and it filled him with a dank foreboding.

"Why the hell not?" Sylv demanded, moodily kicking the table leg. "It's not like she's *important* or anything."

"She won't even hear us out," Deni said, washing her hands rapidly with invisible soap. "She'll tell us not to even try ne—ne—*negotiating* with my brother."

"Ha! Like we ever would!"

"You—you don't understand. He's crazy. He's always been a little mad, you know, but thi—*this*—!" The distraught pooka's fingers were twisting and writhing over each other like a knot of snakes and her tongue thickened, lurching into words like stumbling blocks. "To steal the boy from us to give him to the Unseelie, ye—yes, but then to wi—wi—withhold him from *them* and try selling him back to *us*—! He's cra—he's cra—he's cra—"

"He's fuckin' nuts, okay?" Sylv yelled at her. "Now that we got *that* settled—"

"*Wisdom and sanity need not bed together.*" The voice came out of the corners of the room, a dark, hissing sound that seemed to slip from a thousand different sources and none. The members of the motley looked all around and saw only each other, never the speaker. "*Still our Magloire courts nothing kin to wisdom with his madness.*" Again the voice, everywhere, nowhere, and a gust of damp air that smelled of mold.

The troll Varna got up and went over to a wall where some of Jordan's regular gamers had covered over the plaster with crude sketches of their favorite characters. She cocked her heavy head to one side, rapped smartly at the juncture of three solemnly brooding vampires, and called right at the wall, "Tirall? That you?" Silence answered, then a scratching sound. Varna was satisfied. "Yep. That's him."

Sylv, Deni and Sonnet all eyed the wall nervously and moved away. The she-troll curled her blue-gray lip at them in disdain. "Don't wet yourselves, little ladies; you know Tirall always keeps to his own side of the wall." She rapped at the papered-over plaster again and called, "Isn't that right, sweetworm?"

A hiss like a leaky steampipe answered, and then: "*Do not call me that.*"

"Hoity-toity," said the troll with good humor. "Now why don't you explain yourself, what you meant about Magloire, hey? You saying he's nuts *and* he's stupid too? Smart enough to keep two steps ahead of *us*, that's plain."

"*No great achievement, that. My children too escape you easily.*"

Jordan leaned over to tap Tony on the shoulder and whisper, "He's got *kids* back in there with him?"

"Rats," said Sonnet pertly. "Tirall only calls them his children." She licked her whiskers.

Tony stood and joined the giant she-troll at the wall. Tentatively he rapped his knuckles against the pushpin-starred surface and called, "Tirall? Uh…hi. My name's Tony Lee. I'm Master Lung's apprentice. I'm new to the motley, but I've got a link to Nok-Nok that's the reason—"

"*I knew who and what you were before you ever did, Anthony Edward Lee,*" the sluagh's voice seeped into the room. "*I have watched you and I think well of you.*"

"Well…thanks. Then I guess you know why we're meeting here, and about Magloire's message, and—"

"*Who will blind the satyr?*" the sluagh's voice wove through the room. "*Who need bother, when he is already blind? Does he dream that he deals with witlings when he tries to cheat the Unseelie Court? He sets you a price of glamour to be ransom for the eshu and the eshu's secret, glamour all of you—of us—must pool into a token that he will take for his own, add to his own powers. Fool! Do the Unseelie sleep? While you debate his message, he hides, but to obtain the ransom he must show himself. Will the Unseelie neglect to know this simply because it would suit him that they do? They know, they know! And having in their ranks a Soothsayer great enough to hurl a curse upon the boy at so great a distance, will their Soothsayer be unable to find both the boy and his traitor-keeper now? Or if not now, then soon, soon...*" The sluagh's voice faded away, the sound seeming to ebb off in many directions at once, water trickling away through the holes of a sieve.

Varna clicked her tongue and gave the wall a healthy smack. "Well, that's it. He's gone."

"And a fat lot of help he was while he was here," Sylv said with a little snort of disdain.

"Maybe his idea of help is different from yours," Tony said.

"Mine *and* the dictionary's," Sylv countered. "What'd he give us? Zip. Zilch. Sweet squaddoo. What, so he coughed up the news that Magloire's nuckin' futz? Oh yeah, *big* secret, *big* help."

"Help enough, Sylv." Xia Xiao entered the back room of *Wild Things*. She was still clad in bright red silk, her hair piled in an elaborate design atop her head. Jade ornaments glowed with that special sheen which had once earned the stone its place as the precious gift of heaven, fit only for emperors and gods.

Young Telamon jumped up to offer the elder his chair. She patted his curly head fondly, her wizened brown fingers pausing to caress the small buds of his sprouting horns. "You will all pardon me," she said, sitting down. I have been eavesdropping. I know Tirall; it is sometimes his way to avoid me."

"Why?" Tony asked, genuinely curious. He couldn't imagine why anyone would want to avoid Xia Xiao.

"Because I am the senior member of this motley and because that sometimes makes me, in some small way, its leader. The sluagh do not care for leaders, as a rule." She pressed the palms of her hands together and rested them on the tabletop as if about to say grace before meals.

"So *you* think all that spew of his was a help?" Sylv asked, her color rising. With the sluagh gone, her temper wanted some way to vent a little steam. "Wow. The ineffable wisdom of the Orient."

Xia Xiao let the nocker's sarcasm pass without comment. "Sometimes help brings no new knowledge, but merely reminds us of things we already know, things we might ignore, things we dare not. The Unseelie to whom Magloire first intended to sell the boy do indeed have great weapons on their side, not least of which is this Soothsayer of theirs. As Tirall said, one with the power to curse the boy from such a distance could very well own the power to find him too."

"No," Tony said, shaking his head. "I mean, it doesn't make sense. If their Soothsayer *could* find Nok-Nok now, why didn't he find him *before*, when we were holed up in Master Lung's place?"

"You *know* why not, dummy," Sylv said. "'Cause we were all busting our humps to set up a shield-spell around him, *that's* why!"

"Yeah, which means Magloire's probably got the same kind of shield-spell up around him and Nok-Nok right now. It's gotta be taking a lot of his glamour to do it, but he doesn't dare drop it. He knows he's hunted—not just by us. By now the Unseelie must've caught wise to how he's cheated them."

"Why he'd want to pull a stupid stunt like that…" Sylv grumbled.

"Why?" Deni echoed. Her laugh was thin as an eggshell. "Because whatev—ever rew—w—w—ward they offered him to betr—tray us wasn't enough for hi—him."

"So he tries to sell us back one of our own with a pricetag of high glamour on him," Varna said, her fingers digging into the edge of the table. "Enough glamour to make Magloire so powerful he could put himself way beyond the reach of any punishment the Unseelie could sic on him; enough to set him up soft for *life*." A hunk of tabletop splintered off in her hand.

"Hey!" Jordan protested. A hard look from the female troll hit him right between the eyes. "Never mind," he said quickly.

"Yeah, but *what* life?" Telamon piped up. "Tony's right: It's taking a shitload of glamour for him to keep Nok-Nok under wraps from the Unseelie *and* us. The bastard can't keep it up forever. He wants *our* glamour? I say we don't give him *dick*. I say we wait him out. I say we let him drain himself dry and then when he *can't* hide from us any more—"

"—let the Unseelie find him first?" Xia Xiao asked. "Find him *and* Nok-Nok."

The young satyr twisted up his mouth into a petulant expression, said briefly, "Ah, screw it," and slouched against a wall, sulking.

"So what *do* we do?" Sonnet asked.

"I'll tell you what we *don't* do," Sylv said resolutely. "We don't give that hairy-legged goat butt *anything*. We don't deal with blackmailers. We don't—"

"We do," Xia Xiao said softly, and opened her hands. A disc of pure white jade shimmered in the air an inch above the table, a disc the size of a silver dollar with the coiled body of a dragon cut into the flawless stone with artistry and love.

The old woman closed her eyes and brought the tips of her middle fingers together over the exquisite medallion. Like a drop of honey, an amber tear formed between the pads of her fingers and fell to the disc where it cast up a tiny shower of brightness. No sooner was it absorbed than a second, then a third, then a trickle of that same substance—glamour made visible—poured down into the token that pulsed and rippled as it drank the power in.

And then the trickle stopped. Xia Xiao's hands parted, her head bowed over the white jade dragon. When she spoke, for the first time she sounded older than she looked: "We give him what he wants or we lose Nok-Nok, and if we lose Nok-Nok, Arcadia too is lost."

14

Tony lingered on the threshold of the Wan Sui Herb Shop. "Are you *sure?*" he insisted.

Xia Xiao inclined her head gracefully. "Quite sure. We must do this according to Magloire's instructions, after all, or he will stay away."

Tony got that stubborn look on his face. "I don't like this. None of us do, Xia Xiao."

"Why?" the old one asked, her voice gentle. She was seated on a tall stool behind the herb shop's immaculate, glass-topped counter, and now she unclasped her right hand to let the white jade token with its carved dragon clatter to the shiny surface. "Do you fear I too will betray our motley? Do you think I will take all this captured glamour into myself, rather than giving it Magloire, if you leave me alone?"

"You know that's not it!" Tony was startled by the vehemence of his own reaction to such a suggestion. "And we know you're not gonna give it to him, either, if any of us can help it. What we—what *I'm* afraid of is what if he comes here to collect and he grabs it before you can give the signal? We don't know how much of his own power he's got left. What if he's got enough to take you *and* overwhelm Prinx and Varna?"

"Both of them?" Xia Xiao's eyes slid discreetly from side to side, glancing lightly over the two squat, brass-bound chests that flanked the door. To the casual eye they looked like a pair of giant rosewood blocks, solid as cornerstones in a skyscraper's foundation, but cornerstones were sometimes hollowed out to contain mementos of a building's founding ceremony and these too were not as solid as they seemed. Each covered a trapdoor leading to the herb shop's basement, and when the hour was right and the signal given, each was meant to disgorge a fully armed troll to lay hands on Magloire and put an end to the satyr's career of treachery. "I doubt that, child. Prinx and Varna have the strength of their bodies to back up the power of the glamour still remaining to them. They will be more than a match for Magloire."

Tony scowled. "Yeah, when they *get* here."

"Oh, they will be here in time, never fear." The old woman tried to soothe his misgivings. "It is barely dusk yet, and Magloire will not come until well after nightfall. His message said that he wanted crowds enough to hide him and the boy, but not so many that the Unseelie could use them for cover as well. Most of the tourists have come, seen the parade, and gone off. Say all you will against him, he has a strategist's mind."

"I still don't see why Varna couldn't be here when we need her," Tony grouched.

"We do not need her *yet*. And she could not avoid the event that keeps her from us for these few hours. She still has loving kin among mortals; they have summoned her and she does not dare refuse the call."

"But to a *bar-mitzvah*?" Tony cried, as if begging Xia Xiao to reassure him that there was some mistake, and that Varna and Prinx were both already in place for the night's business.

"These are the matters of Varna's mortal family. They know nothing of her Changeling nature; they only love her. She loves them, too. She will not disappoint them any more than she will disappoint us."

"Okay, fine, so we've got a troll at a freakin' bar-mitzvah. Only in New York," Tony muttered. Then, more distinctly, he demanded: "So why couldn't Prinx be here?"

"I think that was Varna's doing too. She told me that she had to have a…date.

She swore to me that she would fly into full Bedlam if she had to hear her grandmother ask her one more time when she was going to bring a nice boy home with her." A smile flirted over the old woman's lips. "Besides, Prinx is of little use to us without Varna to guide him. Do not worry, Tony, they will come in time."

Tony didn't choose to respond. Instead he mumbled a curt farewell and bolted. He left in such a rush, he almost trod on the little black and white cat who was sauntering up and down the street in front of the herb shop.

"You wanna watch it there, sport?" Sonnet inquired with a forward flick of her whiskery eyebrows.

"Sorry."

"Forget it." The cat settled herself on her haunches and proceeded to wash her face. Between licks she asked, "You catch the parade? Pretty cool, especially all those dragons."

Tony didn't answer right away. There were plenty of people passing by on the street. When the cat-pooka spoke in her animal form, no mortal seemed able to catch the words—they only saw a cat, and of course everyone knew cats couldn't actually *talk*—but if Tony chose to answer, he'd look like a street-crazy, trying to have a chat with an alley stray. Even though he knew the truth of the situation, he didn't like being mistaken for insane.

"Oh, relax," Sonnet purred, giving another lick to her stainless white paw. "I've got my shields up. No one's gonna cart you off to the rubber room if you answer me."

Tony was dubious—pookas were notorious liars, anything for a joke. Sonnet might be waiting for him to start up an earnest conversation just to come back at him with an innocent "Mew?" and make Tony look like a lunatic in front of the tourists.

The cat looked up into his wall of silence, snorted, and with an impatient "Oh, for the love of—!" turned herself human.

Sonnet in human form was a small, deliciously voluptuous young woman with sleek, shoulder-length dark hair, milky skin, and an air of sensuality about her thick enough to peel away in layers. Not even the HELLO KITTY T-shirt that peeked out from beneath her black wool jacket could take that away form her. She linked her arm through Tony's, pressed herself close against him, and crooned, "*Now* will you tell me if you went to the parade?"

"Yeah," Tony admitted. "First time I ever did. Kinda neat, you know? But what do you mean, 'all those dragons'? There was only one."

"Yeah?" Sonnet's eyebrows rose in surprise. "So what were all of those other critters dancing in the streets and charging into all the shops? I mean, I *saw* them."

"Sure you did; so did I. They're lions, not dragons," Tony explained.

"Hey, those things don't look like any lion I've ever met," Sonnet protested. "And believe me, I've met a few. There's this one old pooka grump over in the Central Park Zoo who's found the perfect way to spend his sunset years: Free shelter, free meals, free medical care, and nothing to do all day but sleep and maybe roar at the schoolkids."

"Well, tough, they're *still* lions." Tony held his ground. "*Chinese* lions, okay

PLAYING WITH FIRE   699

by you? Just a coupla guys, lion dancers, doing all kinds of fancy steps, shaking the head, clacking the jaw, even some street acrobatics."

"Since when is rushing into a store in *that* get-up acrobatic?"

Tony grinned. "*That* part of it, Sonnet, is what you call jumping at the chance to pick up some easy money. It's tradition: When the lion charges into your shop you've got to feed him some *hong baos* to make him go away."

Sonnet nodded wisely. "Right, *hong baos*. I love 'em; great with soy sauce."

This time Tony laughed out loud. "*Hong baos* are money packets, Sonnet. You've seen 'em, right? Those red envelopes?"

The pooka scowled. She didn't care to be left looking stupid. "Well, excuse *me*, Mister Wisdom-of-the-Orient, *so* sorry to reveal my ignorance, *such* an honor to bask in your cultural superiority, but it wasn't all that long ago that you couldn't tell a chopstick from a chapstick."

Sonnet's scorn left Tony looking properly humbled. "Sorry. I guess I was showing off a little."

"Forget it. I stand charmingly corrected about the dragons." She squeezed his arm. "Lions, I mean. No wonder I liked them the best. What about you?"

Tony's shoulders rose and fell. "I dunno. There was so much going on: The dancers, the gongs, the music, everyone out there having a good time…But man, you want to talk about *loud*? All those firecrackers going off in the street, it was worse than standing up by the amps at a concert."

Sonnet laughed. "Oh, that's rich. A firemaster who doesn't like firecrackers? That's like me being allergic to catnip."

Tony looked at her quizzically. "Are you?"

"A figure of speech, flamer. Come on, you're not that dumb, no matter what Sylv says."

Tony blushed. "Sylv could learn to shut up once in awhile."

"Not in this life." Sonnet squeezed his arm. "Silent nockers scare the tuna out of me. It's just not natural. If she stopped calling you names and running you down to anyone who'll listen, it'd mean the honeymoon was over."

"Honeymoon?" Tony repeated, confused.

Sonnet chattered on, paying no mind to his question, happy in the sound of her own voice. Words were a nocker's arsenal, but a pooka's playground. "The last guy she went for—not counting Magloire—to hear her talk about him you'd've thought they broke the ugly stick on him, *and* the stupid stick, *and* that he couldn't even find his way to the bedroom let alone—"

"Okay, okay enough already!" Tony tore his arm out of Sonnet's hold and raised both hands in surrender. "You don't have to draw me a picture."

"Maybe not, but how about you giving me a quick sketch or two yourself?" The pooka's eyes twinkled roguishly. "So far the only thing about you that Sylv *hasn't* criticized is the world's oldest, sweetest Art, and I want to know why."

"Sonnet…" There was a warning note in Tony's voice, one the pooka should have heeded.

Pookas were not generally famous for knowing when to stop prying. "The way I figure it," she went on, oblivious, "is that means either you're so good that

ESTHER M. FRIESNER

you made her forget to complain, or you're so bad that it's only a matter of time before—*wow!*"

The single spark of bright pink fire the landed on Sonnet's nose was small, but it hissed and crackled loud as a pine log on a bonfire. It didn't burn—Tony hadn't intended to harm the too-chummy pooka—but it did frighten her clear out of her mortal seeming and back into cat form. The little black and white cat went racing down the block, swearing in the immortal language of her furry tribe. Tony laughed to see her run.

"Oh, *that* was bright," said Telamon. The young satyr had come up behind him while he'd watched Sonnet's flight. "Sure, scare off one of your own fighters, yeah, *that's* how you win battles." He too was in his mortal guise, a gangly boy just into his teens.

"Come on, lay off me, she'll be back," Tony told him. "I just gave her a scare to make her shut up for two seconds. No harm done."

"There'd better not be." Telamon tried to scowl, but his mortal face was still too childish to make the grimace work well.

"There's not," came Sonnet's voice from sidewalk-level. The black and white cat sat at the satyr's feet, smoothing her fur between sentences. "Good one, Tony."

"Thanks, Sonnet, I—"

"Dumb, but good. It's not like any of us have enough spare glamour left to be tossing it around like that."

"You—we could have more," Tony said. He had to struggle to get the words out. He knew he was dredging up a matter that the others thoughts had been settled well before this. Still, it wasn't settled to his satisfaction, it galled him, and he wasn't going to let it lie. "You could have mine."

The cat and the boy-satyr exchanged a look. Tony thought he heard a sigh escape Sonnet's whiskers. "We've been over this before, Tony," she said, sounding infinitely patient when what she really was was fed up with him. "You can't be a part of this."

"Why not?" he challenged. "I've fought before, and I'm the one with the connection to Nok-Nok."

"Which is just why you've got to stay clear," Telamon said. He didn't have as much attitude as a nocker, but he liked the sound of his own voice laying down the law. "We don't know what shape Nok-Nok's in, so what happens if he registers a reaction to your presence? That'd be enough to warn off Magloire and trash the whole sting. Xia Xiao said so."

"Yeah, right, Xia Xiao said so," Tony muttered. He still recalled the first time he'd been told that his active involvement with Nok-Nok's rescue wasn't required. *It's been decided*, that's what Sylv told him. Right. Decided. But not by him. Something about the decision smelled funny, and not just the fact that it'd been made behind his back. He wasn't about to let it go.

"Oh, come on, sweetie, lighten up." Sonnet wove her way around Tony's ankles. "You know the old saying about too many cooks, don'cha? I tell you what, if you want, we'll save you a piece of Magloire's ass for you to kick. Besides, you've got your own stuff to do tonight. Master Lung's counting on you."

PLAYING WITH FIRE

"Master Lung would understand if I took off for this." It was the last of his protests, and it sounded feeble. "If he knew it was to help protect Xia Xiao—"

"*You* protect *her?*" The pooka had the good manners not to laugh. "Look, Tony, we agreed on a plan. Let's not screw it up with any last minute changes, okay? There's too much at stake."

"I know." Tony nodded. "I know." His words were calm, accepting, but his thoughts ran otherwise: *'We' agreed? Where was I when 'we' agreed to anything like this?*

"Good." Satisfied with his response, unable to read the bitterness behind it, Sonnet settled herself comfortably on her haunches. "Okay, boys, who's got a watch on him? When do we take our places for the big production number?"

Tony consulted his wristwatch. "About an hour to go. Prinx and Varna aren't in place yet, and I haven't seen Sylv or Deni." He didn't bother adding *or Tirall*. Sluaghs were seldom seen, seldom desirable to see. If Tirall took part in this venture, it would be as a free agent, on his own terms, and if the sluagh had donated a measure of his own glamour to the bait, no one knew but Xia Xiao, who was saying nothing.

"That's a good sign," Sonnet remarked. "None of us are supposed to *be* seen, remember? Magloire's anything but an idiot. His terms said the herb shop was supposed to be empty, except for Xia Xiao. The rest of us need to hold down watchposts near enough to the pickup zone to sense *him* but far enough away so he can't sense *us*."

"What about the trolls?" Tony asked. "Won't Magloire be able to feel their presence?"

"Trolls go deep enough, you can't tell them apart from the rock around 'em." Sonnet was smug, even for a cat. "That's another reason I love New York: This whole island's built on solid stone."

"It is?" Telamon asked in a voice that betrayed how many science and social studies classes he'd already slept through. "You sure?"

"Well, I always took it for granite," Sonnet said airily. "Pa-dum-*pow!*" Her paw hit a rimshot off an invisible drum set.

Telamon sighed. "Yeah, right, okay. I'm outa here." He slouched off down the street to take up his post and wait for Magloire's arrival.

"Hmph!" Sonnet snorted at the satyr's back. "Give generously to help the pun-impaired," she said for Tony's solitary benefit. "I guess I'd better pick my hiding place too, just in case the big jerk shows up early. It wouldn't do to spook him off."

"Where will you be?" Tony asked.

Sonnet chuckled. "Where *won't* I be? When you're a card-carrying member of the feline tribe, there aren't too many nooks and crannies you can't call your own. Oh, don't worry, I won't get *too* close—Magloire's not blind, and he's got a keen nose on him—but distance doesn't matter to me. See, I'm putting some of my one-shape friends on alert. Magloire knows my seeming, but he's too cocky to go jumping away from every cat in this city. They'll let me know as soon as they spy him, and then, well, you know how fast us cats can move when we want to?"

She switched her tail proudly.

"I guess I'd better move too." Tony glanced up at the strip of winter-dark sky above the narrow street. Few of the stores in the vicinity of the Wan Sui Herb Shop were open nights, and so didn't bother bearing the expense of neon signs. There were a few streetlamps, but only one of them seemed to be functioning, and it stood all the way at the end of the block. "Master Lung will be expecting me. We have to deploy the dragon. Listen, Sonnet, if you need me, if you want me for anything, anything at all—"

"I'll have my people call your people." The pooka's whiskers curved up. "Don't worry, Tony, we can handle this. *Ciao,* mousikins." And by some magic known more to cats than to pookas, she was gone.

Reluctantly, Tony turned his back on the Wan Sui Herb Shop and hurried to his rendezvous with Master Lung. He didn't like the notion of being left out of the affairs of his motley, even if for the best of reasons. He really didn't like the feeling that he was being sidelined in order to protect him.

"I'm not made of glass, dammit," he mumbled to himself as he shouldered his way through the streets of Chinatown. The daytime crowd was gone, but there were still more than enough residents and gawkers remaining to make it slow going. "I can take care of myself in a fight. Shit, I took on a bunch of *redcaps,* for God's sake, and they know it! Think I can't handle a candyass like Magloire…" He was still grumbling when he joined Master Lung on the rooftop.

The old man was just giving the finishing touches to the huge framework that formed the skeleton of the dragon. When he heard Tony emerge from the rooftop door behind him, he turned to greet him with a smile.

"You have done very well, Tony," Master Lung told him. "This one will be the best anyone has ever seen. You ought to be proud of yourself. I could not have done such a fine job without your help."

"I didn't do anything." Tony felt himself blushing, though Master Lung's praise warmed him deeply, made him yearn for more.

"I do not flatter you, I only speak what is true. You have earned every word of it; accept it."

"I don't think I—"

"Accept it," Master Lung repeated firmly. "You have no trouble accepting blame for your faults, even those you do not truly have. Do you feel that blame is the only thing you deserve in this world? Is it so hard for you to learn how to accept praise as well? Accept it from me, if you can not do so from anyone else. I have come to know you, to value you. You matter too much to me for me to do you the insult of false flattery."

Tony met the old man's tranquil gaze. *You matter too much to me…*The words echoed inside his head. Master Lung's face betrayed nothing, but Tony's perceptions were suddenly sharp, able to pierce superficial things. Behind the old man's mask of serenity there crouched a bent, grief-maddened soul that cradled a dead cat to its chest and wailed for loved ones carried off on wings of smoke and fire. *You matter too much to me…*All at once Tony understood why he had been excluded from the motley's plan to take Magloire.

Something alien possessed his tongue as he replied, "Maybe I do burden myself with too much blame, take responsibility for things that go wrong, things that were never mine to control. People I loved died and I got wished into the care of someone who never loved me at all. He tried to make me feel that it was my fault I was born what I was, as if I'd been the reason his daughter married who she did. Never mind how crazy that sounds, he got me believing it. It hurt, but it was better that way, somehow. See, if I believed it was all my fault that my parents were who they were, that they died when they did, then that meant I had the power to control things as big as life and death. I just had to learn how to use that power. If I take the blame, I can claim the power, and once I claim the power I can convince myself that next time I can *prevent* the tragedy. I lost people I loved, but now that I know the—the secret, the trick, the magic, I'll never have to lose any more." He paused for breath, then stared hard at the old man and added, "I'm not the only one who thinks that way, am I, Master Lung?"

Master Lung gasped. His whole body shuddered as if he'd been struck in the chest with a spear made of ice. "What do you know of loss?" he rasped. "What have I ever done to you to bear this?"

"*Are* you the one?" Tony asked softly. "Did you tell Xia Xiao and the others to keep me out of the fight?"

"You are not needed there," the old man said, his voice shaking. "I need you. The dragon—"

"The dragon is done, ready. One touch of your finger to the ignition box and he'll take fire and shape and a skin of glamour. You *don't* need me. Not for the dragon."

"Go, then." Master Lung's face hardened. "You are so wise in the way of reading what another person needs. And what you need? But go. If that is how you think things are, leave. I have done this many times before, alone. I can manage alone now."

Chastened, Tony was quick to say, "Master, I didn't mean any disrespect. If you want me to stay here, I'll—"

Master Lung tried to maintain a mask of stone, but it crumbled before Tony's eyes. The full weight of all the old man's years and sorrows pulled away his stern facade and left the edges of his voice harsh. "You are right, Tony. Yes, you are right, and I will not be the first man who finds the taste of truth bitter on the tongue. I was my word that banned you from tonight's business. Sylv came to me and spoke of what was planned. She too was concerned for your safety, although it was not a fear that came out in words. She would not admit it any more than she would admit to your face how she feels for you. Still, I could tell. Like knows like, my fears were hers, and so I went to see Xia Xiao." The glint of neon from the building across the way reflected from the film of unshed tears in his eyes. "I have offended you in this, and for imagining that you were too innocent to see through it. I ask your forgiveness."

"Innocent? Me?" Tony laughed, a sound that was for once without its usual edge of street-hardened cynicism. He put his arms around the old man and hugged him close as if it were the most natural thing in the world. "No offense taken, no

ESTHER M. FRIESNER

blame given. I only wanted to know that it wasn't some weakness in *me* that was keeping me out of the motley's doings."

"You will join them now?" Master Lung did his best to keep the apprehension out of his question, and he almost succeeded.

Tony shook his head. "Why muddle the plan as it stands? Too many cooks, y'know, like Sonnet says. If they really *had* to have me in on it, Xia Xiao never would have gone along with your request."

"Ah, yes." Master Lung sighed, relaxed. "That is so."

"So okay, then, it's settled." Tony clapped his hands together, then gestured at the framework on the rooftop. "Now let's put on a *show*."

Master Lung chuckled. "A fine show," he agreed. "One I want you to start." He passed Tony the small black control box that would touch off the firework dragon. "I am thankful to Xia Xiao. Despite our time of crisis, she has permitted me to keep just enough glamour to make this year's dragon as magnificent as its ancestors."

"Man, I can't wait." Tony gazed at the dragon with an almost paternal pride. It didn't look like much right now—hell, it didn't look like anything but bundles of fireworks on a skeletal frame, a fugitive from the junkyard—but he could tell just by looking at it that once it was lit, it was going to kick some serious ass. For the first time in his life, Tony understood how a father could look into the red, wrinkly, squished-up face of a newborn and mean it when he said, "She's *beautiful*."

"Now, when I give the signal—" Master Lung began.

"Uh-oh." A new expression crossed Tony's face. He'd been so taken up with the whole business of the New Year's celebrations, of his anger at being kept out of the impending showdown with Magloire, of his recent confrontation with Master Lung, that something had slipped his mind—something simple, yes, but something vital, something he really could *not* afford to forget about any longer, something all the glamour in the world couldn't charm away.

"Tony?" Master Lung tilted his head inquisitively. "Tony, is something wrong?"

"Here." Tony thrust the control box back into Master Lung's hands. "I'll be right back. If I'm not back in time, you set off the dragon without me, okay? And come to think of it, um—um—" He squirmed and fidgeted from foot to foot, then in a tortured whisper asked, "You maybe know where the nearest, um, bathroom is around here?"

"Ah." Master Lung nodded, trying not to smile. "I understand. Go downstairs and cross the street to number five-oh-two, ring the bell for apartment three-C, the Tan family. They are friends. Say I sent you."

Tony sprinted for the rooftop door, then paused and turned. "What if they're not there? What if they're all out in the street celebrating?"

"In that case, Tony," Master Lung replied with mock-solemnity, "I advise you to avoid being startled by the sound of firecrackers."

Tony made a face at him, then dashed away, leaving the old man to share his laughter with the dormant dragon.

PLAYING WITH FIRE   705

15

The Tans weren't at home. Tony had to sprint two blocks before he found a restaurant that would accommodate him. Granted, he had to buy some takeout food for the privilege of using the facilities, but that wasn't too great a burden. Now he sauntered back towards the building where Master Lung waited, munching a spring roll and swinging a small, white pasteboard box full of *bao-tse*, the steamed dumplings that the old man loved.

Dusk had shifted into night, though on this street it couldn't grow dark enough for anyone to notice the difference. Tony's lifesaving restaurant was on one of the tourist thoroughfares, well lit by the signs of eateries and souvenir shops. He liked the honky-tonk atmosphere, the flash, a gaudiness too tawdry to be more than a good-hearted joke on the gawkers.

Walking along like this, alone with his thoughts, he could almost hear the ghosts of goggle-eyed tourists trading whispers: *Look, Mabel, see all that red and black lacquered furniture, all those curlicues and doodads, that big gold plaster dragon, that ceramic god, whatzisname, Buddha? Jesus, he's fat. They've all got that kind of stuff in their houses, that's how they live, that's the sort of stuff they believe. Isn't it weird? Isn't it foreign? Isn't it fun? Oooooh, the mysterious East! Almost like we're not in America any more.*

"Mabel, if that's your attitude, you never were in America to start with," Tony muttered to the ghosts as he licked the last crumbs of the spring roll from his fingers.

The air was thick with the smell of cooking oil and savory food, cut by the acrid scent of powder from the fireworks. The streets were littered with the spent red paper shells of the long 'cracker strings, with here and there an unexploded dud or two. Whatever the legalities, the cops couldn't be everywhere at once and kids were mighty quick when it came to touching off their noisemakers and running away.

Gonna give 'em something even better than this, in awhile, Tony thought, idly kicking aside a gutted strand. *The real thing, the true thing, not some crappy vanilla excuse for a dragon, some sugarcoated refugee from a kiddie show. No way. We're gonna give 'em a dragon they'll always—*

He stopped in his tracks, stared straight ahead of him. There, at the end of the block, was a lion. The two-man costume with its monstrous head and flapping lower jaw, its brightly colored cloth body sewn with golden bells, was as fine an example of the breed as any Tony had seen during the parade today, but there was something about this one, something different, something—

Wrong. The single word set off alarms in Tony's head, loud warning signals that beat at his brain. *Wrong, yes it's wrong, but how?* he wondered, staring even harder. Some instinct restrained him from rushing forward to get a closer look at the lion. He waited until it crossed his path and went down a side street before he dashed to the corner and peered after it.

An old woman coming the opposite way on that same side street thought he was staring at her. She had a face like a dried fig, brown and wrinkled, and her

ESTHER M. FRIESNER

scowl could sour milk that was still in the cow. Tony backed away, mumbling apologies, then scuttled into a doorway to catch his breath.

Whoa! Never thought I could die from seeing too much ugly, he thought, touching one hand to his forehead. It felt clammy. He managed a weak chuckle over the sick feeling still churning his belly from the old woman's glare. *Man, you're an idiot,* he told himself in disgust. *What's with you and that damn lion? So it's a lion, so it's not doing the dance, so it's just sorta slouching along down the street, so what? Maybe the guys inside are tired, ever thing of that, mushbrain? The guy in back's probably drunk, the way his feet're dragging, makes the whole stupid beast look like it's got a thorn in its paw. They did their thing, they raked in the money, and now they're going home. Take the hint yourself and let it go, stupid, just let it go and you go back to Master Lung before his bao-tse turn into a bunch of pork-stuffed ice cubes.*

He moved out of his doorway refuge and took one step back in the direction of the building on whose rooftop Master Lung and the dragon waited. He stopped a second time, a second step untaken.

If they're done for the day, why are they still wearing the costume? That head's one heavy mofo, no one in his right mind'd wear it longer than he had to. But if they're not done, if they're still hoping to collect some more hong bao *from the merchants, then why aren't they dancing? Why are they just dragging it along? Why are they going away from the streets with the most shops, the most chances to score? Only shop I know that's down this street is—is—*

—is Xia Xiao's.

He knew then. He knew, and in almost the same instant he realized that he wasn't the only one who knew.

Their presence was a faint rustling in the air, the whisper of trash being blown along a gutter, the crunch of heavy feet coming down hard on empty firecracker shells, or dry sticks, or bones. The hairs on Tony's forearms rose, and the bristles on his scalp crackled as if he'd turned into a wire alive with electricity. All his blood sang a warning. He darted his eyes left, right, up, down, but saw nothing, no one on the street, no one coming. Even the buildings seemed to have been sucked clean of people. Their windows gaped at him, the gaze of skulls.

His eyes told him that the only living beings here were himself and the lion…the lion…Magloire and Nok-Nok inside the body of the limping lion, the satyr dragging the boy along in his wake, the enspelled eshu helpless to do anything but obey. Vague feelings turned to cold certainties, thrusting themselves into Tony's mind. The lion was already more than halfway down this block. At the corner it would turn, then rush for the shop where Xia Xiao waited.

"…and when it reaches that corner, they'll strike. That's where they wait, Tony, in shadows, in doorways, their archers poised on rooftops, their minions slithering in the sweet darkness beneath the streets."

The whisper fluted up from the sewer grate just under his feet, a sound to prickle his skin. "Ti—Tirall?"

"My street, Tony," the whisperer went on. *"Even mine. They have killed my precious ones, sent their venomed darts deep into the sleek gray fur, the ruby eyes I*

treasure. *They have brought the full complement of their court's greatest warriors, I can not stop them, but you—! Ahhhhhhh."*

"Tirall, how can I stop them if you couldn't?" Tony hissed back, frantic. The lion was drifting farther and farther away, the corner almost in reach of Magloire's feet. "A full Unseelie court's best fighters? Warn the others, tell them, bring them, let Xia Xiao know. I can't stop them alone."

"*I did not say you could, but you will make a pretty death, and I will promise your bones the place of honor in my house.*" The sluagh's voice seemed to trickle away, back into the sewer's clammy depths, his last words falling like chill drops on Tony's heart. "*Make a pretty death for me, little boggan, or scurry off and make for yourself a life that is one long, doleful dying. O master of all fires, in my dead children's name take your choice and take this sword.*"

"Sword?" Tony repeated, looking down. The sewer grate echoed with nothing but emptiness, showed only different shadings of darkness. Then something flashed up through the grating, shot out of the sewer and landed at his feet. Tony knelt, letting the container of *bao tse* drop, his fingers closing around the charred red pasteboard tube of an exhausted firecracker.

Sword…He concentrated his thoughts on the hollow tube's end, and a glow kindled there. The spark grew brighter, a tiny tongue of flame that hardened shape into a blade no bigger than a needle. The needle lengthened, broadened, grew with each passing second. Tony held his breath, willing the growth of the infant fireblade.

The arrow the struck it from his grasp came within inches of piercing him between the fingerbones. The tube tumbled into the gutter, the flame went out with a hiss, and Tony looked up sharply to meet the merciless eyes of the sidhe archer. She wore black leather and russet suede, a constellation of bronze beads seeded through the hundred braids of her raven hair. A second arrow whirred from her bow, singing for Tony's heart.

The shield that flew up to cover his chest was no bigger than a dinner plate, and the sound of shattering crockery startled Tony with the realization that it *was* a dinner plate, the last vestiges of glamour fading from the shards as they fell. Laughter bubbled up from a doorway to his right as Sonnet sprang out. The pooka wore her human form and juggled six more plates with casual grace.

"Not bad, Annie Oakley, but can you do *this?*" she cried at the archer, and whipped all six plates straight at her. The discs glittered green and blue, crackling balefully. The sidhe jerked fresh arrows from her quiver, but there was no way she could fire off a volley fast enough to stop all six of the pooka's missiles.

Six arrows whizzed through the air from six different directions. From rooftops and second-story windows and out of a doorway almost at Tony's left elbow they flew, each twang of a bowstring revealing the hiding place of another sidhe archer.

"Peekaboo, I see you…now," Sonnet muttered, and snapped herself into catskin just in time to avoid a seventh archer's arrow. The little black and white cat shot past Tony yelling, "Move it, fool! Stop Magloire! Deni and I will take care of these Tolkien wannabes!"

Tony hesitated only a moment. He thought he heard a bowstring twang, but it wasn't the fine, high, lethal sound of an arrow taking flight. This twang was dull, lifeless, and was followed by the unmistakable row of a sidhe warrior cursing the eyeblink-swift feet of the mink pooka whose keen teeth had sheared his bowstring in two neat as you please. Tony didn't stay to hear more; he bolted down the street. At his back the din of the first sidhe's curses swelled with the voices of the other elfin archers as Deni and Sonnet and a few of Sonnet's trueborn feline allies did what they could to foil this portion of the Unseelie forces.

Shield them or give them sense enough to run too, he thought as he raced after the lion. *Those sidhe didn't come to fight just with bows. If they've got swords besides— oh, Sonnet, Deni, don't die heroes!*

"Heroes…" Tirall's voice leaked out of nowhere, somewhere, no place Tony had the chance to pinpoint in his flight. "*Run swiftly, my sharp-toothed loves, my sweetings, to teach the heroes how it's done.*"

As Tony sprinted around the corner, he cast on last backward glance down the street where Deni and Sonnet fought the sidhe. He thought he glimpsed a river of small gray shapes with long, naked pink tails come nosing out of a drain. The rats parted into seven chittering streams that rushed deliberately towards the seven sidhe archers. He closed his ears against the first of the screams.

He caught the lion only three storefronts away from Xia Xiao's place. He brought it down by launching himself in a half-assed parody of a football tackle, his arms closing over cloth and bells and a boy's skinny body. There was a loud tearing noise as the cheap satin cloth parted threads. Tony lay panting on the sidewalk, holding a frail form mummified head to foot in a tight cocoon of red fabric, even his face hidden in the shiny folds. The heavy lion's head turned slowly around to stare down at the two of them, paddle-shaped underjaw slack and gaping.

The eyes lit up slowly, first the smoldering gold of the electric lights within, then a deep red the color of blood. The jaw shut with a resounding clack, the great head lowered and the twisted horns of a satyr sprang from the lion's papier-mâché brow. They were black from root to tip, and every ridge of their curved surface had the glitter of a cleaver's edge.

"Give him back, you kithless bastard," Magloire's voice rumbled out of the lion's throat. "My bargain wasn't struck with you."

"With who then, dog?" A new voice, harsh and gurgling, raked the space between the buildings, bouncing from one side of the narrow street to the other. Wild laughter like the mirth of the mad cracked above their heads as the first redcap dropped from his perch on a windowsill, hit the sidewalk rolling and sprang up into a crouch, a dagger in either hand. He came up between Tony and the lion, his attention focused solely of the doubly renegade satyr in his heavy mask. "Pretty bargains, many bargains, struck and paid for with the good gold of our lords and ladies, then pissed away by you like they was no more than weak beer to run through your belly?"

"Run through his belly, ah!" A second redcap tittered as she jumped from hiding. "There's one idea for us to be getting on with."

The man within the ruined lion costume stiffened, the head rose high, then higher still, and a thin trail of yellow smoke began to seep from the painted nostrils.

PLAYING WITH FIRE

The redcaps stared at this phenomenon quizzically, hideous heads cocked to one side as scowls made them more hideous still.

"Wussee doin'?" a third voice demanded, a third redcap crossing the street, having given up a hideaway Tony missed seeing. "Stay back, there's power clinging to this 'un."

The first redcap spat precisely between Magloire's feet. "There's *shit* clinging to this one," he opined. He tossed his daggers lightly hand to hand, making them dance in the air. "A quick carving, snick-snack, and we're done with it." He crept a step nearer, still hunched down like a toad.

Tony pushed himself back with his heels, trying to keep his every move as noiseless as possible, dragging Nok-Nok's shrouded body with him away from the redcaps. He didn't know what miracle was keeping them intent on Magloire alone, but he wasn't going to question it. He cast a nervous look over one shoulder, just to make sure there were no nasty surprises blocking his way. He meant to slide backwards like this, crabwise, Nok-Nok a negligible burden across his lap, until he could reach the relative safety of the corner. Then he'd jump up, sling the boy over one shoulder, and run like hell. It was a simple plan, as long as the redcaps let him keep it simple. His breath was shallow when he let himself breathe at all, and his backward-groping hands fell on more than one unknown sharp object on the sidewalk that bit his palms with pain.

Easy, easy now, he thought. *Don't blow this one, man, keep it quiet, keep it slow. Damn, I wish those nightmares weren't standing between me and Xia Xiao's place! They're gonna snuff Magloire in a minute, maybe time enough for me to get away with Nok-Nok, maybe not, and if not*—he didn't want to think about that; he turned his mind elsewhere. *I could get into the shop, then I could let Xia Xiao take care of Nok-Nok, get Prinx and Varna to come out and help us drive off these redcaps, help Deni and Sonnet clean up whatever Tirall's "kiddies" have left of the sidhe, get Telamon and Sylv in on it too, wherever they've got to, kick all these fuckers' Unseelie asses the hell back to*—

His thoughts were shattered by a sound that reached straight down his throat and clenched talons through his guts. The leader of the redcaps had flung back his head and was filling the night with his ululating battle-scream, a bone-peeling cry that was taken up by not three, but at least a dozen separate voices. Tony's eyes darted from one side of the street to the other, from sidewalks to rooftops. The faces of the old buildings erupted with a company of redcaps, a seething pustulence of monsters that dropped to street level one by one. Mostly they closed in around the lion's head, but there were enough of them to attend to Tony as well as and the pitiful remnant of the lion's body that he still sheltered in his arms.

"Shit," Tony gritted, eyes locked with the eyes of the nearest redcap. Something in the creature's fixed and skeletal leer promised him his choice of agonies. He was going to die, that was all there was to it. And because his death was a settled thing, he felt all fear ebb away, replaced by a great calm, a great resolution. He knew that he had only one thing that he must do; then he could die content.

Still staring straight into the advancing redcap's eyes, Tony tore away the enveloping cloth from Nok-Nok's face. "Get out of here," he said without looking at the boy. "Get on your feet and run. I'll hold them off. Don't look back. Get away. Find someone later, someone of our motley, or let them find you. Go underground, into Tirall's keeping, only get *away*. You understand me? Nok-Nok, *get away*."

"I don't think he can." Magloire's whisper tickled Tony's ear. "No more can you."

Tony gasped as the satyr's knife slashed his side. Magloire leaped free of the entangling red satin and sneered down at his dumbstruck victim. "Masks and mirrors, mirrors and masks," he said coolly. "Not much of a trick, as glamour goes, but enough to serve." He took to his heels.

Just behind him, the lion's head collapsed. The lead redcap pounced forward, daggers raised, as his nearest henchmen dragged the heavy mask away. The redcap's thwarted howl rolled through Tony's pain-starred vision, carrying away with it Magloire's gloating laughter.

"Tricked! Gulled! Cheated!" the redcap bellowed, gnashing his teeth. Tony rolled onto his side and saw the last wisps of Magloire's illusion blow away the limp body that the second redcap now hauled back upright. Nok-Nok's eyes were closed, his head lolled heavily on his slender neck.

"There's the swindler!" the third redcap bellowed, gesturing with his own blade after Magloire's fleeing form. "Stop him!"

"Stop him..." Tony mumbled, forcing himself to his feet. He took a few staggering steps after the satyr, even knowing it was useless. The redcap ring hadn't drawn itself up tightly enough around him and the supposed Nok-Nok. Magloire had speed and agility to take him sailing through the gaps between the shrieking minions of the Unseelie court. He was past them all, at the corner. The redcaps might give chase, but the satyr had terror to add to his natural speed; he'd outrun them because it was that or die. Tony saw him reach the corner, turn sharply, about to be lost from sight as Nok-Nok would soon be lost forever.

"Get out of my way, crone!" Magloire's shout thundered in Tony's ears. The satyr stood still as stone at the corner, arms out, fists raised to strike...what? "Damn you, are you deaf? *Move!*"

"Ha! *You* move, boy, not I!" A biting wind whipped down the street, a grit-laden gust with the power of a thousand fists, beating Magloire back, sending the redcaps nearest him tumbling head over heels like wads of newspaper. And out of the heart of the warring wind hobbled the crabbed, fig-faced old woman Tony had encountered when he'd first taken up the false lion's trail.

His wound throbbed, warm blood oozing through his shirt, but he felt nothing as he stared at her. A strange silence seized the street, all sounds of battle carried away on the back of the wailing wind. The old woman was walking forward, walking towards him, walking through the midst of the redcaps as if they did not exist for her at all in any form, mundane or fey. Each step she took appeared to make her taller, but Tony's weary mind assured him that this was merely an optical illusion. (*It has to be, or else you're crazy, or else she's—she's—what is she?*) Even when he realized that her head was almost level with a windowsill two floors up, he refused to surrender his sanity despite the evidence of his eyes.

Eyes…and how reliable were they now? His vision blurred, softening the lines and creases that scored the old woman's brown cheeks, an aura of delirium that seemed to lend her face an inner glow that charmed away all the outward marks of age. He saw Magloire crouching in the gutter, holding his hands before his face as if protecting his eyes from a light too bright to bear. He saw the redcaps nearest her pale to the color of cigarette ash and back away, sputtering threats while their arms remained powerless at their sides. In the moment she reached him, when her height overshadowed the roof of a three-story building, she turned her placid gaze to him, and in that instant he caught sight of the final ghost of the ugly crone's face melt away into the features of another aged woman he knew very well.

"Xia—Xia Xiao?" His hand trembled as he stretched it out to touch the hem of her trailing sleeve. It was woven of a silk finer than cobweb, rippling with the colors of dawn. She smiled, and Xia Xiao's face was gone. All that was left was the tranquil countenance of an eternally young and beautiful being whose gentle eyes saw misery and meted out compassion, whose heart would not allow her to rest until mercy was served.

Her smile enveloped him in light, and through the light there came unknown words ringing with the sound of the delicate sprays of silver bells adorning the long coils of her ebony hair: *kuan yin, kuan yin, kuan yin…*

She stooped over the redcap who held Nok-Nok's nearly lifeless body in his paws. Her hand was the pale gold of a harvest moon, and from the fingertips a single thread trailed down, a glowing jade pendant spinning slowly at the end. She bent lower and lower still, until the pendant was only a human handspan from Nok-Nok's brow. The redcaps' eyes flared red in the radiance of so much captive glamour.

"Ah!" Tony clapped one hand to his mouth. He hadn't meant to cry out like that, hadn't meant for the swelling pain in his side to get the better of him and break the wonder of this moment. He couldn't help it. The pain was no longer the simple hurt of a knife wound. It burned deep.

He pressed his lips together, but another gasp of agony escaped them. Looking down, he saw that the bright blood had darkened and thickened. A foul smell hit his nostrils and the burning intensified, burrowing its way into his flesh. He swayed unsteadily on his feet, the street whirling around him, then fell to his knees with a moan. Dark clouds swam across his sight and Magloire's long-vanished laughter returned to haunt him.

Somewhere that seemed like leagues away, he thought he heard the first small explosions of the great fireworks dragon. *He couldn't wait forever for me to come back*, he thought. *Oh, Master Lung, I'm sorry. I'm…Sylv, I'm sorry too.*

And in the depths of his pain, Xia Xiao was beside him. The hem of her sleeve fell across his face and body, soothing and cool as the waters of a mountain stream. Something shone before his eyes, a radiant disc that encircled the image of a dragon.

I can heal but one.

Her voice was in the flow of his blood, the harmony of sundered cells rejoining, the discord of a poisoned knife blade being driven out of the body, the sweet accord of a fleeing soul called back, life restored, strength reborn. He opened his eyes to a sky where stars burned clear and bright despite the competing glare of neon signs reflected against the veil of smog.

Something lay heavy on his chest. His fingers closed around the sleek circle of the jade token. Already the spell of the lady's presence was passing—he heard the redcaps shift their feet ponderously, grumbling threats—as her image was melting away before his eyes. Still the voice lingered within him:

Only one, Tony, only one.

"All right, you fuckers, the party's over!" Sylv's voice broke over his head. He sat up quickly, in time to see the nocker spring from around the corner, landing dead-on in front of Magloire and the redcaps that had hounded him. She raised a semi-automatic that carried the unmistakable mark of nocker tampering, fatal bells and deadly whistles. "I capped every one of these bullets with a li'l ol' touch of iron. Wanna play tag?"

"Say yes, assholes," Telamon hollered from a rooftop. The young satyr too held a weapon of Sylv's devising. "My therapist says I've got to learn to play well with others."

"Meat!" one of the redcaps screamed, shaking a fist at Sylv. "We'll have your bones!"

Calmly Sylv leveled the gun between his eyes. "Come and get 'em."

"Sylv?" It was Telamon again. This time the young satyr's voice had lost its brashness. "Sylv, look—down that end of the street—they've got Nok-Nok."

Sylv's eyes turned to slits of rage. She saw what Telamon had seen: The redcaps ringing the boy crowded too close to his frail body for any burst of gunfire aimed at them to leave him living.

"Do what you want with the traitor," the redcap nearest her snarled. "Wear his bloody skin. But this one is *ours.*"

"Ours! The eshu's ours!" the other redcaps echoed, shrieking their triumph. "Ours! A prize of blood and bone!"

No, Tony thought, seeing Nok-Nok's plight, his motley-mates' helpless position. *No. Not yours, blood-drinkers. No one's but ours, in kinship. No one's but his in all else.* He folded both hands over the shimmering medallion on his chest and sent out the call.

The sky crackled with a bolt of light that was never lightning. Scarlet fissures zigzagged across the heavens. Far away, Tony heard an old man gasp and cry out with all the wonder in his aged heart. A blazing shape tore across the rooftops, swept down between the buildings, comets riding the burning golden scales of its back. The dragon came.

He stood to meet it, arms outstretched. Its splendor settled over him like a second skin. He stepped into the fire's heart, meeting it with the fiery power in his blood, the mastery of flame that was his right, his gift, his talent. He felt the ground fall away from beneath his feet, felt the bunching and stretching of new

PLAYING WITH FIRE

muscles, the power of titanic wings at his back. He held his hand before his face and flexed a five-taloned yellow paw.

Air streamed through the rainbow fires sparking from his flanks. He climbed the sky, great tail lashing, and saw all Chinatown, all Manhattan, all the world spread out beneath him. For a time he hovered there above the turning globe, drinking air still unpolluted with the deathly taste of mundanity, then he folded his wings and plunged back into the city's heart.

The redcaps saw his dive and scattered, daggers clattering to the pavement. Nok-Nok collapsed like a ragdoll, abandoned in the wake of their frantic retreat. He sent curls of fire licking after them; the smell of crisping skin sent his head spinning with pleasure. He roared his joy and mounted the sky a second time to loop and soar and dance his victory.

"Tony!" Sylv's frightened cry reached him even there, so high above the streets. He glanced down and saw her. She too had been confounded by his transformation, stunned out of her normal vigilance for a second too long. She'd gone off guard, let the gun hang slack at her side while her eyes followed his wild flight across the heavens.

In that second, Magloire had made his move. Her gun was lying in the gutter, struck clean out of Sylv's grip in her moment of awe-made weakness. The same envenomed knife that had opened Tony's side now lay comfortably close to her throat. Magloire grinned.

"Come down, Tony," he crooned. "Come and claim your prize. The eshu's yours for the taking. Go on, don't worry, I give him back to you freely, much good he'll do you. As for me, I'll settle for safe passage back among the Unseelie."

Sonnet's mocking laughter wafted down over the street. Tony's huge eyes easily spied the cat-pooka and her mink-shaped companion perched on the edge of the roof, beside a fear-stricken Telamon. "'Safe' passage?" she yowled. "To your death!"

"Oh no, my dear, not that, I think." Magloire's face was streaked with grime, but his smirk was just as infuriating as ever. "You see, honor's not a thing the Unseelie hold in such esteem as you fools. A proper price, a little present to let them know I'm sorry for past slips and that they've still got an able ally in me, and they'll be pleased to have me back. I find that most folk are so much more reasonable after a drink, don't you?" He shifted the angle of the blade at Sylv's throat, and the look in his eyes let them know beyond a doubt what sort of drink he'd be pouring out for the Unseelie host.

Dread encased Tony's flaming wings with frost. He felt them crumple away, felt the last of the great fireworks dragon's body falling to ash around him. Human again, he rode the last blanket of sparks back to earth, setting his feet on the sidewalk beside Nok-Nok's body. The jade talisman on his chest glowed far less brightly now, its hoard of pooled glamour almost gone. He cupped one hand over it protectively. Perhaps there would be just enough of it left for him to reach out, destroy Magloire, save Sylv—

I can heal but one.

Tony bent his head. Nok-Nok lay sprawled on the pavement, his hollow chest scarcely rising with each breath. *How can I choose?* he thought desperately. *How can I choose?* But even as his mind howled with confusion, his spirit knew. He knelt beside the boy and touched the power of the dragon to his brow.

It all happened too quickly. Nok-Nok's eyes flew open, knowledge flared, his hand shot out to seize one of the redcap's discarded daggers, he sat bolt upright, jerked back his hand, threw, and the dagger hummed through the air to lodge with a heart-lurching impact at the base of Magloire's skull.

Epilogue

"Yes," Tony said, his eyes fixed on the statue Master Lung showed him in the shop window. "Yes, that's her."

"Ah." The old man nodded slowly. "So she was more than what she claimed, more than mortal or Changeling, and in her mercy she allowed me to dream that I was more than mortal too." Seeing Tony's stricken expression, he added, "When I came down from the roof, when I recovered my breath after our dragon took flight as well as fire, I found this on my pillow." He held out a folded slip of rice paper.

Tony unfolded it and peered at the unintelligible characters. "What does it say?"

"Only what I should have known." Master Lung sighed. "Only that I am not like you, not like the other Changelings, that she wove the illusion and I wore it gladly, like an emperor's robe."

Beside him, wearing her human guise, Sonnet stroked his arm. "Don't feel too bad, Master Lung," she said. "She had a good reason."

"Her reasons are all good," the old man said. He gazed back into the shopwindow, at the small figurine on its rosewood stand. It was no taller than the length of a man's hand, beautifully carved of rare red jade, the shape of a lovely woman whose face held only love. "She is Kuan Yin, the divine one who grants mercy to the suffering."

"Kuan Yin," Tony repeated, remembering the strange words that had echoed inside him, mind and body. Now he knew them for a name, a beloved name. "Kuan Yin."

"That's her name, don't wear it out," Sylv grumbled, slumping against him, arms folded. "Jeez, if I had a face like *that*, no way in hell I'd totz all over this town looking like a dried-up lizard. What, she was maybe testing us, pretending to be Xia Xiao? What for? To see if we'd treat her different 'cause she was old?"

"Oh, no one's got to test *you*, Sylv," Sonnet purred. "We all know how *you* don't care about superficial stuff like looks. Not that anyone broke the ugly stick on Tony, but—"

"*Shut up!*" Sylv screamed in Sonnet's face. Then she gave the pooka a jab in the arm, and stomped off. Sonnet laughed.

"Let her go," she said, catching hold of Tony's arm. "We'll catch up with her at the meetingplace." She checked her watch. "Hmm. Guess I'd better get my fuzzy little butt in gear too. I promised Deni I'd pick her up on the way. You coming, Tony?"

"No," Tony said, looking at Master Lung, not the pooka. "You go on; I'll be there in time."

"You better, or we're not going anywhere," Sonnet reminded him cheerfully. "After all, Nok-Nok's the man with the plan, but you're the geek with the glamour. No use stealing a car that's got an empty gas tank, huh?"

"I said I'd be there," Tony repeated.

If Sonnet sensed anything troubling him, she didn't say. The pooka tilted her head to one side, smiled, and was her preferred black and white self. The cat trotted up the street, tail curved up proudly.

"Master Lung..." Tony began.

The old man shook his head again. "Say nothing, child. Your place is with your people. Come, you too have preparations to make before the gateway to Arcadia can be opened. I will help you pack whatever you might wish to take on this journey." They walked back to Master Lung's place in silence.

Master Lung left Tony to his work while he remained in the kitchen, making tea. It didn't take Tony long to pack—*we're heading for paradise, who the hell's gonna need clean underwear?*—but somehow he felt disinclined to rush. They would all be waiting for him at the meetingplace, they couldn't leave without him. Now that Nok-Nok had recovered his senses, his memories were also restored. Once again the eshu fully possessed the knowledge to lead them all back to Arcadia, but they still needed Tony's command of the firemaster's Art to lend them enough power to open the gate. He could take his time.

He looked around the shabby room, feeling a strange tugging at his heart. He remembered asking Nok-Nok why Master Lung couldn't come with them too, remembered the regret in the eshu's eyes as he explained that the bright realm was not for ordinary mortals. Master Lung was no Changeling, had nothing of the fey blood in him at all. He'd have to stay behind, alone.

Tony squeezed his eyes shut, willing away the image of the old man's sorrow-strained face, the memory of his many kindnesses. Then, perversely, he decided that there was one thing he did want to take with him into Arcadia: a photograph of Master Lung.

The old man was still busy in the kitchen when Tony stole into his room and took out the worn brown album from its hiding place. There had to be at least one spare photo of his friend, his mentor, that he could take. He flipped through the pages swiftly.

Not all the papers in the album were fastened to the pages. Several flew out, fluttered to the floor. Tony cursed silently and dropped to one knee to gather them up again.

The face of a young Chinese man smiled up into Tony's eyes. It was an old wallet-sized photograph, the kind people ordered to commemorate high school and college graduations. This man wore the typical cap and gown, but Tony hardly noticed them at all. He could not look away from the face; it was almost his own. Not so many years on it as he remembered, and his memories were those of a child, but still—still—he turned it over in his palm and read his father's name as it had been given to him, before he'd met and loved an Anglo woman, before he'd turned his back on all he'd been.

Tony covered his face with his hands and let the tears come.

Things were not going according to plan at *Wild Things*. A shriek of indignation from the back room made every browser look up from his or her comic book and trade nervous glances.

At the register, Jordan Avery put on a wobbly grin. "It's nothing, gang; just one of the gamers who takes bad throws a little too seriously. I'll take care of it." He hustled to the back of the shop and stuck his head through the curtain. "You wanna keep it down?" he whispered. "I got a business to run here. Not all of us get to ditch this town on permanent spring break like you guys."

Tony smiled weakly. "Not all of us are leaving, Jordan."

"Huh?" Jordan's gaze skipped from Tony to the rest of the motley. Most of them had taken on their Changeling guises, though the sluagh Tirall for once was in mortal seeming—a skin-and-bones street punk, all Latex and leather, with a pair of pet rats perched on his shoulder—a mercy to the eyes of those who must travel in his company. Even with this concession, this group wasn't a sight for the faint-hearted to bear. Jordan was beginning to regret having allowed them the use of his back room for their departure, but there was no going back on it now. "Who's staying?" He dearly hoped it wasn't Tirall.

"Me," Tony replied.

"You're *what?*" Sylv yelled. "I thought you were bullshitting me before."

"I'm serious. I'm staying," Tony said softly. "I have to."

"Oh *fine!* Just *peachy!* He *has* to," Sylv echoed for the benefit of the rest of the assembled motley. "Oh, that just explains *sooooo* much."

"Sylv, darling, you roll your eyes like that once too often and they're gonna stick that way," Sonnet mewed.

"Fuck you, puss-in-boobs," Sylv shot back. "This guy comes in here, drops a bomb in our lap, and you just lick your hairy butt and say 'Goodie'? Nobody normal just up and decides he doesn't wanna jump on the last train to Eden. He's got a reason and he's gonna spill it, or else."

Nok-Nok came forward. The eshu had been reading one of the comic books Jordan had given him as a going-away present. "If Tony has a reason for his choice, that's his too. He needn't share. He's still granting us the means to reach our dream, Sylv. Let that be enough for you."

"Thanks, Nok-Nok." Tony clasped the eshu's hand, then pulled a thin gold chain from around his neck. The jade talisman spun slowly in the dim light of the back room. "Here. I've put all I can into this. It ought to get you where you're going." He looked at all of them, or tried to. Sylv had turned her face to the corner, her shoulders hunched, her head down. "You've been my friends," Tony said. "You've been my family, but I've just learned that I still have mortal kin on this side of the gateway. I can't leave."

"Tony, you're not the only one," Varna said, touching his arm. "You know I've still got family here, but—but my time with them's all done. There's nothing more for us to say to one another, and Arcadia—"

"Arcadia stands forever, and I *do* have more to say to my kin." He clasped her huge hand in an absurdly gentle clasp. "Goodbye." He spun on his heel and ran, though he heard Sylv shouting a thousand colorful, creative, scurrilous names after him. He didn't stop running until the pain of breathlessness overcame the pain of heartache.

Master Lung was seated at the kitchen table when Tony came in. The photograph of Tony's father lay before him. He looked up at the sound of the young man's footsteps. "I have just received a telephone call," he said without preamble. "My old friend Jiang's granddaughter Elizabeth, very smart, a schoolteacher. She wanted to read me something, a story she had looked up in an old newspaper. She was very happy about it, very excited, even though it was so old. It was about a fire that happened years ago in a two-family house far from here. It was written several days after the fire, the deaths, all about what they found when they investigated the cause." His eyes were shining, steady. "It was in the newspaper for anyone to see, who still had the mind to see it."

"What—what did it say?" Tony asked.

"Wires," Master Lung answered. "Bad wires in the other half of the house. Not the half where I stored my material. Not even a grain of powder left behind in our part of the house, only bad wiring in the other. I could have known then, if my heart had not shattered, if my mind had held strong. It would not have given me back my beloved dead, but at least I could have known that they were not ghosts of my creating." His eyes seemed to bore into Tony. "Why does this woman, Jiang's grandchild, call me now?"

"Because I called Jiang and he said to have her do it, look up the old newspaper stories in the library," Tony confessed, his throat hoarse. "He doesn't read English too well, but she does, and she knows how to run a microfiche reader besides. Just a hunch I had—no, not a hunch: a hope. She was supposed to call me when she found out anything, but I guess I missed the call, huh?" He tried to make it sound like a joke. "Anyway, no harm done. Now you know the truth."

Master Lung laid his hand over the photograph on the table and smiled. "Many truths, Grandson. And many blessings."

"Hello, stranger," Jordan greeted Tony when the younger man came through the door of *Wild Things*. "You taking your business someplace else these days?"

"Yeah, you got that right," Tony replied lightly. He wore shorts and a T-shirt, full summer wear in honor of the hottest late May on record. "Only reason I bothered to show up here again's 'cause I know you turn on the AC as soon as the mercury hits seventy."

"Oh, is that why?" Jordan made a face. "And here I thought it was on account of you maybe picked up another stray."

A shadow passed over Tony's face. He shook his head. "No more, Jordan, no more. Anyway, Grandpa's got me pounding out the college applications, so who's got time for—"

"Funny thing, that," Jordan said as if Tony hadn't uttered a word. "See, I've picked up a stray of my own. Pesky thing. Months and months and *still* hanging around. Comes here every day, hangs out in the back room, reads all my books—doesn't bother to *buy* one, of course—and she keeps nagging me about when the hell you're gonna show your ugly face around here again, because *no fucking way* is she gonna go looking for you, a girl's got *some* pride, a girl's got *some* class, a girl's got *some*—"

Tony didn't wait to here the rest. He bolted through the doorway to the back room as if his feet had taken fire.

Sylv looked up from a dog-eared copy of *Betty and Veronica.* "Took you long enough," she said.

"Sylv! Didn't you—? When the others left, I thought you—what about Arcadia?" Tony finally managed to spit out.

The nocker shrugged. "Arcadia can wait." She threw her arms around his neck and kissed him hard enough for it to be a declaration of war as well as love. "But Mundanity's still good for a few laughs and…maybe something more. Come on, baby, buy me a comic book and let's go home."

Beyond this Book

If this was your first encounter with White Wolf's game-inspired fiction, we hope you enjoyed it. As you have seen, in the World of Darkness monsters can be heroes, and ordinary people, horrific. Those who are brave enough to further explore the personal horror and ambiguous morality of the World of Darkness may be interested in the Storytelling Games that inspired the fiction.

Each of White Wolf's Storytelling Games is a hardcover book that allows you to live the horror and glory of these creatures of the darkness. Available at most book and game stores.

In **Vampire: The Masquerade**, take sides in the constant Jyhad between the manipulative elders of the Camarilla and the guerilla fighters of the Sabbat — fight for power, fight for freedom, or just try to make it through the night.

In **Werewolf: The Apocalypse**, you and your pack strive for honor, glory and wisdom as warriors against the minions of the Wyrm. Combat the ravages of pollution, heal the wounds of Gaia, and punish the evils that men do.

In **Mage: The Ascension**, join the battle for reality — control of outer space, virtual space, and the spirit of humanity. Duel to the death with techno-wizard Technocrats, insane Marauders, and corrupt Nephandi — or become them.

In **Wraith: The Oblivion**, experience the Other Side first-hand — from the grey, decaying ghosttowns in the Shadowlands to the perilous, busy streets of Stygia itself. Get to know your darker half — your Shadow — and conquer it, or fall to Oblivion.

In **Changeling: The Dreaming**, give your inner child free rein — or go Unseelie, and deal with your inner brat. One blink away from the World of Darkness the kings, courts, knights and dragons of the Fae still exist — barely — but it's far harder to stay there than they think.

STEP AWAY FROM THE LIGHT —

AND INTO THE WORLD OF DARKNESS.